SILVER DAWN

C M Debell

The Long Dream Book Two

For Laurie and Dylan, two little dragons.

CONTENTS

The story so far   1

Prologue   11

Part One   17

Part Two   127

Part Three   319

Part Four   409

Part Five   541

Epilogue   629

THE STORY SO FAR

In the first age of the world called Andeira, Tesserion, the spirit of Andeira and the Maker of all life, brought the dragons into the world, the first race. To the dragons she gave half of the elemental magic of the world, control over the pure element of Fire, the rock of her foundation and the skies above, and for thousands of years they were alone in the world. Then men came and the second age dawned. To men she gave the other half of herself—elemental Water, and the earth and the air from which they drew life—but the races remained separate and distinct until they came together to unite their magic and bring the final act of creation to a close.

This union was called the Joining, the linking of man and dragon through which the two halves of the magic of Andeira were made into one. The Golden Age had begun.

The Joining gave elemental mastery to each pairing of human and dragon. There was only one place their magic could not take them, one thing that was forbidden to them, and that was creation, the gift of the Maker alone.

For many thousands of years they were content, until the mage Aarkan and his dragon Srenegar conceived an ambition to take the power of creation for themselves. But their vision, that they saw as a river of power leading to the source of life—to creation—would in fact lead them to their deaths. In attempting to reach that source, Aarkan and his followers would eventually destroy themselves and, by their transgression of the natural order, cause the unravelling of creation itself.

Though Aarkan and his followers refused to acknowledge this, others did. Under the leadership of the mage Lorrimer and his dragon Silverwing, the two sides went to war. At last, realising that Aarkan could not be defeated,

Lorrimer was forced into a dreadful decision—to sever the Joining between the races, and thus destroy the means through which Aarkan sought to realise his ambition. Ending the Joining would rupture the elemental harmony on which Andeira survived. To ensure that it would one day renewed, the dragons created a prophecy that one day the two halves of the divide that had brought them to war would be reconciled, and the child of that union—called by the dragons Æisoul—would recall the dragons from their hiding place and reforge the Joining.

When Lorrimer and Silverwing severed the Joining, the dragons disappeared from Andeira. But their enemy survived. With the departure of the dragons, the elements within their control should have passed from the world also, closing the door on Aarkan's ambition and destroying him, but not all the mages who followed Lorrimer could accept his choice. In secret they created effigies of their dragons that would link with their magic across the divide, and so they allowed a fraction of the elements that should have been lost to remain in the world of men.

The Golden Age passed into a dark time, called the Lost Years, when humanity wandered the changed world, scattering themselves and their knowledge. The dragons were forgotten as the magic drained from Andeira. Mankind was left only with those elements that were their gift from the Maker, and the world with only one half of the magic it needed to survive.

Then the New Age dawned, settlements gradually became towns, town became cities, and nations were born. In the southern continent, three thousand years after the Severing, the vast empire of Caledan is ruled by the Kas'Talani priesthood. In possession of dragon devices—the effigies made before the Severing—they have access to the elements under the dragons' control and believe themselves to be appointed by the Maker as the new guardians of Andeira. What they do not know, however, is that they were given these devices by the ancient enemy, known now as the Arkni, who also founded their Order. Their use of the dragons' magic is what allowed the Arkni to survive, but the dragons to which the priests are linked are slowly dying, their life drained by use of the effigies, and the power of the Kas'Talani is fading.

In their weakened state, cut off from their dragons by the Severing midway through their change, the Arkni possess only a tiny measure of the power they were seeking, and they are seeking it still. Aware of the prophecy, they have been searching for the descendants of Aarkan and Lorrimer, hoping to force the prophecy to fulfilment and control the child who is their only way to recall the dragons.

They enter into a bargain with Vasa, the high priest of the Kas'Talani Order, whose ambition is to bring the northern continent of Amadorn under his Order's control. In exchange for their assistance with this conquest, Vasa agrees to help the Arkni find the child Æisoul, knowing that should the prophecy be fulfilled the power of the Kas'Talani would be destroyed. But Vasa does not know who his allies really are, and that rather than kill Æisoul, they wish to use him to bring the dragons back.

In his efforts to conquer Amadorn, Vasa has made an alliance with the magicians of that continent, a powerful sect that believes as the Kas'Talani do, that the dragons destroyed the old world and then abandoned it; that they are gone and should never be allowed to return. He has also sent Kas'Talani agents to Amadorn, who have been working with the magicians to undermine its kingdoms in preparation for his conquest. Some have been suborned by the Arkni, and one, Darred, has succeeded in finding and bringing together the heirs of the prophecy, and a child has been born.

The Arkni's is not the only treachery brewing in Caledan. The priest Kinseris, sent to the distant, fractious outpost of Frankesh as punishment for courting the affections of Shakumi, Vasa's favourite concubine, is unable to accept the Order's repression of his countrymen. Over the years his efforts to protect them lead him into alliance with Ephenor, a desert stronghold in the southeast of Caledan whose people have been in rebellion against the priesthood for generations. Under their ruler Shrogar, they are the last of what are known as the Lost Houses, a series of fortified settlements concentrated in the region of Sharhelia, guarding, though they have forgotten, the heartland of the ancients' power.

In Amadorn, seven-year-old Aarin's mother Sedaine walks out on him and his father in the remote eastern settlement of Luen, the home of Amadorn's mages. Once a centre of learning for those who survived the great cataclysm, Luen's people no longer hope for the return of the dragons. Only Aarin's father Ecyas retains any belief in the dragons' return, and his belief is so strong it has become an obsession, and it is one that he passes onto his talented, lonely child.

Scorned by the children of Luen and abandoned by his mother, Aarin learns from his father how to control his power. At the age of ten he has his first encounter with the raw power of elemental Fire. Without the dragons, men cannot either harness Fire or survive its contact, but the boy lives. Thereafter his skin is hot to the touch—the dragon fire of the ancients.

Aarin's second encounter with Fire leads to Ecyas's death. Yet when Brannick, his father's friend takes Aarin to the cliffs to burn Ecyas's body, the boy walks into the flames of the pyre and transfers those flames to Ecyas's body. After the fire burns itself out, and thinking Aarin must also be dead, Brannick finds the boy asleep amid the ashes but is unable to accept what he has seen and says nothing.

Wracked with guilt over his father's death, Aarin swears to fulfil Ecyas's dream of finding the dragons, and leaves Luen a few years later to begin his search. On his travels he finds and befriends a mercenary called Kallis. Originally from Caledan, Kallis came to Amadorn as a child and was adopted into the mercenary clans. He tells Aarin about the succession crisis engulfing Lothane after the death of the crown price and the long-ago disappearance of the princess Sedaine—Aarin's mother, though he does not know it. In turn, Aarin tells Kallis about his father and his search for the dragons. They part ways a few months later when Kallis returns to the clans.

Meanwhile, the Kas'Talani agent Darred has insinuated himself into Lothane's court in the capital Rhiannas. On the kings' death, he advises Lothane's council to accept the claim of the Elvelen lord Nathas, knowing the division this will cause when he brings Sedaine out of exile to claim her throne. But he is distracted. The child Æisoul, now a man, has disappeared from Luen, and the Arkni are angry.

Passing through Rhiannas at this time, Aarin meets up with Kallis again. Trouble has been brewing between the locals and the Caledani merchants and Kallis's origins have made him unwelcome. When a tavern brawl breaks out, Aarin manages to extricate himself and Kallis, using his magic to cover their escape. Kallis's already strained loyalty to the clans has reached breaking point, and they decide to head south together.

When Darred arrives at the tavern some hours later, he realises at once who has been there. Preparing to abandon his plans for Lothane, he sends the magician Vianor after Aarin with instructions to take him to his mother in Redstone. Vianor is Sedaine's uncle, and when he realises Aarin is her son, he sees an opportunity to renegotiate the magician's unequal bargain with the Kas'Talani.

Leaving Rhiannas, Aarin and Kallis save a young woman when her party is attacked by bandits. Jeta is Nathas's intended bride, but it is a marriage she has been forced into and she is well aware of the dangers awaiting her in Lothane. Rather than continue her journey she chooses instead to travel south with them. Fearing that Nathas will send men searching for her, Aarin persuades his companions to travel through the Grymwood Vale, an ancient, feared forest in the Istelan Valley, but the pursuit catches them before they can enter.

Vianor is with the soldiers, mercenaries from the clan Kallis deserted. They have come to claim payment for his broken oath, but Vianor has come for Aarin not Jeta. He reveals to Aarin who is mother is and attempts to persuade him to her side, but Aarin refuses. In retaliation, Vianor allows the clansmen free reign, and under their laws Kallis chooses trial by combat. When he wins, the clansmen allow them to make their escape into the forest.

Whilst travelling through the forest, Aarin attempts to explain to Kallis and Jeta why it is so important to bring back the dragons. He creates an illusion to show all the elements working together as they should. In doing so he accidentally awakens the lost elements, which attempt to use him as a channel back into the world. The backlash almost kills him.

Aarin wakes to find himself in Redstone and has a tense reunion with his mother. Darred is also waiting for him there. From Darred Aarin learns about the prophecy, and that he is the subject of that prophecy. He also learns that Darred and the unnamed masters he serves brought about his birth by bringing his parents together and that they intend to control the prophecy by controlling him. But he rejects Darred. In doing so finds himself on the same side as Vianor, who by now has realised that Darred has betrayed everyone. In exchange for his help in escaping, Vianor forces a blood oath from Aarin that he will never willingly help Darred or those he serves. It is from Vianor that Aarin learns of the Kas'Talani in Caledan. Escaping Darred, the three head there.

As Darred leaves to follow them, Sedaine and Vianor return to Lothane where Sedaine claims the throne and works to unite the northern kingdoms. But where Darred sought to destroy the power of the north, Sedaine hopes to strengthen the kingdoms against the invasion she now knows is coming. She sends emissaries to the mages of Luen, requesting their aid, and demands the recognition of her authority from Elvelen, threatening war should they refuse her. Establishing her hold over a single, united northern kingdom, Sedaine and Vianor wait for the arrival of the Kas'Talani.

Meanwhile, in Caledan, the high priest Vasa is finding his alliance with the Arkni increasingly onerous. Hearing of the failure of his plans in Lothane, he realises Darred has betrayed him and begins to suspect that the Arkni are not what they seem.

Arriving in Caledan, Aarin, Kallis and Jeta come to the attention of Kinseris. Although initially distrustful of each other, Aarin and Kinseris quickly realise that their interests lie in the same direction. Kinseris plans to send them to his allies in Ephenor, but before he can do so he is recalled to Kas'Tella by Vasa, and Aarin disappears the same night. Left behind, Kallis and Jeta are freed by confederates of Kinseris, the Ancai Kestel and young guardsmen Trad, who take them to Ephenor as Kinseris wished.

In Kas'Tella, Kinseris is reunited with Shakumi, who offers him information about Vasa's alliance with the Arkni if he will save her and her unborn child. He is also reunited with Aarin, who has been taken there by agents of Vasa and the Arkni. The Arkni Saal'an claims Aarin, intending to force him to return the dragons, but his efforts are hindered by the oath Aarin swore to Vianor. Saal'an's only option is to let Aarin go so he can lead them to the dragons. Vasa finally realises he has been betrayed by his allies.

Fleeing into Kas'Tella, Kinseris and Aarin fall once more into Vasa's power. Furious at Shakumi's betrayal, he has her murdered in front of them. In response, Kinseris destroys the building they are in, fatally wounding Vasa. Fleeing the destruction, they are taken in and helped by an outcast Kas'Talani called Seledar who helps them leave Kas'Tella.

In Ephenor, Shrogar's brother Iarwin brings him a message from Kinseris. The message reveals that Aarin is Æisoul from the prophecy and the man the Kas'Talani believe will destroy them. He begs Shrogar's help to rescue them. When Shrogar expresses his desire to do as Kinseris asks, Iarwin objects, arguing that they cannot risk their people for the sake of a legend. Before they can decide, Kallis and Jeta arrive with their escort, requesting sanctuary in Kinseris's name, and plead with the Ephenori council to go to Kas'Tella. Shrogar agrees.

In Kas'Tella, Vasa has died. Darred watches the Arkni leave with the armies of the Kas'Talani to follow Aarin, and moves to claim power for himself. Promised Amadorn by the Arkni, he prepares to take it by force.

Shrogar's men find Kinseris and Aarin in the desert and take them to Ephenor. There Aarin is reunited with Jeta, where he realises that their feelings for each other have changed. Aware that war is coming to Ephenor, he refuses to accept it.

Aarin and Kinseris discuss the origins of the Kas'Talani Order, and Aarin finally realises that the priests' power comes from the dragon devices they wear. From the old maps in the fortress he also realises that the Lost Houses were guarding the land of Tesseria, the heart of the ancients' power. Knowing now where to look for the dragons, Aarin is desperate to leave the city before the pursuing army traps them there, but he is dissuaded by Kinseris who wishes to defend the Ephenori from their enemies.

The enemy arrives and lays siege to the fortress. Ephenor holds out for two days. Throughout Iarwin makes his dislike and distrust of Aarin and his companions plain. Kinseris and Aarin help where they can, but the Arkni turn their magic against them. Almost losing Jeta as a result, Aarin finally gives in to his feelings for her.

Realising they cannot win, Aarin goes to Shrogar. He believes that if he leaves the Arkni will follow and Ephenor will be safe. He pleads with Shrogar to hold out for one more day to cover their escape. On the point of surrender, Shrogar agrees, and shows Aarin, Kallis, Kinseris and Jeta a secret way out of the fortress. Iarwin follows them, revealing his betrayal of his brother and his people.

In Ephenor, Shrogar and his captains watch the dawn come and find the army still there. Resolving to hold out as long as they can, they launch a night attack within the enemy encampment, destroying their siege engines. Fleeing back to Ephenor through the enemy's camp, Trad and Kestel kill the enemy's general Fader Wedh. The killing is witnessed by another general, Galydon, whom Kestel knows to be sympathetic to Kinseris. Seizing his chance, he persuades Galydon that the Arkni are the true enemy, and Galydon uses his authority to sue for peace with Ephenor and then an alliance.

Shrogar's escape route leads Aarin out near the borders of Tesseria. Realising they are being followed, Kallis hangs back and captures Iarwin, and they discover his treachery. But his betrayal is an unwilling one, compelled by the Arkni to be their eyes inside Ephenor to keep track of Aarin. When he cannot free Iarwin from the Arkni's spells, Aarin realises that the man will remain their spy as long as he is alive. Unable to kill him, they are forced to leave him a prisoner in the desert.

They travel to the ancient mountain range at the heart of Tesseria. An abandoned tunnel that leads them deep within the mountain to the site of the Severing. Activating the magic of the place, Aarin is drawn into the memories of Lorrimer, and watches as Lorrimer and his dragon Silverwing deliberately severed the Joining between men and dragons and ended the Golden Age of the world.

Caught up in the magic, Aarin sees that the Arkni have arrived and calls out for help. His plea is answered by Silverwing, who created the prophecy to bring Aarin to him. But neither Silverwing nor Lorrimer realised then that the actions of their own people in creating the dragon devices would allow their enemy to survive, and Aarin now faces a dilemma. If he returns the dragons to the world, the Arkni will also be returned to their power and Andeira will be devastated once more. Aarin persuades Silverwing that they have only one choice. The Arkni are much more powerful, and the only way to defeat them is to do as they tried to do. They must use the one moment they will have as masters over the power of creation to destroy the Arkni forever. Silverwing agrees reluctantly and shows Aarin where the dragons have hidden the master spell of the Joining. Aarin brings the prophecy to fulfilment as they re-enact that ancient magic. Then they prepare to go even further, as Aarkan once did.

Alone with the Arkni when the Joining is renewed, Kallis, Kinseris and Jeta are taken prisoner by Aarkan and his followers, returned to their power. Aware of their danger, Aarin and Silverwing break free of the dragons' dream and return to the cavern. Aarkan welcomes him as a brother, inviting him to join his cause and recall the dragons to the world. Aarin refuses, demanding the release of his friends, and Aarkan, furious, attempts to destroy him by undermining the fragile basis of his new existence. Driving a wedge between them, he forces Aarin to the brink of death. At the last moment, Aarin reaches out to Silverwing, and in surrendering himself to the magic they have set in motion, brings their change from two to one to completion.

Aarin recalls the dragons, setting the trap around Aarkan and his followers by offering them what they have been seeking. As Kallis and the others flee from the mountain, the Arkni and their dragons reunite. Aarin and Silverwing close the trap. As the Arkni finally realise that life begins and ends in the same place, they are destroyed. But Aarin and Silverwing are trapped and destroyed by the same magic.

In the dawn, as Kinseris watches the newly united armies of Ephenor and Kas'Tella approach, Kallis and Jeta search the ruins of the mountain for Aarin, but he is gone. Aarin and Silverwing watch them. Just as the river flows into death, it also flows out the other side into life, and they have been returned as they were, two individual souls. Yet they are not free to return to their world. Their lives have been given to the dragons, many of whom are still trapped by the devices carried by the Kas'Talani. Together they watch as Kallis, Jeta and Kinseris are met by Shrogar and Galydon. The general offers Kinseris his loyalty if he will take Vasa's place at the head of the Kas'Talani. Kinseris accepts.

In Amadorn, word reaches Sedaine that Darred's fleet has arrived in the south. She orders word sent to their allies to prepare for the defence of the north. Knowing they cannot hope to win, she waits for help to come.

PROLOGUE

THE PRIEST WAS dead when they found him. He had died in his sleep, but it had not been a peaceful death. His body was contorted amid unwashed sheets and his face frozen in shock, as though he could not believe death could come for him this way.

The villagers met this calamity with weary resignation. The man was disliked. He was corrupt, but then so many were, and his greed had caused many families great hardship. But none of that mattered. Nor did it matter how he had died. He was dead and they would be punished for it.

Everyone had heard the rumours of Vasa's death. There was a new high priest in Kas'Tella. Even here, far away from the capital, that news had reached them. But it made little difference to their lives who sat on the black throne. Nothing ever changed, and the priesthood would not overlook the death of one of its own.

So, they took the body from the hut when it was dark and buried it in the hills. With it they buried all the priest's possessions, among them a dull, metallic disc they found clutched in one hand. Then the women stripped the bedding and burned it. And when, a month later, the men from the Order arrived, they told them the priest had left to return to Kas'Tella. And to their surprise, the huge Kas'Tellian captain accepted this unlikely explanation without comment as he stood looking around the priest's empty hut. To their relief, he refused their offer of hospitality, and the soldiers returned the way they had come.

Trad slipped into his place by Kestel's side as the soldiers joined the dirt track leading from the village.

'Well?'

Trad shrugged. 'He's definitely dead, but I don't think they killed him.'

Kestel glanced at him, taking in the dirt under his fingernails and the stains on his clothes. 'Why?'

The boy grinned. 'They didn't do a very good job of disguising the grave. I found this.' He held out his hand.

Kestel looked at the silver brooch. It had acquired a patina that spoke of age and neglect and its face was utterly blank. He sighed. 'Another one. They were warned.'

Trad tossed him the device, harmless now, and he put it in a pouch at his waist where it clinked against others, equally blank. Not all their former owners were dead. Some had handed over the devices willingly, before the dragons they bore had erased themselves, but too many had ignored their high priest's command—and his warning. Some had simply vanished.

'At least we know what happened to this one,' Trad observed, reading his thoughts.

Kestel grunted. There was truth in that, if an uncomfortable one. Better dead than an enemy. But Kinseris would not see it that way, and the mystery of the disappearances gnawed at him. 'We need to know where they are going.'

Trad kicked a stone. 'We already know.'

The Ancai stopped. 'No, we don't. We're guessing. And we've found no bodies.' Not one of the missing priests had turned up dead. So far. Was that just chance? Had they simply left Caledan? Or had they found a way of keeping both the devices and their lives? He took out the brooch they had just collected, turning it over in his hands, ignoring Trad's questioning look and the soldiers milling uncertainly at his back. Every instinct warned him that this was important. 'We're missing something.'

Trad's expression was resigned. 'What do you want to do?'

Kestel looked up, squinting against the sun. 'Frankesh,' he said at last. It was the main port on the Amadorn trading route and, so far from the capital, it had always been difficult to assert Kas'Tella's control over the region as firmly as a high priest might wish. As he had cause to know. More, Darred would take perverse pleasure in using the escape routes established by Kinseris to smuggle his allies out of Caledan. 'If they are going to Amadorn, they are leaving from Frankesh.'

'Frankesh,' Trad agreed. 'And Kinseris?'

The Ancai suppressed a sigh. He knew what Trad was really asking. Detouring to Frankesh would add weeks to their journey, weeks he was reluctant to spend away from Kas'Tella. He had not wanted to leave at all, no matter how important the task, but Kinseris had insisted. *I need someone I can trust completely. I have no one else.* The truth of that was why he had not wanted to leave his lord's side, but someone had to enforce the high priest's edict in the remoter provinces and no matter their oaths, no matter how willingly they might have surrendered their power, no priest could be entrusted with the task. No priest could be trusted to take from another the thing they all craved.

Trust. They had so little of it and needed it so badly.

'Escarian is no fool,' he said at last, wishing, not for the first time, that Kinseris had kept Galydon by his side. 'And if Darred is gathering renegades to him, we need to know.'

If Darred was gathering renegades with their power intact, they were facing a crisis that his presence in Kas'Tella could do little to avert. So they would go to Frankesh, and they would see what they could find. And then they would return to Kinseris and lay before him all they knew of Darred's schemes. And perhaps then they could persuade him to recall Galydon and look first to the defences of Caledan. Because a storm was coming, he could feel it.

PART ONE

ONE

Kas'Tella, Caledan

JETA WATCHED AS the priest, his extraordinary tale told, prostrated himself before the feet of his high priest and begged his forgiveness. She saw Kinseris's expression wrinkle in distaste. If not for her urging, he would have thrown off the trappings of religious rank long since, but both she and the Ancai had argued against moving too fast. His authority was too new—and the demands he must make of the Order too momentous—to risk tearing down the very thing that compelled their obedience. But at moments like this she saw what it cost him to retain the symbols of a man he had hated and continue to rule in the name of a religion he despised.

How do you dismantle a tyranny? How do you restore justice and fair government to a land and a people that have been without it for so long they no longer know what it looks like? And how do you take power from a ruling class, both worldly and magical, who believe it is their sacred right? Slowly and carefully, Jeta had decided. Tempting as it was to burn it all down and try to build something better from the ashes, she suspected that the people who would suffer most if they did that were the very people they were trying to help.

Jeta returned her wandering attention to the high priest's sanctum in time to hear the priest renew his oath of obedience—the new oath, she noted. Then, when he was dismissed from his high priest's presence, she slipped from her hiding place to find Escarian and ensure he placed a watch on the man. This might be a new era of freedom, but there was no sense in stupidity. Until they could corroborate his story—*if* they could corroborate his story—

she would treat this man as the enemy he had been, by his own admission, until very recently.

When she returned, she found Kinseris had not moved, his expression thoughtful as he studied the brooch the priest had given him. He looked up as she entered, then held it out to her. She took it, turning it over as he had done, but it was indeed blank. She handed it back. 'Do you believe him?'

Kinseris smiled ruefully. 'Which bit?' His hair was mostly silver now, the lines on his face etched a little deeper. She did not know if it was the stresses of his new role or the effects of age, so long denied by the dragon device he had worn. She hoped it was the former.

'Any of it. All of it.'

He looked away, hesitating. 'It would explain some things we have wondered about.'

They had wondered if Aarin knew he was killing them—the priests who would not give up their power. She had not liked to think so, but she also knew that he was no longer the man she had loved. She remembered his magic scorching through her in a final farewell, and in its wake was the understanding of everything it had changed. He belonged to the dragons now. And the dragons had been enslaved for centuries by the priesthood they were now destroying. Would their lives even register with Aarin and his dragons as they flickered out? What she had heard today reassured and disturbed her in equal measure. *They had a choice.*

Kinseris sighed. 'But if you are asking whether I believe what he said about Darred, then yes. Or rather, I believe he was telling the truth as he sees it. I take it you have had him followed?'

She nodded. It was not a criticism. Even Kinseris, with his distaste for the less savoury mechanisms of state, could not fail to recognise the necessity. Especially after what they had just heard. Because if this man was to be believed, not only was Darred in active communication with his dissident colleagues across both continents, but he had also somehow discovered the means for them to maintain their command over the dragons enslaved in their devices.

Yet this priest had given his up. Was he telling the truth about that too?

Holy One, the choice came to me, as Darred had told us it would, and I planned to resist. Forgive me, Holy One, for I did not believe. I thought only that you wanted to take away our power to secure your own position. But I saw her—the dragon that was chained to that thing. She asked me to release her, and I knew that if she wished she could break her chains and destroy me before my heart could take another beat. And I knew also that I could stop her, that I could use what Darred had given me to make her a slave once more. But how could I?

He had not, and while Jeta believed that the disgust in his voice had been real, she also noted that he had evading telling his high priest the whole truth. She met Kinseris's eyes, and he smiled slightly. 'Quite. Just enough to convince us of his sincerity, but not enough to damage his master—if indeed that is Darred.'

It was uncanny how well he knew her. The tavern in Frankesh where he had plied her with drink and tricked from her the reason for Aarin's presence in Caledan seemed a hundred years ago. Since then she had lived through a war and seen legends come to life, legends that had taken from her the man she loved. And for a while she had thought they had left her with nothing. When she had returned to Kas'Tella with Kinseris it was because she could not bear to stay in Ephenor, surrounded by memories and smothered by Dianeth's kindness. But when she had stayed here, refusing Kallis's offer to take her back to Amadorn, it was because she had found something to fill that awful void.

'Are you sure?' Kallis had asked.

'Are you?' she had asked in return. Because they both knew what he was going back to. Kinseris had returned to Kas'Tella as fast as the army could travel, but Darred was still one step ahead of them. His invasion of Amadorn was already underway and Kallis was going back to a war. A war he was fighting partly for her, she knew, and partly for Aarin. But mainly because he was a soldier, and it was a war that had to be fought. And she would fight it with him, if not beside him.

Suddenly furious, Jeta expressed just what she thought of Darred. Kinseris's eyes widened a fraction, then he held out his hand. She took it and allowed him to draw her close. So much had changed. When they had first come here, they had been virtual strangers bound only through their ties to Aarin. Thrown together in the chaos of Vasa's downfall and the need to take control, he had come to value her advice and the sharpness of her mind. She had been welcomed first into his counsel and from there to his bed.

It was a funny thing, looking back, how naturally it had happened. There had been none of the agonised soul-searching and desperate longing she had felt for Aarin. Nor, she thought, on his part. It was as if, each knowing the other had given their heart elsewhere, they had taken what comfort they could without asking for more than they knew the other had to give. She might never feel the giddy highs of that brief burst of love, but she felt none of the lows. Much like everything else in her life now, her relationship with Kinseris existed in a place where there was little laughter and fewer tears, and she was content with that. More, she was, in her own way, happy.

And, in helping him to reshape the crumbling empire he had inherited, she had found a purpose. If a desire for revenge played into that at all, it was just another thing they shared. Aarin might have made the magic whole again, but Darred could still make that victory worthless, and she was damned if she was going to let him.

'We need to know how he's doing it,' she said into Kinseris's shoulder. Because if Darred really had found a way to keep the dragons enslaved, Amadorn did not stand a chance. Kallis did not stand a chance. And she was damned if she was going to let that happen either.

Kinseris's messenger found Jeta the next day as she was wandering through the sprawling market in the outer courtyard of the citadel. She came here when she could, her guards trailing after her trying to look as inconspicuous. She had no need of the goods the traders were hawking. She had everything she could want and more. No need of their goods, just their presence, their humanity, the everyday reality of their lives. With her blond hair and pale Amadorian complexion, she would be recognised wherever she went, a magnet for Kinseris's enemies. This was their compromise. He would not allow her into the city proper without him, but he did not deny her this brief contact with life outside the confines of the priesthood's centre of power.

The whole city knew of the high priest's golden whore. The epithet—the assumption—should have offended her. It did not. It was useful, both inside and outside the Order.

The Kas'Talani were an exclusively male order. Women were servants. Or slaves, as Shakumi had been. She was neither. She held no title, had no official standing, yet Kinseris had made it clear, without ever saying so, that he expected her orders to be obeyed. In return she was careful to issue none. Yet she had power here. Everyone knew it and no one acknowledged it. And that suited her fine. The Order would never have accepted her if Kinseris had given her any formal authority. Instead, the ambiguity of both her status and her personal relationship with the high priest ensured wary respect.

She smiled, amused, as the messenger stumbled over how to address her, and allowed her guards to escort her back to the citadel. Escarian was waiting for them just outside the entrance to the high priest's apartments. She felt her heart beat faster at the sight of the tall guardsman who was also Kinseris's spymaster, but she confined herself to a questioning look. He ignored it with his usual lack of expression and dismissed her escort with a curt nod.

As they passed together into the network of rooms that made up Kinseris's private accommodation, she felt a fleeting tingle of sensation brush across her skin. Her unease deepened. The high priest's chambers were guarded by layers on layers of defensive magic, and she passed through those safeguards every day, never noticing a thing. That she should feel even a flicker of sensation indicated powerful precautions indeed.

Kinseris was in his study with another priest, a member of the council that Vasa had disbanded and he had reinstated. Betanas nodded stiffly to her in something approximating a welcome. She smiled sweetly at him in return. And he was one of the better ones. Most of the high priest's counsellors refused to speak in her presence. Jeta took that for what it was. Had they truly believed her nothing more than Kinseris's plaything they would have had no concerns about speaking freely in front of her. Which was why, to save face all round, she usually watched the council meetings from one of Vasa's many secret chambers.

This meeting was clearly something else. Betanas was not just a council member. He was also Kinseris's link to the more disaffected factions within the Kas'Talani, of which there were many. Her heart fluttered nervously.

She perched on the corner of Kinseris's desk as Escarian closed the door and leant against it, arms crossed. She looked between them. 'What's going on?'

Kinseris nodded at Escarian, who said, 'The priest Moralar has been observed meeting with known sympathisers of Darred. It is my belief they are planning a coup against this office.'

In the shock of his stark delivery, it took a moment for Jeta to place the name. Then she remembered. The priest who had told them he had given up the dragon device of his own free will. 'Why?'

'Why?' Betanas scoffed. 'You wonder why Darred might –'

She waved away his protest, her eyes on Escarian. 'No, why do you think it is a coup?'

Kinseris's head of intelligence was not a man to waste words, or emotion. 'Because those sympathisers are on the council.'

Betanas started, clearly shocked. 'That is not possible.'

Jeta met Kinseris's eyes with a slight frown. *He didn't know.* There was something very wrong here.

Escarian shrugged, a gesture that managed to both acknowledge Betanas's objection and dismiss it. 'Nevertheless.'

Kinseris was studying his counsellor. No doubt trying, as Jeta was, to assess his sincerity. 'Why?' he asked at length. 'Why is it not possible?'

'My lord, you have many enemies within the Order, as you well know. Even on the council. Casamir is adamant in his opposition to your chosen path, and he is only the most vocal. It has always been this way. There are always factions. But they are as divided in their course of action as they are united in hatred of your policies. If some consensus had been reached…'

'You would know?' Jeta finished for him. Betanas had known these men far longer and better than Kinseris, who had spent twenty years in virtual exile from the capital. Many of his counsellors were those who had been closest to Vasa, like Casamir, who at almost two hundred years of age was the oldest Kas'Talani still living. Vasa's influence, his daily tyranny over their lives, had made them both wary of whoever held his office and hungry for his power. Their rejection of Kinseris's plans for the Order was absolute, but their ingrained obedience had held them in check, at least until now.

Betanas nodded. 'I am known to favour extreme measures, for this very reason. If any faction were to decide to move against the Holy... the Lord Kinseris, they would seek my help.'

She noted the slip but could not tell whether it was deliberate. Betanas was certainly subtle enough to invoke Vasa's title and everything that went with it to put his loyalty beyond question. She pushed him further. 'Then there are only two possibilities. Either they do not trust you, or you are one of them.'

Betanas stiffened in outrage. 'How dare you? My lord...'

Kinseris stood. 'Enough,' he said, meeting her eyes with a look that said *I need him.* 'I do not doubt you, my friend,' he told Betanas, and Jeta could no more tell how sincere he was than Betanas had been. 'It was our hope that we could use you as a lure for my enemies, but it was only a hope. If Darred can communicate directly with his colleagues, they may know you are not one of them.'

Betanas paled as the implication hit home. His fear, at least, seemed genuine.

Kinseris didn't give him time to think too deeply on that point, turning to Escarian. 'What do we know?'

'My intelligence suggests he will seek a private audience with you, my lord. That he will do so on the pretext of offering information about Darred's network within the Order.'

There was a small silence. Jeta ground her teeth in frustration. 'And?'

Escarian shrugged, emotionless. 'Either assassination or capture. There are benefits to both.'

'Quite,' Kinseris agreed, his voice dry. 'I imagine they will take me alive if they can, but dead I would serve their purposes just as well.'

Control of the Order was all about power, the illusion of it as much as the reality. Kinseris knew that as well as Darred. Kinseris as a prisoner of his enemies would be anything but a figurehead. Nor did Darred have to fear the rallying cry of martyrdom. A high priest overthrown was not a symbol of anything but a failure to wield the power of the office. Kinseris might have changed some things, but he had not changed that.

'Don't grant him an audience,' Betanas suggested, ever practical. And keen, no doubt, to minimise the risk to himself.

Appalled, Jeta realised Kinseris was planning do just that. 'Yes, don't.'

Kinseris shook his head. 'They won't stop trying just because their first plan fails, and next time we might not get any warning. At least this way we know what to expect.'

'You *think* you know what to expect,' Jeta protested. 'What if you're wrong?'

'My information is quite specific,' Escarian told her, though he did not seem happy. Or rather, less happy than usual. Jeta was not sure she had ever seen the man smile. He was one of the handful of Kinseris's agents to survive the Arkni's purge of the city on Vasa's death, and he was loyal to a fault. But he was also ruthless in pursuit of his duty, and protecting the person of his high priest was his primary concern. He would not be pleased at the prospect of allowing a would-be assassin within range of Kinseris. 'Moralar will seek an audience for himself alone. Against one man we can provide adequate protections.'

Kinseris was nodding, and Jeta wanted to scream at him that it was too great a risk. But he would not listen, and she knew he was right. To refuse the meeting would tip their hand and drive any further plots deeper underground. *If* Escarian's information was accurate.

'You are certain he has given up the device?' Betanas asked, hitting on the point of greatest danger. Bound to a dragon device, Moralar could easily overpower Kinseris and any guards he set. It was the only thing that made sense, except it couldn't be true.

Kinseris nodded. 'Quite certain.' With good reason, as Jeta knew. He had made the priest re-swear his oath of allegiance, an oath Kinseris had designed himself that was sourced only through those elements in mankind's priority—Water in its entirety, and those aspects of Earth and Air that humans could touch without access to a dragon device. If those same elements were made whole—if the Fire that belonged only to dragons was present in the swearer of the oath—he would know it. And that posed another problem, because if the priest who had sworn the oath was in fact in league with Darred, it meant that their enemies had found a way to subvert another of their safeguards.

'If he is a traitor, Darred commands great loyalty indeed,' Betanas said, speaking her thoughts, and the ageing counsellor looked reluctantly impressed at the manipulations of a man who could make a Kas'Talani give up the greater portion of their power merely to further his own ends.

'Or offers great rewards,' Escarian added grimly.

It was the great weakness of Kinseris's position. They all knew it. He could only take from the Order and offer nothing in return, not while Aarin and the dragons remained… wherever they were. While some priests had come willingly to his side once they realised the living source of their power, others would never be reconciled to its loss. Watching him now, Jeta realised what Kinseris had always known: this would not stop. Until or unless they could defeat Darred, his enemies would not rest until they had removed him from power. Perhaps not even then. That the magic would be stripped from them anyway did not seem to matter. Jeta wasn't sure they realised that the loss of the dragons' power was not Kinseris's doing. Maybe they didn't care.

She felt Kinseris's eyes on her and knew he had guessed her thoughts. She suppressed a sudden urge to beg him to flee with her, to give up his impossible task, and instead gave him silent permission. His answering smile was brief but eloquent and she found she had to blink rapidly.

'Then we are agreed,' he told them, pretending he had not noticed her rush of emotion. 'If Moralar seeks an audience, I will grant him one.'

TWO

THE DAYS PASSED and no request for an audience came. Jeta found the wait unbearable. She had always known it was possible that the Order would try to depose Kinseris. But to know it was possible and to know it was happening were vastly different things. And she could do nothing but sit and wait, while life and politics in the palace flowed on around her, outwardly unchanged.

She did not see Kinseris for the next two days and infrequently after that for almost two weeks as he attempted to force the selection of lay regional governors through the council. Long delayed by internal disagreement—and outright resistance from many of the most conservative council members— it was one of the key pillars of his plan to transition the government of Caledan from religious to secular rule.

They had spent many evenings together in the early days, talking of Amadorn, of the political organisation of the Golden Alliance, its strengths and its weaknesses, thrashing out between them the beginnings of a way forward for Caledan if the power of the Kas'Talani could be curbed. The city was in chaos all around them, the army keeping order on the streets and inside the citadel itself. They protected Kinseris as he worked to establish his authority within the Order before the shock of Vasa's death and Darred's defection faded and his colleagues realised that the future he offered them would only diminish them further, not return to them the power they had enjoyed before Vasa took it all into his own hands.

It had been a welcome distraction at first, and Jeta suspected that was how it had started. She had been empty of everything after Ephenor, after Aarin left. She had wanted only to escape, so she had left with Kinseris and the

26

army, and all through the journey to Kas'Tella he had kept her by his side, forcing her to think, to talk, refusing to let her retreat into that silent, empty place inside. She had resisted, sitting in silence as he talked with Galydon late into the night. Until one day, as they discussed the merits of different systems of government, she had found herself joining in. Kinseris had said nothing as she argued with Galydon over some detail she had long forgotten, but she remembered the look on his face as he watched them, the barest hint of a smile playing over his lips. It was then she had known she would survive.

They had continued in that way even once they reached Kas'Tella. Exhausted though he was, Kinseris had nevertheless sought her out at the end of each day. Sometimes Galydon joined them, sometimes they were alone. She thought perhaps that by then Kinseris needed the distraction as much as she did. He needed some outlet for his frustration at the task before him, torn between his own hopes and the expectations and demands of a dozen different factions. She could give him what no one else could, not even Kestel, because she was the only one not born in Caledan, that uneasy collection of peoples and cultures forcibly welded together by successive generations of Kas'Talani rule, and she had no ambitions and no agenda other than helping him.

Through it all she had felt herself coming alive again. From an intellectual problem, the future of Caledan and its peoples became something she cared about. *He* became something she cared about. Not in that way, not at first. Then Kallis had arrived from Ephenor on his way to Amadorn, and Kinseris and Galydon had argued. When the dust had settled, and both Kallis and the general had left Kas'Tella, with Trad and the Ancai following soon after, she had felt his despair and loneliness and the effort of will it had taken to keep fighting.

When one night he fell asleep where he sat, she had not called the guards to take him to his quarters. Instead, she had roused him just enough to move him to her bed, intending nothing more than to allow him rest. She still could not explain the impulse had made her climb in beside him, but she had felt his instinctive response, and she had known, without doubt, that it was where she wanted to be. That it was what they both needed.

And it wasn't a betrayal, not really. Aarin might love her, but she had understood enough in those moments immersed in the heady two-way flow of magic between him and the great silver dragon to know that if he ever returned, she would be long dead and the world a different place. Her love for him existed in another time, in another place, walled off inside her and held, sacred and apart, a brightness of memory. It no longer had a place here; she did.

She was reminded of those times now, waiting late into the night for Kinseris to return from the council chambers. And when he did appear, exhausted beyond patience by endless arguments, obstructions and delays, she was there to listen to his frustrations as he drifted off to sleep.

Only it felt different now. There had always been great risk in what they did. At any moment, the resentment that many within the Order felt for their new high priest might have spilled over into outright rebellion. The various factions could have united against him. But, as impossible as it had seemed to her at first, the authority of the office meant something, even to those who disagreed most vehemently with what Kinseris wanted to achieve. Or it had. Perhaps, more than a year and a half into his rule, the fear instilled in them by Vasa was wearing thin and they had realised that dissent would not be summarily punished. Because even the division that had arisen when he demanded the surrender of the dragon devices, ruthlessly enforced by the army, had not felt as dangerous as their situation seemed now.

There was a click as the outer door opened. She sat up as the murmur of voices drifted on the still air from the study beyond. Then she heard Kinseris, his voice rough with fatigue and irritation, and the half-formed fear retreated, leaving her mouth dry and her heart pounding.

Their voices were too quiet for her to make out the words. She slipped out of the bed and padded silently to the door. It stood slightly ajar, enough that she could see a sliver of Kinseris's study, the lamps now lit, but not its occupants.

'… force this through, you will lose half of them.'

She could not at once place the voice, but she didn't need to see the speaker to know he counted himself among the number Kinseris would lose.

Kinseris's voice, when he replied, had an edge that told her he was nearing the limits of his patience. 'And yet you leave me no other option.'

She jumped as a man crossed in front of the door. He paced past her and she saw his face, prominent bones and sunken cheeks exaggerated by the flickering light. Juhael. A man who supported Kinseris in public then used the favour he believed he earned from doing so to barter influence among the council and harangue his high priest in private. Where his true loyalty lay, she could not say, but she doubted he strayed far from his own interests. None of them did.

'And you, Juhael?' Kinseris asked now, as though he could hear her thoughts. 'Where will you cast your vote?'

'When by your own admission you will ignore the outcome?'

'I will not ignore it,' Kinseris shot back. 'On the contrary, I shall think long and hard on the stubborn, short-sighted, self-serving nature of my council. You are there to help and advise me, not to think only of your own ambitions.'

'Even when you are wrong?'

There was a long silence. She wished she could see his face.

'Do you really think this is wrong?' Kinseris asked at last. 'Or do you simply want to preserve your privilege and your power, no matter the cost?'

'It is our right!'

'It is your right,' Kinseris repeated, and his contempt was scathing. 'Tell me, Juhael, when did you last venture beyond the walls of Kas'Tella? Have you ever governed a people so downtrodden they could not pull themselves up even if we left them the resources to do so? Because I have. Everything they make, we tax. Everything they grow, we take. No one can better their situation because we make sure they can't. Outside the cities where we live in comfort, we withhold education, opportunity, wealth, lest the people whose labours provide our luxuries should realise how easily they could take back what is rightfully theirs.' He paused, then after a moment, asked, 'Do you have any idea what life is like for millions of our people who exist at the whim of men who believe as you do, that power gives them the right to do as they please?' There was a crash as something hit the desk. 'It does not!'

There was a pause. She could not see Juhael's face, but she could see he was breathing hard. At length, he said only, 'So you mean to go through with this, whatever happens.'

'I mean to go through with this, whatever happens,' Kinseris agreed.

'And the vote? That means nothing?'

'The decision was always mine alone. The vote is a courtesy.'

'An empty courtesy it would seem,' Juhael sneered.

'As the council is an empty courtesy? Certainly, if you insist on making it so. But never forget, it is one that Vasa would never have offered you. Not in your lifetime has another council met.'

'What Vasa did is not relevant; it is what you do that matters!'

'What Vasa did is not relevant?' Kinseris repeated in disbelief. He must be tired. She had not heard him lose his temper like this, not since Galydon. 'What Vasa did is why we are here, or had you forgotten? It was Vasa who allowed this Order to be suborned by a great evil, whose greed and ambition almost destroyed us all. One man did all that. Perhaps, to undo it, I must do as he did. Should I let a handful of bitter old men dictate the fate of millions? If the council cannot be brought to act in interests other than its own, it is no use to me, and I *will* ignore it.'

'You have already taken from us the wellspring of our power. Now you will take the rest. And you are surprised that we resist you?'

'Never forget that in taking it I saved your life,' Kinseris pointed out. 'Would you rather the dragon had wrested back its life from your control and taken yours with it? That power was never yours, and the other you have abused.'

She didn't hear Juhael's response to that, but Kinseris said sharply, 'I do not seek to destroy the Order, far from it. I merely seek to pull it back within the confines of its original purpose. Let us tend our religion and the worship of the Maker and leave secular matters to those they concern.'

Even before Juhael replied, Jeta knew Kinseris had lost him. He had never really had him.

'So that is your plan? To turn this nation over to the rabble?'

'No, my plan, as I have explained many times, is to build the foundations for a system of government that, in time, will allow the people to govern themselves. Where decisions are not made by one man in one city without knowledge or regard for the differing needs of each region, but where the means is provided to the talented and willing men *and* women of those regions to run their own affairs. This is what I will do,' Kinseris continued quietly after a moment, 'and if you cannot help me, I will do it without you. So I ask again: where will you cast your vote?'

There was something in his tone that told Jeta he would not tolerate further debate. Juhael must have recognised it too, because he did not reply at once, and when he did all the heat had gone out of his voice. 'I cannot support this,' he said at last. 'And I don't believe you ever thought I would. But...'

The word dangled there, waiting for Kinseris to bite. When he did, he sounded so weary her heart almost broke.

'But?'

Juhael's hesitated, then said, 'My lord, we have argued. Not just this once, but many times. I have disagreed with you, and you have let me. I am not unaware of what that means. I would have you take almost any other course of action to the one you are set upon. This you know. But I respect your right to take it. You are my high priest, and your word is law. To me.'

Jeta imagined that Kinseris must feel as stunned as she did at this apparent reversal.

'Juhael,' he said slowly, 'It is late, and I am tired. If you are trying to tell me something, please, do not make me guess.'

There was a rustle of robes and then Juhael passed briefly into view again as he made for the door. 'Only that there are others who may not respect the sanctity and authority of this office as I do. Who do not fear you as they feared Vasa. And it may be that you have pushed them too far.'

Jeta felt a flutter of fear. Then another voice demanded, 'Who?'

Escarian. She had not known he was present, but she was suddenly very grateful that he was.

'I don't know,' Juhael replied. 'Only that one you consider a friend.'

There was a movement she couldn't see, then she heard Juhael's voice, edged with panic, say, 'My lord, I know nothing else, I swear it.'

Despite herself, Jeta grinned. Escarian must have his scary face on. She heard Kinseris say something, then the sound of a door opening and footsteps hurriedly retreating.

'You should not have let him go!' Escarian growled. 'He knows more than he is saying.'

'Maybe, maybe not,' Kinseris replied. Then he was by the door to the bed chamber. She had not heard him get up. 'What do you think?' he asked her as she slipped into the room, a faint flush on her cheeks to be caught listening at keyholes.

Escarian's eyes narrowed as he saw her, but she ignored him. She was used to his disapproval, which appeared to encompass everyone and everything. 'Betanas?' she asked.

Kinseris quirked an eyebrow at Escarian. 'The friend who will betray me, or a rival Juhael wants rid of?'

Escarian shrugged, his expression grim. 'Either. Both.'

'Or neither,' Kinseris said, looking very tired. 'Escarian, whatever you are going to do, do it quietly, and do it tomorrow. I'm going to sleep.'

'You don't seem worried,' she said as Escarian departed, scowling.

Kinseris shrugged and rubbed a hand over his eyes. 'After the last week, half the council wants me dead, if they didn't already. Was that a true warning or just more pressure?'

She opened her mouth to argue, then caught sight of his face and realised that whatever must be done about it, it would have to wait. She helped him out of his heavy robes, suspecting he might otherwise sleep in them, and as he sat on the bed could not help but ask, 'Do you trust Betanas? He knows your plans.'

He lay back, resting his head in the crook of her arm. 'Not all of them.'

Her fingers, which had been trailing circles on his temples, stilled. 'Do I?'

There was a pause as he opened his eyes and twisted his head to see her better. He had almost been asleep. 'All that matter.'

'But not all?'

Eyes clouded with fatigue drooped closed again, despite his efforts. 'Would you have me share my fears?'

'Yes,' she said simply. 'Your fears most of all.'

But he was already asleep.

THREE

JETA WOKE THE next morning to find Kinseris, up and dressed, sitting by the bed. Sleep vanished, replaced by alarm.

'What has happened?'

He was watching her face. His own was unreadable. 'We have heard from Moralar.'

Moralar. The priest whose request for an audience might be the first move in a coup. Darred's erstwhile colleague or current conspirator? 'And?' He seemed more disturbed than she had expected.

'And the request came through Casamir.'

Casamir, his most vocal opponent on the council and the man most rigidly opposed to reform of the Order. 'Not Betanas.'

'Not Betanas,' he agreed.

'But,' she said slowly, thinking it through as he must have done, 'if you wanted to direct suspicion away from Betanas, Casamir is the obvious choice. They hate each other.'

He sighed. 'Or Casamir is the traitor and Betanas is exactly what he seems. Or none of them are. How can we know?'

'What does Escarian say?'

Kinseris grimaced. 'Escarian sees enemies everywhere. As far as he is concerned, they are all guilty. It doesn't matter if he doesn't yet know what they are guilty of.'

'You don't want it to be Betanas,' she said with sudden insight. 'But this makes you think it might be?'

He stood abruptly, turning away from her. 'It's too neat. We know there is a traitor on the council who is in contact with Darred, and possibly Moralar.

Betanas knows we know that. Then Juhael warns me that a friend will betray me, and the very next day the man least likely to be considered a friend passes the message from Moralar requesting an audience.'

She considered this in silence for a moment. Then understanding dawned when he added quietly, 'Juhael has disappeared.'

Which pointed either to his complicity or, more likely, to the fact that his warning had been genuine.

'What does Escarian say?' she asked again, a little desperately. It would have been Escarian who brought the news of Juhael's disappearance.

He was silent, not looking at her. Then said, 'Escarian thinks it is too dangerous now to grant this audience.'

She went cold. 'But you mean to anyway, don't you? Why, Kinseris?'

'Because I don't think I can stand not knowing.' He still wasn't looking at her. 'Because I'm getting nowhere. In all the time we have been here, what have I done? What have I changed?'

She went to him then, slipping her hand over his shoulder and turning him round. 'You have ended the Order's enslavement of the dragons. Surely that counts for something?'

'Or been party to the killing of men I should have been protecting,' he said bitterly, and she pulled away, stung, because that came a little too close to things she did not want to think about.

'And so, what? You just give up? Throw your life away?'

He was angry now. 'That is not what this is.'

'Isn't it?' she challenged him. 'The Order has existed for a thousand years. Did you really think you could change it in two? You have barely started. If you die now, what happens to the Kas'Talani? What happens to Caledan?' She hesitated. 'What happens to me?'

That brought him up short, the anger fading. He took her hands. 'I am not defenceless. Nor am I suicidal. I will grant the audience for all the reasons we have already discussed, because we *need* to know.'

'Escarian…'

'It is Escarian's job to be cautious, you know that. Jeta.' He paused, waiting for her to meet his eyes. 'More than twenty years I have lived like this, surrounded always by enemies, unable to trust anyone. I am tired of it. If there is a traitor on the council, if Darred truly has agents here in Kas'Tella ready to move against me, I must know who they are. I promise you I don't do this lightly.'

He stilled suddenly, head to one side as though listening. She waited, accustomed by now to such absences. After a moment, his gaze focused again, his expression closed down to nothing.

'What?'

'Betanas is outside.'

And just like that she had lost him. For reasons she did not quite understand, the possibility of Betanas's betrayal had shaken him badly. She let her hands fall. 'Will you see him?'

His smile was rueful and fleeting. 'Of course.'

As he turned to go, she called after him. 'It might not mean what you think it means.'

'It might not,' he agreed.

'Kinseris.' There were so many things she wanted to say, something unacknowledged that hovered on the tip of her tongue. But when he looked back, she said only, 'be careful.'

With Kinseris gone, Jeta took her frustrations out on Escarian, which achieved nothing. He might be as unhappy about this as she was, but he had been given his orders and no amount of argument would persuade him to go against them. She did have the satisfaction of eliciting a flicker of reaction when she refused to remain in Kinseris's quarters for the meeting. She was almost certain she heard him mutter something under his breath.

'Kinseris instructed me to keep you safely away from Moralar.'

She smiled, showing her teeth. 'How unfortunate for you that he has also ordered you to allow me the run of the citadel.'

He gave up. In some ways she found that the most worrying thing of all. If he had not been so concerned about Kinseris's safety, he would not have let her have her way so easily. In the ensuing compromise they agreed she would watch the audience from the hidden corridor that encircled the sanctum, built so Vasa could spy on those he had summoned as they waited for him to make his appearance. And she would have a guard with her.

'Two.'

'One.'

Arms folded, Escarian simply stared her down.

'Fine, two. What about Kinseris?'

He gave her a look that expressed quite clearly his views on discussing his security arrangements.

She threw up her hands. 'Don't tell me then. Just keep him safe.'

He left her with the two guards. She did not have to wait long. Determined for his own reasons to get this thing over with, Kinseris ordered Moralar to be brought to the citadel the next morning. Betanas was invited to attend, something that she and Escarian both argued against to no avail.

She watched him now from her hiding place as he talked quietly with Betanas. She could not hear what they said, but she could see the minute signs of strain on both expressionless faces. It could mean something or nothing. Guilty or innocent of this plot, Betanas would not want to be here, and Kinseris never seemed quite comfortable in this room that had once been the heart of Vasa's power. He used it rarely and only for formal audiences such as this one. All other business was conducted in the council chamber or his own study.

Vasa's cushions were gone, as were the gaudy hangings and disquieting portraits. Jeta had never seen the room when Kinseris's predecessor had ruled here, but Aarin had told her about it, and she had seen the wreckage when they returned to Kas'Tella. Kinseris had stripped away all evidence of Vasa's ostentation and in doing so had exorcised more than just the ghost of the former high priest's excesses. Though he spoke of her rarely, Jeta knew Shakumi had been Vasa's concubine, his slave, and that Kinseris's memories of her were inextricably tied to this room and the corruption of the man who had occupied it. And so he had cleansed it as best he could, short of burning it to the ground, which Jeta thought he sometimes wanted to do.

Instead, all that remained of Vasa were the five altars, but where Vasa had shadowed these, directing his Order's adulation from the elements to his person, Kinseris had bathed them in light. The message was clear. Perhaps too clear. She shook off a frisson of fear. Nerves were making her jumpy. It was all taking too long.

From her vantage point she could see only into the sanctum, but as the wards had not yet been raised, she could still hear the activity in the corridor beyond the chamber's magnificent doors. Something was going on outside, and she pressed her ear to the wall as her bored guards watched on. She heard the tramp of feet coming and going and a voice she did not recognise raised in protest, then the reassuring rumble of Escarian giving orders.

She was turning away when the sound came, unmistakeable in the echoing silence. A weapon being drawn. Something was wrong. Inside the sanctum, Betanas glanced nervously over his shoulder. Then Escarian was there, striding across the room. Kinseris turned towards him, a questioning half smile on his face. There was something odd about the way Escarian was holding himself. The feeling of danger now was acute.

Escarian reached Kinseris, one hand on his shoulder as he leaned in to speak quietly in his ear. She saw Kinseris's eyes widen in alarm and he tried to pull away. And suddenly Jeta knew where the threat was. Before she could cry out, a hand clamped over her mouth. Another pinned her arms.

Escarian jerked Kinseris towards him and buried his knife up to the hilt in his side.

Jeta screamed.

Kinseris staggered back a step as Escarian released him, his mouth open in soundless protest, then he collapsed bonelessly to the floor. She screamed again, thrashing against her captor and biting down on the hand across her mouth. There was a pained yelp and the grip slackened enough for her to wriggle free. She felt someone lunge for her in the darkness and tripped, her head slamming into the wall. There was an explosion of pain then nothing more.

FOUR

Lothane, Amadorn

EVERY MORNING SEDAINE looked at the sky. Every morning since *that* morning, when the silvery light of a new dawn had touched something inside her to remembrance of a time long lost. Of a power forgotten, just out of reach. Of a sense of incompleteness she could never after quite shake.

And every morning the sky remained as empty as it had ever been, until even her dreams, soaring aloft on the wings of desperate hope, came crashing back down to earth.

Every mage in Amadorn had felt the moment when the two halves of Andeira's magic were brought back into union. Even the magicians, so far removed in their understanding of the source of their power, had felt it. But nearly two years had passed and the promise of that day remained unfulfilled. The Lost Elements remained untouchable, except to her enemies, and the help she had hoped for so desperately had never arrived. Whatever Aarin had done, he had not brought the dragons back into the world. Was he even alive? Or had he given his life to make the magic whole, as Darred had promised he would? It was the not knowing that was killing her. She thought she could stand anything if only she knew it with certainty. But she could not endure this endless waiting and hoping.

Darred. Even his name left her trembling with rage. She had known he would come. She had helped him lay the foundation for his invasion, however unknowing, however unwilling. And she had felt his hands on her strings when she had taken back her kingdom in blood. But it was in defiance of his ambition that she had stepped from his path and gone further, taking not just Lothane but the whole of the north under her rule—her protection—and turning the military might of the northlands against the oncoming tide of conquest.

So far, it had not come to open conflict, but that day was fast approaching. The first year, the Kas'Talani had been occupied picking off the ripe fruit of the southern states. Only Farnor had offered any real resistance. One of the few kingdoms to possess a handful of naval vessels, her admiral had intercepted and sunk three ships of the invading fleet before the rest had swamped her small harbour and Darred's troops had overrun the coastal capital. After that, the invaders had swept unobstructed across the south coast and up into the Golden Alliance. Now they had reached the Istelan, the great river that marked the border with the north, their numbers swollen with Amadorian conscripts and their power magnified by Darred's coterie of priests, and everything she had done to prepare for their coming seemed suddenly pitiful.

Sedaine turned away from the window, from another cold and empty dawn. If Aarin had made the magic whole again, why did Darred's priests possess the magic of the dragons when neither she nor any of Amadorn's mages could call on that same power in their defence?

Darred, whom she hated but also needed. He was the only man who might be able to tell her what had happened to her son.

There was a soft snore and a rustle of silk, and she saw a flash of pale hair and a plump, white shoulder as Limina turned over in her sleep. Sedaine felt the beginnings of a smile as a shaft of sunlight, escaping for an instant from the clouds, streamed straight onto Limina's face and, half-asleep, she burrowed deeper into the sheets.

Limina, once queen of Farnor, one of the richest royal houses of Amadorn's southern coast. She had ordered her ships to put to sea knowing they could not prevail, just as she had ordered her small garrison to the defence of a city they could never hope to hold. But their sacrifice had allowed many more to flee before Darred's army arrived, and even now, a year later, Farnorian refugees were still trickling into Lothane, following their queen.

Sedaine brushed a lock of hair fondly from her forehead. Into a palace of men, this woman had come. Destitute, dethroned, a refugee and a supplicant. A woman who met her mind to mind as an equal, who had endured the burdens of rule and yet retained her compassion. A woman who understood her pain without need for words and knew better than to believe she could ease it. Instead she had offered friendship and in doing so had shown Sedaine something she had never known and never realised she had lacked.

She perched on the bed, watching Limina as she slowly surfaced. They shared a bed as often as not. Did it make them lovers? She wasn't sure what they were, beyond two women who had lost almost everything and were fighting to keep what little they had left in the only way they could. She did not think she cared to define it, not to herself or to anyone else. In the face of Vianor's stiff disapproval, she offered neither apology nor explanation.

Watching, Sedaine saw the moment when dream slipped away and memory returned, as it did every morning. As she knew too well. Limina had lost her husband in the fighting as she had nearly lost her own life. She had lost the child she had been carrying in her desperate flight. A mother whose child was lost. It was part of what bound them to one another, a shared understanding that required no words because speaking it aloud was too painful.

'Morning, love,' Limina murmured, opening her eyes. She turned over, blinking in the weak sunlight. 'Any word from the mouse?'

Despite herself, Sedaine smiled. 'Not yet. Though I hardly know which of us is the mouse and which the cat.'

'Oh, you are most definitely the cat,' Limina said with a grin, pushing herself up on her elbows. 'Although I must admit there is not much of the mouse about our mercenary. Is that rain again?'

'Not yet,' Sedaine replied without looking. Her years in the east had honed her weather sense to a fine pitch. The day's sullen clouds would not release their rain shower until the afternoon.

Limina pushed back the sheets and slid out of bed, reaching for a robe. It was a cool morning. She looked at Sedaine, taking in her clothes and the open shutters, but she said nothing. She didn't have to. Sleepless nights were something they both understood.

Silently, Sedaine helped Limina dress. After a lifetime spent in the wild eastern lands where there was no place for fine clothes, she had never been comfortable in the elaborate dresses expected of her as queen. But Limina delighted in pretty things, her dresses always the height of court fashion, back when there had still been a court, before Sedaine had suspended the council and sent her lords and their families back to their estates to prepare for what was coming. Sedaine smiled at the thought of the strings of tiny, polished stones the ladies had taken to wearing in their hair in imitation of the ribbons of cowries Limina threaded through her own locks. Everyone knew she was their queen's favourite and the court, such as it was in these times, was scandalised and fawning in equal measure.

They had much to be grateful for. Limina's Farnorians had bolstered their garrisons and what wealth she had been able to save had been freely spent in defence of their borders. Certainly, they preferred her influence on their queen to that of a rival, or even an Elvelian, however politic such a match may have been. *Would* have been. She could never let herself forget Delgar. But in truth it was Limina's gentle wit and compassion that had won them over, so contrary to their queen's prickly exterior.

Against all expectations, Sedaine had to admit that it was what she admired in the woman too. She had lost her softness years ago. Too many hard decisions, made too easily. Ecyas. Nathas. Delgar. Countless others sacrificed to bring these lands together so that the greater portion of her people might be defended. Lives snuffed out, barely heeded. And today she would meet with the current head of Amadorn's mercenary clans to treat for more lives to spend in the defence of her lands and people. If, indeed, she could.

As if reading her thoughts, Limina stopped brushing her hair and said, 'He will listen, surely. The man is no fool.'

Sedaine sighed. 'I sometimes wish he were. Fools I know how to deal with. Maker, I've had enough practice. This man is something else entirely and we are not dealing with him alone but the clans at his back. And what the clans want, other than gold, I do not know.'

'And gold we do not have.'

'And gold we do not have.' None to spare, at least. All the wealth of three kingdoms was committed already to a defence that would likely prove futile yet could not be avoided. *Must* not be avoided. If the clans wished to survive, surely they must see they could not stay out of the fight? But all negotiations up to this point suggested they would do just that unless she offered them gold she did not have to fight their common enemy.

'Deep breaths, love.'

Sedaine unclenched her fists, searching for calm. Limina was right. Anger was no good here. She already knew that Lorac was immune to her rage. And everything else she had tried. Yet he had agreed to return to the table. It told her that there must be something he would accept, short of payment, that would bring the clans to her side. If only she knew what it was.

'Why can't the bloody man just tell me what he wants?'

Limina laughed her husky laugh. 'So said every wife since time began. Why not ask him?'

Sedaine growled. 'Have I not tried?'

'You've asked him to name his price, and he has. Not what he *wants.*'

'They are mercenaries. What else do they ever want but gold?'

Limina shrugged. 'Don't ask me. The clans never did come so far south. But he wants something, and he must believe you can give it to him. Why else is he still here?'

There was truth in that, but Sedaine was beginning to suspect that it was not so much a case of what Lorac wanted, as what he did not want. And if she was right, that was the one thing she could not afford to give up.

FIVE

The Istelan, Amadorn

THERE WAS A time, not so long ago, when Kallis had thought he would not live to see Amadorn again. When the brutal dry heat of Caledan's deserts had made him homesick for the mild northern climate and its overabundance of water. Now, with rain dripping on his face and down his back, his clothes covered in mud, he thought he must have been mad to want to come back here. Throw in the fact that he was effectively trapped in enemy territory with two men who seemed to have no ambition beyond making his life miserable, and he strongly suspected that insanity was the only rational explanation.

The sound of someone tunelessly whistling a popular dockside song drew a muffled curse from his companion. 'Bloody idiot pirate.'

Kallis did not bother to agree. He peered out from under his meagre shelter to see Iraius appear at the top of the bank. The man paused his whistling to wave, then slithered down the steep slope, bare feet sinking up to his ankles in the soft mud.

'Well?' Kallis demanded.

The former pirate grinned as he wiped his hands on filthy leggings. 'I've found us a boat, just as I promised.'

Kallis grunted. 'A rotten hulk no doubt.'

'A rotten hulk?' Iraius put a hand on his heart in mock outrage. 'Pretty as the day I left her.'

'You don't expect us to believe it's your boat, pirate.'

Kallis glanced at Galydon, who was glowering at Iraius from where he crouched amid the roots of a huge willow. Even mud-stained and weary, he had a neatness about him that could only come from decades of military service. Kallis sighed. They had been dodging Darred's patrols ever since they entered the Istelan Valley and this close to the river the area was crawling with them. If they were caught, there was no way Galydon could pass for anything but a soldier. That's if he wasn't recognised on sight. The general might not have had direct command of Kas'Tella's second army, but it was a rare soldier who had not learned to recognise authority when he saw it.

Iraius's grin widened, his good humour calibrated precisely to match the depths of Galydon's irritation. He was another who looked exactly like what he was. Barefoot even in late autumn, his skin tanned deep brown by years spent on deck, everything about him from his long hair to his choice of weapons marked him out as a sailor, and a disreputable one at best.

'And what if it ain't? You going to swim instead?'

Galydon scowled. With the fords heavily guarded, the fast-flowing water and treacherous currents of the Istelan made crossing the great river into unoccupied Lothane impossible without a craft.

Kallis sighed again. He was doing a lot of that lately. Between them they made as conspicuous a group as an enemy could wish for. So conspicuous, in fact, that he had seriously considered the possibility of impersonating Kas'Tellian officers and bluffing their way through the cordon. Had the guards been Amadorian conscripts, they would have done so. But Darred was not so foolish. His interdict on crossing the Istelan was enforced by his own troops, and the danger of Galydon being recognised was very real, quite aside from awkward questions about a Caledani officer keeping company with a desert tribesman and one of Amadorn's most notorious pirates.

Besides, Iraius had promised them a boat and Kallis did not care whether it was stolen. It probably was, if half the stories he had heard about Iraius's startling career were true. Since some of them had been related in a rather different tone by Galydon, whose troops had hunted Iraius's pirates on the Aetelea for years, he was inclined to believe them.

Iraius had appeared one day while they waited for a ship in Frankesh and attached himself to their party, much to Galydon's disgust. He had not explained how he knew where they were going, or how he had found them, but he had made it clear that he was going with them. Kallis had been happy to have him. He liked the pirate and owed Iraius a debt for seeing him and Jeta safely on their way to Ephenor. Galydon had been less impressed with his newest ally, but he was less than impressed by the whole venture, and the more time that passed, the bleaker his mood became. But that was a problem with no immediate solution, unlike their present predicament.

'Is it guarded?' Kallis asked Iraius.

Darred had impounded all craft on the south bank and his soldiers guarded the crossings west of the Grymwood. For more than a year since his army had taken control of Amadorn's southern states, Darred had been seemingly content to ignore the flood of refugees crossing into the north, allowing Sedaine to bear the burden of feeding and sheltering them. But no longer. And Kallis took that as the bad sign it undoubtedly was.

Iraius made an indeterminate gesture. 'Not exactly.'

'And what does that mean—exactly?' Galydon demanded.

'It means it ain't guarded, but they're camping right on top of it.'

Kallis rolled his eyes. 'Wonderful.' So much for slipping quietly into Lothane. He was reminded of his first meeting with Iraius, and absently rubbed the back of his head. He fancied he could feel a dent there as a souvenir of that episode. He did not relish another such. 'Why am I always stealing boats?' He didn't even like boats.

Galydon was already on his feet. 'Show me.'

Kallis followed more slowly, amused by the invigorating effect of the promised skirmish. Galydon was a man who did not deal well with inaction. He was too accustomed to command, to making things happen, and the months of their long journey had chafed at him. What they had found in Amadorn so far had done nothing to improve his state of mind.

In the weeks since their small party had landed on the east coast, far from the Kas'Talani-controlled southern ports, they had gained a rough idea of the lay of the land, and it was not pretty. Their leadership weakened through internal strife, their garrisons depleted, and the magicians long outlawed within their borders, the southern states had crumbled before the advance of the invading army. Even knowing a little of Darred's activities in Amadorn over the years, Kallis still found the ease of his conquest shocking. The invading force was by no means overwhelming. Darred had brought the Second Army with him, and while Kas'Tella's reserve forces were formidable, the coastal kingdoms and the Golden Alliance between them, had they acted together, could surely have held them. There had been rumours of resistance in Farnor, but they could not risk traversing the whole of the occupied southlands to verify those rumours. And resistance in Farnor, real or not, could not help the north.

The north, under Sedaine, which still held out against everything Darred had to throw at it. It was the one bright spot on an otherwise bleak canvas, until you considered that, refugees aside, Darred had not thrown anything at Lothane yet. Whatever he was waiting for, it could not be good, and Galydon was not the only one quietly desperate to reach their destination.

To his surprise, Galydon did not share his disgust at the south's capitulation and had said so bluntly one night not long after they had landed. 'If you had ever seen the Kas'Talani in battle, you would not think so. A handful of priests can destroy a small army by themselves.'

'I was at Ephenor,' Kallis said. 'They fought your priests to a standstill.'

'You faced soldiers at Ephenor. The Kas'Talani barely touched you—those creatures would not allow it. They could have levelled that fortress in a day if they had not wished to preserve the life of your friend.'

There was truth there that Kallis did not particularly want to acknowledge. 'Are you saying this is hopeless?'

'Difficult, not hopeless. The Kas'Talani are formidable, but they have limitations and weaknesses, just like any other enemy.'

'And that's why you're here.'

'Yes,' Galydon had agreed rather grimly. 'That's why I am here.'

Kallis was all too aware of how much that decision tormented him. Galydon had not wanted to leave Kas'Tella. Freed by Vasa's death from a loyalty that had become untenable, he had found in Kinseris a man and a cause to match, at last, his own hopes and desires for his homeland. But Kinseris had ordered him here, to Amadorn, and because he was a soldier, he had obeyed. Not, however, without argument.

Kallis had been present as first Galydon then Kestel argued against this decision. Only with the army behind him had Kinseris taken and enforced his power, and Galydon at the head of that army ensured its loyalty. But Kinseris had been adamant, and whether he was motivated more by guilt or a desire for revenge, it was still a strategic decision. To take back Caledan and lose Amadorn merely moved the pieces around the board. The Order would claim a new power base while Kinseris spent decades undoing the harm they had done in Caledan, and Darred waited for his chance to return.

Kallis understood the reasoning. Galydon understood it too, but like the Ancai, he was wary of the dangers within Caledan that threatened Kinseris's tenuous hold on power.

Kallis had watched Galydon become increasingly withdrawn as the evidence mounted of Darred's ability to retain the power of the dragon device, knowing Kinseris had given up that power of his own free will and now faced an enemy who would never do the same. He was all too aware of the implications for Lothane—and how much they needed someone with Galydon's experience. He just hoped Sedaine would realise it too.

Iraius stopped and Kallis nearly walked into him.

Galydon didn't waste words. 'Where?'

Dropping to a crouch, Iraius wriggled forward to the top of the high bank that surrounded a small, muddy beach where a handful of soldiers in Kas'Talani uniforms were lounging about in varying degrees of inattention. Galydon dropped down beside him, hidden by the thick undergrowth, and made a disgusted noise as he viewed the scene.

'Where is it?' Kallis asked.

Iraius pointed to a canvas-covered mound near the edge of the camp. A soldier was reclining on top of it, one arm behind his head, the other dangling by his side.

Now Kallis knew that he was looking at, the mound did have a boat-like shape, though there was clearly more under the canvas than just a boat. It was probably being used to store the soldier's supplies, and he counted at least four of them in addition to the officer currently draping his portly form over their means of escape into Lothane.

He scowled at Iraius. 'That's your idea of not guarded?'

Iraius shrugged, unabashed. 'He's not guarding it. He's sleeping on it.'

'He is indeed,' Galydon agreed grimly. Glancing at Kallis, he asked, 'What do you think?

Kallis rubbed his hand over a jaw thick with stubble and wished inconsequentially for a shave. 'Kill them all, steal the bloody boat, and get out of here?'

'Direct,' Galydon murmured.

'There might be more,' Iraius pointed out. 'Patrols are thick as fleas on a dog.'

Galydon rocked back on his heels, reaching a decision. 'All the more reason to get this over with before they get back.'

The pirate shrugged. 'They likely to come after us?'

Galydon shook his head. 'They won't follow us into Lothane. Just look at them—they're bored and lazy. Their orders are to guard this bank. They aren't going to want to admit they let us get across by coming after us.'

That was probably true, Kallis conceded, studying the camp. He had rarely seen such slack discipline among professional soldiers. They had the look of men who had been out here for weeks, far away from any meaningful authority, and with nothing to occupy them. Even so, there were five soldiers they could see, possibly more, and they had no idea what condition Iraius's boat was in. It was laid up not too far from the water's edge, but they would need time to unload it and get it afloat, and they couldn't do that and fight off its guards.

'Best to split them up,' he said, thinking aloud. 'Get them away from the camp.'

'That won't be difficult,' Galydon murmured, intent on the camp. He glanced at Kallis. 'That one'—he nodded to the officer—'is mine.'

SIX

THERE WAS A small clearing no more than a handful of paces from the ridge that was perfect for their purposes. Kallis crouched beside Galydon, watching the listless activity of the guards. Then the general cupped his hands to his mouth and called out a stream of insults at the sleeping officer. Instantly, the camp came to life. Soldiers snapped alert, hands reaching for discarded weapons. The officer sat up. He said something to his men that Kallis couldn't hear, and a moment later repeated it at a shout. Someone sniggered. Another pointed up at the ridge that hid them.

Galydon called out again. Kallis had a hard time deciphering the odd mix of low Safarsee and military slang, but he got the general gist. The object of his obscene tirade appeared to understand the details with perfect clarity.

The officer's face suffused with rage as he pointed up the slope, ranting at his men. They obeyed with a slowness bordering on insolence that Kallis recognised as contempt.

Galydon twisted round to ease his sword out of its scabbard and caught Kallis staring at him. 'What?'

Kallis shook his head, suppressing a smile. 'Nothing.'

'They're coming,' Iraius whispered. He was breathing unevenly, trying very hard not to laugh. His command of Safarsee, high and low, was flawless.

Galydon stood. 'Go.'

They went, melting into the trees on either side of the small clearing. It was not long before they heard the soldiers approaching. They were making no effort to move quietly, talking and joking amongst themselves. It was clear they were not expecting to find an enemy lying in wait. This was probably as much excitement as they had seen in weeks.

There was a burst of laughter as a young man stumbled into the clearing, propelled by a shove in the back from the soldier behind, who mocked him good-naturedly as he tripped and nearly fell. The boy recovered his balance, laughing, and backed up ahead of his fellows. Then he was silenced by a grizzled sergeant, who barked at them to be quiet as he stepped out of the bushes, sharp eyes scanning the clearing. Sword out and alerted by the instinct of an experienced campaigner, he brought his men under control.

Now, Kallis thought silently, and Iraius slipped noiselessly into the clearing and let loose a piercing whistle. As all heads turned towards the sound, and the pirate leaning casually against a tree, first Kallis then Galydon stepped out from concealment behind them. The sergeant lunged at Kallis, who turned his blade effortlessly and flicked out with his own. His opponent went down, bleeding from a slash to his thigh, and Galydon disarmed the second with such ease that the fight went out of the rest before Iraius had even put a hand to his own sword. One after the other the men threw down their weapons and milled around nervously.

Iraius peeled himself off the tree and gathered up the assorted collection of discarded blades. A solidly made crossbow he slung over his shoulder with a pleased grunt.

Kallis nudged the downed soldier with his toe and rolled him over. He grimaced. The cut must have severed the big vein in the leg. The man's side was drenched in blood, and it had soaked the ground beneath him. He was obviously and messily dead. One of his companions stumbled and retched and would have fallen if not for Iraius's hand under his shoulder.

Galydon rapped out a command and the men snapped to attention, utterly confused. He looked at them with contempt, his sword hovering at the throat of the man he had disarmed. With a flick, the blade sliced through the stitching of the man's company insignia and it fluttered to the ground. The soldier's astonished eyes watched it fall before returning to Galydon's face as he said with menace, 'You are a disgrace to that uniform. *Take it off.*'

There was a moment of stunned hesitation, then the men were fumbling out of their uniforms and throwing the garments in a heap on the bloody ground.

Kallis watched, bemused. 'Is this really the time?'

Galydon threw him some rope. 'Men are rarely as keen to rush into battle naked. Not that there is much fight in this lot. Get that body out of sight and let's finish this.'

Kallis caught Iraius's eye as the general disappeared down the path to the riverbank. The pirate shrugged and jabbed one of the men in back with his short sword, herding them before him. Kallis followed, and between them they quickly had the three cold, miserable men tied up and secured together against a tree.

As Iraius was about to gag the last of them, Kallis stopped him. He knelt beside the man, knife in one hand.

'How many in your unit?'

The man glared at him in sullen resistance and spat in the mud.

Kallis sighed, and pricked the man's neck with his knife, forcing his chin up. He leaned in close. 'How many?'

He could see the fear in the man's eyes and the rapid pulse in this throat, but he stayed stubbornly silent. There was a muffled protest on his right, and without taking his eyes off the first man, Kallis moved his knife to the throat of the young man next to him, who instantly stilled.

'Let's try again,' he suggested. He had not missed the resemblance between the two. 'How many?'

The man's eyes flicked to his left. Kallis increased the pressure on the knife, drawing a choked cry from his victim. Iraius grabbed him by the hair, holding him still against the knife.

Kallis raised an eyebrow.

'No more,' the man growled out. He spat again. 'Traitor.'

'Hardly,' Kallis replied, holding his eyes for a long moment. Then he sheathed his knife and stood. Iraius released the young man, who was shaking and sobbing, his breathing ragged against the leather strap in his mouth.

Kallis stood, watching in silence while Iraius tied the final gag, then they gathered up the weapons and headed to meet up with Galydon.

'You believe him?' Iraius asked.

Kallis shook his head. 'You?'

'Nah,' Iraius replied happily. 'If they're as useless as that lot, ain't going to worry us much.'

Kallis had to admit that thus far the opposition had not been too taxing, and they arrived at the beach to find Galydon already had the officer at sword point. The man's dark face had paled to a sickly hue and he was quivering with fear. There was a bald patch on his uniform where his badge of rank had been and a suspicious stain on his breeches.

'The others?' Galydon asked.

'Hog-tied and out of sight,' Kallis confirmed. He nodded to the prisoner. 'How's our friend doing?'

'He pissed himself,' Galydon said sourly, shoving the unfortunate officer to his knees in the mud while he quickly tied his hands together. 'Are we expecting more?'

Kallis shrugged. 'They say not. They're probably lying. What did he say?'

'You'll get no sense out of him. He thinks I'm a punishment from Darred.' His mouth twisted over the name.

Iraius called out, and they turned to where the pirate was standing by the canvas-covered mound they had come for, his face a mirror of the disgust on Galydon's when confronted by his countrymen's incompetence.

About twelve feet long, the boat was tilted to one side, resting deep in the soft, sticky river mud. Iraius dragged off the canvas and hopped over the side. With Kallis helping, he began unloading the half-empty crates the soldiers had placed inside while Galydon hunted around for oars. As Kallis rummaged through the crates, transferring a few useful items to his own pack, Iraius inspected the hull, muttering to himself.

'She's sound enough,' he announced eventually. 'They must have dragged her down here recently, because she'd warp and rot quick enough if left like this for long.'

Galydon returned holding the cracked shaft of one oar. 'No sign of the other.'

Iraius jumped down. 'One will do. Let's get her afloat.'

Tossing the captured weapons and the oar into the boat, Galydon and Kallis put their backs under the side that was tilted downward, heaving the boat upright while Iraius rocked it from the stern, trying to break the suction of the sticky mud. Just when Kallis thought something in his back was going to burst, the hull came free with a gurgling pop and Iraius shouted with delight as the boat tipped level.

'Time to go,' Galydon said as he scrambled to his feet to push the boat towards the river's edge.

They were halfway to the water when the rest of the patrol returned.

There was a shout of alarm and Galydon swore. 'There were more of them.' He dropped down behind the boat as a hail of crossbow quarrels slapped into the boards. Kallis ducked down beside him, regretting the captured crossbow lying out of reach in the bottom of the boat. Iraius, caught on the exposed side of the boat, vaulted over the side and tumbled down in the mud, half-stunned and bleeding from a gouge on his temple.

Kallis shook his shoulder, receiving a vague response. Galydon was peering cautiously round the stern. 'How many?' Kallis asked.

Galydon flinched back as an arrow hit the wood inches from his face. 'Only three that I can see.' He shifted into a crouch to draw his sword. 'Iraius?'

Kallis glanced at the pirate. He was conscious, barely. 'Out of it for now.'

There was frantic yelling and Kallis risked a look over the side to see the fat officer rolling in the mud screaming at the new arrivals, whose bolts were vibrating in the ground all around him. He saw the advancing men check as they recognised the officer as one of their own, and one of them hurried to untie him. The others continued their cautious advance.

'Two each,' he murmured as the officer pushed himself to his feet. 'Oh no, he's off,' he amended as the fat man turned stumbling towards the safety of the trees. He grinned at Galydon. 'What did you say to him?'

'Another time,' Galydon replied. 'Ready?'

Kallis nodded, sword in hand, and as one they rose screaming from their shelter. Kallis leapt onto the boat and as it rocked under his weight, threw himself into the closest soldier, taking them both crashing to the ground. Straddling the man, he punched him in the face and lurched to his feet. A wild swing came at his head and he jerked back, his sword cutting up and into his assailant's unprotected side before he could recover his guard.

Breathing hard, Kallis looked around and saw Galydon put the last solider down with a slice that nearly took off his arm. On the ground, the man Kallis had punched rolled over and groaned. A well-aimed kick knocked him out again.

Wordlessly, they wiped down and sheathed their swords and returned to the boat, pushing hard against the stern. Iraius swore and flopped out of their way.

A quarrel slammed into the ground, then another.

'Only *three*?' Kallis shouted, straining his shoulders as he heaved against the heavy hull. Then he was on his back as the boat slid the last few inches and nosed into the water.

Galydon grabbed Iraius under his shoulder, dragging him through the mud and into the boat as Kallis pushed off from the shore. The autumn had been wet and the river was high. He could feel the tug of the current around his legs even in the shallows and almost lost his grip on the boat as the swirling waters tried to take it. The river was up to his chest now, and arrows were slapping into the water around him. One thudded into a plank next to his hand and he grabbed it, hauling himself up and into the boat as Galydon took charge of the tiller and guided them out into the main current.

Galydon looked down at him as he lay gasping in the bottom of the boat. 'Are you hurt?'

Kallis sat up, steadying himself with one hand as the little craft careened down the fast-flowing river. No more arrows fell near them. The current had carried them out of bow shot, but there was an ominous roar of white water ahead. He glanced at Iraius, sitting half-dazed where Galydon had propped him against a bench, and back at the oncoming rapids. 'This is not good.'

Galydon followed his gaze then nudged Iraius with his foot. 'You with us, pirate?'

Iraius mumbled something unintelligible. Kallis reached down and turned his head so he could see the rapids.

Iraius blinked and shook his head, then looked again. 'Oh.'

'Yes, oh,' Kallis retorted, hearing his voice rise. 'Time to make yourself useful.'

Iraius shoved himself to his feet, one hand pressed against his head in a way Kallis did not find at all reassuring. But the pirate managed to shamble over to Galydon, who gave up his place by the tiller.

The general joined Kallis in the waist. 'What can we do?'

Iraius grinned. Some of the brightness had returned to his eyes. 'Sit down and hold on. And get rid of those.' He nodded at the collection of blades at Kallis's feet. 'Don't want anyone to get cut.'

Kallis was more than happy to comply, tossing the Caledani weapons into the river before bracing himself in his seat. He risked a glance over his shoulder at the fast-approaching white water and quickly looked away. Water sloshed around his feet. He looked down and saw the river seeping between the boards. 'The bloody thing's leaking.'

Iraius spared him a brief glance. 'She's old. Of course she's leaking.'

Kallis glared at him in disbelief but had no chance to give full vent to his feelings as the boat hit the start of the rapids and it was all he could do to keep his seat. Within seconds he was soaked as the boat slapped against the furious water. One spectacular splash drenched him from his head down, and he saw Galydon grinning as he shook the water out of his hair.

Iraius called a warning as they hit the main section of the rapids and the buffeting began in earnest. Joints screaming and teeth aching, Kallis's whole attention was focused on staying in the boat as the wildness of the water lifted it up and dropped it down, throwing its occupants from side to side.

The rapids smashed them against a rock. There was a crack and the tiller lurched out of Iraius's hands as they stuck fast, water pouring in. He cursed, shaking a wrenched wrist. 'Rudder's gone.'

Galydon tossed him their broken oar and the pirate shoved hard against the rock to send the boat spiralling back into the current.

Kallis rocked back, only just keeping his balance. He had time to register what the collision with the rock had cost them—the boat, already awash, was sitting far too low in the water. The bottom scraped against submerged rocks and he was sickeningly certain they were not going to make it.

'The water's too fast,' Iraius shouted. 'She'll break up. I'm going to take us in. Get ready to jump.'

Soaked to the skin, Kallis gripped the side of the boat for dear life and looked incredulously at the churning water. 'Jump? Into that?'

Iraius grinned, black hair whipping around his face. 'Trust me.'

Galydon's dark eyes glittered with laughter.

'Maker save me from lunatics,' Kallis muttered, then he was thrown to one side as the boat was buffeted through a narrow channel between the rocks. Galydon's arm shot out, steadying him as he almost tumbled out.

Iraius stood balanced in the stern, their one oar reversed in hands, his eyes narrowed in concentration as he watched the water. The boat skipped across the white-tipped rapids as he edged it towards the northern bank.

Glancing ahead, Kallis saw a tangle of branches caught around a fallen tree. They were heading straight for it. He closed his eyes.

'Get ready,' Iraius yelled, and plunged the long oar deep into the water. The little boat spun violently on its axis, nearly spilling its passengers as it shot out of the foaming rapids into an oasis of calmer water.

'*Now*,' Iraius shouted, leaping nimbly onto the side of the boat and into the pool without waiting to see whether the others followed.

Kallis rolled out of the boat as Iraius's momentum tilted it on its side, and the river closed over his head. As he broke the surface, coughing, he could feel the swirl of the eddy trying to drag him back into the main current, but Galydon had hold of him, and with that iron grip on his arm he managed to get his feet under him. Together they staggered out of the water to where Iraius waited.

Safe on the bank, his heart racing and his breathing ragged, Kallis turned and watched as the boat spun lazily around the edges of the eddy. Then it leapt up as the current caught it once more and dragged it back into the maelstrom. Unmanned, it was smashed from side to side as it hurtled through the foaming water, and he could hear the creak of its stressed hull giving way even over the roar of the rapids. By the time the boat was lost from sight around the bend of the river it was little more than splintered wood.

'Merciful Maker. I hate boats.'

Galydon laughed and clapped him on the back before throwing himself down beside Iraius.

Kallis glowered at him. 'Don't tell me you enjoyed that.'

The general grinned. It made him look years younger. 'I grew up near the Aetelea. Reminds me of some of the rapids I used to run as a boy.'

'Aye, she has some rare runs,' Iraius agreed, wistful. 'Nothing to match this old girl in full flood, mind.'

Galydon choked on a laugh. 'You're quite mad, pirate.'

'It gets worse than that?' Kallis asked with a backwards glance at the churning water.

'Aye, you should see the river run through the Grymwood in the spring. It's almost like it's alive.'

Kallis shivered, remembering his journey through that ancient forest with Aarin and Jeta. 'Now that I can believe.'

He shivered again as the chill set in

Galydon saw it and stood. 'Come, we need a fire, and dry –'

As if summoned by his words, a line of flame erupted at their feet and within seconds they were encircled in a wall of fire.

Kallis stepped back smartly. 'What the –?'

'Company,' Iraius murmured, hand on his knife, and through the flickering flames Kallis saw figures stepping out from the tree line.

'Well, that answers one question,' Galydon observed. 'At least we know someone is guarding the river.'

'A pity they seem to think we're the enemy,' Kallis retorted, edging away from the spitting flames until he was back-to-back with the others.

The figures drifted closer. There were five of them, all cloaked and hooded but curiously unalike.

'Magicians,' Kallis muttered, hand flexing on his sword hilt, something nagging at him.

Galydon did not take his eyes from their silent watchers. 'Magicians?'

'Interfering, power-hungry tricksters.'

Kallis glanced at Iraius. 'Met some, have you?'

The pirate smiled grimly, still fingering his knife. 'Aye, one or two.'

Then one of the cloaked figures pushed back their hood, revealing a spill of long, blond hair. Not magicians, or at least not all of them. Which was when Kallis remembered what his brain had been trying to tell him.

Kallis did not consider himself an expert on magic. Quite the opposite. But he had travelled with Aarin long enough to know two things: neither magician nor mage could control fire, and magicians were masters of illusion.

'It's not real.' He kept his voice low and his eyes on their watchers, who seemed in no hurry to make their next move. Quite possibly, they didn't know what their next move was.

Galydon's head shifted in his direction. 'What isn't real?'

Iraius chuckled and waved his hand close to the fire. He stepped forward, grinning back at Kallis and Galydon. 'No heat.' Then he walked through the wall of flame, the woman made a chopping motion, and the pirate dropped to the ground.

Things went a little crazy after that. Galydon, whose experience of magic very definitely included mastery of fire, followed Kallis through the flames with a determined grimace. The illusion broken, the fire winked out, but they had not taken a handful of steps before the world seemed to explode in a cacophony of sound and dizzying force. Thrown to his knees by a punch that seemed to come out of thin air, Kallis clamped his hands over his ears and fought to stay conscious against the sudden greying of his vision.

As he passed out, he realised none of their assailants had even moved.

SEVEN

KALLIS WOKE WITH a start. It was dark and his head ached like the worst sort of hangover, but the bout of drinking that had preceded it was gone from his memory.

He closed his eyes, taking stock. He was lying on his back on the ground by a fire. His muscles ached like he had been in a fight. *The bloody boat.* And then it came back to him.

He turned his head to the side. An old man was sitting on a log at the edge of the firelight, watching him. Beyond him, in the darkness, Kallis could hear sounds of quiet conversation and the occasional rustle of movement. He tried to sit and found his hands were tied at his back, forcing him to roll on his side and rock himself upright. As he did so, he caught a glimpse of Galydon, apparently still insensible. Iraius he could not see at all.

Kallis turned back to the old man, who had watched his efforts in silence. Shaggy white hair framed a weather-beaten face and deep-set dark eyes that were naggingly familiar.

The man smiled grimly at his scrutiny. 'You don't remember me, do you? Let me remind you—where is Aarin?'

The question caught him off guard. Then he remembered. Redstone. 'Brannick.'

'Kallis. You haven't answered my question.'

'And I should? Last time we met, you betrayed him to Darred.'

Brannick stretched out booted feet closer to the warmth of the fire. 'I did not, but I realise why you might think so.'

'Then you will also understand why I am reluctant to tell a man who is now working with the magicians.'

Brannick gave a thin smile. 'War makes for strange bedfellows, does it not? Before you question my loyalties, you should examine your own, travelling with a Kas'Talani officer. Perhaps I should not be surprised, given who you are. Is that why you will not tell me where Aarin is?'

'I cannot tell you what I do not know,' Kallis ground out. A movement at his back told him that Galydon was awake and listening. 'And if you think we are in league with Darred, why aren't we dead already?'

'Because I wanted to ask you that question. And others.'

'Such as?'

But Brannick did not reply, his unfocused gaze looking past Kallis at something only he could see, and the mercenary remembered the man who had come to Aarin in Redstone and pleaded for forgiveness. And he remembered that this was Aarin's father's friend, a mage who would have felt the change in the magic that Aarin had wrought. He knew what the questions were, he just did not know the answers.

'I was with Aarin when he healed the magic,' he told Brannick. 'I was with him when he found the dragons. That is all I can tell you, because what happened then, and where he is now, are things beyond my understanding.'

There were tears in the old man's eyes and on his cheeks. 'Thank you.'

Galydon nudged him, and Kallis cleared his throat. 'Untie us?'

There was a crunch of footsteps and the woman from the riverbank stepped into view. Iraius stood behind her looking sullen. 'Not quite yet. Some of us have more questions.'

'Which I have answered,' Iraius observed to no one in particular. He was unbound and appeared none the worse for whatever had been done to him, but he acquiesced without protest as she told him to sit down and shut up.

'Which your friend has answered,' she agreed, turning back to Kallis and Galydon, who had abandoned his pretence at sleep. 'I'm interested to see whether your answers match.'

She sat down next to Brannick. Close to, Kallis could see she was older than he had first assumed. Her fair hair was almost grey and fine creases were etched around eyes that were clearly more accustomed to smiling than she was letting on at present. She wore a thick fur jacket over a man's worn tunic and leggings, and she carried no weapons that he could see. She had no need of them.

'My name is Needa. You, Kallis, we know. But you,' she nodded at Galydon, 'make us a little nervous.'

'Good,' Galydon replied. 'It would be disappointing if I didn't.'

Needa raised a sardonic eyebrow. 'Really?'

'You wouldn't be much good as border guards if you let a senior officer from your enemy's army through your ranks without first testing his claims of friendship.'

Needa flicked an irritated look at Iraius who returned one of his devastating smiles, all teeth and no warmth. 'And you are claiming friendship with Lothane? Why?'

'Because I was ordered to.'

Brannick, who had had been paying little attention until now, asked sharply, 'By Darred?'

Galydon looked amused. 'I would hardly say so if that was the case.'

'Then who?' Needa demanded. 'You understand we cannot simply accept your word?'

'Then accept mine,' Kallis suggested. He knew this woman must come from Luen—there were no female magicians, though clearly she kept company with them. And he guessed her to be no more than a handful of years older than Sedaine. She would have known Ecyas and Aarin, and from the ease of her manner with Brannick, there was every chance she had followed Sedaine to Redstone. Either way, what Aarin had done had to mean something.

She studied him coolly. 'Because of your friendship with Ecyas's child?'

Or perhaps not. He tried again. 'If you accept that, you must know I would never ally with Darred.'

'On the contrary,' she replied, ignoring Brannick's protest. 'We know that Darred offered the boy a deal.'

'Which he did not take,' Kallis retorted, growing angry.

'Did he not? Because from where I am sitting, the only beneficiary of what he has done is Darred.'

Brannick shifted uncomfortably. 'Needa…'

'No, Brannick, I'm sorry. Your friendship with Ecyas clouds your judgement. It is for his son to answer these charges, but he is not here.' She looked at Kallis. 'Why is he not here? If, as you maintain, Darred is his enemy, why is he not here, with you?'

Why is he not here? Despite the level tone, Kallis heard the appeal in those words. Where Aarin was, and what he was doing, were questions he too would dearly like answered. Aarin might have achieved his aim, but Kallis could not deny that what he had left behind him was little changed—and not for the better. From where Needa was sitting, he could indeed see how the circumstances seemed damning.

Healing the magic of Andeira had always been an abstract concept to Kallis. The dragons had been more foreign still, and only the sheer scale of the power arrayed in opposition to the mage had convinced him that it was more than just a young man's dream. But then the dragons had appeared. He had seen them. He had felt the vastness of their power and the power of their enemies. He had seen Aarin take that power for himself, and while he had not seen what happened next, he knew that the man he had glimpsed when the dust had settled was utterly altered.

And so, he had expected… something. That the world would change also? That it had changed in ways he could neither see nor feel he had no doubt. The Kas'Talani had been like men waking from a dream in the aftermath of that conflict, both transported and bereft. But for Kallis, the soldier who dealt only in tangible, everyday realities, nothing had changed. They had exchanged one enemy for another, and Darred seemed a much more immediate threat to the things Kallis cared about than the Arkni had ever been.

He looked up. Needa was watching him. The resignation in her eyes made something inside him twist painfully and still he had no words.

It was Galydon—Galydon who had never known Aarin—who broke the fraught silence to defend him. 'Be thankful you are facing only Darred and not his former masters. I cannot speak for a man I have never met, or his motives, but I do know that his actions saved us all from an enemy much worse than this one.'

Needa studied him intently and Kallis sensed her *need* to believe. 'Tell me,' she said at last. '*All* of it.'

EIGHT

SEDAINE FOUND VIANOR waiting for her when she emerged from yet another frustrating meeting with her chancellor and the heads of Lothane's banking families. Money. There was never enough of it, and there was forever some delay in getting hold of more. She had grown heartily sick of the laconic shrugs and commiserating head shakes that greeted her every request for funds, and this morning her patience had come close to snapping. Only the skillful negotiation and careful flattery of her chancellor had secured yet another temporary loan on terms that would not cripple the crown for a generation.

'Bloody fools,' she snapped by way of a greeting. 'Do they imagine they will be spared when this war finally arrives? If their penny pinching leaves us exposed, they will die just as easily as the rest of us.'

Vianor blinked, taken aback. Then he shrugged. 'Money has protected them before. They imagine it always will.'

'Bloody fools,' Sedaine muttered again, gesturing for the old magician to walk with her. It sometimes seemed that her days were just a succession of such conversations as an endless line of officials and those of her nobles who remained in Rhiannas tracked her steps through the palace wanting a moment of her time, a word in her ear, a small favour. She had hoped to snatch an hour for herself this morning, to prepare for a third and possibly final meeting with Lorac, the mercenary captain-of-captains, but she resigned herself to its loss. 'At least Derias knows how to handle them. The crown would be mortgaged thrice over by now otherwise.' Or she would have throttled the lot of them, one or the other. 'What do you need, uncle?'

Vianor did not answer directly. 'Derias is doing well, then?'

Sedaine nodded to a guard who rushed to open a door as she approached. 'You know he is.'

'He is certainly competent,' Vianor agreed. 'He has proved that before now. You are fortunate to have such a harmonious relationship with his office. Your father was rarely so lucky.'

'My father's reign made his lords rich,' she retorted. 'And the richer they have become, the tighter they hold onto their money.'

'All the more reason to keep the Morvens close,' Vianor pointed out. 'Their pockets are deep.'

Sedaine spared Vianor a suspicious glance. Her uncle was notoriously sparing with his praise, and this was not the first time he had commented favourably on her chancellor. Derias Morven, the youngest brother of the new Lord of Morven, was fifteen years her junior, good-humoured, clever, and undeniably beautiful. She suspected he was a little bit in love with her, but then Derias was a little bit in love with so many people it was hard to be sure. Certainly, he owed her everything he had—one of the highest offices in the land and an estate just outside Rhiannas. It was one of the reasons she had appointed him rather than his brother or some other great lord. He had no wealth and no land to protect that had not come from her hand. But his rewards had been earned, and he had served her well in the months and years since she had taken the throne.

'No,' she said abruptly. 'We are not discussing this, Vianor. Not again.'

The magician's face darkened with anger and frustration. 'You take thought for everything else but this! You too can die as easily as the rest of us. And if you do, who will take up the reins and keep fighting? If you will not take a husband, you must make clear the succession.'

Sedaine stood still, fists clenched and trying to control her breathing. It was an old argument between them. An old, tired argument that had become an obsession for a man who had schemed so long and so hard to put her where she was. He might have accepted that she would not marry and reproduce, but he would never forgive her.

This time, however, she had an answer for him. 'I have named Limina as my heir.'

Vianor's outrage was scorching. 'Your lover?'

'She's not my…' Sedaine stopped and pinched the bridge of her nose. 'She is an experienced ruler, and she will be a good queen.'

'She is a foreigner, from Farnor,' he hissed. 'Lothane would become nothing more than a vassal of the south.'

Sedaine smiled mirthlessly. 'Unless something momentous happens, there is no south to be a vassal of. What do you care about more, uncle? The future of Lothane, or that whatever is left of this nation, someone of your blood should rule it?'

'I care more about Lothane than you seem to! You have squandered every chance to give this nation an heir. Even Delgar –'

'Careful, uncle,' she warned. 'Delgar served his purpose and met the fate he deserved, as you intended—as you planned. You cannot now berate me for failing to marry him when you yourself warned me of the dangers of the match.' She took a deep breath. 'I know you cannot understand, but I have a son. I will have no other, even if I could.'

The son she had loved, then abandoned, only to find him again when she had thought him—hoped him—lost forever. The son who had left again of his own will to pursue his fate with her enemies and his following after. She had let him go because she had no choice, because she had forfeited her right to a stake in his future, but it had haunted her ever since—the not knowing. That he was out there somewhere in the world and she was unable to offer help or comfort. Even had the choice still been hers to make, she could never have endured the heartache another child would bring.

'Who will never rule here,' Vianor snarled, too angry to be careful. 'Even if he still lives.'

Sedaine met his rage with a calm that was entirely superficial. 'Who will never rule here. So I have named Limina my heir.' A raised hand cut off his protest. 'The documents have been drawn up and witnessed. It is already done. Unless you are planning to outlive me, I fail to see why you need to concern yourself with this further. The matter is closed.'

Her elderly seneschal was approaching. She dismissed Vianor and went to meet him.

The man stopped several paces from her, giving her a bow that was correct in every aspect. 'Highness.' He had served her father and her grandfather, and he refused to let her lack of ceremony relax his own.

Sedaine obliged him with the forms he was expecting and held out her hand to receive the messenger pouch he was carrying. She opened it as she walked, the old man scuttling along beside her.

'It just arrived, your highness. From Brannick. It is marked urgent.'

Brannick. She had not heard from him for months. She only knew vaguely where he was—somewhere along the Istelan. Ever since *that* day, when the world had changed and stayed the same, when the promise of something perfect had been dangled before them only to remain unfulfilled, Brannick had drifted away from her. Where Vianor had taken refuge in anger, unable to comprehend the enormity of what had happened, Brannick had retreated within himself, diminished. She understood. How could she not? They bore the scars of the same guilt, and had felt the same soaring, dizzying hope. The difference was that she had somewhere to focus her energies. She had a country to defend, an enemy to hate. For Brannick, who had only started to believe in Ecyas's dream after his death, all that remained after this partial fulfilment was *absence*.

Sedaine unrolled the message, recognising Brannick's crabbed hand. It was written in cipher, and she paused, taking a few moments to unravel the code. Then she read it again, painful hope spearing through her. She raised her head, the movement instinctive, the message unheeded in her hand.

The seneschal cleared his throat.

She looked at him. How long had she been standing there?

He tried again. 'Your highness?'

Sedaine tucked the message back in the pouch and resumed walking, thinking about what the message had said, and what it had not. The things Brannick would have written if he could. Hope receded but did not entirely die. She reached a decision.

'Send my apologies to the mercenaries' captain and tell him we must delay our meeting. Then I need you to send a message to Brannick.'

NINE

Kas'Tella, Caledan

WHEN JETA WOKE she was lying on a dirt floor in a dark room. Her head ached fiercely, and after the first attempt to sit up, which set the world to spinning and made her stomach revolt, she lay still. Memory returned in flashes. She remembered watching Kinseris and Betanas as they waited for Moralar to arrive. Escarian entering the room, Kinseris smiling as he turned to meet him… She was sick then, as her mind replayed over and over the look on Kinseris's face as Escarian had murdered him.

She was retching, gasping for breath and head pounding, as her stomach emptied itself. A door crashed open and someone ran into the room. Slim arms wrapped round her shoulders and braced her against the spasms. Furious, weeping, she tried to wrench herself free, and a voice said, 'Jeta, it's me. You're safe. You're safe.'

'Trad?' She pulled away, trying to focus on his face. It really was him. She sagged under a wave of relief so intense that she did not even wonder how he was here.

Trad smiled, brushing her filthy hair back from her face, frowning as his fingers touched the source of her pain. 'I'm sorry about your head. I didn't mean to trip you.'

'You! That was you?' Then she was hitting him, shouting incoherently as tears streamed down her face.

He fended off her blows, trying to calm her, but it took a long time for his words to penetrate her rage. And when they did, they brought understanding but little comfort.

They had gone to Frankesh, Trad and Kestel, chasing down the Order's missing priests, and they had discovered that their enemy was far, far ahead of them. 'We arrived back yesterday,' he told her. 'We heard rumours that Darred was preparing to move on Kas'Tella and we nearly broke our necks to get here in time.'

Except, of course, they hadn't. Aware that the conspiracy involved those close to Kinseris, rather than go directly to the citadel, they had gone instead to the First Army's camp where the Ancai had sought out Galydon's officers—those men whose loyalty to their old general and Kinseris might persuade them to take a hand in something in which the army traditionally took no part. And they had, just too late. When they arrived at the citadel, Escarian had already pulled all the high priest's personal guards from their stations. Trad had gone to find her, while the Ancai had led the officers to Kinseris's apartments. Where they had found what they had found. Which changed everything.

Too late to prevent the transfer of power, their hands now tied, the soldiers had returned to the camp. Which was where they were now, protected for a while by a loyalty that *should* have died with Kinseris.

So close. They had been so close. In time to save her, but not Kinseris. She couldn't hold back her tears as she looked at Trad. 'He's dead.'

Trad stood and offered a hand to help her to her feet. 'Not yet,' he said grimly. 'Not yet.'

Trad led her into another room. The Ancai stood just inside the door, so solid and reassuring a presence that she would have hugged him if he had not looked so grim. Behind him, as he moved to one side, she saw Kinseris. He lay on a cot in the corner. Someone—Kestel, she guessed—had stripped him of his bloodied robes and covered him in a thin blanket. He was not conscious, but she could see the faint rise and fall of his chest that told her he was alive. *Alive.*

The relief made her dizzy; she wobbled to her knees. Kinseris wasn't dead. She wasn't a prisoner. As the memories of Frankesh retreated, she felt the panic ebbing, replaced by a hollow fear deep in her belly.

She crawled across the floor to his side and reached out tentatively to touch his hand. There was no response. His face, half-turned from her, looked almost bloodless. If not for the faint pulse in his throat, she would have thought he was dead.

Exhausted, sick, she rested her forehead on the pallet. Her initial relief was fading under the onslaught of despair. She curled her fingers around Kinseris's cold hand and tried not to think about herself. About what this meant for her. To lose another… to have the new life she had built for herself ripped so cruelly away. To be once more alone in the world.

No! She shut down that line of thought. Kinseris was not even dead yet and she had already buried him. And while he lived, she still had a purpose. An enemy. She groped for anger to rescue her from grief and found it readily enough. Darred had done this. But Darred was far away. Her immediate enemy was closer to home. Escarian. Escarian was the traitor. 'Why? Why did he do it?'

Kestel looked up. He was sitting hunched up in the corner. For such a huge man, she had never seen him look so small. He knew at once who she meant. 'He had the spark, but the Kas'Talani would never have accepted him. He was bitter.'

'But why?' It made no sense. Kinseris was working to reform the Order, to break its stranglehold on the magic. Why kill the man who might have given him what he wanted? Maker, her head hurt.

'He felt he had been betrayed.' The Ancai's voice was dull and flat. Had she been feeling less terrible, the utter absence of emotion would have worried her. 'He fought for years to bring the Order down. And then, just as that goal was in sight, Kinseris took away the very power in which he had hoped to share.'

And Darred, of course, would have known just the lever to use on a man like that. But how… She sat up, cursing as the movement made the pounding in her head worse. 'How do you know?'

There was a flash of something very dark in Kestel's eyes. 'He told me.'

'He told you? When?'

He met her sharp gaze. 'After I asked him and before I killed him.'

Jeta looked from the huge, strong hands resting on the Ancai's knees to his blank eyes and decided she did not want to know any more. 'Good. He deserved to die.'

The Ancai did not answer. Trad had disappeared, where and to do what she did not know or care. Later, she would. Later, they would have to gather their shattered wits and make plans. Later she would have to think of the future. But not now, not yet.

Her mind kept flashing back to the moment Escarian had struck. To Kinseris's face as his protector had become his killer. And before that, as Escarian had whispered in his ear. The shock. And something more.

'What did he say to you?' she murmured, her hand on his cold one.

Escarian, whom they had trusted without question. The one person, other than her, who could pass freely through all the wards in the citadel, the one person who could get close enough to Kinseris while armed. And whom no magical defences would detect. Because Escarian had told them the attack would come from Moralar, they had never even considered physical violence. Because they had trusted him, they had let him lead them one way and then another, never seeing what was right in front of them.

One of them you consider a friend.

They had been so blind.

Lost in misery, Jeta found her thoughts spiralling down tracks she usually refused to tread. To Aarin. To *before*. And where always there had been a searing pain, of loss and rejection, now she felt a stirring anger. Because this was his fault. Because he had been so fixated on his goal he had never considered the consequences, for her or anyone else. For Aarin, finding the dragons had been the only thing that mattered, and even his love for her had not made him hesitate, even for a second, in his pursuit of that goal.

Except, of course, he had hesitated. She thought back to her frustration and hurt at the way he had kept her at arm's length, at how he had refused to admit his feelings. She understood a bit better now the reasons for that hesitation. Because he had always known what he would do if he could, and he had never pretended otherwise.

She knew also he'd had little choice. She would never forget those final days. The intense heat of his skin, the fire that seemed to be burning him away from the inside out, wearing him down until at times it seemed he wasn't really with them anymore. The convert concern of the others, even Kallis, who had held onto his anger over Iarwin longer than he should have as a shield against what was coming. And then how the magic had taken him, at the end, as though welcoming him home. Before *they* had come, and nearly destroyed everything.

She had thought afterwards that they had won. Even through her own pain, the price she had paid, she had thought it a victory. But sitting here in the dark, one hand resting lightly on Kinseris's chest so she could reassure herself he still breathed, she knew the price was much higher than she had realised. And it was being paid by the survivors, all of them. Kinseris, desperately hurt, fighting for his life. Shrogar in Ephenor, still grieving his brother and all his people who had died because Aarin had come to them. Kallis in Amadorn— if he was still alive. Amadorn itself, ravaged by Darred's invasion.

She knew it wasn't fair, but, *Maker*, she hated him then. She hated him for abandoning them, for making them vulnerable when they needed so badly to be strong. For not being here when they needed him.

Oh, Aarin.

A tear splashed onto her knees, and she realised the Ancai was watching her. She turned her face away. She could not bear his scrutiny or his despair. Later. Not now. Without even noticing, she fell asleep.

An army physician had been and gone while she slept. He had left her a salve for her bruises. Kinseris still had not awakened. She felt the urgency of time passing throbbing in sympathetic beat with the ache in her head.

She looked over at the Ancai, sitting silently in the corner. 'They will search the camp.'

He turned his attention on her with a visible effort. 'Yes.'

'When they do, they will find us.' She wanted to shake him. 'How hard can it be to find a fugitive in an army camp?'

'Harder than you might think,' the Ancai said, 'if the army chooses not to cooperate.'

'They will hide him, but they won't fight for him?' Jeta asked in disbelief. 'Why won't they fight for him?'

He did not answer. She felt cold. 'Because they think he's dying?' She looked away, blinking back tears. 'And if he's dying, why should anyone else die for him, is that right? Doesn't it matter that he was betrayed, that they tried to *assassinate* him?'

He endured her anger in silence. Then, after a while, asked, 'Do you know how many high priests have died of old age?'

She shook her head, scrubbing the tears from her face.

'I don't either. Too few to be worth remembering. If there was civil war every time the office changed hands by murder, the Kas'Talani would have destroyed themselves centuries ago.'

'But this is different. *He* is different.'

The Ancai shrugged. 'To you, maybe. To the people, if only they knew it. But to everyone here within the shadow of Kas'Talani influence, he is just one more ruler who could not hold onto his power.'

'They brought him to that power,' she retorted, furious. 'They chose to put him where he was. Doesn't that mean anything?'

'And they will hide him now he is fallen from it. Be grateful,' the Ancai said harshly, 'for small mercies.'

She looked away. It was the truth. The army had always been the lynchpin. Standing behind Kinseris, they had forced the surrender of Kas'Tella to him, formality though it had been, and it was the army that had backed up his demand that the priesthood relinquish the dragon devices. But Galydon had been here then, and the abuses of Vasa and the horrors of Ephenor fresh in their memories. Without the charismatic general to show them how to navigate the line between loyalty and honour, the most powerful military force in two continents was simply going to sit on its hands. If they were lucky.

'Someone will give us up.'

'Eventually, yes.'

Jeta bit back an angry retort. It was not just the army that thought Kinseris was dying, she realised abruptly. His captain, his *friend*, wasn't refusing to act.

He was doing nothing because he didn't know what to do. All his life Kestel had served Kinseris, supporting him, protecting him, their lives so entwined that Kinseris's aims and ambitions must have become Kestel's own. If Kinseris died now, everything he had hoped to achieve still unfulfilled, where would that leave the man who had given up his own life to serve him?

The Ancai was not simply grieving, he was paralysed. Unless she could snap him out of it, this temporary reprieve would turn out to be exactly that. And she was not going to die here. She was *not*.

She was awake the next time the doctor came. He examined the bruise on her temple and asked briskly about dizziness. She was careful not to shake her head. Then he tended to Kinseris, carefully changing the stained bandage for a clean one. Through all the handling, Kinseris stayed frightening still.

Jeta brushed a strand of hair from his face, wishing for some sign, anything, to tell her he was fighting. 'Why doesn't he wake?'

The doctor finished tying the new bandage and sat back. 'Because the drug I have given him is keeping him asleep.'

Startled, she looked from him to the Ancai. 'You're keeping him unconscious? Why?'

The doctor did not bother looking at her. 'Because awake he would be in terrible pain. This way he does not need to suffer.'

'While he dies?' Jeta demanded, rigid with anger. 'Are you so convinced he will die that you won't even give him a chance to live?'

'Jeta.' It was Kestel. His tone was very gentle. 'A wound like this… it kills men.'

She glared at him, tears streaming down her face. 'He deserves to know what is happening, to decide his own fate. This isn't a kindness.'

The Ancai shook his head. 'I have seen men die from such wounds. I have seen their agony. You don't know what you are asking.'

'No,' she hissed. '*You* don't. You've given up on him, but I haven't.' She turned to the doctor who was carefully packing away his things. 'Can you say for certain that he will die, or is it possible he will live?'

'Yes, it's possible.' Finishing his packing, he stopped to look at her at last.

'If the blade was clean, if it didn't hit anything vital—unlikely, but I have seen it happen—if he can survive the blood loss, if there is no infection. He's still alive, so yes, it is possible. But if he does survive, he will likely be in pain for the rest of his life. And the rest of his life might not be very long.'

But she had stopped listening. She turned to the Ancai. 'He might live, Kestel. He *might*. And even if he doesn't, this isn't just about him. We have to think. We have to decide what to do next. We can't just sit here, waiting. You must let him wake, please.'

Kestel looked away, but not before she saw the conflict on his face.

'You've assumed he will die. You have not even considered the possibility that he might survive—that changes everything. If Darred regains Kas'Tella, he controls the Order on two continents. What happens to Amadorn then? To your people and mine who are fighting there? You know Kinseris better than anyone and you know how much –'

'Kas'Tella is lost,' the Ancai broke in. 'Don't tell me Kinseris would want us to start a war to retake it!'

Good. He was angry. Anything was an improvement over paralysing despair. 'I'm not suggesting that. But he would want to keep fighting. And he would want us to keep fighting if he could not.' She took a deep breath, tears threatening again. 'He would not want this, Kestel, you know that. Please give him a choice.'

She saw her words hit home, saw him turn in query to the physician, who shrugged as if he did not care one way or another. 'If you want him to live, stillness and freedom from pain are what he needs most. That is what I am giving him.'

'I know that,' she said quietly. 'But you are taking everything else.'

TEN

IN THE END she got her way, but not for another day. Another day in which it seemed to her that they existed within a bubble of time quite divorced from the rest of the world. Confined within the walls of the hut, she had no idea what was happening outside. Alone with the Ancai, she was the only one who seemed to care.

She had argued that Kinseris had a right to decide his own fate. And Kestel, whose loyalty was deeply ingrained, had reluctantly agreed. The saturnine little physician had acquiesced, but he had advised them to wait a day. *The more time you give him, the better his chances.* And she had agreed. What else could she do?

Trad appeared at intervals, speaking quietly to Kestel and checking on Kinseris. The first time he returned he handed her a pile of neatly folded garments and told her to change. Jeta inspected the smartly tailored uniform doubtfully, imagining trying to squeeze her curves into garments made for much narrower hips. But she was grateful for clean clothes. The hut was stifling and her Caledani silks were filthy with dirt and sweat.

The army's physician returned the next morning. She tried to look away as he removed the old bandage and uncovered the ugly wound, but he made her watch, showing her what she would need to do if he could not come again. Struggling with nausea, she did not ask why he might not be able to come again. But when she asked him why he had not stitched the puncture closed, he had rounded on her with a vehemence that shocked her.

'If you want him to live, you leave that wound alone! I have been putting soldiers back together for thirty years, and I know a thing or two about it. If that blade had severed any major blood vessels, he would have died on the floor of his sanctum. If it had cut anything else vital, he would already be dead. It is a miracle he has survived this long. Keeping that wound clean and open is the only chance he has. I have seen men die of infection from a cut on their finger. If I start fiddling around in there, it *will* kill him.'

She nodded mutely and waited as he finished his work and left. But she thought perhaps he was not quite as uncaring as he pretended.

Then she sat down to wait. The doctor had been unable to say how long it would be before the drug wore off. 'He may not wake at all,' he had warned her. 'You must be prepared for that.' And all through the interminable hours of that long morning she worried that he would not wake, and then that he would. She knew the risk she was taking with his life. She had argued he had a right to decide his own fate, and he did. But that was not the only reason. Nor was it the instinct screaming at her that they could not stay here, doing nothing, waiting to be discovered.

They needed what he knew. They needed his knowledge—of Darred, of the Kas'Talani, of decades of political manoeuvring. And she needed to know what Escarian had said to him. Kas'Tella might be lost, but they were still alive and so was Darred. And, Maker forgive her, she needed every advantage she could get against that one.

She looked at the Ancai, hovering in the corner. He was another whose knowledge she needed. 'Why did you go to Frankesh?' she asked him now. They had received his message weeks ago, but of necessity it had said nothing of his reasons, only his destination. From his lack of surprise at the time, she thought Kinseris had known, or at least guessed.

Would you have me share my fears?

The Ancai tore his gaze from Kinseris with an effort. 'Because I thought Darred might be using the port to smuggle priests to Amadorn.'

'And is he?'

He nodded. 'Kinseris sent us to enforce his edict among those priests most distant from Kas'Tella. Many were dead already. Their deaths persuaded others that it was safer to comply. Others we could not find.'

'And they have gone over to Darred, to Amadorn?'

'Some, yes. The new Vela'Frankesh, certainly.'

The Vela'Frankesh. Once that had been Kinseris, and this man had been his captain. Together they had worked against Kas'Tella for years, protected by distance from the scrutiny of their superiors. It was why Kinseris had chosen his replacement with such care. Not quite enough, it appeared.

She told the Ancai about Moralar, and what he had revealed of Darred's ability to retain the dragon device.

'It is true,' he confirmed. 'In Frankesh we encountered at least one former priest in possession of the device. It was from him we heard the rumours that Darred might be moving against Kinseris.' He paused, his gaze flickering to the still form on the stretcher. 'We immediately despatched a messenger with a warning while we tried to find out more.'

She stared, eyes wide. 'We never received a warning.'

He looked back at her. 'You wouldn't have. We sent it to Escarian.'

Oh, Maker! No wonder he was falling apart. But they had all trusted Escarian. They had all made the same mistake. She started to tell him as much when a sound from the cot drew their attention to Kinseris. His eyes were still closed but his face was no longer still, a frown creasing his forehead. His lids fluttered open and she smiled into his eyes. But it was an instant only, then they closed again. She took his hand, wanting to give him the reassurance of touch, when there was a rush of movement outside the hut, the sound of raised voices and footsteps. She froze, her eyes locking with the Ancai's. She wanted to scream. *Not now!* To bring Kinseris to consciousness just as his enemies found him was too cruel.

The Ancai uncoiled, reaching the door just as Trad ducked inside. He was breathing hard, his hand on his sword. 'We need to move him, *now*.' He stood aside as two soldiers filed in after him and took up position at either end of the cot.

Jeta squeezed Kinseris's hand. 'What's happening?'

Trad nodded to the soldiers, then took her arm and pulled her away. 'They're searching the camp.' He looked over her head at the Ancai. 'They know he's here.'

She did not hear the Ancai's reply as the soldiers lifted the cot and Kinseris cried out. 'You're hurting him!' she snapped, frightened and furious.

'Jeta.' Trad pulled her to face him, hands on her shoulders. 'We don't have time to be careful. I need you to do what I say and not ask questions. Can you do that?'

She nodded, swallowing panic. He gave her an apologetic smile and reached down to smear mud from the dirt floor over her face and hair. He took off his cap and pulled it down over her head, tucking the dirty coil of her hair underneath, then he gave her a gentle push and she followed the soldiers as they carried their burden from the hut. Not through the door Trad had used, but back through the room where she had woken and out the rear of the hut, where she found herself standing in the shadows between a row of identical buildings. Supply depots, she guessed.

The Ancai was already outside, talking to a tall officer who looked vaguely familiar. One of Galydon's captains, though she could not remember his name. He gave her an abstracted nod, his eyes flicking over Kinseris's half-conscious form before returning to the Ancai. 'It's not safe to try to leave the camp. They are watching the perimeter. We will do our best to slow the search, but you will need to keep moving.' He winced as Kinseris moaned. 'Can you keep him quiet?'

The Ancai nodded. 'Where are they now?'

'They have searchers moving in from each corner. They will try to trap you between them.' He made a beckoning motion and five more soldiers stepped into view. 'These are my best men. They have volunteered to do what is needed.' He took a deep breath. 'If you find yourselves with no other option, make for the command pavilion. It has already been searched.'

The Ancai raised an eyebrow. 'If they don't find him in the camp, they will search it again.'

The officer looked bleak. 'I know.'

There was a pause as the Ancai and the captain locked gazes. Jeta held her breath. Trad shifted nervously behind her, anxious to be moving. Finally, the Ancai shook his head. 'He would not want it.'

The captain let out a breath and looked away. Jeta sensed his profound relief. But a beat later, he said fiercely, 'He has a right to ask.'

Jeta felt a rush of exhausted gratitude. Perhaps the army was not so unwilling to fight after all. But she caught the Ancai's warning glance and knew he was right, no matter how much she wished otherwise. If they sought the formal protection of the army now, it would unleash a bloodbath. There must be as many factions within the military as there were in the Order. If she forced them to take sides, here, now, it was possible none of them would survive it. She looked into the captain's pale, determined face and knew he would give her that protection if she asked and that doing so would almost certainly kill him.

She put her hand on his arm. She had him now—Captain Fylian. 'He would not ask it, Captain.' She gave him a moment to compose himself, then said gently, as much for her own wavering resolve as for his, 'You need to go now.'

He swallowed and nodded. 'I understand. Good luck. We will do our best.' Then he turned on his heel and walked away.

Trad rapped out an order and the soldiers melted away as silently as they had appeared, to keep watch and give warning. The Ancai followed, only to return a minute later and confer briefly with Trad before gesturing for them to follow, decisive once more. Jeta walked beside the cot, one hand resting on Kinseris's chest, Trad hovering on her other side. Kinseris was drifting in and out of consciousness, coming closer to waking, and she could see the lines of pain deepen on his face. She bit her lip. Stillness and freedom from pain, the doctor had said. They had taken that from him now.

'Where are we going?' she whispered to Trad. Even in the tension of the moment she had grasped the tactical problem—with searchers closing in from all sides, they would be forced to retreat deeper and deeper into the camp, until there was nowhere else to go. And then, what? With Kinseris unable to walk, they made a conspicuous group moving around the camp. They could not fight their way out. They could hide, but for how long?

Trad frowned, his eyes on the Ancai's back, and she knew the decision making had passed firmly back into Kestel's hands. She had never quite grasped the intricacies of rank where these two were concerned. As Kinseris's personal guards, they held no military rank. She was not sure if they held any rank at all. She thought of Kestel as the Ancai still, though he had left that role behind when they had fled Frankesh two years ago. Yet she had the unmistakable impression that, in some subtle way, even Trad outranked all but the most senior officers here—while Kinseris lived, anyway. There was no doubt, however, of where the authority lay between the two of them, even if it was only in moments like this that it became apparent.

'We cannot avoid the searchers forever, and we cannot risk leaving the camp,' he said at last. 'But if we want them to stop looking for Kinseris here, we must convince them he is out *there*.'

'How do we do that?' But before she had even finished speaking, she knew. Her mind returned inexorably to their escape from Darred in Frankesh. To the man and woman who had died in their place. *Decoys.*

Trad nodded, not quite meeting her eyes. 'They have volunteered.'

Ah, so that was what Tylian had meant. Once, she might have protested. But she had been prepared—*almost!*—to throw them all on the army's mercy and start a civil war that would have killed thousands. She could hardly object to this. The expedience had appalled her then, now it was merely the lesser evil.

But if the decoys could leave, why couldn't they? 'Why stayed trapped in here? Surely we should leave if we can?'

Trad shook his head, glancing at Kinseris as he stirred restlessly on the makeshift stretcher. 'There's no guarantee we would make it through the cordon, and even if we did, where would we go? He is too weak to travel and carrying him we could never stay ahead of a pursuit.'

'We could hide in the city.' Kas'Tella was huge and sprawling, far bigger than the camp. 'It would take much longer to search.'

'But they would search, and we would have to keep moving, always looking over our shoulders. Besides, who could we ask to hide us? Most of those loyal to Kinseris were murdered by Vasa and the Arkni. The rest have no reason to risk their lives for him and every reason to give him up. We are at much greater risk of betrayal out there than we are in here. How would we know who to trust?'

Who indeed? Escarian's name hung unspoken between them. Escarian who, by his own admission, had turned traitor because the outcome he had fought for his whole life had failed to match up to his personal ambitions. How many others might feel the same, for similar or different reasons? *Oh, Kinseris. You have fought so long and so hard to help these people, and this is how they repay you?*

The Ancai held up a hand and they stopped. As Jeta crouched beside Kinseris, she saw his eyes were open and watching her. She put a finger on his lips as the Ancai hunkered down beside them. They had not gone far, sticking close to the rows of supply huts with their shadowed corridors between buildings, but they must be closer to the heart of the camp now, because she could see soldiers moving to and from a brick building further down the line, and beyond them neat row after neat row of canvas tents.

And moving between those rows, some way away but getting closer, were parties of searchers. Even at this distance she could pick out the midnight robes of the priests accompanying the guards searching the tents.

She glanced back at Kinseris. His eyes were closed again. When she looked up, Kestel was watching her. 'What now?'

He pointed to the building as a small group emerged and separated. Two men, one leaning heavily on the other, limped slowly away from them, heading north. A minute later, the remaining figures resolved into two men carrying a third between them on a stretcher. They set off at a fast walk in the other direction, cutting across the lines of tents. Soldiers nudged each other as they passed. A man called out. She tensed. They couldn't be caught so soon!

A hand closed on her arm; she was shaking. Taking a deep breath, stilling the panic, she met the Ancai's questioning look and gave him a sharp nod. He held her gaze a moment longer then, satisfied, gestured for the small party to follow him.

Keeping to the shadows, they made their way to the last but one hut in the little row and filed quickly inside. Piled up crates filled most of the cramped space. There was barely room for the stretcher on the patch of bare earth by the entrance. A tiny, smeared window did little more than reveal the gloom. Kestel crouched beside it with Trad. The two soldiers positioned themselves by the door to keep watch. Jeta sat by Kinseris, trying not to think about what would happen if the searchers came upon them here. Trying not to think at all.

'Jeta.'

She looked up to see Trad beckoning her and climbed to her feet. Kestel moved to one side as she joined them. It took her a moment to register what she was seeing. Outside, the ordered search was starting to unravel as the confusion caused by the decoys and their enthusiastic spotters eroded the discipline of the priests' guards. More importantly, they were heading away from their present hiding place and towards the outer camp.

'You wanted them to be seen.'

'They wouldn't be much use to us if they weren't.'

The relief was fleeting, their discovery delayed not averted. 'And us?'

Kestel pointed to the brick building. 'That's the camp's infirmary. It will have been the first place they looked. We will hide him there.'

It had been his plan all along. Where better to hide a sick man than with other sick men? Except this man's face was too well known to be missed. 'When they realise they've been tricked, won't they search again?'

'They might. That's why we must make sure no one will recognise him.'

'But how?' Then she realised what he meant. 'He can't.'

'He has to.'

She looked at Kinseris. His eyes were closed but his face lacked the stillness of drugged sleep. Beneath his lids, his eyes were moving, and lines of tension and pain were etched around his mouth. He would wake soon, but would he be able to do what was needed? And even if he did, surely his colleagues would know?

'There is another way,' the Ancai replied when she pointed this out. 'A trick Aarin showed him Ephenor.'

And then she remembered. How they had cast a web of illusion over Ephenor, repairing damage to its walls, concealing soldiers in some places, bolstering their numbers in others, and hiding the magic from the Kas'Talani and the Arkni by anchoring it with their own lives.

It is little enough, Aarin had told her. *But there is little enough we can do that they cannot use against us.*

84

And she remembered all too vividly how they had used Kinseris's protective spells against those they protected. She remembered Aarin coming to her in that room of blood and bone, how he had soothed her horror and taken her from the slaughter. And how, later, he had taken it from her...

She clamped down hard on that train of thought and looked instead at Kinseris. He had been healthy then. Could he now, holding onto life by such a fragile thread, strain that thread still further?

A heartbeat later it ceased to matter.

ELEVEN

AS JETA CROUCHED by the grimy window, a voice, magically enhanced to carry across the camp, called out, 'Soldiers of the First Army. You have hiding in your camp a traitor not just to the Order, but to you, its loyal servants. A man who has plotted against his own people for years, and who planned to destroy this great empire you are sworn to protect. Your commanders betrayed you when they brought him here, and they betray you now by making you complicit in his treachery. Do not let them! The men who bring this traitor to us will be rewarded with rank and privilege.'

Jeta turned to the Ancai in dismay as the voice repeated the message in Renallan and was shocked to see he was smiling. Beside him, Trad was doubled over in silent laughter.

'What?' she hissed.

Kestel shook his head. 'They've given the army permission to mutiny.'

Her eyes narrowed. 'They offered a reward for giving him up!'

'Have they? Most of these soldiers don't want an officer's rank and responsibilities. They want a warm bed, food to eat, and money in their pockets, preferably in return for doing as little fighting as possible.'

But something was happening. As the words echoed through the camp, the message repeated over and over, all around them soldiers started to move. With a growing sense of despair, Jeta watched as they coalesced into small groups and started to spread out. Searching. She looked away, eyes burning, and reached out blindly to curl her fingers around Kinseris's slack hand. 'You're wrong, they're going to find us.'

'They might, if they were looking,' the Ancai replied. 'Look again.'

She turned back to the small window. Outside, the camp had started to resemble a battlefield after a battle. The soldiers who had been standing patiently outside their tents now threw themselves into playacting. They were not searching, she realised, they were joining the decoys. Men carried their fellows, writhing and groaning, in one direction after another. Others supported those limping painfully—but with remarkable speed—as they threaded their way through the neat tents towards the edges of the camp. Still more chased after them, calling out to the priests and their guards, who were quickly besieged by clamouring soldiers.

The swell of unexpected emotion brought tears to her eyes. It was ridiculous and it was wonderful. It could not possibly fool anyone, but it could and would provide the distraction they needed. The Ancai appeared to come to the same conclusion as he exchanged a look with Trad, then crouched down next to the two soldiers and exchanged hurried whispers. They stood and headed to the door and Trad and the Ancai took their places at either ends of the stretcher.

At her questioning look, Trad said, 'We're not going to get a better chance than this. If we're going to leave, we must go now.'

'I thought you said we couldn't –'

'Plans change. Come.'

He plucked at her sleeve, pulling her to her feet. He took one end of the cot as the Ancai picked up the other, sweeping her up in their sudden, hopeful urgency.

But they had gone no more than a dozen yards before voices sounded nearby. Too close. Kestel backed up, the movement catching Trad by surprise. He stumbled, almost dropping the stretcher. Then they were running the few yards to the infirmary and the cover of its shadowed outbuildings. Seconds later, a group of guards in palace livery rounded the end of the nearest row of tents.

'Jeta…?' Kinseris, jostled by the rough movement, came fully awake. Confused, he struggled to sit, the unexpected motion upsetting the stretcher. It tipped and he slid to the ground, caught by the Ancai who ruthlessly smothered his cry as Jeta dropped to her knees by his side. Her eyes met Kestel's in horrified silence, waiting for the shout that would herald their discovery. When the seconds passed and it did not come, she closed her eyes, dizzy with relief.

Then Kestel cursed and she saw the bright blood covering his hands. Her eyes flew to Kinseris, pale and gasping, blood beginning to pool around him from the reopened wound. His own eyes were open and fixed on hers, dulled by pain but cruelly aware for the first time since his wounding.

She felt the desolation of utter despair grip her by the throat. They had been so close! She snatched the dropped blanket from the ground and pressed futilely against his side. There was so much blood. He jerked and went rigid under her hands and tore his head free of the Ancai's restraining hand.

'Jeta... leave...'

'No!' She pressed down harder, tears streaming down her face.

A door opened and a resigned voice said, 'Bring him in here.'

She looked up into the face of the little army physician, standing in the shadow of a door she had not noticed. The Ancai reacted first, gathering Kinseris into his arms and lurching to his feet. Jeta and Trad scrambled to follow. The doctor stood aside as they stumbled past him into the temporary sanctuary of the camp's infirmary. Rows of bunks lined one wall, a few occupied by soldiers who ignored their entrance with studied disinterest.

Overwhelmed by the abrupt reprieve, Jeta followed limply as the Ancai carried Kinseris to an empty bunk and laid him down. He was immediately displaced by the doctor who muttered under his breath as he peeled back the wadded blanket. Fresh blood started leaking from the wound.

He thrust the stained cloth into Trad's arms. 'Get rid of this and bring me some clean towels.' Then he looked up at Kestel. 'They have searched here twice already. They will come back.'

Trad returned with a bundle of cloth. The doctor took it, his attention still fixed on the Ancai. 'You need to decide, and quickly.' Then he turned at last to Kinseris, wadding the clean towels to slow the blood flow.

Kestel knelt by Kinseris's head. Kinseris's pain-rinsed eyes followed him sluggishly, but Jeta knew he had grasped enough of their situation when he clumsily reached for his friend and whispered, 'Go.'

The Ancai's eyes closed for a moment, then he covered Kinseris's hand with his own. 'I will, my lord. But first I need you to do something for me. Your enemies are searching for you. There is nowhere for us to hide you, so I need you to hide yourself. I need you to change your face, and I need you to do it so no one can tell.'

Kinseris's head rolled to the side, searching for her. She brushed past the doctor to kneel beside the Ancai. 'Jeta… can't hide… you.'

She started to tell him it didn't matter but the Ancai cut her off. 'You don't have to. It's just you. I know you can.' It was almost a plea.

'If he's going to do anything, it needs to be soon,' the doctor said. 'He's not going to be conscious much longer.'

Jeta tore her eyes from Kinseris's face to the spreading stain. 'Why aren't you *doing* anything?'

'I am doing something,' he retorted. 'But you have more immediate problems.'

He nodded towards the window as Trad hurried towards them. 'They're coming back. We've only got a few minutes.'

The Ancai gripped Kinseris's hand. 'Now, Kinseris, please.'

And as Jeta watched, Kinseris's face seemed to ripple, his features fading in and out, until they settled into a new form, one that was uncomfortably familiar. She cursed silently, measuring the despair that would have led him to choose *that* face. His eyes closed. The doctor reached for his wrist, then peeled back an eyelid. 'He's out—will it hold?'

Kestel straightened. He too was frowning at the likeness Kinseris now wore. 'I think so. I saw him hold such illusions for days in Ephenor, even in sleep.' He crossed to the window, one hand on Trad's shoulder. 'We cannot stay, we are too well known. Jeta –'

'I'm staying.'

To her surprise, he didn't argue. There wasn't time. Instead, he looked over at the doctor. 'Can you hide her?'

'Do I have a choice?' the doctor snapped, then waved them away. 'Go! You put us all in danger.'

The Ancai nodded. 'We'll come back as soon as it is safe,' he promised.

Then he and Trad were running through the infirmary and she was alone with the doctor.

He held out her hat. She hadn't even noticed it had fallen off. 'Cover your hair.' Then he turned to the soldier sitting on the nearest bunk. 'Storeroom, both of you. Now. Keep her out of sight. I don't care how.'

The soldier unfolded from the bunk with a notable lack of urgency and the look he gave Jeta came very close to a leer. Dark hair flopped over a face that would have been entirely forgettable if not for the scar on one cheek that pulled his mouth into a permanent sneer. It was not a face that inspired confidence, but she had no choice except to follow as he led her through the door into the network of tiny, windowless storerooms.

There was barely room for one person let alone two in what was little more than a series of adjoining cupboards. The soldier kept one hand on her wrist as he twisted between two shelves and through an opening into another room, the sliver of light from the infirmary door dwindling until she had to feel her way by touch. Behind her she could hear the dull thud of booted feet and the rising murmur of voices and expected at any moment for the door to open. But the darkness remained undisturbed, and she forced herself to breathe evenly. There was no way you could hide an injured man in this claustrophobic warren, as no doubt the searchers had already established, and it was Kinseris they were hunting. It did not make her safe, only safer.

A sharp tug on her wrist brought her to a halt. Eyes adjusting to the gloom, she saw they were standing uncomfortably close between two rows of shelves. He put a mocking finger to his lips. She pulled a face then forgot him, her whole attention focused on the sounds coming from the infirmary. She heard a harsh voice rapping out orders, but whoever it was spoke in Renallan, which she did not understand. There was movement in response, none of it urgent. The sound of something—a bunk?—dragged across the floor. More orders, and then another voice, quieter than the other. She heard the doctor's voice raised in protest, then go silent. Her heart raced.

She caught a flicker of movement and turned just as the soldier leant forward and snatched the hat from her head. Her golden curls spilled down her back, bright even in the dim light. She froze as their eyes locked, then the man tossed the cap away and spat at her feet.

Realising his intent, she threw herself to one side, but he was quicker, grabbing her arm and twisting it behind her so she had to stop struggling or risk breaking it. She stilled, crouched at his feet, her mind utterly blank. The flurry of footsteps in the infirmary receded.

Suddenly his face was very close to her ear. 'Up, bitch.'

She stood carefully, guided by his lock on her arm. There was a roaring in her ears that blocked out everything else. A sharp prick to her neck brought tears to her eyes. She felt faint.

Knife at her throat, the soldier nudged her forward. 'Move.'

She obeyed, threading her way back through the storerooms. Voices sounded from the infirmary and this time she recognised one of them. Then they were at the door and it was all about to end.

The knife disappeared as the soldier leaned past her to shove open the door. Then it was back, urging her forward.

As she stepped out into the infirmary, three men turned to stare. Furthest from her, Captain Fylian's face paled in dismay. On the doctor's, anger turned quickly to fear as the soldier stepped out after her.

And on the third face, that of the priest, there was nothing at all.

TWELVE

JETA'S EYES MET those of Betanas across the silent room and encountered not a flicker of recognition. She knew then that it was over.

A sharp shove, a flash of pain. She stumbled forward. The soldier let go of her arm and took a handful of hair, wrenching her chin up, knife held across her throat.

'Shall I kill the whore, my lord?'

Jeta saw the horror on the captain's face, the arrested movement of his hand to his sword. There was nothing he could do, and they both knew it. She felt strangely calm.

The doctor rounded jerkily on Betanas. 'Not in here!'

And Kinseris's counsellor said, without expression, 'By all means, let us not make a mess.'

He looked straight into her eyes then, and she saw *something*. Her captor's breath was hot on her cheek as he leaned close and said to Betanas, 'He is here. I can show you. But I want my reward.'

Betanas raised an eyebrow, his eyes never leaving her face. 'Of course. Captain, take the girl.'

Fylian took a step forward. The soldier lowered the knife, but his hand remained tangled in her hair and she felt the sudden spasm as he went rigid and began to choke. Wrenching herself free, she tripped and sprawled to her knees. When she looked up, her captor was clawing at his throat, knife hanging limp from one hand.

She turned to Betanas. 'What have you done?'

He watched her, head tilted to one side. 'Given him his reward.'

Then he reached out and took the knife from the soldier's hand. As the man's knees folded, his hands still grasping at his throat, Betanas placed a steadying grip on his arm, drew back his hand and plunged the knife into the soldier's belly. The man's eyes widened in shocked agony, blood spilling over the fingers he pressed to the wound. He choked and gasped as Betanas released the stranglehold on his airways, then toppled sideways to the ground, his life flowing out with the pumping blood.

Jeta stared at the contorted face in frozen horror. Beside her, the army's physician stared down at the body with a more clinical shock. Betanas merely stepped over the corpse as though it wasn't there. He nodded to Jeta as she looked shakily around for somewhere to sit. Behind Betanas, Fylian seemed in similar condition, torn between relief and indecision, his hand hovering on his sword hilt as he tried to make sense of what had just happened.

Betanas appeared oblivious to the tension, the dead man already dismissed. 'We don't have much time.' He nodded at the unconscious form laid out on the bunk. 'I assume this is him? How is he?'

The doctor looked up from the body at his feet, his face carefully blank. 'Better than this one, my lord. But only just.'

If Betanas noticed the accusation in that dry tone, he ignored it. 'Can he be moved?'

'Does it matter? It's only a short walk to the scaffold.'

Careful, oh, careful. Betanas's eerie calm was unnerving, and right now she would bet no one's life on whose side he was on, despite the man lying dead between them.

The old priest raised an eyebrow. There was a *ripple* and the dead soldier's features transformed into the likeness of Kinseris. Jeta gasped. Betanas's wintry eyes held hers for a moment before settling on the doctor. 'Can he be moved?'

The doctor shrugged. 'You can move him. I can't tell you whether he will survive it.' He nudged the corpse with his toe. 'Do you really expect this to fool your colleagues?

Betanas asked with chilling sarcasm, 'Why? Is the wound in the wrong place?'

The doctor's eyes narrowed and Jeta thought for a moment that his anger would get the better of him. 'No, my lord,' he grated at last. 'Your aim was excellent.'

'Then it's up to you. And you had better do a good job, because it is your life if they find out. Strip him. My colleagues won't be able to pierce the illusion with their eyes, but the feel of his uniform will give him away.'

Ignoring the doctor's towering fury, Betanas turned to Jeta. 'You can't stay in the camp any longer. The army has shown itself to be remarkably loyal, but there will be more like that one.' His glance skimmed the corpse as Fylian helped the doctor lift it onto an empty bunk and strip the dead man's clothes. 'You need to leave now, while my colleagues are unlikely to notice one more stretcher-borne body.'

As she groped for a reply, Jeta realised she was looking at a stranger. She had underestimated Betanas, as she had underestimated all of them. She had thought them bitter old men who resented the curtailment of their power. She had not realised the strength of their hunger for that power, and she should have. She had seen it in Aarin every day. And Betanas… Betanas she had not known at all.

'What about you?' she asked him now. 'When they find out what you have done, they will kill you. Come with us.'

But Betanas shook his head. 'If I leave now, this'—he gestured at the body, his lips curling in disgust—'will have been for nothing. It will take them time to discover the truth, time you need to get away from here.'

Jeta stared. She had not thought him capable of… *this*. 'Why?'

Betanas turned back. 'I am one hundred and seventy-six. I thought that life under Vasa had shown me the worst the Order could become. I thought Kinseris was an idealistic fool. I thought a lot of things I now realise were wrong. I am one hundred and seventy-six,' he said again. 'And in all those years I have done nothing I can look back on with pride.'

He hesitated, as though he might say more, then he turned and was gone.

Things moved swiftly after that. As Jeta sat on a stool, shivering in the aftermath of violence, a blanket round her shoulders, Fylian disappeared to fetch the Ancai and Trad. It was only after he had gone, as she watched the doctor scrub the blood from the floor, that she realized the infirmary was empty but for the two of them, Kinseris and his double. Betanas must have cleared the place deliberately, which told her he had known Kinseris was there. How much else had he known? They would never know now whether he had been complicit in the conspiracy to bring down his high priest, only that in the end he had saved him. She found she no longer cared.

Kestel came in, his assessing glance taking in every detail of the scene. He crouched before her so he could look her in the face. She managed a limp smile, which freed him to go to Kinseris.

Trad took his place. Less restrained, he hugged her. 'Are you all right?'

She nodded, her eyes on the Ancai. He was talking to the little physician whose usually taciturn countenance had given way to a rather pallid complexion. His hands were shaking too.

She turned back to Trad. 'We need to leave.'

'I know. We will. Kinseris…?'

She shrugged helplessly. She was beginning to realise just how precarious his condition was.

Light footsteps heralded Fylian's return. He paused in the doorway. 'We're ready.'

'We?' Jeta asked Trad.

He grinned. 'We have an unofficial escort.'

'Is that safe?'

It was Fylian who answered. 'If we go quickly. It's chaos out there.' He nodded at the doctor. 'You should come too.' Because whichever way events played out from here, he was guilty. It had happened in his infirmary.

The little man looked at them, his expression faintly appalled. 'Thank you, no.'

He handed a neatly packed bag to Kestel, who said, 'Are you sure?'

'Completely,' he replied firmly. 'Now, please leave.'

Jeta stood, handing him back the blanket. 'Thank you,' she said quietly, meaning it.

He nodded. 'Remember what I told you. Keep the wound clean and keep him still. After that, it's up to him.'

Then the Ancai and Fylian transferred Kinseris back onto a stretcher and they left. Jeta walked beside them as though in a dream. Fylian's escort seethed around them, a crowd of soldiers moving in all directions but never in their way. Like water flowing round a stone, the crowd parted for them at every step, surrounding them in a confusion of movement and the clamour of raised voices.

In that way they passed through the centre of the camp, past the command tent where the Kas'Talani were gathering, past Betanas at the head of a party of guards making their way back to the infirmary, past the disordered perimeter where their escort peeled away until they were alone in the empty streets outside the camp.

She cried then. Under the open sky and the cleansing heat of the Caledani sun, another life behind her. Another future stretching out before her. She did not know what it would hold, but she knew now where she was going. There was only one place to go.

Back home. Amadorn.

THIRTEEN

Lothane, Amadorn

THE ROYAL PALACE in Rhiannas was famous throughout the north.
Parts of it were older than Lothane itself, or so local legend claimed. It was
vast, sprawling across the centre of the city towards the rich, eastern suburbs.
Many of the older sections had been largely abandoned as a succession of
kings had rebuilt and expanded in their own styles. The southernmost section
had been converted into a barracks for the city garrison, and it had also
housed the mercenary troops Darred had hired in Nathas's name after King
Kaefal's death. Kallis remembered it as being damp and drafty for all its
decaying grandeur. So he wasn't prepared for the splendour of what was now
the main palace when the elderly steward led him through the courtyard,
surrounded by its elaborate porticos, and up the sweeping steps.

Inside, the corridors were laid with marble slabs and gold leaf covered the
intricate ceiling carvings. But as he looked around, the clip of his boots loud
in the echoing silence, he realised the place was empty. Not just of people
but of everything. The niches and plinths lining the corridors were bare, and
there were marks on the floor where things that had stood for decades had
been removed. And the bustle of courtiers and servants was almost entirely
absent, replaced by the silent presence of guards in royal livery at almost every
door.

The seneschal stopped outside a set of grand but ageing doors. He nodded
at the guards flanking them, who stood aside with a curious look at Kallis.
Then they were inside a small antechamber, surrounded by yet more guards
who stood beside another set of doors, slightly ajar. Through the sliver of an

opening, Kallis got the impression of a large room with a cluster of people at one end. He could hear the murmur of voices, rising and falling.

He turned to the seneschal and raised an eyebrow.

The elderly man cleared his throat. 'The queen asks you to observe the discussions. She said you would know when to announce yourself.'

Kallis's eyebrow climbed higher. 'And do what?'

The steward shrugged. 'I'm told you will know.'

'That's it? I'll just know?'

The steward cleared his throat again. 'Perhaps if you listen, you'll understand.'

Kallis glared at him, but he turned back to the doors. He was looking into what must be the great hall of the palace. A high vaulted ceiling, richly painted, enclosed a room bigger than any he had been in before. Like the rest of the palace, it had been stripped of everything of value. Discoloured walls showed where hangings had been hauled down or paintings removed. Sold, he guessed, to fund the coming war.

He shifted so he could see the occupants of the room, four of them seated around a table with Sedaine at its head. A woman sat on her left, a look of polite boredom on her face, giving Kallis the distinct impression of a discussion that had been going nowhere for some time. Wine stood untouched in the middle of the table, and a greying man sat alone at one end, the mercenary captain-of-captain's band on one arm. Kallis grinned as he recognised the defiance in the man's posture. He could guess what they were arguing about. The evidence of Sedaine's pecuniary hardship was all around them, but if she had asked him here because she thought he could persuade the clans to accept less than their due, she would be disappointed. They never, ever compromised on their fee.

His eyes drifted around the table. He recognised the old magician who sat on Sedaine's right and felt a flash of anger on his own account. Because of Vianor, he had killed the man who had been his captain and could, in time, have been his friend. He wondered how Vianor had wormed his way into Sedaine's favour, and if she knew just how poisonous his presence would be to any negotiation with the clans.

Irritated, Kallis was about to turn away when the mercenary captain pushed himself back from the table and stood. Fists on the table, he flung Sedaine's terms back in her face. Kallis froze, rocked by unexpected, painful recognition. His hand touched the sword at his waist as a voice he had not expected to hear again suddenly brought a lot of things into focus. He knew why he was here now. What he could not fathom was why, if Sedaine knew what she must know, Vianor was here too.

'And if not us, who will you fight for?' the magician demanded, standing in his turn, and Kallis winced as he saw Lorac's back stiffen. 'You think life will be better under the Kas'Talani? You're a fool.'

'Do not think that we care either way which of you wins this war,' Lorac growled. 'If you want the clans to fight for you, you must offer us terms we can accept. You cannot compel us.'

Kallis grinned. He could wait a lifetime and never be offered as good an opening as that. He strode into the room. 'But I can.'

All eyes turned to him. He saw Sedaine's widen in relief—and something else—then she too stood.

Lorac, controlling his shock, watched his approach narrowly. 'Kallis.'

Kallis nodded to him. 'Lorac. The Ravens have risen high, I see.'

The mercenary regarded him stonily, understanding his intent. 'You cannot command us, Kallis. You don't have the right.'

'Oh, but I do,' he replied, unbuckling his sword and tossing it on the table. He was conscious of Sedaine's eyes boring into him and hoped she would have the wisdom to stay silent. 'That sword says so.'

Lorac's expression hardened as he recognised his cousin's blade. 'You killed my captain, but I told you then what I tell you now—*we will not follow you.*'

Kallis gave him a feral grin. 'Yes, you will, because I can offer you something you want even more than gold.'

'And what would that be?'

Kallis's glance flickered to Vianor. 'Revenge.'

Lorac followed his gaze, anger replaced by confusion. Then he tensed, hand on his sword, suspecting a trap.

'Revenge,' Kallis repeated, and saw Sedaine's fingers brush against the magician's arm, telling him to hold. 'The man who engineered the slaughter at the Istelan. Is that not why you are here?'

Fury and suspicion flooded Lorac's face, and Kallis shook his head. 'No, my friend, it is not who you think.' He met Vianor's gaze. 'Is it, my lord?'

The magician's face was expressionless and for a moment Kallis thought he had missed his guess, then the old man gave him the barest of nods.

'Despite what you believe,' Vianor told the mercenary captain, 'my people were there in good faith. It was not by our design that we left the field.'

Lorac looked between them, unsure where to direct his anger. 'If not you, who?'

'It was Darred who ordered us to withdraw at the critical moment.'

Kallis watched the emotions play across his former oath brother's face. Lorac's knuckles were white as he gripped his sword. 'The same Darred who heads this invasion?'

'The very same,' Kallis replied, and something in his voice seemed finally to penetrate the other man's suspicion.

Lorac stepped back, running a hand through thinning hair, buying time. 'We still need a contract.'

Kallis held up a hand to silence a retort from Sedaine. This was a matter for the two of them. 'There are no more contracts. You're not a fool, Lorac. You never were. If you have any thoughts of securing a contract with the Caledani you have grossly misjudged them. Darred ensured the slaughter of the clans for this very moment. He needed to break your fighting strength because you were—*you are*—the biggest threat to his plans. Go to him now and he will finish the job. The only chance you have to secure the survival of your people is to join with us and fight him.'

'Us?'

The question was asked by a chorus of voices and Kallis enjoyed the moment. 'Why else do you think I am here?'

Visibly shaken, Lorac withdrew with no offer made or accepted. Vianor watched him go, his expression scornful. 'There goes our army.'

'He'll be back,' Kallis replied, allowing some of his own hostility to leak into his voice as he said, 'You cannot expect the clans to abandon their way of life overnight. Nor their hatred of you. I might have killed his captain, but he would be alive today if not for your interference. And let's not forget whose interests you were serving at the time. If the clans find an alliance with you abhorrent, you only have yourself to blame, *my lord*.'

Sedaine's voice cut across the rising tension. 'The Lord Vianor has earned my trust and his place by my side,' she told Kallis. 'As you have yet to do.'

'Pardon me, *your highness*,' Kallis retorted. 'I thought I just did that. Exactly how long have you been trying to persuade the clans to fight for you? And if you want to know why they would not, just look at your pet magician.'

'The clans have taken our gold before,' Vianor snapped as the woman beside Sedaine turned away to hide the twitching of her lips.

'But you're not offering them gold, are you? You're asking for an alliance. Have you truly no idea how *hated* you are?'

Sedaine held up a hand. 'Enough.'

Say what you would about Aarin's mother—and Kallis, in his time, had said plenty—there was no denying her authority here. As Vianor subsided, Sedaine fixed Kallis with a gaze that was frightening in its intensity and asked the question he had been both expecting and dreading—the more so since his encounter with Brannick and Needa. 'Is Aarin with you?'

Kallis sighed, reaching for his sword belt. 'No.'

Sedaine took a pace towards him, vibrating with tension. 'Where is my son, Kallis?'

He understood her need for answers, but he had none to offer. He still wasn't sure he trusted what he had seen that day amid the ruins of the mountain. 'Honestly, I have no idea.'

'Is he alive?'

'He was alive when I last saw him. As was his dragon.'

Sedaine turned her face away, but not before he had seen the wetness in her eyes and heard the hitched intake of breath.

Vianor's face turned to stone but his old eyes burned. 'His dragon? He found them?'

'Oh, he found them,' Kallis agreed. There were some things about that day he would never forget. Aarin sitting astride the great silver dragon. The sky above ripped apart and swarming with dark wings. The Arkni shedding their human forms and becoming something *other*. The explosion that had collapsed part of the mountain in on itself.

'Where are they?' It was the woman who asked. The woman whose fingers had curled around Sedaine's.

Kallis registered the oddity as he met her clear gaze. 'I told you, I have no idea. All I know is that he's gone, and his dragon with him.'

'Is he coming back?'

Kallis hesitated. Then he shook his head. 'I don't think so.'

There was no mistaking Sedaine's reaction this time, and she leaned into the other woman's touch. For her part, the woman gripped Sedaine's hand even tighter and said fiercely, 'So, we are on our own.'

Irritated and tired, Kallis studied her. Soft and round next to Sedaine's lean restlessness, her pleasant face was neither old nor young and her wispy, mousy hair was threaded with what Kallis had assumed to be beads, but now saw were tiny shells.

'We, my lady?'

She acknowledged that with a faint smile and Sedaine returned from wherever she had been to say briefly, 'This is Limina, Queen of Farnor.'

The woman smiled. 'Queen of not very much, but Sedaine is kind to pretend.'

Sedaine. No honorific. Equals. Friends. Kallis snorted. He could not imagine Aarin's mother being friends with anyone. Let alone… 'Farnor?' It had been so long since he had thought of the politics of Amadorn that he had not immediately made the connection. 'The Petticoat Revolution?'

Her smile was sharp-edged. 'An unfortunate name that has unfortunately stuck. Some old men died. I appointed some women in their place. Hardly a revolution. There were no petticoats and very little embroidery—unless you count embroidered facts. Not that it matters now. Farnor is lost.'

'Rumour has it Farnor doesn't think so,' Kallis replied, sketching the few details they had heard on their journey west.

A spasm of something indefinable crossed Limina's face, but she said only, 'My countrymen are stubborn, but not, I fear, very realistic.'

Kallis shrugged, letting it go, and instead addressed her original question. He turned to Sedaine. 'Will you accept help if it comes from Caledan?'

She had regained her composure, although her eyes were still too bright. 'From Caledan? Or from the Kas'Talani?'

Vianor hissed at the name. Sedaine ignored him.

'Both, in a way. Darred does not control the Kas'Talani in Caledan. The man who does has his own problems, but he has sent what help he can. You need it.'

She frowned but didn't disagree. 'This help, where is it?'

'Outside the city. I didn't want to risk your soldiers slaughtering them on sight.'

'Them?'

Kallis grinned. 'You'll see.'

FOURTEEN

GALYDON AND IRAIUS were brought in, and if they were not exactly under guard, they were certainly heavily escorted. The Caledani general's eyes were bright with amusement at this wary treatment. Iraius wore his usual look of casual insolence.

Sedaine had chosen to receive them in her private audience chamber rather than the great hall, with only Vianor in attendance. And Limina, who sat in the corner doing embroidery. Kallis gave her a sharp look, which she returned blandly, and he was almost sure she was mocking him.

Kallis watched Sedaine as Galydon and Iraius entered the room. She looked composed, but her hands gripped the arms of her chair with a tension he was sure had nothing to do with the meeting about to take place. His news had shocked her, badly. A part of him was glad. It made her more human.

She did not rise when they entered. Galydon, whose observant gaze had taken in the understated elegance of the furnishings and the deliberate lack of adornment of the seated woman who watched him, offered her a precisely calculated bow. Even out of uniform and divested of his glittering insignia, the general carried himself with a military bearing that made even his peasant garb look like a parade uniform.

Iraius, more in deference to Amadorn's advancing season than the elevated company he was entering, was actually wearing boots. His own bow was also carefully calculated. Kallis sighed.

Galydon straightened. 'Highness, I bring greetings from the Lord Kinseris, high priest of the Kas'Talani Order, to you as Queen of Lothane. He has sent me to you as a gesture of friendship between your people and mine, and I am to offer you my services, to use as you see fit.'

Sedaine studied him in silence for a long moment. 'And how should I use your services?' she asked at last.

And Galydon, who had endured her searching regard without any sign of unease, said simply, 'To lead your army.'

Sedaine checked Vianor's spluttering outrage with a raised finger. 'And why would I do that?'

'Two reasons, your highness,' Galydon replied. 'First, because I know your enemy better than you do.'

Sedaine raised an eyebrow. 'Because you have commanded their army? An interesting point. You could be a sword at my side or a knife in my back.'

He shrugged. 'My lord weakens himself by sending me here, at a time he can ill afford to do so. That is no small thing.'

'So you say. And the second reason?'

'Because you need me.'

'We do not!' Unable to contain his anger, Vianor ignored Sedaine's sharp look. 'Do you think us such fools that we would take our enemy into our confidence and simply place our defences in your hands?'

Galydon's eyes never left Sedaine. 'Then into whose hands will you place them?'

'We have our own commanders,' Vianor spat. 'We don't need you.'

'Do you?' Galydon asked, finally facing him. 'Men who have fought campaigns, not just hired mercenaries to fight for them? Who have led armies not just their household guards? Who understand what it is to fight an enemy that may call fire out of the sky or rupture the ground beneath your feet? If you have such men, you have no need of me. But if you don't, you should beg me to help you, because without me you are finished.'

He had not raised his voice, but Vianor recoiled as though he had.

Kallis looked at Sedaine and saw her watching Galydon. When the general looked calmly back at her, she merely nodded to him, deferring the discussion, before transferring her attention to Iraius.

'Captain Iraius. Do you also come to offer me assistance?'

In the corner, Limina looked up.

Iraius grinned. 'Like the general here, my talents are at your disposal.'

105

'Piracy?' At Iraius's surprised look, she added, 'Your reputation precedes you, captain.'

Iraius's grin widened. 'If you like, your highness. But there's something we both need first.'

Sedaine fixed Iraius with a speculative look. 'You can give me ships?'

'Boats, your highness,' the pirate corrected.

Kallis rolled his eyes. 'Things that float. Which you need.'

She glanced at him. 'I know. And the price?'

Iraius seemed taken aback. 'Price?'

'Yes, your price,' she repeated. 'None of you has reason to love me or my country. Quite the opposite, in fact. And yet here you are, apparently making a gift of yourselves to my cause. Why?'

'None of us are here for you,' Kallis said. 'Your enemy is our enemy, and this is where the fight is.'

A ghost of a smile flickered across Sedaine's face. 'I can believe that is your reason, Kallis. But you do not speak for these men.'

'He's right, your highness,' said Galydon. 'What happens in Amadorn affects us all. What happens in Lothane will decide the fate of Amadorn.'

Sedaine tapped her fingers on the arm of her chair. 'Self-interest then.'

'Call it whatever you like,' Kallis said, impatient. 'You need us, and you need the clans. We both know the Lords of the North have spent a generation getting fat on trade. They don't know the first thing about war. Put them in charge and this will be all over by spring.'

Sedaine looked amused. 'As it happens, I have suspended the lords' council.'

Kallis couldn't hide his surprise. 'You have?'

'Of course, I cannot prosecute a war by committee. And who among them could I raise above the others?'

She rose, signalling the end of the audience and the end of the discussion before Kallis could demand to know who was currently in charge of Lothane's defence. But he suspected he knew the answer.

Galydon bowed again and turned to leave as Limina laid aside her embroidery and drifted over to Sedaine's side.

'Captain Iraius?' she called.

The pirate paused, eyeing her warily. 'My lady?'

'You don't remember me?'

'We've met?'

Limina smiled, an expression edged with steel, and Kallis saw Iraius's gaze flicker to the doors as if he were planning his escape.

'Not met exactly. I was not much more than a child. I believe you were a prisoner of my husband once.'

Iraius licked dry lips. 'And who is your husband, lady?'

This time Limina's smile was positively wolfish. 'Admiral Hanlon.'

That was name even Kallis had heard, though his time in Amadorn had been spent far from the southern coast where Farnor's small navy under its ruthless admiral had hunted the pirates who terrorised the shipping lanes. Iraius had turned a sickly shade of grey, but Limina's amusement had already evaporated.

'Relax, captain. We are a long way from Farnor, and I have no desire to rake over the past. Besides,' she added with a twisted little smile, 'he *was* my husband.'

Iraius's head came up at that, his expression pained. 'Was?'

'He died in the defence of Farnor,' Limina told him. Her eyes were dry. It was only her voice that betrayed her.

'As he would have wanted it,' Iraius murmured with a bow. 'I'm truly sorry, my lady. He was a fine sailor.'

Limina gave a strangled laugh. 'Yes,' she agreed. 'He was a fine sailor.'

Kallis caught Sedaine's eye and steered Iraius towards the door before he could say anything else.

'I like her,' Galydon announced after they had been ushered out into the corridor.

'Of course you do,' Kallis muttered. 'Bloody dictators, both of you.'

There was a cough, and Kallis found the elderly steward at his elbow.

'The barracks?' he asked, with a certain amount of resignation.

'By no means,' the seneschal replied. 'If you gentlemen will follow me, I will take you to your quarters.'

'Well, well,' Kallis murmured as they fell in behind him. 'I think she liked you too.'

Sedaine watched her unlikely allies as the doors closed behind them, then turned to Limina as she packed away her embroidery.

Sedaine held out her hand. 'Let me see that.' She turned the hoop over in her hands, studying the mass of random, crude stitching. Her lips twitched. 'You've never done a day's embroidery in your life, have you?'

Limina looked offended. 'According to some that's all I did in Farnor.'

'Ah yes.' Sedaine grinned. 'The Petticoat Revolution. What would you have done if he had asked to see this?'

Limina laughed. 'As if he would ask.'

Sedaine handed back the abused hoop. 'And the pirate! What was that?'

Limina looked up. 'Hmm? Oh, just something my husband once said.'

'What did he say?'

'That pirates were more use to him alive than dead.'

Sedaine looked at her curiously. 'More use to him? How?'

'I never thought too much about it,' Limina admitted. 'It was Hanlon's job to protect the shipping, and he was good at it. I didn't interfere. He hanged one from time to time, but he always said it was wasteful. I never wondered before where they disappeared to. The others, that is.'

Intrigued, Sedaine asked, 'The others?'

'The ones he didn't hang, like Iraius. But we know now, don't we? He went to Caledan.'

Sedaine stared at her. 'What are you saying?'

Limina shrugged, frowning. 'Nothing. But he wasn't happy, was he? When I told him Hanlon is dead.'

It was with Limina's words echoing in her ears that Sedaine went looking for the Caledani general. She had questions she would ask him, in private.

She found Galydon alone in the upper gallery, standing by a window. She studied him in the fading light. Tall and lean, his body hardened by a lifetime of soldiering, he wore his years on his face. Skin the brown of a deep summer tan was creased like old leather and his black hair was streaked with silver. It was a handsome face for all that, sculptured features still sharp despite their weathering, and he held himself with the confidence of a man secure in his ability and authority.

He must have felt her scrutiny because he turned, his eyes searching. When he saw her, he inclined his head a fraction, offering respect but not subservience. 'Your highness?'

'General,' she replied in the same tone.

When she said nothing more, he raised an eyebrow. 'Do you need something from me?'

'Yes, General. I need to know why you're here.'

She saw she had surprised him, but not unduly. He studied her in his turn, and she knew what he was seeing. A woman well into middle age, her black hair starting to silver at the edges. Handsome once and still striking, attired in a man's clothes rather than the royal robes of a queen. But she did not need them, and she knew it. Watching him, she saw that he knew it too.

'I already told you. I am here because I was ordered to come.'

'By your high priest?'

He nodded. 'And here, in private, you wish to ask whether you can trust his motivations?'

She did not reply at once, moving instead to stand beside him by the window. It faced south, towards the Istelan. Towards Darred. 'You serve the priesthood, is that right?'

'I am sworn to the office of the high priest.'

She noted the correction. 'And when your high priest is not present?'

He turned towards her. 'Whom do I serve?'

She met his eyes squarely. 'Yes. Forgive me, general. But out there is another priest of your Order. One who has led an army of conquest to these shores—a conquest that, as I understand it, has long been desired by the Kas'Talani. Whom you serve. So, I ask you now: if Darred were to command you, would you obey?'

Something stirred in his dark eyes. A flicker of anger perhaps, though none showed on his face. 'My lord Kinseris sent me to you, to place myself and my skills at your disposal, to fight against this invasion, which is none of his doing. I will not lie; I did not come willingly. My place is by his side, and his need is as great as yours. But for the sake of a friendship, here I am.'

'And Darred?'

There was definite anger this time, though not, she thought, directed at her. 'Darred is no longer of the Order. I am yours to command.'

She believed him. He did not want to be here; she believed that too. But while he was, she could trust that he would put his considerable skills at her service, and she had great need of those. She was not blind to the deficiencies of Lothane's defences. She felt a lessening of the unbearable tension Brannick's message had brought. 'Very well, General. I command you to see to the defence of Lothane.'

Galydon acknowledged that with a bow, and a smile that crinkled his eyes in a way that made her heart flutter.

She smiled back and turned to leave, then said, 'You must have known each other a long time.'

The comment took him by surprise. 'Kinseris? Not long, in fact.' He hesitated a moment before adding, 'That was not the friendship that brought me here.'

She paused, her heart thudding painfully. 'Then who −'

'Your son, highness. Kinseris sent me to you because of your son.'

It was only after she left that she realised she had forgotten to ask about Iraius.

FIFTEEN

IT WAS CURIOSITY and old loyalties that prompted Kallis to seek out Lorac and his kin when he made his escape from Sedaine's steward. That and a persistent itch between his shoulder blades, despite his confident words to Vianor.

Lorac at the head of the clans was a gift he had not expected, but one that might still prove dangerous. The Lorac he had known as an oath-brother was level-headed and practical. A solid tactician if given enough time to think things through, but he had none of the flamboyant, spontaneous brilliance of his cousin, whom Kallis had killed to secure his freedom from the clans. Nor any of the dangerous violence of some of the mercenaries' more ambitious leaders. But that was two years ago. The man he had known then would never have wanted the position he now held. Kallis could only guess at how he had come to take it, and why. There had been a strung-out tension to the man today that spoke of more than the usual stresses in the complicated clan command structure.

The clans had been on the brink long before this invasion. Ever since the disaster of the Istelan Vale, in fact. Lorac might believe that Vianor and the magicians had not enacted a deliberate betrayal, but whether he could convince the clans was another matter. And if he couldn't, there was no chance he could persuade them to fight for Sedaine with the magicians by her side—with or without a promise of gold. And they had to have the clans. They were the largest force of professional soldiers in the whole of Amadorn. Their training and discipline made each clansman worth any three of Rhiannas's garrison-trained guardsmen, let alone what passed for soldiery in the south, and a generation of over-reliance on mercenaries had weakened

Lothane's defences to the point where the country was not defensible without them. Sedaine knew that even if she would never admit it. Darred knew it too, since he had engineered it.

Darred. His fingerprints were all over this. The man had spent decades patiently scheming, exploiting weaknesses, playing up prejudices, creating a hundred little fractures that kept the peoples of Amadorn from allying effectively against him.

Maker, how he hated that man, hated him with the sort of dark, poisonous hatred that made rational people do stupid things. Professional that he was, Kallis recognised the danger, and part of him wondered whether Darred provoked such a reaction deliberately, as he had provoked the hatred between the clans and the magicians. For of all possible alliances, that was the one he must fear the most.

The itch between Kallis's shoulder blades increased in intensity as he approached the tavern where the mercenary leaders were holed up. He might have settled his quarrel with the Ravens, but his life was still forfeit by clan law, and any of the mercenary clans in Rhiannas could take it at will and no punishment would befall them, at least not from their own. Her situation as precarious as it was, he doubted Sedaine would stir herself to vengeance on his behalf. She didn't even particularly like him.

The last time he had been to this particular tavern, Aarin had dragged him out by the back door semi-conscious after a brawl that it was just possible he might have started. The last time he had been here he had begun the severing of his connection to the clans that had ended in Leumas's death in the shadow of the Grymwood. That memory was likely at the forefront of Lorac's mind tonight. Checking his numerous blades were within reach, Kallis squared his shoulders. Aarin and his tricks would be very useful right now. But since he was on his own, he would just have to brazen it out.

As he approached the tavern, he adopted the clansmen's sword language— left hand on his hilt and his right open and palm facing away from him. It signalled to the mercenaries milling around outside that he was not looking for a fight but that he came ready to defend himself if they insisted on it. It also told them precisely who he was, but that could not be helped. He watched them watch his approach. There were no faces he recognised, but the hostility in their expressions was eloquent warning of the state of his welcome.

A large, bearded clansman wearing a faded hawk emblem rose to block his way. Kallis stopped a few paces from him so he wouldn't have to look up.

'Let me guess, I'm not welcome here?'

The clansman folded his arms across his chest and smiled, showing teeth. One at the front was missing.

From inside the tavern, Kallis could hear raised voices, Lorac's among them. He nodded at the door. 'I have business with your captain's captain.'

The man's grin grew wider. He was missing more than one tooth. Kallis's hand twitched and he curled his fingers round his hilt. The watching mercenaries seemed content not to interfere for now, but he did not want to put their tolerance to the test by letting this come to blows.

He smiled, showing his own full set of teeth. 'Perhaps you'll let Lorac know I'm here?'

The clansman spat at his feet.

'I'll announce myself then,' Kallis sighed, and took a step forward.

No one moved. Then, to his astonishment, the man shifted to let him pass. It was so unexpected, and his nerves drawn so tight, that Kallis almost turned and drew on instinct. Instead, he forced himself to keep going and felt the huge mercenary fall in behind him, padding like a shadow through the low door of the inn.

Inside, the place was filling up with mercenaries from numerous clans. Kallis recognised several Ravens as well as faces from other clans. A couple of Ravens nodded as he passed. Most ignored him, but a few sets of eyes followed his progress as he pushed through the throng, the Hawk menacing his shoulder.

The argument he had heard had broken up, and Lorac was alone at a back table. Even in the dim light he looked tired and irritated, and Kallis was abruptly aware that his presence here was more likely to hinder than help the clan leader. But the shadow at his shoulder shoved him forwards. It was too late to change his mind.

Lorac looked up, saw him, and sighed. 'Go away, Kallis.'

He smiled, pulling up a bench and signalling the innkeeper. 'No.'

When the drink arrived, his shadow leaned over and picked it up. Moments later the empty tankard was slammed back down in front of him. Kallis ostentatiously wiped at the splashes on his vest and waved his hand for another. When the innkeeper hesitated, Lorac snapped, 'Give the bloody man a drink. And back off, Meinor.'

This last was directed at the clansman behind Kallis. Kallis swivelled to face him. 'You heard the man,' he said sweetly. 'Now, back off.'

Meinor glowered down at him, then flicked a scornful look at Lorac. 'Baran will hear about this.'

Lorac put his drink down with a long-suffering sigh, and informed Meinor succinctly just what the Hawk's captain could do with the knowledge. Kallis raised an eyebrow.

Meinor's face darkened. 'You're making a mistake, Lorac. You should be killing this man, not talking to him. If you don't, we will.'

The mercenary's captain-of-captains pulled a braided strip from his arm and slapped it down on the table. 'It's my mistake to make, Meinor. When your captain wears this armband, he can do whatever he likes. Until then, fuck off.'

Then, ignoring the fury of the man he had just dismissed, Lorac picked up his tankard and took a long drink. His back to Meinor, Kallis forced himself not to flinch as every instinct screamed that he was about to get a knife in the back. The moment stretched out, then the barely perceptible tension in Lorac's shoulders lessened and he realised the man had left.

Lorac met Kallis's amused relief with irritation. 'This had better be good because you've just caused me a bastard of a headache. Baran is a pig's arse, and he's been looking for a reason to challenge me ever since I got this bloody thing.' He retied the stained braid around his arm. 'It's not like I wanted it, but I'll be dead before I see the clans in the hands of a man like that.'

'That's usually the way it works,' Kallis agreed. Here, among his own, Lorac was a different man. 'Girion's dead, I take it?' The captain of the Eagles had not been a man to let go of power this side of death. He was just surprised

Lorac had been the one to take it from him. If, in fact, he had. That was partly what he wanted to find out.

Lorac sat back and gave him a considering look. 'Why are you here? You made your case back at the palace and you will have my answer when I'm ready. There's no need to repeat yourself.'

Kallis shrugged. 'I can't visit an old friend?'

'We're not friends, Kallis. You killed my captain, you broke your oath, and lost us a contract −'

'Which you didn't want anyway.'

'− which saddled us with a tax on all future contracts for a year.'

Kallis winced. For the clans, breach of contract was the ultimate crime. Punishments hit the offending clan where it hurt most—their pockets. 'Girion's dead, I take it?'

Lorac snorted, the ghost of a smile twitching his lips. 'All right, Kallis. Let's hear it. You didn't risk dismemberment by the likes of Meinor for a cosy drink with a man who would gladly gut you just to pass the time of day. So, *why are you here?*'

Kallis laid his hands palms up on the table. After hesitating a moment, Lorac did the same. He fixed Kallis with a penetrating look. 'Truth, then. What haven't you told me?'

'You're not going to like it.'

Lorac rolled his eyes. 'I rarely do. Now spit it out before Meinor gets back with Baran and I'm mopping your brains off my best jack.'

Kallis slid his hands off the table and took a sip of beer. It was better than he remembered, or maybe he was just thirsty. He took a moment to order his thoughts, then said, 'You remember the lad I was with when you caught us by the Grymwood?'

'The mage? I'm not likely to forget. That old bastard Vianor was burning to get his hands on him.'

'Do you know why?'

'Are you going to tell me?

'Because he's the queen's son.'

Lorac put his drink down. 'Do you say so?' Kallis watched him file that information away. 'What happened to him?'

'Ah, well, that's where it gets interesting.'

SIXTEEN

'DRAGONS.' LORAC'S FACE had an ashen tinge as he took that in. 'You saw them?'

Kallis nodded.

'But they're gone?'

He shrugged. 'They're not here, that's all I know. Gone? I don't think so.'

Lorac considered this. 'Pity,' he said at last. 'Because it sounds like we're going to need all the help we can get.'

Kallis opened his mouth then thought better of it. He took a long drink.

Lorac was looking at him with an unreadable expression. 'You think we want to sit by and watch the north overrun?'

Kallis had the sense not to answer that, since that was exactly what they had been doing.

'As it happens, you were right.'

Kallis choked on his drink. 'I was?'

'You think you understand us because you fought beside us. But you always were an outsider.' Lorac held up a hand. 'That's not an insult, it's a fact. You were not born of the clans. You did not have two centuries of tradition drummed into you before you could walk. You adopted those traditions, but they were never yours. To you the Istelan was just a battle that went badly. To us it was a mortal wound, a wound that went bad and spread its poison all through us.'

'I understood better than you think,' Kallis said, remembering his long-ago words to Aarin that echoed those Lorac spoke now. Then, because it needed to be said, 'I didn't want to fight him.'

'Why do you think you're still alive? The magician made you fight, as they made us fight that day in the Istelan Valley. *They* have been our poison, and we could never fight for your queen while that man stands at her side and his people at her back.' His eyes fixed on Kallis. 'And you knew that.'

Kallis returned the look without flinching. 'I did not lie to you.'

Lorac searched his face a long moment, then he nodded. 'So, we share an enemy. That's good, because I didn't want to have to kill you. But you understand this is one decision I can't make alone? If I can't bring the clans with me, what use is my agreement?'

Frustrated, Kallis leant forward. 'You also realise, I hope, that we need the magicians? This is just what Darred wants. How else do you expect Lothane to stand against the magic of dragons?'

'That,' said Lorac, sitting back and staring over his shoulder at something, 'is your problem. And you'll have your chance to make your case.'

It was then that the sound, or lack of it, penetrated Kallis's awareness. He met Lorac's eyes as the mercenary captain looked back at him. 'Baran?'

'Who else?'

Kallis put down his drink. 'How do you want to play this?'

Lorac gave him a level look. 'With sweet reason and an exercise of my authority.'

'Same as always then,' Kallis sighed, unbuckling his sword belt and looking around for a less lethal weapon. All around them mercenaries were climbing to their feet, many a little unsteady, as the new arrivals stood framed in the doorway. The clanging of metal indicated a growing pile of weaponry as the clansmen shed their blades in preparation for the brawl. By clan law, you did *not* draw blood against your own except by formal challenge. Kallis hoped it would not come to that. He was more than half drunk himself.

He turned back to find Lorac still seated. 'You're not joining the fun?'

Lorac flicked a speck of dust off the filthy armband. '*You* are sweet reason, and *they*'—he waved his empty tankard at the clansmen on their side of the room—'are the exercise of my authority.' He shouted for the innkeeper to bring him another drink. The man was cowering behind his bar, but the bag of coins Lorac threw on the table had him scurrying over with a refill. Lorac slid the bag towards him. 'For the damage. Now get out of here.'

As the innkeeper hurried to obey, abandoning his tavern without a backward glance, the captain-of-captains picked up his drink and settled back. 'I said you would have a chance to make your case.'

Kallis smiled through his teeth. 'You bastard.' Then he forgot Lorac as he turned to face the danger striding towards him, Meinor's massive bulk at his shoulder.

The Hawk's captain did not stop for pleasantries. Reaching the table, Baran jabbed his finger at Kallis. 'This one is a traitor and a murderer. You fail in your duty every minute he still breathes.'

Kallis's hand was reaching for the sword he had discarded before Baran finished speaking but Lorac shot him a look of such icy fury that he stepped back.

'Leumas was killed in formal challenge,' Lorac told Baran in a tone of quiet menace. 'His debt to the Ravens is paid.'

'But not to the clans!'

The captain-of-captains slammed his hand down on the trestle. 'I *am* the clans! And I say his debt is paid.'

Kallis gave him a sharp look, undecided whether to be grateful or angry. Lorac's protection now only made his own position more dangerous. Because they both knew what was coming, and the former captain of the Ravens was playing for deadly stakes.

At a gesture from Baran, the Hawks fanned out behind him, each one armed with a club. The sword in their captain's hand told a different story.

Trapped between them and the table, Kallis cursed silently. Baran was about to challenge his captain for command of the clans, and if he won, Sedaine lost her army, and they lost their lives. Which was why, of course, Lorac had just done what he had done.

Not looking at the sword, Lorac said to Baran, 'Leave now. You have one chance to think better of this.'

'Or what?' Baran sneered. 'Are you frightened to face me? You got lucky with Girion. I am neither old nor injured.'

Well, that was one question answered, though Kallis found his curiosity on that point had waned somewhat. Then Baran's sword arm was rising to issue the challenge, and Lorac, sighing, turned to Kallis. 'Over to you, sweet reason.'

Baran blinked, confused. And Kallis punched him in the face.

Kallis staggered out of the tavern at dawn, stomach sour and head pounding. He squinted as the light hit his eyes and had to put out a hand to steady himself until his head stopped spinning. Maker, he was out of practice. Then he dunked his head in the horse trough by the entrance and the icy shock dispelled the worst of the fog.

There would be sorer heads than his this morning, but no bodies to bury. His blow had knocked Baran out of the fight before he could complete his challenge, and his men had proved reluctant to take it up on his behalf. Of course, the insult to the Hawks could not be allowed to pass unanswered, but a deadly confrontation had been turned at the last moment to a merely bruising disagreement.

A shadow fell across him as he straightened. He blinked the water out of his eyes and found himself looking up into Meinor's ugly face. Kallis groaned, then the air whooshed out of him as Meinor's fist drove into his stomach. He folded, going down hard, and for a horrible instant couldn't catch a breath. Then he was puking his guts out on the cobbles and taking distant satisfaction from the way the vomit splattered on his assailant's boots.

Somewhere above, Meinor snorted with laughter, then offered Kallis his hand. He waved it off, still gasping, deciding it was safer to stay down than get knocked back on his arse. He leant back against the wall and closed his eyes. His stomach threatened to empty itself again. He had forgotten how the mercenaries could drink.

'Ah, man, I'm not going to hit you,' Meinor's voice rumbled, amused.

Kallis cracked open one eye. 'You just did,' he complained. 'So forgive me if I don't believe you. That was you trying to kill me last night, wasn't it?'

'Man, if I was trying to kill you, we wouldn't be having this little chat. Last night was for my captain. *That* was from me.'

Kallis took a tentative breath. 'And how is your captain this morning?'

Meinor laughed, holding out his hand again. 'Reordering his priorities,' he said, as he hauled Kallis upright. 'Thanks to you and our twisty chief.'

Kallis stepped back and propped himself up against the wall. He squinted at Meinor. 'You seem rather less upset about that than I would have expected.'

The huge clansman shrugged. There was dried blood around his lips and what looked like a chipped tooth. The man was *hard* on teeth. 'He's my captain. That doesn't mean he isn't a fool. Clan law says you're free to go. Baran lost his chance to change that. I don't like Lorac, but he's no fool.'

Kallis took that in amid a wave of nausea. He leant to one side and vomited again, feeling a lot better. Apart from the deep ache in his belly. He forced himself to focus on Meinor's face. 'You know what he will propose? That the clans set aside their feud with the magicians and fight for the queen?'

Meinor growled deep in his throat. 'I know.'

Kallis waited, but nothing else appeared to be forthcoming. 'And?'

'And I don't like it. But I'll hear him out.'

'We have a mutual enemy,' Kallis reminded him.

'Aye, so you say.'

Kallis raised his hands in defeat. Wincing, he pushed himself off the wall. 'Tell Lorac I'll be waiting. He knows where to find me.'

Galydon was waiting for him when he returned to the palace. Impeccably turned out in new clothes, the Caledani general's gaze raked him from head to foot, taking in the tears, vomit stains, and pinched brows. Kallis forced himself to straighten but could not quite hide the wince as the movement pulled at sore muscles.

Galydon's eyebrow arched. 'It went well, then?'

Kallis grunted something unintelligible and shoved past him. He wanted clean clothes and a bed, not necessarily in that order. To his annoyance, Galydon peeled himself off the wall and followed.

'The queen wants to see you.'

'Are you her messenger now?'

'No, only her general.'

At Kallis's sharp look, he smiled. 'So, go and clean yourself up. We have work to do.'

SEVENTEEN

KINSERIS STOOD ON deck as the ship slipped out of the harbour, watching Caledan recede in the hazy dawn. He braced his feet against the gentle sway, measuring the weakness in his legs, the deep ache in his side. The weakness left by pain and fever, of weeks hovering between life and death that remained to him only as flashes of memory, barely trusted.

The Ancai hovered somewhere behind him, ready to steady him should he falter. Jeta stood beside him, her fingertips brushing his. They had saved him. They had taken him from the midst of his enemies and carried him to safety. To freedom.

He had been drowning in Kas'Tella, sinking under the weight of a responsibility that had seemed impossible to fulfil, under the exhausting necessity of constant distrust, his every decision questioned and every colleague suspect. And the one man in Kas'Tella to whom he had given his trust was the one who had betrayed him. But their loyalty, their faith in him, had saved more than his life.

Jeta had told him how the army had come for him—too late, maybe—but they had come. How they had hidden him, defended him when he could not defend himself. How they had come within a hair's breadth of fighting for him. He could not be other than thankful that it had not come to that, but it meant something, nonetheless.

Yet, for all that, Kas'Tella was lost. Caledan was closed to him. He had tried and he had failed, and though he regretted everything he now could not do, he was also free. The relief of that was something he could not deny.

But one battle lost did not end the war. And it was to that war they were heading. He had done what he could. Fylian had come to him in the city before they left, had found, in fact, a place for them to hide while he recovered enough strength to travel. From the captain he had learned that Betanas was still alive, still free, apparently, of suspicion. He did not know if that meant the Order believed the deception or whether they wanted the world to believe it—that he was dead, and his changes with him. Fylian could not tell him.

'What do you wish me to do, my lord?' the captain had asked him, and Kinseris had made two requests. He did not know whether Fylian could do the first—whether the loyalty of the army was strong enough to permit it— and he dreaded that he should ever have to do the second, but it had been necessary to ask. Because replaying in his ears every moment were the last words Escarian had spoken to him. The warning he now carried to Amadorn.

You would take away our power. Darred will bring us dragons.

PART TWO

ONE

The Long Dream

THE MAN WHO had been Aarin and was now Æisoul wandered through the corridors of Lorrimer's memory, seeking answers to questions he hardly knew.

He watched a man stand alone in a sea of people. A sweep of black hair hid his face, but his hunched shoulders and clenched fists spoke of unbearable pain.

Memory gave him a name, called from a distance. The man looked up, his face a mask of unheeded tears. A little girl ran to him, her red hair pulled askew from its plait, and wrapped her arms around his knees. He saw the man stagger as her weight hit him, then his hand unclenched and he laced his fingers through her hair.

Their eyes met for an instant over her head, then the man knelt, gathering the sobbing child in his arms and rocking her against him. Rocking her, over and over, in a grip so tight his knuckles were white.

He turned away, unwilling to watch… and the memory *shifted*.

They were alone. The child was asleep at last, the tears giving way to exhaustion. Now the black-haired man sat in silence, head bent, a storm-cloud of anger darkening the room.

Lorrimer/Æisoul felt an unaccustomed helplessness. He had an immensity of power on which he could call and yet here was something he could not mend. The other man's depthless grief robbed him of words and arrested every impulse to give comfort. They had been as close as brothers, but this had erected a barrier between them that he did not know how to breach.

At length, that dark head looked up. 'Why?'

Lorrimer thought of the body on the cliff, lying like a broken doll on the rocky slope, long red hair fanning out around an energetic face, now forever stilled. He remembered the frozen edge of panic he had felt, looking down, as above him a dragon screamed and wheeled in a frenzy of grief. And he remembered the laughing, open face of his friend when he had gone to tell him. The way the laughter had died in his eyes, replaced by shock then raw, unchecked grief. Then anger. Something dark and ugly now resided where laughter had been, and he feared what it might do.

He could not say what had happened, no one could. A moment's inattention, one unsteady step. A fatal plunge so quick that not even the vast power of their pairing could prevent it. But that was not the question, and he did not have an answer.

Why her?

They had become so unaccustomed to death, except among the very old for whom even the regenerative power of the dragons could no longer hold back the inevitability of age. There was little else short of death that they could not, given time, heal from within. Only the death that came instantly, unexpectedly, as hers had done, were they powerless against.

'Why, Lorrimer?' Aarkan demanded again.

Because he could not answer, he did not, and felt the memory slip and start to fade away, to be replaced by another, sharper recollection. Riah was older now, almost a woman. She stood beside him as she greeted her father, her back stiff with hurt and anger that Aarkan barely seemed to notice, let alone understand. He had been gone years. Years in which his daughter had grown up without a mother or a father, grieving the one and resenting the other. Precious years that could never be recovered, but they had not been without love. Lorrimer had seen to that.

Aarkan seemed bemused by his daughter, almost as though he had no idea how long he had been gone. He treated her as the child she had been though his eyes must see the woman she was becoming, and there was something in the way his gaze slid always past her that told Lorrimer that what he could not bear was the resemblance she bore to Ashlea, her mother.

Riah must have sensed it too. When he looked for her again, she was gone, and he was alone with Aarkan. Or maybe time had slipped. It did that in memory. And this was not a memory he wanted to relive.

They were in Aarkan's home. He had gone there, he remembered, to speak to him of Riah, but he had found his friend pacing the room in agitation, muttering to himself. For a minute it seemed like he had not noticed Lorrimer's arrival, but then the—madness?—dissipated and he was himself again. Almost.

'I'm so close,' Aarkan said in answer to a cautious query.

'So close to what?'

Aarkan shook his head. He sat, his foot tapping on the stone floor.

Lorrimer/Æisoul looked from the foot to his friend's face, losing himself in the memory as the hazy edges sharpened. 'Where have you been?'

Aarkan's hand waved vaguely. He had always had such expressive hands. 'Away. Not far. Looking for answers.'

'To which questions?'

Aarkan frowned, head tilted to one side. 'You know.'

'No, Aarkan, I don't. Tell me.'

His friend gave a bark of harsh laughter. 'To why. To going back. To undoing. To freeing us from this tyranny.'

Alarmed now, Lorrimer tried to hold Aarkan's gaze but could not catch it any more than Riah could. 'Tyranny, Aarkan? What tyranny?'

The foot stopped its tapping. 'Death, Lorrimer. The tyranny of death. An unjust and jealous limit on our power!' He surged to his feet, as though he could no longer contain the urgency of movement. He paced to the end of the room and back. 'All other powers are ours, why should this last be denied us? Why should we suffer this pain when we need not?'

Lorrimer/Æisoul felt his first taste of real fear as he looked into the flushed, manic face of his friend. An awful suspicion was forming. 'Death comes to all of us eventually, even the dragons,' he said quietly. 'As it must. As it should.'

'As it came to *her?*'

That one word held an ocean of rage and pain. It battered against him, drenching him in a tide of emotion that was not entirely human. There was a change in the feel of the air as Aarkan drew on the power of his bond with his dragon. Lorrimer felt Silverwing stir in response to Srenegar's sudden anger, felt his dragon's confused query. Never before had a quarrel between them provoked such a reaction.

Calmly, deliberately, Lorrimer disengaged from his active link with Silverwing. It was akin to laying aside a weapon. For several heartbeats more Aarkan held Srenegar's power against him, then he seemed to realise what he had done and let it go in a rush, a rueful smile on his face.

The echo of it hung between them as Aarkan spread his hands in apology. 'Forgive me, my friend. Her death… it is still raw.'

His attention rivetted on that echo, Lorrimer brushed his friend's apology aside. Because he had had his second taste of fear.

There had been two ghosts, not one, standing between them in the moment of confrontation. Two women who had commanded the emotions of the man before him.

There was a difference to second pairings, as Aarkan's had been. Dragons who had already lived one human lifetime in partnership retained the memory of grief. Some never did Join again after the death of their mage; others sought the comfort of another pairing almost as soon as the madness lifted. Srenegar had been one such, Joining with Aarkan a mere ten years after the death of his first partner, Lelana. At first that thought had been a comfort to Lorrimer—that Aarkan, lost in his own desperate sorrow, should share this with a creature who understood what it meant to lose someone loved beyond measure. But now he feared the combined weight of their loss had broken his friend's mind.

It was Lelana, standing beside Ashlea, he had sensed in that moment.

His third taste of fear came close on the heels of the second. Aarkan was talking again, the words coming so fast that Lorrimer, distracted, could not at first follow them. But as the sense of them reached him, he felt a cold dread.

Flush with excitement, the latent violence of seconds before forgotten, Aarkan was inviting him to share in his discovery. Lorrimer tried to speak, to stem the flow, but Aarkan could hear nothing but his theories and see nothing but his vision.

A terrifying vision. Of a magic taken far beyond its natural limits to challenge the Maker for the power of creation, to unmake death. It was a vision that could lead to….

A barrage of images flashed before his eyes—*their* eyes. Lorrimer/Æisoul staggered, losing control of the memory as Aarkan's face was replaced by a flood of future awareness. Of memories yet to be made, of things Lorrimer could guess and things he could not possibly know. Of a future Aarin had glimpsed, and one he had lived.

Impossible now to separate one from the other. He was neither Lorrimer nor Aarin. Neither an old man's memories living again in another, nor a young man reliving an old man's life. Instead, he was Æisoul, and Æisoul *knew* the consequences of this path. He had lived them as Lorrimer had not— not yet. And he only now realised the danger.

That awful premonition—*from which of them did it come?*—prompted a violent denial. Aarkan stepped back, shocked hurt on his face. Then his expression shuttered, the mania draining out of him as the vision faded.

The eyes that met Lorrimer's were empty of all emotion. His hand moved, a gesture of entreaty started then abandoned. 'I thought you would understand. I was wrong.'

Appalled, Lorrimer found he could not speak. Aarkan's eyes held his for a moment longer, then he turned his back and walked away.

Æisoul watched him go. Distant, remote, he could feel the thudding of Lorrimer's heart and the weight of the old man's fear and regret. And he knew, somehow, that this was the moment—the chance to persuade Aarkan from his path—and it had slipped through his fingers.

TWO

THERE WERE NO days in the Long Dream, no nights. For three thousand years it had been dusk. Now it was dawn. And with every dragon that was freed from Kas'Talani control, that silvery light grew brighter and brighter, bringing with it the promise of a new day to come, and another after that. Of a future where the dream was no longer needed, and the races once more existed together on Andeira in harmony.

It had been Ecyas's vision. Then it was Aarin's. Now it was for Æisoul to bring it about. And so Aarin left Lorrimer's memories and returned to the task that was his alone, and the haunted dreams of the dragon he wanted most to wake.

Yet the harder he tried, the more elusive this one mind became. Eiador's dream shifted around him. The unpredictable trance defied his attempts to hold it steady and form a connection with the mind at the centre of the fast-disintegrating dreamscape.

Aarin cursed silently. One moment he was soaring on the winds, almost within touching distance of the dragon's consciousness, the next he was tumbling through nothing, cut off. He exerted his control, pitching his call once more to the unique signature of the shackled and dreaming dragon, but barely a flicker of recognition answered him. It was almost as if the creature did not want to hear, that it no longer had the strength to break free of its prison. He tried once more, shaping his entreaty with all the promise of the new dawn, but even as he felt the mind he invaded stir in sudden response, he felt a sharp tug and then nothing...

Aarin opened his eyes. 'Why did you do that? I almost had him.'

No, Æisoul. You almost followed him too far.

He frowned, replaying the encounter in his mind. And then he saw it—the point at which he had stopped calling and started following. The point at which the dragon's power had been called upon by an external agency. That was where the danger lurked. It was why Silverwing watched over him but never added his call to Aarin's. The draw of the dragon devices was strong, seductive. They could not risk it luring them too far. All the shackled dragons posed this risk, but it was different with Eiador.

Aarin leant his head back till it rested on Silverwing's scaled haunch, enveloped in the queer exhaustion of the dreamworld that touched his mind but never his body. 'His hold is too strong.'

Silverwing did not respond, and Aarin knew his thoughts were following the same dark track as his own. From the first time he had felt this creature's presence, it was as a cry of pain. Sucked deep within the swirling magic of Darred's near-fatal spell in Redstone, he had heard Eiador's agony as the renegade priest had drawn perilously deep of the dragon's faltering reserves. Yet, time and again, Eiador had resisted his efforts to free him from Darred's control. It was an unsettling thought, but he could no longer deny the possibility that somehow Eiador was colluding in his own captivity.

Not knowingly. Not willingly. It is not possible.

'And yet he won't let me in.'

No matter how far they were sunk in their weakness, or how deep they were dreaming, the minds of the other dragons he had freed had eventually opened to him. He had but to touch them to gain access to their consciousness. Some were harder to reach than others, but once wakened to awareness of their plight, they could act—with his help—to free themselves. But that was changing.

He had woken Kinseris's dragon first, an ancient female so old she surpassed even Silverwing's years. But even though Kinseris had set aside the device willingly, she had been so weak that even now she had yet to unfold her wings and take flight. Aarin worried that she never would.

They were all like that, to some degree, the dragons he had wrested from the priesthood's control. Some awakenings came easier than others, where the humans who shackled them gave them up freely. Others he had to fight for. Still more, like Eiador, displayed a subtle resistance, and their numbers were growing. But all of them, on waking, were like helpless babes, drained of even the natural strength of their kind.

It was why he was here. Together with Silverwing, linked through the great knot of the Joining, they were righting the flawed balance of Andeira. Through them, all five elements were pouring back into the world, and in the silvery light of that new dawn the dragons could regain what they had lost. Safe in the Long Dream, hidden thousands of years in the past and cocooned in their own minds, the dragons could recover from the unwitting depredations of humanity. But first he had to free them and sometimes it felt like centuries had passed and there was still so much more to do.

Patience, Æisoul. We have time.

But his uneasiness was not something Silverwing could understand. After millennia away from the world, possessed of a longevity many times a human span, even a human Joined and sustained by the magic of his kind, what did a few months or years mean to a dragon? Hidden away with him, Aarin had lost much of his sense of time. Its passing meant little; it barely touched him. But his anxiety did not come from within.

As a boy he had dreamed of the dragons; as a man he had searched for them in growing desperation. Reeled in on the coattails of prophecy and Silverwing's Fire, he had done the thing he had been born to do, and he had followed Silverwing into the Long Dream and into a world where memories were given form and substance through the healing he brought with him. But those memories were not his. Fascinated though he was, try though he might to lose himself in the faces and events of a time long past, awareness of his *now* hovered always at the edges of his mind.

It was why he kept returning to Eiador, why he kept trying to reach the dragon's awareness. For behind Eiador was Darred, and Darred threatened everything he held dear in the life he had left behind.

Yet it was not Darred he had seen in Eiador's mind.

In the moment the priest had flexed the leash and called on the dragon's power, it was the echo of another man that Aarin had glimpsed. Fair-haired and ageless, flawless in the way of memory. Loved.

Cadyr.

The name came from Silverwing. Or at least he thought it did. Sometimes Lorrimer's memories clung to him even after he had stepped from them. He opened himself to them now, allowing the old man's knowledge to fill the gaps of his own.

Cadyr had been Eiador's mage before the Severing. His first. And Cadyr, like those other dead men and women whose dragons had become enslaved by the Kas'Talani, had been unable to face the finality of the Severing. Like Kasandar, for whom the Kas'Talani Order had been named, he had given a part of himself to his dragon, and taken a part of the dragon in exchange, in the hope that something of their partnership would endure past the ending of the world.

And like those others, he had died, leaving Eiador vulnerable to the machinations of Aarkan and his followers as they fed off the power he had caused to remain in Andeira long after it should have vanished. It was that power that had founded the Kas'Talani, under the secret aegis of the Arkni. It was that power in the Order's hands that had enslaved Eiador and hundreds like him for a thousand years while the Arkni clung to their half-life and waited for their chance to reclaim the river of power they believed would lead them to life without death, to power over all things, and the chance to remake the world as they thought it should be.

But the Arkni were gone. Their river of power had drowned them in its flood, as it had drowned Silverwing and Aarin in their turn. That they had survived where their enemy had perished had been for one reason, and one reason only—to free the dragons from their captivity and restore the elemental harmony of Andeira. And now the memory of a dead man stood in their way and blocked their path.

THREE

ÆISOUL WAS BACK in Lorrimer's memory. He could not remember if he had come here willingly, or if he had been pulled here. It was like that sometimes in the dream. The barriers of self could be fluid.

He knew at once that time had passed. As he slipped deeper into the memory, he could tell that Lorrimer felt — older. Not simply in years. He felt aged, tired. Worn down by secret cares.

For a moment Æisoul hung suspended between past and present, as his awareness blurred with the mind held open for him. Then a voice—once loved, now feared—called his name, and two became one.

'Lorrimer! You came.'

Aarkan was walking towards him, arms spread wide in welcome. He was smiling. The smile transformed his face, banishing the harsh aspect that had become so much a part of him, and Lorrimer felt a smile of his own drawn from him in response.

'Why should I not?' he asked carefully. 'When did I not?'

Aarkan reached him, hands clasping his shoulders. 'I feared —' He shook his head. 'It does not matter. You are here. Come.'

Aarkan started back the way he had come, heedless of the sheer drop just a stone's throw from the path. Lorrimer followed more cautiously. They were on a narrow track rising into the mountains that clung to the edge of a river gorge. The air was heavy with water mist and the rich smell of soil. Distant thunder through the close-packed trees spoke of a waterfall ahead. The place was a reservoir of raw power.

Lorrimer drew in the elements with every breath, his lungs expanding and the tightness disappearing from muscles and joints. He felt light, fresh, suffused with the energy of a youth he had left behind long, long ago.

Aarkan turned and grinned. 'Glorious, isn't it? You wanted to know where I have been. I have been here. And other places like it. Do you know why?'

And Lorrimer, who had long since guessed why, found he did not want those fears confirmed.

Aarkan laughed and turned back to the trail. 'You will see.'

Before long he did see. The incline increased, and the roar of water grew louder as the track emerged from the trees. The mist was heavier now, but not even blindness could have hidden the waterfall from Lorrimer's sight. Jutting darkly through the cloud of vapour, the foaming water poured off the cliff edge hundreds of feet high. Standing by the edge of the gorge, no more than halfway to the top of the falls, Lorrimer was drenched in the power of Water—the one wholly human element, the opposite and essential power mankind brought into union with the dragons' Fire.

A shadow swept across the sun. A dark shape now clung to the rocks by the edge of the falls. As Lorrimer watched, Srenegar shook out his great wings and folded them against his flanks, sitting calmly amid the spray as steam rose from his scales to mingle with the mist.

And he knew that the first step had already been taken.

The Joining had given the dragons the ability to bear the touch of water, but once the novelty wore off, few would willingly seek it out. Srenegar's choice of perch was as unnatural as it was disturbing.

If you asked it of me, I too could endure that.

Silverwing's thought in his mind told Lorrimer that the dragon sensed his fears and, like him, did not want to believe them.

But I would not ask it, and neither would the friend I knew.

Aarkan saw the look on his face and misread it. He smiled, the years falling away. 'That is nothing.'

Lorrimer could feel his euphoria, heightened by the vast concentration of power, and knew that, in this place, there was no argument that could match it.

Aarkan was watching him. 'You would not hear me once before. Will you hear me now?'

'What do you want me to hear?' Lorrimer asked sadly. 'Can you really not see where this will lead?'

Aarkan frowned, sensing rejection. 'Let me show you –'

Lorrimer reached out and grasped his wrist. 'Please. Please, Aarkan. Will you first listen to me?'

Aarkan looked from his hand to his face, frown deepening. And underneath the euphoric glow, Lorrimer saw the tell-tale signs of strain that foreshadowed the cost of his chosen path.

'Are *you* going to lecture me, Lorrimer? They are your footsteps I'm following.'

Shame quickened to anger. 'Then you know it is past time to turn back,' he snapped. 'The power you are seeking is not meant for you, or for me. It will destroy you—both of you. Power must have limits, and this is ours. Creation is for the Maker alone.'

He had expected anger, but Aarkan's tolerant smile was far more frightening. 'Thank you for the warning, my friend, but your failure to harness it does not mean it cannot be done.'

'But it should not! Just think of what you will have to do—what you must sacrifice—to do this thing. And what will you gain? Ashlea is dead. You cannot bring her back. *This* cannot bring her back.'

The mention of her name brought storm clouds boiling across the sky, their darkness reflected in Aarkan's eyes. Lorrimer did not need Silverwing's urgent warning to know he stood now in grave danger, the power held against him by the man who had once been his closest friend already far outstripping anything he could bring to bear. But he did not back down, seeking instead some sign of the friend he had lost the day Ashlea died.

Aarkan had wept for her just once, when Lorrimer brought the news of her death. Then he had smothered the grief, locked it away where it had festered like a wound until the poison of it drove him first from his daughter and his home and finally to this. Srenegar, who should have tempered the extremes of his mage's grief, had instead fed it with his own. And somewhere along the way, whatever Aarkan believed, this had ceased to be about what they had lost and had become all about what they thought they stood to gain.

All traces of warmth, of friendship, had vanished from Aarkan's face. 'I don't do this for me,' he snarled. 'I do it so no others need suffer like I have. I do it for *you!*'

'Then for me, stop,' Lorrimer pleaded. 'I do not want this.'

But Aarkan was already backing away, the sad smile on his face twisted by incipient madness.

Desperate now, memory tainted by the knowledge of the catastrophic consequences of Aarkan's choice, Lorrimer reached out to stop him leaving, to plead with the man who had been his friend, to make him understand…

…a *ripple* in the dream. A sharp pain. A formless sense of loss.

Lorrimer's memory splintered and faded. Æisoul was back in the Long Dream, but it was not as it had been. In that changeless place, something had changed.

Silverwing flew high above, and his was the warning.

Eiador is gone.

For an instant, he did not understand. *Dead?*

Could it be that Darred had, finally, taken too much?

But it was for an instant only.

Not dead. Gone.

As the Long Dream settled around him, Aarin felt the change and knew it for what it was, because only he and Silverwing had crossed that barrier before.

Darred had indeed taken too much, taken what was not his to take. He had taken Eiador from the dream back into Andeira. And suddenly everything had changed.

Lorrimer's urgency was still on him. The sense of teetering on the edge of a precipice, of failure and regret. Lorrimer had been unable to save a friend from himself, and Aarin, reliving those memories, had failed to heed their warning.

He thought of Aarkan and the transfiguring power of loss. Of how unchecked grief, finding its companion in the lingering madness of his dragon, had turned a friend into a monster. And he thought of Cadyr, alive in Eiador's sleeping mind. Alive *again*.

Though he did not understand how, Darred had used that power to keep Eiador shackled to the dragon device. That he had manipulated the dragon's enduring sorrow for his lost mage to keep him in bondage.

Eiador had resisted all attempts to free him, because freedom meant once more losing the man to whom he had Joined, and to whom he had given a part of himself in tragic denial of the Severing.

And now, somehow, Darred had called the dragon to him, across the barrier of the Long Dream. A dragon was once more free in Andeira, but a dragon whose conscious will was still bound to the silver effigy, and whose power was at the beck and call of a man who would use both to exert his influence over the world they had left behind them.

Silverwing, who could read his thoughts as though he had spoken aloud, said, *You are not done yet, Æisoul.*

Æisoul looked up as silver scales flashed in the brightness of the endless dawn.

No, he was not done. He had barely even started. And he was in the wrong place.

It was time to go back.

I must be Aarin again.

FOUR

Amadorn, the south

HANLON SHUFFLED THE short distance from his tent to his captor's, the butt of a spear jabbing him in the kidneys every time he stumbled. He kept his rage tightly bound, enduring the humiliation as he had endured it for months, committing the faces of his tormentors to memory. He had not considered himself a vengeful man, but it was the thought of revenge that sustained him now, that kept him alive.

They stopped outside the tent and he pulled himself upright, stretching cramped and aching muscles. This captivity was making him old, his once strong body hunching over and powerful muscles giving way to useless fat, slowing him down. It made him angry. It was meant to.

'The prisoner, my lord,' the guard called, and the hated voice summoned him.

Hanlon was shoved inside and forced into the chair facing the man he swore to kill each night, and each morning. The scar where his eye had been flared with irritation, and he resisted the urge to scratch the empty socket. The wound was almost healed and it itched unbearably, but he would not give Darred the satisfaction of letting him see the injury bothered him. Besides, scratching just left it sore and weeping and he was too experienced a campaigner not to fear the possibility that even now the wound could take a poison and kill him. And he had too much left to do to die now.

Watching Darred through his one good eye, Hanlon could tell the Caledani was rattled. He had come to know Darred in the months of his captivity, well enough to see past the smooth-as-glass exterior to something of the man beneath. Well enough to know when it was safe to speak his mind and when it was not. It was his misfortune he could not always hold his tongue.

'Bad news?' he asked acidly. He had been dragged from camp to camp for some time now, after Darred realised it was unwise to leave him locked up in Farnor. It hampered his activities, but not unduly. Though there were shackles on his wrists and guards at his door, he remained who he was, and men remembered.

His urbane captor glanced up from his desk as though he had only just noticed his prisoner's arrival. It was a game they played, and just the fact they were playing it was a small triumph in an existence without much scope for victories.

'On the contrary,' Darred replied. 'An unlooked-for success.'

Hanlon weighed that in silence. The very blandness of Darred's manner was a warning he had learned to heed. It was in just such a cold fury that Darred had taken his left eye. He did not want to risk the other. On the other hand, he never could resist the opportunity to needle this man.

'Shall we celebrate?' he asked after an interval. He gestured with his bound wrists to the bottle on Darred's desk. 'I've a thirst for strong spirits these days.'

Darred's eyes flicked to the bottle and back again. 'So you can drown your sorrows, Admiral? I hardly think so.'

Hanlon bared his teeth. 'It takes the edge off your hospitality, *my lord*.'

'I apologise. Is there some comfort you're lacking?' Darred spread his hands in mock contrition. 'Speak, and it shall be yours.'

'You know what I want,' he growled, provoked despite himself. He had a son grown from his first marriage. Darred claimed to have him. It was that threat, and that only, that kept him from killing this man with his bare hands. It had paved the way for their dance, as each tried to draw from the other the intelligence they needed to advance their plans. But he had been allowed no sight of the boy, and the uncertainty shackled him tighter than any knowledge could have.

'Alas, that request I cannot grant, but there is a matter on which I do wish to consult you. My men have apprehended a spy in this camp. What would you say is a suitable punishment for such a crime? Should I take his tongue or his eyes?'

Helpless rage flooded him, accompanied by the phantom agony of his own maiming.

Darred raised an eyebrow at his taut silence. 'You do not wish to choose? Very well.' Without lifting his eyes from Hanlon's face, Darred called back the guard who waited outside. 'Take both.'

Hanlon nearly killed him then. Muscles bunched on instinct, before the colder, rational part of his brain kicked in. Darred *wanted* him to do it. The man was in a killing mood, angry enough to sacrifice even his most valuable prisoner. And he could do nothing for his people if he was dead.

'Your success makes you generous,' he sneered when he could control his voice. 'What victory could have inspired such a depth of mercy?'

Darred shrugged, though his eyes spoke of something much darker. 'There is no reason you should not know. I defy even you, Admiral, to turn an assassination in Caledan to your advantage, especially as it leaves me master of the Kas'Talani on both sides of the sea.'

The shock almost betrayed him. Hanlon forced himself not to react as months—*years!*—of careful scheming unravelled at a stroke. An invading force cut off from its homeland with no hope of reinforcement was an enemy he could fight, no matter how annihilating its apparent advantage. But if what Darred said was true, Hanlon's enemy was no longer isolated in a hostile land. He now had the resources of an empire behind him. It was an astonishing triumph, yet the man was furious. He wanted very badly to know why.

'Allow me to congratulate you,' he said at last. 'But if you have the whole of Caledan, what do you need with Amadorn?'

Darred stiffened, cracks appearing in his self-control as he said with unaccustomed violence, 'Amadorn is *mine!*'

Hanlon sat back, a smile flickering on his lips. 'Not yet, my lord.'

He was prepared to suffer for that. There had been something close to madness in his enemy's eyes as he had grasped the only lever he had. But it was gone as quickly as it had come, and he had gained nothing beyond the satisfaction of seeing that mask slip for a bare instant.

'Careful, Admiral,' Darred admonished. 'You can serve me just as well blind. I advise you to stop trying to provoke me.'

Hanlon bit down on his instinctive response as Darred rose and walked around his desk. Perching on its edge, one leg dangling, he said, 'As enjoyable as this, I did not call you here to fence with me, but rather to discuss strategy. I feel it is time to take the fight to Lothane.'

Hanlon grunted. 'About time.'

Darred's smile was fleeting. 'Indeed. My officers have drawn up plans for an invasion. I require you to study these plans and give me your opinion—your *honest* opinion.'

'I'm a sailor, not a soldier.'

'Come now, Admiral. I also have my spies. I know your history, and your legend.'

He shrugged. 'Legends are untrustworthy things, my lord. As you should know.'

Darred seemed genuinely amused. 'Oh, I think not. Neither mine nor yours. I will not ask again.'

They locked stares. Hanlon looked away first, as he was meant to. He could not allow himself to forget the cost of defiance. 'You have vastly superior numbers. Cross the Istelan, take Rhiannas, and the north is yours.'

'That would be a lot easier if they didn't control the river.'

Hanlon forced himself to meet that knowing gaze without betraying so much as a flicker. 'If you had not dallied so long in Farnor, perhaps they might not.'

'Dallied so long in Farnor,' Darred repeated, rolling the words around thoughtfully. 'Rather revealing, don't you think, Admiral? After all, you were responsible for that dallying, and now I must ask myself—why?'

Hanlon ignored the veiled accusation, sticking stubbornly to his point. 'You could have been sitting in Rhiannas months ago.'

Darred's fingers played idly over the charts on his desk. His eyes never left Hanlon's face. 'So you have said. And yet I find myself unwilling to place my complete trust in any strategy you urge on me.'

Hanlon shrugged. 'Makes no difference to me.'

'No, it doesn't, does it?' With a faint, sardonic smile, Darred pulled the bottle towards him and poured a drink. He placed the cup at the edge of the desk but made no move to cut the cords around Hanlon's wrists. 'Tell me, Admiral, have your spies succeeded in discovering why I don't?'

There was no point denying it. It had taken him months and almost all his considerable fortune to find out why the Caledani were not pushing their advantage. And the answer his efforts had bought him was a garbled nonsense of legends and children's tales. A story planted by Darred, no doubt, though for what purpose he did not like to guess.

His mouth dry, Hanlon glanced the cup.

Darred tracked the movement, lips curling into a sneer. 'I see that you have. But you are not sure whether you can believe your spies?'

'I wouldn't call your men spies. Armies gossip worse than old women.'

Darred smiled. 'They do, don't they? Makes it so hard to keep a secret.'

It's a dance, Hanlon reminded himself as he met that penetrating gaze. His capture was one of those secrets, and one he had his own reasons for wanting to keep. News reached him, even in the heart of Darred's camp. He knew his wife was alive, that she had taken up with the northern witch and had brought what remained of Farnor to the aid of Lothane. But he did not think Limina knew he lived, and he wanted very much to keep it that way. While she had married him for sensible political reasons, she also was who she was, and she would move mountains to free him. They were, after all, rather fond of each other. Better by far that she think him dead, and that the snippets of news he sent her way came merely from what was left of Farnor's resistance. He made very sure she could not follow those snippets back to their source.

'I see we understand one another,' Darred said when Hanlon did not reply. He slid the plans across the desk. 'Now, you have work to do.'

Hanlon looked from the stack of papers to Darred's face and raised his bound hands. The cords fell away to drop in his lap, and he repressed a shudder as he massaged chafed and bleeding wrists. A life spent in the south, far from the magicians of the northern courts, made him deeply uncomfortable in the presence of magic, and this man's even more so.

'In your own time, Admiral,' Darred murmured as he walked back behind his desk. Hanlon ignored him. A slender knife lay on the desk between them, and he knew it was there to tempt him. He also knew such an attempt would end in his death, and calculated the odds of taking his enemy with him as he stretched cramped shoulders.

A glance at Darred showed the man lounging back in his chair, his attention focused on the casual play of light across his fingers—a temptation and a warning.

With a mental shake of his head, Hanlon pulled the plans towards him. He could not forget his son. All he could do was take what he learned and put it in the hands of others who might be able to use it.

Eventually, he sat back, studying Darred from across the desk. He tapped the topmost sheet of parchment. 'Either your officers are fools, or you think I am.'

Darred let the lightshow dissipate and sat up. 'I assure you, neither of those things is true.'

Hanlon raised an eyebrow. 'Then this is pure fantasy.' He hesitated, struck by an unpleasant thought. 'Unless…'

Darred cocked his head. 'Unless?'

That smile. Hanlon felt a chill run down his spine. He thought again about what his spies had told him. About the creature rumoured to have been seen in the skies, far to the south and east. Every rational instinct told him it could not be true, that Darred was playing him and his network, and yet the plans he had been shown were utterly worthless, unless there was a missing piece, something he had not been told. If that something…

He shook his head. 'You're mad. You cannot believe…'

'It's not a question of belief, but of knowledge. So, tell me, Admiral. If you add that knowledge to what you see here, what do you think of these plans now?'

Playing for time, his mind ablaze with something close to panic, Hanlon looked again at the strategies he had dismissed, committing them to memory and adjusting for the unthinkable, the impossible, that Darred clearly believed he could bring to bear.

'It's untidy and inefficient,' he said at last. 'You'll take Lothane, but you will sacrifice men needlessly and leave yourself open to attack from Elvelen.'

Darred looked at him thoughtfully, fingers drumming on the desk. 'My commanders believe Elvelen will surrender if Lothane falls.'

Hanlon shrugged. 'Maybe. Maybe not.'

'What would you change?'

He leant forward. 'Tell me the whole plan, and I'll tell you what I would change.'

Darred barked a laugh. 'I'm sure you would, Admiral. But I am not convinced it would be to my benefit. Here,' he pushed the untouched cup of spirits across the desk. 'Let us drink to success—yours or mine. You have given me much to think about.'

Hanlon reached for the cup, his mouth parched, and choked as the fiery spirit hit the back of his throat. 'What is this filth?'

Darred laughed. There was no humour in it. 'Caledan's finest rotgut. I used to drink it once, with a friend.'

Hanlon wiped his mouth on a filthy sleeve. 'Now I know that is a lie. A man like you never had any friends.'

'No,' Darred murmured. 'I expect you're right.'

FIVE

Ephenor, Caledan

AARIN SAT WITH his arms wrapped around his knees, shivering in the early morning chill, watching the sun rise over Ephenor.

He was alone. Silverwing had left him here in the pre-dawn darkness, gone to find a place of concealment before the sun rose. Behind him lay Tesseria, before him the dusty hinterlands that surrounded Ephenor on three sides. Beyond the fortress on the western edge, the harshness of the deserts brushed up almost to her walls. Or it had done. Did it still? The light of the new sun revealed a scattering of outlying farmsteads, replacing those that had been stripped and dismantled before the siege. He imagined he could still see the scars on the land. He could have reached out and read them if he wished, but he was reluctant to tap that well and all it would show him.

He had no idea how much time had passed since he had left this world for the Long Dream. No idea what he would find when he walked up to the gates of the city. He had little sense of the passing of time in the dragon dream. It could have been a day since he left. It could have been a hundred years. And what then? If everyone and everything he knew was gone, if the world he had left no longer existed?

The sense of *feeling* rocked him to his core. For the first time—in how long?—he had a physical awareness of himself he had not realised he lacked. It was only in returning that he realised how utterly he had been removed from this reality.

He looked at his clothes—the same clothes he had been wearing when he had confronted Aarkan, the same clothes he had worn during the siege of

Ephenor. His fingers traced the stains and rips in shirt and leggings and the fine tracery of corresponding scars beneath. He flexed his right hand, feeling the deep ache across his palm of the healing cut. It looked only a few days old. It was only a few days old when he'd left. Did that mean no time had passed, or that time itself was meaningless? He had been gone an eternity. He had *lived* an eternity.

Transported into the Long Dream with Silverwing, Aarin had never questioned how he was there, or even *where* he was. The memories he had inherited from Lorrimer understood the nature of the dragon dream without need for explanations. But here, back on Andeira, that understanding was as ephemeral as the morning mist. Here he was connected to himself and the world in a way that was absent from the reality spun by the dragons' collective unconscious.

The sun rose higher, the chill dispersing as the temperature started to climb, but still he did not move. The fortress was some five miles distant, five miles under a baking sun, and he was intensely conscious of his thirst. He had no water, for he had none to bring. When had he last had a drink, or eaten food? His stomach contracted painfully at the thought, yet he did not feel weak from hunger. Something had sustained him.

Aarin knew he should move, start the long trek before the heat of the day reached its peak. The memory of his flight across the desert with Kinseris was suddenly vivid and awful. But not knowing what—or who—he would find at the end of it stole his resolve. The ties of friendship, of love, which had been but a memory in the dream, returned to him now. He both longed for and shied away from encountering the people they connected him to.

In the end it was thirst that propelled him to his feet and put one foot in front of the other. Silverwing could have taken him to the gates of the fortress and spared him the walk, but every instinct warned him against the sudden appearance of a dragon. If Eiador had indeed returned to the world, Aarin needed to know where he had gone and what he had done before he dared risk exposing Silverwing's existence. His own was another matter, and there was only one way to find out what that would mean.

As Ephenor drew nearer, Aarin could see that some time must have passed.

The walls had been repaired, but he could not tell how recently. The gates had been replaced. He had held the fortress gates together by sheer force of will against the armies of Kas'Tella and he knew them intimately. These new gates, standing open in the morning sun, had never withstood a siege.

The gates were open but not unmanned. The lookouts on the walls had spotted him some time ago, and the guards at the gate watched him approach with caution tempered by curiosity. He was, after all, only one man.

The challenge, when he reached them, was polite but firm. He hesitated over Shrogar's name. His use of it would mark him one way or the other. Then he heard running footsteps and a voice he did recognise. The guard gave him an odd, searching look then stepped aside and ushered him past. His heart hammering, Aarin walked through the gates of Ephenor and prepared to confront the world he had left behind.

He emerged from the shadow of the gateway to see a man standing there, arms crossed and an impish grin on his face. It was the grin that identified him and took away the worst of Aarin's fears at once.

'Lysan.' His voice cracked over the name, but Ephenor's captain of archers did not seem to notice.

A moment later he was swept into an embrace and when he was released Lysan had been joined by another. Identical in aspect if not in disposition, Lysan's twin brother Callan regarded him with a reserved smile and a degree of justifiable apprehension.

'Welcome back,' Callan said at length. 'We didn't expect to see you again.'

'I see you've learned nothing about walking the desert under the sun,' Lysan laughed. 'You look only slightly better than you did when you arrived here the first time.'

Aarin flinched. He imagined he looked almost exactly as he had when he first arrived, with the marks of that fading sunburn still on his face. He felt Callan's questioning gaze and knew the man was comparing his memories with the present. Whatever conclusions he drew, the tightening of his expression told Aarin they were not entirely comfortable.

'I didn't expect to be back,' Aarin admitted. 'At least, not yet… not now. Kallis and… are they still here?' He couldn't bring himself to say her name.

The brothers exchanged a look. Then Callan said, 'Come. Shrogar will want to greet you himself, and then we can talk.'

Shrogar welcome him with warmth but there was a caution in his eyes that mirrored the look that had passed between Callan and Lysan. They had found him with Dianeth and his daughter, a sturdy toddler with her mother's fine blond hair and her father's piercing eyes. Seeing her, Aarin could measure the passing of time, though he still could not match the two years he guessed must have passed with his sojourn in the dream.

Dianeth's greeting was more restrained than her husband's. Aarin felt a vague sense of guilt as she welcomed him gravely before gathering the child in her arms and leaving the men alone.

Shrogar leant back in his chair, studying him as Callan had done. 'I admit, I am surprised to see you. Kallis and… your companions tried to explain what happened…' He shrugged, sharp eyes fixed on Aarin's. 'You are most welcome here, but I must ask –'

There was a hesitation in his manner that made Aarin uneasy. It came to him that they were treating him very carefully. 'Why I am here? My lord, I –' He stopped. What could he say? 'I'm not asking for shelter,' he said at last, answering what he assumed must be their first concern. After the last time.

He knew he was not making much sense. Shrogar was watching him with an expression of polite puzzlement and Callan with open concern. Everything was a jumble of sensation and he understood that he was still not firmly rooted in this reality. It made coherent conversation difficult as his past collided with his present and he tried to find his way back into a skin that no longer fit.

'Shelter you will have, whether you need it or not,' Shrogar replied. 'I well recall why Ephenor still stands.'

It was Callan, leaning against the wall, arms crossed, who asked, 'Where have you been?'

Such a simple question. Such a complicated answer. 'With the dragons.' That was honest. 'They needed me.' That too was honest, though it surprised him how much it sounded like an apology.

Shrogar exchanged a look with Callan over his head. 'And now?'

'Something has happened. Something has changed. Something here.'

Lysan stirred, about to speak, but something—Callan possibly—made him think better of it. Shrogar flashed his captain an unreadable look before asking carefully, 'What has changed?'

'They stopped waking up.' He did not know how much Kinseris had explained about the Kas'Talani's relationship with the dragons, but from the dawning comprehension on Shrogar's face, he guessed the priest had revealed the whole unpleasant truth. Knowing Kinseris, it did not surprise him. What did surprise him was the shadowed pain in Shrogar's eyes.

He recalled the scene he had witnessed through Silverwing's eyes, of the soldier who had knelt to the priest and the standard that had been lowered then raised up again. As, one by one, the sleeping dragons had been coaxed awake, he had guessed he had Kinseris to thank. That some of them had been harder to wake than others was not surprising. Few among the Kas'Talani would choose to give up such power willingly. 'Kinseris took Vasa's place? The Order accepted him?'

Again that slight pause. 'They had little choice. He had the backing of the army and Vasa had concentrated power in his own hands for so long that when he died there was no one to take control.'

Aarin examined the memory again. 'You made him take it.' Although Shrogar could not have known it, Iarwin's death would have been the lever to compel Kinseris to accept a role he must hate.

'I did.'

It sounded like an admission, but he made no excuses. It had been necessary, even Aarin could see that. The man who had brought down the Order had a responsibility to clean up the wreckage, and Kinseris would never have forgiven himself if he had walked away.

'What of the Order now?'

Shrogar hesitated, his gaze darting to Callan. Aarin felt a flicker of fear. Now they were coming to it, whatever it was.

'What has happened?'

Shrogar cleared his throat. 'We thought it was why you came back…'

Aarin looked between them, seeing at last the signs he should have read at once, and it took him a moment to realise Shrogar was speaking. Still longer to process his words.

'Kinseris is dead. He was assassinated a few months ago, by his own bodyguard. Darred's faction has retaken Kas'Tella.'

Aarin froze. The cold, logical part of his brain, the part that remained with the dragons, understood that Kinseris's death was the reason the dragons were no longer waking so easily. The rest of him was howling his grief. 'Kestel? Kestel killed him?'

Shrogar shook his head, his own face stripped bare. 'No, a man called Escarian. Kinseris trusted him. I trusted him. He worked for us for years. I do not know why. Aarin...'

There was more. Oh Maker, there was more. He met Shrogar's eyes and recoiled from the pity in them. 'What?' It came out as a whisper.

'Jeta was with him. I'm sorry.'

'You're sorry?' He did not understand, he refused to understand. The blood was roaring in his ears. His head felt like it might explode. 'Why?' he demanded. 'Why are you sorry?'

No one answered him. He was not sure he had spoken aloud. He felt Silverwing's questing concern and shut the dragon out, hard. Jeta was dead. Kinseris was dead. And he had abandoned them. He had walked away, knowing better than anyone the threat that Darred posed. Worse, he had stripped them of the protection of the dragons' magic and left them defenceless against him. He had thought he was serving a higher purpose but all he had been doing was running away. He had thought he was saving them, instead he had killed them. Was Kallis dead too? Sedaine?

At some point his thoughts cleared enough to realise he was alone. He was still sitting at Shrogar's desk. Hours must have passed. It was dark outside. And cold. Everything was ashes.

He could feel Silverwing hammering at the edges of his awareness, demanding admittance. Someone was knocking at the door.

SIX

DIANETH STOOD FRAMED in the open door, her expression unreadable. She waited for him to say something. When he did not, she closed the door and entered the room.

'The men are frightened to intrude. Are they right?'

He looked up. He did not understand what she was saying.

Dianeth studied him in turn and there was little of sympathy or even friendship in her face. He understood that. His presence could only mean loss for her, as it had last time.

As if she could read understood his thoughts, Dianeth shook her head, the gesture irritated to the point of anger. 'This helps no one.'

'It's too late anyway.'

'For them, yes,' she agreed. 'But you did not come back for them.'

That piercing insight, delivered without pity, made his face burn as if she had slapped him. Because he had not come back for Jeta, or Kinseris. It was the threat to the dragons that had brought him here.

'I killed them.' He had made them vulnerable then left them.

Dianeth sighed. She swept up her skirts and sat in Shrogar's chair, watching him. She looked cold, her face pinched and the fingers of the hand that reached across the desk for his were white with chill.

'This is not a question of blame,' she told him. 'Responsibility, maybe. And yes, some of that is yours. But no one can be completely responsible for another's fate. You cannot hide behind guilt. Give her your honest grief then let her go.'

Let her go.

He had let her go once before, reluctantly but willingly.

'Will you not cry for her?' Dianeth asked gently. 'She cried for you.'

And he dropped his head in his hands and wept.

As soon as the dam broke, the savage cold broke with it and sunlight streamed back into the room. Dianeth sat back, the relief leaving her trembling. It had taken all her courage to enter this room, to confront this man who was *other* and whose grief had stolen both warmth and light and chased the men from the room.

She watched him look up and around. As the sunlight hit his face, he turned to her, eyes wide and dark.

'Did I do that?'

She nodded and saw some expression she could not interpret chase across his face. There was a pause during which his attention turned inwards, away from her. When he came back to himself there was an altogether more human vulnerability in his eyes.

'I'm sorry. I'm not used to this…' His hand gestured vaguely. 'We have not been together in this world for long and everything is different here.'

Nothing about that made sense. 'We?'

A fleeting smile. 'I'm sorry. The dragon to whom I am Joined.'

Her fear must have shown on her face because he reached out a hand as though to touch her, then thought better of it and let it rest on the table between them.

'You don't need to be afraid, truly. Despite…' He looked away, at anything but her face. 'It is hard to explain, but where I have been—it is like I was standing in the shadows and now I am in the sun. Everything I feel, it is stronger here, and I have not yet learned to control it.'

Dianeth took a shaky breath. 'No harm was done, except to the men's pride.' She forced a smile. 'They are waiting outside.'

Aarin nodded, and she fled from the room with as much dignity as she could muster.

Shrogar brushed aside his apology, and if Lysan's smile was rather fixed he did at least look Aarin in the eye. Only Callan seemed undisturbed, though his gaze held a painful mixture of compassion and curiosity. No one mentioned Jeta or Kinseris, but there was one other name still unspoken.

'Kallis?'

Shrogar exchanged a look with his captains. Aarin felt a flutter of panic. Callan saw the thought and said quickly, 'It's not that.'

Aarin frowned, suddenly sure that whatever trouble Kallis had found, that was where he needed to be. 'Then what?'

Shrogar sighed. 'Those in the Kas'Talani who resisted Kinseris's authority rallied around another standard.'

Darred. He had been almost sure when Eiador disappeared from the dream, but now he was certain. He knew where Kallis was. Because Darred had made no secret of the prize he had craved and Aarin knew exactly how long he had plotted to make it his, and who his schemes had entangled.

'Darred. Darred has gone to Amadorn. And Kallis has gone after him.' Because Kallis hated Darred with a passion that went far deeper than anyone but Aarin realised.

Shrogar nodded. 'The first thing Kinseris did once he was secure in Kas'Tella was strip the priesthood of much of its power. Those who would not give up that power have flocked to Darred, and many have joined his army in Amadorn.'

His army. An army backed by the power of the dragons. The very thing he had tried so hard to prevent. Amadorn would be defenceless against such a threat, and even if his mother somehow managed to bring the mages of Luen to her side, they could never hope to match the might of Darred's forces. And now, if what he and Silverwing believed was true, they did not just have the power of the dragons, but dragons themselves.

His mouth dry, Aarin looked up to see Shrogar watching him. 'What can you tell me?'

Lysan handed Shrogar a map and the lord of Ephenor spread it out on his desk, briskly outlining what intelligence he had. 'You will appreciate that our news is months old by now. We know Darred controls the entire south of the continent, but the last word we had from Kas'Tella indicated that the north continues to hold out. If that is still the case I cannot say.'

'It won't be for much longer. I have to go to Amadorn.'

Lysan raised his head. 'I will come with you.'

'Lysan!'

There was a fraught pause as Lysan met his brother's anguished gaze. Then he said, 'You don't have to come.'

For a frozen moment no one moved. Then Callan walked out, the door slamming behind him. Left behind, Lysan cursed and kicked the desk. Then he looked at Shrogar. 'My lord…?'

Shrogar nodded. 'Go.'

And Lysan was running after his brother.

As the door closed behind him, Aarin turned to Shrogar. He had seen Callan and Lysan disagree before, but not like that.

Shrogar sighed, answering his unspoken question. 'No one survived the siege unscathed. Callan perhaps least of all. He hasn't touched a weapon since.'

Aarin thought back to the quiet, contained man he had known two years before. The soldier who had fought beside him and the captain who had led his men with such easy competence. And the brother who could so easily shatter his calm. Then he remembered the look he had just seen on his face, the echo of a trauma that had gone bone deep, and understood that Lysan's impulsive decision to throw himself into the middle of another conflict had just ripped away whatever measure of peace his brother had found since.

'I did not come here recruiting,' he said quietly. 'Neither of them has to come.'

Shrogar looked away. 'Lysan will go with you. So Callan will go too. If you want to help Callan, keep Lysan safe.'

Aarin was on the walls when Lysan found him and told him they would both go with him.

Aarin turned slowly. 'Why?'

'Because it isn't finished. I thought we had won the war here, but we didn't. If we turn aside from this fight, how long before we have to defend these walls once more?'

Aarin studied his face, hearing the words he did not say. The unfamiliar anger, frustration and worry that was eating at him. He poked the wound. 'And Callan?'

Lysan did not reply at once. He moved to stand beside Aarin, looking out into the desert's night. 'My brother is weary of war,' he said at last. 'Too many died here, too many at his orders. He cannot forgive himself.'

Aarin said nothing, knowing there was more, and after a moment Lysan sighed. 'We were coming to help you. But we were too late. You did whatever it was you did and all the priests… it was like they lost their minds. Some of them fell to their knees, others were laughing like madmen. And my brother…' He looked Aarin in the eye for the first time. 'My brother just stood there, weeping. He has never been the same since.'

Aarin met Lysan's stricken gaze. Callan was not the only one who had lost something. His brother was also hurting. 'I'm sorry.'

Lysan looked away first. 'I'm sorry, too. I think I know what she meant to you; I saw what you meant to her.'

Aarin swallowed. He dared not think about Jeta, or Kinseris.

'And that's why you're coming?'

Lysan shrugged. 'That's one reason.' And Aarin flinched as he added fiercely, 'You took my brother's peace. Maybe you can give it back.'

Aarin called to Silverwing and felt the dragon answer. He was close, and it was not long before the dark speck in the sky grew larger and took shape.

There were unshed tears in Callan's eyes as the dragon landed on the plains to the north of the city, great wings sweeping down to curve around powerful flanks and his scales ablaze in the morning sun. Lysan's eyes were as wide as a child's and for once he did not notice his brother's distress.

Leaving the brothers to wait, Aarin crossed the distance to Silverwing, mentally and physically. The connection that had overwhelmed him in Ephenor, that he had suppressed so desperately ever since, yawned wide and deep as Silverwing welcomed and rebuked him.

'I'm sorry,' Aarin murmured, head resting on the dragon's flank.

Your pain is mine, little brother. Do not shut me out.

I lost control.

We will learn, Silverwing assured him. *Together.*

Aarin opened his eyes and looked up, then back at Callan and Lysan. *Will you carry them?*

Silverwing followed his gaze. *One of them…*

I know.

The dragon shifted his bulk, unfolding his wings. Aarin sensed a feeling of intense satisfaction. Then Silverwing reared up, wings flaring outwards. Lysan leapt back and nearly fall.

I will carry them.

SEVEN

Amadorn, Lothane

KALLIS COULD NOT remember the last time he had felt this tired. He glanced at the man beside him and saw the same fatigue on Meinor's battered features. How long had it been since he had slept? One day? Two?

'That's the last of them,' Meinor said gruffly, as the filthy, exhausted men filed past.

Kallis scrubbed a hand over his face, feeling the building ache behind his eyes. He turned to Lorac. 'Watch your right flank. They nearly came past us the last time.'

Lorac exchanged an amused look with Meinor and slapped Kallis on the back. 'Get some rest. I've fought once or twice before.'

Not like this, Kallis wanted to say, but he did not. They were all of them unaccustomed to this kind of fight, hunkered down in ditches, wading through mud and blood to hold an enemy advance that should not have been possible.

He waited while Meinor spoke with Lorac, giving him the names of the clan dead. The big man looked as tired as Kallis felt, and his Hawks little better. There wasn't a man or woman among them not bleeding from somewhere. He watched as one stumbled to the side and puked his guts out into the mud. Kallis offered his water flask to the woman crouching by his side, and she nodded her thanks, her own face drawn and dirty as she turned back to the soldier with possessive concern. Kallis watched them with distant curiosity. The clans took a practical view of women in the fighting companies, as long as they weren't married and had no children. They took a practical view of securing new generations as well. Even so, there weren't many who chose that life, and fewer still who chose to mix it with romantic entanglements. But he had seen more women with the companies in the last few months than he had seen in all the years he had fought with the clans.

He had been in Lothane for six months. It felt like six years, and that was just the last two days. Whatever Darred had been waiting for, he was waiting no longer. The attack had come from nowhere and had made it almost to the gates of Rhiannas. Only meticulous preparation—and a mercenary clan in the wrong place at the right time—had given them enough to warning to hold Darred's troops between the Istelan and the city and save them from a siege that would have pinned down the heart of Lothane's forces and left the enemy free to ravage the rest of the country.

The clans had come to Sedaine late in the autumn of the previous year, after what Lorac had described as 'an ugly bloody brawl' that had seen the fall and rise of several captains. They had been promptly put to work by Galydon, along with what seemed like most of the country after the harvest was safely gathered in, building a network of fortifications up and down the river and behind it all the way to Rhiannas. Whole villages had been cleared, their people sent to Rhiannas and from there further north or east, away from the fighting to come and to join what would become a national effort to secure food supplies for a country that might well lose half its good farmland to war. There had been hard choices, small and large, as Galydon had decreed which towns could be defended and which could not, and Kallis had seen enough anger and misery and defiance to last him a lifetime.

Sedaine had begun the process, fortifying the main river crossings and garrisoning them with a skeleton force, but without the mercenaries she didn't have the manpower to do more. They were there to give warning, not to repulse an invasion. With greater numbers behind him and an energy that Kallis found dizzying, Galydon extended that network from the Grymwood in the east to the Grey Mountains in west, which marked the border with Elvelen. And he had sent three clans into Elvelen to assist King Elian's efforts to guard the mountain passes. Every ford was manned, and even those sections of the river that ran through steep gorges had signal towers.

Wherever Darred tried to make his crossing, they would do so under the eyes of Lothane's defenders and Rhiannas would know in short order.

And that was not their only defence. Iraius had been as good as his word. He had turned the small riverside settlement of Carter's Ferry into a temporary boatyard and its residents into what he half-jokingly called his navy. Up and down the Istelan, rivermen had flocked to him, unable to safely work the river since Darred's forces had claimed the southern bank, and he had set them to work, building the sleek, dangerous crafts he had used to such devastating effect on the Aetelea. As far as Kallis could tell, he was having the time of his life.

As the boats left the boatyard, they took up station at the main forts on the northern bank, from where they patrolled the river and stood ready to harass any attempt at a crossing. With them went the mages and magicians who made up the magical cordon Sedaine had placed around her nation, an extra line of defence against the power of the Kas'Talani. Though no match for priests in possession of a dragon device, they would have the Water of the Istelan to draw on, and they would be both safer and more effective for it.

So there should have been no way that Darred could ferry enough troops across the Istelan without triggering Galydon's defences. But he had. As Kallis trudged back from the maze of earthworks the Caledani general had dug across the main land route to Rhiannas, his exhausted mind continued to worry that problem. Because if Darred could do it once, he could do it again, and though Galydon's lines were holding, the sudden appearance of small army between them had still caught them unprepared and cost them more lives than they could afford.

'We might have a week or a year,' Galydon had told Sedaine that first day as he had outlined his plan. 'But I think we will have until the first thaw.'

Three months. It had seemed an impossible task, but Galydon had an iron will and knew exactly what he wanted.

'I have fought on the other side of such conflicts enough times to know what works and what doesn't,' he told Kallis, who was beginning to realise just how reliant they were on his experience. The mercenary clans were superb soldiers, but they did not know this kind of warfare, nor did they have any concept of the power they would be facing. Galydon did, and he used that knowledge to minimise the enemy's advantage wherever possible. Only the river forts were bare wood. The redoubts that stretched across the southern plains of Lothane between the Istelan and Rhiannas were banked with earth or covered in clay and surrounded by earthworks. Of all the powers the Kas'Talani possessed, it was their use of fire as a weapon that Galydon feared most. And his decision to dig in rather than build up their second line defences was as much from fear of the destructive weather the priests could conjure as the need to conserve wood for Iraius's enterprise. Kallis had seen how effective's Aarin defensive use of Air had been in Ephenor. He did not want to see what the Kas'Talani could do with it in an offensive capacity.

They had bargained on three months. They had got six, and they had made good use of them. And still Darred had got past them.

Galydon met them as they straggled into the camp. Iraius was with him.

Kallis stopped dead. 'What are you doing here?' The enemy was between them and the river. If ever Iraius was needed there, it was now.

Galydon looked Kallis critically up and down. 'Later. Come.'

And Kallis sighed and followed when he would much rather have dropped where he stood and slept for twelve hours.

A few minutes later, a cup of steaming hot *kafe* in his hand as he gave his report, he felt marginally more human. Where Galydon had managed to find the prized Caledani beans in Lothane more than two years since the departure of the last caravan he did not know, but it had never been more welcome. He shook his head in frustration as he finished. 'I still don't understand how they managed to get so many across the river without alerting us. Or how they made it so far north.'

That was almost as bad. Neither Sedaine nor Galydon was under any illusion that they could prevent the invasion when it came. But all Galydon's preparations were designed to slow it, to make it impossible for a large-scale movement of Darred's troops across the river at any one time. To divide his much larger army into smaller units that could be trapped and crushed between Lothane's lines.

Well, that was the plan. But the division currently pinned down two miles south of where he sat had apparently floated past the river's defenders like ghosts and the two-sided trap had not closed. Galydon had decided against drawing the best part of the Istelan's garrison two days north to attack from the rear. If, as seemed likely, the invasion had begun, they could not risk weakening their first line of defence. Which was why Kallis was so surprised to see Iraius here.

Iraius was staring at the distant Istelan, one arm resting on his bent knee. He said, 'She's a big river. We can't be everywhere. What's worrying me ain't how they crossed the river, it's how they got past Needa and her people.'

Galydon glanced at Kallis. If the Kas'Talani had sent priests with the troops, the mage cordon could not hold, but it would not have gone down without a fight. They would have had some warning.

But if there were priests with this vanguard, they had not yet made their presence known.

'Do you think they're dead?' Kallis asked. That was a blow that would be hard to absorb.

Galydon looked doubtful. 'All of them? Let's hope not.' He was watching Iraius. 'No, we're missing something. There have been no reports of troops massing on the south bank?'

Iraius shook his head. 'We've seen nothing. It's all quiet on the water.'

'Too quiet?' Kallis asked. 'But it's been too quiet for months. Magic?' That was an uncomfortable thought.

'It's possible,' Galydon conceded, 'but that's why the magicians are down there. Vianor was certain that illusion on that scale would be impossible to conceal completely.'

Kallis grunted. Sedaine trusted Vianor. He had no opinion on the matter. But he knew what Aarin thought of the magicians and their magic. 'I've seen Aarin hold unbreakable illusions. It can be done.'

Galydon shot him an unreadable look. 'He's not here, and I can only go by what I know of the Kas'Talani. Such an illusion, I am told, involves potentially fatal exposure. I do not believe they would risk it.'

'So what then?' Maker, he was tired.

'Elvelen,' Iraius said.

'What?' Kallis set down his cup, looking between them.

Galydon, the fingers drumming on his leg the only visible sign of enormous stress, said, 'It's possible this attack is either covering the movement of troops into Elvelen or is the result of Darred already having done so. If this division did not cross the river, they may have crossed the mountains. We cannot afford not to find out.'

Kallis leant back, suppressing a yawn. 'And if they have? Do you think Elian…?'

'I don't think anything yet,' Galydon said firmly. 'But nothing about this makes sense. I don't like the chance we could be looking in the wrong direction when the moment comes. I have sent scouts west, to the mountains. Iraius will go by the river, and he will check in on Needa and Brannick, find out what they know.'

So that's why Iraius was here. Kallis was about to ask about the clans already sent west when the yawn he could no longer hide overtook him.

Galydon smiled. 'Enough for now. Go, sleep. We'll talk in the morning.'

Someone kicked him awake much earlier than that. Kallis opened his eyes to see Lorac standing over him, a mug of *kafe* in each hand.

Kallis blinked. The sky was just on the turn from black to grey, which at this time of year meant it was still far too early to be awake. 'What?' he growled, rolling over and onto his knees. Then, more urgently, 'What's happened?' Lorac should have been enjoying a night in the trenches. He should not have been back in the main camp.

'Here.' Lorac thrust the *kafe* into his hand as Kallis made it to his feet. He started walking. 'They're withdrawing. Galydon isn't happy.'

'He's not?' Kallis asked, rubbing the sleep from his eyes as he fell in beside Lorac. It was cold and every muscle in his body ached. 'Why not?'

'No reason to pull back now. And he doesn't like the thought of so many enemy soldiers running around Lothane. Neither do I.'

'Where is he now?'

'Everywhere,' Lorac replied laconically. Then added, 'He's sent the Eagles and the Falcons after them. Make sure they go in the right direction.'

Namely, onto the swords of the river garrison. Kallis glanced at Lorac. The mercenary captain-of-captains had brought the clans into this alliance, but he had refused to place them directly under Galydon's command. With so many of the mercenaries still hostile to the magicians, he could only go so far. But the two commanders appeared to understand each other. As long as Galydon did not overstep and give the clans a direct order, Lorac would see he got his way. Kallis suspected Lorac was happy enough to let Galydon take charge, but he would also do what he could to ensure the clans did not shoulder a disproportionate risk.

'Is Iraius still here?'

Lorac shrugged. 'Haven't see him.'

Kallis sipped the scalding *kajf*. 'You know where he's going?'

'Yes,' Lorac replied as Galydon came striding towards them, a ripple of frantic activity fanning out in his wake. If he had slept since Kallis had last seen him it was not immediately obvious.

'I need you to go back to Rhiannas,' he told Kallis. 'Report to the queen. We'll follow once we've cleaned up here.'

'Then what?'

'Then we'll see,' Galydon called over his shoulder as he kept walking.

Kallis watched him go, head still thick with sleep, then turned to Lorac. 'What about you? Will you go west?'

Lorac stared straight ahead. 'Maybe. Might have to.'

If this had been merely a feint to hide an invasion of Elvelen, the three clans Galydon had sent west were at best at risk, and at worst they were already dead. In between were a range of other possibilities that Kallis would not be the one to voice. From Lorac's brooding silence, he did not have to. When the scouts returned, they would know more.

The camp was coming to life as weary men arrived to rest and others prepared to leave with Galydon in pursuit of the retreating army.

'Who's staying here?' Kallis asked.

'I am, for now. Meinor's taking the Hawks to check the western routes into Rhiannas, make sure everything's still quiet.'

Kallis shivered, and it had little to do with the pre-dawn chill. There was something unnerving about this inexplicable flare of activity after months and months of waiting. 'None of this makes sense.'

The mercenary captain-of-captains drained his *kafe* and threw the dregs onto a fire. 'None of it makes sense *yet*. I reckon we won't like it any better when it does.'

Kallis grunted. 'That's truth.' Then his nose caught the smell of cooking and he said hopefully, 'Any chance of something to eat before I go?'

EIGHT

AARIN HAD NEVER thought about a dragon's range. How far could they fly without rest? How far, when carrying three humans rather than one? Once they left the land behind, it suddenly became a pressing concern. The world had changed since Silverwing had withdrawn from it, and the dragon had no concept of human systems of measurement. Even worse, Aarin had only limited knowledge of the geography between Caledan and Amadorn. There were island chains strung out between the two continents, including the volcanic Illeneas archipelago that was the major trading stop between Frankesh and Farnor in Amadorn, but he had only a vague idea of where and no way of finding them. And they had to find land. None of them would survive a dunking in the ocean.

They sighted land just as it seemed to Aarin that neither of them could make it much further. Silverwing's exhaustion was dragging at him, making it harder and harder to stay alert, to stay awake, and it was only when Callan's frozen fingers gripped his shoulder and steadied him that he realised he had drifted off.

Callan pointed, his face pinched, and Aarin saw the speck of land through the clouds. Silverwing was already dropping down towards it, the intensity of his fatigue making his descent fast and clumsy. Aarin gave the last of his remaining strength to the dragon and felt himself almost pass out, but their descent steadied enough for Silverwing to bring them in smoothly.

As he touched land, Silverwing sank down in surrender, head resting on the sand of the small beach, his sides heaving. Aarin rested his own head on the dragon's neck and would have stayed where he was but for his passengers. He could still feel the touch of Callan's ice-cold fingers and see the blue tint of his lips. They needed warmth, and quickly, and he managed to summon enough concentration to draw on Silverwing's fire and wrap the heat around them. He heard Lysan's sigh of pleasure as cold limbs were suffused with warmth, and then they were slithering stiffly down the dragon's wing to land in a tumbled heap in the sand. He was vaguely aware of Callan saying something, and then he was curled up against Silverwing's flank and the world faded away.

Callan shook him awake sometime later, pressing food into his hand. It was dark but a fire was burning close by and he could smell… Someone shook him, and he opened his eyes to Callan's concerned frown. He must have drifted off again, food forgotten. He tried to speak, but the next thing he knew the fire was cold and the only sound was someone snoring gently in the darkness.

Aarin struggled to his feet, flexing cramped muscles, then staggered off into the darkness to relieve himself. When he came back, he found Callan awake, arms wrapped around drawn-up knees.

It was cold, but rather than draw on more of Silverwing's depleted reserves, Aarin squatted by the fire and began to build it back up, shaping a spark of Fire to kindle the driftwood. Callan watched him in silence, and the weight of unspoken things hung between them.

At length he was rewarded by a quiet question. 'You take from him, and he takes from you?'

Aarin sat down, drawing up his knees to mirror Callan's pose. 'Yes. Or rather, I give to him, and he gives to me. It isn't usually so extreme.'

Callan considered this for a moment. 'It was hard to wake you. What would have happened if we hadn't found this place when we did?'

Aarin half smiled. 'We did find it.'

Callan looked away, towards the place where Lysan lay curled up asleep. When he looked back, there was a terrible yearning in his eyes. 'What is it like?'

Such a little question. Such a dangerous, impossible answer to give a man with that look on his face. But truth, or as much truth as could be contained by mere words, was the only possible response.

'It is like being whole for the first time in my life. It is like I am only now truly alive, and that everything else is alive in me. Like a river that was dry and now is in flood.'

For a long moment, Callan just stared back at him. Then his gaze dropped, and Aarin saw dark lashes sweep down to cover the sudden brightness in his eyes.

'Thank you. I think.'

'Things were different in the dream,' Aarin told him, understanding his need to *know*. 'Here, everything I feel... In Ephenor...'

'You don't have to explain.'

'But I do have to understand. I have to learn to control this power. Before, it was a conscious thing. I had to *choose* to use it. Now, my every thought, my every emotion... I have to choose *not* to use it.'

We are something new. There has never been another pairing like ours.

The thought was Silverwing's and it was for him alone, but Callan's head jerked around to look at the dragon, apparently deep in slumber.

This one can almost hear me.

Shaken, Aarin focused on Silverwing. *That is not possible.*

How do we know? The dragon sounded amused. *There has never been another pairing like ours. All this is new.*

'Please, stop.'

Callan was looking at him across the fire, a plea in his eyes.

'I'm sorry,' Aarin said helplessly.

And Callan got to his feet and walked away.

The morning dawned clear and cold. Aarin woke, his head thick with sleep, to find Callan and Lysan were already up. He blinked in the brightness of sunlight reflected off the water and experienced a moment of unsettling disorientation as he remembered where he was, and where he was no longer. Silverwing was a reassuring bulk at his back, anchoring him here, now, as he had done in the dream he had yet to shake off.

Lysan was grumbling as he looked for kindling. After one fleeting glance that consigned their conversation of the night before firmly to the past,

Callan joined his brother, leaving Aarin precious minutes to gather his disordered wits.

By the time they returned, carrying a collection of driftwood and bamboo and bickering good-naturedly, Aarin had managed to get himself together and had even made it as far as the gently lapping waves to splash cold seawater on his face.

Lysan dropped his bundle on the sand. 'Breakfast?' he said hopefully.

Aarin's stomach growled and he realised he was starving.

Callan held out a chunk of bread. 'Eat.'

Lysan took another and eyed it with distaste. 'Will we be moving on today? Because if not, I'm going fishing.'

Aarin tried to measure the depths of Silverwing's exhaustion against the regenerative nature of the dragons and the uncertainty of their location. They had left the coast of Caledan due north of where he thought he remembered the islands of Illeneas were positioned. If they had not reached them yet, they must be close. If they could make the outer edges of the archipelago today, they could rest there before making the last, long flight that would take them to Amadorn.

Lysan was looking at him, waiting for an answer.

'We go on,' Aarin said, his voice rusty.

'Eat,' Callan insisted again, frowning at him. 'You look… thinner.'

Aarin took the bread, his eyes drawn like Callan's to the sharply defined bones of his wrist. With a stirring of disquiet, he shook back his sleeve to look at his arm, disquiet changing to alarm as he saw the bones and muscles clearly delineated under pale skin. And now he thought about it, he felt lighter, less substantial, as though the vast expenditure of energy had melted the flesh from his bones.

He looked up. Callan pushed the rest of the food towards him.

Behind him, Silverwing stirred from his slumber, drawn to wakefulness by his mage's concern. Aarin felt his wry amusement.

This one knows what he is talking about, Æisoul. Eat the food. The energy must come from somewhere.

This insight delivered, the dragon reared up, sending Lysan flying backward in shocked surprise. Then, stretching his wings, Silverwing launched himself into the air, wheeling high above them before diving down to skim low over the surface of the water, his silver scales sparkling in the morning light.

Lysan picked himself up, grinning ruefully. 'What's he doing?'

'Hunting,' Aarin replied around a mouthful of bread, struck by a memory that wasn't his—of newly-Joined dragons cautiously testing the waters of the Aetelea. 'Watch.'

Wings spread wide, Silverwing glided over the surface of the ocean, his shadow rippling below him. Then, quite suddenly, he arrowed downwards, breaking the water with barely a splash and disappearing below the waves. The seconds ticked away, the surface of the water giving nothing away. Then the ocean exploded in spray as Silverwing powered upwards from the depths, something large and still-thrashing held tight in his jaws.

Aarin grinned as Lysan's mouth fell open. Callan laughed in delight, and the sound drew his brother's gaze like a lodestone.

Callan didn't notice Lysan's thoughtful expression as he said to Aarin, 'I did not think a dragon could do that. They are such creatures of fire.'

'They couldn't, if not for the Joining,' Aarin replied, watching as Silverwing glided down to land on the beach, his catch still twitching feebly. A shark, and not a small one. The dragon pinned the shark with his talons and efficiently put an end to its struggles with a snap of his jaws.

He turned back to Callan. 'Dragons have no natural affinity with Water. They gain it only through the link, just as the link gives me the ability to control their Fire. If we were not Joined, such immersion in water would be deadly.'

'If you can control fire,' Lysan interrupted with a pointed look at last night's ashes, 'why are we sitting here shivering?'

It *was* cold. Wrapped in the warmth of Silverwing's Fire, he had not felt the chill. With an apologetic grimace, he reached out to remedy the lapse.

Callan put a hand firmly on his shoulder. 'My brother is more than capable of tending a fire.'

Lysan grinned. 'Yes, mother.'

He threw up an arm as Callan sent a stone flying towards him and bent good-naturedly to his task. And as the flames of the little campfire warmed them, Aarin felt Silverwing's warmth seep into him, closing his eyes again. Acquiescing to the dragon's gentle urging, he allowed himself to drift back to sleep.

NINE

THE FIRST SCOUT returned to Rhiannas from Elvelen a day after Galydon and Lorac brought the news that Darred's advance forces had been pushed back into the river. It was a victory with little to celebrate, because, as Lorac grumbled, it felt like it had been handed to them.

'There has been no sign of any other activity?' Galydon asked for the third time as he studied the maps laid out on the desk in his small office. 'Nothing at all?'

'Nothing at all,' Kallis confirmed from his perch by the window. 'Meinor has sent regular reports. All the positions between here and the roads in from Elvelen have been quiet.'

Lorac stabbed a finger down on the place where the soldiers had appeared. 'How did they get there? We're as sure as we can be that they didn't cross the river, so they must have come from Elvelen.'

'Unless they came from the east,' Galydon said, looking up from the map. He pointed to the dark outline of the Grymwood that marked the unofficial south-eastern border with the wilds. A series of pen sketches had filled in previously unmarked settlements in the eastern lands, but most of the broad sweep of coastal land between what had been Naveen and the sea was uninhabited, although not entirely unguarded.

Kallis shook his head, remembering the one time he had passed through the ancient, forbidding forest. Aarin had said the Grymwood had welcomed him. If it welcomed Aarin, he reasoned now, it would not do the same for Darred.

'Darred knows his way around the east,' Galydon pointed out. The poor defences on the eastern border had long worried him. 'Why not use that?'

Kallis moved to the table. 'He might,' he agreed. 'But I don't think he could come through the Grymwood, even if he wanted to. So if he has taken the eastern route, his troops would have crossed into Lothane here.' He indicated a point on the map to the east of Rhiannas and north of the Grymwood Vale. 'They could not have marched from there to here, where we fought them, without passing half a dozen outposts. And why would they? Our defences are concentrated to the south and west of the city. They could have attacked Rhiannas from the east and hurt us badly.'

Galydon studied him, grim-faced and thoughtful. 'Why could he not go through the forest?'

Kallis sighed, frustrated. 'I don't know. Instinct. I can't explain it. But if the Kas'Talani are unlikely to risk themselves casting illusions our mages cannot see through, I don't believe Darred would risk this enterprise by testing that forest. It is something else.'

'For what it's worth, I would not send my men through there, not when there are other options,' Lorac said.

There was a taut silence, then Galydon nodded. 'Very well. Then we must assume it is Elvelen.' He looked at Lorac. 'I need you there.'

The mercenary captain nodded. He had been expecting it.

There was a knock at the door.

'Come,' Galydon called, and the door opened to admit a travel-stained and weary clansman, one of the scouts sent west to the mountains.

The man offered Lorac the clan greeting, soldier to captain, with clipped urgency.

Lorac returned it, his eyes studying his scout intently, and took the message scroll he held out. A series of quick gestures passed between them, half seen, and Kallis felt a thrill of alarm as he saw Lorac's face change.

Galydon patiently waited out the silent conversation. Kallis had never seen a man exercise his authority so effectively by *not* exercising it.

Kallis was not possessed of the same patience. 'Did you find them?'

The clansman looked to Lorac, who signed his permission as he passed the scroll unopened to Galydon.

The scout turned to Kallis. He was visibly exhausted and must have ridden through the night without pause to bring them his news. 'We found them. They are where they should be.'

Galydon paused as he opened the scroll. Like Kallis, he had caught the dissonance between words and tone. 'And? The enemy, where are they?'

The man's eyes flicked to Lorac. 'We did not see an army.'

Kallis restrained the impulse to pluck the message from Galydon's hands. Whatever it was the scout did not want to say, there was nothing to be gained by delay. Then something in the man's pale face prompted Kallis to look closer, and he realised he wasn't just exhausted. He was terrified.

He glanced at Galydon just as the general finished reading, his face suddenly grey. He handed the message to Kallis. 'Tear up your strategies. This is no longer the war we thought it was.'

'A dragon?'

There was shock in Sedaine's voice as Galydon relayed the news the scout had brought—of the creatures glimpsed amidst the peaks of the Grey Mountains.

She shook her head firmly. 'No, they must be mistaken. There *cannot* be dragons here. We would know.'

'How?' Galydon asked, his tone careful. 'How would you know?'

Kallis watched Sedaine struggle with the question, moved to sharp sympathy by the look on her face. A look he had seen so often on her son's. And he experienced again the disbelief he had felt when the scout had finished his report.

'We would know,' she insisted. 'And they would not be with Darred.'

Galydon, who was by no means unaware of the cause of her distress, said gently but firmly, 'They are sure. They *made* sure before sending word.' He glanced at Lorac. 'I cannot imagine the courage that took.'

The mercenary captain acknowledged that with a faint nod, but Sedaine turned away from Galydon's understanding as though it hurt her.

She looked at Kallis. 'You told me the Kas'Talani are killing the dragons with their magic. *Why would the dragons help Darred?*'

He shook his head helplessly. 'Sedaine, I don't *know*. Aarin –'

'No!' She cut him off, hands clenched by her side in a visible struggle for control.

She was alone. Galydon had requested that she come to him, unwilling to allow this news to leak out too soon, but it meant that Limina, who might have offered comfort in this moment, was not here.

Instead, Galydon offered her a new focus. 'You are still determined to defend Elvelen?'

It had the desired effect. 'Yes,' she said icily. 'I am still determined to defend *all* my people. And if we give up Elvelen, Lothane will be surrounded. I will not abandon them.'

'Very well,' Galydon agreed. 'But this changes everything. We cannot continue as we have been.'

Sedaine nodded, calmer. 'You will tell me there must be sacrifices.'

Kallis saw the flicker of a grimace cross the general's face. 'Your highness, this is a war. Sacrifices are unavoidable. I am telling you I no longer know what we are up against. I know the Kas'Talani. I know what they can and cannot do. No one knows the dragons, possibly not even Darred. How he will use them, *if* he can use them—until we know these things, I can make you no promises, and give you no strategies that are not guesses.'

He sighed, looking all of his years and more. 'Darred has not done what we expected. Now we know why, although we do not yet know what it means. It forces us to react before we know all the facts, and that I do not like.'

It was an uncharacteristic display of doubt, and Kallis saw Sedaine liked it about as much as he did.

'React how?' she asked.

Galydon smoothed out the map. He drew her attention to the Grey Mountains where the scouts had seen the dragons. 'We could not understand how Darred managed to cross the river and move troops so close to Rhiannas without us seeing them. We thought the recent attack might be a distraction to hide the movement of troops into Elvelen. It was in an attempt to verify this that we sent out the scouts who brought word of the dragons.'

Sedaine looked up from the map. 'Were you right?'

'We cannot be certain, but we now think he may have used the dragons to move men, in which case it is reasonable to assume their presence in Elvelen indicates that at least some of Darred's forces are there too. But what we do not know is whether this play for Elvelen is genuine or whether we are meant to think so. Unfortunately, we have no choice but to react according to what we think we know, and we cannot hope to defend both Lothane and Elvelen from here. We must split our forces and send part of our army west to support the king.'

'And if it is feint?' she asked. 'What then?'

'Then we have made ourselves vulnerable. But if it is your intention to defend Elvelen, and I believe we must, then we have no other option. It is what we must do now in any case. Now Darred can call on dragons, splitting our forces becomes urgent. We cannot risk concentrating our main army in any significant number.'

'We need smaller, more mobile forces,' Kallis added, before she could dwell on that. 'We propose sending Lorac and half the clans into Elvelen to join up with King Elian and prevent Darred from entering Lothane via the Grey Passes. Galydon will remain here at Rhiannas with most of the army of Lothane, because we cannot risk losing the city.'

'And you?' Sedaine asked.

Kallis glanced at Lorac. 'I will take the rest of the clans east. We must defend Iraius's enterprise if you are to make use of the river—and we need those boats. From there we will be well placed to harry Darred's forces as we can and keep him from focusing all his attention on Rhiannas.'

It sounded good, but Kallis knew Sedaine would see its weakness as clearly as Galydon. Against an attack on multiple fronts it was a viable strategy. Against an army with dragons on its side, all strategies were worthless. All they could do was avoid presenting their enemy with a single, vulnerable target. And they had to protect Iraius. The dragons might give Darred the means to avoid their patrols, but unless he had hundreds of them, he would still need boats to take an army across the Istelan. And if they lost control of the river, it was only a matter of time before they were pushed further and further back. Assuming they could hold onto the advantage of the Istelan now Darred could attack their little fleet from the air.

Sedaine held his gaze, eyes searching, before she released him and turned to Galydon. But not before Kallis had seen in her face the same question that was tormenting him.

There was a distant shout from out in the courtyard and the sound of horses on the cobbles. Another patrol returning, doubtless with the same news. Beside him, Kallis saw Galydon pause as he too registered the disturbance.

Lorac had wandered to the window and now he signalled to Kallis. 'You should see this.'

Kallis peered down into the courtyard and swore under his breath. This could *not* be good news.

'It seems to me that I recognise that face,' Lorac murmured. 'Coincidence, you think?'

Kallis shook his head. 'That she should turn up here, now? I don't think so. Do you?'

Behind them, the discussion had petered out. Kallis turned to see both Galydon and Sedaine watching him. He swallowed.

Galydon quirked one expressive eyebrow. 'Well?'

Kallis managed a thin smile. 'I hope you have enjoyed your freedom because it just ended. Your master's here.' And he had the dubious pleasure of seeing Galydon utterly thunderstruck.

TEN

AS THEY APPROACHED Rhiannas, it occurred to Jeta that it was more than three years since she had turned aside from her journey to this city—and an unwanted marriage to a man about to succeed, however temporarily, to the most powerful throne in the north—and made the decision that would change the entire course of her life. A decision that would bring her back here, now, in the company of a man who had once ruled half the world. It was fear that had driven her then, fear of the repercussions of Lothane's uncertain succession, but it was not fear that drove her now. It was something else entirely, something much darker.

It had taken five long, hard months to get here. When they had left Kas'Tella it was in the back of a farmer's cart, Kinseris unable to walk more than a few steps at a time, his recovery still uncertain. It had taken weeks just to reach Frankesh, stopping to rest every hour, then every two, until they finally limped into the northern port at the sweltering height of the southern midsummer and had to wait out the three-day festival in the tense, airless confines of a room at one of the most unsavoury sailors' taverns.

Those were dark days. Exhausted by the journey and the stifling heat of the tiny, cramped room, Kinseris barely conscious and feverish beside her, Jeta found herself returning to the terror of the army camp. She would wake unsure where she was, confused by the darkness of the windowless room, and almost choking as panic closed her throat. Then she would remember, and it was worse, because the fear was still there. It never went away. When, finally, they had boarded a ship to leave Caledan behind them, she could hardly bear to go into the small cabin she shared with Kinseris. On the deck, with the wind in her hair and the salt spray drying on her skin, she could at least pretend to forget for a time what she was running from and where she was going.

Kestel touched her arm and pointed. Shading her eyes against the afternoon sun, Jeta could see the dark smudge of the city ahead. She glanced at Kinseris, riding beside her, his head bowed against his chest. The Ancai had quietly taken the reins of his horse some time ago. She looked back at Rhiannas, hoping their arrival would give him time to rest, to recover the strength that Escarian and months of ceaseless travel had taken from him, but a part of her knew that might never happen.

If he does survive, he will likely be in pain for the rest of his life, the army doctor had told her in Kas'Tella. The rest of what he had said she preferred not to think about. But the hatred rose, even so, and she embraced it, as she had embraced it before, on the ship, when it had seemed that the fear would drown out everything else.

Though she had not known it then, it was Darred she had escaped from when she had fled her impending marriage. Darred who had wanted to take from her something she had not then given to any man. Darred who had trapped Aarin in his twisted schemes that had nearly destroyed him. Darred who had reached out from across the sea to so nearly kill both her and Kinseris, and Darred who threatened her homeland.

Three times she had been helpless before him, powerless, and though he had succeeded in taking neither her body nor her life, no action of her own had saved her. For a time the fear had made her sick. It had controlled her, day and night, until she realised she could either surrender to it or she could face it, control it. Over the months of travel, of hardship and worry, the core of hatred that burned inside her had grown and sharpened into something much more deadly. She was not running anymore. She knew exactly where she was going, and what she was going to do when she got there. She just didn't know how. Yet.

Trad reached over and took her reins, his face puzzled, and she realised that the others had stopped a few paces behind. Nudging her placid mare, she walked the horse back to the Ancai. He had his hood pulled down low despite the mild weather, as he had almost every day since they arrived in

Amadorn. Until she stepped ashore, she had not thought how conspicuous a group they would make. The Ancai in particular, with the black skin and imposing height of the people of central Caledan, would stand out in a crowd even in the more multicultural ports of Amadorn's south coast, and they had come ashore far to the east of those Caledani-controlled ports. They had as much to fear from Amadorian citizens bent on revenge as they did from Darred's army, or they would have, if they had not been protected so carefully since the moment they stepped ashore.

When Kestel had found the fugitive Farnorian sea captain in the Illeneas Isles she had thought it was luck. That captain, as she learned over the course of a voyage spent largely on deck and under the sun, was a survivor of the very first engagement of Darred's invasion and had been hiding out in the archipelago ever since. When he had smuggled them safely ashore and handed them over to the first of their guides, who had followed each other in seamless succession across the south of the continent, she had realised it was not the coincidence it seemed. And she wondered how long Kinseris had had this escape route planned, and what else he had not told her.

He was awake now and watching her, concern in his eyes. For her. Jeta clamped down on the anger and managed a smile as the Ancai scanned the horizon. They had circled round into Lothane from the east, where the last of their guides had left them. She had answered question after question about the land they would travel through, questions she had answered as well as she could, but her time in Lothane had been brief. Most of what she knew of the northern kingdoms came from books concerned with their politics and ruling families, not with geography. Armed with scant information, the Ancai had led them north for two days before turning at last south again towards Rhiannas, hoping to by-pass whatever defences Galydon had put in place between the capital and Darred's army. Though he did not say so, she knew he was more concerned with keeping Kinseris's presence here secret than the risk that they might be mistaken for the enemy. The longer Darred was unaware his assassination attempt had failed, the safer they would be.

Then they were moving again as the Ancai satisfied himself that the way was clear. They would be there in half a day at most. Half a day. After months of travel, it hardly seemed possible. And then she would have to confront whatever they found when they got there. In Caledan, she had thought she was coming home. Now she was here, she knew that home was not a place, it was people. So she worried. Because Amadorn was at war and she knew what happened to people in war.

ELEVEN

AS SEDAINE SWEPT out of the room issuing a stream of orders, Kallis followed Galydon as the general jogged through the palace corridors. Kallis could not imagine what he was thinking, but they both knew that Kinseris would not have left Caledan unless he had no choice. Whether that meant a crisis there or here, he did not know.

The organised chaos in the courtyard as the palace made the urgent transition from military headquarters to diplomatic welcome reminded Kallis of what Rhiannas had been in better times. He caught sight of Jeta's blond head through a knot of palace officials, the looming bulk of the Ancai behind her. She looked tired and tense, and he quickly identified the source of her concern in the rapidly converging figures of Kinseris and his general. The crowd parted as Galydon reached him, dropping to one knee, head bent.

He caught Jeta's eye over the general's head, her expression anguished. She had witnessed the arguments that had preceded Galydon's departure, all the more bitter for the friendship that lay at their heart. But that alone could not account for her visible distress, and Kallis felt a growing sense of unease. Then Kinseris held out a hand to raise Galydon back to his feet, a smile on his face, and Kallis relaxed a fraction.

Kinseris looked exhausted, they all did. And no wonder, if they had travelled from Caledan through enemy-controlled territory, and quickly enough to outpace any rumour of their coming. He had no chance to ask Jeta, or even greet her, however, before Sedaine arrived, looking for once every inch the queen. Limina stood a handful of paces behind her. Kallis saw Jeta tense at the sight of Aarin's mother, but she made the proper curtsey as Sedaine's eyes glanced over her and came to rest on Kinseris.

'My lord, we are honoured,' she greeted him. 'On behalf of Lothane, I welcome you to Rhiannas. Forgive the lack of ceremony, but we did not know to expect you. When you have rested from your journey, I hope you will join me. I think we have much to discuss.'

Galydon on one side and Jeta hovering close on the other, the Ancai at his back, Kinseris took a step forward and bowed to Sedaine. 'Your highness, please forgive our lack of warning. It was necessary, and our business urgent. We would welcome an audience at your earliest convenience.'

Well, that couldn't be good. Kallis looked again at Jeta, but she avoided his eyes. Worse and worse.

Sedaine took in their weary, rumpled state, and appeared to reach the same conclusion. 'I am at your disposal, my lord.' And she signalled to her steward to lead them inside.

As Kinseris and Jeta were swept inside by the seneschal's staff and the courtyard cleared, Kallis was left alone with the Ancai and Trad. They stood looking at each other in silence, then Trad grinned, breaking the tension. Kallis laughed, embracing the younger man and exchanging a friendly nod with Kestel.

He ruffled Trad's hair. 'It's good to see you both, though I suspect whatever news you have will change that.'

Trad opened his mouth to reply, but the Ancai cut him off. 'We have news, but it is for your queen to hear it first.'

Kallis made a face. 'Don't expect her to take it well, whatever it is.' They had all had enough news for one day.

The Ancai didn't reply, and Trad averted his eyes from Kallis's enquiring look. He sighed. 'Come on. I'll find you somewhere to bunk down. And you can tell me how you managed to across the length of Amadorn and avoid all Galydon's patrols, not to mention a bloody enemy army, because you can be sure he's going to want to know.'

'With great difficulty. How did you manage it?'

'With great difficulty,' Kallis agreed. 'It if wasn't for Iraius, we might not have made it at all.'

The Ancai looked round sharply. 'Iraius is here? Why?'

'You didn't send him?'

'Did he say that?'

Kallis shook his head. 'No. But I assumed…' Someone had to have told Iraius where they were going and why, and the Ancai was the only link between them that he knew. He filed the question away to ask Iraius another time. He had a rather more pressing concern.

'What happens to Galydon now Kinseris is here?'

The Ancai frowned. 'What about him?'

'His first loyalty is to his high priest. He was sent here to serve Sedaine as he would Kinseris. But now Kinseris is here…?'

'To whom does he owe his loyalty?'

'It matters. She will want to know.'

The Ancai and Trad shared a glance and the Ancai sighed. 'We shall see, but I think Galydon must decide that for himself.'

Kallis thought about that for a while. 'That's good,' he observed. 'Because I think he rather likes her.'

'I thought we were fighting a war,' Kallis grumbled to Lorac as they waited in Rhiannas's throne room for the new arrivals to appear. Despite Kinseris's professed urgency, Kallis was not surprised that 'at your earliest convenience' had turned into a delay of several hours. The queen's fussy little steward was a stickler for protocol, and he was not doubt enjoying the opportunity to organise a royal welcome after months of what he clearly considered a deplorable lack of ceremony. From what little Kallis had observed in the last few hours of frenetic activity, he was glad he had safely installed Kestel and Trad with Lorac's Ravens in the barracks.

Not that this was like any reception for visiting dignitaries that Kallis had ever seen, which he had to admit was not many. The stripped hall, with its sad empty spaces where the riches of royalty had once adorned its walls, was not crowded with the who's who of the court. Sedaine, with practical efficiency and no little relish, had dispatched all those of her nobility who didn't fulfil a useful purpose—which appeared to be most of them, Kallis noted—back to their estates where they could see to their own interests, which is largely what they were good at. Instead, the room held only military officers and essential officials—though neither Sedaine nor Galydon were yet present—and its only furniture was the single long table around which the queen conducted her councils.

Lorac nudged his elbow. The steward, looking as pleased as Kallis had ever seen him, announced the arrival of the guests. Kinseris walked in behind him, looking out of place in formal Caledani robes. If the man had rested in the few hours since their arrival, there was little sign of it. He had exchanged his travel-stained garments for clean ones, but he looked quite as haggard as he had when he had greeted Sedaine on the steps of the palace.

Then Kallis's attention was caught by a shimmering apparition at his side. Clad in layers of draped Caledani silks, her face veiled by the elaborate arrangement of her headdress, Kallis could not at first reconcile this stranger with the girl he had known. Then she turned, sweeping aside the concealing veil, and met his gaze with a crooked smile that was all Jeta.

Gone was the scrawny wraith who had said good-bye to him in Kas'Tella, her cropped hair bleached almost white by the sun and skin tanned a deep brown. Before him now was Jeta as he had met her three years before, not twenty miles from where they stood. And yet not. Her blond curls were piled high on her head and draped in gossamer silk after the fashion of Kas'Tella, and her skin had a luminous quality that spoke of skilled artifice. Yet the fragile, entitled pride of the girl who had been sacrificed to a political marriage was replaced by a confidence that came only from the experience of real power. And that *was* interesting.

'She's a beauty,' Lorac murmured.

Kallis snorted. 'And you're married. What would Magra say?'

Lorac laughed. The formidable matriarch of the Raven clan was famously unforgiving of campaign indiscretions. 'She'd tell me I could be her father, though it looks to me she has a liking for older men. I thought you said she snuggled up with the boy.'

Kallis frowned. 'She did.'

'Well, I think you would need a lever to pry her from your priest's side now.'

'He's not…' Kallis looked between Jeta and Kinseris, eyes narrowing in suspicion.

Feeling his gaze, Jeta glanced towards him, arching an eyebrow at his dark look.

'I hear you know our esteemed guests,' said a smooth voice by his ear.

Kallis turned to the elegant young man at his elbow. He was watching Kinseris and Jeta as he sipped from his glass. Kallis grunted. He rather liked Derias Morven, Sedaine's chancellor, despite his fancy clothes, smooth manners, and inherited privilege that the soldier in Kallis resented and distrusted as a matter of principle. He was competent and loyal, which were the qualities they needed right now, and he could actually use the sword that hung at his waist. Lorac said he drove a hard bargain, and he should know. The clans were the North's best negotiators. They always got their price. Except this time. Looking round for Lorac now, Kallis saw the mercenary captain beating a hasty retreat.

'Is that a yes?' Derias enquired. 'I'm afraid I'm not familiar with mercenary slang.'

'Very funny,' Kallis retorted. 'I know them. Why?'

'Professional curiosity. The young lady looks expensive. And money is rather tight. Unless you think they might bring some funds with them?'

Kallis snorted. 'I don't suppose they stopped to pack their valuables.' He might not know why they were here, but he would bet Derias's personal fortune that they had left in a hurry. Whatever Sedaine's steward wanted to pretend, this was not a state visit. He glanced at the chancellor. 'How bad is it?'

'Oh, we're completely beggared,' Derias replied without any sign of concern. 'I've borrowed against the value of the crown's assets a hundred times over. After a certain point, it all becomes rather meaningless.'

'There speaks a rich man,' Kallis observed.

'Formerly, alas,' Derias murmured in a sorrowful tone as he examined his beautifully manicured hands.

Kallis ignored that. 'So, we're broke?' It was a worrying thought. While Sedaine was not paying the clans their usual exorbitant fees, the mercenaries still had to be fed and housed, as did the city's garrison and the levies from the lords' estates. And a hundred other things besides. The financial demands of war were enormous, and war on this scale even more so. To run out of money when things had barely started would make a hard task next to impossible.

'Oh no, we have funds. I've borrowed as much as I can get my hands on. It's only a problem if we have to pay it back.'

Kallis gave him a sharp look. 'It sounds like you're not expecting that will be necessary.'

Derias's smile was bleak. 'Are you?'

Jeta appeared by his side and he was spared the need to answer that.

'I once hoped I would never see this place,' she said with a smile of greeting. 'And I certainly never thought I would be so glad to see your face.'

Kallis grinned. 'If you'd like an escort south, I'm afraid I'll have to pass this time, jewels or no jewels.'

'Jewels?' Derias asked hopefully.

Kallis shook his head in disgust as Jeta gave him an enquiring look.

'Introduce me?' Derias murmured, amused.

Kallis eyed him sourly. 'Meet Derias Morven—younger son, not *the* Morven.'

'Thank you for that,' Derias said, a laugh in his voice. 'And you…?'

'Jeta Elorna,' she replied. 'Of *the* Elornas.'

There were several reactions this could have elicited from a noble of Lothane, given Jeta's role in the succession crisis. The chancellor, a practical man who had benefited from Sedaine's crowning, brightened considerably. Jeta's father was one of the richest men in the South, though much good that would do him with the South under Darred's control.

Derias gave her an extravagant bow. 'It is my pleasure to welcome you to Rhiannas, Jeta Elorna. And is your father…?'

'I have no idea,' Jeta replied with a brittle smile.

'Get lost,' Kallis growled, and Derias laughed, waving airily as he disappeared.

Jeta watched him go. 'Who's that?'

'The queen's bean counter. He's worried you're going to cost too much to keep.' Kallis took her by the arm and dragged her a few steps away. 'What are you doing?' he hissed. 'He must be four times your age.'

She shook his hand free. 'Almost five. And that's between us.'

'And Aarin?'

For the first time he saw the flash of real emotion in her eyes, something dark and deep. He could have kicked himself. 'I'm sorry.'

'Aarin left, Kallis. He *left*. How long would you have me wait for him? He's not coming back.'

There was nothing he could say to that, so he sensibly didn't try. But the damage was done. Jeta turned her face away, but not before he had seen the sheen of tears.

'Jeta, I '

'Don't, Kallis. Not now.'

Before he could think of something else to say, Jeta gave a little sniff and walked away.

Jeta walked away from Kallis, angry at him and herself, and almost collided with a blond woman in a rich silk gown embroidered with pearls. As she stumbled through an apology, Jeta recognised her as the woman she had seen with Sedaine on the steps of the palace. She could not remember her name.

The woman smiled. 'Forgive me, we have not had a formal introduction. I am Limina, and you are Jeta, yes? Such a pretty name. Are you very tired from your journey? Such a long way you have come. I would be *so* exhausted.'

Her head spinning from the smiling barrage of niceties, Jeta searched for a response.

Limina took her hands with a smile, rescuing her. 'Your dress is beautiful. I have never seen anything like it. You must tell me how you do it. And so flattering. I'm afraid I am growing sadly stout and these dresses Lothani women favour do nothing for me.'

Jeta let the comfortable prattle wash over her, smiling and murmuring polite comments at the appropriate intervals, grateful for the kindness.

Limina drew her towards where Kinseris was standing, talking awkwardly to an elderly man in the long robes of a magician. Jeta's eyes narrowed as she recognised the long white hair and lined face. Vianor. His name conjured memories she would rather not relive, and she felt a surge of anger to see him here, apparently trusted—*rewarded*—for his past treachery. Aarin had told her Vianor had helped him in Redstone. She knew him only as the man who had tried to engineer Kallis's death, who would have returned her to a doomed wedding, and who had tried to ensnare Aarin in his schemes for Lothane.

Then she remembered those schemes had been Sedaine's too, at least in part, and that they had succeeded for she was now queen. And that Lothane stood alone against Darred.

Sensing her tension, Limina tucked her arm through Jeta's. 'Will you introduce me?' she murmured, leaning close. 'The Lord Vianor forgets himself. There will be time for serious discussion once the queen arrives.'

The magician glanced at them in irritation. When he saw Limina, irritation turned to outright scorn, and Jeta returned the pressure of her new companion's arm with more warmth, a fierce smile on her face.

'My Lord Vianor,' Limina said. 'Allow me to introduce the Lady Jeta.'

'We've met before,' Jeta said acidly. 'Haven't we, my lord?'

The magician gave her a disdainful look. 'Have we? I barely recall.'

Jeta's smiled through clenched teeth. Kinseris was watching her, his expression caught between amusement and mild alarm. 'I am surprised, *my lord*. If *I* recall, you were very insistent that I should come to Rhiannas. But no doubt you prefer to forget that when we met you were in the service of Darred?'

Limina made a choked sound. Fury glittered in the old man's eyes. For an instant Jeta thought he would lash out, then he seemed to remember where he was, and managed to rein in his tongue.

'Darred has fooled many over the years, myself included,' Kinseris said, smoothing over the awkward moment. The look he shot her promised questions later.

Vianor's face was still savage with anger. 'Indeed.'

Limina, who Jeta suspected had just achieved her objective, coughed delicately. 'Are you going to introduce me?'

The scorn in the magician's eyes morphed into something close to hatred. Jeta wondered what her companion had done to deserve such disapprobation and immediately liked her for it.

'My apologies, my lord,' Vianor said to Kinseris. 'Allow me to introduce Limina, formerly Queen of Farnor. If you will excuse me, I will see what is keeping *our* queen.' And he left them.

Jeta stared at the woman. *Queen of Farnor?* Limina winked at her.

Shock rippled across Kinseris's face, and just as quickly disappeared. 'Your highness,' he said with a bow. 'It is a pleasure to meet you. I have had some correspondence with your husband over the years. I would welcome an opportunity to meet him. Is he also in Lothane?'

Their arms still linked, Jeta felt the tremor that ran through the other woman.

Then Limina smiled and said, 'I'm afraid my husband is dead.'

Jeta started to offer her condolences when she caught sight of Kinseris's face. The polite smile had slipped, and in its place was an expression she had not seen since the darkest days in Kas'Tella. Stomach churning, she stumbled through the meaningless platitudes that politeness required of her, and Farnor's exiled queen accepted them in the same spirit. By then, Kinseris had regained enough composure to offer condolences of his own, but his eyes were distant, and she wondered once again just how much she still didn't know about the man whose life she had chosen to share.

He must be four times your age.

Suddenly, those words took on a meaning Kallis had not intended. The difference in their ages had never seemed important, had been irrelevant to the comfort they gave each other, but since that life had been wrenched away, she had been coming to realise just how little she knew him.

Four times her age. *Almost five.*

A lifetime lived that she had not shared, could never share. People, plans, hopes, fears she would never know.

And in amongst them, somehow, somewhere, was Limina's husband.

A lifetime, unknown.

Did it matter? Did what had gone before mean anything when what lay ahead was still to be made? She had not thought that it did, but all of a sudden she felt uncertain, as if in losing Kas'Tella she had lost the convenient fiction that the choices she had made there existed only in the moment, that they had no permanence, no consequences. That they were not, in fact, choices at all.

That she had not given up on the man she loved.

That even that was no longer as simple as it had been.

Kallis's reaction had shaken her. She had known, coming here, what she would face. Not just Kallis's disapproval, but the scorn of a society that saw only scandal and ruin for women who dared to engage in such a relationship outside marriage. She had not and did not care what they thought. She *did not*. But that did not prevent her from feeling lost in a land that should have felt like home. Or from longing for the purpose she had lost when Kas'Tella was stolen from them. And she wondered, not for the first time, how much more acute those feelings must be for Kinseris.

Then the doors opened again and Galydon entered, followed by Sedaine, and there was no more time for her doubts. They had a warning to deliver.

TWELVE

'WHY ARE YOU really here?' Kallis asked.

The formal welcome having concluded, Kinseris now sat with Sedaine and her advisors. And Jeta, who made it quite clear she would not be left out.

Kinseris addressed his answer to Sedaine. 'Your highness, it is not just an offer of aid that I bring, but also a warning, if you will hear it.'

'A warning that you felt necessary to bring yourself I would be a fool not to listen to,' Sedaine replied. 'Tell me, how does one address the High Priest of the Kas'Talani?'

'From one ruler to another, your highness? I don't believe it has ever come up,' Kinseris answered truthfully. 'And now we are alone, I must tell you that it does not apply. That is no longer an office I hold.'

Galydon lurched forward in his seat. '*What?*'

'I did not abandon my role, I promise you,' Kinseris told the general. 'It was taken from me.'

'You lost *Caledan?*' Kallis asked in astonishment. 'All of it?'

'Yes, Kallis, all of it.' That was Jeta, acerbic with impatience.

A faint smile twitched Kinseris's lips as he answered ruefully, 'And almost my life.'

'Assassination?' Galydon asked sharply, eyes raking his former high priest. 'How close?'

Kallis saw the lines of illness and pain etched on the man's face. How close? Too close. He shivered, his eyes drawn to Jeta. Had she been there? Of course she had, or she wouldn't be here now.

Kinseris shook his head slightly, dismissing the question as irrelevant, but Kallis saw the look on Galydon's face and knew the fallout from this was going to be spectacular. He made a mental note to keep out of the general's way until he had a chance to vent his anger elsewhere.

'And that is why you have come to us?' Sedaine asked.

Kinseris smiled wryly. 'For shelter? No. But why—yes. Because that concerns you closely. Your highness, your enemy and mine has gained a terrifying advantage. Darred no longer simply has the magic of dragons. If what I believe is true, he now has dragons.'

'Yes,' said Kallis with a certain amount of satisfaction. 'We know.'

The news from Caledan was every bit as grim as Kallis had feared. It had not taken long for Kinseris to impart the gist of everything he knew and guessed about the activities of Darred and his followers in Caledan, or the implications for Amadorn, including what the Ancai and Trad had discovered in Frankesh.

Galydon listened to the recital in brooding silence, interrupting only twice. Once to ask about the fate of the army doctor (they could not tell him) and again about Fylian. Kallis did not miss the way Kinseris avoided answering that one directly and he knew Galydon had also noted it. When Kinseris and Jeta retired soon after, visibly exhausted, the general followed close behind.

Sedaine let him go with a distracted nod. Kallis watched her uneasily, aware of what was coming. Lorac shot him a sympathetic look as he made his escape, excused to begin organising the redeployment they had agreed on only hours before.

Tempted to disappear before she had a chance to notice him, Kallis found that unexpected compassion held him where he was. He cleared his throat. 'Sedaine…'

She turned, eyes focusing on him with an effort. 'Kallis. Where is Aarin?'

Kallis swallowed his frustration. He had known this was coming. From the moment the messengers had brought the first warning of the dragons, he had felt her eyes burning into him. Kinseris's confirmation of what they already knew had made it inevitable. It didn't make it any less difficult. 'I already told you, I don't know.'

Sedaine clenched her fists. 'How can you not know? You were with him!'

'What can I tell you? I have no idea where he is, or if he is even on Andeira. Wherever the dragons have been for the last three thousand years, that is where Aarin is. I can tell you no more than that.'

That brought her up short. 'Not on Andeira? What does that mean?'

Kallis fumbled for the words to describe what he had seen more than two years ago. 'I saw him open some kind of gateway to another place. We were in a cavern, deep inside a mountain. And then it was like the ceiling was ripped away and the sky was full of dragons. And Aarin was with them.'

'You left him.'

'He left *us*. To fight a bloody great battle—*in the sky*! What else were we to do?'

'You left my son alone?'

'Your son needed no help of mine,' Kallis shot back, remembering Aarin as he had last seen him, vibrating with a vast ocean of power and glowing an eerie silver, arms flung wide astride Silverwing as he challenged Aarkan to take his prize. 'And I don't think he even knew we existed, at the end.'

He could see the anguish on her face as she took that in, and everything it might mean in light of what they had learned.

'Then why?' she demanded. 'If Aarin found the dragons, why are they fighting on the side of our enemy? Why are they not with us when we need them?' And in her voice Kallis heard an echo of the quiet desperation that had been so much a part of Aarin, and something more—the agony of abandonment, by her son or the dragons, he could not tell.

'He died,' a quiet voice said from the doorway, and they spun around to see Jeta standing just inside the room. 'They sacrificed themselves to stop the Arkni, and they died.'

Sedaine's face was ghastly. 'My son is dead?'

Jeta shook her head. 'No, he's alive. He passed through death and out the other side.'

Limina slipped her hand into Sedaine's as she sagged. 'Don't play with us,' she told Jeta fiercely.

'I'm not. I'm trying to explain. Kallis is right. Aarin is with the dragons. He was *given* to the dragons.'

Recovered enough to speak, Sedaine asked faintly, 'Given?'

Jeta shrugged. 'They need him somehow. That's why he's alive. It's the *only* reason he's still alive and it's why he can't come back.'

'And now?' It was Limina who asked the question no one else dared. When no one ventured an answer, she followed the thought to its logical conclusion. 'If Aarin is with the dragons, and the dragons are with Darred, whose side is he on?'

Kallis winced, but Jeta just looked troubled. He looked from her to Sedaine. Both had good reason to know what Limina could not—that there was no inducement possible to make Aarin join with Darred.

'You can't really think that,' he protested when the silence stretched on.

Jeta sighed. 'I don't. But only because I don't think he would recognise a side. Kallis, the Kas'Talani are dying to give up their power. Kinseris ordered them to relinquish the dragon devices, and those who did not—they *died*. I don't think Aarin is on Darred's side. He couldn't be. But I don't think he's on ours either.'

THIRTEEN

'I SHOULD NEVER have left.'

Kinseris turned from the window to regard his general—his former general—rigid with something very close to fury. They were in the room that had been prepared for him in one of the older sections of the palace. He could see dust sparkling in the light streaming through the small window, and marks on the floor where furniture had been dragged around in a hasty effort to transform a storeroom into a bed chamber. Jeta had disappeared to the women's apartments, giving them this moment together. He could wish he was not so tired, but Galydon was entitled to his anger, and his concern. 'Is that your way of telling me you were right, and I was wrong?'

Galydon's shoulders relaxed a fraction. 'That was never in doubt.'

Kinseris laughed. 'Have you achieved nothing here?'

Professional pride bristled. 'Lothane is as secure as I can make it. But to lose Caledan –'

Kinseris shook his head. 'That is my loss, not yours.'

'It is mine too!' Galydon cracked back.

Kinseris silenced him with a raised hand. 'You misunderstand me. Yes, Caledan is lost to us, but Darred is our enemy and Darred is *here*. Defeat him in Amadorn, and Caledan can be reclaimed in time. But not by me. That is *my* failure.'

He looked for a chair and pulled it towards him. The ache in his side, his constant companion, was always worse when he was tired.

Galydon, who missed nothing, refrained from comment. 'Why come here? Why put yourself in more danger? You could have sent others with your warning.'

Leaning on the chair to take the weight off his side, Kinseris considered his next words carefully. 'This is where Darred is, so this is where I must be.'

The general's eyes narrowed. 'Why?'

'Because I might be the only person other than himself that Darred has ever cared about.'

'He tried to murder you!'

'That,' said Kinseris, 'is far from clear.' Over Galydon's furious objection, he said, 'Someone tried to murder me in his name. That's not the same.'

'And what do you think you can do? Call on your friendship and persuade him to surrender?'

Kinseris shrugged. He wanted very badly to sit but pride would not allow it. 'I don't know. But we were friends once, good friends, and that might yet count for something. We have precious few weapons left with which to fight him. If I were anyone else, would you fail to use this one?'

Galydon regarded him in drawn-out silence. 'You realise, of course, what you are asking of me?'

'I am asking you to use your judgement, which I trust, and not hesitate to use every means at your disposal to win this war. As I will use mine.'

'You still think we can win?'

'I think we must.'

The general nodded. 'What have you not told me?'

Kinseris sighed. It was too much to hope that Galydon had missed his evasions, but the news he had received tonight made the plans he had laid in Kas'Tella irrelevant. When they found the Farnorian captain in the Illeneas Isles he had allowed himself to hope, but the man had been ordered from the doomed sea battle outside Farnor by his admiral in its opening stages. He did not know how it had ended, though he had promised to bring word of their arrival should anyone still live to receive it. But fate had taken even that chance from him. He had asked two things of Fylian. The first, it seemed, was now impossible.

My husband is dead.

'There are certain… things… I had hoped for. I do not believe now that they are possible. It is better, perhaps, that you don't know.'

Galydon exhaled a long breath, clearly dissatisfied. But he said only, 'We can argue that point another time.' He looked pointedly at the chair. 'I will leave you to rest. Tomorrow, the queen will want to speak with you again. She at least will not hesitate to use you.'

Jeta watched Galydon leave Kinseris's room wearing a worried frown. The general paused when he saw her and she thought he would say something, but perhaps he saw enough on her own face that it was not necessary.

Kinseris was still standing where Galydon had left him. She saw the strategically placed chair. The lines of pain. The guarded look in his eyes.

It was the first time they had been truly alone in months. A chance to take a breath, to let down her guard, to rest. For both of them. So why was it so hard?

'He's gone,' she said without inflection. 'It's safe to sit down now.'

Kinseris gave a long-suffering sigh. 'I am not –'

'Of course,' she agreed, and waited.

His hands tightened on the chair, but he did not sit. Instead, he watched her expectantly, cautiously.

Now they were here, there was something between them that needed to be spoken, but she did not know how.

'This doesn't feel like my home,' she said eventually. It was not what she had meant to say, but it was something.

He smiled tiredly. 'And Kas'Tella did?'

'Not home, but I felt like I had a purpose there. Here…?' She gave a small shrug. 'Here, I don't know what I am. Or even who I am.'

'You are worried about what they will think?'

She dismissed that with a toss of her head. 'Let them think what they like. It is no concern of theirs.'

'No?' he asked, faintly amused. 'I didn't realise Amadorn took such a relaxed view of such things.'

'I don't care,' she said fiercely, and saw his expression change, saw the worry and doubt, and knew what he was going to say.

'Jeta, we are not in Kas'Tella any longer and I doubt we will ever return.

What was then, who we were… I will not presume to simply expect that to continue.'

She went to him then and silenced him in the only way she knew how, because she could not put into words all that she was feeling and did not want to try. Then he allowed her to lead him to the bed and lie, as they had so often in Kas'Tella, with his head resting in her lap. But it was not the same. Somewhere along the way, their roles had shifted. In Kas'Tella he had been a protector, carving out a place for her in his life through his power and influence. But that was half a world gone, and here in her homeland he was just another refugee from Darred's war. As she was.

It should not have changed anything. In many important ways it did not. In others, it changed everything, because *she* had changed. And that scared her a little—the anger and hatred that were ever present, just beneath the surface, colouring everything. Sometimes she felt she was losing herself, just as she had on that journey from Ephenor after a war had been won and lost, and she needed again what he had given her then, but she did not know how to ask.

Something in her silence must have alerted him to her distress. He sat up, eyes raking her face, trying to understand. 'Jeta, we are safe. You can let go now.'

She drew in a breath. Her chest hurt. It scared her sometimes, how well he could read her. 'Are we?' she asked, her voice cracking. 'Because we can't be, can we? This is where he's coming.'

Kinseris caught her hand and held it between his. There was a warmth in them that spread through her, calming her. 'If you want to go, we will go.'

She gave a shaky little laugh. 'Go where?'

'I don't know,' he replied, honest. 'We can keep moving, keep running…'

'No! No more running.'

He smiled. 'Or we can stay and do what we can to help. Defeating Darred is the only way we can truly be safe again.'

'We won't be safe until he's *dead*.' The words were fierce, full of her anger and hatred.

He did not reply at once, a look on his face that she could not interpret.

Then he said, 'I once hoped it would not need to come to that. I hoped that I could help Aarin preserve the dragons without sacrificing my colleagues, most of whom have no idea the harm they have done. When they started dying…' He looked away and she felt his hands tighten their grip. 'I was angry. But I did not understand the danger. As long as the means exists for us to possess a power that is not our own, someone will try. It is not just Darred who needs to die. The Kas'Talani Order must die with him.'

He had no love for his brotherhood, she knew that. But she heard the bitterness and knew it stemmed from a sense of failure, as though he was in some way to blame for letting it come to this. 'There never was any other choice,' she told him. 'You tried to spare them.'

Kinseris met her eyes, his own bleak. 'May Tesserion forgive me, I have tried to destroy them.'

She froze. 'What have you done?'

He dropped his hands and stood, walking to the window. 'It doesn't matter now. What plans I had made… they will come to nothing now.'

She watched his back, stiff with tension. 'Why?'

'Because information has no value if there is no one to receive it, and the one man who could have done something with it is dead.'

'Who?' But then she knew. She remembered the Farnorian captain who had brought them here, and Farnor's widowed queen, saying tonight 'my husband is dead'. The look that had flashed in Kinseris's eyes.

'What have you done?' she asked again.

So he told her.

Kestel was saddling the horses when Kallis walked into the stables. He had been looking for Meinor, worrying over details of provisions and supply lines, and he stopped in surprise at the scene before him.

Kestel acknowledged him with a brief glance as he tightened a girth strap. Kallis returned the wordless greeting as he stood in the doorway. The Ancai turned away to saddle the second horse. Behind him, crouched in the straw, Trad was checking their packs.

'Going somewhere?'

Kestel gave him an inscrutable look and said nothing.

'What?'

Trad grinned, brushing straw from his leggings as he handed a pack to Kestel. 'Not much to do here. Kinseris wants us to have a look around.'

'Look around at what? Where?'

Kestel silenced Trad's reply. The boy shrugged at Kallis.

Suspicion bloomed. Kallis grabbed a bridle as Kestel moved to lead the horses out of the stables, stopping him. 'You're going south.' It wasn't a question. 'Does Galydon know?'

He wouldn't put it past Kinseris to be acting on his own initiative. The man had acted alone for too many years to lose the habit now and Galydon was sworn to Sedaine, not matter how conflicted he might feel. Just as Kestel and Trad were sworn, body and soul, to Kinseris.

'Ask him,' Kestel said.

Which Kallis took to mean that Galydon was aware of what they were doing, but that if he disagreed it would not have stopped them. And it did make sense, he could see that. Who else could insinuate their way into Darred's camp and perhaps learn something of his plans? And they needed that intelligence. But it was also a risk. They might be recognised, and with them their connection to Kinseris. If it came to it, there were more damaging secrets they could reveal than simply Kinseris's continued survival.

Kallis let go of the bridle reluctantly and stood aside. 'Be careful.'

Kestel nodded, leading the horses out, Trad behind him.

Kallis followed them out. 'I mean it,' he said, as he clasped the Ancai's arm in farewell. 'We have heard things… and he knows your face.'

'We will take no unnecessary risks,' Kestel assured him as he swung up into the saddle. Trad was already mounted and waiting to leave. 'We will send word when we can.'

Kallis watched them leave and part of him wished he could go with them. Doing something, not waiting for something to happen. Then he brushed off that thought and headed to the barracks. It would take two days to get to the boatyard and he had things to discuss with Iraius.

FOURTEEN

LIMINA LOOKED AT the body lying in the filthy alley behind the palace. The man had been dead for days, long enough for the corpse to take on a waxy, bloated look. The smell of decay was thick in the air and she imagined she could see maggots wriggling around in his part-open mouth.

She had seen bodies before. Men had died to get her out of Farnor and more had died on the journey north. She had buried some of them herself. But this… she looked away, covering her face with her sleeve, trying not to breathe.

Crouched beside the corpse, Galydon's eyes were fixed on her face. 'Do you recognise this man?'

She shook her head. 'No. I don't think so.'

The general raised an eyebrow. 'You don't think so?'

She looked again, but between the bruises and the pooling blood, the man's face was too disfigured for her to recognise his features. 'I'm sorry. There is something about him…. But I cannot say I have seen this man before.'

Galydon rose, taking her by the elbow and walking her some distance away. Behind them, two soldiers began the unenviable task of removing the body. As Galydon led her out of the alley, Limina took a deep breath, trying to clear her lungs.

'I'm sorry to bring you here,' Galydon told her. 'But it was important to know.'

'Why?'

'Because we think he was trying to reach you, to bring you a message.'

She glanced back at the body, now veiled under a linen shroud. 'Why?'

'He had these on him.' Galydon held out two message cylinders of the type used by couriers. Both were blackened and broken. And empty.

Limina looked from the cylinders to his face in confusion. 'I don't understand. Why do you think they were for me?'

Galydon, who had been studying her intently, hesitated before saying, 'This is not the first. Iraius pulled a body out of the Istelan a month ago. One of these was found in his possession. We believe they were both Farnorian.'

'I'm sorry, I still don't understand.'

Galydon handed her a drawing. 'Both had this tattoo on their arms.'

Limina stared at the sketch of a leaping fish crossed with a cutlass. Her heart was beating very fast.

'Do you know what this is?'

'Yes,' she said faintly. 'It is Farnor's naval symbol. My husband's symbol.' But Hanlon was dead. She had watched his ship go down, ablaze with unnatural flames, and knew he would not have left it. None of Farnor's ships had survived that day, or so she had been told. But some of their crews clearly had.

Galydon waited as she gathered herself, then asked, 'Have you had received any contacts, any news from Farnor?'

She took a deep, steadying breath. 'Of course. My presence here is no secret and my people in the south send what intelligence they can. Most is of little consequence to the war—news of people, of families that became separated. We have reunited as many as we can. Anything of interest I pass to Sedaine, and Sedaine to you.'

'And you have never received a message in this manner?'

She shook her head. 'No, never. I know…' She paused. *Rumour has it Farnor doesn't think so,* Kallis had said when she told him Farnor was lost.

'What do you know?' Galydon asked.

Limina looked again at the sketch in her hands, her fingers tracing the familiar design. 'Can I keep this?'

Galydon made a gesture of assent. 'What do you know?' he asked again, gently.

She looked away as all the trauma of a nation so brutally lost rushed back. 'I do not know,' she said at last. 'Not for certain. But I believe there is a network of Farnorians in the south, working against Darred. I don't know any details, but there is a precision to the way information reaches me that doesn't feel random.'

'Can you access this network?'

She stepped to the side as the soldiers carrying the body edged past them. Her eyes followed them, fixed on the shape shrouded in old linen. 'I have never tried. They contact me. I think that is how they want it. Captain Iraius found the body a month ago?'

Galydon nodded. 'It had been in the water for a while.'

Limina chose not to think about that. She looked at Galydon. 'I can tell you one thing. No contact has been made for at least two months, possibly longer. Perhaps there is a connection.'

He took her back to the palace after that and made her promise to inform him should she hear anything. She agreed, only half a mind on his words, the other on the sketch she held tight in one hand. On the men who had died trying to reach her, and why. On the man who had inspired their loyalty. She was very close to tears.

She left Galydon on the palace steps and walked without seeing through the empty corridors to the room she sometimes shared with the queen.

Sedaine was inside, sitting crossed legged on the bed, a stack of documents in front of her. She looked up with a guilty start as Limina entered, then saw her face and was halfway across the room before Limina had closed the door. 'What has happened?'

And Limina fell into her arms and wept.

FIFTEEN

WHEN HANLON WAS next ushered into Darred's presence there was no trace of the rage that had simmered below the surface of their last meeting. Instead, there was something much worse, a sense of satisfaction that made him deeply uneasy.

He accepted the watered wine Darred offered him, too tired and parched to do otherwise. His captivity was a torture of small cruelties and humiliations, designed to break him by inches, but it also gave him purpose. He was not done yet. Not while this man lived.

He replaced the empty cup on the desk, and said with a sneer, 'I take it your conquest goes well.'

'It does,' Darred agreed, ignoring his tone. 'Thanks to you, Admiral.'

Hanlon regarded him narrowly. He knew of nothing of great import that had occurred to the north, and while his sources were neither infallible nor omniscient, they were many, and he distrusted this mood, as he distrusted everything about the man.

'Don't you want to know why?' Darred asked him. 'After all, you are so very *involved* in my affairs.'

Hanlon offered him a tight smile. 'You do keep asking for my help.'

Darred laughed, leaning back in his chair and propping his feet on his desk. 'As ever, a matter of perspective and interpretation. Did I ever tell you how much I enjoy our chats? No? But alas, indulging my enjoyment of your wit is not why I called you here—not primarily at least.'

He paused to refill his cup and Hanlon forced himself not to look at his own empty one. Not to give Darred the satisfaction.

'You are right, of course. But success is not always a matter of victories on the battlefield. Sometimes it is just as satisfying to tease your enemy and see how he responds.'

'How *she* responds, surely. Or have I missed something vital?'

'I feel sure even your spies would have reported that,' Darred replied, the hardness of his eyes belying the ease of his manner. 'I was speaking of her commander—or perhaps you have missed something vital after all?'

Hanlon ignored the dig, his concentration on what went unsaid.

'Sedaine has had the services of the Kas'Talani's most celebrated general these last months. After Wedh, of course, but he is dead, and perhaps celebrated is the wrong word for such a...'

'Butcher?' Hanlon offered. 'My intelligence was up to that, at least.'

Darred raised the cup in mock salute. 'Wasteful would have been my word, but as ever you cut straight to the heart of it, Admiral. And this one, I think, is not so inclined. I have allowed him enough time to prepare, and to feel confident in his preparations, and now I have shown him a hint of what is to come. And much depends on how he reacts. So, tell me, Admiral. What would you do, in his place?'

His one good eye fixed on a point behind Darred, he asked, 'What manner of a man is this general?'

'Galydon? I know him only by his reputation, which is much like yours, Admiral. Formidable. A soldier's soldier. Ruthless but not reckless. Men follow him, even when they should not.'

There was no mistaking the warning, but Hanlon ignored it. What else could he do? If Darred thought he compelled the actions of free men while blindfolded and shackled to a chair all day, he was crediting him with a power far beyond any he possessed. He applied himself instead to the question, for the answer mattered to him very much.

'Your general will seek first to preserve lives. Lothane's strategy is defensive. Their efforts are focused on resisting your invasion, not taking back the lands you have already claimed. You have only changed the rules, not the stakes.'

'Their strategy is defensive *for now*,' Darred corrected. 'Sedaine will know she cannot hold out forever, and she will not come to an accord. Therefore, her ultimate aim must be to drive me out of Amadorn.'

Hanlon shrugged. 'Might be her aim, doesn't mean she can do it. And it doesn't change my answer. Defend or attack, they need men. So, they need to keep them alive. If this general is the man you say he is, he will buy time and lives by splitting his forces to avoid presenting you with an easy target.' He eyed Darred with suspicion. 'Which is what you want him to do.'

Darred smiled. 'Of course. Only a fool would underestimate the mercenary clans, especially under such a skilled commander.'

'Seems to me the opposite should be true,' Hanlon pointed out. 'You could take them out in one strike, or enough of them to force a surrender—if you really have what you say you have.'

Darred raised an amused eyebrow. 'I can't admire your stubborn refusal to accept the truth. Would a demonstration help convince you? Perhaps it is time to put Lothane's little ship-building enterprise out of action for good.'

'Why bother?' Hanlon asked, his mouth dry. 'If you control the skies, all the boats in Amadorn won't save them. And you lose the element of surprise.'

Darred laughed. 'You are almost convincing, Admiral. But the dragons are not a secret there is any advantage in keeping. I *want* to lose the element of surprise.'

'Then you will do what you please,' Hanlon growled. 'But don't pretend you are doing it to prove anything to me.'

'Am I not?' Darred asked. 'You underestimate the esteem in which I hold you, Admiral. But you are right on one score.' He leaned forward, eyes blazing with sudden emotion. 'I don't just want to win the northern kingdoms. I want to crush them. The whole of Amadorn will see and understand the cost of defiance, of *her* betrayal. I want to draw this out until they are on their knees and then I'm going to grind them into dust beneath my feet—one after another—and then, and only then, will I take what is mine.'

He stopped, his breathing gone ragged, and Hanlon watched as the mask that had been shaken loose was slipped back into place. But not before he had seen the rising tide of madness that lay beneath it.

'And if you destroy them utterly?' he asked with more calm than he felt. 'If you crush them under your heel so they cannot rise again, what will be left at the end for you to claim?'

But the moment had passed. 'My revenge,' Darred replied briefly. 'And I have an appetite for it. I would not like to extend it to Farnor, but you test me, Admiral. More than is wise.'

Hanlon stifled his instinctive retort. The ache in his eye flared. This threat, like the others, restrained him. He did not doubt for a moment that Darred would carry it through. The veneer of sanity grew thinner and thinner. Something deep and ugly swirled beneath the surface, something that cared nothing for what he claimed as his, only for possession of it. Jealous. Irrational. Yet cold and calculating.

Abruptly, Darred tired of the conversation. Whatever he wanted, he either had it or had decided he did not need it.

Hands grabbed him, pulling him to his feet. He shrugged them off, reclaiming Darred's attention. 'There is always an advantage in surprise, whatever your ultimate goal.'

Darred spared him a fleeting glance. 'Oh, I know. But this is a personal message I wish to deliver, and I want to make sure it is clearly understood. More than is wise, Admiral. More than is wise.'

Something snapped. He lunged forward, hands straining against his bonds, and met an impenetrable barrier.

'I'm right here!' Hanlon snarled as the guards fell on him, but he was a powerful man, and angry. 'You want to punish me, then do it. Only a fool throws away an advantage for revenge!'

More soldiers entered. A vicious blow to the back of his legs dropped him to his knees, then his head exploded with agony and he was on his side, blood masking his eye. Two guards piled on his back, pinning him to the ground. His vision cleared enough to show him two black boots inches from his face. He spat a mouthful of blood and heard a mild curse. Then he was dragged upright and hauled to his feet, pain spiking through his head.

Darred reached down and casually cleaned the muck from his boots. He did not look up.

'Move, you stinking ship rat,' growled a guard, following it up with a blow to his back.

He staggered a step, then doubled over and vomited, sour wine and blood splattering across the rich carpet. A barrage of blows followed, driving him back down, and he let them come, smiling savagely.

Someone, another guard, stepped between him and the violence. 'You dumb fucking shit. Get him out of here, then clean that up.' More hands grabbed him, manhandling him back to his feet. He didn't fight it this time, letting the soldiers haul him away.

'Oh, Admiral,' Darred called after him. 'We caught one more of your messengers yesterday. But you need not worry about sending another. It's too late to warn them.'

Hanlon could feel his face burn with the heat of his rage even as his insides froze. He did not turn. He did not trust himself and he knew that if he tried anything now, he would be killed. He ducked out of the tent, putting a barrier between himself and the man he wanted to murder. *Needed* to murder. There he found the body, discarded in his path like so much trash, his face so mutilated that Hanlon did not recognise him at first.

The rage threatened to burn him from the inside out. But he also felt relief and was sickened by it.

Because this was not the face he had feared to see.

They had passed over the southern coast of Amadorn sometime the night before. Aarin had not been able to see the land, but he had felt it.

The draw of Earth like a lodestone. The receding call of Water. An abstract sense of homecoming.

Now they were here, a growing urgency was drawing him north, and he had fretted away the daylight hours spent hidden in the dense forests of the south-eastern coast. Darkness would not conceal their presence from another dragon, but it would hide them from merely human eyes.

That sense of coming home increased the closer they came to the Istelan and the ancient forest that separated the eastern lands from the rest of Amadorn. Aarin felt Silverwing respond to the call of the Grymwood, altering course by inches as though dragged by an invisible force.

Then he felt it too. The pull of like to like. The thrill of proximity.

There are dragons here.

The swell of euphoria was not entirely human; the grim warning that followed came solely from Silverwing.

They are hunting.

Aarin felt a flutter of anticipation. He drew back, trying to separate his thoughts and emotions from Silverwing's overwhelming physical response to the presence of another dragon. Over the Istelan. Hunting. Into Lothane. Hunting what?

Splintered images came to him through Silverwing's eyes. A dragon's vision, day or night, was vastly superior to a human's, and he borrowed Silverwing's sight now as they ducked beneath the cloud cover, scanning the landscape below.

A hand touched his shoulder and he remembered their passengers. Turning, he saw a question on Callan's face, and realised the man would have felt the abrupt shift in focus. It was a reminder, too, that they could not take the brothers into whatever was about to happen.

Closer. West.

The dragon was coming in from the west, closing fast. Was it hunting them?

Hunting, Silverwing said again, and Aarin understood that the concept Silverwing conveyed applied only to prey. But what did a dragon controlled by Darred consider prey?

Enemies.

The dark mass of the southern edge of the Grymwood was below them now, the river coming up fast. Silverwing aligned his flight with the snaking line of the Istelan…

… and the night exploded in a burst of raw power.

The backwash shivered through him from his head to his toes, permeating his body with pinpricks of sensation. Far ahead, the darkness was shattered by the glow of flame. Dragon fire.

The dragon had found its prey.

SIXTEEN

NIGHT WAS FALLING as Kallis watched Iraius tie up the boat and hop onto the jetty, exchanging a cheerful stream of greetings, orders, and insults with the men and women who had drifted over to welcome him back. He raised a hand to Kallis and gestured towards his boat, so Kallis ambled over and waited while Iraius dealt with the numerous small problems that had accumulated in his extended absence.

When he finally joined Kallis, his expression was unusually serious. 'Thought I might see you here. Where are you camped?'

Kallis jerked his head to the northwest. 'Sitting across the road to Rhiannas, currently. We move about.'

Iraius gave him a sharp look but said nothing as he dropped down the ladder into the tiny cabin.

Kallis followed. By feel, he perched himself on the edge of the narrow bunk while the former pirate lit the small lamp then searched the untidy desk until he found cups and a bottle of spirits.

'You're running low,' he remarked as Iraius emptied the bottle and handed him a cup.

'Don't you worry. There's more where this came from.'

Kallis tipped back the cup, gagging as the raw liquor hit his throat and started to burn. He coughed, eyes streaming at the affront to his senses, and it was a full minute before he could speak. 'What is this filth?' Then he sighed, wiping tears from his face with his sleeve. 'Don't tell me. There's more where this came from because you're making it yourself.'

'I won't tell you then,' Iraius replied, knocking his own cup back as if it was water and reaching for a refill. 'Take some back with you if you like.'

'No, thank you. You've seen Galydon?'

Iraius shook his head. 'Needa went. I wanted to get back. Reckon you know why, since you're here.'

That was two of Kallis's questions answered. 'You saw the dragons?'

'Didn't see 'em. Saw plenty of folks who did. And I believe it.'

'What did you find out?'

'Not enough. There's troops in Elvelen right enough. Don't know how many or how they got there, but I reckon the dragons have something to do with that. There's at least two, maybe more. Needa and the others ain't seen 'em either, but they were as tense as I've ever seen. Like they could *feel* 'em.'

Kallis thought about Sedaine's instinctive denial of what Galydon had told her, of her insistence that she would have known if there were dragons. Needa and Brannick would have been that much closer. He could easily believe they had sensed something. And he couldn't quite keep the grimace from his face when he imagined Needa's reaction to this development.

Iraius lifted his cup to his lips. 'She wasn't happy,' he agreed. He eased back, wincing, and Kallis caught a glimpse of a bandage beneath a rip in the sleeve of his jacket.

'What happened?'

Iraius followed his gaze and tugged his sleeve down. 'Little run-in with the other side. Nothing to worry about.'

'You were attacked? Where?' If there were more soldiers on the northern bank, they needed to move quickly. 'Does Galydon know?'

But Iraius waved away his concern. 'Ain't nothing to know. They weren't in Lothane. Needa took care of it.'

'Needa who doesn't like you much?'

Iraius flashed him a lascivious grin. 'She's coming around.'

Well, that was as unexpected as it was unlikely. But it failed to distract Kallis from the pertinent detail. 'You crossed to the south bank? What were you doing there?'

'Trying to find out what's going on,' Iraius said irritably. 'Why do you think?' Then he seemed to realise that wouldn't cut it, because he added, 'Pulled a body out of the river a while back. Didn't think much of it at first.

Plenty of folks trying to get out of the south. But now I'm wondering whether someone was trying to warn us.'

'Someone?'

'If I knew, I wouldn't have gone looking.'

Kallis scrubbed a hand over his face as he considered that. 'Someone was. But Kinseris brought his warning himself. He made no mention of messengers.'

Iraius sat up, cracking his head on the low ceiling. He swore. 'Kinseris is here? In Amadorn?'

Kallis cocked his head, curious. 'Yes. He arrived a few days ago.' And he relayed the gist of Kinseris's news. By the end Iraius was looking as grim as Kallis had ever seen him. It reminded him why he had come. 'What is this fight to you, Iraius? Why are *you* in Amadorn?'

The frown vanished. 'Same as you. I've no more wish to see these bloody priests in my homeland than you do. Alliance patrols ain't got nothing on that lot for making life difficult for free traders.'

'If that's the case, what were you doing in Caledan in the first place?'

Iraius grinned. 'Got a bit too hot for me at home, didn't it? Thought it best to disappear for a while. Then, all of this…' He waved his arm in a gesture meant to take in more than just the cabin. 'Seemed like as good a time as any to come back.'

Kallis raised an eyebrow. 'In the middle of a war? How did you know about that?'

Iraius winked. 'I have my sources.'

'Kestel?'

'Might have been.'

'It wasn't.'

Iraius frowned, his expression guarded. 'Does it matter?'

Kallis shrugged. 'It doesn't. But I'm curious. Why the secrecy?'

'There's a reason, and it don't concern you. Won't hurt you either.'

Kallis recalled the hunted look on Iraius's face when Limina had teased him about her husband. The regret. And he realised that this man might well have ties he knew nothing about.

'This is my home too,' Iraius added, after a pause.

Kallis raised his hands. 'Fine. I don't need to know.'

A wave lapped against the boat, rocking it gently, then another. Iraius stilled, hand reaching towards his cutlass.

Then a powerful gust of wind slammed into the boat, sending them both crashing to the boards. There was a flare of light, and Kallis saw through a tangle of limbs that the lamp had fallen and smashed, flames already licking across the desk. Iraius cursed, and the pirate threw himself at the small fire, snuffing it out with his jacket, plunging the cabin into darkness.

Outside there was a shout and the sound of running feet. Kallis swore, hitting his head against a beam as he struggled to his feet. The boat rocked again, and the night exploded in screams. Kallis followed Iraius's swearing out of the cabin and onto the deck where a wall of heat hit him in the face. He cursed, appalled, as he saw the flames rising from the newly launched boats as they bobbed on the water. Including the one he was standing on.

Iraius was off the burning boat and onto the dock before Kallis had recovered from his shock. Instinct made him look to the side. He called a warning to the pirate. Iraius pivoted and parried a blow from a Caledani soldier who had appeared out of nowhere. Iraius's cutlass flickered in the queer light of the inferno. The man fell, forcing the soldiers behind him to pause and back up to avoid their fallen comrade. Kallis crashed into them from the side, sending two sprawling to the dock. Rolling over and upright, he used his sword like a club to take out a third, then scrambled backwards to join Iraius as the floating dock swayed underfoot.

The pirate had blood running down his forearm from a cut near his shoulder and there were tears of rage on his face. His short-bladed cutlass was fast and lethal as he threw himself into their attackers, the only one of them unaffected by the rocking of the jetty. Kallis fought his way to Iraius's side, using his elbows and knees to force a space for his sword in the close press, all the while fighting to keep his balance. His sword snagged in flesh. He yanked it free, spilling his assailant to his knees, and lashed out with his foot. He felt bone crunch under his heel. Then he spun away, blocking a wild swing, and kicked out to send his attacker flying into the man behind him.

Iraius's blade took one in the throat, and Kallis finished the other.

Iraius's cutlass dripped blood onto the dock, some of it his. The vibration of pounding feet reached them through the wood. More soldiers. Kallis had no time to wonder where they were coming from, and why they were so focused on the two of them. He yanked Iraius back as he was about to throw himself at the oncoming soldiers. There were too many and they were trapped between the water and land, burning boats on both sides.

There was an unearthly screech and Kallis was almost knocked from his feet by a powerful rush of air. Instinct sent him sprawling into Iraius, sending them both crashing to the ground as a monstrous black shape passed overhead. The pressure of its wings flattened his face into the dock and he could not draw a breath, then a dragon—a bloody dragon!—was past them and Kallis, lifting his head, watched in horror as the creature spewed flame across the boatyard until the ferocity of the heat forced him to look away.

Faint shouts reached them above the roar of the flames and the awful screaming. The conflagration would be visible for miles, and the mercenaries camped nearby might already be here. He hoped Meinor would have the sense not to come in after them. The boatyard was already lost. He watched the curve of the dragon's wing as it swept lazily overhead, angling north—towards the mercenary camp—and bitter rage choked him. He was here to protect Iraius, instead he might lose the boatyard and his men.

Iraius grasped his shoulder. The advancing soldiers were scrambling to their feet. Kallis got his elbows under him and accepted Iraius's hand. They backed up until their heels hit the end of the jetty. Kallis looked at the dark water of the Istelan, glowing an eerie red in the light of the flames, and back at Iraius, who jerked his head towards the river.

With a sigh Kallis sheathed his sword and followed Iraius as he dived into the black water.

He swam down under the burning boat, hampered by the long scabbard against his legs, looking up through the pitch-black water at the flickering orange glow. He broke the surface on the far side of the hull and saw Iraius's head do the same a few metres away, long black hair slick against his head and eyes glowing in the light the fire. Before Kallis could speak, he turned and started swimming—not in the direction of the shore to the west and safety, but back towards the burning boatyard.

Kallis swam after him, catching him easily, and grabbed him by the shoulder. 'Where are you going?' he shouted over the roar of the inferno. 'It's gone! There's nothing we can do!'

Iraius shook him off. Kallis swallowed a mouthful of water as his head dipped below the surface. He came back up, spitting curses, and shouted after Iraius. The pirate ignored him.

'Bloody fool!' Kallis swore, as Iraius's head disappeared into the gloom. Then, with a backward glance at the burning boats, he started swimming.

Iraius was a stronger swimmer, but the injury to his arm was slowing him down, and Kallis caught sight of his dark head as they drew level with the slipway. But Iraius swam on, letting the current take him past the ruins of his boatyard. The glow from the fire no longer reached the level of the water and Kallis almost missed the splash as Iraius exited the water.

Kallis swam to shore and pulled himself out of the river, water pouring from his clothes. The wind had changed. Smoke and sparks billowed in his face, and he clamped his arm across his nose and mouth as he started after Iraius. The pirate was running silently through the flickering darkness and Kallis saw the dim outline of a building ahead, some way behind the main boatyard. More of a shack, he realised when he reached it, rough planks nailed together with a flat roof and a small opening with shutters barred against the night. Iraius fumbled with the lock before slipping inside.

Kallis followed him. 'What are we doing here? What is this?'

The hut was filled with boxes, piled high on either side. A storeroom. A *locked* storeroom hidden away from the main yard.

Iraius was shifting boxes, blood dripping down his arm, his movements urgent. Kallis took hold of the other side of a crate and helped him drag it into the centre of the floor. Something like fine soil leaked out from a crack in the corner. He dusted it off his leg. 'What's in this that's so important?'

Iraius was levering the lids off the other crates one by one. Several were filled with boatbuilder's tools, metal hammers and wedges, drawing knives and other implements Kallis didn't recognise.

He didn't pause as he replied, 'Hanlon called it black sand. He thought he could make a weapon from it for his ships. Put fire to it and...' He made a gesture that needed no explanation.

Kallis stepped away from the crate. '*Admiral* Hanlon?'

Iraius looked up with a grin. There was no amusement in it. 'Have to go a lot further than that.'

Kallis scowled at him, acutely aware that he could only see what Iraius was doing because there was a huge fire not far behind him. 'What's it doing *here*? And what are you planning on doing with it?'

'Sent to me,' Iraius said tersely, moving from one box to the next, checking their contents. He had pushed the two crates of black sand into the centre of the hut and started stacking the boxes of tools on top. 'Safe keeping.'

Kallis rolled his eyes. 'Yes, very safe. Who sent it?' Then he decided there were more pressing concerns. 'There's a bloody great inferno out there in case you had forgotten.'

'Ain't forgotten.'

Kallis glanced nervously over his shoulder. The hut was some way from the burning boatyard, no doubt to avoid just the kind of disaster that Iraius was apparently determined to induce. What he didn't understand was why.

He crouched beside the pirate, an arresting hand on his arm. 'What are you doing, Iraius? What good will this do?' If this black sand was a weapon they could use, they should take it to Galydon. But there was a part of him that did not want it anywhere near their side, not after what he had seen the dragon do tonight.

Iraius's expression was savage. 'It killed my people!'

Kallis winced, remembering the screams as the dragon-fire swept across the yard. Then his eyes narrowed as he considered the pile Iraius had created with the black sand at its centre. It was not hard to imagine the unpleasant consequences if the fire should reach it.

'What are you doing?' he repeated, more sharply. 'The dragon has gone.' At least he hoped it had. *Maker, not to the camp!*

'Maybe' Iraius retorted. 'But maybe not so far I can't tempt it back.'

'Iraius...'

The pirate shrugged him off. 'That thing could burn Rhiannas to the ground and there's nothing you can do to stop it! This might, and we can't leave it here for them to find. We ain't getting another chance like this.' Then he added, 'If Darred wants the river, he needs to kill me. The dragon will come.'

Kallis stared at him. 'You don't know that!'

An inhuman screech echoed across the boatyard and Kallis jerked to his feet. Not gone, after all. Every instinct was telling him to run as far from this place as possible, but there was cold, hard logic in what Iraius was proposing. This might be their only chance to strike back at a creature that would otherwise be far beyond their ability to fight.

The sound came again, accompanied by a blast of wind that stirred the hairs on the back of his neck. The dragon was circling above the yard. Waiting. For Iraius? He found that hard to believe. Yet the Caledani soldiers on the dock had come straight for them, ignoring the boatyard and everyone in it. Almost as though Iraius had been their target.

Iraius was watching him expectantly.

Kallis swore. 'Whatever you're going to do, do it fast. I don't want to be anywhere near this place when it goes up.'

Iraius's face split into a savage grin. 'You won't be.' He dragged the final box of tools towards his lethal cairn and stood back to admire it, wiping his hands on his leggings. 'Let's go.'

Kallis peered out into the uncertain night. He tried not to look at the boatyard, but the fierce flames blazed their imprint across his vision, blinding him. It was impossible to discern where the dragon was on its circuit.

He edged out into the shadows, Iraius at his heels. He wanted to put as much distance between them and the hut as possible before… *You won't be.*

Kallis stopped dead. 'Where will you be?'

Iraius nodded his head at the roof with a careless grin. 'Up there.'

Kallis felt a hard knot form in his stomach. He shook his head. 'There must be another way.'

Iraius shook his head. 'No sense in risking us both if it's me it wants. Get back to your men and get them away from here.'

'Iraius…'

'Go! I ain't planning on dying here.' Then he swung himself up onto the roof of the hut, crouching down to shoo Kallis away. 'Go,' he repeated. 'Far as you can.'

Still Kallis hesitated, even as he felt warning signs of the dragon's approach. Iraius was already running in a crouch along the flat roof. The dragon screamed as it saw him, and the sound jolted Kallis into motion. There was nothing he could do now except get caught in the blast. But it *hurt* to turn his back on a friend and walk away.

The rhythm of those powerful wings was at his back, forcing him on. He went as far as the riverbank before he looked back to see Iraius capering across the roof, every movement a taunt, and the dragon a dark shape against the red of the boatyard's dying moments.

The dragon swept down.

Kallis clenched his fist so hard he drew blood. *Jump!*

Iraius turned and ran across the roof, leaping from the shed just before the dragon opened its huge mouth.

The wall of flame hit him as he somersaulted through the air. Kallis heard his own voice screaming in fury, then the building exploded with a force that ripped the night apart.

The explosion slammed him into the ground. The night faded in and out in a burst of searing light. A dragon screeched in pain and fury, once, twice. He rolled onto his back, his vision swimming, and for a moment he was sure he could see two dragons not one, then the two came together and the vibration that thundered through him almost emptied his stomach. He coughed, choking on smoke, and tried to pull himself away from the brawling, screaming mass overhead, but something was wrong with his head. His face was wet. He slipped from his elbows onto his shoulder, his face hitting soft mud. Then nothing.

SEVENTEEN

KALLIS FELT COLD, chilled to the bone, as the heat of the fire subsided. He was aware of the murmur voices, drifting in and out, and the vague sensation of stumbling, half carried. The movement hurt and he must have cried out because he felt something touch his face, something warm, and he turned into the touch. Then all feeling melted away.

When he opened his eyes sometime later it was to a memory of another time. Aarin's anxious face looked down at him and he knew he was remembering an empty road in the borderlands and the stranger who had stopped to help him.

'Go away,' he mumbled, turning his head. 'This wasn't any fun the first time.'

The vision gave a choked laugh and said, quite clearly, 'Nor the second. If you want me to stop saving your life, you'll have to take better care of it.'

And Kallis realised, belatedly, that this wasn't a dream. The face from his memory was subtly changed. Older, thinner, more remote. But the expression of irritated concern was the same as ever.

He tried to push himself onto his elbows but Aarin's hand on his shoulder kept him firmly on his back. Head swimming from even so slight a movement, Kallis conceded the point. 'If you're here,' he asked at length, 'where am I?'

Aarin grinned. 'Is that supposed to make sense? But if you mean, am I with you or are you with me, the answer is we're in your camp.'

Kallis glared. Someone laughed, then another face swam into view. Kallis blinked, now completely confused. 'What are you doing here?'

'Well, there's a welcome,' Lysan laughed. 'And after we pulled you out of that ambush, bleeding all over the place, and my brother patched you up. Not even a thank you.'

Kallis looked around and saw Callan sitting cross-legged on the ground, an almost identical smile on his face. He sketched a wave and Kallis flapped a hand in reply. 'I've been spared your dreadful sewing skills at least,' he said to Aarin. 'The Maker is merciful indeed.'

'And no one is happier about that than I am,' Aarin replied with a look at Callan, who unfolded from the floor to come and squat on his heels by the cot.

'Will I live?' Kallis asked him, then Lysan's words penetrated his foggy brain. There was a small silence as he remembered what he had forgotten. 'What happened?'

'The boatyard was destroyed,' Aarin told him, watching his face. 'Burned to the ground.'

Kallis cleared his throat, his voice suddenly gruff. 'Iraius?'

'The pirate?' Callan asked. 'He's dead, I'm sorry.'

Kallis looked away. He had known his friend was dead. Nothing could have survived that conflagration. But it did not lessen the sharp pain of hearing it confirmed. He blinked, eyes stinging, and tried to measure the cold, strategic cost of the attack, but jumbled emotions clouded his thoughts. He was aware of movement as the others withdrew, giving him space, and he must have drifted off for a time because when he came to again, the change in light told him several hours had passed.

By the time things had resolved back into some kind of focus, Kallis decided he had spent more than enough time on his back. Groaning, he pushed himself upright and sat with his head in his hands as the world tilted in an unpleasant fashion.

'You would be more comfortable lying down,' a voice told him, and he looked up through his fingers to see Aarin watching him from a chair.

'You really are here then? This isn't a dream?'

Aarin laughed. 'You dream about me? I'm flattered.'

Kallis made a face. 'You shouldn't be. Things have gone to shit here. Where have you been?'

Aarin's expression shuttered. 'It's complicated.'

'No doubt,' Kallis agreed. 'But we needed you.'

He was saved from the awkward silence that followed by the return of Callan and Lysan.

'You would feel better lying down,' Callan said after a critical look at his face.

Kallis grunted. 'So I've been told.' He stayed sitting up.

Callan shrugged, casting a speculative look at Aarin.

Lysan, oblivious to the tension, flopped into an empty chair. 'Who's the toothless giant? I thought he was going to take my head off when we brought you back to camp.'

'That's Meinor,' said Kallis. 'He has trouble with first impressions.'

Lysan laughed. 'He said to tell you the boatyard has been secured and they are salvaging what they can.'

Kallis digested that in silence. Without Iraius and his craftsmen, they could not replace the boats they had lost. Without those boats, they could not maintain their control of the river. But Darred had already shown them how meaningless that was. Lothane's southern border was wide open. It always had been. The only difference was that now they knew it.

'They won't find much,' Aarin said quietly. 'Dragon fire burns hot.'

Kallis glanced at him. His head was aching fiercely now and the fury of the assault on the boatyard, the horror of Iraius's dying, was abruptly too close. 'How are they here? And why are they with Darred? We were holding our own, but the dragons have changed everything.'

Aarin frowned. 'Not through their free choice. They are enslaved.'

'What does that mean?' Kallis demanded, his headache making him irritable. 'Can you free them? Make them fight for us instead?'

'I can't *make* them do anything,' Aarin snapped. 'This is not their fight.'

'Tell that to Iraius,' Kallis retorted, too angry to watch his words, too angry to care. 'Is your dragon with you?'

'How else do you think we pulled you out of that mess at the boatyard?'

Kallis shivered and decided not to think too closely about that. 'Good. Because we're going to need a dragon of our own.'

'That's not why we're here,' Aarin said. 'This is not our fight.'

Kallis stared at him in astonishment. 'You brought the bloody things back into the world. And now you're just going to stand aside and let them slaughter us? Jeta was right—you're not on our side.' He stopped as sudden stillness fell. He took a deep breath, anger draining away as quickly as it had flared. 'I'm sorry. That was unfair.'

There was a tense silence. Kallis decided that perhaps he would be more comfortable lying down after all. He leaned back and closed his eyes. When that failed to erase the last few minutes, he sighed and opened them again. Aarin was staring at him, an odd expression on his face.

'Does Jeta even know you're back?' Kallis asked cautiously, unsure what, if anything, Aarin knew of her relationship with Kinseris. 'What is it?'

Aarin's expression closed down to nothing. Without a word, he stood and walked out.

Kallis watched him go with a confused frown, then fixed Callan with a stern look. 'Is there something you're not telling me? Something more?'

Callan tracked Aarin's departure with a worried frown, then turned back to Kallis. His face was grave. 'Yes. I'm sorry. Jeta is dead.'

Kallis just stared at him. That made no sense. 'She can't be.' He had seen her only days ago, safe in Rhiannas.

Callan shook his head. 'I'm sorry,' he repeated, hesitating before adding, 'Kinseris too.'

Stunned, Kallis squeezed his eyes shut. No wonder Aarin's temper had been so brittle. 'Who else?' If Jeta and Kinseris were dead when they should have been safe within Galydon's cordon, Rhiannas itself might be lost. *Oh, Maker!* His eyes snapped open. 'Sedaine?'

Callan, watching him closely, cocked his head in confusion. 'Sedaine?'

'The queen,' Kallis clarified, then stopped. He sat up. 'When did this happen, Callan? How did they die?'

'Several months ago, in Kas'Tella. There was an assassination –'

Kallis fell back with a bark of relieved laughter. 'Get Aarin back in here.'

Callan exchanged a look with his brother. 'I don't think…'

'Just get him. Jeta and Kinseris aren't dead. They're in Rhiannas.'

For a startled second, no one moved. Then Lysan shook himself and dived out of the tent. Callan, his face suddenly drained of blood, lowered his head in his hands. When he raised it again, he was smiling. 'You have no idea…'

Kallis grinned. 'Oh, I think I do.'

Lysan returned, Aarin on his heels. He looked from Kallis to Callan with a frown. 'What's happened?'

Kallis glanced at Lysan who was grinning from ear to ear. 'I thought you would want to tell him.'

'Tell me what?'

Kallis could feel the smile creeping over his face. 'That you're an idiot,' he said affectionately. 'Jeta's alive. Kinseris too. They're here, in Lothane.' Time enough to break the other news when emotions weren't so fraught.

Aarin said nothing.

Kallis started to repeat himself when Callan put a hand on his arm. Aarin unfroze. He took a half a step forward, mouth opening to speak, then turned on his heel and left. Again.

Lysan looked at his brother, a question in his eyes, but Callan shook his head. 'Leave him.'

'What was that?' Kallis demanded, unnerved by the absence of human emotion in Aarin's response.

'That was a desperate effort not to feel,' Callan replied absently, his unfocused gaze still on the place Aarin had been.

His brother shuddered. 'In Ephenor…'

'Lysan.'

Callan gave his brother a warning look and Kallis decided he was too tired to deal with whatever they were keeping from him. He lay back, eyes suddenly heavy.

'What happened?' asked Lysan. 'We received word in Ephenor that Kinseris was killed in his own chambers, by his own guards. Our contacts were certain they were both dead.'

Kallis winced as he shifted in search of a comfortable position. 'Only nearly dead. Kestel and Trad got them out in time. The army hid them until Kinseris recovered enough to travel. Then they came here.'

'Why didn't they send word?' Lysan demanded. 'Why let us believe they were dead? Shrogar was nearly out of his mind. If we had known...'

Callan laid a hand on his brother's arm. 'He was protecting us. You know what Shrogar would have done. Ephenor cannot withstand another campaign.' He turned to Kallis, who was finding it increasingly difficult to keep his eyes open. 'How is Kinseris now?'

'Well, he's not looking his best, but better than a corpse.'

'Bit like you,' Lysan said with a grin, and got another quelling look from his brother.

Callan stood. 'Get some sleep. We can talk later.'

Kallis tried to reply, but he was asleep before they left the tent.

EIGHTEEN

HE WOKE TO a voice shouting his name.

'Kallis! Get out here!'

Rain was falling on the tent, sending a staccato beat through his aching head.

'Kallis!'

He groaned, pressing his hands into his face. Then he rolled off the cot and staggered out into the rain.

Mercenaries were milling around uncertainly. Kallis couldn't blame them. He caught a glimpse of Meinor standing at the back, arms folded across his chest as he looked on with casual interest. Kallis shot him a pained glance, and in response he got a shrug and a wry grin and no help whatsoever.

He sighed and turned his attention to the bedraggled figure standing in the mud outside his tent. Needa's fair hair was plastered to her face by the rain. A small pack lay discarded by her feet, soaked and filthy. Her skin was black with soot, sluiced into rivulets that dripped grey streaks down her clothes. Her eyes, when they met his, were red with it.

'I went to the boatyard,' she told him, her tone hollowed out.

She would not, he realised, ask what she desperately wanted to know. What she must already have guessed. *She's coming around,* Iraius had said, with a grin that conveyed his meaning in full. Kallis wasn't sure he had believed it then. He did now. *Maker.*

'He's dead, Needa. I'm sorry.'

He thought she was going to strike him, then her face crumpled and it was worse. He heard his own voice stumbling over inadequate phrases as the rain fell harder, thundering into the mud.

Then her expression changed, from grief to rage. He turned. Aarin stood just behind him, staring at Needa in astonishment.

Her face twisted with anger, Needa advanced toward the mage. 'You,' she said harshly. 'You did this.'

Shocked, Kallis moved on instinct to cut her off. She shoved him aside, jabbing an accusing finger at Aarin.

'Your father always thought he was better than everyone else. You're no different. Look what you've done! We were fine! We might not have had the power of the ancients, but we didn't need it! What did it bring them but war and death? What has it brought us if not the same?'

Aarin recoiled from her anger, eyes wide in a colourless face. He said nothing, and into the space left by his silence Needa poured the furious torrent of her grief. Kallis saw the words fall like weapons on the open wound he himself had inflicted, and yet he did nothing to stop her. When at last the storm of words had run dry, they stood there staring at each other, frozen in place. Needa made a disgusted sound. She turned abruptly away, then spun back and spat in the mud at Aarin's feet. He flinched but made neither move nor sound, and Kallis found he could not look at his face.

Needa hooked the bag she had dropped by her feet. Without another word, she flung it over her shoulder and disappeared into the crowd of mercenaries. Kallis watched her go, his chest strangely tight. When he looked back, Aarin had gone.

His head aching, Kallis watched Aarin as the mage stood looking out over the river. He had found him here only minutes before, having quartered the camp looking for him, and was surprised by how much he felt like an intruder.

'Why are you here?'

Ignoring the distinct lack of welcome, Kallis responded in kind. 'I was about to ask you the same thing.'

Aarin gestured at the river. 'Water.'

Kallis duly observed the broad expanse of the Istelan and sighed. 'Not what I was asking.'

A slight smile told him Aarin had not entirely lost his sense of humour. 'The dragons.'

Kallis massaged his aching head as he stifled a flare of irritation. 'I want to understand, but you're not making it easy.'

'I'm here because the dragons are here,' Aarin said at last, his voice remote. 'Because their lives and freedom are my responsibility and Darred threatens both.'

Kallis studied him, and it was like looking at a stranger. It was more than a little unnerving. Two years were not enough to account for the change. Two hundred, maybe. But it was more than that. There was a reserve, a distance, that was hard to breach. And a reversal in roles that Kallis found disconcerting. For all his power, Aarin had always been a boy to him, someone who needed his protection. The man before him needed no one to protect him. Though he was clearly hurting.

'Aarin, what Needa said… She was angry and…'

'And right.' The mage had half-turned to him, though his eyes were fixed on river. 'You said it yourself—I should have been here.'

Kallis scrubbed a hand over his face. 'Yeah, well, I was angry too. You were doing what you had to do. But you're here now.'

Aarin flinched as though Kallis had struck him. He hunched his shoulders, arms clasped tight across his body, and didn't answer.

Kallis thought about what Jeta had said, about sides. He thought about what Callan had said the night before. *That was a desperate effort not to feel.* None of it made him very happy.

'You need to go to Rhiannas,' he said brutally. Then whatever this was would be someone else's problem.

Aarin sighed. 'I know.'

Then Kallis kicked himself, because Sedaine was in Rhiannas, and that was a fraught enough relationship all by itself. But Jeta was there too. There was nothing he could do to warn Jeta, but he could not let Aarin walk into that without knowing what he would find.

'Aarin, before we go, there is something you should know.'

'What?'

'Jeta is there. *With* Kinseris.'

The emphasis was subtle enough that it took Aarin a moment to understand. Kallis watched a flicker of something cross his face, then the mage met his eyes, his expression unreadable. Eventually, he asked, 'Is she happy?'

Kallis shrugged. 'It's hard to tell. Look, Aarin…'

But he had already walked away.

'Well, that went well,' Kallis said to Lysan who had appeared silently beside him.

'What did you expect?' Lysan asked, sounding more like his brother than Kallis had ever heard him. 'You just made a hard thing even harder.' Then, sounding more like himself, 'When you said "with" did you mean…?'

Kallis threw him a disgusted look. Then he stalked back the way he had come, his head throbbing in time with the rain.

NINETEEN

THEY MOVED THE camp. The boatyard was a burnt-out husk. The mercenaries had spent two days combing through the wreckage, salvaging whatever they could, searching for survivors. They found no one alive. Aarin had seen the expressions on their faces as they returned from that grim duty, and memories that were not his supplied the images of what they had seen.

Kallis returned with a face like thunder and Aarin had stayed out of his way as the mercenaries struck the camp and loaded wagons with an efficiency born of long practice. When the clansmen had found them, dragging Kallis between them away from the fire the night the dragon had struck, he had not known whose side they were on. He had seen no raven badges—the looming captain whose men had surrounded them wore the tattered emblem of a hawk—but he remembered the sentence that had been handed down that night three years ago in the shadow of the Grymwood, and knew that if the mercenaries recognised him, Kallis's life would be forfeit.

It was only when the captain—Meinor—had threatened to shoot him if he did not release Kallis that an unpleasant misunderstanding had been averted. Since then, the mercenaries had largely ignored them, tolerating their presence as long as they did not get in the way.

Kallis stood to one side talking to Meinor and a scout. Riders had been out screening the road in both directions since dawn. It was now midday. They would have to move soon if they were to make camp again before it got dark, and he wasn't surprised when Meinor started the wagons moving a few minutes later.

Far overhead, Silverwing flew in great looping circles that skirted the river to the south and the land around them. Kallis feared another attack by the dragon, but the more mundane danger was that the Caledani army massed on the far bank would begin to cross in numbers now their ability to control the river had been so severely hampered. Alone, there was not much Kallis's force could do to prevent that. A messenger had left for Rhiannas straight after the attack, but it would be days before any they could expect any kind of response, let alone assistance. In the meantime, they had to go where they could be most useful but least vulnerable—and rely on Silverwing's eyes to give warning.

Part of Aarin rode with Silverwing now, sharing his sight and his joy, allowing it to soothe the turmoil of his own emotions. Since their return to Andeira, the dragon seemed younger, lighter, somehow. No longer the weary creature, shackled by prophecy and burdened by the consequences of the Severing, who had first called Aarin to him in the Dream. Who had answered Aarin's call.

Even far beyond sight, Silverwing heard his thoughts. *Andeira makes me young again.*

Aarin remembered the intensity of feeling he had experienced on his own return—a sojourn of just two years against the immensity of three millennia—and felt the dragon's unleashed exuberance flood through him. He grinned like a child as somewhere high above an ancient being turned somersaults in the clouds, filled with the joy of living after an eternity of merely existing.

Then Kallis was shouting at him to get on a wagon or be left behind, and Aarin dragged his attention from the skies to run after the convoy. Callan reached out his hand and hauled him up and onto the wagon bed, and for a while he just sat there, half here and half there, with the sun on his face and the wind in his hair, sharing the exquisite pleasure of life lived in perfect harmony. Of the fulfilment of the dream he had longed for all his life. And forgot, for a time, everything that still stood in its way.

They didn't go far. An occasional mercenary encampment half a day's march to the east and north of Forthtown offered a defensible base within reach of the river while they waited on word from Rhiannas—or for Darred to make his next move.

Aarin jumped off the back of the last wagon as it rumbled into the camp. Miles to the west and high above the fast-flowing waters of the Istelan, Silverwing flew over Forthtown. Aarin recognised the river town. He had passed through it several times in the years after he had left Luen. As the main river crossing between Lothane and the Alliance states it had always been busy with travellers and merchants, even with the Alliance tolls. But that had been before the Caledani invasion. The toll shacks had gone, replaced with fortified towers either side of the crossing, and many of the townsfolk had shuttered their homes and gone north. Not all, however. As Silverwing flew through the gathering twilight, Aarin saw a twinkling of lights in the tavern windows and heard voices drifting up on the wind.

There were lights too in the towers, muffled and eerie, and a subtle weaving lay in the air and over the soft rush of the river. Light and deft, it created no barrier, offered no resistance, as it drifted almost unnoticed through the currents of the night, but Aarin recognised the touch of his countrymen, of Luen, in that delicate casting. Should anyone, friend or enemy, attempt the crossing here, the defenders would be well warned.

Silverwing flew on, and Aarin found his feet taking him on a path towards where the dragon would pass overhead. All around him the clansmen moved quickly and efficiently to establish picket lines, unload the wagons, and erect the tents. Others tended the small cooking fires that Kallis had permitted, and the camp sprung into being with deceptive ease.

Darkness was falling in earnest now and Aarin borrowed Silverwing's sight once more as the landscape sped by below the dragon. There was a scattering of hamlets between Forthtown and what had been Carter's Ferry, where Iraius had made his boatyard. Crossing the river here in any numbers would require boats, and lots of them, and Aarin knew Kallis did not think it was likely that Darred would try his luck on this section of the river.

Clearly, the local people felt the same. Where Forthtown had been all-but deserted save for its new garrison, the handful of dwellings east of the town showed lights and activity.

Too much? They had been watching for soldiers crossing the river. They had not considered the ones who might have already slipped across, unnoticed and beyond the reach of the mage-wards at Forthtown, in the days and weeks before the attack. Directing Silverwing to fly lower, Aarin looked around for Kallis and saw him duck into a tent on the far side of the camp, Meinor by his side.

'Aarin?' Callan was beside him, looking at him curiously. 'What is it?'

Aarin frowned as he hurried after Kallis. 'Maybe nothing.'

Callan had to jog to keep up. 'Maybe?'

Silverwing's flight took him over a clearing east of the small village. Several men emerged from the trees, moving with purpose towards the tree-lined road that led into Forthtown from the north. Their clothes were dark—too dark to make out any details even with a dragon's sight—and Silverwing flew lower.

'Something,' Aarin said grimly as they reached the tent Kallis had entered.

Maps covered a small camp desk. Kallis was leaning over them in close conversation with Meinor. Lysan was with them.

Kallis looked up when he entered. 'What is it?'

Aarin started to say something, then his splintered awareness tagged movement on the road. More men. They were making no effort to conceal their presence, and Silverwing's eyes caught the flash of steel.

'Aarin?' Kallis asked again.

Closer, lower. Only at the last moment did Aarin, through Silverwing, catch a fleeting glimpse of another group of men, hidden until now, swarming around a wooden contraption. He caught a glint of metal and hands working a crank handle as the dragon swept past.

Instinct screamed warning.

And something ancient and familiar rose in the night.

Silverwing tried to twist away, huge wings beating frantically down, reaching for height.

The machine released with a thud.

The heavy bolt cut deep into the dragon's flank, tearing through scales and thick muscle. The blow sent Silverwing tumbling through the air, screeching in outraged agony. The thud of his wings brushed against the shaft of the bolt…

...and back in the camp, Aarin cried out, his hand flying to his side as Silverwing's white-hot pain ripped through him.

TWENTY

CALLAN WAS HALFWAY towards him when Aarin held out a hand to stop him. He raised his head, said clearly, 'Not me.' Then he fainted.

Callan dropped to his knees beside him, hands searching for injury. Then he rocked back on his heels and met Kallis's eyes. He shook his head and Kallis felt a surge of alarm.

Not me.

The dragon.

Then he was running, Lysan and Meinor beside him, shouting to the men to form up. Because if the dragon was where it was supposed to be, and if it had been attacked, it meant the enemy was not safely contained across the river, they were *here.*

As the camp erupted into action, Callan joined him, Aarin beside him. Kallis spared the mage an assessing glance. 'Are you up to this?'

Aarin nodded, his face tight, and behind him Callan shrugged. That was good enough for Kallis, and he was already turning his attention back to his men when Aarin shouted, dragging him to the ground. A wave of flame engulfed the camp. Kallis felt the heat of it roar against his back, then a flood of freezing cold. He twisted out of Aarin's grasp and rolled over, expecting to see the men and tents aflame. Instead, ice crunched under his elbows and knees as he pushed himself to his feet, and ice crystals clung to everything in the camp.

He glanced at Aarin, still on his hands and knees, then up into the sky as a black shadow screeched overhead. There was a roar of sound followed by a clash of metal from the southern perimeter, then a long scream as the dragon swooped down.

Aarin's head jerked up. 'Go,' he said fiercely, then did *something* and the dragon pulled up, screeching its rage.

Kallis did not wait to see what followed. Beside him, Meinor was bellowing orders and men were pelting through the camp. He ran with them, screaming at them to form a line as Darred's soldiers materialised out of the trees. Too many were already loose in the camp, killing and burning. Then Lysan was there with a handful of archers, and Kallis spun away, leaving Meinor in charge.

He ran after the marauding soldiers, grabbing his own men as he passed them, forcing their attention on the human threat and not the inhuman menace in the skies above. Let Aarin deal with that. There was nothing anyone else could do.

It was a bloody chaos amid the tents. Men caught completely by surprise were gutted as they stumbled into the open, and the blackness was punctuated by blinding bursts of flame that stole precious seconds of sight, making it hard to identify friend from foe. Kallis shouted till he was hoarse, using his voice to draw his men to him, to penetrate their panic.

He felt something whistle past his head and threw himself to one side in time to avoid the follow-up. His opponent stumbled, overbalanced, and Kallis kicked him, driving him into the mud. He knelt over his attacker, one knee in the small of the man's back, and yanked his head up. But the man coughed, and blood gushed from his mouth. Cursing, Kallis rocked back and turned him over to find the broken shaft of an arrow embedded in his chest. He swore, then lurched to his feet and grabbed a passing soldier. 'We need a prisoner!'

The man stared at him blankly for a beat, then nodded and disappeared. Kallis looked around. Already the intensity of sound was lessening as his officers imposed order on the chaos and the attackers were isolated and dealt with. Not all fatally, he hoped. An unpleasant suspicion was forming, and he began to jog back to where he had last seen Aarin.

He caught sight of the mage through a gap in the tents and started towards him. A huge shadow swept silently overhead and disappeared into the blackness. Someone cheered, then a wave of hysterical relief thundered against his ears, and Aarin staggered, falling to his knees.

Someone touched his arm, arresting his instinctive movement.

'You wanted a prisoner.'

Kallis saw Callan run towards Aarin and shifted his focus to the soldier. 'Yes. Where?' A man with bound wrists stumbling along between two of his men. He caught sight of Meinor hurrying to join them and gestured to the command tent. With a backward glance at Aarin, he flexed his fingers on his sword hilt and started walking. 'Bring him.'

The crescendo of noise hit like a wall. The danger was gone. The wave of exhausted relief shattered Aarin's focus for a bare instant and the pain was overwhelming. Unable to let the link go dark, aware of Silverwing's urgent need to draw on his power to heal the wound, Aarin had fallen back on his mental defences to block the dragon's pain. As the adrenalin drained out of him, the block failed, and *something else* hit him like the scream of a thousand voices.

He lurched forward, reaching for a tree to steady him. Then the dragon fire roared through him in a sickening wave and he slipped to his knees, guts cramping as he vomited. And the scream went on, an echo through the land that washed through him and over him and left him sick and weak.

He heard footsteps and the murmur of voices. He rested his forehead on the damp trunk, struggling for breath. Then someone's hands were holding his shoulders and easing him back and cool fingers were pressed into the burning skin at his wrist. Callan. He felt a tug at his tunic and cried out. Then something wet and icy cold was pressed against his side. The shock pushed back the pain for a split second; Aarin seized the respite, gathered his wits, and slammed his shields back into place.

The relief was instantaneous. The pain wasn't gone, but it was no longer a searing agony. Held at bay behind his mental shields, Silverwing's wounding was reduced to a throbbing ache. The roaring tide of heat ebbed away. In its absence he could track the dragon's urgent warning and through Silverwing's eyes saw the danger—Darred's scouts, sent to finish what their ballista bolt had started.

Aarin dragged his attention back to himself. He was shaking, wrung dizzy by the massive power of the shields he had wrought to deflect the dragons' fire, but it would pass. He could feel the fingers still on his wrist, measuring the slowing of his pulse, and gently pulled his arm free. He opened his eyes to see Callan watching him.

'Thank you.'

Callan nodded, holding out his hand, and Aarin allowed himself to be levered upright to sit with his back against the tree. The ice that had shocked him back into control was already melting and soaking his tunic, but the cold was locked away as tightly as the pain.

The world came back into focus, slowly. Lysan flitted out of the darkness and said something to Callan, then disappeared again. Behind him, the camp seethed with shadowy motion. It made his head spin and he shut his eyes.

When he opened them, Kallis was on one knee beside Callan. 'Darred is going after the dragon. Where are we going?' Then, 'Can you walk?'

Aarin nodded, unable to speak past the sudden rush of gratitude. Kallis had realised the danger. He would have understood at once that Darred would follow through on his attack on Silverwing and that the dragon, injured and separated from Aarin, would be at risk. He might view Silverwing as a strategic advantage, but it was one he would not want to lose.

Aarin held out a hand and Kallis hauled him to his feet. He rested his hands on his knees for a long moment as his vision greyed in and out. Silverwing's drain on his resources was lessening. The dragon would know he had little left to give. Silverwing's wound was painful and debilitating but not dangerous—if they could give him the time to heal. If they could get to him first. He formed a mental picture of the dragon's location and oriented himself in the darkness.

'Not far,' he told Kallis. 'About ten miles. Northeast.'

Kallis eyed him dubiously, no doubt weighing his appearance against the prospect of a ten-mile trek. Then he nodded. 'You lead. We need to go now. They have a head start.'

TWENTY-ONE

TEN MILES FELT like a hundred. No, two hundred.

Kallis fell in beside Aarin a couple of miles out from the camp. 'What are we facing?'

Locked in wordless communion with Silverwing, his own vision blurring with tiredness, it took an effort for Aarin to order his thoughts.

'Two groups. Thirty, maybe more. Further to walk.'

Kallis eyed him warily. 'They are behind us?'

Aarin nodded.

'Just men?'

'For now.' He did not think Darred would send the dragons against Silverwing. Even hurt, the link with Aarin made Silverwing far too dangerous. And, as he had just discovered, conventional attack, so unexpected, was effective enough. Darred being Darred, he would have no qualms about sending a patrol of soldiers against a wounded dragon on the sliver of possibility they could prevail. If they failed, he lost only men, and he had plenty of them.

Through his anger and Silverwing's pain, Aarin took stock of this unanticipated danger. The dragon's wound was not life-threatening, but it was debilitating, however briefly. Darred did not need to kill Silverwing to vastly reduce his threat. He just needed to keep the dragon out of the fight and force Aarin to shoulder the burden of channelling their shared power. It would tire him faster and shrink the sphere of his influence. Their greatest strength—their greatest threat—was their mobility. Without it, Aarin could defend only his immediate surroundings. And Silverwing could not challenge Darred's dominance of the sky.

He would make their strength their weakness. A hurt to one was a hurt to both.

But Darred, like Kallis, had made the mistake of assuming Aarin was here for him.

Then he thought of the scream he had sensed, that had almost overwhelmed him at the camp, and felt nausea rise in his throat.

That whiplash of raw power—the haunting echo of the death it left in its wake—was more than a warning. He knew what it was now, or thought he did, the fading shockwaves of devastation on a scale that dwarfed the destruction of the boatyard. Something, many days ago and hundreds of miles distant, had been destroyed by dragon fire. A provocation and a taunt. A promise of what was to come. A trap that would bind him once Kallis knew. And he had to know.

Aarin searched for the words that could explain such a thing but when he tried to speak he realised Kallis was gone and there were still many weary miles ahead.

The night was nearly done when they reached the place where Silverwing had hidden himself. Without his certain knowledge of where Silverwing was with every breath he took, Aarin might have walked right past the dragon. His very presence was mazed in thoughts of concealment and misdirection, instinct shaping the elements around him to his need.

Aarin felt Kallis hesitate, his step faltering as the huge form of the dragon came into view, ancient scales rippling like armour across muscled flanks. It was one thing to see a dragon from a distance, another to see one close up and feel the heat of its fire. Each rumbling breath sent vibrations through the ground at their feet, like the purring of a giant cat—a cat with talons longer than a man's forearm and teeth that could rip a horse in two. Aarin could almost hear what Kallis was thinking; he could feel his fear.

The ballista bolt protruded from Silverwing's flank, sunk deep into the powerful muscle of the dragon's leg. Trails of dried blood stained the silver scales, but the wound was no longer bleeding. Aarin ran his hand over Silverwing's neck. *I'm sorry.* The weapon would have to come out.

Do it quickly, little brother. This splinter hurts my pride.

Smiling, Aarin turned to Callan. 'Can you remove it?'

Callan nodded, his eyes meeting Silverwing's, seeking permission, before he stretched his hand out to gently probe the injured muscle. A shudder swept through the dragon's side.

'I'm sorry.' Callan spoke directly to the dragon. 'This will hurt.'

Silverwing snorted, smoke curling in black wisps from his nostrils, and Aarin felt his amusement even through the pain.

Callan smiled wryly; he had sensed it too. Then he looked directly at Aarin. 'What about you?'

Aarin grimaced. There was no way he would be able to block *that* out.

Callan frowned, his gaze drawn to something behind Aarin's shoulder. Suddenly Kallis and Lysan were there, one on either side of him. They each took hold of an arm as Callan gripped the shaft of the spear.

'What…?'

Callan *pulled*; someone screamed. The world splintered and went dark.

When he came to it was full light. He was lying with his head on a folded cloak, his own draped over him, and his limbs were stiff with cold.

'That makes us even,' Kallis observed with a grin. Then added more seriously, 'Fun though that was, don't make me do it again.'

Aarin sat up. The pain was distant, controlled. 'Silverwing?' He must have passed out when the bolt was removed, but not for long.

'Sleeping.' Callan dropped into a crouch beside Kallis. 'He also appears to be healing. Faster than I would have thought possible. Is this some other function of your bond?'

Aarin glanced at Silverwing, deep in healing sleep. The dragon was no longer drawing so deeply on the link, but energy was still trickling in a steady flow from mage to dragon, accelerating a process that would have been slower but no less certain without it. He shook his head. 'That is theirs alone, I think.'

But even as he said it, he knew that was not quite true. A memory came to him, of Aarkan's shocked grief and inability to accept the death of his wife— *because it should not have happened.* Because death, except from great age, was almost unknown to Lorrimer's people, whose lifespans stretched into centuries paired with their dragons. And he thought of Vasa, the former high priest of the Kas'Talani. *He has ruled here for more than three centuries,* Kinseris had told him so long ago in Frankesh when he had revealed his own advanced age. Old yet not aged. It was not simply an extended lifespan the link bestowed, but an extended youth—the unconscious capacity to defy the effects of age, to survive illness and injury that would otherwise kill. And, with time, healing and renewal.

Kallis listened with a darkening frown. 'So whatever damage the explosion did to that dragon, it has probably already recovered?'

So Iraius died for nothing were the words he did not say, but Aarin heard them nonetheless and felt a twinge of irrational guilt. 'I don't know,' he said honestly. He did not know how badly the dragon had been hurt and neither did Silverwing, but it was unlikely to be more than a temporary hindrance.

A shout from a sentry saved him further explanations. Kallis jumped to his feet. 'Stay here.'

Aarin looked at Callan. 'What's happening?'

'I imagine our pursuit has caught up. They don't seem to have been in any hurry.'

Kallis returned. 'We have company at last. Are you up to a few tricks, or do we have to do this the hard way?'

Aarin grinned. 'What do you need?'

Kallis glanced at Silverwing's impressive bulk. 'Nothing fancy. We can fight them. They have the numbers, we have the ground, but it will still be costly. Or we could take this opportunity to sow a little confusion, muddy the waters a bit. I'm thinking an angry, aggressive dragon might accomplish both aims without anyone getting hurt.'

Aarin followed him to where Lysan waited, half-hidden by a screen of trees. Their position higher up the valley gave them the advantage over the approaching soldiers, fanned out in a ragged line and moving cautiously. As Callan had predicted, they did not seem particularly keen to find their quarry. They were armed with lances and crossbows but only lightly armoured and in nothing more substantial than hardened leather or gambesons. It would give them no protection but at least it would do them harm. Someone had clearly been thinking, and he doubted Darred would care enough to warn his soldiers not to wear metal armour.

Kallis tapped him on the shoulder and pointed. Away to the left, further down the valley, a second group was making its way slowly upward. It was clear they knew roughly where Silverwing had hidden himself. Now the sun was up, the landscape showed a trail of destruction from the dragon's heavy landing. Unimpeded, there was little chance they would not find him eventually.

'They look ready to soil themselves,' Lysan observed happily. 'Just shoot them and be done with it. More merciful.'

Kallis snorted. 'You have an interesting concept of mercy.'

Lysan laughed. 'I know which one I'd rather face.'

'You do realise the dragon's asleep?' Kallis asked him. 'Aarin's only going to scare them a little.'

Aarin tuned out Lysan's reply as he shaped Earth and Water to confuse sight and hearing, sending fine, questing tendrils of power out towards the soldiers, rustling the leaves around them and reflecting flashes of silver in the sparkling dew.

He heard Lysan's soft laughter as the first nervous shouts passed between the searchers.

'Now they're on alert,' Kallis growled in his ear. 'I was thinking something a little more dramatic.'

'Oh no, this is better,' Lysan said. 'Creepy.'

'And you have a cruel sense of humour,' Callan murmured. He was standing beside Aarin, his face taut with strain as half-felt snatches of sensation taunted him, just out of reach.

Aarin looked away, focusing on the soldiers. The gentle rustling became a sudden crashing in the undergrowth. Lysan jumped and swore, and distantly Aarin heard his brother's gentle teasing. He spread his net wider, creating a disturbance further to the right and another to the left, louder this time and accompanied by a trembling in the ground.

Already razor-thin, the cohesion of the searchers dissolved into panicked chaos. The advance checked as the lines broke and the soldiers converged on one another. He saw several span their crossbows, aiming wildly, trying to cover all possible directions. An officer batted one down, shouting and pointing at the other group of soldiers, but fear was eroding whatever discipline his men had left.

Kallis pulled him back deeper into the trees, the others following. 'This could get ugly fast. No sense getting shot by accident. Maybe it's time to stop playing with them.'

Aarin closed his eyes, shaping an image of Silverwing in his head, giving the illusion form and texture, then unleashed it.

The dragon reared up out of the trees, huge muscles bunched and ready to strike, scales glinting silver-bright in the dawn. Its enraged screech echoed across the valley.

'Merciful Maker!' Lysan breathed.

Then another dragon, blackened and battle-scarred, took to the air from the other side of the slope. Srenegar, with all the cold menace both Aarin and Lorrimer recalled too well.

He heard Kallis's startled shout and grinned at him, wiggling his fingers as the dragon dived down towards the soldiers, who scattered in terror back down the slope. The dragon swooped low over their heads, talons extended, and several soldiers threw themselves to the ground as Aarin pummelled them with powerful beats of Air.

Kallis looked from his hand to the dragon. His face relaxed. 'Clever. That will confuse things.'

As the black dragon circled around, illusion-Silverwing powered upward, wheeling high above their heads. The prone soldiers scrambled to their feet and hurled themselves in a stumbling run.

A gout of fierce flame tore up the undergrowth in their wake, the intense heat burning the land to ash in an instant.

'Huh,' said Kallis. 'That's a bit too convincing.'

Aarin sighed, stopping the flames before the fire could spread out of control. *We don't actually want to kill them.*

Nor did I, Silverwing replied lazily. *But I feel sure they would expect me to try.*

Kallis was still watching the smouldering vegetation as smoke and ash drifted over them. 'Aarin?'

'That wasn't me.'

The mercenary turned to where Silverwing rested; watching through the slit of one eye, and could not disguise his start of surprise.

Overhead, the illusion dragons pursued the fleeing soldiers down the slope before breaking off and flying north, deeper into Lothane, until Aarin let the magic dissipate and fade away.

Kallis watched the soldiers go, half an eye on Silverwing. 'I don't think they'll be back, but we should stay here no longer than necessary.'

Aarin nodded, understanding that his concern was not just for Silverwing but for his command. And already he could feel the dragon's pain lessening, the damage starting to repair itself. *When can you fly?*

Soon. You need not fear leaving me.

Aarin frowned. It was not another attack by men that he feared.

We are not like you, Æisoul. We do not hunt each other.

You did once.

This is not the same.

'Aarin?'

Kallis was watching him, waiting for a response.

Go.

With a sigh, he stood. He did not want to leave Silverwing, but already he could feel the pull of divided loyalties. If he stayed, he left Kallis's camp undefended and desperately vulnerable to another attack. And if Kallis had not asked it of him, it was because he assumed that Aarin's help would be his, and why shouldn't he? But if he made their war his own, the death he had sensed in that silent scream would become the weapon Darred used against them. He would do it again and again, trapping Aarin in an endless, hopeless defence that foreclosed all other choices he might make. Worse, if he made their war his own, dragon might be called on to fight dragon, and Lorrimer's memories shied in horror at the thought. He could not afford to forget why he was here. The dragons were only a danger because of what Darred had done to them. Freeing them had to be his first concern, and yet…

'Let's go,' he said wearily. Because he could not leave them so exposed. He could not fight their war for them, but he could not stand aside and watch them die.

TWENTY-TWO

MEINOR WAVED KALLIS over as they straggled back into the camp. He indicated the cluster of tents. 'Your general's here. Came as soon as he got your message. Wants to see you the instant you get back.' He grinned, looking Kallis up and down. 'Are you back?'

Kallis sighed. Galydon must have ridden hard to get here so soon. It had only been four days—or was it five now?—since he had sent his message. 'That man sees everything. I'm here.'

He looked over his shoulder at where Aarin trudged between Callan and Lysan and debated the wisdom of delaying that meeting until the morning, but decided he was unlikely to get away with that either. 'Where is he?'

'Over yon,' Meinor replied. 'Here, there, everywhere. He'll find you.'

'Of that I have no doubt.' He clapped Meinor on the shoulder and set off to find Galydon. He had a good idea where he might find him.

As they neared the tent where Kallis had left their prisoner, he saw the general emerge, talking intently with Meinor's second-in-command, a taciturn clansman known by his fellows as Surly. What his real name was, Kallis had no idea. Galydon saw their approach and came to meet them. The usually undemonstrative general put a hand on his shoulder. There was sympathy and regret on his face. 'How are you?'

Kallis nodded, swallowing hard. He had tried not to think about Iraius in the chaotic events that followed his death, but Galydon brought it back. 'The boatyard is gone,' he said now, focusing on the impersonal. 'I'm sorry.' It had been his job to protect it.

Galydon shook his head. 'I've been there. You could not have saved it.'

'Sedaine?' His message had been pointed and urgent.

Galydon sighed. 'I've arranged to move her out of the palace. She won't leave Rhiannas.'

That was no surprise, even if he had hoped Galydon would convince her otherwise. The palace was just too tempting a target.

By his expression, Galydon agreed, but he asked instead, 'What happened here? Meinor said…'

Then something behind Kallis caught his attention, and his hand dropped back to his side. Kallis turned to see Lysan with his brother, a smile plastered on his face. Aarin was doing his best to disappear into the background.

Galydon said to Kallis, 'Your message said nothing about this.'

He greeted Lysan with a friendly handshake and nodded at Callan. 'You're a long way from home.'

'So are you,' Lysan pointed out. 'But we did have an alliance, or had you forgotten?'

'Indeed. How fares Ephenor?'

'Ephenor fares well,' Callan replied with considerably more reserve than his brother. 'It's good to see you, General. But we are not here on behalf of Ephenor.'

Galydon's eyes lingered on Callan's face, searching. Whatever he found there, he said simply, 'I expect nothing. I hope for friendship.'

'You have that, always.'

Galydon nodded, his gaze turning to Aarin. Kallis saw his eyes widen in recognition. What was it Vianor had said the first time he laid eyes on Aarin? *You are the very image of your mother.*

Typically brisk, the general did not wait for an introduction. 'I hoped we might see you eventually,' he told Aarin. 'It hardly feels my place to welcome you, since I am the stranger here, but welcome, nonetheless.'

Aarin, who looked rather hunted, acknowledged that with a silent nod.

Undeterred, Galydon said, 'I would let you rest. I can see you need it. But I have not much time and there are things we need to speak of.'

Aarin watched the Caledani general warily. Kallis had offered his tent for this meeting then made himself scarce with almost palpable relief. There was a long silence, in which his searching regard was returned in full measure. Aarin felt like a child hauled before his elders for some misdeed, and he felt a flush of guilt for the thing that he knew that he had not shared.

It was Galydon who broke the uneasy silence. 'I will not presume to treat you like one of my soldiers. But I would like to know why you are here and what you intend to do.'

First Kallis, then Needa. Now this man. 'Are you asking whose side I am on?'

The general's steady gaze held his. 'Do I need to?'

Aarin choked back a bitter laugh. Their suspicion *hurt*. 'I had not thought so, but apparently no one is quite sure.'

'You misunderstand me,' Galydon said mildly. 'It has been made clear to me that what you did was necessary for reasons quite separate to what is happening here. If Darred has used that to his advantage, it is no fault of yours. What matters is what you intend to do now.'

Aarin felt a knot inside him loosen at those words. 'I'm here for the dragons.'

'So I assumed.'

'Darred is my enemy.'

A slight smile twitched Galydon's lips. The man's calm acceptance was unnerving. 'I rather hoped so. You do not need to justify yourself to me. But you do need to trust me.'

'Because you serve my mother?' It came out before he could stop it, and he winced at the childish words.

Galydon regarded him in contemplative silence. 'Your relationship with your mother is between the two of you,' he said at length. 'It is no concern of mine. The prosecution of this war is, however, and a lack of trust between us makes my job more difficult.'

That was nothing less than truth. Suddenly very tired, the dragging fatigue of Silverwing's injury clawing at him, Aarin dropped onto a stool and rested his chin in his hands. 'Of course, I'm sorry. But it is not simple. Darred is my enemy; his dragons are not. They are my *duty.*'

Galydon sat in his turn, perching on the edge of Kallis's cot. 'Explain.'

'Darred has enslaved them. I am here to free them.'

'How?'

Aarin spread his hands helplessly. 'I don't know. Yet. But they are not my enemy. I will not fight them for you.' He felt again the echo of that long scream.

Dark eyes studied him for a long moment, weighing those words. 'Very well,' Galydon said finally, standing. Neither face nor tone gave away a hint of his thoughts. He looked down at Aarin. 'Will you come to Rhiannas? We have much still to discuss.' He did not say 'to see your mother', but the words hung between them just the same.

Rhiannas. Jeta was there too. With Kinseris. His feelings about both were too conflicted for the prospect to fill him with anything but dread. But some things could not be avoided. He nodded. 'Soon.'

Galydon rose to leave. 'Soon then.'

He couldn't bear it. 'Wait,' he called. They would find out anyway and the result would be the same. They would expect and need him to protect them, never realising that his protection was the very thing that put them at risk.

Galydon was watching him, waiting. Aarin took a breath, then another. 'There has been another attack.'

TWENTY-THREE

'RHIANNAS HAS ALWAYS been a target. Nothing has changed. I will not run away!'

Jeta tried to pretend she could not hear the raised voices in the next room, but the argument was loud and the walls were thin.

'No one is asking you to run away, Sedaine. Just move out of the palace.'

That was the pretty young man she had met a few days ago. The queen's bean counter, Kallis had called him. Her chancellor. When Galydon had left to attend to whatever calamity had prompted Kallis's urgent message, he had stayed just long enough to make arrangements to move the queen to a house in the city—she had refused to leave Rhiannas. And it had fallen on Derias's shoulders to see those arrangements through, a task that was causing him no small headache. That much was clear.

'It is the same thing! What message does it send?'

'It is a sensible precaution. And you know it.'

He sounded like he was running out of patience. Accustomed to the extreme deference shown to the office of the Kas'Talani high priest, Jeta found the lack of formality of Lothane's court disorienting. Or perhaps the pointed lack of an honorific was a sign of Derias's spiralling frustration. She had been listening to this same argument for some time.

'Yes, Rhiannas has always been a target,' he agreed with forced patience. 'But the enemy didn't always have the ability to strike against it in the way they do now. Please, at least until Galydon returns and we know what we are facing.'

It was good advice, but Jeta could understand Sedaine's reluctance. It would feel like a defeat.

'There, what do you think?'

Jeta jumped, a guilty flush rising in her cheeks as she returned her attention to Limina, who was standing in front of her, awaiting her verdict.

'It's beautiful.'

Limina swished her hand through the layers of shimmering fabric. Farnor's queen-in-exile had been fascinated by Jeta's Caledani silks and had immediately set about trying to mimic the look, a project in which she had commandeered Jeta's assistance. The resulting fusion of Farnorian and Caledani fashions that Jeta was dutifully admiring was undeniably striking—and also entirely frivolous, given the current crisis.

'Oh, I'm staying here,' Limina said absently as she turned to admire her reflection in the long mirror. She pinched the silks either side of her waist. 'I think just a little tuck here and here, don't you agree?'

Jeta blinked. It was too surreal. 'What? Why?'

Limina sighed. 'To give the illusion of a waist, since my own has sadly departed.'

A door slammed. It was followed by something that sounded very much like an elegantly booted foot kicking a wall, then Sedaine stalked into the room. She stopped short in surprise when she saw Jeta, then her eyes latched onto Limina, who gave an obliging twirl, and a look of utter bewilderment flashed across the queen's face. She seemed to find the abrupt shift from crisis to couture as disconcerting as Jeta.

Limina gave her an expectant smile. 'What do you think?'

Sedaine stared at her, bemused. 'What are you doing?'

'What does it look like?' Limina asked moved a pile of unused fabric from a chair and steered Sedaine to it. 'What are *you* doing? Apart from tormenting poor Derias.'

Sedaine sighed. 'I cannot go along with this. My place is here. I cannot run at the first hint of danger.'

Limina gathered Sedaine's long hair in her hands. 'Galydon would not ask it of you without cause, and you did agree.'

'How can he know? Whether the danger is real or not, the damage this does is irreparable. If I run now, how can I expect my people to stand firm?'

Limina combed her fingers through Sedaine's hair, clever fingers teasing out knots, soothing away agitations. 'The solution is simple, love. You have left Rhiannas many times with Galydon to inspect the defences and give heart to your people. You will appear to go on just such a trip now. I will remain here, as I always do…' A firm hand on Sedaine's shoulder forestalled her objection. 'And no one will suspect anything is amiss. Go with Derias. Poor boy, he is quite dispirited. Let him take you to his family's house in the city. It would cheer him up no end.'

'No.' Sedaine gently disentangled herself from Limina's ministrations and stood. 'You cannot ask me to leave you here to face danger in my place.'

'Oh, tsk. But I will not be in danger, love, because you won't be in Rhiannas, remember?'

Sedaine gave an exasperated sigh and Limina turned once more to her reflection. 'Perhaps not,' she mused, playing with the fabric. 'Perhaps a looser fit is more flattering. What do you think?'

'I think,' said Sedaine, 'that you are trying to distract me. And it will not work. What about the lords? Their wretched delegation is due any day. What will they think if I am not here to receive them?'

'That you are busy with the defence of the realm, as they should be, and think themselves lucky to miss you. And you will be keeping Derias out of his brother's way, which is better for both of them. Leave the lords to me, love. You are altogether too harsh with them. You should at least pretend to consider their concerns before you dismiss them. Flatter them a little. Now, do I put a dart in here or not?'

Sedaine shook her head, but she was smiling now. 'Not,' she said firmly, and reached round to tuck in the fabric under Limina's bust. 'Here, if anywhere. It suits you better. Though when you think you will wear this ridiculous thing, I don't know.'

Limina laughed in delight. 'You are right. That is perfect.' She winked at Jeta, who was beginning to suspect that Limina did nothing that was not deliberate. 'I thought I might wear it for the lords.'

Sedaine choked on a laugh. 'No, please, I beg you. And you say I am too harsh with them.'

'Too stern, then,' Limina amended. 'You treat them like children.'

'I –'

'Yes, yes, and so they are. But you also need them on your side, so leave this to me and go and prepare.'

'I don't want to leave you here alone,' Sedaine said, and there was real affection underlying the protest.

'You won't be. I'll have our guests to entertain me, and Jeta has promised to show me how to tie those beautiful veils.'

Jeta started. Had she?

Sedaine glanced at her but did not otherwise acknowledge her presence. It had been that way since the first evening. She guessed that Kallis had told Sedaine where things had stood between her and Aarin. Now she was here, with Kinseris, and she sensed that Aarin's mother simply did not know how to treat her. Once or twice she had caught the queen staring at her, a hungry expression on her face as though she wanted to ask her about Aarin, but something always held her back. Fear of offending Kinseris, perhaps, though it would not. Or perhaps just fear of what she might hear. Whatever else she was, there was no denying she was also a mother.

There was a knock at the door. Derias called, 'Your highness?'

Sedaine rolled her eyes at Limina's smug smile. 'Come.'

It was only when Derias entered, accompanied by the grizzled clan captain Galydon had placed in charge of Rhiannas in his absence, that it became apparent that he had not come to continue their argument. The chancellor's face was unusually grim.

Sedaine saw it at once. 'What is it?'

Derias gave way to the clansman, who offered the queen the briefest of bows, little more than a nod. 'We've received word from Kamarai, your highness.' He hesitated, then added, 'It is gone.'

Jeta felt a little flutter of fear. Limina turned from the mirror, her gaze flicking between Sedaine and Derias.

'Gone?' Sedaine demanded. 'What does that mean?'

It was Derias who answered. 'Burned to the ground. We think it must have been…'

'The dragon,' Sedaine finished for him, her voice brittle.

Jeta gripped the sides of her chair. The fear twisted, close to panic. Had Aarin freed the dragons so they could do this? She could not believe so, but what then did this mean for him? She had felt the force of his dream—she had lived for seconds in the heady glory of the link—and this had no part in it. She was sure of it.

Jeta saw a reflection of her anguish on Sedaine's face, stealing her resolve when she needed to be strong.

She knew Aarin's mother to be brave and decisive. She had to be, to do what she had done. She had thought her cold and hard for the same reason. She was starting to know better. Hard perhaps, but not cold. She had realised that the first night they arrived, and she saw it now. The agony of doubt that was paralysing her. Sedaine did not know Aarin as Jeta had known him. She did not know the man he had become, only the child he had been and the wrong she had done him. She had seen only his hurt. And now the creatures to whom he had devoted his life—to whom his life had been given—were turned against her. Of the two possible explanations, Jeta did not know which his mother dreaded most. That he was dead and she had lost him, or that hurt had turned to hatred and revenge.

And Jeta thought that Aarin would be appalled if he could see her doubt—and she wanted to say as much—then she remembered all the priests who had died, and the words would not come.

The clan captain cleared his throat. 'Your highness. With Kamarai gone, the passes from Elvelen are wide open.'

'But Elvelen is our ally,' said Limina. She had moved next to Sedaine, standing close against her side. Offering support. 'Your chieftain is there, and four of your clans.'

'Are they?' the mercenary asked bleakly. 'Your highness, we have not heard from Lorac since he left. We do not know where he is. Where any of them are.'

Maker, he thinks they're dead. Jeta felt sick.

'Galydon…' Sedaine said faintly.

Derias was practically hopping up and down with agitation. 'Petrik has sent word,' he said, and the mercenary captain nodded his confirmation. 'But we can't wait for him to return.'

The captain, Petrik, added, 'I have sent scouts west, but it is six days ride to Kamarai. They will try to locate Lorac, find out if... find out more information. But we must secure Rhiannas, and that means you, your highness.'

'We must go now,' Derias urged. 'Galydon will come to you when he returns, but we cannot wait. We should leave Rhiannas...'

'No. I will not leave the city.'

Petrik exchanged a glance with Derias. 'It would be better —'

Sedaine silenced his protest. 'I said no. This changes nothing. I cannot leave. How can I expect my people to stand and fight if I will not do the same? Make what arrangements are necessary to defend Rhiannas, but I will not leave.'

TWENTY-FOUR

WHATEVER PETRIK THOUGHT of the queen's refusal to leave the palace, he wisely kept it to himself. Derias was not so easily defeated, however, and Jeta could hear the results of his latest attempt to change Sedaine's mind from the upper gallery, where she stood with Kinseris watching the mercenaries' preparations.

'What can they do?' she asked him now. All she could hear was Petrik's shocked voice. *It is gone.* Burned.

Kinseris was leaning against the stone of the arch, dark eyes intent on the activity in the courtyard, already soaked by the relentless rain. He had done little but sleep for the first two days after their arrival—and she had spent most of that time curled up next to him—and though he was still too thin, still showing the lingering strain of their journey in the hollows of his face, he nevertheless looked better than he had in months.

'Probably very little,' he admitted. 'Not on their own. But I do not think we will see a dragon here, not yet.'

There was a calm certainty to the words that she could not share. The threat was too huge, too inconceivable. Kamarai, a city of no small size and significance, had been completely destroyed. Her fear was as formless as it was overwhelming.

Kinseris saw it and one hand reached out to snare hers. 'Jeta, he's not coming here, not yet. Darred is not interested in a quick victory. If he were, Lothane would have fallen a year ago. He doesn't need the dragons to take it. He never did.'

'You don't think he will attack Rhiannas?'

He hesitated, studying her face. Then said, 'He'll come. Eventually. But he hasn't made Lothane or her queen suffer enough yet.'

Jeta pulled away. 'He's playing with us?'

'Nothing so benign, I suspect. I have witnessed Darred's revenge many times. It is never just about balancing the scales, not to him. It's about punishment. About making sure his victims know never to cross him again, that they never *can* cross him again.' He rested a hand on the stone arch, and his eyes had a distant look, as though he was not seeing the palace of Rhiannas but the sun-baked courtyards of Frankesh and Kas'Tella. 'Vasa thought he could use him, so did the Arkni. Vasa is dead, his power broken. And the Arkni…'

'That was Aarin's doing,' Jeta insisted. 'You were there.'

'I was,' Kinseris agreed. 'But Darred could have stopped him, could have stopped us. In Kas'Tella. But he let me go, he let *Aarin* go. And he knew exactly what he was doing when he did so.'

He straightened, frowning in irritation at the close-fitting garments that still looked so strange on him. Clothing in Caledan was loose and light, and with the exception of the priesthood, almost entirely unadorned. The clothes they had arrived in, given to them by the ship's captain who had brought them to Amadorn, had not been fit for anything but burning, or so Limina had declared when she appeared on their first morning here with maids carrying neat piles of fresh, clean clothing. The silks Jeta had brought with her had been purchased by Trad in the markets of Frankesh at Kinseris's insistence, as had the robes Kinseris himself had worn that first night. It had not been vanity. Even as ill as he had been, Kinseris had known it was important that they did not arrive here as refugees. They came as allies, as equals, and Kinseris, who had lived the politics of power for so many years, understood the role that appearances played in such things.

Limina understood it too and she had dressed him in the clothes of a Lothani noble. 'Derias won't miss them,' she had said to Jeta with a wink. 'The man must have a hundred outfits.'

Jeta had laughed at Kinseris's confusion when confronted by the complex array of layers, buckles, and brocade, and he had quickly discarded the more elaborate aspects of local dress and adapted the rest into as simple a display as possible, and she had to admit, it suited him well, even if the deep brown of his complexion ensured that he would never quite blend in.

She thought of Sedaine, determined to fight this war she must know she could not win. 'Do we have a chance?'

She felt his eyes on her and could not bring herself to meet them. She knew by now that though he never lied to her, the things he did not say were legion, that the evasions and the secrecy sometimes skirted the edges of dishonesty. She had accepted it, she understood that it was a habit of decades. And she also understood that he was protecting her, that perhaps there were things she did not want to know, and though he might not always judge correctly, those judgements were never made from a desire to deceive.

She did not know, at this moment, whether she wanted the unvarnished truth, or a truth with its hard edges blunted and made bearable.

In the end she got neither.

'There you are,' Limina said brightly, arriving by her side and slipping a warm hand through her arm.

Jeta cast a slightly desperate look at Kinseris. His answering smile, faintly amused, erased whatever expression had been there before.

Limina pretended not to notice. 'I've been looking for you everywhere.' Then, to Kinseris, 'May I borrow her? I find there is so much to do, and I simply cannot manage it all alone.'

Amusement crinkling his eyes, Kinseris said lightly, 'Neither of you needs my permission.'

As Limina dragged her away, Jeta could hear only those words and what lay beneath them. She looked back at Kinseris, still standing in the shadows of the gallery, suddenly without occupation or purpose for the first time in decades. She didn't want to leave him alone, but there was nothing she could do to erase the hard truth: that now they were here, his warning delivered, he had no influence, no say, in the events that would follow, save what the queen and Galydon allowed him.

'Give him time,' Limina murmured with uncanny perception. 'He has to find his own place.'

Jeta looked at the woman beside her, another displaced ruler who had had to find a new role in a world where all her former power and influence counted for nothing. 'Or accept the loss of it?'

Limina patted her arm. 'Oh, I don't think so. The queen will let nothing of value go to waste. Now,' she said decisively, before Jeta could decide whether that was ominous or reassuring, 'seeing as Derias has all but stripped us bare, I need your help bringing a little luxury back to this dreary place.'

Jeta trailed Limina through the hallways to a wing of the palace she had not yet seen, where the servants were busy airing rooms and sweeping away dust and cobwebs.

'Are we expecting visitors?' she asked as she stepped aside to allow a maid carrying fresh linens to enter a bedchamber that was being hastily restored to something like its former glory—or as close as it could come with its finery stripped and sold.

'Alas,' Limina sighed, catching the maid by the shoulders and turning her around. 'What did I tell you? These are for the blue rooms.'

Jeta watched the maid scuttle down the corridor, the pile of linens wobbling dangerously. 'Who?'

With a final survey of the room, Limina followed the maid. 'We are to have the pleasure of the Lords of the North. Come to make their displeasure felt, I have no doubt.'

'Their displeasure?' In the shock of Kamarai, she had forgotten that the delegation was due. 'About what?'

'Oh, everything. If they feel anything else, I have never seen a sign of it. But mainly because they feel they are not listened to. Ah, there you are,' Limina said as she found the steward, and issued a stream of instructions that Jeta.

'Aren't they the queen's council?' Jeta asked. Her parents had made her study the workings of power in Lothane ahead of her ill-fated betrothal to Lord Nathas. The Lords of the North had acted as the regency council after the king's death and had formed the inner circle of his government while he was alive.

'Certainly,' Limina agreed, pausing by a window. 'From a distance.'

Jeta grinned. 'You mean she's ignored them?'

'She has not ignored them,' Limina retorted. 'She just gave them important roles to play elsewhere. She could not have them here, underfoot, questioning everything, insisting on doing things their way. And they would make Galydon's life impossible. A Caledani general in Amadorn? That they would never accept. And it would be far better if she's not here to meet with them now. There is an epidemic of stubborn old men in Lothane,' Limina said absently, her eyes on Vianor crossing the courtyard below them. 'And the best thing to do in such circumstances is to get rid of them.'

Jeta stared at her in sudden suspicion. This was, after all, the queen famously rumoured to have organised the Petticoat Revolution. 'Is that what you did? In Farnor? Got rid of them?

'No, love,' Limina said brightly. 'Those stubborn old men died.'

'Limina!'

Limina laughed and squeezed her hand. 'They were old. They died. Honestly, what do you northerners think of me?'

Jeta flushed, aware she was being teased. 'I'm not a northerner. I'm from Situra.'

Limina said, a little wistfully, 'Everywhere is north of Farnor. Sometimes I fear I will never see it again.' She looked at Jeta. 'Do you ever think of Situra? Of your family?'

Situra. Part of the alliance of southern states that bordered the Istelan. Situra, her home for most of her life, now taken by Darred, like all the lands to the south. Home to the parents she had not seen in three years, to all the people she had known when life was different, safer. Situra, that she had abandoned without looking back and yet in some ways had never left.

But there were some doors Jeta was not prepared to open, because if she did, she did not know if she could close them again.

'No,' she lied, but already she could feel the hairline cracks opening in the wall she had made between her present and her past. Between her present and what must lie ahead.

Limina nodded, as though she understood everything that lay behind that one word. And then, with unspoken compassion, kept Jeta busy for the rest of the day with a hundred little tasks until her feet ached and her fingers were raw, and she was too tired to think of anything but how soon she could tumble into bed and sleep. And when she woke in the morning, aching and sore, the cracks were safely papered over, and she could once again go about her day without feeling like she was about to break open at the slightest touch. Some part of her was aware that what was behind that wall would burst through eventually, but not *now*. She could not bear it now. There was something she had to do first.

TWENTY-FIVE

GALYDON RETURNED THE next day, his clothes caked in mud and his face like thunder. Jeta was with Limina in the guest wing when they heard the clatter of hooves and saw the general and his escort ride into the courtyard.

Kinseris was already there by the time they reached the palace's grand steps, and he squeezed her hand as she stopped beside him, the fleeting pressure warm and reassuring.

Galydon didn't waste time on greetings. As soon as the groom had taken his horse, he came striding towards them. 'Darred sent a dragon against the boatyard. Iraius is dead.' He took the steps two at a time, handing off his ruined cloak to the guard at the door. 'I need to see the queen. This is not the first attack; there has been another.'

'Another?' Limina asked, hurrying after him. 'Not just Kamarai?'

Galydon stopped dead. 'So, it was Kamarai. We suspected as much.'

'We? Did the messenger not tell you?'

He shook his head, stripping off his filthy gloves and discarding them. 'I've seen no messenger, but I came by the river. The roads to the east are impassable past Forthtown.'

Limina frowned. 'Then how do you know about Kamarai?'

Uncharacteristic hesitation flitted across Galydon's face. Then he said, 'Darred sent a raiding party against the boatyard, and another against the camp. There were prisoners.'

Jeta heard him through a daze, her eyes on Kinseris, whose face betrayed the impact of yet another blow. She had asked him, the night they arrived, what he had done. And he had told her, thinking those plans dead. Iraius was, perhaps, the only one who could have revived them, and now he was gone.

There was sadness on her own account, too. She remembered him, vividly, from her time onboard *Situran Dawn*. She had liked him, though she would not have admitted it at the time. He and Kallis had been friends.

Kallis. The boatyard. She felt a flutter of fear. 'Kallis?'

'Is fine,' Galydon assured her, already moving on, heading to the small office that adjoined his quarters in the palace. 'The queen?'

'Still here,' Limina told him, and at his raised eyebrow added, 'She would not leave.'

Galydon did not address that directly, though his face expressed his frustration. 'I must speak to her. I need you,' he said to Kinseris, eyes narrowing as he noticed the rapidly fading shock. 'There are things we need to discuss.'

Jeta glanced at Kinseris, unnerved by Galydon's urgency. She had not missed the brisk evasions, and she wanted to insist that she go with them, but if Kinseris had no status here, she had less. Once again, she would be left to wait, to worry, and suddenly she was back in that windowless room in Frankesh, back in the filthy hut in the army camp…

Limina leaned in, slipping an arm around her waist. The touch grounded her, but the cracks were growing again, and the rest of the conversation was lost as she concentrated on holding those cracks at bay.

She managed a smile for Kinseris as he left with Galydon and let Limina hustle her away, chatting a shade too brightly as she busied them both with tasks that could have been left to others. But even Limina's amusing stories and scandalous gossip about Lothane's noble counsellors, soon to arrive among them, failed to distract her from the certainty that *something* was coming, and she had been kept deliberately in the dark.

When night came and Kinseris and Galydon still had not emerged from their interview with Sedaine, she made her way to his room rather than her own. She would not sleep, she knew that already, so she would wait for him, as she had waited so many nights in Kas'Tella. And it surprised her that those memories carried a sense of happier times. Yet even there she had been forced to wait. Unable to take action of her own, only react to the actions of others, and she did not know how much longer she could do it.

It was very late when Kinseris finally returned, slipping quietly into the dark room, hesitating as he realised she was there. Some instinct kept her still, feigning sleep, some sixth sense that warned her not to break that silence, that something irrevocable lay behind it.

She felt him walk towards the bed, the hitching stutter in his steps betraying his tiredness. He paused, looking down at her, and she gathered her courage and rolled over, opening her eyes. 'What's happened? How bad is it?'

Kinseris sighed, rubbing a hand over his face. 'Bad enough.'

She sat up, drawing her knees up to her chest. 'Tell me. Is Kallis really all right?'

'Yes.' He sat down heavily on the edge of the bed furthest from where she sat. 'You should not be here.'

She had not expected that, and she had no time for it now. 'Tell me.'

So he told her the news that Galydon had brought. How a dragon had killed Iraius and destroyed the boatyard. How it had attacked the mercenary camp. That Darred had men inside Lothane already.

She listened in silence, hearing the things he did not say, and it did not surprise her when, at the end, he said quietly, 'There's more.'

Of course there was more. She wasn't stupid. She could feel it in the careful distance he left between them, in the withdrawal of the closeness they had shared. And she was perfectly able to read between the lines. The mercenary camp could not have survived the onslaught that had destroyed the boatyard unless it had been protected by something capable of turning aside dragon fire. By someone.

She waited for him to say it. Was that a cruelty or a kindness? She could not tell. She could barely breathe. *You should not be here.*

'Jeta,' he said, and she did not know whether his reluctance was for himself or for her. 'Aarin is back. He is here, with Kallis.'

And just like that, the thread that bound them together was severed.

'Why?' She hardly recognised her own voice, tight and thin, as though she were suffocating on too little air.

Beside her, Kinseris was very still. 'Why?'

'Why is he back?'

She could sense his confusion, that this was not the reaction he had expected. 'The dragons…'

She lay back, feeling the last of her breath leave her, grateful to the darkness for hiding her face. 'The dragons.' Because Aarin had not come back for her, because she had never been a factor in his decisions. But even knowing that, she could not prevent the longing from drenching her. She could not stop it hurting Kinseris, who understood better than anyone what this would mean to her, and who had already pulled away to protect them both.

It was too late to get up, to leave and return to the rooms she had been given. And she did not want to. In the end, he lay down beside her, because he was tired, but the distance between them already stretched endless, and she didn't know whether to be angry or sad. She could feel his breathing, too even and controlled for sleep, and wanted to reach out, to touch him, but she did not. Instead, they lay there together, not sleeping, through all the long night.

She must have drifted off sometime before dawn. When she woke hours later to the bright sun of mid-morning, he was already gone.

TWENTY-SIX

IT WAS RAINING again. Kallis brushed the streaming water from his eyes as he peered around the tumbledown wall. The village looked quiet, its main street churned into thick mud and the shutters on the houses closed and barred against the weather. But appearances were deceptive, and his men had already marked the locations of the Caledani sentries and even now should be moving to take them out.

Kallis turned to the shivering prisoner behind him. 'You're certain—no priests?'

The man nodded, his shoulders hunched uncomfortably against the cold, his wrists tied at his back. 'Never even seen one of them,' he said sullenly, his Taslorian accent thick with resentment.

Lysan slipped in beside them, a grin on his face. He shook his head.

Kallis grunted, satisfied. Aarin had said there were no Kas'Talani close by, but Aarin was not here, and Kallis wasn't taking any chances. The damned priests had to show their hand at some point, and he had no intention of being taken by surprise.

He turned, making a gesture over his shoulder, and saw Meinor pick it up and pass it along the line. At least the heavy cloud had given them the cover of bad light as his men stole into position. They only awaited confirmation that the sentries had been dealt with before they moved in.

There was a flicker at the end of the muddy street. One of his men ghosted into view, one hand held up, flashing four times.

Kallis swore.

'I'll go,' Lysan murmured.

Kallis gave him a grateful nod and Lysan disappeared. Galydon had been adamant that he wanted Darred's men out of Lothane, and Kallis was only too happy to oblige, but they had to do this as quickly and quietly as possible. Their prisoner had been as forthcoming as he was able—he didn't know much, something Kallis could readily believe—and as a result they did not know for certain how many of these riverside hamlets had been taken by the Caledani. They could not risk a survivor escaping to cry warning, and one of the sentries had apparently eluded his men.

Kallis glanced at Meinor. If luck was with them, Lysan would track down the sentry before he could cause a problem. He did not have enough men with him to send more after one man. If all went well, this wasn't the only settlement they would be taking back today, and missing sentry or no missing sentry, he couldn't jeopardise that by delaying further. The rain had already put their bows out of action, and the unseasonable cold would numb the fingers and slow the reactions of his men the longer they waited, even as their enemy sheltered in the warmth of the cottages.

Meinor replaced Lysan at his side. 'We moving?' The big man's expression was fierce and eager. The clansmen were itching to avenge the attack on their camp and the massacre at the boatyard. The memory of the aftermath still made Kallis's stomach churn. Neither the sight nor the smell of the devastation would leave him.

'We're moving,' he agreed, as his mind replayed the moment the dragon's flames had caught Iraius in mid-leap.

He fretted impatiently as the mercenaries edged past him, wanting to get this over with and get back to Rhiannas. He needed to speak to Galydon about Iraius, about the black sand that he had forgotten in the crisis that followed. Kallis had been worrying that detail ever since and he had come to some conclusions of his own, not least among them the suspicion that Galydon had known a lot more than he had shared about Iraius. And he was having a hard time deciding whom he was most angry with—the general or Iraius himself, whose silence had certainly contributed to his death. Because if they had known that he had made himself such a target, they would not have left him so exposed.

As the last of his men slipped past, Kallis followed, reaching the closest dwelling just as the first shouts erupted from the buildings and the soldiers hidden inside came tumbling out, pulling on armour and fumbling for weapons as they came.

The clansmen fell on them with cheerful savagery, surprise and professionalism giving them an easy advantage. And several of the Amadorians among the Caledani soldiers, finding themselves under attack from their own countrymen, simply laid down their weapons and surrendered.

The blow to his chest that sent Kallis staggering back came out of nowhere, and his vision greyed out for an instant as he lost his breath.

There was a growl and a rush of air, and Kallis stumbled to the side to avoid a strike that would surely have felled him as a quarterstaff whistled by his head. He got a brief impression of greying hair and a ragged beard in a too-pale face, before he was forced to duck again, retreating until the heel of his back foot connected with a wall.

Right hand pressed to his throbbing ribs, Kallis stepped to the side, blocking the next blow with his sword high, and the force of the impact vibrated down his arm. He hated bloody quarterstaffs. And he didn't have time for this.

He was lucky that his attacker was not accustomed to using the staff as a weapon. The next wild strike he caught from above and forced the staff down, then twisted and lunged, letting his momentum carry him forward in the second he had bought himself, and felt his blade pierce muscle even as the staff pulled across and took his legs from under him. Kallis rolled, the mud sucking at him, slowing him, but his assailant was also down, bleeding from a wound in his shoulder.

Hands on his knees as he cradled screaming ribs, Kallis took in his attacker's lined face, filthy homespun and worn-through boots and had an uncomfortable suspicion that this was not, in fact, an enemy.

Hoisting the man upright by his collar, he propped him against the wall.

'You live here?' he asked.

One hand pressed to the shallow cut in his shoulder, the man treated him to a look of pure hatred. 'Till you lot kicked us out, we did.' And added a word Kallis hadn't heard in years, but which did at least explain his aching ribs.

'Watch your tongue,' he snapped. 'This one's on your side. How many are there?'

The man spat. 'Like you don't know.'

'No, I don't,' Kallis said, losing patience. 'That's why I'm asking you.' He held his sword out behind him, pointing to where the mercenaries were mopping up the last of the resistance. 'See my men? We serve the queen and we just freed your village. So perhaps you could help us, and maybe we'll patch you up before we go. But if you prefer, I can leave you out here to bleed to death.' Which was unlikely, since the blood flow was already slowing, but the wound had to hurt. Well, good. He was angry. 'Call me that again, and I'll show you what it really means, understood?'

The old man's eyes flicked warily in the direction Kallis had indicated, and he nodded.

Kallis released his grip on the man's shirt and stepped back, sheathing his sword. 'Thank you. And, er, sorry…' He waved his hand at the bloody shoulder.

There was a bright peal of laughter from somewhere behind, and he turned to see Lysan escorting a rather dishevelled missing sentry, chatting happily in fluent Safarsee, to his prisoner's evident confusion and dismay.

'Who's the leader here?' Kallis asked his assailant, keeping his voice low. 'Do you know his name?'

The old man gave a pained shrug. 'Heard a couple of them talk about an Ottil. Don't know if he's the leader, but they sounded scared of him.'

'That'll be him,' Kallis patted the man on his good shoulder. 'Play along.'

'*You!*' he called at Lysan's prisoner in Safarsee as they drew level. '*You're one of Ottil's?*'

When the man's only response was to stare at him with his mouth hanging open, Lysan snapped, '*Answer the captain!*'

That got a frantic nod and a sideways look in the direction of the huddle of disarmed prisoners being hustled inside the largest of the hamlet's buildings.

Kallis snapped his fingers under the man's face, trusting Lysan to pay attention to what he couldn't see. '*Look at me, not at him. You're in enough trouble. Why did Ottil ignore his orders? What are you still doing here? Quickly, boy,*' he snarled, as the sentry's gaze slid back to the other prisoners, '*and maybe you won't share his punishment.*'

'*Punishment?*' *We were to hold this position and stay out of sight until further orders. We haven't had further orders.*'

A touch of defiance entered his tone. Kallis didn't give him time to think. '*Who told you to shoot the dragon?*'

The poor sentry gaped. '*That's why we're here!*'

Kallis shook his head in mock disgust and gave the man a shove towards his fellows. '*You shot the wrong bloody dragon though, didn't you?*'

'Any idea which one's Ottil?' he asked Lysan, as a clansman grabbed the sentry and shoved him after the others.

Lysan was grinning at the look of pure terror that had flashed across the Caledani's face. 'Curly hair, short. Shouty.'

Kallis gestured to the man he had wounded, who had watched the exchange in suspicious silence. 'This is one of the villagers. Get him inside and patch him up.'

Lysan gave him a pained looked as he slung the wilting farmer's arm over his shoulder. 'Do I look like my brother?'

'Very funny. Just do your best.' But he wondered, and not for the first time, why Callan wasn't here with his brother. The man he had known two years ago would never have let Lysan come alone.

Then he pushed that thought to one side as he watched his men herd the last few stragglers into the main building. Most of the small villages in this part of Lothane had somewhere like it. Not quite a meeting hall, less than a tavern, it nevertheless offered somewhere for folk to gather, and sometimes as a place to get a hot meal.

He waited a few minutes before following, giving their bewildered sentry an opportunity to spread a bit of panic and confusion. Then he snapped out an order in Safarsee to the clansman outside, who grinned and opened the door.

He was met with tense silence, evidence that rumours were already circulating, and Kallis allowed himself a grim smile. Their reluctant Taslorian conscript had confirmed what he had suspected—that this advance force would be largely Amadorian under Caledani officers—and his entrance had just thrown their assumptions about who had attacked them and why into confusion. It wouldn't last long.

Meinor had Lysan's short angry man up against the far wall, a knife at his throat. The dusky tone to his skin betrayed his Caledani origins—somewhere north of Kas'Tella, Kallis guessed—and the scowl on his face betrayed his uncertainty.

'*Ottil,*' he bawled. '*What have you been doing, you incompetent piece of shit?*'

The Caledani captain was not as easily intimidated. He glared at Kallis defiantly over Meinor's blade. *Who the fuck are you?*

Kallis stalked across the room, kicking a chair out his way. '*The last thing you'll see if you don't answer me, and quickly. Why are you still here? Where are the others?*'

Red rage flushed Ottil's face. '*We are where we were ordered to be. And we took down the silver dragon. Again, as ordered. I don't know who you are, but you're mistaken if you think you can walk in here and threaten me. My orders come direct from Darred.*'

Kallis bunched his fist in the man's tunic and leaned in close. '*So do mine, and you shot the wrong one, Ottil. So, tell me, what do you think* my *orders might be?*'

Kallis almost laughed at how quickly red faded to a sickly grey. The depths of Ottil's terror told him this man must have had some personal dealings with Darred. And that he might be in possession of some useful intelligence. If so, Galydon would extract it from him.

'*I'll ask you one more time. Tell me what I want to know, and maybe I won't send you back to answer for this mess in person. Where are the others?*'

Fear of Darred's wrath unlocked Ottil's cooperation. He nearly fell over himself spilling the positions of the companies sent over the river.

Kallis listened to the flow of words, relieved that the incursion hadn't gone any further—unless something went badly wrong, the men he had sent to the other hamlets should be able to handle the rest of the clean up—when he became aware of a man watching him with disconcerting intensity. Very fair, he was crouched in a corner a little way away from the other Amadorian prisoners, and something about the quality of his gaze was unsettling.

Kallis focused his attention on Ottil, who was watching him hopefully as the words finally ran out.

Kallis smiled and patted his cheek. 'Thank you,' he said in Amadorian. 'That's just what I needed to know.' And watched as confusion turned to furious realisation.

Meinor, his bottom lip swollen and bloody, grinned in satisfaction as the Caledani captain erupted into an angry tirade.

'Gag him,' Kallis ordered as he turned to leave. He was almost at the door when there was an urgent shout. He turned on instinct, and a knife buried itself in the wood of the fireplace not a handspan from his shoulder. He looked from its vibrating hilt to the man who had thrown it, his blood already pooling on the worn boards of the floor as Meinor straightened up.

In his corner, the blond man paused half-way to his feet. It was his shout that had delivered the warning.

Kallis ignored him, staring at the Caledani officer as he gurgled his last breaths. Then he swore, slamming a fist into the wall.

Meinor gave him an unapologetic shrug. 'Not like you needed him for anything else, is it?'

Kallis stared at him for a long moment, breathing hard, trying to contain his anger. Then he turned on his heel and walked to the door. 'Send someone to check on the others. We destroy the ballista and then we head back. We've been here too long already.'

Kallis watched from the village as his men rolled the ballista to the riverbank. The Istelan was deep here, the bank falling steeply towards the fast-flowing waters, deep enough to swallow the weapon and leave no trace of it.

By his side, Meinor spat in the mud. 'Still think we should keep it.'

Kallis glanced at him, his anger at the death of Ottil still simmering. They had already had this argument and he had no intention of rehashing it. It was not that he disagreed. He had seen what the thing had done to Silverwing, what it could do to Darred's dragons. And he had watched, helpless, as the dragon had destroyed the boatyard and killed Iraius. It went against his every instinct as a soldier to destroy such a weapon when they had no others. But he also knew, with certainty, that Aarin would never forgive the use of this weapon against any dragon, ever.

But it wasn't friendship that made him deaf to Meinor's arguments—that was a changed and uncertain thing—it was a cold calculation that they needed Aarin more than they needed a physical weapon. To keep this ballista, much less use it, would be to forfeit whatever help and protection the mage could offer them.

Meinor spat again, saliva tinged with red as he worried a broken tooth.

'Why don't you just pull the bloody thing out and be done with it?'

In answer, the huge clansman gave him a gruesome grin, full of his jagged front teeth.

Kallis shook his head and looked away. 'Point taken.'

The men pushing the ballista stumbled to a halt as its left wheel sank into the mud and the machine tilted dangerously to the side.

'You sure about this?' Meinor asked after a while, as they watched the mercenaries swarming over the ballista with ropes to pull it free. 'Your boy doesn't seem that keen to help. He's not here, is he?'

Kallis sighed. 'It's complicated.' Too complicated for him at any rate. Whatever conflict Aarin felt, it seemed clear to Kallis that they shared an enemy in Darred, and while the dragons killed his people, they too were the enemy. He understood that Aarin didn't see it that way, but that was as far as his understanding extended.

Meinor grunted his contempt for such ambiguities and nodded towards the ballista, teetering now at the edge of the steep bank. 'That ain't.'

'No, it isn't,' Kallis agreed, waving his assent to the men on the bank, who sent the ballista tumbling over the edge to be lost in the churning waters of the Istelan. 'But it's not going to win this war for us either.'

There was an angry growl beside him. 'And the boy will?'

'I don't know,' Kallis admitted, heading back to the village where his men waited with the prisoners. 'But he's worth more than that thing.'

TWENTY-SEVEN

CALLAN WAS WAITING when they made it back to the camp two days later with their prisoners in tow. Eyes scanning the ragged group for a sign of his brother, Callan picked his way through the mud to Kallis's side.

Kallis looked at his tight face then back down the line to where Lysan trudged beside the prisoners, demonstrably alive and well. Not Lysan then. He sighed. 'What now?'

Callan's eyes flicked back to him and the lines of strain on his face faded. He shook his head, mutely dismissing Kallis's concern, which failed to have the desired effect. Or it would have failed, if Kallis hadn't been too tired to worry about anything else right now. Still, he filed it away for later. He might have been distracted virtually every moment since Callan and his brother had arrived in their midst, but he wasn't unaware of the tense undercurrents in their relationship.

Nor the fact that Callan had chosen to stay with Aarin rather than accompany his brother.

He looked for the mage and couldn't see him. 'Where's Aarin?'

'Sleeping.'

'Still?' The attack had been days ago.

Callan shrugged and said, 'The dragon's still healing,' as if that explained everything.

Kallis didn't have time to worry about that either. Meinor was bellowing orders and he knew he needed to see their prisoners secured. He just needed a minute.

Lysan appeared beside him, grinning at his brother. 'See? Back safe and sound, and barely a scratch among us for you to fuss over.'

Callan looked unimpressed. 'Barely?'

Lysan's eyes twinkled. 'Perhaps a cracked rib or two.'

Kallis rolled his eyes as Callan turned to look at him. 'I'm fine,' he insisted, ignoring the persistent throb of abused ribs, and took his leave before either of them could pursue that line of enquiry any further. All he needed was a chance to close his eyes for longer than two hours at a stretch. And perhaps a drink.

He hadn't gone more than a dozen steps when Meinor found him.

'Prisoner wants to talk.'

Kallis sighed and tried not to curse out loud. But they needed information, and they needed it badly, so he changed direction to follow Meinor and tried to not to think about his bed.

When Kallis entered the tent where Meinor had stashed the prisoner he found the fair-haired Amadorian trussed up inside. Despite cords that were tied painfully tight around wrists and ankles, and the chain that secured him to the tent pole, the man was the picture of serenity.

Kallis surveyed him with irritation. 'If you're expecting me to thank you, you're wasting your time and mine.'

The man raised an eyebrow. 'Of course not. You are Kallis?'

Kallis was unimpressed. 'Any one of my men might have told you that, intentionally or otherwise.'

The man acknowledged that with a slight smile. His eyes were very blue. 'Your men—Hawks, I believe?—are not exactly chatty.'

'Fine.' He remembered the man's intense gaze back in the village. His timely warning. He hooked a stool towards him and sat down with a groan. It had been a long day, his bruised ribs were throbbing in time with the ache in his head, and he didn't have the patience to play games. 'You know my name. What else do you know?'

'I know Iraius was your friend. Is he dead?'

Kallis felt a flash of anger. 'You were there,' he guessed. 'What do you think?'

The man cocked his head, his blue eyes curious. 'You survived.'

Anger flashed to something darker, and Kallis felt his hands ball into fists. He forced himself to relax, unclenching his fingers to grip the seat of the stool.

His reaction did not go unnoticed. 'I'm sorry,' the man said. 'We tried to warn him.'

'We?'

A fleeting half-smile. 'Not everyone in the south is your enemy. There are those of us who are fighting our own kind of war.'

Kallis stared at him, the words fitting too neatly with his own suspicions. 'And you're telling me Iraius was working with you?'

The man made a vague gesture that was painfully reminiscent of Iraius. 'In a manner of speaking. How well did you know him?'

'Not as well as I thought, apparently.'

His prisoner smiled. 'Better, I think, than most. Only Hanlon really knew him.'

And now they were coming to it. *Hanlon called it black sand.* He could feel the prisoner's gaze on him, waiting, watching, assessing.

'Admiral Hanlon,' the man repeated. 'Have you heard of him?'

'The scourge of the pirates? I've heard of him.'

The man laughed, his expression disarmingly open. 'Only the ones who got too greedy would call him that. My admiral was half pirate himself. We took our fair share of Caledani merchants ships together. But he kept piracy under control—that is true. No one touched Farnor's ships, nor those of the other coastal kingdoms that paid for his protection, not if they wanted to avoid the noose.'

Kallis grunted, far from surprised. 'So, the great admiral was a brigand himself. Did his wife know?'

The prisoner grinned. 'Have you met her?'

Kallis had to allow it was unlikely Limina had been unaware of her husband's activities.

There was a pause, then the prisoner asked, 'Is she well?'

Kallis nodded and took a chance. 'She would be heartened to hear news of her husband. Is he well?'

The man's face closed down. He looked away. 'Hanlon's ship went down with all hands. If he survived, no one has seen or heard from him since.'

Kallis studied him. The emotion, he was sure, was genuine. The words he was less sure about. 'You survived,' he said, throwing the other man's accusation back at him.

Anger flashed in those blue eyes. 'I was not with him that day.'

Kallis heard the toxic mix of regret and guilt and did not push. Instead, he asked, 'Was it Hanlon who sent Iraius to Amadorn?'

The man shook his head. 'He could not have done. It must have been Vasa's successor. Hanlon had dealings with him for years. But he too is dead now.'

Kallis stared at him, feeling the throbbing anger build like an ache behind his eyes, cursing himself for his stupidity. Because who else could it have been? And Kinseris had said *nothing*. How much of this could have been avoided if he had not kept them in the dark? How much more had he not told them? But even through his anger he was careful not to correct the man's assumption that Kinseris was dead. 'Which one of you sent the black sand to Iraius?'

The man grimaced at his harsh tone. 'We had to get it out of Farnor. We couldn't risk it falling into Darred's hands.'

Kallis thought about the explosion that had killed Iraius as surely as the dragon had done. 'No, I see that.'

'But we didn't know then, about the dragons.'

There was nothing to say to that. None of them had known about the dragons.

'When we did, we tried to warn you. Tried to warn Iraius. Make no mistake—Iraius was its target. Darred never cared how many boats you had. Now we know why.'

Kallis frowned. 'If he didn't care about the boatyard, why kill Iraius?'

The man started to reply, then shrugged. 'I don't know.'

Kallis had sensed the presence of half-truths in much of what he had been told so far but that, he was certain, was an outright lie. He let it pass. He would have the truth from Kinseris one way or another.

'We think—we *believe*—that the dragon knew how to find Iraius,' the man said. 'I think it would have found him anywhere. If it can do that once, it can do it again.'

Kallis felt a chill tingle down his spine. He remembered how the dragon had come straight for them. How it had circled overhead while they had hidden in the storage hut, waiting for Iraius. 'What do you mean?'

'I mean,' the man said precisely, 'that Darred could send a dragon to kill you whenever he wished. You, your general Galydon. Even your queen. And it would find you.'

That was a thought to keep him up at night, and he didn't need any more nightmares. Galydon said he had arranged to hide Sedaine somewhere in the city. If what this man said was true, that would do them no good at all when Darred decided he was finished playing with them.

'How many are there?'

'Three that we know of.'

Three. That was not what he had wanted to hear. Aarin had barely held off one. What could he do against three? What *would* he do?

Kallis scrubbed a hand over his face, suddenly very tired. He looked at his prisoner, this self-confessed Farnorian pirate, his blond hair bright even in the gloom of the tent. 'What's your name?'

The man smiled. 'Best you don't know that.'

'Why's that?'

Still smiling, his prisoner said, 'I hope you will let me go. I'd rather you couldn't name me, just in case.'

Just in case he found himself a prisoner of Darred. What a charming thought. He shook his head. 'Can't do that.'

The man's eyes narrowed. 'Can't?'

'How would that look to your fellow prisoners?' He had taken out his small knife and was using it to clean the filth from his fingernails. 'I assume you don't want them to know about your activities?'

The prisoner shook his head, watching him intently.

Kallis stood, the knife falling to the ground within reach of the man's bound hands. Long, agile fingers curled around it, tucking it out of sight.

'We'll be moving as soon as the weather clears. Heading to Rhiannas. We'll pick up the road at Forthtown.'

The man nodded and Kallis left.

TWENTY-EIGHT

KALLIS FOUND CALLAN tending a cut one of his men had taken to his arm. It was the only injury any of them had sustained, if he didn't count his bruised and aching ribs.

'How bad?' he asked as Callan finished what he was doing and started to pack away his things.

'Not bad as long as he keeps it clean. What do you need?'

'Wake Aarin. I need to speak to him.' As Callan opened his mouth to object, he added, 'Now.'

Ten minutes later they joined him in his tent. Aarin looked half asleep still, his face thin and drawn.

Kallis's eyes narrowed. 'What's wrong with you?'

When Aarin didn't answer, Kallis decided he didn't have the energy to pursue it. Whatever it was, Callan could deal with it. 'You said the dragons are enslaved. What did you mean?'

Aarin frowned. 'Why?'

'Because I want to understand what we're up against,' Kallis growled, too tired and sore for patience.

There was a pause as Aarin searched for the right words. Then he said, 'The power of the priesthood comes from the dragons, from the devices they wear—you know that?'

Kallis nodded. He understood that much. He also knew that Kinseris had forced the Kas'Talani to set aside the dragon devices, and that not all of them had complied. Jeta had said those who refused had died. Except, presumably, those with Darred. And Darred himself.

'Each device is linked to a living dragon,' Aarin continued. 'They were forged before the Severing, meant to act as a link between mages and their dragons once the magic that joined them was broken. But the mages who made them died, and the Arkni gave them to the Kas'Talani so their use of them could sustain the Arkni's existence until the magic could be rejoined.'

'And now the magic has been rejoined…?' Kallis prompted.

Aarin looked troubled. 'I don't know.'

'You don't know?'

The mage sighed. 'Those devices existed before the Severing. They exist after the reJoining. They are unchanged. Everything else is different, and they remain constant. That changes everything. I have been helping the dragons to wake, to throw off their chains, but if the Kas'Talani do not give up the devices willingly…'

'They die?'

Aarin winced and looked away. 'Yes.'

'Then why,' asked Kallis, 'is Darred not dead? And why is his dragon *here* instead of… wherever you have been?'

'The Long Dream,' Aarin murmured, his voice tight. 'Because his dragon does not want to be free. You must understand—each of those devices was created out of love. A love that joined dragon and mage, but every mage that made one died, and you cannot imagine what that means.' His gaze drifted again. 'If Silverwing died, I would die with him, instantly. Even his hurts… But a dragon does not die when its mage dies; they are not granted that kindness. And the grief when that bond is broken—it's like a madness, a madness that can last a hundred years. I'm not sure it ever fades.'

This time, Kallis had the sense not to push him, uncomfortably aware of how close they had already come to disaster, understanding now the exhaustion that clung to Aarin like a shadow. And he was relieved beyond measure that the ballista was now rotting at the bottom of the Istelan.

At length, Aarin gathered himself. 'The device Darred possesses once belonged to a mage called Cadyr. The dragon to which it is linked is called Eiador. I knew if I could wake Darred's dragon—if I could take from him the source of his power—then he could not do what he has done. But Eiador would not answer my call. I didn't understand why until it was too late.'

He looked at Kallis as though asking for his understanding, his forgiveness, and Kallis found he had could not hold his gaze. *Where have you been?* he had asked. *We needed you.*

'Eiador would not answer me because Darred has used his memories against him. He has taken on the guise of Cadyr. To Eiador, Darred *is* Cadyr, and he could no more give up his mage than Silverwing could set our partnership aside. And, through the device that enslaves him, Darred can draw on Eiador's power as easily as I can draw on Silverwing's. More easily, for his will is dominant. In a true pairing, the connection flows both ways— my thoughts, my memories, everything I am, I share with Silverwing. Eiador shares only a ghost with Darred. In many ways, he is still sleeping. Darred is in control.'

Aarin's voice cracked with fatigue and Callan, who had been silent until now, said, 'Sit down.'

Kallis blinked at him in exhaustion, unsure who he was talking to.

When neither of them moved, Callan sighed. 'Both of you.' He steered Aarin to a stool and gestured pointedly at the cot.

Kallis sat, all at once aware of how tired he was. He winced, one hand straying to his ribs. He wondered briefly if he had cracked them, but he had broken ribs before, and this was nothing to that. He rubbed his eyes, aware his mind was wandering.

'There are three dragons here,' he said. 'Three at least.'

Aarin did not seem surprised. 'There were others who resisted. Eiador will not be the only dragon to be trapped by its memories, not now Darred has realised it is possible. And now the magic is healed, the way between our time and the dragons' dream stands open. They do not come, because…'

And Kallis thought *they do not come because you won't let them.* He tried to imagine a world with the dragons suddenly unleashed upon it, even dragons who intended no threat to humanity. He imagined the horror and fear, and the inevitable violence and death—on both sides. And he realised, again, that far from abandoning them, Aarin had been protecting them. But could he protect them now he was here? Could he see past what Darred had done to the danger it posed?

Darred could send a dragon to kill you whenever he wished. You, your general Galydon. Even your queen. And it would find you.

'That was no opportunistic attack on the boatyard,' he told Aarin. 'That dragon came for Iraius, and it did not leave until he was dead. It *knew* him. It was *aimed* at him.'

Aimed, like a weapon. Surely Aarin had to see that.

The words, and their implication, echoed too loudly in the fraught silence. Aarin's expression was a frozen wasteland.

Callan was watching them both with open concern. 'Is that possible?' he asked Aarin, drawing the mage's attention away from Kallis. 'That the dragon could target Iraius specifically?'

Aarin's face unlocked with a visible effort. His voice was strained and distant. 'Silverwing would know any of you, could find any of you, if I asked him to.'

It was the confirmation Kallis needed, if not what he wanted. He understood better now the heart of Aarin's dilemma, the conflict he felt. Jeta said he had been given to the dragons, and so it was for them he had returned, and if what he said was true, then the dragons needed to be saved from Darred as surely as they did. But he also had to see what Darred had made them—the perfect weapons.

'Don't you see what this means?' he pressed. 'Darred has all the powers of the dragons and none of the restraint. He can make them do *anything*. A dragon could come for you, or me, or the queen at any time. It could burn Rhiannas and everyone in it. They would have no choice, I understand that, but that does not, cannot, change what they are.'

'And what are they?' Aarin asked him, his voice cold.

Kallis felt a spasm of pain, knowing he had lost him. 'They are Darred's weapons. They are the enemy.'

'Not my enemy!' Aarin's eyes blazed, and for a moment Kallis saw the flash of silver that echoed the not-quite-human mage who had faced down Aarkan in the caverns of Tesseria half a lifetime ago.

He drew back, unnerved. 'Suit yourself. But if they are yours, they are your responsibility. So, what are you going to do about them?'

He didn't really expect an answer, and he found he couldn't endure the tense silence. He knew what he had done, the weakness he had exploited, and he wasn't proud of it, but it had been necessary. He stood, not looking at Aarin, and not quite able to hide the hitched breath as the movement pulled on abused muscles. He could feel Callan's eyes on him, but he didn't look at him either. He said, to no one in particular, 'I must go to Rhiannas. Galydon needs to know.'

For a long moment he thought he had failed, that the ties were not as strong as he had believed them to be. Then there was a rustle of movement and Aarin stood. 'I will take you.'

TWENTY-NINE

KALLIS WAS GLAD to have his feet back on solid ground. It wasn't that he didn't like flying on the back of a dragon, he decided, it was just that it was bloody terrifying and not something any sane man should enjoy. Not to mention cold, in every sense of the word.

Beyond brief instructions before they left, Aarin hadn't spoken to him since their confrontation in the camp. But Kallis sensed that it was not so much anger on Aarin's part—though he suspected he was still not forgiven—more an intense reluctance to come to Rhiannas, and Kallis couldn't really blame him for that.

Not that he was actually in Rhiannas, at least not yet. Aarin had refused to bring the dragon within sight of the city, and Kallis couldn't disagree with that either, even though it meant trudging several miles through rain and mud with aching ribs and gave Aarin the excuse he needed to delay difficult reunions for a while longer.

Kallis was met on the palace steps by the elderly steward, who eyed his filthy, dripping clothes with distaste. He had been hoping to find Galydon here and save his aching feet another walk, but he was surprised when the steward informed him that Sedaine was also in residence.

'She didn't leave?'

'Leave? Certainly not. And you cannot go in —'

Ignoring his protests, Kallis pushed the old man gently aside, and proceeded to track mud through the pristine corridors. Limina appeared, looking flustered and inexplicably sporting the remains of a cobweb in her hair. 'She wouldn't leave,' she said, hurrying after him. 'You won't persuade her.'

'I'm not going to try,' Kallis growled, pressing himself against the wall as a procession of servants walked past, an assortment of furnishings in their arms. The empty corridors of Rhiannas's palace were empty no longer. 'What's happening here?'

Limina frowned at the dirty steaks his wet clothes had left on the wall. 'The Lords of the North.'

Kallis swore. That was all they needed.

'Yes, quite,' Limina observed dryly. 'It would have been far better all round if she had been persuaded to leave.'

Kallis snorted. 'And leave us to deal with them? No, thank you. Is Derias here?' He'd had dealings with Derias's brother in his time with the clans, though Leodad had not been a lord then, only the heir. Kallis did not relish renewing the acquaintance. Not that there was much chance such a man would remember a mere mercenary.

Limina sighed. 'He's another who would be better off away from here.'

'Let me guess. They don't get on.' Derias was as different to his half-brother as black was to white.

'On the contrary,' Limina murmured as she left him at the suite of offices outside Sedaine's private rooms. 'Derias is very fond of him.' Her tone made it clear what she thought about that.

Derias himself looked up as Kallis entered. Though he was as immaculate as ever, Kallis could see the strain on his face and wondered which was causing him more anxiety—the fact that Sedaine would not leave, or that his brother was coming. Despite Limina's assertion, the younger brother's elevation to chancellor must have been a point of contention.

Derias's brow creased in surprise when he saw Kallis; the frown deepened when he saw the mud. 'Where did you come from? A swamp?'

Kallis grinned. 'Near enough. Is the queen in there?' He nodded towards the door to her private chambers.

'It speaks,' Derias observed with mock surprise. 'Perhaps it is a man after all. And no, she is not here, so you can go and wash, or whatever it is you mercenaries do to achieve your idea of cleanliness.'

'We wait until it dries and then roll around on the ground until it comes off,' Kallis retorted, throwing his filthy pack at Derias's chest, where it left a muddy stain. 'There. Now you can try it for yourself.'

Derias held out the pack in distaste and brushed ineffectually at the mud on his tunic. 'Thank you for your suggestion,' he said, sarcasm heavy in his cut-glass aristocrat's accent.

Kallis grinned and slapped a dirty hand on his shoulder. 'Has there been any word from Lorac?'

Derias peered at the muddy handprint with resignation and shook his head. 'Petrik sent riders out searching as soon as we had word of what happened at Kamarai, but we don't expect them back for at least another week. More, if this weather holds.'

Kallis nodded. He did not say what they were both thinking—that if the mercenary force had not been in Kamarai when it was attacked, they should have had news of them by now. He did not want to think about the crisis they might be facing in the clan power structure if Lorac was dead. He was too far removed from clan politics, even now, to know which way that would go, or whether a new captain-of-captains would honour the alliance Lorac had made with Sedaine.

But that would have to wait. Just now, he had more pressing concerns, and a few things he wanted to get off his chest.

Leaving Derias looking mournfully at his mud-stained floor, Kallis went in search of Galydon. The general was in his office with Kinseris, which was just fine as far as Kallis was concerned. He had had plenty of time to think since his chat with the Farnorian prisoner—since Iraius's death—and he had a few things he wanted to say to Kinseris.

Kallis kicked the door shut as they turned to face him. 'It was you who sent Iraius,' he said to Kinseris by way of a greeting. If it sounded like an accusation, he didn't much care. He half meant it as one. Iraius was dead.

Galydon forestalled Kinseris's reply. 'What's happened?'

Kallis dragged his attention from priest to general. 'We took an interesting prisoner. From Farnor. He had a lot to say about Iraius—and who he was working for.'

'Then you will know it was not me,' Kinseris replied evenly. In the shadows of the dimly lit room, his face betrayed nothing.

'No?' asked Kallis dangerously. 'You didn't send him?'

'Only one man has ever sent Iraius anywhere, and it was not me,' Kinseris told him. 'I don't deny that I informed him of what was happening here, and where he could find you. What he chose to do with that information was entirely up to him.'

Kallis was not so easily satisfied. 'And you said nothing to us? Iraius is dead! If we had known what he was doing, perhaps he wouldn't be.'

'Perhaps,' Kinseris admitted. 'But Iraius's silence was his own choice. I can only guess he had his reasons.'

'But you know what those were, don't you?' Kallis persisted, sick of the secrecy, angry with them both for their silence. 'If we are all on the same side, it makes no sense to keep us in the dark.' When Kinseris said nothing, he growled, 'Are we? On the same side?'

Galydon took a deliberate step forward, placing himself between them. 'Be very careful,' he told Kallis, 'what you say next.'

Kallis gave a bitter laugh. 'And you are not his general anymore, you are Lothane's. And you should be just as angry. But you're not,' he added in sudden realisation. 'Because you knew, and you kept it from me.'

'You are mistaken,' Galydon said icily. 'I had my suspicions, but that is all they were. It was not my intention to keep them from you. Events overtook us. I know more now.'

Kallis glared at him, unwilling to let go of his anger. 'And why's that?'

It was Kinseris who answered, and he sounded suddenly very tired. 'Because I told him. Despite what you think of me, I did not set out to deceive you. Out of respect for a long-standing alliance, I alerted Iraius to the threat to his homeland.'

Kallis folded his arms over his chest. 'And that alliance would be with Admiral Hanlon?'

Kinseris offered him a twisted smile. 'Whose ships do you think carried you to Amadorn?'

An impatient retort died on Kallis's lips as he realised Kinseris was not talking about his most recent journey. It was a reminder of a debt he had never acknowledged, that to Kinseris likely did not exist. A reminder, too, that this was a man who had spent decades in quiet rebellion against Vasa's oppressive regime, and whose intrigues had stretched across Caledan. It should not have surprised him that they had reached into Amadorn as well. He should have guessed who had sent Iraius, if not why, and he should have asked the right questions. But it was too late for that now.

'The Admiral and I came to a mutual agreement many years ago,' Kinseris explained, saving him from the burden of responding to that revelation. 'His ships brought my fugitives to Amadorn, and I turned a blind eye to the activities of Amadorian pirates on the Aetelea, an enterprise that was very profitable for Farnor, in both goods and intelligence. Iraius was skilled at ferreting out both, and yes,' he added a trifle defensively at Galydon's thinly veiled disapproval, 'we traded information that might once have led you to brand me a traitor, but Hanlon was concerned only with defence. He could see how tempting a target Amadorn must be to Vasa, and he guarded against that as best he could.'

Which had not, in the end, done him or Farnor much good, Kallis reflected. By now he knew the stories of Farnor's brave defiance, of her little navy's doomed fight. How none of her neighbours had come to her aid. A victim of the coastal states' deeply ingrained rivalry and the South's chronic inability to organise and defend itself. Impenetrable barriers, even to a man like Hanlon who seemed to draw men's loyalty like moths to a flame.

He sighed, much of the anger draining out of him. 'You should have told us.'

'You forget that Farnor had already fallen,' Kinseris replied. 'I had no idea whether the admiral had survived. I hoped so. I wanted to believe so—that man is nothing if not resourceful. I knew Iraius would find out, one way or another, because if Iraius ever called any man his master, it was Hanlon. But Hanlon is dead.'

Galydon, who had listened to the exchange in silence, said carefully, 'Limina believes he is, but I think Iraius suspected otherwise. We know there is a resistance network in the south, probably Farnorian or at least connected with Farnor. There is evidence they have tried to smuggle information to

Limina—Iraius found an empty message cylinder on a body in the Istelan some weeks ago. Another turned up in Rhiannas just after you left.'

Kallis stared at him in disbelief. *We tried to warn you.* 'Why didn't you tell me?'

'Because so much was guesswork. Until Iraius brought word of the body in the river, and his suspicions about who this man was trying to reach and why, he said nothing of his motives for being here.'

Kallis walked restlessly to the window, leaning his hip against the sill. 'They were trying to warn us about the dragons. Our prisoner knew my name. He knew more than that. He claimed to be a friend. If he was telling the truth, and I think he was, we might have found valuable allies in the south.'

Galydon asked, 'Did he say whether Hanlon is alive?'

Kallis shook his head. 'He told me no one knows what happened to Hanlon, but if he was honest about the rest, I would swear he was lying about that. And that's not the only thing.' He told them what the prisoner had said about the dragon targeting Iraius, and what it meant. What Aarin had said— and where *he* was. Because although he would never say so, would never admit that the dragons were their enemies, Aarin had come to Rhiannas to give them the protection of his presence. And Kallis knew how much he did not want to be here.

'He's certain?' Galydon asked when he finished. He sounded resigned, as though this revelation was just one more thing to add to their long list of disadvantages. Perhaps it was. There was no way to counter the threat it represented. No deception they could use to hide any one of them from Darred. In a way, it made things simpler.

Kinseris was silent, and Kallis didn't like to speculate about how he must feel about Aarin's return. As far as Kallis had any views on the matter, Aarin had left and Jeta was free to do as she pleased. He certainly wasn't getting involved.

'He sounded certain. But why would Darred send a dragon to kill Iraius? If it is true that he never cared about the boatyard—and now we know he has dragons, it explains why he ignored it all this time—what made him go after Iraius? And why now?'

Galydon's eyes narrowed as he caught Kallis's meaning. 'You think Hanlon is alive?'

'I think,' said Kallis, recalling his prisoner's evasions, 'that there was no reason to kill Iraius except for his connection to Hanlon.'

Kinseris had turned away so Kallis couldn't see his expression. His back was rigid with tension, but his voice, when he spoke, was perfectly calm. 'If he's alive, they will keep that close, to protect him. And if he's dead, they will not want it widely known. His is a name that gives men hope.'

Galydon was also studying Kinseris. 'There's a third possibility. If he's a prisoner…'

'Then they are also protecting Limina,' Kinseris finished for him, turning back. Some of the tightness had left his face, replaced by grim determination. 'We need to talk to your prisoner.'

Kallis sighed. He should have anticipated this. 'You can't.'

'Why not?'

'Because he escaped.' Or at least he should have done by now, if he was half as capable as he appeared.

'Escaped,' Galydon repeated flatly, his anger carefully controlled.

Kinseris's was not, and his thwarted fury reminded Kallis, yet again, of who he was, and everything he had been. 'You let him escape? Knowing what you have just told us? Do you realise what you have done?'

'Why don't you tell me?' Kallis shot back, angry in his turn. 'Just for once, explain yourself.'

'It matters,' Kinseris said with cold anger, 'because if Hanlon is alive, then perhaps something can be salvaged from all this. If we knew he was alive— if we knew how to reach him—there are those still in Caledan who could help him, help us. But without access to his network, there is nothing they or I can do.'

'I couldn't know that *because you didn't tell me!*' Kallis retorted. 'Perhaps if both of you had trusted more, we would not be in this mess.'

'Don't forget the world in which this alliance was made,' Kinseris snapped. 'Vasa's spies were everywhere, and Hanlon would have faced charges of treason if his activities in Caledan had been discovered.'

'Limina would not have condemned her own husband,' Kallis scoffed, thinking of all Hanlon's other activities she had overlooked.

'He was not her husband then, and she was not the queen. And Farnor under Limina's father was a different place.' Kinseris took a deep breath, wincing. 'What's done is done. I have done what I can, before we left Caledan and since we arrived, to get word to Hanlon or any of his crews who survived.'

'Kestel and Trad.'

Kinseris nodded. 'Them, and others. By now, they will have found Darred's army. If Hanlon is a prisoner, there will be rumours. If he's alive, they may be able to find him. And if we can find him, it might change everything.'

There was a short silence, then Galydon said to Kallis, 'Satisfied?'

He nodded. Much as he wanted to hold onto his anger, there was nothing to be gained from it, and he was not blameless. 'There's more,' he admitted, remembering the hut on the edges of the boatyard, and the boxes of black sand that Iraius had hidden there, and where he said it had come from. *He thought he could make a weapon from it for his ships,* Iraius had said of Hanlon. Not for the first time he wondered what else he might have done with it.

Galydon listened as Kallis relayed the events that preceded Iraius's death. Then he asked, as Kallis had known he would, 'This black sand. Is there more?'

'I don't know.' He had not thought to ask. Another mistake. 'I hope not.' Then, in answer to Galydon's curious look, snapped, 'It didn't do us much good, did it? Iraius hoped the explosion would kill the dragon, or at least disable it. He was wrong, and now he's dead. When our enemy uses fire as a weapon, that stuff is a danger to us.'

'You are right, of course. But if that is not all of it, where is the rest? If it is as destructive as you say, then I want to know it won't be used against us.'

'It won't be.'

They both turned to Kinseris, who had gone rather pale.

Kallis stared at him with dawning, awful suspicion. Because what else Hanlon might have done with it had just occurred to him. 'Why won't it? What have you done?'

Galydon was looking at Kinseris with a similar expression. 'If you know where it is, tell us.'

Kinseris turned away from the combined weight of their gaze. 'It's in Kas'Tella,' he said bleakly. 'Under the citadel.'

THIRTY

IT WAS GALYDON who broke the appalled silence. 'Who else knows?'

Kinseris flinched at his tone. 'Betanas.'

Betanas. Kallis remembered that name. He shook his head in frustration. 'The man who may or may not have betrayed you?'

Kinseris nodded.

'Who else?' Galydon asked.

'Fylian.'

Galydon stared at him for a beat, something unreadable on his face. Then he exhaled a long breath. 'You know that if they question him, he will tell them.'

Kinseris looked away. 'I know.'

Galydon sighed. 'Why?' he asked at last.

Kinseris shrugged. 'Insurance? If I couldn't stop them… couldn't keep control. Losing Caledan was always possible. Not just possible, probable.'

Maker. Kallis swore under his breath as he realised what Kinseris was saying. As he glimpsed the kind of desperation and despair that would lead someone to even consider the course of action he had just confessed to.

Galydon looked horrified. 'You would have destroyed the citadel?'

Kallis had Kinseris by the throat before he was even aware he had moved. 'You bastard. What about Jeta? Would you have killed her too?'

Kinseris did nothing to free himself, as he certainly could have done. 'Of course not,' he rasped. 'I would have seen her safe.'

Kallis shoved him back into the wall. 'I don't know if you have noticed, but she does nothing she doesn't want to. And she would *not* have let you send her away.'

A blade touched his throat, and Galydon said, very calmly, 'Let him go.'

Breathing hard, Kallis gave Kinseris one last shove and stepped back. 'He could have killed her,' he said to Galydon.

'But he did not,' the general replied, the knife disappearing. His face reflected a sentiment not too different to Kallis's own.

Kinseris still slumped against the wall, his face tight. Kallis remembered the assassination attempt and knew he had hurt him, but he was too angry to care. Too horrified by the thought of the death hidden beneath the citadel in Kas'Tella.

Galydon was looking at Kinseris with something akin to disappointment, his breathing controlled and even, and Kallis realised he was struggling to keep his temper in check. 'You should not have kept this from me,' he told his former high priest in a sharper tone than Kallis had ever heard him use with Kinseris. Then, with a burst of frustration, 'When will you realise you are not in Frankesh anymore? You do not have to assume everyone is your enemy.'

'No, indeed,' Kinseris said with bitter sarcasm and it was Galydon's turn to flinch. 'In Kas'Tella I was surrounded by men I could trust. How foolish of me not to realise that.'

He pulled himself upright, pain spasming across his face. 'I did not ask Hanlon to send me his weapon. But he did, and what was I supposed to do with it? I put it where I knew it would be safe, and yes, where it might serve me if all other avenues failed. You underestimate my colleagues—all of you. This is not just a question of power, though they crave power in all its forms. It is *need*. Physical, burning need, every single day, to take back what I took from them. I have felt it, and I set that power aside of my own free will. You might think that Darred and his rogue priests are your enemy, but you would be wrong. They are just the start. While the Kas'Talani Order survives, this war will never end.'

Kinseris stopped, breathing hard, one hand pressed to his side. 'It took me too long to see that. I did not want this, and I did not plan it, but if Fylian or Betanas uses that weapon, I will not weep either.'

That is exactly what you'll do, Kallis thought, but he did not say it. He didn't need to. Galydon, a kind of appalled compassion on his face, rested a hand on Kinseris's shoulder. 'I will never believe that.'

Someone cleared their throat, and Kallis saw his guilty start echoed by his companions as they turned to see Sedaine standing in the open doorway, Derias by her side. Absorbed in their argument, they had not realised they were no longer alone.

'Am I interrupting anything important?' the queen enquired with a sarcastic bite, and Kallis wondered how much she had heard.

'Your highness,' Galydon said calmly. 'What can we do for you?'

It was Derias who answered, with none of his usual poise. 'Darred has offered a truce. He wants to talk.'

THIRTY-ONE

JETA WATCHED AARIN as he stood in an arch of the upper gallery, looking down on the courtyard. He had been here for hours, barely moving. There had been precious little opportunity for solitude in the turmoil of the last few days, and his stillness did not invite intrusion. And he had not sought her out.

He looked different. Physically he had not changed much. Thinner maybe, his hair a little longer. Yet there was something about him that was subtly altered. A new confidence in the way he carried himself, though she doubted he was aware of it. A sense of power, tightly coiled, that almost made the air around him ripple. And a new guardedness where before his face had been an open book. A distance that kept everyone at arm's length, including her.

His eyes had sought hers and held them, just briefly, that first day when Kallis had brought him to the palace. And before he had looked away, she had felt a hunger so intense it had burned her and then… nothing. Like a breath blowing out a candle, it was gone so completely she could not be sure she had felt it at all.

Since then she had not seen him. Darred's offer of a truce had broken the uneasy waiting of the last few weeks. For two days the men had been locked in frantic meetings, all the clan captains in and near Rhiannas coming and going in a steady stream as plans were revised and strategies discussed. Even Limina had abandoned her preparations for the imminent arrival of the queen's erstwhile counsellors and had been closeted with Sedaine and Galydon as often as not. Where Aarin had been, she had no idea.

For two days, Jeta had been virtually ignored, left to observe the fierce debate from a distance. Where once she would have gone to Kinseris, and he would have given her both knowledge and comfort, she found herself now strangely adrift, their closeness lost behind a formality that masked a confusion of feelings on both sides. He would not turn her away if she went to him—if she needed him—but she knew it was not fair to take her comfort at the cost of his, even though his absence left her exposed and vulnerable, and the cracks too close to the surface.

A distant roar reached her, the sound of the crowd that had been gathering outside the palace gates since first light. It had started two days ago. Only a few at first, a handful of those displaced from their lands to the south of Lothane, and now a packed throng of angry, desperate people demanding… something, *anything*. She did not know what, exactly, they wanted. She had stayed away. It felt like cowardice, but she could not endure their fears on top of her own.

Aarin still had not moved; he did not seem to hear the noise. She didn't know where he had been, but she knew why he was here now. Below, in the courtyard, she saw Galydon walking swiftly towards the gates. Rhiannas's clan commander was by his side. She glanced back, towards the palace steps, and caught a glimpse of movement in one of the upper windows. She was not the only one forced to watch from a distance.

Jeta looked again at Aarin. As far as she knew, they had not yet spoken, Aarin and his mother, other than the stiff, formal greeting in front of others that she had witnessed on his arrival. Hard enough to rebuild that relationship—to find a way through all the years of separation and hurt— without having to do it in full view of a royal court. The place where his mother had been born, where she now ruled, a place as far removed from the life he had lived as anything could be, and a reminder of the cost of Darred's meddling in both their lives. The very strangeness of it reinforced how little they knew each other, and how little they had in common except blood.

But how much did he have in common with any of them anymore?

And that, she was certain, was the real issue. She felt his isolation like a wound. But he would not seek her out. She had known that with certainty after that brief, intense glance. So she had come to him, only to find herself unwilling to break this moment of silence, unwilling to intrude where once she would have been welcome.

Indecision held her fast too long and resolve deserted her. She was about to retreat when he finally turned. She realised he had known she was there, that he had been waiting for her to leave. But that was not what shook her. It was the look on his face, or rather the lack of it. She had expected hurt, even anger, but she had not expected this utter absence of feeling.

Tears pricked her eyes. 'I'm sorry.' She was suddenly desperate to get away. 'I don't care if you hate me; I can survive anything but your indifference.'

'Indifference?' Surprise and confusion flickered in his eyes; the frozen mask melted away. 'Jeta…' The pause stretched on, the words tangled around something deep and painful. He looked away. 'I thought you were dead. You can't know… And then not dead, but also not –

'Not yours?'

He said softly, 'You were never mine. You shared yourself with me for a time, and it was precious. But I left, and it is your life.'

The tears were falling freely now. 'I would have stayed.'

And suddenly his need was clear in his eyes. She longed to reach out and touch him, but it was not just his reserve that made her hesitate. 'Aarin…'

He took a deep breath as a shudder rocked him where he stood. 'Jeta, I can't… I'm sorry, I can't do this.' His voice was like broken glass.

'Don't walk away from me!' she snapped. 'Not again.'

He stopped. His back rigid with tension. 'Nothing has changed. Even if you had not….' He cast around for the right words and could not seem to find them. 'I am here for the dragons, and I cannot stay, not for you, not with you. What good would it do either of us to rekindle that flame for so short a time? And it would not just be ourselves we hurt.'

It was as close as he would come to speaking of Kinseris. Was he angry? She couldn't even begin to tell. Once, he would have been quite unable to hide his emotions from her, but that was a different time, and he had been a different man. They had all changed since then.

'Does it matter what I want?' she asked. Why did they both think they could make her choices for her? Did they think it was kindness?

A frown kinked his brow as he recognised her tone. 'I did not –'

'Think of anyone but yourself? No, you never did.'

The apprehension that crossed his face was so perfectly *Aarin* that she almost smiled. Almost. 'But no doubt it doesn't matter, because *you* have already decided.'

That wasn't entirely fair, but Kinseris wasn't here, and right now she was just angry.

Aarin started to say something then thought better of it. She met his eyes with a defiant tilt of her chin. He sighed and asked, 'What do you want?'

Defiance crumbled and misery washed back. 'I don't know.'

She saw hurt then, and regretted it. She had not wanted to hurt him.

A shout from the courtyard shattered the awkward silence. She recognised Kallis's voice, the sound drawing Aarin's attention.

He cocked his head towards the noise of the crowd, resurgent now the bubble around them had burst. 'They know. Someone told them.'

It took her a second to catch his meaning. 'Told them what?'

'That Darred has offered peace. They want to go home.'

She shook her head. 'He hasn't –' *Oh.*

A wry smile crossed his face. 'This meeting is a trap. Galydon knows it. Kallis certainly does, my mother too. But she will go anyway, she has no choice.'

Jeta knew it too. Even without the growing unrest, Sedaine had never had a choice. Not since the moment Darred had shown how easily he could hurt them, and how badly. 'What will you do?' Because he was the only thing standing between them and Darred now, and only she understood that was not his place.

And yet it was. And *he* knew it.

He looked away. 'If anyone else…' Then, with resignation, 'What choice do I have?'

'Not one you could make,' Jeta agreed. 'But you've never let Darred force your hand before, and I don't think you will now.'

Tense stillness relaxed, almost to a smile. 'Then make sure you don't give him any leverage.'

THIRTY-TWO

IT TOOK MOST of the morning to disperse the crowds, and at times things had been tense enough to threaten Galydon's injunction against violence. Tense enough that there had been moments when Kallis had feared the desperation of the crowd would become a full-scale riot.

He was under no illusions about why they were there. The steady stream of refugees from the South had swollen Rhiannas's population to twice its normal size, and it had grown still further with the influx of Lothani displaced from their towns and villages on the vulnerable southern plains. Yet there had been remarkably little unrest until now. In the first year, the example of the South had been all too close, and the refugees had carried with them tales of the invading army's atrocities. Now food was starting to run short. Not critically, not yet, but the loss of Kamarai and potentially Elvelen meant that could change, and quickly. And the people knew it.

They had also heard the rumours. They knew how Kamarai had burned. Fear was coiling through the crowded city like a poison.

The rain had finally paused its relentless assault, but the muggy heat that had replaced it promised more to come and left Kallis sweaty and irritable as he regarded the bedraggled figures of the morning's apparent ringleaders.

'Find out what they know,' he told Petrik, impatient to return to the palace and the discussions taking place within it. 'More importantly, find out how they know, and if possible, who.'

Fear and unrest had been deliberately stoked by rumours of a rejected peace offer. A peace that would save them from Kamarai's fate. If they did not stop it now, that rumour would grow and spread, and before you knew it, the city would turn against Sedaine. And if that happened… well, wars had been lost before now for want of unity at home, and they didn't have enough men to fight Darred and keep a discontented, terrified populace in check.

'But do it *politely*,' Kallis added, with a glance at Petrik's grim face. Two of his men were nursing broken bones after the morning's work and the clan commander looked like he was itching to repay those injuries. Which was the last thing they needed.

To the two men and one woman glaring at him from the cell, he said, 'There has been no peace offer. Do you understand? You have been lied to. The only terms Darred will offer are for Lothane's complete surrender, and I promise you that is not an outcome you will enjoy.'

'So *you* say,' one of the men growled, and Kallis rolled his eyes, too hot and tired to take offence.

The woman spat. 'Better to surrender than burn alive.'

'I wouldn't be so sure of that,' he said grimly. His presence wasn't helping, and he needed to report to Galydon and Sedaine. He nodded to Petrik. 'Do your best.' And left him to it.

When he reached the council chamber, it was apparent that discussion had already descended into argument. Of course it had. Because Darred knew this game and he knew the players. Kallis had seen what he had done to Lothane after the old king's death. If he could do that to a prosperous country at peace, it was nothing to stir a desperate, exhausted nation into chaos, and the people outside the gates were not the only ones who were frightened. Darred knew exactly what pressure to apply, and when. This offer came too hard on the heels of the news from Kamarai and the destruction at the boatyard, hitting them when they were still reeling from the worst of their losses.

'We cannot trust him,' Vianor growled, angry and insistent, as Kallis entered the room. 'Darred has betrayed every loyalty he has ever pledged, broken every promise. I will never believe he offers this meeting in good faith.'

'Of course it's not in good faith,' Kallis muttered, nodding to Aarin who was standing apart by the door. 'That's why you've got a mob at your gates.' In response to Galydon's silent query, he added, 'They're dispersed—for now. But they will be back. They are terrified of sharing Kamarai's fate, and who can blame them?'

Sedaine was frowning. She was no fool. She understood what Darred was doing. Kallis could not help but admire the woman who had taken the three northern kingdoms and welded them together to resist this invasion. She had done it to protect what she could, having accepted there were so many she could not save, but Darred had made her choice clear. She could fight him, but it would be at the cost of everything she had tried to save.

'What do you suggest?' she asked him. It was a genuine question. How far they had come.

Kallis shrugged. 'What choice do you have? You can't let this get out of hand. You have to play his game, at least for now.'

'You cannot consider meeting him!' Vianor snarled, shoving himself to his feet.

'I must consider it,' Sedaine replied, turning to her uncle. 'Good faith or not, this meeting gives us breathing space we badly need. And, for the sake of all the peoples of the North, I cannot turn a deaf ear to any offer of peace. It is not what I want. But this is not the enemy we expected to face, and he has already shown us how badly he can punish us.' She sighed. 'The people are not the only ones who want peace. The Lords of North want it too. I cannot ignore them forever. We need their cooperation.'

Kallis cast a sideways glance at Derias. His brother was first among those lords. If they were calling for peace, the Lord of Morven would be at their head. Derias, feeling his look, returned one of bland innocence, and Kallis concluded that either he did not share his brother's views, or more likely, he had no intention of being drawn into the middle of a destructive quarrel between his sovereign and the head of his family.

'So you will let them force your hand? Accept an offer you know is a lie?' Vianor demanded.

'Did I say so? But, in their absence, you have apparently forgotten how much our survival relies on their goodwill. Their lands produce food, their households provide men, and weapons, and horses. Their coffers provide money—money that is dwindling the longer this drags on. Of course they want peace, and so I cannot afford to reject this offer out of hand. But if what Darred offers us is not peace and freedom, but conquest and enslavement by another name, they will understand why I do not accept—and so, my lord, that is why I must meet him.'

When Vianor's mutinous silence was his only response, Sedaine added acidly, 'Perhaps you have allowed your hatred of Darred to cloud your judgement, uncle. In times past, you would have given me that lecture.'

'It is not my judgement that is clouded,' the magician growled, turning his back and walking away. 'Give your nation away if you wish. Don't ask me to watch!'

The door slammed in Vianor's face so hard the frame creaked and almost gave way. A piece of plaster came loose and tumbled to the floor, a sprinkling of dust coating the startled magician's shoulder. Kallis looked from Vianor to Sedaine and saw her eyes locked on Aarin's. He hadn't moved, and his expression was unchanged, but Kallis knew who had blocked Vianor's exit. He was careful not to let his amusement show.

Vianor turned, his expression both shaken and furious, but before he could speak, Sedaine waved a hand to his empty chair.

'If you please, my lord, we are not finished here. I do not wish to lose your counsel just yet.'

The polite phrasing did not disguise the threat. Vianor's back stiffened. Kallis thought he would refuse, then he bowed. 'As you wish, my queen.'

When he was once again sitting, Sedaine said, 'If I refuse to meet him, what then? You know this man as well as any of us.'

Vianor scowled at the reminder. 'This is no negotiation with an overreaching neighbour. This is a man who seeks nothing less than total dominion over the entire continent. Whatever he might promise, he will never allow Lothane to maintain its autonomy, not when he holds the means to crush you into submission—and he does. So, this offer of a truce must be false. There is something else that he wants.'

Vianor did not look at Aarin, but Kallis could feel the weight of the room's collective attention focus on him nonetheless. Because what else had changed?

'It seems to me there is a simple solution,' Kallis said into the pause, only partly to distract their attention from Aarin. Because *that* wasn't happening. 'We can trust nothing Darred offers. We agree on that at least. He is counting on us honouring the truce. But what is the point of playing by the rules when your enemy has no intention of doing so? I say we betray the truce before he can. Accept the offer, go to the meeting. Then kill him.'

Silence greeted this suggestion. Seven pairs of eyes were staring at him with very different expressions. Then Limina laughed, drawing a smile from Sedaine. Jeta was looking at him with fierce approval, and he knew the women at least would have no problem with such a plan.

'You might not find that so easy,' Aarin said quietly.

And Kallis managed—just—to resist voicing his frustration. Killing Darred was the only way he could see to end this, and Aarin had to know that. If he had to break a truce to accomplish it, it seemed a small price to pay.

Sedaine pointedly didn't look at Aarin. 'As attractive as that idea is, Kallis, I must first hear what he has to say. No, he knows I will go. It is just a question of where and when.'

'And who,' Galydon said, quietly but firmly.

Sedaine frowned. 'I —'

'Will not meet him. Whatever the truth of Darred intentions, if you meet him as an equal you legitimise his claim to the South.'

There was a short silence, then Sedaine asked, calmly but with dangerous precision, 'Before whom?'

Kallis flinched. He recognised the look and the tone, but Galydon, who knew both well enough by now, chose not to heed them. 'You will not go.'

Something swirled between them, unspoken and fierce, but the eruption Kallis expected did not come. Across the table, he saw Derias Morven watching the queen, a slight frown on his face, and knew he was not the only one to sense the deep currents at work here. Feeling his gaze, the chancellor looked over at Kallis with a rueful smile and a small shrug.

It was Kinseris who broke the awkward silence. 'I will meet him.'

Jeta's head snapped up. 'No,' she said, the word drowning out Galydon's equally emphatic refusal.

Kinseris looked between them, a slight smile tugging his mouth. 'Yes. Why else am I here?'

'To hide,' she said flatly.

To give Kinseris credit, he did not react to that. Instead, he said patiently, 'Jeta, Darred held my life in his hands for years. He could have betrayed me to Vasa a hundred times, but he did not. We were friends for fifty years before he ever set foot in Amadorn. Perhaps something of that friendship remains, even now.'

'He tried to have you killed!'

'Perhaps—we don't know that for certain.'

'Yes, we do,' Jeta insisted. 'Escarian was his creature. He said so.'

Kinseris shook his head. 'He did it for Darred. He did not say he did it at his orders.'

'What difference does that make?'

'Jeta's right,' Galydon said. 'You cannot risk it.'

Kallis saw the conflict on his face. Galydon had been right about Sedaine, though his reasons were not nearly as simple as he would have them believe, but it was friendship talking now. Cold, hard logic argued that Kinseris was right, and Galydon knew it. He just didn't want to admit it.

'This is a war. It is not a question of risk or no risk, but of which risk to take when. Who else knows him so well?' the former high priest asked his former general. His friend. 'And if my presence throws him off balance, even a little, it gives us an advantage. And you said it yourself—we have precious few of those.'

'So you're giving him the chance to finish what he started?' Jeta objected. Logic was not going to hold any sway with her. 'You cannot go,' she insisted, her voice very close to a plea.

Kallis glanced at Aarin, saw the tightness around his eyes, and looked away only to find Sedaine's eyes on him. She tilted her head towards Kinseris, her face holding a question as her fingers drummed on the table. He sighed and nodded. She returned it, before glancing at Derias, whose eyes widened slightly in surprise. Then he too nodded.

The queen directed her attention to Kinseris, ignoring the ongoing argument. 'Your offer is accepted, my lord, with thanks.'

Galydon's head whipped around, his expression a mix of shock and anger. She held up a hand. 'But you cannot go alone. My lord chancellor will accompany you to speak for Lothane.' She gave Galydon a sweet, vengeful smile. 'And Kallis will go with you both, since you, my general, can no more be risked than I.'

Kallis flinched as Jeta shot him a look of pure betrayal. 'Jeta –'

She didn't give him a chance to speak. Her chair flew back from the table as she stood, reaching the door just as it opened to admit one of the clan mercenaries he had left on the gates.

The man dodged to one side as Jeta brushed past him, looking from Kallis to Galydon, then nervously taking in the rest of the room's occupants.

'What is it?' asked Galydon, already on his feet.

Kallis was a second behind him.

'A Raven. From Elvelen.'

'We were not in Kamarai when it burned,' the Raven scout told them. He was young, not much more than twenty, but his face was grey with exhaustion and his eyes bore the haunted look of someone much older. 'But it was chance only. We were delayed on the road—a grain convoy had been attacked. There were several injured. Lorac ordered... But we were close enough to see it, and the next day...'

The scout trailed off, his facing paling at the memory, and Kallis winced in sympathy. They had survived, by sheer chance, an attack that was almost certainly aimed at them as much as Kamarai, but judging by the look on the Raven's face, they would still carry its scars.

'Some stayed in Kamarai. To help. We couldn't just...' He swallowed, looking away.

'Of course,' Galydon asked, gently steering him past the memories. 'The rest of you?'

'We continued into Elvelen, to meet up with the other clans.'

'And did you?'

'Some of them.'

There was another pause. It was plain the boy was so tired he was struggling to order his thoughts.

'Elvelen is overrun,' he said eventually. 'The borders are anyway. Word is that Korva and the Valan Lakes are holding out, but we couldn't spare the men to check. And we can't help them even if they're still fighting.'

Galydon paced the length of his small office, frowning. 'Why didn't anyone send word?'

The scout looked up. 'They did. They thought that's why we came.'

Kallis exchanged an alarmed look with Galydon. They had had no word from the clans in Elvelen since well before Kamarai had burned. It was one of the reasons Galydon had sent Lorac west. If those messengers had been intercepted, what else didn't they know?

'Where is Lorac now?' he asked. If Elvelen was lost, there was little they could do but hold the mountain pass. Lorac would know that.

'The borders. He was near Darlan when I left him. But they are hard-pressed. There are survivors from the Lynx and Grey Fox clans, but they're scattered. He wants to give them a chance before we pull back to the pass.'

Kallis grimaced. Lorac knew he couldn't help Elvelen, but he was not going to abandon his men, and they could not reinforce their western border to help him. They were stretched thin enough as it was, and Galydon would have to strip Rhiannas of much of its garrison to accompany Sedaine to meet Darred. But he hadn't tried to prevent the meeting, because he knew—they all knew—that she couldn't let another city burn.

'Can they hold the pass?' Galydon asked the scout, evidently having made the same calculation.

The scout shrugged. 'For how long?'

How long indeed? That was the question. Something needed to happen, and soon. No one willingly sought a pitched battle if it could be avoided, but they needed to engage Darred's forces somehow. Otherwise, by sheer, creeping attrition and the threat of the dragons, Lothane would be lost with barely a skirmish to show for it.

'Go and rest,' Galydon told the scout. 'We'll talk more later.'

Kallis waited until the exhausted clansman had left in search of food and a bed, before dropping into a chair with sigh. Galydon was staring after the scout with a thoughtful look on his face.

'I don't like this,' Kallis complained. 'He's drawing our focus south when we need to be looking west.' When that failed to illicit a response, he added irritably, 'We have no one to send.'

Galydon snapped out of his daze. He looked at Kallis with the beginnings of a smile. 'That's not quite true.'

THIRTY-THREE

JETA RESTED HER cheek on the cool stone, one hand braced against the wall as black spots danced across her sight. She forced herself to breathe through the tightness in her chest until her vision cleared, but it was several moments before she dared relinquish the support of the solid stone.

No one had followed her. No one would. They would hear only her fear. They would not see what she knew—Kinseris was not rational, not about this. He might believe what he said about Darred—he might even believe that was his true motivation—but she knew him better. She knew the guilt he carried for the Kas'Talani's role in bringing about this conflict, for what they had done to Caledan and what he had failed to stop them doing. And she could not let it drive him to this. She would not.

Sedaine would see only the apparent advantage Kinseris offered her. Only Galydon would not want to allow it, for reasons less rational even than hers. So it was Galydon she sought out hours after the council had broken up.

She found him with Sedaine and Limina. They had been arguing. Good. If Galydon was prepared to fight, he would be more likely to listen to her.

'Send me,' she said into the silence that greeted her arrival. 'I will go. I will kill Darred.'

Galydon turned to face her. '*What?*'

She lifted her chin defiantly. 'You heard me.'

'On the contrary, I did not,' he said. 'And let us leave it there.'

'Do not treat me like a child,' she snapped. 'Vianor is right. You know this is a trap, and whatever Kallis wants to believe, none of you has a chance of touching him. Aarin will not help you murder him. But I will—use me!'

Appalled, Galydon shook his head. 'I cannot.'

She would not convince him, but it did not matter. It was Sedaine who had made the final choice, and it was Sedaine who could change it. It was the queen she needed on her side. 'You cannot send Kinseris,' Jeta told her now. 'He is wrong about Darred. If you send him, you play straight into Darred's hands. It is what he will expect you to do. It gains you nothing and loses you an ally. He will not be expecting me.'

Sedaine regarded her in silence for a long moment, then she turned to Galydon, one eyebrow quirked in question.

'No.' Galydon cut off her unvoiced thought. 'I will not consider this. And neither will you.'

'Why not? Because of what she means to Kinseris?'

'No,' Galydon snapped. 'Because I do not send my men to their deaths needlessly and I will not start now.

'I am not one of your men,' Jeta retorted. 'And this is not needless. It is *necessary.*'

He shook his head. 'It is suicide. What makes you think you have a chance? There have been five attempts on Darred's life that I know of, and you can be sure there have been many more. Why can you succeed where everyone else has failed?'

'Darred wants me,' she said, saying the words but refusing to hear their meaning. 'He has always wanted me. He might kill me, but he will try to take me first. That is how I will kill him.'

Galydon greeted this pronouncement in silence, his face frighteningly grim. At length, he said, 'If that is meant to persuade me, you have missed your mark by a very wide margin. And this discussion is over.' He walked to the door. 'You have no idea what you are asking,' he said more gently, pausing there. 'And you cannot imagine the consequences.'

Jeta felt her back stiffen. 'I will bear those consequences.'

Galydon turned, his hand on the door, his expression caught between anger and something else. 'No,' he said. 'You won't.'

As the door closed behind him, Jeta turned to Sedaine.

Aarin's mother shook her head as she followed Galydon from the room. 'Don't look to me to sanction this.'

That left Limina, who took her hands and kissed her on the cheek. 'My dear, you are braver than you are wise. But this is not the way.'

'I hate him,' Jeta said bitterly, tears threatening. She wasn't sure, in that moment, which of them she meant.

Limina shook her head sadly. 'You think I don't? My husband is dead at his hands. But sacrificing yourself only makes us weaker.'

'And if you still had a chance to save him?' Jeta demanded, unthinking. 'You wouldn't take it?'

Limina dropped her hands. 'Not like this.'

'What else do I have? What else can I do?'

'You think you will save the lives of the men you love by killing Darred and dying with him? It won't save them, it will destroy them—both of them.'

'But they would *live*,' Jeta insisted. 'If Kinseris goes, Darred will kill him. And Aarin…'

Aarin. She did not know what Aarin would do, now he was here, but she knew what Darred would do to him if he could.

'I cannot stay behind and wait, not again,' she told Limina. 'Don't tell me you would have let your husband go to his death if you could have done something to stop it.'

Limina's face hardened. 'I *sent* him to his death. I sent him out to die and I would do it again, because it saved countless lives.'

'I'm sorry,' Jeta whispered, meaning it. 'But this is not the same.'

'Isn't it?' Limina asked, more gently.

Jeta closed her eyes, a sob catching in her throat. She would find no help here. 'I'm sorry,' she said again, and fled the room.

Limina called after her; she did not look back. She did not stop until she found the one person who would help, the one person who would not lose a moment's sleep over the risk to her life if there was even a sliver of a chance it would achieve his end. Wiping her eyes, she hurried after him. 'Lord Vianor, a moment.'

PART THREE

ONE

THEY LEFT RHIANNAS five days later.

Jeta felt Galydon's eyes on her as they rode, his brows drawn together in a frown. He did not want her with them, and she couldn't blame him. After all, he knew what she wanted to do. It was Sedaine who had intervened, to her surprise and Galydon's consternation, by asking Jeta to attend her on the journey. The decision had caused a sharp exchange with Limina, but Sedaine was quietly adamant.

That first night on the road, in her entirely fictitious role as attendant and companion, Jeta dared to ask Sedaine why.

The queen was standing by the window of the small bedchamber that was all the roadside inn had to offer. 'Would you rather be left behind to wait and wonder?'

She shook her head. That was the last thing she wanted.

'Well then, neither would I. And so here we are.'

There followed an uncomfortable silence, in which they had both contemplated that proximity did not change their roles, only made the distance between wondering and knowing shorter. She had been turning to leave when Sedaine said quietly. 'I cannot protect him. I never could. But don't think I don't want to.'

It was an understanding she had not expected, but the worry in it curled her toes.

'What do you fear?' she had asked the queen, standing so rigid and controlled in her misery, separated from Aarin by wood and plaster and twenty years of lost time.

Sedaine didn't answer. Then Derias arrived, looking very fine in clothes more suited to a court function than a meal in a crude inn. His appearance brought an amused quirk to Sedaine's lips, and he endured her teasing with a grace that suggested he had invited it as he asked her permission to escort her to dinner.

On the second day out of Rhiannas, they joined up with Kallis's mercenaries, who pitched their spartan camp around the inn where Sedaine's party was staying, and the evening was soon filled with many voices and cheerful fires.

Jeta looked longingly out of the grimy common room window as the clansman went about their business, wondering vaguely whether Aarin was with them. She was acutely aware of Kinseris behind her, head bent in conversation with Galydon and Derias. He had come to her in Rhiannas, after the council. She had not thought he would, but she had forgotten how well he knew her. He had come to explain, to calm her fears, but he had been unshakeable in his resolve, no matter how much she begged him to reconsider. Since then they had not spoken. It was a distance she needed, for so many reasons, but it hurt all the same.

The door crashed open and mercenaries spilled into the common room. She heard Kallis bellowing pointlessly, 'No one gets drunk!' Then he appeared in the doorway, scanning the room. When his eyes lit on her, he grinned and said something over his shoulder, and after him came friends she had not thought to see again. After them came Aarin.

All at once she wasn't in a damp, roadside inn in Lothane, she was back in the dry, dusty streets of Ephenor, the horror and bloodshed behind them, and they were all alive. She didn't remember standing, but suddenly Jeta found herself surrounded by smiling faces as Lysan swept her into a hug, laughing, and his brother, more restrained, smiled his welcome.

Kinseris was beside her, surprise and delight on his face, and everyone was talking at once. Kallis, looking very pleased with himself, hooked an arm around Aarin's shoulder, saying something she couldn't hear, and she saw Aarin smile.

It was the reunion that the aftermath of Ephenor had denied them, a moment of spontaneous joy amid the strain and fraught nerves of the past weeks, and the clansmen were more than happy to get into the general spirit of things. She suspected they would drink the place dry whatever Kallis said. He didn't seem terribly inclined to stop them.

As Callan took Kinseris aside, she found herself standing with Lysan, who was surveying with room with the air of someone deciding where to seed chaos first.

'Who's that?' Lysan asked, looking at Derias. 'The one in the ridiculous…' He trailed off, gesturing to his clothes.

Jeta giggled. 'That's Derias, and don't let him hear you say that.'

Lysan grinned, mischief in every line of his face. 'Why not?'

'Because… oh, never mind.' He *did* look a bit ridiculous in this crowd of scarred, travel-stained mercenaries.

Derias soon joined them, plainly delighted by company and the promise of merriment. He immediately found a kindred spirit in Lysan. Which, Jeta reflected, was not at all surprising.

Even Sedaine relaxed in the jubilant atmosphere. At one point, Jeta saw her laughing with Galydon and Kallis. *Kallis.* Having listened to him express his less-than-complimentary opinion of Aarin's mother more than once between Redstone and Caledan, Jeta found the sight a little disconcerting, and instinctively looked around for Aarin. He too was watching Kallis and Sedaine, but there was no telling what he thought about it. Their eyes met for a moment over the heads of the others before he looked away. It was an exquisite form of torture, Jeta decided, to be so close to the man she had loved—whom she had believed she would never see again—and for him to be as out of reach now as he had ever been.

What good would it do either of us to rekindle that flame for so short a time? Aarin had said, and he was right. But that didn't stop the flame from burning them both.

Dropping her own gaze, she glanced at Kinseris and saw him watching her watch Aarin. There was nothing to be read on his face, but the slight crease between his brows, to her, spoke volumes. It was an added cruelty that she should hurt two men she loved, and estrange them from one another.

At some point in the evening, Sedaine disappeared, and Galydon, after a brief conference with Kallis, soon followed her. Derias, who had spent the last half hour drunkenly trying to teach the clan's fiddler to play a particular tune, abandoned his efforts in mock disgust and the man, grinning, started up a reel. Jeta was dragged to her feet by Derias, who with cheerful determination adapted the court dance he had wanted to the faster speed of the jaunty tune. Then Lysan, laughing so hard he could barely stand, attempted to copy the complicated steps, and somehow Derias ended up dancing with him instead.

Jeta, breathless with laughter at the sight of Sedaine's urbane young chancellor twirling Lysan across the filthy boards of a cheap tavern common room, collapsed beside Callan, who made room for her on the bench. The mercenaries were stamping their feet as Derias attempted to guide Lysan through a particularly complex sequence and the fiddler upped the tempo, trying to trip them up.

'I wondered how long that would take.'

Still laughing, she asked, 'How long what would take?'

Callan nodded towards his brother's antics, one eyebrow raised.

Oh. *Oh.* 'I don't think…' she began, and then stopped, looking again.

'You don't?' Callan asked innocently.

She blushed, flustered, and he laughed.

The mercenaries erupted into a cheer as the music reached a feverish pitch and the defeated dancers ended up in a tangled, gasping heap. A position from which, she noticed, they were in no hurry to untangle themselves.

In the end it was Kallis who stepped in, wading between them and hauling them both to their feet. He said something to Derias that Jeta didn't catch, but which made Callan choke on his drink. Derias and Lysan drifted off to a corner, heads together. When she looked for them a little later, they were nowhere to be seen.

Kallis pulled out the bench opposite and sat. She looked around for Aarin. She realised she hadn't seen him for some time.

'Where's Aarin?'

Kallis paused, his gaze sweeping the room. Then he shrugged.

She gave him an irritated look.

He frowned back. 'I'm not his keeper.'

'No,' she agreed acidly, 'but you are his friend.'

Kallis looked at her in silence for a moment. Then he sighed, about to stand, when Callan said, 'No, stay.' He nodded to Jeta. 'You go.'

She found Aarin not far from the inn, sitting in the pool of darkness between the lights of the tavern and the fires of the mercenary camp. There was something in his stillness that made her look up. If the dragon was near, she could see no sign of it in the night sky.

'Silverwing?' she asked.

He tilted his head, off towards the west.

'Is that why you're out here?' It wasn't, but she wanted him to say it.

He rested his chin on his knees, a pose so familiar from the months they had spent together.

'Aarin?'

He sighed. 'What do you want me to say? I can't... I don't belong here anymore.'

She studied his outline in the darkness, shoulders hunched. 'Where else should you be?'

He didn't have an answer for that, but he didn't move when she sat beside him.

'No one is pushing you away, Aarin. You are doing that yourself.'

He made a frustrated sound. 'I'm not...' Then, 'You all expect me to be the same, but I'm not. I can't fit back into a space that is a different shape.'

She waited, and eventually he said, 'I can still touch the person I was. I still care about the things I used to care about, still feel the things I used to feel, but it is like looking through a cracked mirror. I *died,* Jeta. I remember it, the feel of it, of coming apart and being knit back together. We were there, in the heart of everything where all things are one. And I could *see* everything. All the links in the chain that ties this world together—our place in it, the dragons'. We *need* them. I thought I understood before, but...' He shook his head. 'Kallis thinks I'm refusing to see the obvious. You all do. But I have memories in me now that stretch back thousands of years, and they are not all human memories. The dragons—they don't see things the way we do, or think the way we do, and I see the world now through eyes that are not solely mine. I am not the same. I am not *free*.'

His distress was real, and it hurt because she could not ease it. It was the price he had to pay for the choice he had made, and he would make the same choice again.

'Aarin…'

'It's not just that. It's not easy to see what I left behind, what that meant. What I've done.'

She frowned. 'What you've done?'

Instinctively, his head turned to the west, towards the dragon. 'I did what needed to be done, I *know* that. But I didn't think about the consequences. I never imagined…'

'What would happen?' She had thought the same, in her dark moments, even in anger. But it wasn't fair. Even if he had known, what else could he have done? And if he thought anyone blamed him for that, for this, he was mistaken.

Hugging her own knees, she tried to make him understand. 'Do you think any of us would be here now if not for you?'

He flinched. 'You don't need to tell me that,' he said bitterly. 'I know this is my fault.'

'That's not what I mean, and you know it,' she snapped. 'Kallis –'

'Kallis is here because he hates Darred. And where else would he be if there's a war on?'

'He hates him because of what he did to the clans, and to you.' *And would have done to me.*

Aarin looked at her in disbelief, and she wondered what Kallis might have said to him, in his own unguarded moments of anger.

'Kinseris,' she took a deep breath. 'Kinseris might still be in Kas'Tella if he hadn't sent Galydon to your mother—for you, Aarin. For friendship. Have you even spoken to him?'

'I –'

'And Sedaine –'

He shoved himself to his feet. 'Stop.'

But she didn't stop. Why couldn't he see? 'Do you think Sedaine would have taken this path if you hadn't stumbled back into her life? She would have gone along with Darred's schemes, even if she hated them, because she thought she had no choice. But then you showed up and she realised it was you he wanted all along and she wanted to protect you more than she feared defying him.'

He was silent a long time and in the darkness she couldn't tell what he was thinking.

At last, he said, 'I should not have left.'

She remembered the feeling of his power thundering through her, tied to the dragon, and the realisation of what it meant, of the inevitable parting and his acceptance of it. 'Did you have a choice?'

'Yes... No.' This time even the darkness couldn't hide that hesitation.

So, he'd had a choice, but not one he had felt able to make. She understood that. And she could understand his guilt, because she felt it too, weighing heavier on her with each mile of their journey. 'We all have things we must do that will hurt others,' she said quietly. 'But that doesn't mean we shouldn't do them.'

She could feel Aarin's eyes on her, feel the half-formed question, and she did not want to lie to him, so she said, 'She's your mother, Aarin. She loves you. Talk to her.'

TWO

SHE'S YOUR MOTHER. *She loves you. Talk to her.*

Jeta's words carried him to Sedaine's door, but once there he found he could go no further. He could hear the murmur of voices in the room beyond, and it gave him the excuse he needed to retreat—again—from an encounter he was not brave enough to face.

Then he heard a laugh, a woman's, his mother's. It was a sound straight out of his childhood, and it wrenched him back with sudden longing.

A floorboard creaked under his faltering step. There was a silence, then Sedaine called, 'Come.' And it was too late to retreat.

Lothane's queen was sitting in the room's only chair, her feet tucked up beneath her, long hair hanging loose around her shoulders. She looked towards the door as it opened, a query on her lips, and her eyes widened as she saw him. 'Aarin.'

Galydon was with her, perched on a stool by the fireplace. He too was looking at Aarin, his expression carefully neutral. Two cups of wine stood on a low table between them, a scattering of papers attesting to the fact that this was not quite the casual meeting it appeared.

Sedaine uncoiled from her seat, every movement strung through with nervous tension. 'Aarin,' she said again.

Galydon stood, the barest hint of a smile on his lips. 'It's late. I must go.' The general offered his queen a short bow and took his leave, nodding to Aarin as he passed. Then the door clicked shut and they were alone.

Sedaine stood at one end of the empty room, watching him warily. His mother, the Queen of Lothane. A title that meant so little and so much between mother and son.

He did not know what to do, what to say. His memories of his mother were so distant, so indistinct, so detached from the woman who stood before him. What time they had spent together since the day she had left him, aged seven, was even more so, his memories blurred by drugs, exhaustion, and despair. And yet he had clung to them. She had been drunk and angry and hurt. By his anger and rejection, by his father's disappointment, by Darred's manipulations, by her own ambition. By the conflict she could not deny between love for her child and love for her country.

He had thought she had chosen her country. He realised later that she had done it to protect him. Caught in a web she could not escape, she had tried to keep him free of it, and torn out both their hearts in the process. But that knowledge, hard won, could not erase the lost years, or change the fact that they were, to each other, little more than strangers.

He did not know how to breach that distance, only that he wanted to. Only that there were too many emotions in this encounter to be safe.

But if he found that words would not come, it was clear she suffered the same affliction, and the silence became like a live thing, twisting torturously between them.

Sedaine reached for a cup. Her hands trembled. Not from too much wine this time, from fear. The weight of suppressed emotions battered him, threatening to throw his link with Silverwing wide open, as it had done in Ephenor, and his ability to hold that power in check was still so tenuous.

Sedaine set the cup down. It clattered as it left her unsteady fingers, the sound harsh in the silence. She righted it before it could fall, taking a deep breath, and said without looking at him, 'I have been told that I cannot ask you to fight for me. I want you to know that I would not.'

He winced to hear the hurt she tried to hide behind a mask of formality. *I have been told.* By others, not by him.

'But I need to know why.'

'Why?'

'I looked for you,' she told him, her face neutral, her voice not quite steady. 'The day the magic changed. And then, when you did not come, and Darred did, I feared…'

'That I had chosen him after all?' he asked, unable to disguise the rawness of the wound Needa had opened.

'I thought you were dead!' she cried, echoing the words he had spoken to Jeta in Rhiannas. Maker, he had made a mess of that too. Every encounter with the people had known seemed to cause only heartache, to widen the rift between who he had been and what he was now. To hammer home a painful truth—that he no longer belonged.

A sliver of feeling slipped through the cracks in his control.

You are lonely.

Aarin drew in a harsh breath as Silverwing's care intensified the misery of isolation among the people he loved.

I am lonely, he agreed, gently pushing the dragon out of his thoughts.

Sedaine was looking straight at him now, a look in her eyes that was oddly familiar, and he saw the changes of two hard years on her face. The fine lines. The grey in her dark hair. 'I thought I had lost you, Aarin, finally lost you, and I would never…' She blinked, turning away. 'And then the dragons came.'

He heard the things she did not say. The dragons had come, and he had not. Worse, they had come as creatures of her enemy, and he knew she had doubted him. Even her.

It shook him, more than the others. *I need to know why.* So many questions disguised as one.

'I realise I cannot ask you to forgive me, that I do not have the right,' she told him, surprising him again. 'But I need to know that it is not because of… because of what I did, that the dragons…' Her voice cracked. 'That they have not returned to us.'

His heart lurched. He knew what it was now. Callan. She looked like Callan. But where Callan was tortured by an absence he could not understand, for Sedaine—for all those who could touch the elemental power of Andeira—to feel that power made whole and yet be excluded from it must have been an enduring torment.

But to think it was his doing, to believe he was withholding from them the thing they longed for… as a *punishment?*

'Do you think I have a choice?' he demanded, incredulous. 'That this is within my gift and I have withheld it?'

'No!' She sounded surprised, shocked. 'But I *need* to know. Surely you can understand?'

He could. He did. Aarin felt again Needa's furious grief, her rejection of the dragons, the blame she laid on him, and knew it all stemmed from the same fear—that *they* had been rejected. That the heritage they had lived in the shadow of their whole lives had come once more into the world and they had no part of it. And to have no idea *why*.

But what was the truth? Because he did have a choice, just not the one she thought he had. And when Darred's threat was ended—if he could end it—what then?

Then we return. There was fierce yearning in Silverwing's thoughts.

But how? The world was so changed, the dragons so alien. A partnership that was sourced in harmony would cause only discord. The dragons would be a power to be feared, or exploited, all knowledge of the healing they promised lost forever—except to these few, who already feared they had lost it.

Silverwing and his kind longed to return to Andeira, but there was nothing the dragon could hide from him, and Aarin knew that the future would never be like the past. It was a truth they had both accepted when they had taken up the task to which their lives had been dedicated. The future would be different. The future would be lonely.

'Aarin?'

The plaintive note, so jarring, reminded him he owed her an answer. 'It was not you. It was never you,' he told Sedaine, and saw her fingers tighten on the edge of the table. 'But it is us and everything we have become. The dragons have not chosen Darred; they have not rejected you. And this war is not just about freeing Amadorn, it is about freeing the dragons. And then,' he paused, unable to meet her eyes. 'And then... I don't know.'

Sedaine was silent a long time. Then she nodded, accepting that half-truth, unable to argue with what she did not understand and felt she did not deserve. It was Sedaine, after all, who had walked away from everything that Luen had once stood for when she had left his father. That it was Darred who had instigated it meant nothing—and everything.

But that was not all. He watched her change, from one moment to the next, from a mother to a queen.

'There's one other thing we must discuss. Once it becomes known who you are, there will be expectations of you from certain quarters.'

She stopped, waiting for his protest.

Aarin met her gaze steadily. 'Then they will be disappointed.'

The barest of smiles twitched her lips. 'Bitterly, no doubt.' And there was an undercurrent there that twisted her meaning. 'So, when the Lords of the North return to Rhiannas, it would be better for both of us if you are nowhere to be found.'

For both of us.

She would not ask for what he could not give, and he would, by his absence, refrain from complicating what must already be a fraught succession.

'I understand.'

She smiled again, but it was edged with bitter sorrow. 'Thank you.'

Then there was nothing more to say and a mere ocean of words left unsaid. Like a single sip of water to ease a burning thirst, it was so very far from enough, but sufficient, in its way, for now.

He was halfway to the door when she called after him.

'What about Jeta?'

He stopped, shoulders tensing. 'What about her?'

Sedaine searched his face, looking for something. She wouldn't find it. For everyone's sake, those emotions were buried deep. 'She deserves better, Aarin.'

'Than me?' His voice was light and airless. 'Isn't that what she has?'

'Does she? She deserves better than to be treated as though she does not know her own mind. She deserves better than to be ignored, Aarin.'

He clamped his jaw on an angry denial that would have been a lie. And instead, said, 'Yes, she does.'

Then he did leave, before he could damage this fragile beginning that meant so much and in the end had cost so little.

THREE

LOTHANE WAS NOT a small nation, but its main population centres were concentrated in the south, within two to three days of the navigable section of the Istelan and along its many tributaries, where the climate was milder and the land more fertile. Rhiannas itself had been founded along the route of a tributary that had dried up too many years ago for anyone to remember, and it had maintained its status as the capital only because it also sat at the junction of the other main trade routes, linking the road to Kamarai with the heavily travelled merchant routes to the Istelan's major ports—Forthtown in the east, and Vannarai in the west.

All this Jeta knew from the lessons drummed into her by her tutor in Situra, but she had never been to Vannarai, which was famous even among the merchant families of the Golden Alliance for its vast wealth. Sitting almost at the farthest extent of the Istelan that was navigable by ships of any size, and only three days by road to Rhiannas, Vannarai was the only city in Lothane with a permanent bridge. Unlike the seasonal pontoon bridge at Forthtown that linked north with south when high water made the natural ford too dangerous, Vannarai's stone bridge had, in peacetime, been a thoroughfare for trade. That bridge was now mostly rubble on the riverbed, its ancient piers standing forlornly between broken arches, sacrificed in the defence of Lothane.

Galydon had not chosen Vannarai as the location for its wealth, though that had its advantages. The city had stout walls, and it was one of the most heavily defended in Lothane—its own garrison, funded by rich merchants, had been bolstered with two companies of mercenaries, who manned the walls and the series of small forts that had been built along the bank to the east. Rather, it was Vannarai's natural defences and its position between the rugged, mountainous country to its west and the rolling plains of southern Lothane that made it the ideal place for such a meeting—or so Derias cheerfully explained to her as they approached the city, pointing out the city's strategic advantages as though they were on a tour of the sites.

She already knew from Galydon's maps that Vannarai was built on a broad expanse of flat land along a deep curve in the river. To the west, steep cliffs created a sheltered meadow where the meeting would be held. It was close enough to where the old bridge had stood that a small boat could ferry passengers easily between the north and south banks, but the cliffs and the city's defences protected the routes into Lothane should parley turn into attempted invasion.

A memory tugged at her as she looked at that sunny meadow. 'This is where they hold the summer fair.'

'Have you been?' Derias asked.

She shook her head. Her father had attended, of course, but he had never taken her, though she had begged him every year. Vannarai's summer fair was famous across Amadorn. It would not have been fitting, or so he told her, even though many merchants took their families. Ferlan Elorna had thought that his wealth set him apart from common traders, and the daughter he intended to marry into the upper echelons of society must not be seen as a mere merchant's daughter.

She let her attention wander as Derias described the many wonders of the north's great gathering of merchants. After the sprawling markets of Frankesh and Kas'Tella, Vannarai's fair, something she had dreamed of experiencing as a girl, would likely seem small and insignificant.

Derias looked wistful. 'Perhaps next year,' he said, and she wondered who he was trying to convince. There would be no fair here next year. They both knew that. Would there ever be again?

Derias lapsed into silence, his unguarded expression betraying his own worries. She thought she could probably guess what they were. Not just the fact that his queen was riding with them rather than remaining in Rhiannas, even if she had promised not to attend the meeting itself. Not just his fear that they were riding into a trap. Much more mundane problems were mounting up. Food shortages, already a problem, could soon become critical if Elvelen was truly lost, as would shortages of other essential supplies. The destruction of Kamarai might have torn open a hole in Lothane's defences, but it had closed an important trading route.

Or perhaps it was just the headache he couldn't quite hide, in which case her sympathy was limited. That was entirely self-inflicted.

She did not want to think about Kamarai as they passed within the safety of Vannarai's walls, but still it haunted her. Even with Aarin's reluctant presence, Galydon had taken no chances. He had brought with them as many mercenaries as could be spared from Rhiannas and her immediate defences without leaving the city completely exposed. They would camp in the meadow, in plain sight, but if an attack came, Galydon would not try to hold the meadow. Kallis's larger force had dug in several miles back where the cliffs sloped down to meet the road to Rhiannas. If it came to it, they would hold the enemy there.

That was as much as she knew. Sedaine was staying in Vannarai, protected by its strong walls, and Derias and Jeta were there with her. The city leaders fell over themselves to offer their queen the most comfortable accommodations, and their arrival was followed by a bewildering few hours of ostentatious welcomes and flattering speeches as a family was hurriedly moved out and their apartments made ready for royal guests.

Safely out of the way. And out from under Galydon's eye.

Left to herself at last, Jeta looked down at the black cloak laid out on the bed in the rooms she had been given, grander even than her father's house in Situra. A magician's cloak. A magician's cloak laced through with its owner's skilled craft of illusion. She ran her fingers through the thick pile of the velvet, steeling scattered nerves. Once she put it on, Vianor's spells would wrap themselves around her, masking her from those whose notice she wished to avoid, showing to those she wished to see her the face of a magician of Lothane. *If* she put it on, she could use the gift of those spells to slip out of the house in which she was staying, out of the city itself, and down to the camp where there was a boat that could take her across the river.

If she put it on, she would have a chance to do what she had pleaded with Galydon to sanction. If she did not, Kinseris would meet with Darred tomorrow and there was only one way that would end. She did not think she could stand it.

Before she could change her mind, Jeta unfurled the cloak and settled it around her shoulders. The magic came to life and settled into *her*. She felt it, like gossamer threads resting against her skin, light and caressing, and as unlike its creator as she could imagine.

There was no going back now. Vianor had been clear. She would have only this one chance. Once worn, the illusion would be spent. Now she was wearing it, she must use it.

There was no going back.

Working quickly but with care, Jeta pinned her hair close to her head and checked the tiny knife strapped to the inside of her wrist. Satisfied, terrified, she turned her back on the safety of inaction and its intolerable cost and walked quickly towards the danger she had spent too long running from.

FOUR

THEY HAD GIVEN her the finest lodgings in all of Vannarai, and in a city like this, that was saying something. Sedaine smiled in silent amusement. She wondered which merchant family had been turfed from their home to make room for this unexpected royal visit as she made a mental note of the riches around her. Had they known she was coming, they would have hidden their wealth away. Derias had no doubt already taken his own inventory, and that merchant family would be cursing her twice over before she left them. Well, more fool them for not stripping this place and sending their valuables north as so many others had done. Did they not know what was coming?

Amusement faded. Vannarai was closer to the centre of the conflict tonight than it had ever been. If Darred turned his dragons against them—and Aarin could not protect them—this city and its people would burn as Kamarai had burned, and the army camped just across the river would swarm overs its cooling bones into Lothane and the North would fall.

Sedaine shivered in the cool breeze from the open casement. An unease she could not identify had plagued her all evening, a sense of something *not right*. That coaxed a bitter smile. Nothing about this was right.

Her thoughts turned to Jeta, isolated from those who should have supported her by the tangled, strained bonds of love and friendship. Sedaine could not do anything to resolve that, but she could ensure the girl was not entirely alone, that she didn't have to endure the agony of waiting, far away and blindfolded. It was why she had not challenged her over the thing she carried, the resonance of which Sedaine had felt on the edge of her senses since they had left Rhiannas. She could guess what it was. She didn't need to guess where it had come from—she had known that signature her whole life.

If it gave the girl comfort to have the means to do something, who was Sedaine to take that away from her? As long as she was not foolish enough to actually use it.

Were they so different? Why else was she here, if not because now she had found him, she could not bear to let Aarin out of her reach? That she could not, again, let him go away from her into danger that was partly of her making. Danger that she could not protect him from, no matter how much she wanted to.

That she could not give up on the promise of reconciliation.

The cool evening was turning chill. As she reached out to close the window, she finally realised what was bothering her. Not a something, but an absence. The absence of Vianor's needling conjury that Jeta had carried with her since Rhiannas.

A surge of alarm took her to the door and she flung it open, almost sending Derias flying as he raised his hand to knock.

He saw her face and his smile faded. 'What is it?'

'Jeta—where is she?'

His eyes narrowed in confusion. 'Jeta? I don't know. Why –'

'Find her!'

Her urgency was infectious, and he backed away. 'Stay here,' he said as he walked quickly down the corridor to Jeta's chambers.

Sedaine stepped back inside, closing the door and leaning against it. The room felt airless, starving her lungs and making her dizzy. How could she have let this happen? What had been meant as a kindness had been exposed as an appalling error of judgement, and Jeta would not be the only one to pay the price.

Derias returned a few minutes later. 'She's not in her room. And she's not downstairs. The groom thinks he saw someone leave the grounds at dusk. It could have been Jeta, but he's not sure. He did not see their face. He did not even remember it until I questioned him.'

'He would not have,' she said grimly, striding past him. 'She was wearing a glamour.'

'What?' Derias hurried after her. 'A glamour? I don't understand.'

She didn't waste time trying to explain, already half-way down the mansion's grand staircase. Dusk was more than an hour ago. Jeta would be out of the city by now. If they didn't act fast, it would be too late.

Derias took the steps two at a time to block her path. 'Where are you going?'

She tried to go round him, but he held out an arm to stop her.

'Talk to me. Please.'

She took a deep breath. He was here to protect her, which in Galydon's view meant keeping her within the relative safety of the city and as far from Darred as possible. But it was Galydon she needed now. She had to warn him.

She had spoken aloud. Derias's frown deepened. 'He's here.'

'Indeed I am,' came Galydon's voice from above, and she turned to see him standing at the top of the staircase, looking down at her with a frown of his own. 'What is so urgent that you must leave the city, and against my express instructions?'

Of course. He had promised to report to her this evening. Relief stole her balance and she grabbed the handrail to steady herself.

He saw it and took two quick steps towards her. 'Your highness?'

Sedaine shook her head, hand raised to stop him. 'Not here.' And started back up the stairs to the privacy of her rooms.

Derias and Galydon followed close on her heels. Inside. She was too restless to take the chair Derias offered her, pacing to the window and back, searching for the words.

'Please,' Galydon said, his dark eyes studying her face, seeing the strain. 'Tell me.'

She faced him. There was nothing for it. 'Jeta has gone. Vianor has given her a glamour of some kind. I think she intends to kill Darred.'

Derias's shocked inhale barely registered. Her eyes were fixed on Galydon, who closed his eyes, leaning his weight on balled fists. 'You need to leave, now. Derias will take you back to Rhiannas.'

She shook her head. 'I –'

'You will go, now,' he repeated, and she could not mistake it for a

337

suggestion. 'I won't ask if you let her go. I don't want to know. But now she has gone, you cannot be here. My lord—see to it. You leave tonight.'

The flare of anger was all-consuming. For a moment she couldn't speak. Then Derias touched her arm, murmuring her name, and she snapped. 'I don't know what you think I have done,' she told Galydon coldly. 'But I did not encourage or allow this.' But she had known what Jeta carried with her, and what it meant, and not told him. Of that she was guilty.

His fist slammed down on the desk. 'You let her come with us, knowing what she wanted to do. She should never have been here!'

'She had the right to be here!' Sedaine shot back. 'You dismiss her, all of you, but she knows exactly what she is doing and why she is doing it.'

Galydon shook his head, his words a growl. 'I don't care what her intentions are. Don't you understand? She has betrayed the truce. That is all the excuse Darred needs. So, you will go, tonight, and you will not argue. And I will deal as best I can with what comes next.'

And then she did see. Not just the awful risk to Jeta and the destructive hurt to those who loved her, but the opportunity it would hand to Darred. To the potentially deadly consequences. For all of them.

'I don't want to leave.' It was an admission. It was also acceptance.

Galydon's face eased a fraction. 'You must,' he told her, more gently. 'If you are here, you tie my hands. I must protect you at all costs, and I assure you, you will find that cost too high.'

His anger she could withstand. His understanding undid her. She nodded, not trusting herself to speak, and he turned from her to Derias, moving swiftly from one problem to the next, organising her departure in the time it took to cross the room. Derias followed him with a backward glance that tried to both reassure her and ensure she remained where she was. Then they were gone and she was all alone.

FIVE

KALLIS TRUDGED EMPTY-HANDED back to where Galydon waited. His boots were slick with river mud, and water had seeped through the worn leather, the discomfort adding to his black mood.

Galydon appeared out of the gloom. He was alone. 'Anything?'

Kallis shook his head. 'The boatmen said they took a magician over an hour or more ago, but when I pressed them they could not be sure.' And they had not thought to question the magician, a lapse for which Kallis had berated them at length. Their confused response had only fuelled his frustrated anger, but at least they hadn't seen Jeta, and there was no other way she could have crossed to the far bank.

'Sedaine said she was wearing a glamour.'

It took only a few heartbeats to put it all together and he felt a flash of rage. 'Vianor.' The magician would have no compunction about sending Jeta to her death if it served his ends, and no one but a magician could have given her the means to disguise herself so perfectly as one of them. And Sedaine had *known*. 'What was she thinking? How could she?'

'She did not,' Galydon said tiredly. 'The fault here is mine.'

'Why? What did you do?'

Galydon sighed. 'Jeta came to me, in Rhiannas. She asked me to send her to Darred. To kill him.'

'And you let her come with us?' Kallis asked, incredulous with anger. 'Did you think she would just give up because you said no?'

'I did not want to. The queen insisted.'

'You let her come,' Kallis said again, the words grating through clenched teeth.

'As I said, the fault is mine.'

Kallis turned away, disgusted and furious with all of them, Jeta included.

'Where are you going?' Galydon called after him.

'Where do you think?' he replied without looking back.

'You can't go after her, Kallis.'

Something in Galydon's tone stopped him short. 'Why not?'

'Because it's too late to bring her back. She'll be in the camp by now.'

'You're saying we just abandon her?'

'No, I'm saying we don't hinder her.'

The angry protest died on Kallis's lips. 'You mean to let her try.'

'Since it is too late to stop her, yes, I mean to let her try,' Galydon retorted, his own anger finally stirring. 'Whatever you think of his methods—no matter how angry you are with me—Vianor has given her the means to get close to Darred. If you go after her now, all you achieve is both of you in his hands.

'And when she fails?' Kallis demanded. 'What do you suppose he will do to her then?' His own imagination shied away from the answer, his anger a convenient shield.

Galydon didn't flinch. 'Nothing you could save her from.'

The words hung between, cold as a northern winter, and it was Kallis who looked away first, his shoulders slumping in defeat. He drew a hand over his face as despair replaced anger. 'What do we tell Kinseris?' And Aarin. Maker, that was not a conversation he wanted to have.

Galydon didn't reply at once, his expression equally bleak. Then he sighed. 'Nothing. Not tonight.'

'*Nothing?*'

Galydon stared out over the black expanse of the Istelan as though he see into Darred's camp. 'How do you propose we stop them, either of them, if they decide to go after her?'

Kallis closed his eyes. Not if, when. Galydon was right, and he hated it. He hated his own helplessness more, but they were not ready, this moment, to deal with the consequences of rash action. They had come here under a flag of truce. That was their shield, however flimsy, however likely it was that

Darred had no intention of honouring it, but thanks to Jeta's precipitous action, that was gone now. Galydon must weigh the risk to an entire nation against the life of one woman.

Why Jeta? Why did you do this? But he knew the answer, because he knew her, and he should have paid more attention—they all should.

'Very well,' he said at last. 'As long as you understand what this means.'

Galydon looked at him then. 'I know.'

Kallis wasn't sure which of the possible calamities he was referring to.

SIX

SHE KEPT HER hood up and cloak held tight around her as Vianor had instructed. The glamour would hold until she dropped her hood—and she meant to use that moment to maximum effect.

She hailed the sentries as soon as she was close enough to see them, holding her hands—and the message cylinder bearing Ordaine's forged seal—high above her head. Her heart was thumping in earnest now and her mouth was dry as her shout set the perimeter of the camp into urgent motion. Two guards approached while behind them more soldiers appeared and spread out along the picket line.

The two sentries stopped around twenty yards away and one called out in broken Amadorian. She pretended not to understand, repeating her request, holding out the message cylinder. A third, an officer of some sort, pushed his way through the gawking line of sentries and joined the first two.

'State your business,' he called in Amadorian. His accent was Situran. The flash of outrage helped steady her.

She repeated the words Vianor had given her, trusting her life to his illusion and his assurance that the phrases he had taught her would gain her the audience she needed.

The officer snapped his fingers and a soldier approached, moving cautiously. At another gesture, the men on the perimeter spanned their crossbows and pointed them in her direction. 'Don't move,' he told her. 'Don't speak.' She did not.

The soldier reached her and held out his hand.

'Give it him. Slowly,' the officer commanded, and she had no choice but to obey.

The solider backed away until he reached the Situran officer, who glanced at the markings on the cylinder before sending the man running back into the camp.

'You will wait here,' he told her. Then repeated his warning as her legs wobbled and the crossbows twitched. 'Don't move.'

Their fear of her was palpable and shocking, until she remembered the guise she was wearing. For an instant she feared Vianor had played her false, and her stomach churned dangerously. If she had dared to move, she would have turned and fled. But that option had gone. Her legs were shaking so badly she was worried she might collapse and the sudden movement would get her killed. A thudding in her temple matched the thudding of her heart as she waited, eyes locked with the Situran officer.

A shout drew his attention back to the camp, where another officer flicked his wrist, beckoning.

The Situran repeated the gesture in her direction, stepping aside to let her pass before falling in behind her. She didn't need to see him to know he had a weapon drawn at her back.

She could not retreat. She could only go on.

This was what she had come for. It was what she had wanted ever since Escarian had betrayed them in Kas'Tella. Yet now she was here, she knew it for the foolish impulse it was.

The night deepened as they led her through the camp, soldiers surrounding her on all sides at a respectful distance. She wondered what they were seeing. Certainly not a girl in a dark cloak much too big for her. Did she look like Vianor? Tall and stately and radiating power?

A pavilion came into sight, dominating the centre of the camp. Two soldiers stood guard at the entrance, more milled about in the space around, a steady coming and going even at this late hour.

The Situran ordered her to stop and advanced to exchange a quiet word with the guards before ducking into the tent. He returned a few moments later, beckoning her forward, but her legs would not move. He repeated the gesture, more forcefully, and she stumbled a step toward him, then another, until she was standing just outside the entrance.

'Inside. He's waiting.'

And she went inside.

Darred was reclining in a chair, his booted feet resting on a camp desk as he turned the message cylinder over in his hands. He was just as she remembered, everything about him from his clothes to his mocking smile neat and controlled.

He leant back further as she entered, studying her with sardonic amusement. She felt sure he would see through the glamour, but it must have held because he tapped the cylinder with a finger as he said lazily, 'So, the magicians are regretting their hasty betrayal? I imagine you must have more to offer, something you think I might find to my advantage, because I'm struggling to see why I should care, one way or another. It's rather too late to regret choosing the losing side when your treachery makes so little difference.'

The voice and the manner touched off a spark of anger.

'No?' he enquired of her silence. 'Nothing? I expected at least the proffer of some intelligence, a secret or two, the revelation of a weakness... What can you possibly give me that I do not already know?'

The spark spread, igniting the core of molten fury that had burned since Kas'Tella. She pulled back her hood and saw Darred's eyes widen as the threads of Vianor's glamour fell away.

He sat up, boots hitting the floor with a thud. 'Jeta. Well, well, I was wrong. This is... unexpected.'

'I imagine it is,' she said coldly, locking down her fear behind hatred, red-hot and burning. 'After all, I'm supposed to be dead.'

'Yes,' he agreed, watching her with an unblinking gaze. 'You are.'

'Then how disappointing it must be for you to find I am not.'

Darred's lips quirked as he leant back in his chair. He was recovering his composure. 'My dear, I am ecstatic to see you. But I am somewhat surprised, given your memorable declaration last time we met. Something about death being preferable to my company?'

'I am not here for me.'

'No, really?' he murmured. 'Don't tell me—you're here for Aarin?'

'Aarin can take care of himself, as I think you know.'

'Perhaps.' He stood, walking around the desk until he was facing her, arms crossed. 'I shall certainly enjoy finding out. But if not Aarin, what else is so important that it requires such a desperate sacrifice?'

She would not play his game. 'I think you know. After all, you've already tried to kill him once. But you failed, didn't you? Kinseris is alive.'

She saw the words hit him, hard, shattering his cool mask for the second time. Something flashed behind his eyes, a storm of emotion she could not read, and suddenly the certainties on which she had planned her course shifted beneath her feet.

'Escarian failed,' she repeated. '*You* failed, and I won't let you succeed this time.'

Darred's eyes were very dark. His silence was unnerving.

'I know your offer of truce is lie,' she said, a little desperately. His reaction was all wrong. 'I know you're planning to kill him.'

'You do?' he asked with a puzzled frown. 'Oh yes, the meeting. How clever of you.'

Her eyes narrowed. 'You don't deny it.'

'Of course not.' He had recovered from his shock. 'Frankly, I'm amazed anyone would believe otherwise. I assumed there was some sort of counter betrayal on the cards, but perhaps I was wrong. Or am I to believe *you* are that counter move?'

She lifted her chin. 'I am here to bargain for his life.'

Darred's dark brows curved expressively. 'Really? How interesting. And what will you offer me in exchange?'

Her mouth dry, Jeta found that now the moment had come, she could not say the words.

'Well?' Darred drawled, closing the distance between them. 'You must have had something in mind.'

She flinched and turned her head away. She tried to hold a picture of Kinseris in her mind, of Aarin, to remember why she was here, but it was filled with memories of Redstone, of the last time she had been alone with this man.

Darred laughed softly. 'Come now, my dear. You do not seem very willing. Am I supposed to give up my vengeance for such a reluctant exchange?'

He was mocking her. Furious, she said hotly, 'That didn't seem to bother you before.'

'Ah, but that was then. Now you would like something from me. This is a bargain, is it not?'

'I will not pretend to offer what I cannot give,' she told him with fragile dignity. 'I offer you my body for Kinseris's life. Nothing more.'

Darred made a show of considering her words. Then he shrugged. 'Very well.' And he reached out to run his hand through a loose strand of hair.

She could barely breathe. Her heart was pounding so fast she felt dizzy. *Closer. Come closer!*

Pain flared as his fist bunched in her hair. His lips brushed her ear. 'As it happens, my dear, your sacrifice is quite unnecessary. I never wanted Kinseris dead. Why should I? I wanted him alive in Kas'Tella doing exactly what he was doing. I wanted an Order that would be ready to beg me to restore their glory when I return after making this land my own. No, Kinseris alive and in Kas'Tella was more important to me than you can imagine. But now? Now I know he's alive, he's just another obstacle to my plans, so as generous as your offer is, I find I must decline.'

He released her and stepped back as she reeled from disbelief to shocked understanding—*he had not known!* Far from saving Kinseris, by coming here she had doomed him.

'No!' She reached out in desperate entreaty. 'Please! I am not unwilling. Let me prove it to you.'

She fumbled with the thick coil of her hair, pulling free the pin that held it confined so it tumbled in a golden wave down her back. She reached trembling fingers to slip down her dress, exposing one pale shoulder.

His gaze roamed from her shoulder to her face, and she let the fabric drop still further.

'Please,' she said again, voice shaking.

Darred shook his head, all trace of amusement gone. 'No, my dear. I think not.'

Something clamped hard around her wrist, twisting it. She yelped and dropped the long pin.

Darred crossed the space between them in three short strides and scooped the pin from the ground. 'Well, well,' he murmured, turning it around in the light as she struggled against the restraining force of his magic. 'I'm impressed. Who gave you this, I wonder? Not your general Galydon. This is not at all his style. And Kinseris would never allow you to come. Sedaine, perhaps? But no, she would be more direct. Ah,' he said with a sardonic smile. 'Vianor. Of course. I can feel him now. He does hate me, doesn't he?'

'He's not alone,' she said bitterly, masking despair with defiance.

'I'm sure you're right, but hatred is such a useful thing, don't you think?' He smiled and pinched her chin. 'It brought us together.'

He called for his guards, and two soldiers in Caledani uniform entered the tent. Darred handed one the hairpin. 'Get rid of that—carefully. It is coated in a rather nasty poison. And put her with the other prisoner.'

One of the soldiers took her elbow as Darred let his hold on her fall away, dismissing her into the custody of his men without a backward glance. She allowed herself to be dragged one stumbling step after another, then stopped dead. The guard tugged hard, and she let him jerk her from her feet to her knees. She shook her wrist, feeling the little knife drop into her hand. As the soldier dragged her upright, she struck with all her strength at the man she had come here to kill.

Darred caught her movement a second too late and twisted to one side. Even as his power lashed out to arrest her thrust, the deflected knife sliced down through the thin fabric of his shirt and scratched a faint trail of blood on the skin of his forearm.

He raised horrified eyes from the scratch. She saw fear, real fear, on his face.

She laughed wildly and spat at his feet. She knew she was about to die.

Darred's face spasmed in rage. With an incoherent scream, he grabbed her by the throat and flung her across the tent. She hit hard against metal and her head exploded.

The world faded and returned in splintered fragments. Through a spreading haze, she saw Darred stagger into his desk. A flailing arm swept papers and charts onto the floor. The desk toppled after them and he crashed to the ground. Sound roared back, filling her ears with the frantic yelling of the guards and Darred's furious ranting. He shrugged off their help, rolling onto his hands and knees and dragging himself through the debris to where she lay.

Then he was on his knees before her, his breath hot on her face. She closed her eyes.

Darred's hand in her hair yanked her head back. He sagged, half-falling, and his voice was slurred as he hissed, 'You think you can kill me that easily? You think poison can kill me, little whore? *I am dragon!*'

He released her with a shove and she fell back and down, and down, into darkness…

SEVEN

Caledan, New Age 2022
A memory

'WELL, THIS IS NICE.'

Kinseris's undignified start provoked a soft laugh, and he let out a long breath as he turned to see Darred reclining on his bed, booted feet dangling above the rich carpet that covered the floor of his room.

He closed the door, removing his cloak and hanging it carefully as his heart rate returned to normal. 'What are you doing here? How did you get in?'

Darred swept an arm around the small room. 'I came to see your new accommodations. So very fine, compared to what we have been used to.'

And what you still have, Kinseris finished for him silently, thinking of the cold, spartan cells where the lower-ranked priests resided. He knew better than to offer platitudes, much less sympathy. Nothing provoked Darred's blistering scorn more surely than an effort to pretend his circumstances were anything other than deliberate insult.

'It is very comfortable,' he agreed as he sat. 'But you expected nothing else. Why are you really here?' His new rank, so recently bestowed, placed him far above his friend in the Order's hierarchy. Contact between them, other than for the provision of such services as his position required, was now actively discouraged.

There was a flash of irritation as Kinseris failed to rise to the bait, then Darred nodded. 'Very well. I delivered your message.'

Kinseris's eyes flicked up in alarm and Darred laughed. 'Am I a fool? No one is listening.'

Alarm turned to fear. 'What have you done?' There were listening wards in every room in the citadel. Vasa's paranoia was out of all control, and to interfere with those wards was to provoke an accusation of treason. There were several reasons Kinseris did not want to invite scrutiny of his activities, quite apart from a healthy desire to hold onto his life.

Darred was grinning like a child who had learned a new trick. 'You should see your face. Don't you trust me?'

'What have you done?' Kinseris repeated, already feeling out the wards, hoping he could undo whatever meddling his friend had wrought before it was noticed.

'Stop that,' Darred said. 'I haven't disabled them, I just turned them outwards. If anyone is listening—and why would they be?—all they will hear are the sounds from the corridor, or the courtyard. We are quite safe.'

Kinseris saw it was true. He grinned, noting the subtle manipulation and filing it away for future use. 'A clever trick, but even so...'

'Even so, nothing,' Darred retorted. 'You will happily risk both our necks in your misguided efforts to build alliances outside the Order, and you worry about a simple trick like this?'

Kinseris conceded the point. 'Very well. You delivered my message. Do you get a reply?'

'Of a sorts. They don't trust you.' Darred's mouth twisted. 'Or maybe they don't trust me. They have no reason to. If you want to convince them, you'll have to meet with them yourself. And we both know you can't do that.'

Kinseris raised an eyebrow. 'I can't?'

Darred stared at him, his dark brows drawn together in a frustrated frown. 'No, you can't. Do you have a death wish? Why are you even doing this? What concern is it of yours how the guilds are taxed or what happens to the street brats or the farmers in the provinces? It is beneath you, beneath us. And it will get you killed.'

'Beneath us?' Kinseris asked, watching his friend. 'Beneath us how? As governors of this city and this land? We should have no care for the people who live in it, who feed us, and pay for our luxuries? Isn't that, in fact, our duty?'

'Our duty,' Darred scoffed. 'Listen to yourself. The Kas'Talani do not care and will never care for the lot of *chattan-ai* and you can't change that.' He used the derogatory Renallan word for those who could not touch the magic. 'So what is the point of meeting with the guilds? There is no promise you can make them that you can keep, no influence you can exert on their behalf. All you do is risk your own position, and perhaps your life. For nothing.'

'*Not* for nothing,' Kinseris said, sitting up. 'You are right, there is nothing I can do *now*, but I can learn, I can understand, and I can build…'

'A powerbase among the people?' Darred sneered. 'That is exactly what *he* will think you are doing.'

'I don't want a powerbase,' Kinseris snapped. 'I want to help.'

Darred shook his head, pushing himself to his feet. 'You can't help them. And I won't help you throw your career away, or mine, such as it is.'

Kinseris stood in his turn. 'If that is how you feel…'

'It is.'

The words were spoken with force, but Kinseris knew he was not finished, and it did not surprise him when his friend hadn't gone two paces before he stopped.

'You don't think,' Darred berated him. 'Vasa does not even have to find out for this to destroy you. If any of the elders discover what you are doing, if any of our superiors even suspect, they will use this to control you. Simply the threat of exposure will tie you in chains so tight you will never escape. Imagine a life bound to someone like Casamir? Even I could do this, and still you keep trusting me!'

Kinseris cocked his head with a bemused smile. 'Why would I not trust you? We are friends.'

Darred looked backed at him, distraught. 'You are such a fool.' He took another step towards the door, and stopped again. 'If this will destroy your career, Shakumi will destroy your life.'

Kinseris felt a sick fear coil through him. 'What are you talking about?'

'You *know*,' Darred insisted. 'If she is just another strand of your pathetic rebellion, forget her. It was fun for a while, but it has to stop. Now.'

'She is not. I –'

'Do not say you love her,' Darred sneered. 'Haven't you been listening? She is a weakness. If all your other transgressions are enough to ruin you, what do you think knowledge of your little dalliance with Vasa's favourite whore would do? If someone threatened her harm, is there anything you would not do?' His anger faded. 'I hold too many of your secrets, my friend.'

Kinseris put a steadying hand against the wall. 'You would not –'

Darred's face twisted with disgust. 'That is what makes you doubt me?'

And instantly he felt ashamed. 'Of course not. But I will not end it.' He could not meet Darred's eyes. 'I cannot.'

There was a long silence, then Darred shrugged. 'On your head be it, my friend.'

Why would I not trust you? We are friends.

The look on Darred's face as he had spoken those words had haunted Kinseris for thirty years. That was the moment their friendship had started its long, slow unravelling. It was the first time Darred had warned Kinseris not to trust him, but not the last. And yet he would swear that the betrayals that lay ahead were still entirely in the future. It wasn't until their exile to Frankesh—the consequence of Kinseris's refusal to heed Darred's warning about Shakumi—that decades of discontent had been exploited by Vasa to finally and irrevocably break that bond.

Except it hadn't. Not quite. Kinseris had last seen Darred in the corridors of Kas'Tella after he and Aarin had escaped Vasa's cells, and his friend had met him with words of alliance on his lips. He had never understood why, after all that had gone between them, Darred had made that offer.

Now, as he contemplated the meeting to come, only hours away now, Kinseris thought perhaps he had found the answer.

Trust.

It had always been the chink in Darred's armour. It was what Kinseris had offered him, simple and unquestioning. It was what he had craved from the Order and never been given. And it was the trust, however self-serving, that Vasa and the Arkni had shown him, that had turned him at last. But Darred had never, as far as Kinseris knew, broken *his* trust. Darred had held his life in his hands for years. Enough secrets to destroy him ten times over, and he had never used them, even when their paths and ambitions had diverged so completely.

Kinseris had taken Darred's lesson too much to heart. No one person knew a fraction of his secrets now and what good had that done him?

Was trust still Darred's weakness? If he had changed since that day three decades ago, Darred certainly had. And this time Kinseris wasn't just trusting him with his secrets, he was trusting him with his life. But what choice did he have? What other purpose did he have? Stripped of his power and influence, he had now only what others chose to give him. If he could not do this, what was he?

He did not believe Darred was behind the assassination attempt. That was not sentiment, it was logic. Darred would not hesitate to move against him if he thought Kinseris stood in his way. But he had not, quite the opposite. In forcing the Kas'Talani to relinquish their power, Kinseris had given Darred all the allies he needed in Caledan. He knew it; it was why he had taken the direst of precautions. Nor did he believe Darred would send someone else to do his killing for him. Of that Kinseris was certain. If it came to it, *when* it came to it, the killing blow would come in plain sight.

Kinseris blinked against the glare as the sunlight hit the water, trying to banish Jeta's face from his mind. It was entirely possible that moment had come. He could not pretend otherwise, nor could he hide it from her, and it hurt him in ways he had not expected to cause her pain. But he had not come here to hide. More than that, if it was on anyone's shoulders what Darred had become, it was on his.

Footsteps behind him. He turned and greeted Galydon with a muted smile. It would be pointless to pretend he was not afraid. 'Is it time?'

His former general regarded him gravely. 'Not quite.'

Something in his voice made Kinseris go very still. 'What is it?'

And Galydon showed him his worst fears realised as yet again a woman he loved placed herself in danger for his sake and *he could not save them.* All at once he was back in that room with Darred, thirty years in the past. *If someone threatened her harm, is there anything you would not do?*

He could barely breathe. After Shakumi, he had not thought he would ever find himself here again. He had never wanted to. But Jeta had breached his defences without even trying.

He had cherished her for her courage, for her honesty, and the balance she had given him. It was because he cherished those things that he had not wanted to stand between her and the man she loved, or make her choice to leave him harder than it had to be. He had not realised until this moment, on the brink of an entirely different kind of loss, that he *needed* her.

Galydon was standing there, watching him, compassion and defiance on his face.

He answered both, his voice barely above a whisper. 'You should not have kept this from me.' If he known, he would have gone, last night. He would have done anything to spare her.

If someone threatened her harm, is there anything you would not do?

Kinseris closed his eyes. It was a pain sharper even than Escarian's sword thrust to know that she had gone for him, and he could not help her. That he dared not, because of what he knew and what he could be forced to do. Because his friendship with Darred cut both ways, and Jeta was now in the hands of the man who knew him best, who knew exactly how to break him. And the price of his sanity was far too high.

If someone threatened her harm, is there anything you would not do?

Galydon's gaze was too sharp, too knowing, and he looked away. Because this was why he had not been told, and they both knew it. At least Galydon did him the kindness of not saying so.

'Aarin?'

'Kallis is telling him.'

So, Kallis had known too. It would have taken a restraint he had not thought the mercenary possessed to let what Jeta had set in motion play out. He could not guess what Aarin would do. Because Kinseris understood in a way no one else seemed to, save perhaps Jeta, that his hands were also tied.

'What will you do?' he asked Galydon.

His general spread his hands in a helpless gesture. 'What will *he* do?'

He could guess the answer to that and wished he couldn't. Darred would never spend a coin if it might be saved to serve him later. And he would not waste the opportunity Jeta had handed him by killing her, not yet. But there were worse things he could do, to all of them.

EIGHT

THE FIRST THING Jeta was aware of was damp ground beneath her cheek and the earthy, pungent smell of soil and human waste. Then there was pain, a pulsating wave of agony in her skull. She tried to move and the ground moved instead, disappearing out from under her and sending her spiralling back down into the darkness.

The second time she woke, the pain was less. Her head still felt like it was trapped in a vice, but she could move it without setting off an avalanche. But when she tried to move her arms, she awoke a new monster as muscles screamed in protest at long hours of restraint.

She was tied up. She was a prisoner. Darred's prisoner. Panic blossomed from one instant to the next, her breathing coming quick and painful as her vision started to tunnel. *Not again, not again, not again.*

'Easy, girl,' a gruff voice said. 'Just breathe.'

Her eyes snapped open. The darkness was complete. She tried to speak but could only manage a breathless gasp.

'Easy,' the voice said again. 'Don't think, just breathe. I'm not going to hurt you. Breathe.'

The words continued in a comforting stream, the deep voice non-threatening, and she felt herself slowly calm as she latched onto the sound and let it wash over her. She lay like that for a while, just breathing, not thinking, and eventually the man stopped speaking.

She opened her eyes. It was lighter now, slivers of pale light giving texture and contrast to the darkness inside what she realised was another tent. There was a man sitting there, watching her with one sharp eye. The other was a mass of ugly scarring, still raw and red in places. He was a big man, broad across the shoulder with a chest like a barrel and a belly that strained against his filthy clothes. There were chains at his ankles and his arms were out of sight behind his back. Chained too, no doubt. Another prisoner.

The light was brighter now. She felt ashamed of her panic. 'Thank you.'

The man grunted. 'Feel like that myself sometimes. You one of mine?'

Her head hurt. That made no sense. 'One of yours?'

The man waited as she closed her eyes and breathed through the pain. When she opened them again, she could see him more clearly. She must have drifted off. 'One of yours?' she asked again.

He smiled slightly. It made him look a little less grim. 'Farnorian.'

Farnorian. It should mean something. Oh yes. 'Like Limina.'

There was an odd silence, then the man said, '*What* did you say?'

'Limina,' she said again. 'She's from Farnor.'

'Who are you?' the man demanded.

Who was she? It was so hard to think. She felt sick. Time passed.

'Girl, stay with me,' his voice called. 'Tell me who you are.'

'Jeta Elorna,' she said, pleased with herself.

He made a frustrated sound. 'Jeta Elorna, where have you come from?'

So many answers to that question. As she drifted off, she heard herself say, 'Caledan.'

'Jeta Elorna, wake up.'

Jeta opened her eyes. The words were running through her head on loop and she guessed the man who spoke them had been repeating them over and over.

'Jeta Elorna, wake up.'

She screwed up her eyes and rolled on her back, her shoulders screaming in protest. 'I'm awake.'

There was an explosive sigh. 'You've been out for half a day.'

That shocked her. Half a day? How long had she been here? By now both Kinseris and Aarin would know what she had done… She struggled upright, urgent as she realised what they might do—what she might cause to be put at risk. 'I have to get out of here!'

The man laughed. It rippled through his belly like a wave. 'You and me both, girl.'

Her head pounded but at least her mind was functioning. She rested her head on her knees. 'You don't understand.'

'Oh, but I would dearly love to. You have a story to tell me.'

She looked up. 'What do you mean?'

'Who are you, and why are you here?' He was staring at her intently. 'Rumour says someone stabbed Darred. Did you do that? Because if you did…' He shook his head, his voice trailing away.

She lifted her chin. 'If I did, then what?'

He laughed again, in pure delight. 'Then I could kiss you, girl, that's what. But he's not dead, not that one. So, tell me who you are and why and I might be able to help you.'

Jeta looked at the chains around his ankles. 'How can you help me?'

His head jerked around, towards the tent opening. 'Lie down, close your eyes.'

Jeta obeyed. There was a rustle of canvas and someone entered the tent. She heard the clank of metal and risked a look through her lashes to see a Caledani soldier unlock the chains around the man's wrists.

'You stink of shit, Admiral,' the soldier sneered, throwing a wineskin into the man's lap.

'That's because you shit yourself every time you come near me,' her companion growled, flexing his scarred hands. The skin around his wrists was raw and weeping.

The soldier spat at his feet and said something in Safarsee that Jeta hoped her fellow prisoner did not understand.

A second guard entered, and she shut her eyes, head spinning. *Admiral.*

Something heavy hit the dirt near her head. Footsteps shuffled closer and a rough hand shook her shoulder.

'Wake up, bitch.'

'Careful,' a voice called, harshly mocking. 'She might stick you too.'

She jerked as though waking from sleep and the soldier standing over her swore and jumped back.

The man in the chair laughed.

'Bitch,' the soldier said again, raising his hand.

The other guard caught his wrist. 'He wants her undamaged,' he warned, speaking in Safarsee. 'Bring in the food. I want out of this wretched stink.'

Red-faced, the reprimanded soldier passed crude commentary on Darred's intentions, to which his partner, laughing, added a few obscene observations of his own about his commander. Jeta glanced at her companion. If he understood their conversation, he gave no sign of it.

A bowl of thick brown stew was placed on the ground beside her, slopping some of its unappetising contents onto her feet. She waited patiently as the cords around her wrists were untied so she could eat, then nudged the bowl suspiciously with her toe when the guards retreated back outside.

'It's not poisoned.'

She sniffed at the contents. 'Not intentionally, perhaps.' She reached for the wineskin and took a drink, only to spit out the rancid water in disgust.

The man in the chair snorted with amusement. 'You get used to it.'

'Do you?' she asked, staring at him. 'Admiral?'

He shook his head, and mouthed, 'Not now.' Aloud, he said, 'Eat. You need your strength.'

She glanced at the part-open tent door and back at the food, forcing herself to eat a mouthful. She was chewing laboriously through her third when the guards returned to take the bowls and filthy water away.

'Wait,' she called, suddenly aware of an urgent need. Her faced flushed. 'I need the privy.'

The guard laughed. 'Piss yourself. He does.'

Jeta did not look at the man in the chair but she could feel his rage and humiliation. Her own anger was a cold fire. She knew who he was now. In rapid and flawless Safarsee, she repeated the soldiers' comments about Darred, with a few additions of her own, then smiled sweetly and repeated her request.

The men stared at her, stupid with shock. Then the older one snapped out a command and she was dragged to her feet. They tied her hands and pushed her roughly out of the tent to the camp latrines. The experience made her glad she had barely touched the food and water.

Her guards wasted no time returning her to the filthy tent. A shove sent her sprawling to her knees and the soldier yanked her across the muddy ground by her hair and retied the bonds around her ankles, kicking her in the belly for good measure. Not hard, but hard enough.

'You keep your mouth shut, bitch,' he hissed in warning.

She nodded, tasting vomit, and lay still until she heard him leave.

She let her head drop until it rested on dirt as the first flush of reaction set her muscles twitching. Tears burned against her closed lids, shame for the fear she could not hide.

Eventually, the shaking stopped and breathing grew easier.

'Back with me, girl?' the rumbling voice asked. 'Are you hurt?'

Jeta shook her head and struggled upright. She met the man's one-eyed gaze, her tired brain struggling to recall what she knew of him. The precious knowledge she could share or withhold, and the service Kinseris had intended to ask of him. 'Admiral Hanlon? Limina's husband?'

He looked away.

'She thinks you're dead.'

'It's better that way.'

'No, it's not.'

'What would you know about it?' he asked savagely. 'Will knowing the truth—*this truth*—make her feel better?'

Jeta blanched under his anger. It was her turn to look away. 'She misses you.'

'And how do you know that?' he demanded. 'Jeta Elorna, who speaks Caledani like a native but is no native of that land—who are you and how did you get here? *And how do you know my wife?*'

'I –' But thinking of Limina brought other thoughts tumbling to the surface—the realisation, yet again, of just how dire her mistake. Because Darred had not been intending to kill Kinseris, but now he could use her against him. She had to believe he would see the danger, that Galydon would not let him come. She forced herself to breathe, to stay calm. 'You said you could help me. Did you mean it?'

He studied her, smiling faintly. 'You don't need to bargain with me, girl. I will do what I can, but I can make no guarantees.'

'Thank you.' It was something. 'I need to send a message to the commander of Lothane's army. Darred offered a meeting under a flag of truce, but he lied. He means to attack.'

Hanlon was silent for a long time. At length he said, 'Of course he lied. Why would your general believe him?'

'He didn't. He doesn't. But he didn't have a choice.'

'So he sent you?' His disbelief was clear. And something more. Something that hadn't been there before.

'No one sent me,' she retorted, stung. 'They do not... they did not know.' But they would all know by now, and she could not let her mistake undo everything she had come here to save. 'They cannot try to rescue me. You have to tell them that—they must not come for me. Please.'

Hanlon leant forwards as far as the chains would allow, and now she could see the suspicion on his face for what it was. 'But why, Jeta Elorna? Tell me why.'

Her evasions had aroused his suspicions. That her sudden appearance here, with Limina's name on her lips, might not be what it seemed. 'Darred is my enemy,' she said fiercely. 'I came here to kill him, not spy for him.'

His eyes narrowed. 'You haven't answered my question.'

She met that penetrating gaze without flinching, Kinseris's name hovering on the tip of her tongue. It was a name that would unlock Hanlon's help, she was certain of it. The things she knew, the things Kinseris had told her, could do a lot more than that, but she had to be sure that by telling Hanlon she would not be placing that knowledge into Darred's hands. That she was not doing exactly as Darred had intended when he had put them together.

But if she did not tell him, she would be squandering a chance that would never come again. *Information has no value if there is no one to receive it,* Kinseris had said to her in Rhiannas. *And the one man who could have done anything with it is dead.*

Well, he wasn't dead. He was sitting in front of her right now. She did not know what he could do with the knowledge, but if he could help her send a message, she had to believe he could do *something*. And something was a lot better than nothing.

She took a deep breath. 'I came because if I did not, someone else would have come and Darred would have killed him.'

'Who?'

'You know him, I think. His name is Kinseris.'

Hanlon's eyes widened in surprise and shock. He had thought Kinseris dead. Did that mean the plans Kinseris had set in motion so many months ago might still be intact? Because that was the other unknown, and it would remain so until—*unless*—a man in chains in the heart of the enemy camp could find the means to use what she could tell him.

That man was watching her now, the shock receding to be replaced by something that looked suspiciously like amusement. 'So you thought you would kill Darred and save him?' Hanlon threw back his head and laughed until tears streamed down his cheeks, indifferent to Jeta's fury. 'Girl, that is the single most stupid idea I have ever heard, and the bravest. What is this man to you? No, don't answer that, Jeta Elorna from Caledan. I can guess.'

Cheeks burning, Jeta fixed him with a haughty stare. 'Can you get a message out, or was your offer of help just an empty boast?'

Hanlon shook his head, still chuckling. 'I can do better than that. You will deliver your message yourself. But now I do want something in return.'

'I thought I didn't need to bargain with you.'

'This is not a bargain. It is an exchange of intelligence between allies. But first I need your promise that my wife will never hear my name from your lips.'

Heart aching for Limina, Jeta nodded.

'*Say it!*'

'I promise.'

He sat back, tension draining out of him. 'Well then, Jeta Elorna from Caledan, *friend* of Kinseris. Tell me what you know and leave nothing out.'

NINE

AARIN WAS FLOATING, detached from himself, as the conflict raged within and without.

In Ephenor, Shrogar had told him Jeta was dead. Then, in the shadow of Vannarai's great walls, Kallis had given him worse news—that Darred had her. That she had gone to him of her own free will, to kill him, to protect Kinseris. Not just Kinseris. She had gone to Darred for all of them, and he could not stand it.

The argument raged around him, but it did not touch him. He could feel Kinseris' frantic worry, Kallis's anger, the rapidly unspooling thread of Galydon's patience, but he was apart from it, protected from it by Silverwing's vast and ageless calm. It was both like and unlike Ephenor. He had learned better how to control the power that came with breathing, with feeling. How to make the use of it a conscious effort, not an unconscious instinct, and he needed that distance, that calm. The greatest danger—to Jeta and to everything she wanted to protect—lay in giving into emotion, because Darred was a master of manipulating emotion.

But he was close, so close, to losing control.

'We cannot just leave her there!'

Kinseris' voice was tight with desperation, with the memory of another woman he had not been able to save. Her death was seared in Aarin's memory too. Her death and what came after.

'No one's suggesting that,' Galydon snapped. 'But we can't simply react.'

And Aarin knew he should say something, that he should intervene before this spiralled out of control, before Kinseris's desire to go after her overrode his understanding of just how disastrous that would be.

'You made sure of that,' Kallis snarled to Galydon, and his anger was like a furnace, ready to explode. There was even greater danger there, Aarin realised. For all that he loved her, decades of hard decisions, of weighing consequences and choosing the least-worst option, at least gave Kinseris the ability to see clearly. Kallis just wanted to act, so Aarin would have to act for him.

And once he did, he would have intervened in a way he could not walk back from.

'We're wasting time.' The words cracked in his dry throat. 'Get everyone out of here—pull the army back to Rhiannas.'

He felt their attention like a weight falling on him.

Kallis crossed his arms, his face closed, dangerous. 'Why?'

'Why?' Galydon asked, in an entirely different tone.

He was the only one of them who retained any semblance of calm, and Aarin didn't know how much was down to long years of training and how much to the impossible position he now found himself in. In his brief interactions with the Caledani general, he had come to understand that he had dedicated himself completely to the task Kinseris had given him, and that he would place that duty above personal loyalties. He already had, in fact, when he had stopped Kallis going after Jeta last night. When he had deliberately kept them in the dark.

That decision might have staved off immediate disaster, but it also meant their window to act on their own terms was closing fast. So, ignoring the seething emotions, he put words to Galydon's dilemma. 'You cannot take her back by force. Not with the resources you have, not without my help, and if that happens…' He shrugged. If that happened it meant all-out war, right here, right now, and they were not ready for that. He glanced at Kinseris. 'But you cannot allow Darred to use her as a bargaining chip and you cannot abandon her.'

Galydon nodded. 'Go on.'

'So leave now,' he begged, even Silverwing's steadying presence unable to drown out the sense of time slipping through their fingers. 'I will get her back, but I cannot do that and defend you. And if you're here, you –'

'No,' Kallis said emphatically, before Galydon could say a word. 'No one goes in alone, not even you.'

'He doesn't have to go alone.' Kinseris said to Aarin. 'I'll come with you.'

Kallis's furious denial was drowned out by Galydon's. Kinseris ignored them both. Aarin knew what he was thinking, what he was remembering.

'None of you are coming with me. Not even you,' he said to Kinseris. 'You cannot help, you can only make this more difficult. So, please, go back to Rhiannas and *get out of my way!*'

'Not happening,' Kallis growled. 'I might not be able to stop you, but don't ask me to just walk away. Darred has an army with him. While you're busy with Darred and the dragon, what do you think his army will be doing? You need us.'

'No, what I need –'

But time had run out. There was a scratching at the tent door and Galydon pulled back the canvas to admit a nervous soldier. The man held out a message cylinder and the silence was profound as they all looked at it and silently measured what it meant. Then Galydon dismissed the soldier and turned back, the scroll balanced on his palm.

Aarin felt the blood pounding in his ears. 'What does he say?'

Galydon opened the slim cylinder and shook out its message. 'Let's find out, shall we?'

He read the message in silence. Beside him, Kallis vibrated with tension. Aarin didn't look at Kinseris. He didn't need to. Kinseris knew as well as Aarin that it was not Jeta's death they needed to fear in this moment, it was what she would be used for. Darred would bargain for something or someone, it just remained to be seen what he would ask for.

Kallis's patience snapped. 'What does he want?'

Galydon looked at Kallis and held out the scroll. 'You.'

'What?' Kallis looked as surprised as Aarin felt. 'Me? Why?'

Galydon gave a small shrug. He was still holding out the scroll. Kallis took it and scanned it before handing it to Aarin. There was little enough to be read in the terse phrases. Darred proposed an exchange—Kallis for Jeta.

There were no extravagant flourishes or elaborate threats, nothing of Darred's usual manner at all, merely a simple demand and instructions for carrying it out.

Aarin looked up. He felt cold, a coil of dread escaping his careful control. Darred knew him too well, and he knew Kallis. 'He's lying.'

Galydon nodded. 'I agree.'

Kallis snorted. 'Of course he's lying. But he knows we'll go along with it anyway.'

'Why you?' Kinseris asked bluntly. He would see the trap. 'Why would Darred ask you when he could ask for…'

'You?' Kallis finished for him.

'Or Galydon, or my mother,' Aarin murmured, eyes still on the message. He did not add himself. Because Darred would never be that direct when he could play with them first. 'Any one of them is worth more to Darred than you.' He had to make Kallis understand. Darred could have demanded Kinseris and Aarin did not know if they could have stopped him going, even knowing what would happen. But it was a bigger prize he was reaching for.

Kallis folded his arms across his chest. 'You tell me.' And the freezing antagonism between them was all the worse for the friendship it sprang from and obscured. Aarin understood that the anger was not directed at him, that he was just a convenient target, but it hurt all the same.

'Because it is not your value to Darred that signifies here, Kallis. It is your value to *me*. Of everyone, he is gambling that you are the one I can least afford to lose. If you go, he will have you and Jeta, and he has used you both before to try to force my hand. He will do it again. Don't make me make that choice. I am *not* free to choose.'

But it was no use. Kallis was too angry to hear the warning. 'If it's you he wants, why not just ask for you. He must know you would go.'

That was like a punch in the gut. Through his choice of proxy, Darred had shown he understood Aarin far better than Kallis did. 'But would I?' he asked, avoiding Kinseris's troubled gaze. 'I left her once. She's moved on. And she did not go to him to save me. No, he cannot be sure I would make that sacrifice for Jeta. He is gambling that I will not risk both of you.'

'And you would risk her life on that guess?' Kallis demanded. 'What if you're wrong?'

'What if you are?' Aarin shot back, perilously close to losing his own temper. 'Since when did you start trusting Darred to keep his word?'

'I don't,' Kallis growled. 'But if he's lying, I pay the price, not you. Because as much as Jeta means to you, to me, to all of us, her life is not worth yours. And if she were here, she would tell you the same thing.'

Aarin forced himself to breathe. 'You're not listening to me. If Darred has you both, the greater his leverage. If you leave now, if you take the army with you, you take away that leverage. But you won't, will you? Because you *want* to go. You want your chance to kill him.'

'And you don't?'

'Not like this!'

'Why not?'

'Because I don't know what he has done!' The words were an angry shout. 'I don't know what he has done,' he said again, more quietly. 'And I don't know what will happen if he dies.'

Galydon silenced Kallis's angry retort. 'Explain.'

Aarin forced his rapid breathing to calm. Memory recalled Belegast's mindless, destructive grief after his son had died at Aarkan's hands. No, not his son. Lorrimer's. They could not risk that, not here, not now.

'If I die, Silverwing will go mad with grief. That is the price of the bond. If that death is violent and sudden, the greater the risk that madness will be utterly out of control. This dragon lost his mage in the Severing and ever since has been trapped by the device Darred now wears. There has been no recovery, no healing. He believes Darred is Cadyr. Break that illusion—kill Darred—and you risk breaking that dragon's mind.'

'So you would sacrifice Jeta for the sanity of a dragon?' Kallis asked.

'Don't you understand? Haven't you seen enough of what they can do? Do you want to unleash a mindless, savage creature to seek revenge?'

Galydon was frowning. 'Are you saying we cannot kill him?'

'I'm saying it is too great a risk, at this moment, when we do not know what will happen.'

Kallis shook his head in disgust. 'Let me get this straight. If Darred dies, the dragon loses its mind. But if the dragon dies, so does Darred.'

'Is that true?' Galydon asked. 'The dragon's death will cause Darred's?'

'It's true,' Kallis said grimly. 'But he won't harm the dragon or let anyone else do so.'

'I can't,' Aarin retorted. 'Why won't you understand? Their lives are in my charge. They are the only reason I'm alive. Please, listen to me. Get everyone out of here—pull the army back to Rhiannas. Do it now while you still can.' Because the presence of that army constrained his ability to act and Darred *would* use it against him.

'You should do as he says,' Kinseris said, and Aarin flashed him a grateful look.

Galydon looked between them, then shook his head. 'I'm sorry,' he told Aarin, regret in his voice. 'I understand, but Kallis is right. I can no more let you go up against Darred on those terms than I can leave Vannarai defenceless and allow the enemy to walk into Lothane unchallenged.'

'I will go,' Kinseris said into the fraught silence. 'If someone must go, let it be me.'

Aarin felt of stab of guilt. Of all of them, Kinseris would understand Aarin's impossible dilemma, and he was trying to give him a way out. As though Kinseris in Darred's hands would mean nothing to him, as though their friendship meant nothing. And he knew he had no one to blame for that but himself.

But his protest was lost as Kallis said, 'No. It must be me. Because of everyone, my loss is the least damaging, as you have pointed out.' Now he had won, there was no bitterness in those words. No satisfaction either. Just simple fact.

The light flickered for an instant, making Aarin dizzy, as the weight of that decision cracked the shields he had built. 'Kallis, please. It's a trap.'

But Kallis was immovable. 'I'm sorry, Aarin. I *am* going.'

TEN

AARIN HEARD KALLIS calling after him, but he didn't stop. There was nothing more to say.

As he walked, he threw his link with Silverwing wide open, each footstep taking him deeper within the coil of their magic. By the time his hands gripped scaled ridges to pull himself astride, he was back in the Dream and the First Age was alive around them. He felt the ripple of their passage spread outwards, touching the dragons still caught here, waiting, and he felt their response as a great swell of yearning for the place he had come from.

Silverwing flew through clear, open skies even as Aarin felt his own substance fading. *Why are we here, Æisoul?*

For Eiador. Because it was the only thing he could do. The only option he had left.

But he is not here.

Yes he is. And he let the vision unspool before them.

In the space where Eiador had been—before Darred had taken the dragon out of the dream and into the *now*—an imprint remained. A memory. That part of the dragon that was not wholly free, that remained trapped within the device that contained its essence and its will.

Aarin felt his resolve falter. Because it was a vision of joy, of freedom. As Eiador soared and rolled through the skies of a world that was gone forever, scales the deep red of iron ore burnished by the morning sun, he saw a creature transfigured by joy. Where before his existence had been an endless cry of pain, Darred's deception had given the dragon back the appearance of life.

He watched and knew he had lost.

He will not hear me.

Then let me try.

The dream shifted. The landscape did not change, but it was subtly altered as Silverwing took control of the vision and the dragon reshaped the world through his eyes.

Through Silverwing's farsighted gaze, Aarin saw Eiador transformed. The shadowy outline of chains laced around his outstretched wings, tethered to a point just out of sight, and joyful somersaults were rewritten as the recoil of those chains pulled taut each time the dragon sought to fly free. The proud head drooped, eyes like dull river stones, dimmed of life and brightness.

He will not listen, said Silverwing, *but maybe he will* see.

And Aarin felt his feet touch the shifting ground of the Long Dream as Silverwing left him behind, and could only watch as the dragon took to the air, silver streaking towards rusty red. The call that went out, dragon to dragon, echoed deep in his bones, as two ancient creatures met in flight, one free and one shackled to a destructive lie. He watched as Silverwing led Eiador on a twisting dance, forcing the other dragon to the limits of its chains, again and again, stretching its endurance to the point of exhaustion as it tried to follow the eldest.

But no matter how Silverwing pushed, how he coaxed, no matter how hard he tried to lift the blinkers from Eiador's eyes, the dragon remained enthralled, tugged sharply back over and over from the freedom it craved.

The sun moved through the sky, marking the rapid progression of the hours, the cold morning light transforming into the warmth of afternoon. And all the time Aarin was seeking Eiador's mind, trying to find a way in, a chink through which he could forge a connection. And break one. He summoned his memory of Cadyr as he had glimpsed him in Eiador's mind and came up against a projection of the man so strong, so solid, that he knew Eiador had already gone far beyond his reach.

And then Cadyr was no longer there, he was *here*.

Pale hair glowing like fire in the setting sun, whipped into tangles by the powerful beat of the dragons' wings, the long-dead mage faced him across the empty landscape of an age before Men. A smile hovered on his lips, faintly mocking, and though he wore a different face and stood far out of his own time, Aarin knew him.

Great wings eclipsed the orange glow of sunset, casting the man into shadow. Then Silverwing was there, a blast of dragon-fire engulfing the false mage where he stood. But the flames licked harmlessly at the edges of his shield, flickering and dying even as Silverwing wheeled around for a second pass.

Cadyr/Darred spread his arms, looking straight at Aarin, a question in his eyes.

Silverwing's jaws opened, dragon-fire burning deep in his throat.

Darred opened his hands, flashes of silver falling through his fingers, and Aarin screamed, *Stop!*

The silver disks revolved as they fell, the rising moon glinting on the dragons engraved on their surface. Behind him, the outlines of those dragons were drawn in ghostly relief against the cloudless sky. Hostages to hatred.

A long screech ripped through the air. Chains snapped taut, bringing Eiador tumbling through the skies to Darred's side, where the rust-red dragon unfurled its fettered wings to encircle its mage in their protective shadow.

Silverwing's fury and hatred flooded Aarin's mind as the dragon landed beside him. He laid a hand on a silver flank and felt the dragon-fire surge within as the moon continued its remorseless journey through the sky. The beat of his heart sped up to match the urgent march of time.

Darred mimicked his gesture, eyes glittering with vicious laughter as he set the silver disks spinning once more. And this time it was not dragons that Aarin saw reflected on their surface, but different likenesses. Friends.

The threat was unmistakable, the implications unthinkable.

This must not be. Silverwing's hatred was a visceral thing, something primal and deep and utterly inhuman.

Each life in Darred's hands tied their own a little tighter. They could not help Eiador. The dragon had made its choice, the choice of a mind lost too long to the madness of grief. But they could and must protect those creatures whose choice yet lay before them.

To do that he needed the freedom to act without fear of the consequences to the people he loved.

He stepped out of the Dream, banishing Darred from it, and emerged into the first dull glow of the new dawn.

They could not allow Darred to take the other dragons, and he could not endure Kallis and Jeta in Darred's hands.

It was time.

'He's not here,' Kallis growled, stalking back into the clearing. He had quartered the mercenary camp looking for Aarin, but there was no sign of him. 'If he's gone…'

'I doubt it,' Callan murmured. 'You made that impossible.'

Kallis narrowed his eyes. 'And what should I have done, Callan? Let Aarin give himself to Darred, just like Jeta did?'

'Is that what he was going to do?' Callan asked with maddening calm. 'Isn't it what you're doing?'

'No, it's not!'

Callan cocked his head. 'Isn't it?'

Shaking his head in disgust, Kallis threw himself to the ground on the far side of the fire. But within a few moments he was back on his feet, pacing from one end of the clearing to the other. He should be resting before the exchange at dawn, but Aarin's absence gnawed at him. They had not spoken since the disastrous confrontation that morning. He had not even *seen* him. One minute he had been walking away through the camp, and the next he was gone.

Callan watched him from his perch on a tree trunk that had been dragged into the camp to serve as a bench. 'Time does not move faster just because you do.'

Kallis bit back a scathing retort. It would do no good to take out his uneasy conscience on Callan. He knew this was a terrible idea. But when all your options are bad, the least terrible idea becomes the best.

As if he could read his mind, Callan said, 'Aarin is far from defenceless.'

'I know that,' he growled. 'But there are three dragons out there, Callan.

Three! And an army. And defence is all he has.'

'If you understand that, why make this harder?'

And good intentions were forgotten. 'You think I should have let him go?' he demanded. 'You've been stuck closer to his side than your own brother since you all arrived, and you're telling me we should just have pulled out and left him to Darred?'

'I'm telling you to listen!' Callan snapped, as close to anger as Kallis had ever seen him, and he knew he had touched a nerve, he just had no idea which one. 'Just for once, listen to what he's trying to tell you. Don't do this.'

Kallis glared back. 'When he says something worth listening to, then I'll listen.' And he snatched up his sword belt from where it hung from the tree trunk.

Callan's hand closed on his wrist. 'Where are you going?'

He jerked his arm free. 'Where do you think?'

'It's not time. There's hours yet till dawn.'

'And?' Kallis snarled. 'You know where I'll be.' He couldn't just sit around any longer. If the plans changed, they knew where to find him.

He heard Callan call after him as he walked away, but he didn't look back.

ELEVEN

JETA WOKE TO the murmur of voices, low and hurried. It was dark and she was careful not to move or make a sound. Her back was to the chair where Hanlon sat chained, day and night, but she had a sense of another beside him, a man, crouching down. It was this other who was speaking, and though she could not make out his words, his tone was urgent not aggressive. A friend, or at least not an enemy.

A cramp flared in her leg and she twitched. Silence fell. Then Hanlon said, very quietly, 'Jeta Elorna. If you're awake, it is polite to say so.'

Heat flooded her face and she was glad of the concealing darkness. 'I'm awake,' she said, just as softly, turning onto her side and sitting up with an effort.

There was a shifting behind her, in thought and space, as the men adjusted to her waking presence.

'We do not have much time,' Hanlon told her after a pause, and though his tone was calm and unhurried she sensed an urgency to match the words. 'Darred has been ill but he is recovering, and when he does, you cannot still be here. But there are things we must know before we can act. Do you understand?'

She nodded. 'I understand.'

'This is one of my captains. He has just come from Lothane and he has questions for you.'

She took in Hanlon's visitor, no more than an outline in the darkness save for the bright halo of his hair. But she could feel his eyes on her, studying, assessing. She could feel his doubts.

'You claim Kinseris is alive?'

'He is.' To Hanlon she said, 'It was another of your captains who brought us here. Gerain.'

The men exchanged a look over her head. 'Gerain is dead,' the fair-haired man said. 'He cannot speak for you.'

She felt a spark of anger at his implication. 'Do I need someone to speak for me?'

'Yes, you do. How many in your party? Describe them.'

'Why?' she asked defiantly. 'How do I know I can trust *you?*'

'You must answer,' Hanlon told her, but it was less command than request, and it reminded her that they were not enemies, and that she needed him.

She told Hanlon's captain what he wanted to know, and again felt the men exchange an unseen look. The tension in the tent relented a fraction.

'What was the name of the man who betrayed Kinseris?'

'Escarian,' she said, surprised. 'Why −?'

'How did you escape?'

Suppressing her irritation, Jeta repeated the tale she had already told Hanlon.

'The captain's name?' her interrogator demanded.

She told him that too. She knew now what he was doing. With each detail, his hostility eased. 'Are they here?' she asked. 'Kestel and Trad?'

She heard a muffled chuckle, but neither man answered. Kinseris had sent the Ancai and Trad south to find out what had happened to Hanlon. But no, Hanlon had said this man had come from Lothane. She tried again. 'What will you do?'

It was like she had ceased to exist. Though she could not see their faces, she could feel the intensity of their silence.

'How long?' she heard Hanlon ask at last.

The blond man shrugged. 'Four months. At least. Too long.' He sounded frustrated. 'And we would have committed everything.'

Her heart fluttered, a tantalising sliver of hope after months of despair. 'Please. You have to −'

'We don't *have* to do anything,' the man cut her off, low and harsh. 'Understand, if we do this—if we abandon all our plans, as we would have to do—and this hope you offer is not real, we lose much more than a simple gamble. We lose everything we have worked for to this point, and more besides.'

The words reminded her of a council in Ephenor, when Shrogar had sought to persuade his doubting captains to risk everything on a wild gamble to rescue Aarin and Kinseris from Kas'Tella on just such an uncertain promise. And these men now faced the same choice, to give up all their small, hard-won gains, that together could never deliver the victory they sought but might at least blunt the force of their eventual defeat—to give up the small war they could control—and risk it all on her word that what they stood to gain outweighed what they could lose.

Like Shrogar before him, Hanlon had sufficient trust, or desperation, to take that chance. It was his captain who did not know her who needed convincing. And this time she was horribly aware just how flimsy the hope she offered them was.

'They'll come,' she said fiercely, hoping she was right. Hoping that a promise made so many months ago could be fulfilled. That those who could fulfil it were still alive and free to do so. 'If you go, they will be there.'

There was a rustle of movement as the man stood. Then Hanlon's voice, barely more than a whisper. 'Davi.'

His companion went very still. 'Admiral.' It was a plea.

Hanlon ignored it. 'I need you to go.'

'My place is with you. Sarelle can go.'

'No, Davi,' Hanlon said gently. 'It must be you.'

The captain, Davi, exhaled a long breath. Then he nodded. 'Yes, Sir.' Captain to his admiral.

Hanlon turned to Jeta. 'We sent something to Kinseris. A weapon. Do you know where it is?'

She thought of Kinseris' anguish the day he had learned of Hanlon's supposed death. The day he told her what he had hidden deep under the citadel. *May Tesserion forgive me, I have tried to destroy them.*

'I know,' she said to the man who had sent it to him, and she told him. It was the second of the two things Kinseris had asked of Fylian before they had fled Kas'Tella. To safeguard something he hoped would never need to be used; the means to use it, if it did. It was the first request that had seemed so very far out of reach that might now have a chance of being fulfilled.

Hanlon said nothing for a long moment, and she could not tell whether he was relieved or disappointed. 'Then it is out of our reach and out of our hands.' He turned once more to his captain. 'Davi, go now. Don't wait. Do what you need to do, but I must know nothing further.'

Davi muttered something under his breath, then said explosively, 'They have to hold. Do you understand?' He was talking to Jeta now. 'If we do this, you have to hold.'

'Daviyan.' Hanlon's voice rapped out, as close to an order as she had heard from him yet. 'Go.'

His captain snapped to attention, responding to the tone of command. Then he knelt before his admiral, head bowed. They did not touch. They did not need to. Hanlon, his hands chained at his back, inclined his own head. Then, without a backward glance, the man stood and was gone.

Hanlon turned to Jeta. His voice, when he spoke, was curiously light. 'Jeta Elorna. There is one more thing you must do for me.'

Jeta blinked back the sudden wetness in her eyes. She concentrated on Hanlon's shadowed form. 'One more thing, then you get me out?'

He laughed. 'You can hardly help me from here, can you? Now, listen. In a few hours you will be free. It's all arranged. And you will take with you a message for Kinseris. Because Davi is right. They must hold.'

Kestel watched as the fair-haired Farnorian exited the tent that housed Darred's prisoners. Some distance away, in the darkness between the dying campfires, Trad was waiting, ready to cry warning should a patrol come too close. But discipline was slack here in this camp, and the officers either complacent after two years of unchallenged occupation or disinclined to exert themselves in the service of an invader, despite their reluctant assimilation into its military ranks.

And Darred, though more than dangerous enough, was not a military commander. Everywhere around him the Ancai saw evidence of his failure to impose the kind of discipline Galydon had done in Lothane. The army feared him, but the command structure required to weld these disparate groups into an effective force was almost entirely absent. And, as it happened, Darred was not currently in a position to punish any dereliction of duty.

He still could not believe how close Jeta had come to killing him, if rumour could be believed. If indeed it was Jeta inside that tent, and if she was, in fact, still alive. He itched to find Darred, to try to finish the job she had started, but Darred had sealed himself within a circle of wards none but another Kas'Talani could break. And his duty to Kinseris compelled him to do what he could to protect the woman who had put herself at terrible risk to protect him. Not that there was much he could do without the help of the man standing casually outside what should have been the most heavily guarded tent in the camp as if he didn't have a care in the world.

The man looked around him in an unhurried way, before moving away from the tent. He caught Kestel's eye and the Ancai fell in beside him as he strolled through the sleeping camp as though he didn't have a care in the world. These Farnorians conducted their small, needling rebellion with blithe confidence, despite the horrific fate that awaited them if they were caught. The corpse of Darred's most recent victim, mutilated almost beyond recognition, still decorated the southwestern corner of the camp. Almost beyond recognition but not quite. Kestel had, after all, spent several weeks on the man's ship on the voyage to Amadorn.

It had not been hard to insinuate their way into the sprawling camp, hiding in plain sight among so many of their countrymen. It had been harder, much harder, to find the threads of resistance and trace them back to some kind of authority, which he now knew resided in this man, absent for many weeks and only now returned, and the man in whose long shadow he stood.

They had never met before, despite Kinseris's extensive dealings with the Farnorians, but the Ancai knew who this was. Daviyan. The captain of Hanlon's flag ship. His second. If he could not deal directly with Hanlon, Daviyan was the next best thing.

'She's here,' Daviyan said eventually as he sidestepped a snoring soldier. 'She hasn't been hurt. That might change.'

'Can you get her out?'

Kestel caught a flash of white teeth in the darkness. 'Not me, I'm to head south. But yes, we'll get her out.'

Finally. Kestel looked away, hiding the force of his relief. 'South?'

There was a not entirely happy silence, then Daviyan said, 'She corroborated your story. He's convinced. You're to come with me.'

Kestel raised an eyebrow at that. 'Am I?'

'Yes, you are. Both of you.'

It was not so much a command as a condition, and Kestel knew he had no choice. His duty to Kinseris was clear. He had come here to find this man or his master, to use their ships to do what no one else could. But it was Jeta who, in the end, had done what he and Trad had not been able to do alone. And it was Jeta who had put herself in danger to protect Kinseris. If he left now, he had to entrust her release to people he did not know, and whose ability to protect her was equally unknown. Kinseris would never forgive him if harm came to her that he could have prevented.

They reached the Amadorian quadrant of the camp, and his companion crouched down by a smouldering fire, soaking up the last of its fading warmth. Figures crept out of the darkness to join them. Trad appeared like a wraith at Kestel's side, and two more, both women, knelt in the drying mud by Daviyan.

'Jeta?' Trad asked.

Kestel shook his head, glancing at Daviyan.

'Safe for now,' the man said briefly. 'She's not your concern any longer.'

Kestel gripped Trad's wrist, silencing his retort. 'She will always be our concern,' he told Daviyan.

'This is a war, and she chose to be a soldier,' Daviyan said, his voice harsh with his own losses. 'My people will do what they can—my admiral wants her safe. But there are more important issues at stake, and you know it.'

He turned away, dismissing the matter, and Kestel tightened his grip on Trad's wrist. This was not the time, and the man was right.

Daviyan looked at the woman on his right, lean and weathered with iron-grey hair tied in a sailor's queue. 'Sarelle, get word to your crews. We're going south—all the way to Caledan—and we're going to need your ships. All your ships.'

The woman called Sarelle nodded. 'Aye, Davi. Where?'

Daviyan rocked back on his heels, thinking. 'We can't risk anywhere in Farnor. Somewhere east of Taslor would be safer.'

She shook her head. 'Safer but slower.' Taking a stick from the fire, she sketched a map into the dried mud and Kestel tried to match the rough scratches to his scant knowledge of Amadorn's southern coast. 'Taslor offers the most direct trade route to the islands. If we go far enough to the east to avoid the Caledani garrisons, we lose the island current and add an extra week to our journey.'

Daviyan swore. 'Taslor is as heavily garrisoned as Farnor's major ports. You take your ships in there, they'll be impounded and your crews strung up.'

Sarelle grinned. 'Ah, Davi, you forget who you're talking to. I've been taking my ships in and out of Taslor's waters for longer than you've been at sea, and never paid a silver in duty on their cargo. Plenty of safe berths along that stretch of coast. We time it right, they can come in at night and pick you up and be gone before anyone knows we were there.'

'When do we leave?' It was the other woman, a younger, rounder version of Sarelle.

Daviyan stood. 'Now. Tonight. Get your people out, but do not tell them why. Two weeks from now we must be under sail.'

Trad shook off Kestel's hand as he surged to his feet. 'Jeta?'

'That is a task for others,' the captain told him. 'You must leave, now, with us. You know too much. I cannot let you stay here and put everything at risk. And I will need you when we get there.'

'You do not command us!' Trad told him furiously.

Daviyan smiled once before turning away. 'I do now. You want me to do this? Then we do it my way.'

TWELVE

THEY CAME FOR her two hours before dawn with the change in the guards outside their prison. At first she thought they were Darred's men, come to take her. Then one of them, slipping inside, whispered a greeting to Hanlon while the other knelt to undo her bonds, and she knew they were friends.

As the ropes around her ankles gave way, she caught a glimpse of dark-lashed eyes and a curl of dark hair. The woman helped her to her feet, steadying her as she stamped feeling back into cramped limbs. Then she handed her an old cloak. 'Put this on. Hide your hair.'

Jeta turned to Hanlon. 'What will he do to you?'

He looked her in the eye with the one that remained to him. 'He won't touch me. He needs me.'

It was a lie and they both knew it. 'Come with me.'

He shook his head. 'I can do more from here.'

The woman tugged at her arm. 'We have to go.'

Jeta shook her off. 'More than you could do if you were free?' She did not believe him, and from his scowl she knew he had heard it. 'Come with me,' she said again.

Hanlon turned his head away, his eye bright. 'He has my son.'

'There's no time,' her rescuer said urgently. 'Admiral…'

'Go,' he said fiercely, not looking at her, and she let herself be led to the door. But she kept her eyes on him as her rescuers held a hurried conversation over her head.

There was a pressure on her arm, insistent, and she turned her attention to the woman. 'Follow me, but do not run. If we are separated, keep heading

381

northeast until you get to the perimeter. Don't stop for anyone. We'll find you. Understand?'

Her companion hissed, 'Now.' And the woman pulled her out of the tent and into the night, brushing past the two men standing this guard duty, who ignored them as if they did not exist. They had gone only thirty yards or so when she heard a shouted query and risked a backward glance.

A hand on her neck forced her head back round. 'Don't stop. Don't look back.'

It was too like Frankesh. At any moment she expected to hear an alarm, a cry of pain, the sounds of a struggle, but none came. Instead, she heard relaxed laughter, fading with every step she took towards freedom.

No one tried to stop them, and her fear grew with every step. It could not be this easy. Then they were through the perimeter and her legs were trembling, so fierce was her relief. She barely remembered the walk to the river, as black spots danced in her vision and her breath came in short, painful gasps. At some point her guide dropped back to walk beside her, and Jeta was aware she was talking but the words did not register. It wasn't until the cold water was swirling round her ankles and hands were helping her into a boat that the pressure in her chest started to ease.

The boat pushed off. The first dull glow of the dawn was visible on the horizon, enough to let her see the faces of her rescuers, bent to the oars. She looked past them, eyes straining to the distant shore, but it was little more than black shadows in the pre-dawn darkness.

Something made her turn back. And there, standing on the southern bank, a man watched.

A smile on his lips, Darred raised a hand in mock salute.

She froze, heart thudding painfully, as the boat pulled further and further away and Darred did nothing to stop it. As he let her go.

The woman called out a soft warning as the little craft was jostled by the fast-flowing current in the main channel. She lost sight of Darred as the sharp movement tossed her about and when she looked back he was gone. But she could still see his face. Smiling at her.

The world narrowed to pinpoints of awareness—the slap of oars on the water, the sound of her breathing, sawing in and out—but her mind was utterly blank.

'Out,' the woman ordered, and thought snapped back. They had reached the other bank.

Jeta clambered over the side, gasping at the cold as the waters of the Istelan lapped at her knees. The boat was already disappearing into the gloom, leaving her alone in the shallows.

The splashing must have alerted a sentry because suddenly there was a line of silhouettes on the beach and arms were reaching to pull her out of the water.

Someone snapped a question and she threw back her hood. 'I need to see Galydon.' She had already been gone too long. They had to know she was safe.

She ignored the clamour of questions, repeating her request, all the time seeing Darred's knowing smile, terrified of what it meant. The camp was in motion all around them as her escort led her to where Galydon was already up and deep in conversation with the clan captain Petrik. His expression morphed to horror as he caught sight of her, and he grabbed a passing soldier. 'Get a message to Kallis. Now! Tell him Jeta's back. And find Aarin.'

Fear crushed her chest. 'What's happening?'

He ignored her, issuing a stream of orders she didn't understand, long strides taking him away from her.

'General!' she shouted after him. 'Please, I must talk to you.'

Usually so controlled, Galydon's fury was plain on his face, and some of it was at her. At any other time she would not have dared test that anger, but this was too important. She had made a promise and it had secured her freedom. Braving Galydon's fury was a small price to pay.

She caught up with him, stumbling as the cold, wet skirts of her dress tangled her legs. 'I have a message for you. From Limina's husband.'

Galydon's face stilled. He let out a long breath. 'Darred has him?'

She nodded. 'He got me out.'

'You escaped?' His face was strangely bleak.

'Yes. No. He helped me, but Darred let him.'

He stared at her in silence for a beat, then took her arm. 'Come with me.'

He set a fast pace and she struggled to keep up. 'General, you must listen. He lied about the truce. He never meant to honour it.'

'We know,' Galydon said shortly, not slackening his pace.

No, you don't she wanted to tell him, but Galydon was bundling her into a tent and Kinseris was there, and the sudden rush of relief pushed everything else aside. *He was still here!*

His face froze as he saw her and she saw something of the general's shock in his eyes.

'I've sent messengers,' Galydon said as he released her. He sounded tired and grim. 'There is nothing else we can do.'

Relief turned to uncertainty. She took a hesitant step, and he was *right there,* holding her, and at last she felt safe. 'Why?' he murmured. 'Jeta, why?'

Her eyes filled with tears. She felt weak and shaky, her heart fluttering too fast, and there was a tremble in her voice as she said, 'I'm sorry, I could not let him kill you.'

He took a shuddering breath, his grip tightening. 'Jeta…'

Behind her, Galydon said impatiently, 'You said you have a message from Hanlon?'

And Kinseris released her, eyes flaring with sudden hope. 'Admiral Hanlon? He's alive?'

She nodded. 'He's alive. He's Darred's prisoner, but he's alive.' She tried to sort her thoughts into some kind of order. 'He knows… I told him. But he needs four months, perhaps more.' She turned to Galydon. 'You have to hold on for that long.'

'Why?' Kinseris asked, his voice not quite steady.

She smiled. 'Because they're going. They're taking the ships to Caledan. They're going, Kinseris.'

She saw the impact of those words hit him, but his reaction was muted, distracted. Something was wrong.

'That's all?' Galydon demanded. 'He said nothing else?'

'It's not all.' Hanlon's warning echoed in her ears, the message he had given her for Kinseris. *Listen to me, girl. He hates the queen. He hates her with an all-*

consuming passion that is twin to madness. He wants to break her more than he wants Lothane. He won't end this until he's had his revenge. 'I was wrong,' she admitted. 'This wasn't about Kinseris. It isn't even about Aarin. It's about the queen. It's about Sedaine.'

There was a small silence, then Galydon said, his voice tight, 'About Sedaine how?'

Jeta looked at Kinseris, who knew Darred better than any man alive, and saw that he understood. *It is never just about balancing the scales, not to him. It is about punishment. About making sure his victims know never to cross him again, that they never can cross him again.*

She returned her attention to Galydon. 'Sedaine betrayed him. That's why he's doing this. He can take Amadorn any time he likes, but he doesn't, because he is punishing her for reneging on their bargain.'

Kinseris rubbed a hand over his face, suddenly looking every one of his years. He avoided Galydon's eyes. 'Everything he does will be to punish her. *Everything.*'

He wasn't looking at Galydon, but Jeta was, and she saw his face go grey. She felt faint as she realised what she had missed. 'Where's Aarin?'

Galydon glanced at her without really seeing her. 'He was right.'

'Who was?' And then she realised who else was absent. 'Where's Kallis?'

It was Kinseris who told her, drawing her attention away from Galydon and the look on his face. 'He has gone to meet Darred. He offered an exchange—your life for Kallis.'

She felt dizzy. 'But… why would you let him?' Then, more urgently, 'Aarin would not let him.' Because Aarin would know how Darred would use that leverage. Kallis should know too, but Kallis wouldn't be thinking straight. And Darred would know that, he would use that. He *had* used it.

Maker, if Kallis went… Aarin would go.

I've sent messages.

Darred smiling at her from the bank.

What better way to punish Sedaine than to kill her son?

And then she was screaming at them.

THIRTEEN

DARRED WAS WAITING in the clearing. He was not alone. Two priests stood a few paces to his right while behind him soldiers fanned out in a half-circle.

'Really?' Kallis asked as he stepped from the cover of the trees and strolled forward, hand on his hilt. 'I'm flattered.'

Darred smiled. In the fickle shadows of approaching dawn he looked pale but composed. A sweep of his arm encompassed his silent entourage. 'I did not get where I am by underestimating my enemies. And you, Kallis, would happily murder me, truce or no.'

Kallis grinned, baring his teeth. 'I can't recall that we ever got to negotiating that truce.'

'Indeed not,' Darred agreed. 'I can only admire your determination to strike the first blow, and your delightful choice of weapon.'

Kallis forced himself not to react, but his fingers clenched in a painful grip on his sword. 'You were never going to honour a truce.'

It wasn't a question, but Darred answered it anyway, clearly enjoying himself. 'Of course not. Just like this is not an exchange. Frankly, I'm rather surprised to see you here. I thought you knew me better than that, or did you really think I would just give her back?'

He raised his hand and the two priests moved to stand close on either side. He looked at Kallis, one eyebrow raised in a question.

Kallis sighed and shouted a command into the shadows behind him. Then he unbuckled his sword and tossed it on the ground as Darred's soldiers stalked forward to surround him, weapons drawn. The familiar cold touch of magic settled into his bones, binding him tight. A sudden, familiar breeze fanned his cheek. He smiled savagely, and said, 'No one expected you to just give her back.'

There was utter, frozen silence. Then the darkness was momentarily complete as an even darker shadow swooped overhead. An instant later Aarin walked into the clearing.

Glittering silver eyes swept over Kallis without expression before coming to rest on Darred. Their eyes locked, and Kallis had the distinct impression of wordless communication. Then Darred smiled, and there was such satisfaction in his expression that Kallis felt a chill run down his spine.

'Master of dragons.' He offered Aarin a mocking half-bow. 'I was not sure you would come.'

Then Aarin said quietly, 'No.' The cold menace in that one word froze Kallis to the spot even as he felt the touch of Darred's magic dissolve.

'No?' Darred asked. 'But you do not even know what I'm offering.'

Aarin ignored him. 'Release them.'

Darred spread his hands. 'You've already released the mercenary. As for the girl, I'm afraid it's no longer within my power to return her to you.'

Kallis was moving before his brain had fully processed the words, a red haze in front of his eyes. He snatched his sword from the mud as the soldiers melted uncertainly away. But Aarin, one arm held out behind him, stopped him in his tracks.

'Release them,' he said again.

Darred laughed. 'Ah, I see I was not mistaken. But the answer is still no. In fact,' he added silkily, twisting his wrists to shake two blades into his hands, 'I rather think it is time I took them, don't you?' And before Kallis realised what was happening, Darred turned the daggers on the priests on either side, slitting their throats in two swift movements.

Through his own stunned shock, Kallis felt Aarin tense, the hand on his chest clenching as a sensation like static brushed over his skin.

Darred turned from his contemplation of the bodies, his eyes laughing. 'Oh, you don't need to worry about that,' he told Aarin, nudging aside the cloak of the nearest priest with his foot. He leaned down and unhooked something from the man's tunic, holding it up to the light in fingers stained red. Silver glinted dully in the insipid dawn. 'I already have them well under control.'

Kallis watching in growing horror as Darred removed the device from the second priest. 'He's mad.'

But Aarin didn't seem to hear him, his whole attention riveted on Darred. He said, in urgent warning, 'Don't do this.'

Darred's half-smile was tinged with madness. 'But I already have.'

There was a distant thrumming and the air around them began to pulse. Kallis took a step back. 'What the −?'

Then Aarin's hand was on his shoulder, forcing him to turn.

'Go!'

Kallis stared stupidly at him. Aarin shoved him, hard, and they were both running, back towards the trees and their illusion of shelter. As they reached them, the mercenaries Kallis had brought with him fell in behind them, and Kallis his own fear reflected on their tight faces—because they all knew what was coming.

Aarin's eyes kept flicking upwards. Kallis twisted his head to follow his gaze and tripped and nearly fell. The mage gripped his arm, hauling him on. Kallis realised he was furious. He stopped dead in shocked surprise as Silverwing dropped out of the sky just ahead.

'Aarin…'

But the mage didn't turn as he swung himself up the dragon's wing. Only as Silverwing's muscles bunched to take off did he look at Kallis, his face empty of emotion. 'Get out of here. Don't let this be for nothing.'

Then they were gone.

Kallis hunched his shoulders as the powerful downdraught beat against him. When he could open his eyes, the lightening sky was empty and he could not shake a feeling of dread.

He confronted his present predicament. Darred's soldiers were still out there, the Maker knew what else was coming for them, and they were on their own. He split his men into pairs, sending each pair off in a different direction. Separated, they had a better chance of evading both threats.

Then he was running too, as his mind replayed the image of Darred removing the dragon devices from the dead priests. He had felt Aarin's shock.

Don't do this.

I already have.

But what had he done?

He collided with a warm body and twisted, knife in hand, and bore his assailant to the ground. As he brought his knife up to the man's throat, another hand gripped his wrist.

'Kallis!'

Callan. He sat back, releasing his grip on the man beneath him, and Callan let go of his wrist. Lysan sat up rubbing his elbow and grimacing.

Callan asked, urgent, 'Did the messenger find you?'

'What messenger?'

'From Galydon,' Lysan said. 'We sent him after you.'

Kallis shook his head. 'He didn't reach me.'

There was a hesitant silence. Then Callan asked, 'Where's Aarin?'

Horrified realisations cascaded through his mind.

It is no longer within my power to return her to you.

And he *knew*. Spinning around, he ran back the way he had come, Callan and Lysan behind him.

I was not sure you would come.

Kallis swore. Darred had been after Aarin from the start. And they had played into his hands with every decision they had made.

The pulsing grew in intensity and a dragon's shriek—too close—was answered by another, then another.

'Kallis!' Callan caught up and grabbed his arm, forcing him to stop. 'What's happening?'

But all Kallis could hear was the last thing Aarin had said to him. *Don't let this be for nothing.* He looked up to see the three dragons flying in from the south and heard his own words, spoken in anger weeks ago. *What are you going to do about them?*

He stopped running, hands resting on his knees as he sucked in lungfuls of air. It was too late now to stop what his error had set in motion. All he could do was watch the consequences play out and hope it did not end in tragedy.

FOURTEEN

AARIN WATCHED KALLIS dwindle into a dark speck below him as Silverwing flew higher and higher, circling upwards to give them the advantage of height. He felt the wave of alarm swell over Silverwing and an instant later he sensed it too as the dragons rose after them *as one,* with a single controlling influence. An impossible, single mind.

He glanced back in a kind of frozen panic, seeing the outline of Galydon's camp behind and below him—too close—and all plans unravelled. They would be given no chance to escape. Darred had engineered this conflict and he meant to force it to its devastating conclusion. He had to. The power of their pairing was the only thing that stood in his way. And he had stacked the deck against them, because Aarin had just shown him that he placed the lives of the dragons above any others.

The dragons were on them faster than thought. Aarin surrendered to the creature he rode. Silverwing knew this dance. Lorrimer knew it too, but his memories carried such a weight of sorrow that Aarin shied away from them, relying on Silverwing's millennia-old instincts to keep them clear of their attackers. Yet for all the dragon's skill, for all his grace in the air, Silverwing was old now, and Aarin could feel the dull ache in his flank as newly knitted muscles protested the exertion.

On instinct, Aarin reached out to smooth away the pain and felt a grunt of exasperated amusement from Silverwing.

It will not hinder me, Æisoul. These are children.

But they weren't. Every dragon still living was a survivor of the war that had ended their age. Every single one of them knew what it was to face another dragon in battle. And the dragons they were facing were still trapped in that war, hostage to the memories of men and women long dead, their desperate resolve fuelled and channelled by the man who now held their reins.

Aarin stretched himself flat along the curve where Silverwing's neck met his massive shoulders as his dragon looped and dived through the dawn.

They are linked, Silvering said grimly, confirming the suspicion that had been growing since Kallis had told him how Iraius had died. He wheeled through the air to avoid the slashing claws of another dragon. Aarin almost choked on the heartbreak of it.

Focus, Æisoul.

He pushed back the anguish, shutting his mind firmly on Lorrimer's leeching despair. He tagged Cadyr again. It was why he was here. He could not give up. And felt Eiador's grip tighten on the image of his dead mage. Millennia spent in grief-wracked enslavement had blurred the edges of the creature's sanity.

Linked, but not joined.

There was a difference, and it mattered. They had seen that in the Dream. Darred was not Cadyr. He could have tried to join with Eiador as himself, but he had chosen the surer path—to meld minds with the dragon under the guise of another. To manipulate, not partner. And in the process he had wrought an almost-Joining, a link that was forged from the memory of the magic of the Joining, not its substance. It gave him the powers of the link with none of its constraints. It gave him control. It gave him freedom.

Freedom to do it again, and again. To split himself once, twice, three times. He was no longer just Darred and Cadyr. To control three at once he must sustain four identities, a division of self no human mind could support.

And it had made him quite mad.

We cannot escape them like this.

Silverwing was tiring. Aarin needed to act.

But do what? His life had been spared in exchange for the freedom of the dragons. He *could not* turn his hand against them without breaking faith with Andeira. And these dragons were not free, whether they knew it or not. Their will had been stolen by another and it was a threat that hung over every dragon still bound to a Kas'Talani device. They were not his enemy.

A spiked wingtip brushed so close it tore a strip from the back of his tunic. They were being corralled closer and closer to the cliffs that sheltered Rhiannas's forces, but even if they could break out, to the south was Darred's camp. And Jeta. Darred had said he could not return her. Aarin refused to let his mind dwell on what that might mean.

He lies with every breath.

I know.

But whether she was there or not, whether she was even alive, he dared not unleash the kind of storm this could become over the heads of thousands of human lives. Lives that could be used to force his hand as long as Darred believed he was a threat. Somewhere far below, he was sure he could hear Darred laughing.

Two dragons wheeled towards them. Eiador hung suspended behind them, huge wings beating, then he dived straight for the camp.

In desperation, Aarin extended the shield of his power over the army camped below, and the destructive force of Darred's will hammered mercilessly against his hasty defences. They held. Just. And the scorching wave of flame passed harmlessly over the encampment, Eiador following in its wake, powerful wings taking him past and away. But in defending those below Aarin had left himself perilously exposed, and suddenly there was nowhere to go, nothing more to give, and Silverwing's panic pulsed.

Behind them was only the bleak, unforgiving rock of the cliff face. Above and ahead, the two remaining dragons waited.

To escape, they had to go *through* the enemy's attack. There was no choice, only a flicker of suspicion and the barest hint of an idea. Only an old man's memory of regret over a death that should not have happened.

Silverwing, understanding his intent, drew on his vast reservoir of energy. The dragons did not wield the magic. They *were* the magic. With every movement, every thought, they drew in and expended the power gifted by the link, as natural as breathing. Aarin breathed in the dawn now, the grey clouds heavy with rain to come, drawing to him the power of elemental Water as a desperate, final defence.

Eyes closed. Silverwing *flew*.

The fire burst over them.

The pain was white hot and molten.

It seared away thought. His control splintered and broke, and defence turned deadly.

Kallis stood on the cliff top, watching the lethal dance in awed silence. Callan and Lysan were beside him, and those others of his men who had managed to rejoin them. No one said a word. There were no words for what they were seeing.

Again and again, Aarin and Silverwing refused to engage, refused to fight. And again and again, the dragons got between them and freedom, stopping them from flying free.

They watched a dragon come so close that Kallis feared it had gored the mage from Silverwing's back. He felt Callan's arrested movement, his instinctive urge to *do something*.

'Come on, Aarin!' he growled. They could not win this way.

One of the dragons broke off, wheeling around and down. And with a jolt of horror Kallis realised they had forced the confrontation directly over the army's encampment. His heart thudded, almost to a stop, as the flames roared out, sheeting towards the unprotected troops, before it was turned at the last moment to glide harmlessly overhead. Then the trap sprung closed.

They heard the scream, man and dragon, as they were engulfed in a billowing wave of flame that came from above, below and all sides. Kallis could not tear his eyes from the sky, could barely hear past the hammering of his own heart and the harsh sawing of each in-drawn breath.

Out of the deadly burst of fire, Silverwing emerged, trailing black smoke, one wing burned almost through.

'Merciful Maker,' Callan breathed, horrified, as the pair tumbled through the sky, and Darred's dragons dived after them. Dived and caught them, coming together in a tangled mass of claws and teeth.

Then they were blind.

The pulse of light was bright enough to burn sight. The power sheeted out and Kallis was on his knees, hands shielding his eyes. The force of it rocked him where he knelt, and he braced himself against it. Then it was gone, rushing out like the tide, his ears popping as the pressure lifted. He dropped his hands to see the others doing the same, exchanging looks of shaky relief. But Kallis felt only dread.

The dawn had been cloudy and grey, but not a shred of cloud remained in the sky, as though they had been seared out of existence by the intensity of that burst of power. The light was oddly splintered, the rising sun suspended in pinpricks of brilliance. Of the dragons there was no sign.

Kallis drew in a shaky breath. Whatever they had done, whatever Aarin had intended, they had swept the board clear of Darred's most deadly weapons, but at terrible cost. The deaths that Aarin had been so desperate to prevent seemed certain, the clearing skies emptied of all life, and the one life he wanted to preserve above any other might even now be lost. As for his own… Kallis knew that this time there could be no last-minute reprieve. Nor could he wish for one. Not from that.

Don't let this be for nothing.

His throat closed, a tightness in his chest robbing him of breath. Of all the bloody stupid things he had done...

He had to move, to think. But just for the moment he could only stand there, his hands clenched in tight fists and his vision blurring.

All around him was silence. Disbelieving, as shocked as he felt. His breathing quickened. That it should end like this…

'Kallis.'

It was Callan. With an effort, Kallis tore his gaze from the sky to a face as stricken as his own. They were alone.

'We need to find them.'

Kallis nodded. His throat ached and it hurt to speak. 'Where?'

Callan pointed along the cliffs to where a wisp of smoke trailed from a distant crash site, trees and undergrowth scorched and flattened.

Kallis closed his eyes. He did not want to go to that place. But he had to. He owed it to Aarin. 'Let's go.'

FIFTEEN

THE SMELL HIT them first. A sickening stench of roasted meat. Kallis faltered and stopped. Beside him, Callan was bone-white under his fading desert tan. It took Kallis greater resolve that anything he had ever faced to force himself to keep walking, scrambling over the wreckage of the trees and scrub, walking the path the downed dragon had torn through the undergrowth.

Then they felt the heat and heard a creature's rasping breath. Kallis pushed his way past a screen of gorse, Callan behind him, and saw a broken sprawl of silver in the centre of a circle of scorched earth.

The great dragon turned his head towards them with an effort that was painful to watch. His scales were blackened with soot and his sides torn into ribbons by cruel talons. One wing was nothing more than tattered fragments of skin and fine, flensed bone. And on his back…

Kallis looked away. Nothing could have survived that inferno. For mercy, nothing *should*.

There was an agonised scraping as Silverwing dragged the ruined wing around, his eyes fixed on Callan, beseeching. Callan stumbled to his knees by the dragon's head, his fingers resting on the scarred scales of the creature's neck. A shudder rocked Silverwing's body and the … thing… on his back stirred.

Awakened to new horror, Kallis started forward. 'Callan…'

Callan turned, his face white. 'He's still alive.'

Swallowing bile, Kallis forced himself to take a step, then another, but Callan held him back. Ashamed of his relief, Kallis watched as the other man scrambled up the proffered wing, trying and failing not to cause pain. He looked away, finally, as Callan reached the charred figure at the base of the dragon's neck. He could not bring himself to think of it as Aarin.

It was the dragon who called him back, shifting its bulk once more to ease Callan's descent with his gruesome burden. He cradled the body across his chest and legs as he slipped and slid down the wing, his eyes anywhere but the horror in his arms. Reaching the ground, he laid Aarin as gently as he could next to Silverwing's flank. Then he lurched to his feet and took three unsteady strides before falling to his knees to be noisily sick.

Propelled at last by shame, Kallis moved towards the body of his friend, but Callan's out-flung arm stopped him in his tracks. 'Don't!' He took a breath, then another. 'Don't,' he repeated, and as Kallis hesitated the dragon dragged the remains of its wing back to enfold the body of the mage in tatters of silver scales. Then the great beast's eyes closed and its body heaved a shuddering breath and relaxed. The message was clear.

Kallis crouched beside Callan. 'We're just leaving them?'

Callan's face was very pale and Kallis could see the rapid pulse in his throat. His arms and clothes were streaked black and red where he had held Aarin against him, and the hands resting on his knees trembled violently.

'There is nothing we can do for them,' he said at last, rising to his feet.

Anguished, Kallis heard what Callan was really saying. And he needed no one to tell him that from such horrific injuries there could be no hope of recovery. And yet... 'We just leave him here to die?' He wouldn't, couldn't, accept that. Not after everything.

Callan looked from the pair by the cliff edge then up at the bright, empty sky. 'But where else should he die, Kallis?'

They had expected to die, all of them. Looking around the camp, Kinseris could see the same shaky relief on every face. His own hands were trembling with it. As the great dragon had broken through the clouds and its fire swept down, he knew he was watching his death, that there was no defence he could summon that could withstand the ferocity of that onslaught. And yet every shred of power he possessed was concentrated over one precious point in the camp.

But it never reached them. In the split second between life and death, something had deflected that deadly fire. As it poured harmlessly over their heads they had glimpsed, for an instant, the distant battle in the sky above. Then the light had burst, blindingly bright, and stolen their sight. And now there was nothing. He felt sick.

'Leave as soon as you can,' Galydon said as he mounted his horse. He looked down at Kinseris, his face grim. They both knew what that empty sky might mean. 'I will not be far behind you.'

Kinseris nodded, thinking of the woman in his tent, utter exhaustion dragging her under despite her fear. What would he tell her when she woke? What could he tell her?

The clan commander at his side shared a final, hurried conversation with Galydon, but Kinseris couldn't focus on the words. All around them, exhausted mercenaries were waking from the nightmare, their officers chivvying them out of their shock, making them move, think.

Time passed. He looked for Galydon, but he was gone. The clan captain, Petrik, was talking to him.

Kinseris shook his head. 'I'm sorry…' He had not been listening.

'Get some sleep,' the man told him gruffly, not without understanding. 'We move at midday.'

They all needed sleep. He should get back to Jeta. He should be there when she woke and wanted to know what had happened. But he stayed where he was a few minutes more, unable to tear his eyes away from the sky, searching for something, anything.

He must have moved eventually because he found himself outside his tent and the curve of the sun was higher in the sky. It was silent within, the girl still sleeping.

He ducked inside and stopped dead.

A figure stood in the shadows by the cot, looking down at Jeta. At Kinseris's indrawn breath he turned, the light falling on his face, and Kinseris felt his heart stop.

Face pale and eyes bloodshot, his hair tangled and filthy, Darred met his horrified look with the barest hint of a smile, for once utterly devoid of mockery. His clothes were in disarray, one sleeve torn and bloodstained. Below the turned-back cuff Kinseris could see the red rawness of a new scar. The scar Jeta had given him.

Darred saw the direction of his gaze but did not cover the cut. 'You nearly let another one die for you,' he murmured with a last look at Jeta. 'Really, Kinseris, you should not be so careless.'

But the weary tone did not match the needling words, as though the taunt was mere reflex. This was Darred as Kinseris had not seen him in decades, stripped of the manipulation and cruel wit that he placed between himself and the world. Exhaustion clung to him like threads of fading power. He was drenched in it.

Kinseris glanced at Jeta, asleep on the cot, painfully aware that there was *nothing* he would not do to keep her safe.

'She will not hear us,' Darred told him. 'No one will hear you. And there is nothing you can do that will touch me.'

Kinseris could feel the weight of his power all around them, surrounding the tent and its occupants in an impenetrable shield. 'Why are you here?'

Again that half-smile. 'For you.'

Kinseris felt strangely calm. He had always known, in the end, that it would come to this. It was, after all, why he had come to Amadorn. 'You have me. You don't need to hurt her.'

Darred laughed softly. 'You do not change. Such self-sacrifice. But it's never you who pays the price, is it? How many have died for you? Did you ever stop to count? And you look at me as though I am the monster.'

The words burned as they struck, too close to his own thoughts. Too close to truth. 'I look at you and see a friend I lost. But it is not too late.'

'Is that why you're here?' Darred asked, and he sounded genuinely curious, almost distressed. 'Do you think you can save me?'

'Do you need saving?'

Darred's mouth quirked. 'Not by you, Kinseris. Never by you.'

'Then why are you here?' he asked again.

Darred looked down at Jeta as she stirred in her sleep. His eyes were miles away. 'It was not me.'

'What was not you?'

'Escarian. No order of mine turned his hand against you. You did that all by yourself.'

Kinseris looked away so Darred would not see what that meant, what it cost. 'I never thought you did.'

For some reason that made Darred angry. 'Then you're a fool,' he sneered. 'A sentimental fool. Don't think it was friendship that stayed my hand.'

'I never thought that either.'

They stared at each other, too much and too little left unsaid, but there were no words to bridge the gulf that had opened where once there had been friendship. Too many things had passed in between. Darred broke the contact first, looking away and up through the half-open tent door. Then he crossed the space between them, slowing as he passed. Kinseris watched him, both wishing him gone and regretting the chance that was slipping away, however slender, to call this man back from the path he had chosen.

But Darred surprised him. He paused in the entrance, the grey light of morning already moulding itself around him. 'Good-bye, Kinseris. For the sake of the friendship we once shared, I will give you one last warning, and then we are done. Stay away from Rhiannas.'

Then he was gone.

Kinseris followed him out of the tent. He almost called out to alert the camp, but caution held his tongue. They would not find him, and if they did, they could not take him. Too many would die if they tried. He looked back at Jeta, still asleep. She could never know how close Darred had come.

Stay away from Rhiannas.

Kinseris began to walk back toward the command tent.

Stay away from Rhiannas.

His steps quickened, and then he was running, hand pressed to his side as dull ache flared into sharp stabs of pain.

Stay away from Rhiannas.

He burst into the tent. The grizzled clan commander, Petrik, was alone. He looked up from the lists he was writing, his hand paused in mid-air as he saw Kinseris's face.

'What?'

'Darred is moving against Rhiannas. *Now.*'

Petrik stared at him. 'Are you certain?'

Kinseris nodded.

The man looked down at his careful plans and swore. Then he was on his feet, striding out of the tent. Kinseris caught his arm. 'Send someone after Galydon.'

Petrik nodded, grabbing a passing soldier and sending him to wake his officers. He kicked a couple of clansmen still dozing by the remains of fire. 'Up, wake your units. We leave in an hour.' He turned to Kinseris. 'Tell me what you know.'

SIXTEEN

THE LONG WALK back to the camp was silent. There was nothing to say. Or rather, there was lots to be said, but it was altogether too painful, so they said nothing. Even so, Kallis felt that silence was not his friend. In his head, Jeta was screaming at him, and behind her Sedaine. Someone would have to tell them. A wave of nausea engulfed him as he let himself remember what they had left behind.

'Kallis?'

He concentrated on breathing. Not that. He could not tell them *that*.

They started walking again. It was not a journey he was anxious to finish. Getting back meant making decisions he did not want to make. Like who was going to take the news to Rhiannas.

In the event, that decision was taken from him, as he should have realised it would be. Ducking into his tent, he walked straight into Galydon, who wasted no time on greetings and instead demanded, '*What has happened?*' And he knew Galydon had come himself because he feared bad news.

Kallis ignored the urgent question, divesting himself of his sword belt and filthy jack and throwing them carelessly in the corner. Then he sat heavily on the cot and looked up at Galydon. 'The dragons are gone.' But not *the* dragon. Not Darred's dragon.

He saw Galydon take that in and knew the general was also reading his face, which reflected something very far from triumph.

'And?'

There was a rustle of canvas and Callan ducked inside. Lysan must have told him Galydon was here. The general spared him a brief glance before turning back to Kallis. 'And?' he repeated.

'And so is Aarin,' Callan finished when Kallis found that he could not.

Galydon paled. 'Are you sure?'

Kallis thought of the devastation they had left on the cliffs. He nodded.

Bracing himself for questions he had no wish to answer, he was surprised when they did not come. But Galydon hadn't spent years leading men not to recognise when a soldier had hit his limits.

'I'll stay here tonight and leave in the morning,' Galydon told him gruffly. 'Before I go, we need to talk.'

Kallis nodded again. The general left. Callan lingered, a question in his eyes. Kallis lay back on the cot, arm over his eyes, and Callan took the hint and left him alone.

When he rose the next morning, Kallis spent an hour with Galydon, and at the end of that difficult interview it did not surprise him when the Caledani general did not, after all, leave as intended. Some news you did not rush to share, even if perhaps you should. Instead, he took from Kallis for the space of a day the necessity of doing what had to be done in the wake of disaster. And he took from him also the need to carry the news to Rhiannas.

Kallis took that day and spent it getting drunk and no one said anything. Not until Lysan found him that evening and demanded impatiently, 'Are you done yet? Do you think you 're the only one who cares?'

Kallis opened his eyes, groaning. 'Go away.'

'Much as I would like to let you continue to wallow in whatever this is, I need you sober.'

Kallis closed his eyes again. 'Tomorrow.'

Lysan growled. 'No, not tomorrow, now.' And kicked him, with some force, in the ribs.

Kallis swore, curling around his bruised side. 'Why are you here? Where is your brother?'

'That,' replied Lysan, 'is a very good question. And one I was hoping you could answer.'

Kallis cracked open an eye, peering at Lysan's face through the blur of spirits. He did not look his usual happy self. 'What's wrong?'

'Are you capable? I need your help.'

Kallis levered himself up onto his elbows. 'To do what?'

'To find my brother.'

Kallis sat up with an effort and held his head in his hands, waiting while the pounding subsided to a more distant hammering. 'Why are you so worried? He's a grown man.'

'He is,' Lysan agreed. 'And he's just lost something more than a friend.'

Too tired to untangle the implications of that, Kallis regarded Lysan irritably between splayed fingers. 'What are you talking about?' And was surprised to see Lysan's face crumple. 'What is it?'

Callan's brother didn't answer at once. He threw himself into the tent's only chair, where he stared at Kallis miserably. 'I can't explain it,' he said at last. 'I think maybe Aarin understood. I lost my brother after the siege. When Aarin came back, and the dragon with him, I started to find him again. Now…' He stopped, and Kallis saw the real fear in his eyes before he turned his head away. 'Now they are gone, I'm afraid I will lose him again.'

Kallis sat in silence, watching him. Then he sighed and pushed himself to his feet. 'Right. I didn't understand any of that. But let's go.'

As it happened, Callan was not hard to find since he was in his tent, but they wasted a good hour looking elsewhere. An hour in which Lysan grew increasingly agitated and Kallis wanted very much to be lying down. By the time they thought of looking in the obvious place, he was quite sure that lying down had become more of an inevitability than a choice.

He sat with a groan as Lysan greeted his brother with a stream of worried complaints, which Callan ignored. Never talkative, he gave his brother a look that was positively clam-like, and continued with what he was doing. Which, Kallis noted through slitted eyes, appeared to be packing.

He sighed, resting his head in his hands. 'What are you doing?'

Callan barely glanced at him. He did not reply.

Lysan, belatedly coming to the same conclusion, grabbed his brother by the shoulders, forcing Callan to look at him. 'Where do you think you will go?'

Callan shook off his hands. 'Anywhere. I can't stay here.'

'So you just leave?' Lysan demanded. *Leave me,* was what he did not say, but they both heard it, nonetheless.

Callan looked at him with tormented eyes. 'You should come with me.'

Lysan shook his head, distraught. 'I can't. You know I can't. This—it matters, Callan. It should matter to you too. It did.'

'It doesn't,' his brother replied. 'Not anymore. Nothing matters now.'

There was a fraught pause. Kallis wished he was anywhere else.

'Because he's dead?' Lysan asked eventually, his hurt barely concealed. 'Or because what he could have given you died with him?'

'Lysan –'

'No, I won't let you do this. Do you understand? I won't let you give up.'

Callan turned his head away, towards Kallis, who flinched from the desolation in his eyes. 'But how do you expect me to go on?'

Lysan looked at Kallis in mute appeal, but he had no answer to such a depth of despair. Not now. He had not understood before. He had not seen what was right in front of him, but he should have, because he had seen it before. In Aarin.

In the silence that followed, Callan returned to what he had been doing. As he reached for a neatly folded bundle of clothes, Lysan tore them from his hands and threw them across the tent. Then he snatched his brother's small pack and emptied it onto the ground. 'I won't let you!'

Anger bloomed in Callan's eyes. 'Don't *you* understand? Everything we fought for has just been wiped out. Everyone who died at Ephenor just died for nothing! It makes no difference now how this war ends. Either Darred wins, and his corruption destroys even the possibility of reunion, or you defeat him, and break the Kas'Talani, and all means of accessing the dragons' power is gone—forever. Aarin is dead!'

Callan looked directly at Kallis, who found he could not hold his gaze. His head pounded mercilessly, but it was not the distraction he had hoped it would be, and all the drink in the world could not drown out the truth of Callan's words—though he had tried. Maker, how he had tried.

'So, what then?' Lysan shot back. 'We just let Darred win? What he is doing—what he will do, to this land and its people, doesn't matter, because the dragons—which he has!—are lost to us? Callan, we have been on our own for thousands of years. You cannot tell me it doesn't matter what happens to these people because something they have never known is gone! You can't tell me you don't care.'

'Why?' Callan demanded. 'Because it's not what you want to hear?'

'Because I *know* you!'

Something in Callan seemed to crumble at that. He dropped onto the narrow cot as if his legs would no longer hold him. 'How can you?' he asked, his voice dead. 'When I don't even know myself?'

Lysan gave a strangled sob and fell to his knees, taking his brother in his arms as dammed up grief broke free at last.

Kallis watched them for a few moments, then stood and slipped out. It wasn't tomorrow yet and there was still plenty of wine left in his tent. If that failed to knock him out, he could always bludgeon himself unconscious with the bottle. Anything to not deal with this for a few more hours.

PART FOUR

ONE

THE GREEN AND gold flag of Morven flew over the gates of Rhiannas. Below it hung the flags of five more of Lothane's noble families. Sedaine noted them as she passed through the gate on her return to the city, matching the flags to the men they represented. Some did not surprise her, but two gave her pause, and one she had expected was not present, though that could mean anything.

Derias's mouth thinned as he recognised the blue and white of his brother-in-law, Andras Taith, ever Morven's faithful ally. There was no love lost between those two, despite the affection in which Derias held his little sister, Sofiya. Perhaps because of it. A joyless tyrant, Derias had called Sofiya's husband, and worse, once or twice. Sedaine wondered what he thought of his own brother, whose bitterness at Derias's appointment as her chancellor he had never bothered to conceal. But she had never asked him and it was too late now.

'To the palace?' he asked, as the gate guards raised the royal standard for her return, and she felt a petty satisfaction as it fluttered in the breeze above the green and gold.

Derias was also watching the flag, his expression tense, and he made no move to match words with action.

'To the palace,' Sedaine reminded him, because where else would she go? She was tired and travel-worn. Derias had set a faster pace on their return, no doubt at Galydon's orders, and as she contemplated the imminent audience, she wished she had insisted on a slower pace and a change of clothes. But it was too late for that too, and the lords would have to take her as they found her. That also was faintly satisfying.

The palace, when they reached it, was a bustle of activity, the courtyard filled with the inevitable entourage that accompanied her nobles wherever they went. She looked for Limina as Derias saw to the handing off of their mounts and baggage. They had not hurried through the city. Word would have reached the palace well ahead of them, but Limina did not appear. The grooms went about their business with silence deference but there was *something* in their manner that prompted her to countermand Derias's dismissal of her guard. She ignored his surprised look and swept up the steps, anxious, suddenly, to get this over with.

Inside, the palace was even busier than the courtyard. She suppressed a sigh. There had been distinct advantages to sending her nobles and their endless retinues out from under her feet this last year. It could never have lasted, but she had cherished the quiet, and the freedom. That was gone too now.

She dismissed her steward outside the throne room, to his grievous disappointment, and they entered without a herald. The better to see the reactions that would greet her arrival.

'Leo,' Derias exclaimed happily as he saw his brother standing in the centre of a knot of his household guards. Sedaine recognised the long, unsmiling face of Taith at his side, and the scattering of the other lords whose flags had flown with Morven's.

Leodad Morven turned. He was a heavyset man in middle age, with thick brows, craggy features, and none of the good looks or easy charm of his younger brother, whom he greeted now with a grim nod.

'Derias. It's time you returned.'

Derias's steps faltered at his tone, but then he reached his brother and embraced him.

There was an odd tension in the room. A watching stillness. Sedaine, studying Morven's face over this brother's shoulder, saw what Derias had not.

It was happening. She had always known it might. And she was alone.

As Morven met her eyes, his own hostile and determined, she reached out with her power—the power she had never formally acknowledged to her people, the power she hoped they had forgotten—drawing it to her, holding onto as much as she dared, until she felt herself trembling as singing energies filled her to the brim.

'Will you not greet your queen, my lord?' she asked, cold and deliberate.

Morven stiffened, releasing his younger brother, and Sedaine did not know, even now, where Derias would stand in what was coming. He had been reluctant to come to the palace, but that might mean everything or nothing.

Derias's smile slipped as the heavy tension finally registered. His sharp eyes quartered the room, seeing the lords' men standing around them, grim-faced, his brother in half armour. In the throne room. He backed up a step and Taith put a heavy hand on his shoulder, holding him in place.

Derias looked from the hand to his brother. 'Leo, what is this?'

Leodad Morven made a gesture and his men moved to disarm their small guard. 'This,' he said, 'is something that should have been done long since. Take her.'

Sedaine's guards, realising what was happening, drew their swords. Morven's men did the same.

'Stop!' she cried, before the latent violence could explode. 'Put away your weapons, all of you.' She faced Morven, Derias standing frozen beside him, Taith's hand still on his shoulder. 'Leave now and I will forget this happened. Lothane needs you, my lord. I do not want to lose you.'

She would not persuade him, she knew that, but for his brother's sake she had to offer him a chance. Because, in rejecting it, Morven would force Derias to choose a side. To betray his queen or betray his brother, his family. There was no going back from either choice, but without Derias she was unlikely to make it out of this room alive. She *needed* him.

For an answer, Morven drew his own sword, raising it until the tip stopped just inches from her chest. 'Lothane needs me. It does not need you.'

'You fool,' she hissed. 'What did he promise you?' Because why else had Darred asked for a meeting that would draw both her and her commanders out of Rhiannas at this precise time, if not to clear the way for this sordid rebellion? And she should have expected it. She knew what he did to those who betrayed him, and he knew how much she loved Lothane and how much she had sacrificed to gain it. He had used it to control her for too many years. Darred could never allow her to lead her country to a glorious defeat. That country must reject her, cast her out, before he would take it.

Derias's face was white. He shrugged off Taith's hand. 'What have you done, Leo?'

Morven spared him a fleeting glance, his attention focused on Sedaine. 'Autonomy for Lothane in exchange for you. If we make peace he will respect Lothane's independence.'

'You fool,' she said again, the words grating against her dry throat as she drained the moisture from the room and directed it upwards, into the ancient, crumbling plaster. 'He will break you.'

'You already did that,' Morven snarled. 'Once when you made your filthy bargain and then again when you betrayed it. You claim you are defending us against the Caledani threat, and yet your commanders are Caledani. You take advice from one of her priests. I am not the fool you take me for. You have betrayed your country and you are not fit to sit on its throne.' He spat at her feet. 'Take her away.'

'No!' Derias had his sword in his hand. He dodged Taith's attempt to hold him and was at her side in three quick paces. 'Get behind me.'

She ignored him, her eyes fixed on Morven. 'You forget who I am, *my lord.*' And she lashed out with the power she had hoarded, flattening a path through the soldiers behind and before her, slapping them aside like flies. As Morven fell back, his mouth hanging open, she grabbed Derias and pushed him back, out of range. 'Get behind *me.*'

And the ceiling of the room exploded as she ripped it apart, raining down huge slabs of the old plaster amid a shower of thick dust. She did not wait for it to settle. Derias was tugging at her sleeve, dust thick in his hair and on his face, urging her to move.

Several of her guards were picking themselves up and following, and then they were at the doors, two men in Morven livery standing nervously between them and their escape. She saw the indecision on their faces, clearly unsure what would anger their lord more—allowing them to escape or attacking his brother. Derias did not give them a chance to think about it. He shoulder-barged one, his sword coming up as he twisted past to deflect a half-hearted blow from the other, then they were through.

Morven's furious bellow followed them out of the throne room and his soldiers spilled out into the corridor. Summoning Air to her need, she wove a barrier between them. Not strong, it would not last, but it stole them precious distance as she followed Derias.

Her guards did not follow. As Derias dragged her down the hallway, they turned to face Morven's soldiers, standing between their queen and her enemies. Frantic, she forced what strength she had left into the obstruction, trying to give what advantage she could to her handful of protectors.

'They'll kill them,' she gasped.

'Then they will have died in defence of their queen,' Derias said savagely. 'Run.'

She ran, too exhausted to argue. Her strength was in fine control, not brute force. What she had done in the throne room had emptied her; it could not be repeated.

They rounded a corner, coming out onto the upper gallery. Instinctively, she turned to her right, towards the palace's main door, and saw Morven's men advancing toward them. Derias swore, pushing her ahead of him as he backed up, sword drawn.

Sedaine tripped as she spun, falling heavily against a doorframe, and remembered where she was. 'This way.'

Derias followed her into the series of interconnected rooms that had once been her mother's receiving suite and bedchamber.

'We don't want to get trapped in here,' Derias warned, close at her heels, weaving his way between the old furniture.

'We won't.' She found what she was looking for. On either side of where her mother's four-poster bed had stood were two doors cut into the papered walls. One was the servant's stair, leading down to the kitchens in the basement. The handle was stiff with disuse, the door swollen and warped by damp. Derias pushed her to one side and set his shoulder against the door.

'Leave it open,' she told him, already at the other. This one opened more easily. It was not as old as the servants' door. Her Farnorian mother had had the private closet it led to installed soon after she had married Sedaine's father. Tucked into a mezzanine floor just below her bedchamber, it too connected to a servant's stair to the main floor below, but it had not been used for decades. She doubted anyone remembered it was there.

Derias followed her as their pursuers reached the room beyond. He closed the door quietly, his fingers closing firmly on her arm to arrest her movement down the stairs. He canted his head to the door, and she knew the soldiers would hear their feet on the stone steps. She was almost sure they must hear her breathing, so loud did it sound in her own ears. But a clattering of booted feet and armour descending the other stair told her they had taken the bait.

Derias nudged her down the steps. She wove a trickle of power around the door behind them, holding it tight against casual inspection, and conjured a small sphere of light to guide them down into the darkness. She heard a hiss of expelled breath behind her but Derias made no other comment until they reached the closet and she started toward the servant's stair.

'I go first,' he said firmly. 'Where do these come out?'

She had to think about it. It had been thirty years at least since she had played on these stairs with her brother. 'The main service corridor,' she said at last. 'It runs parallel to the long gallery one floor door.'

'The other stair?'

The one their pursuers had taken. 'Opens onto the same corridor, but the steps continue down as far as the kitchens.'

He nodded grimly. 'Let's hope they don't stop to look around.'

She did not think they would. Their only way out was down. Their pursuers would know that, so they waited, tense and barely breathing in the tiny closet, until the sound of descending footsteps told them Morven's soldiers had indeed carried on down to the kitchens on the lowest level of the palace.

The brief reprieve made her dizzy. Derias pretended not to notice. 'Where now?'

She gestured along the service corridor. 'Down there. It will take us to the back of palace.' To the stables and servants' quarters and, if they were lucky, to the tenuous safety of the city beyond.

'Easy,' he smiled, trying to reassure, trying not to hurry her. 'Ready?'

It was not easy.

As they passed a storeroom, its door ajar, a muffled gasp made her turn. Limina, her dress filthy, her hands chained, *chained*—Sedaine felt a hot pulse of fury at the sight—was standing just inside the room. There was a gag in her mouth.

She stopped dead. Limina gave her head a tiny shake, her eyes filled with desperate warning, and Sedaine froze as she felt a hand grab her hair and the point of a blade press against her ribs.

Derias, several steps ahead, jerked to a stop at her shocked hiss.

Sense and thought returned. Anger sharpened into pinpoint focus, but the hesitation had cost her. Before she could free herself, a man walked out of the shadows behind Limina, his sword unsheathed at her back.

'*Don't*, your highness.'

She didn't. She could not strike fast enough to save both herself and Limina. Once, she might have done—she was certain Aarin could have done—but she had put aside her power for too long, and spent too long before that denying its source and its strength. And she was already tired.

Derias, caught mid-step and unable to act without endangering her life, turned to face Limina's captor, his tone flat and wary. 'Andras.'

'Put your weapon down, boy,' Taith ordered, hard eyes never leaving her face. 'They both die if you don't.'

He would do it, too. She was sure of it. There was a coldness to the man that foreclosed any appeal Derias might make. He tried anyway, his voice cracking on useless entreaty. 'Andras. Please.'

'Now, Derias.'

The command cracked like a whip, and Derias's shoulders slumped. With a helpless glance at Sedaine, his sword clattered to the ground.

Taith sneered. 'It's about time you remembered where your loyalties lie, boy. Come here.'

Derias didn't move, and Taith's cold eyes turned in his direction at last. He raised his sword until the tip rested against Limina's back. 'Come here.'

Sedaine caught the minute flicker of a glance before Derias's head dropped and he went to stand meekly by Taith's side.

Something cold and hard settled in the pit of her stomach. Limina's terrified gaze was locked on hers, and Derias, unable to meet her eyes, stood just behind his sister's husband, his hands clenched into fists, knuckles white with tension.

Taith put up his sword. 'Take them –'

He stiffened then staggered. Derias shoved Limina forward and down as his other hand, holding a bloody dagger, stabbed again into Taith's side.

The suddenness of it saved her life. As the hand locked in her hair jerked her back, Sedaine concentrated all the force she had gathered and lashed out, hard, sending the man sprawling to the floor. Then she was kneeling by Limina, who fell shaking into her arms.

Over Limina's shoulder, Sedaine stared without flinching into the eyes of her would-be executioner as Taith gasped out the last of his life through the blood bubbling from his lips. Then, as Derias stepped past her, scooping his sword from the ground, she raised a shield around them that blanketed the sound of what he had to do.

Limina gasped around the gag, tears streaming down her face, and Sedaine fumbled with the knot before dragging the stained cloth free and hurling it away.

'He's dead, he's dead,' she soothed, stroking dirty blond hair, keeping herself between Limina and what was happening behind her. It didn't take long.

Derias dropped down on one knee beside them, his dark hair in disarray and a splatter of blood across one cheek. He hacked at the chains with his reclaimed sword, frantic with urgency. 'We have to move.'

Sedaine didn't look at him. She ignored the pounding of footsteps and the distant shouts, her eyes locked on Limina. 'I'm not leaving you.' If Taith would have killed his queen, what chance did Limina have?

She felt Derias's desperation, for her and for himself after what he had done, but he didn't argue, just doggedly attacked the metal links.

She followed the chain with her eyes, but it was secured around one of the line of columns that ran down the centre of the room. If she could…

Cold metal touched her hand. Limina said, 'You have to go.'

Sedaine shook her head. 'No. Don't ask me to leave you again.' She was sure she could solve this. But she was so tired. Her thoughts were all jumbled and the calm she needed was nowhere to be found.

'You don't have time. You have to go now.'

Derias was on his feet. 'She's right. We must go.'

Already the sounds of pursuit were louder. It would not be long before they realised what they had missed, or whom they were missing.

'They won't hurt me,' Limina insisted. 'Not when they can use me against you.'

A scream was rising in her throat. Desperation, denial, fear. But she pushed it back, held it in, until the back of her mouth ached with suppressed emotion. She glanced at Derias, standing an agitated watch by the door. He hesitated for an uncomfortable second, then shrugged. He didn't know.

Limina took her face in both chained hands. 'Please,' she begged. 'If they take you, they will kill you. What use will they have for me if you are dead?'

She closed her eyes, feeling tears, hearing the words for what they were but unable to deny the truth in them. 'I *will* come back for you.'

Derias was tugging her to her feet and there was no more time for words. The hand on her arm forced her to run, feet skidding on worn flagstones as they hurtled down the hallway, and she did not look back—she could not allow herself to look back or she would have been unable to go on.

Then they were out of the palace and stumbling across the cracked paving of the back courtyard towards the stables, and it wasn't until there was a shout behind them that she realised she should have cast a glamour to hide them.

TWO

SEDAINE BUMPED HER hip against a stall selling the dried remnants of last summer's apple crop. She caught the trestle as it wobbled and muttered her apologies to the stallholder, her eyes flicking from one stall to the next, each of them bearing mute testimony to the worsening food shortage.

'You never told me it was this bad,' she hissed at Derias as he caught her by the elbow.

He pressed her to move, glancing back over his shoulder. 'What would you have done?' Then he swore, backing up a step.

She peered past him. 'What is it?'

He turned her around, cutting off her view. 'Don't look, keep walking.' And he hustled her ahead of him, back into the tangle of stalls. 'My brother's soldiers. Blocking the lane.'

Her heart beat a bit faster. 'Did they see you?' They wore only the lightest of glamours, turning her hair from black to silver, Derias's dark head to blond, and hiding the bloodstain on his sleeve where a blade had slipped through his guard. The spring rains still hung heavy in the air, giving her a well of power to draw on, but a glamour was delicate work and she was too tired to trust herself with anything more complex. It would be enough from a distance, but it would not fool anyone who knew their faces if they got too close.

As Taith's men had done as they fled the palace. She eyed the bloody fingers that gripped tight to her elbow, and the growing stain on Derias's wrist. If she was tired, he was exhausted and hurt. They badly needed to find somewhere they could hide, rest, but first they needed to shake Morven's dogged pursuit.

Derias's hair brushed her cheek as he leant in close. 'Haggle,' he murmured, fingers twitching on her arm.

She risked a glance and saw men in Morven's colours threading their way through the market a couple of rows over, and she bent her head over the bolts of undyed cloth on the stall before her, letting her long hair fall across her face. The cloth was coarse under her fingers, but she made interested noises and the stallholder obligingly made the opening moves in the negotiation. And all the while she could feel the thud of Derias's heart as he pressed close to her side, eyes scanning the crowds.

The stallholder's smile was tight as he countered her offer with one at least twice what she guessed the cloth was worth. She noticed his own clothes were worn, the signs of careful mending just visible when he moved. A cloth merchant's attire was an extension of his wares, a display of quality. This man's garments were as poor as his cloth, a stark reminder of the cost of two years of closed borders, high taxes, and a city overwhelmed with refugees.

There was a tug on her arm. 'Enough. We're moving.'

She smiled regretfully at the stallholder and shook her head, letting Derias guide her towards the edge of the crowded marketplace. They had been heading for the old centre, hoping to lose their pursuit in its maze of narrow streets and interconnected buildings, but at every turn they found their way blocked by soldiers in green and gold. Either Morven had guessed their intentions or he had far more men with him than she had realised.

She cursed her stupidity. Of course he did. This was a coup, and he had staked everything on it. That she had returned to the city alone but for Derias and a small escort was pure chance. Morven had been expecting to have to hold the city against Galydon and her mercenary army. He and his allies would have brought every last man they could spare. Lose this gamble and they would certainly die.

But they hadn't won yet, and that was solely because of the man by her side, the wild card Morven had misjudged so completely. The brother he had forced to choose between two loyalties, and who had chosen her and risked his life doing so. Who had killed for her.

Derias nudged her to the right, between a row of busy stalls that led to the western edge of the market. As the crowd swirled around them, he said, 'We can't stay here. We must get past them. Can you distract them?' And he drew her attention to the group of five guardsmen by the entrance to the alley opposite.

Raised voices came from their right, a wave of anger that rose and fell swiftly, and she saw the guardsmen's eyes turn briefly to where two men were engaged in a minor dispute by a cart piled high with empty barrels.

She nodded, focusing her attention. 'When?'

Derias shifted position so he was no longer pressed up against her back, but was walking on her right, giving himself more space to move. His left hand slid down till it clasped hers and gripped tight. As they reached the second-to-last stall he whispered, 'Now.'

There was a loud crack. The overburdened cart shuddered and collapsed, spilling its contents across the market, upsetting several other stalls as it did so. The shouting started, and Derias gripped hard, pulling her towards the alley as the guards were distracted by the commotion.

She tightened her grip on the glamour, focusing attention on the grey hair that rendered her beneath notice, and they slid between the soldiers, her heart pounding in her throat. No one spared them a glance as the uproar from the market swelled into a cacophony of outrage and accusation.

The mouth of an alley opened on their left and Derias swung towards it, pulling her with him—and came face to face with one of his brother's guards who had been relieving himself against the wall.

The man checked in surprise, then he registered the familiar features beneath the false blond hair. His eyes widened, his hand going to his sword, his mouth opening to cry warning. Derias was faster and the soldier collapsed. His sword clattered to the cobbles with a distinctive ring just as the sound from the market died down.

A voice called out in query from behind them, followed by another of the soldiers coming to investigate. Her eyes met his as he rounded the end of the alley and it was too late.

The solider backed up, calling to his fellows, and Derias shoved her hard. 'Run!'

But she was frozen, unable to move. Unable to leave him.

Four men appeared at the soldier's side, weapons drawn.

A grey-haired man with a ribbon of rank on his tunic stepped forward. 'We don't want to hurt you, my lord,' he said to Derias. It was clear they knew each other. This man had probably been in Morven's service longer than Derias had been alive.

'Then let us go,' Derias said quietly. 'I can't let you take her.'

The man shook his head, looking pained. 'Please, my lord.'

'She's your queen,' Derias hissed. 'This is treason.'

'Only treason was hers!' one of the others called out, and there was an angry murmur of agreement.

A howl of anguish rose in her throat as she felt the words stiffen his resolve. He would die before he surrendered, and she couldn't let him.

'Derias…'

'Run, your highness, please,' Derias begged her. He used her title, which he almost never did, to remind these men who she was. But it was hopeless and he knew it. It did not matter how skilled he might be. They were five; he was one. It did not matter that they did not want to kill him. He would make them, because he would not give her up.

The grey-haired sergeant saw it too. He looked past Derias to her. 'You could give yourself up, highness. Then no one need die here.'

'She will not,' Derias shot back. 'You will not!' And his head half turned to where she stood.

It was enough. In that instant when his attention was diverted, they were on him, two at once, the others circling round. Round him, to her.

She saw Derias's desperate parry as he too realised the danger, but two on one kept him pinned down and he could not help.

She thought of his shock in the throne room when he had realised what his brother had done. Of his laughter as he had danced that ridiculous dance with the Ephenori captain. Of the look on his face when he had killed Taith. And she could not stand it.

The wind of her rage whipped through the narrow alley, hurling the approaching soldiers from their feet, then she hardened it to a killing pitch and *pushed,* driving them back with the force of hammer blow, hard enough to break bones. She saw one man collapse, blood leaking from his nose and ear, and he did not get up. Another staggered to his knees, his shoulder bulging oddly against his stained surcoat, a scream on his lips.

The two facing Derias, furthest from her, were still on their feet. She dared not strike against them directly for fear of hurting him too. Instead, she let the storm-wind die away, drawing it back into her, gently at first, then in a fierce rush. And then, with surgical precision, she took the air from them entirely, so that one moment they were standing and the next they were sinking to their knees, their hands reaching desperately for their throats as their eyes bulged with terror.

She held that death-grip on their lungs till they dropped, unconscious or dead she neither knew nor cared. She staggered as the power rushed out of her, almost blinded by release, and when she could see again Derias was on his knees, cradling his left arm, his sleeve a sodden mess, and his eyes were locked on her in disbelief and fear. She took a step towards him and the world blurred and went black.

When she came to, she was being dragged across the cobbles, someone's harsh breathing by her ear. Anger pulsed, hot and deadly, and she tried to pull herself free. *She would not let them take her!*

There was a muffled curse and the arm that held her strengthened its grip, but the pace never slackened. With a sob of frustration, she reached for power as she had done in the alley, but she was husked out, dry, and it skittered away from her.

Then her stumbling feet caught on a missing cobble and the momentum sent her to her knees, taking her captor down with her, and they sprawled together on the filthy ground. She bit the hand that reached for her, rolling desperately to one side and into a crouch, and saw wary brown eyes looking back at her.

Derias was on his hands and knees where he had fallen. He held out a hand. 'Sedaine, it's me. You're safe. It's me.'

Breath left her in a rush and she had to put an arm out for balance. She let her head drop, her hair hanging long and black onto her knees. Black. The glamour was gone. She shot a frantic glance up and down the narrow street, but the soldiers were nowhere to be seen and they were no longer where they had been. The cobbles beneath her feet were older and in disrepair, and the buildings that lined the alley were largely wood, not stone, and leaning badly. The people passing by on either side cast wary glances at Derias's sword and stepped quickly around them. No one here would know their faces, but their clothes and weapons marked them as trouble, and these folk would not see trouble they did not need.

'Where are we? How long…?'

Derias had pushed himself from his knees and was slumped against the wall. He looked exhausted. 'I'm not certain. West of the old town, I think. We should…' He waved his arm vaguely, pressing his back against the wall as he tried to rise.

They should get off the street, find somewhere to hide.

'The soldiers?' she asked, her voice cracking on the words. 'Did I…?

His eyes held hers briefly, a dark tangle of emotions in their depths. Then he shook his head, looking away. 'I don't know.'

And she remembered that he too had killed, and why. On impulse, she reached for him. 'Derias…'

But he would not look at her, his head turned resolutely down the street. 'They won't be far behind and we can't go much further.' His voice was remote, impersonal. 'We need shelter.'

She stood, the dragging weakness already fading. 'Where?'

For an answer, he started up the street, putting his shoulder to each door they passed until one cracked inward under the pressure, opening onto the dusty chaos of an abandoned cloth merchant's workshop. Most of the contents had been picked clean by the locals, but Sedaine could make out the remains of draper's tools amid the general disorder of stripped panelling and broken furniture. Two boys, the knees of their ragged leggings patched and their faces pinched with hunger, came running out of the back room, their arms full of broken oddments. Derias held the door wide and jerked his head at the street. 'Out.'

The boys took one look at the sword and scuttled past him. He caught the tallest as he passed and said something to him that she didn't catch. The boy gave him a terrified look and scampered after his companion.

Derias slammed the door closed. The bolt on the inside was misaligned and would not move. He cursed. 'Cover the window,' he ordered as he dragged an upturned table over as a barricade.

She glanced at the window, a small opening that had once been boarded over, but now let in shafts of light through the cracks of successive break-ins.

'I don't think…'

'Just do it!'

She gave up and scrounged through the dusty mess for something that could cover the cracked window. But there was little enough in the main room that had not been scavenged, and she wandered through the door the children had emerged from to find the remains of the storeroom. The bolts of cloth had long since gone, but a pile of discarded ends lay in one corner and she dug through it until she found a few larger scraps that might serve.

She gave them to Derias, who took them without a word, his back turned to hide his face. She watched, heart aching, as he secured the scraps of cloth as best he could over the small window.

'Derias,' she tried again, but still he would not look at her.

Eventually, he said, 'I did not know. I swear it.'

'I believe you.'

She saw the tremor that ran through him. 'If I had…'

If he had, what would he have done? She did not want to dwell on that. It was one thing to turn against your brother in the act of the treason, another to turn him in for thinking it. But it did not matter, because in the end he had not betrayed her. He had killed his sister's husband for her. The little sister he adored. As she had killed for him.

'I owe you my life,' she told him now, reminding him why he had done it. 'Thank you.'

He looked round then, a wry smile on his lips. 'I owe you mine, twice over. I had forgotten. I did not realise…'

Her smile mirrored his. 'I meant you to.' Not to deceive. That had not been her intention. Or, at least, not with malice. But she had come to the throne at the machinations of the magicians and the Kas'Talani, tainted in her country's eyes by her time in the eastern lands and her part in the danger facing her nation. She had needed her lords' acceptance, craved her people's. So she had put aside her power, letting go of a lifetime of unconscious use of magic. She had set it aside willing, but not without pain. Not without regret. And with no evidence of their queen's power to remind them, her lords and her people had gradually forgotten she had ever held it.

Save for that day, when she had risen from her throne in the middle of an audience and walked out of the palace to stand in the grand, stone courtyard and look up into the sky, tears on her face, searching for creatures she had not known she had longed for until that instant.

Save for that day, her people had forgotten.

Until now. The day she lost them, along with her crown.

'What will you do?' Derias asked.

The question surprised her, a reminder that even driven from her palace, even in hiding, she was still his queen and she had to fight. If she didn't, she threw his sacrifice back in his face. Because what use in defending her, in turning against his own brother, if she just gave up?

Blood dripped from the cut on his wrist onto the floor. She looked from it to his pale face. They were safe for the moment. It was time to see to his hurts.

'Tomorrow,' she said gently, taking his arm and guiding him to the floor until he sat with his back against the wall. 'We'll decide tomorrow.'

THREE

'THEY'VE DONE WHAT?' Galydon paused in the act of removing his gloves as Petrik's words sank in.

'Taken Rhiannas,' Kinseris confirmed, studying his former general for some sign of the news he carried that must now wait. 'They say they have the queen and they intend to surrender her to Darred in exchange for independence for Lothane.'

'I think not,' Galydon said with grim certainty and drew Petrik's map toward him. The clan commander had covered it in notes marking what information he had about the numbers and disposition of the occupying forces. 'Do we know for certain they have Sedaine hostage?'

Kinseris exchanged a glance with Petrik. They had arrived a day ago to be met by barred gates and walls lined with soldiers dressed not in the royal livery but an assortment of colours of Lothane's most prominent noble families. Dialogue had been short and hostile and a request for the queen to be brought to the walls had been denied.

'They have not let us see her,' he admitted. 'We know she arrived here.' There were plenty of witnesses who had seen Sedaine's party pass through the gates, but his fledgling network in Rhiannas was too new and too fragile to tell them much more than that. He hesitated, and because it had to be said, added, 'They have taken the palace. We cannot be certain she still lives.'

A tensing of muscles in Galydon's jaw was the only sign he had heard that. Without looking up, he asked, 'Who are we dealing with?'

Petrik rattled off a list of names and likely numbers with the casual familiarity of a man who had fought for or against most of them at one time or another over a long career. 'Morven leads them.'

Galydon's head came up. 'Morven?' Then he slammed his fist down in a rare loss of control. 'And I sent Derias with her!'

Petrik turned his palm up in a gesture Kinseris recognised from Kallis but could not quite interpret. Honesty, perhaps. 'I do not think Derias is involved.'

'And I would have said the same until I found his brother holding the city against us,' Galydon growled.

'I've had dealings with his brother, and they are… unlike. I would say he is loyal. If he was with her –'

Galydon shook his head. 'And we can afford to make no such assumptions. If we find him, arrest him and then we will see.' His gaze turned to the camp, assessing their numbers, which were few. 'Tell me again what he said.'

Kinseris repeated the warning from Darred that had brought them back to Rhiannas at speed, leaving the bulk of their forces to follow. Jeta was with those travelling behind them. He had not wanted to leave her, and she had not wanted to be left, but they had no idea what they would find here, and for once she had not argued. Seeing Galydon's brittle tension, and dreading its cause, he was grateful she was not here, not yet.

Galydon listened intently, his frown deepening. 'So, we must assume they are in alliance with Darred, or they think they are.'

Kinseris thought of the self-righteous conviction of the man who had shouted down to them from the walls, and his claim that they were saving Lothane from enemies within and without. Arrogance or delusion? 'I doubt they would see it that way.'

'Then they are fools. Are there priests in the city?'

Kinseris shook his head, understanding at once what Galydon was really asking, bracing himself for it. There were pockets of power within the walls of Rhiannas, but he was as certain as he could be that Darred had sent no Kas'Talani to the conspirators. Magicians he could handle, should it come to it. It was unlikely any of the mages would ally with the lords against their queen, who was, after all, one of them.

But the lack of Kas'Talani was an omission that niggled at him. *Stay away from Rhiannas.* It had been a warning that did not align with the threat. By leaving the lords unsupported, Darred was not acceding to their demands for independence, he was betraying them to their fate. Because he had to know what Galydon's response would be. Unless the warning had been meant to keep Kinseris away. But he did not believe that. They knew each other too well.

Galydon must have made the same calculation. 'So, he leaves them vulnerable, and they are expecting negotiation, not an attack. We go in hard and we end this, now. I want as many of your men mounted as you can manage,' he said to Petrik. 'I don't care on what. I just need them to move quickly. Have them follow us as closely as possible. We take the palace and secure the leaders as our first priority. The rest of your men will come behind and hold the gate.'

The clansman was looking at him as though he had lost his senses. 'Just like that? Even supposing we can persuade them to open the gates, there will be hundreds of their men between us and the palace.'

Galydon flashed him a fierce smile. 'But we have something they don't.'

Kinseris schooled his face as images flashed before his eyes. Of the streets of Frankesh awash with blood after the Kas'Talani had suppressed the food riots a lifetime ago; of the horror of the walls of Ephenor, so recent and vivid. He knew only too well how the Kas'Talani went to war.

But Galydon was not—*would not*—ask such things of him. He forced himself to listen, pushing the memories aside, as the general outlined what he wanted and Petrik watched him with an expression that veered between awe and aversion.

When he had finished, Kinseris said only, 'There will be damage.' There would be no avoiding that, however precise his instructions.

Galydon's keen eyes were trained on his, too observant to miss what he tried so hard to hide. 'Damage can be repaired. If we let this come to fighting in the streets, there will be worse than damage. Can you do it?'

That was not concern from a friend, but a blunt question of strength. Once, there would have been no question, but he had set that power aside. The thought brought with it a surge of loss. He had put it aside freely, and there wasn't a day that went by that he did not wish it back, did not yearn for it with a visceral longing. He took a deep breath, banishing that line of thought. He had now only what he had been born with, and it would be enough. It *was* enough.

Galydon was waiting for an answer. He nodded. What else was he good for? What else could he offer? He had no power left but this, no other weapon he could bring to their war, and the hope he had clung to—that his friendship with Darred could be turned to some advantage—had led them here.

Galydon scrutinised his face for a moment longer, then tapped the map, tracing the path of the city's main avenue. 'This is the most direct route to the palace.'

Petrik dragged his eyes from Kinseris and sucked his teeth. He indicated a point to the east of the palace. 'Morven's city mansion is here. He might not be in the palace.'

'He'll be there. If he hopes to hold the city, he must establish his control from the outset, and that means taking the palace. So we must take it back.'

'Aye.' But the clan commander looked troubled. Eventually, he said, 'Would it not be prudent, given the mood, to do this quietly?'

Kinseris heard the things he did not say—that they were Caledani, and these were Lothane's own lords in Lothane's capital city.

Galydon appeared to consider this for all of a few seconds. Then he shook his head. 'We have no time.'

Petrik sighed. 'Very well. When?'

'We go now,' Galydon decided. 'Waiting just gives them more time to establish their hold.'

Petrik looked like he wanted to argue, but then he shrugged. 'I will ready the men.' And left them alone.

Galydon sat with a sigh, suddenly looking very tired. Kinseris, who had some idea what was driving this single-minded focus other than the discharge of his sworn duties, finally asked the question that had hung unspoken since the general had ridden into the camp little more than an hour before to be confronted with this latest crisis. 'What news will you have for the queen when we find her?'

Galydon's eyes closed briefly as he ran his hands over his face. Then he straightened, looking bleakly at Kinseris. 'Nothing she would not gladly give up her kingdom to undo.'

And across the yawning chasm of loss, he heard Galydon say, 'If it comes to it, take them all down.'

FOUR

WOOD WAS ONE of the easiest materials to work magic on. Grown from the earth, nurtured by water, sun and air, wood was the embodiment of mankind's innate elemental mastery. Even for Kinseris, who had spent two years in forced rediscovery of both the limits and potential of that innate mastery after decades of reliance on the dragon device, manipulating wood was the work of moments.

The gates of Rhiannas were made of wood. They were old and strong, layers of criss-crossed solid planks reinforced with iron strapwork that had lasted a hundred years and would last a few hundred more, and he could turn them to dust in the blink of eye. But doing so would leave the city wide open to attack. Only if they could not persuade the would-be usurpers to open the gates for them would they resort to such tactics.

Galydon's plan was deceptively simple, but far more complex to carry out, and Kinseris thought wryly that it was a long time since he had juggled so many threads of power in his hands. So many interlaced layers of deception and misdirection, so directly.

The light armour Petrik had found for him sat uncomfortably across his shoulders, and he felt a sudden longing for the simplicity of Caledan's loose robes. But at least the mercenary leathers meant that clothing was one thing he did not have to alter. The face he wore now was one he knew well, that he had worn before, always as penance. Galydon retained his own features, with just the dark brown of his skin pared back to match the tan most mercenaries carried year-round. Easier to hold the glamour that way. Petrik was himself. That was, after all, the whole point.

The clan commander had managed to round up fifteen horsemen. The mercenaries did not generally fight from horseback and their mounts were reserved for scouts and their wagons, which had mostly been left with the forces that followed behind them. Kinseris was faintly relieved there were not more. Holding the glamour to disguise their origins was one thing. To do that while hiding the mounted clansmen from notice was infinitely more complex, and that was before they even entered the city and the second part of Galydon's plan came into play.

'I want maximum chaos with minimum damage,' the general had told him. 'These men will never have encountered such power used against them. It will take little to send them running. Keep them back and off balance, and we will do the rest.'

Simple to say, so much harder to do. At least, Kinseris reflected, as he concentrated on controlling his horse, once they were inside the city he could drop the glamours and focus on the chaos.

Yet the first part was simple enough. The officer who came to their summons apparently found nothing suspicious in a mercenary commander changing sides. Secure in their hold on the city, he seemed to find it perfectly natural that the clans would abandon the queen, who famously was not paying them, to negotiate a contract with those who now held the reins of power in Lothane. The clan lined up behind Petrik and his two silent officers, presenting itself for inspection, was neither threateningly large nor insignificantly small, and the great gates swung open.

The horsemen surged through. The blur of movement caught the gate guards completely by surprise, and by the time the enemy emerged from the dissipating glamours and they understood they were being attacked, it was too late.

The gates clear, Galydon kicked his horse forward, Kinseris following. On Petrik's command, the horsemen peeled off to follow them, leaving the rest of the mercenaries to secure the gate. Outnumbered, they could not hope to hold it long, and Galydon's plan had no contingency should they become trapped within the city. They must strike fast at the palace, take Morven and his fellow conspirators prisoner, and deprive this rebellion of its leaders. They lacked the numbers, so all they had was surprise and fear.

Their charge scattered the townsfolk and traders gathered to either side of the thoroughfare that stretched from the gates to become the broad avenue leading to the palace. A troop of household guards in green and gold emerged from the mouth of that avenue. They ranged into a line across the street, pikes planted to deter the horses, as more soldiers appeared behind them to deepen their ranks.

Galydon did not slow down. It was Kinseris's job to clear their way.

Behind him, Kinseris could hear the violence of the mercenaries' defence of the gates as a wall of noise. Before him was eerie silence but for the pounding beat of the horses. But where there should have been fear, there was instead a well of calm, of memory, as something inside him that had been cast down and suppressed suddenly threw off its chains.

He had been lost, his power, his rank, his purpose, even his country gone. All of it had been stripped from him, so many long years and careful plans turned to ashes. Everything he had fought and schemed for slipping through his fingers like water. He had been lost; he had not known himself. But here, amid the chaos, he remembered who he was, what he was. And *why*. This was just one more battle in what, for him, had been a lifelong war.

He let the power surge, absorbing the sharp pain of what he had lost and would now forever lack. This was what he was. No longer Kas'Talani. No longer defined by a stolen, corrupted power, but a vessel for the pure, undiluted energies of Andeira that were mankind's alone, that through Aarin…

Flat rage seared through him, and he reached deep into the earth beneath the paved street. The ground heaved and shook, and the soldiers arrayed against them stumbled and broke apart. Buildings shuddered, dust cascading down their façades as they slumped and groaned. He heard cries of alarm and knew there were people trapped in the buildings. He channelled his will into them, holding them steady, even as the quake shook the street and sent the soldiers scattering in terror.

But he stopped short of the destruction he had seen his colleagues cause. What he did was much harder. This was no rupturing of the earth, meant to maim and kill. And this was no enemy city to be destroyed. Even if Galydon had asked it of him, he could not have done that. No one would die here by his hand if he could help it.

His horse shied at the unstable ground, snorting with fear, and he knew he could not hold it. Riders pressed close on either side, and a hand reached out to take the reins as they surged through the splintered ranks of Morven guardsmen.

A clash of blades on either side told him they did not make it through cleanly. The rider to his left fell away and another took his place. Grit choked his throat and stung his eyes, and he called a wind to clear it away so that they rode out of the thick cloud of dust, caked and inhuman, and the reinforcements just arriving fled from them in terror.

The earth settled. Shouts rang out as discipline kicked in, and he set fires amid the rubble. Flames leapt skyward as a ferocious blaze roared up in their wake, cutting off the street behind them, sparks swirling out of thick black smoke.

Galydon, looking over his shoulder, grinned fiercely.

It would not hold them long. Fire without heat would reveal itself as illusion, but they were through and the palace lay ahead.

Warning had run ahead of them, the smoke and dust clouds of the havoc in their wake enough to alert the men in the palace. A hasty line of soldiers formed across the great arch into the palace courtyard even as the iron gates swung closed.

'Hold them!' Galydon shouted.

He sent a gale that lifted the men from their feet and forced the gates shrieking back on their hinges. The effort nearly cost him his seat as that burst of power seemed to take some of him with it. But he could not fall. They were too close-packed as they rode through the arch and willing hands held him steady.

Galydon rode his horse up the steps to the very doors of the palace, Petrik and his clansmen at his heels, where they wheeled their horses around in a stamping semicircle to face the stunned defenders. There was a strange stillness, despite the confusion of sound and movement, as all around them men weighed their choices.

Suddenly, Galydon was beside him, a hand on his arm, helping him down. He would not wait for them to make a decision. 'Come with me.'

As his feet touched the ground, the power drained away, leaving Kinseris hollow and wrecked. Pain returned as the world frayed at the edges.

A hand gripped his elbow. '*Can* you walk?'

Kinseris forced himself to focus, to push back the rising ride of exhaustion, aware he had stretched himself beyond wise limits, but to falter now would leave them fatally exposed, surrounded by their enemies.

He let Galydon lead him through the corridors of the palace, all else inconsequential beside putting one foot in front of the other. He was vaguely aware of shouting, of running feet, of panic rolling out ahead of them as their remorseless march took them to the doors of the throne room. There he stopped, pulled up short by the resonance of spent power and the pattern of violence it left behind.

Galydon checked, alert to his tension. 'What is it?'

His vision blurring and side aching, Kinseris let his senses quest outward, tracing the echoes. 'She fought them.'

Galydon's eyes narrowed, his fingers tensing on the hilt of his sword. 'And?' So much in just one small word.

Kinseris shook his head. He could feel the resonance of magic wielded in anger, in fear, not the outcome. But he had her now, the signature of her power, and he would know it again.

The door was closed, the corridor to either side of them empty. Beyond it he could hear frantic movements and hushed voices. Galydon exchanged a weighted look with Petrik, then the clan commander grinned and stepped forward to knock solemnly on the door.

Silence, instant and complete. Then Galydon turned to Kinseris, one eyebrow raised.

The doors exploded inward, a great cloud of dust billowing out to shouts of dismay from within. Galydon had him by the arm, keeping him on his feet, as Petrik's clansmen poured through the gaping doorway into the ruined throne room.

Galydon waited until the dust had cleared before he followed, Petrik and

Kinseris a step behind. The Lord of Morven sat on the throne on the centre of the dais, protected by his personal guards, weapons bare but their faces white and drawn. The mercenaries surrounded them in a loose ring, their numbers evenly matched. Neither side made a move.

Sedaine's circlet hung lazily from Morven's hand.

Galydon's gaze snap to the slender gold band. The queen had carried it with her to Vannarai.

Morven held the circlet aloft, letting the light catch its polished contours. 'The crown no longer requires your services,' he said to Galydon in gloating triumph. '*Lothane* no longer requires your services. Leave now, willingly, and I will overlook the damage you have caused. Refuse, and the witch will lose her life along with her throne.'

Galydon's fierce gaze swung to face him. 'You attempt to bargain from a mistaken position. I hold the power in this room, and I do not bargain with traitors. The crown requires your surrender. Give it now, willingly, and I will leave you to your queen's justice. Refuse, and you will face mine.'

Morven surged to his feet, his face flushed an ugly red. 'Yours? This city is burning by your hand, and you accuse *me* of betrayal?'

'Only one of us has attempted to usurp the throne,' Galydon said, the words deceptively calm. Only Kinseris could hear the frightening rage that lay beneath them.

'Usurp?' Morven demanded. The hand holding the circlet clenched into a fist. 'An illegitimate ruler cannot be usurped! The witch betrayed us all when she bargained with your masters, then she mocks us with this ruinous war while giving the country into your hands! What is this if not Caledani invasion in the guise of defence?'

'This,' Galydon replied evenly, 'is treason. Make your choice.'

Morven gave a bark of laughter, unable, it seemed, to recognise his danger. He turned away from Galydon, dismissing him, as his eyes scanned the mercenaries and fell on their commander. 'Petrik. I hear the witch is not even paying your contract.'

Petrik, leaning his elbow casually on the hilt of this sword, nodded. 'Aye, that is so, my lord.'

'The clans do not fight for free,' Morven scoffed. 'She dishonours you, all of you, when she asks for your swords while she betrays Lothane to your enemy.'

The clansmen at his back shifted restlessly, and Kinseris heard a rumble of discontent. Petrik did not reply, but a series of quick hand gestures quelled the unrest. He looked at Morven. 'Speak your piece, my lord. I will listen.'

Galydon turned an outraged look on the clan commander, and Kinseris had a sense of the ground shifting beneath him. Perhaps it was Galydon who had not recognised the danger.

Morven, sensing weakness, went for the kill. 'Surely you must see this for what it is? These men are not even Amadorian, let alone Lothani. These are not allies, they are conquerors!'

Kinseris felt a swell of alarm. Petrik had warned them, but Galydon had not listened. The room was suddenly rigid with tension—and he noticed, for the first time, the damage all around them. Damage he could not have caused. Something else had happened here.

'They are but two,' Morven said, wheedling now. 'Join your men with ours, and we will end the Caledani threat in Lothane once and for all. And I will pay your contract in full.'

The reaction, this time, took longer to settle, and Kinseris felt the subtle shift in the mercenaries as they looked from him to their commander and to Morven. He took a step to one side, giving himself space, reaching deep for whatever reserves remained. Galydon's fingers tightened on his arm, holding him fast.

Petrik waited in silence until the muttering subsided. 'I admit, I am tempted. And it is true that you have paid well in the past, my lord, but when my captain accepts a contract for all the clans, it is not for me to break it.'

The clan commander turned to Galydon with a regretful shrug. 'Unfortunately, the queen offered no contract.'

As one, the clansmen pivoted to direct their threat towards Kinseris and Galydon as Petrik, sheathing his sword, walked towards the dais with his empty hands spread palms out before him.

Morven gestured for his men to let Petrik through as he hurled Sedaine's circlet contemptuously at Galydon's feet. 'I rescind my offer. For the damage you have done to this country and this city, you will share the witch's fate.'

Galydon looked down at the royal band and back up at Morven. He said nothing, did nothing.

A flash of rage twisted Morven's face. 'Do you understand? You've lost.'

Galydon said dryly, 'So it appears.'

And Kinseris realised that the men around him, who should have been terrified of the power he held, were grinning. He looked again at the room and realised what he should seen at once if he had not been so tired—that if Sedaine was not here, with a knife at her throat, she was likely still free. Or already dead.

'Get them out of my sight,' Morven ordered, his tone a sneer of disgust.

The clan commander drew his sword, but he did not extend it towards Galydon. 'What the queen offered,' he said conversationally, 'was an alliance. And that we accepted.' He held out his left hand as Morven stared at him blankly. 'Your sword, my lord.'

Morven's hands went on instinct to his belt before he realised what had happened. Then he snarled with rage, jerking back out of Petrik's reach, his own sword held out not in surrender but in challenge.

There was a clatter of steel and Kinseris dragged his eyes from the confrontation to see the Morven guards dropping their weapons. He had not even noticed the mercenaries move to disarm them.

Their lord ranted at them in incoherent fury, but it was too late. 'Your sword?' Petrik said again, and Kinseris watched in fascination as pride, anger, and disbelief fuelled a hopeless, final burst of defiance.

It did not last long. As the blade lowered, Petrik reached out and snagged the hilt from Morven's nerveless fingers. He handed it to Galydon, who tossed it aside with the same contempt with which Morven had discarded the queen's circlet. This he now lifted carefully from the floor.

'I promised you your queen's justice,' he said to Morven. 'Be grateful you do not face mine.'

A clansman entered the throne room. He saluted his commander, and reported to Galydon, 'We've searched the palace. She's not here.'

Galydon's eyes snapped to Morven. 'Where is she?'

The intensity in those words made Kinseris's hackles rise, but Morven threw back his head and laughed. 'You're too late. She's dead.'

Galydon was halfway to him, blade in hand, when a clear voice cut across the room. 'You lie. She's alive.'

Limina stepped out from behind the clansman. Her face was bruised and filthy, her hair a tangled mess, but her chin was tilted in defiance as she glared at Morven. A chain dangled from a cuff on one wrist, the other was red and raw. 'You lie,' she said again, then looked directly at Galydon. 'She's with Derias. She's alive.'

'Where?'

And Morven, still wheezing with laughter, said, 'You'll have to hurry. My men are already looking. They may have already found her. And Derias has his orders.'

FIVE

LORAC BLEW ON his fingers, rubbing frozen hands together in a vain attempt to regain some feeling. Even in late spring, snow still clung to the higher slopes of the Grey Mountains between Elvelen and Lothane, and when night fell it was bitterly cold even in the lower passes. He eyed his former second Sem, the Raven's new captain, in the flickering light of distant torches. Even after two years, Lorac had to keep reminding himself that the Ravens were just one more clan now, not *his* clan any longer. Sem's pinched features were muffled by a spare shirt tied as a scarf, reminding Lorac his men fared no better.

'One more day,' he said in answer to Sem's question and saw the man frown. One more day would see a few hundred more refugees through the pass, and a few more stragglers from the Fox and Lynx clans, assuming there were any more left alive. Behind Sem, a steady stream of human misery stumbled past the ragged line of his men. Families, some with babes in arms wrapped tight in rags, the old leaning on the young as the treacherous mountains took their toll. All fleeing the brutal occupation of the borders and the spectre of Kamarai. All trying to escape into Lothane through the pass his men were holding open. But every day they delayed here in the lower pass was another day for the Caledani invaders to come against them in force. Every day they saved precious lives here, they risked the lives of not just the survivors of Kamarai but all of Lothane. They should have pulled back to the narrow defiles of the upper pass three days ago. The look on Sem's face said as much, yet here they were.

'One more day,' Sem repeated. Then he turned and disappeared into the confusion of refugees.

Lorac turned away, leaving the dispositions in his captain's capable hands. There were some advantages to his present position. If he had to make the hard decisions, at least he didn't have to deal with the human cost of seeing them through. Not yet, at least.

And they were hard. The clans had always held themselves apart, never involving themselves in the lives of the northern peoples. They took contracts, did the job, and got paid. They did not consider moral questions, nor concern themselves with the fate of the people caught up in lords' squabbles. They did the job, they got paid. When their own code pitted brother against brother too often, what was it to them if others suffered similar tragedies? They had thought themselves hardened to it, but in fact, bound tight by tradition, they had just not let themselves *see*. The scene before him was not unfamiliar, just many times worse. How many times had clan fighting sent local people running from their homes?

Now our eyes are opened. Not one of his captains had challenged his decision to hold open the lower pass for the refugees, nor would they challenge the delay, though they knew as well as he did the danger it brought them. Kamarai had changed them. Or perhaps it was just that here, at last, was a fight worth fighting. They were all, finally, on the same side.

Lorac sighed, feeling the heaviness of a command he had never wanted settle on his shoulders. Whatever it was behind this impulse, it was his responsibility to ensure it didn't get them all killed, not when they were all that was currently standing between Lothane and an invasion from the west. Hard decisions.

'Captain!'

There was an inflection in the word that told him *captain* meant him, not one of *his* captains. There was another note too, that spoke of urgency but not imminent threat.

He turned, squaring his shoulders, hiding his doubt.

Sem was striding towards him, a pair of muffled figures trudging wearily behind him. Lorac gritted his teeth. Refugees. Perhaps prominent local figures come to harangue or complain. He felt his irritation rise. He had had enough of that these last few days and no patience for more. As far as he was concerned, they had left their rank behind when they fled. Sem knew better than to bother him for this.

He opened his mouth to say as much when the Raven's captain flashed him a series of hand signals. Lorac's eyes narrowed. *Here?* He looked more closely, seeing what his eyes had missed in the torch-lit dark—fur-lined cloaks over thick coats, sturdy boots, neat packs. No refugees, even the rich, were half as prepared as these two. And, beyond them, further up the slope, he could see a handful more. *Up* the slope. They had come from Lothane.

He closed his eyes briefly. *Thank you, Lady Mother.* A messenger had got through. At last.

Lorac walked to meet them as the lead figure dropped his hood and he found himself looking into the craggy face of one of Sedaine's mages, and had to force back a flash of revulsion. These were not magicians. His memory dredged up a name. *Brannick.* They had met once. Behind him, a fair-haired, sharp-featured woman emerged from the deep folds of her cloak. Her, he knew better. She had come several times to Rhiannas.

'Needa,' he nodded at her. 'Brannick.' Both of them should have been guarding the Istelan. If they were here instead…

Needa answered his questioning look, her voice brittle. 'Galydon sent us. Said you need help.'

Sem bristled on instinct. They didn't need help, they needed reinforcements.

'Aye.' What use denying it? He looked past her to the cluster of figures who had accompanied them. 'Just you?' They needed men, soldiers, not court tricksters. No, not court tricksters, he reminded himself. But not fighters.

'Just us,' Needa agreed, her mouth a thin line, her tone a challenge.

He frowned. She had never been brimming with warmth in their prior dealings, but she had not been hostile either.

'If your general could have spared men, he would have sent them,' Brannick told him. He sounded tired. 'But I think you will find we are all you need.'

Lorac resisted the urge to point out that Galydon was not *his* general, nor did he care right now why men were so scarce that none could be sent. There would be time for that later. His problems were immediate and here, and he would take what help he could get, but all they needed? He shook his head. 'We've got hundreds of refugees need guarding, and a small army behind us. We can't hold this pass with the men we have, your power or not.'

'Then close it,' Needa snapped, and he was struck again by her hostility.

'Close it?' That was Sem, scorn in his voice. To his men, the difference between mage and magician might as well not exist. 'You gonna make it snow?'

The heavy snowfalls of winter blocked the pass to trade for months at a time, but winter was a whole fighting season away. They could not count on snowfall to do the job for them.

Brannick forestalled the woman's angry retort. 'You don't need more snow. You've got more than enough of it already.' He gestured towards the glittering white of the high slopes. 'And snow is Water.'

Lorac bit back an irritated response. Of course snow was water. Even a child knew as much.

Needa muttered something about ignorant clansmen, and he chose not to hear her. A sharp sign to Sem made that an order. The last thing he needed was a fight between his men and these newcomers.

'Water,' Brannick said patiently. 'Water is our element.'

Dawn light was creeping into the sky when Lorac woke the exhausted mages from their brief sleep and led them a short distance up the main path. He made them scramble up a scree slope to a raised outcrop that afforded them a view in both directions—down to the foothills, painted dark green and purple with heather, and up to the higher slopes of the mountains that towered through the morning mist on either side of the defile. Sharp turns hid the trade road from their sight, but he wasn't interested in the trade road right now. It was the looming menace of the upper peaks and their burden of snow that he wanted them to see.

'There.' Belly-down on the sharp stones, he pointed to where the side of the most distant peak seemed to shear straight down as though it had been sliced by a giant sword. Distance and angle magnified the illusion. Up close, the drop was neither so precipitous nor so clean, the scar of a rock fall almost a decade before that had reshaped the pass and altered the route of the trade road. 'That's the top of the pass, more or less, and its narrowest part. Used to be you could get two caravans abreast through there, now one is tight. That's where we hold them. Close that gap and they're stuck this side till it clears.'

There were other paths through the mountains—higher, narrower, more dangerous—but they were good only for scouts and goats. An army had to take the lower, easier trade road. So did refugees. It was the trade road they had to close.

He heard the creak of Brannick's joints as the old man lowered himself onto the rocks. Needa perched in a neat squat, wrists crossed and dangling from her knees, her shadowed gaze intent on the distant rock face. Neither spoke for a long interval, and he waited with wary patience. There was that in their silence that was not simply the absence of speech, and he found it unnerving.

At length, Brannick stirred. 'How long?'

Lorac looked back down the mountain. He had sent men in the night to relieve those skirmishing with the Caledani advance in the foothills and taken the reports of those returning. So far they were holding, but the line of refugees straggled for miles and there would be more behind them. He could not save them all. 'One more day,' he said gruffly, turning his back on the sight. 'We start pulling back tonight. We've already waited too long.'

He saw Needa's quick glance take in the decision and its consequences. She did not protest. He didn't think she cared. Brannick, lost in contemplation of the distant snow-capped peaks, had not yet realised the cost.

'Can you do it?' Lorac asked him. If their magic could really bring down the snow from those high peaks, they need not wait for the winter storms to close the trade road. And it would free some of his men to return to Rhiannas, where it seemed they would soon be needed, if the news he had had from Brannick was anything to go by. If Darred had called a truce, someone had forgotten to tell his forces in Elvelen.

Brannick nodded. 'We can close the pass once you are through. How far behind is the army?'

Needa made a derisive noise. 'Filling the pass with snow protects no one. Summer is almost on us. The snow will melt, and the pass will reopen unless we stay here to maintain it, and we cannot do that. We buy a week or so at most, nothing more.'

Lorac frowned. Even a few weeks was a grace he had not thought to receive a day ago, but she was right.

Brannick was shaking his head, his face pained. 'Stone is the dragons' domain, not ours.'

Lorac winced at the word 'dragon'. Kamarai was too fresh.

'Did you take nothing from your friendship with Ecyas but a slavish devotion to his son?' Needa sneered, and Lorac realised her hostility was all encompassing. Aimed at no one and everyone. 'I do not need to speak to stone to make it do my bidding, and neither do you.'

'That is not…'

Needa pointed to the cliff. 'There is a weakness there, in the rock. Perhaps another five years, and the rest of that cliff will come down.'

Brannick stirred uneasily. 'Needa…'

She ignored him. 'Snow gets into the cracks, it melts, it freezes, and the fault widens.'

Lorac looked from her to the sheer rock face, his eyes narrowing. *Water is our element.* He was starting to feel distinctly uneasy.

She looked at him and laughed. It was an odd, brittle sound. 'If we want to protect Lothane, we must bring down the mountain, and bring it down on *them.*'

Brannick's face was pale and appalled. 'Are you mad? Our power is not made for killing. We can guard, protect, but never kill.'

Needa gave a snort of disgust. 'Did you see Kamarai? That power you revere burned Kamarai to the ground and it will kill us too if we don't fight back! If their dragons don't get us, their cursed priests will, and you want to politely object without taking lives? What did you think we would have done if they had come across the river in force?'

As Brannick recoiled from her anger, she snapped, 'Are you relying on the boy to save you? He's the reason we're here. And once again he is not.'

Brannick looked at her sadly. 'Taking your revenge won't bring the dead back to life.'

'It's not revenge,' she hissed. 'It's justice!'

Lorac closed his ears to their argument to look once again at the cliff face. A rockfall such as Needa proposed would stop the Caledani force in its tracks. It might very well block the pass for good, but he could not worry about the wisdom of that now. Yet his stomach turned at the thought of the deliberate slaughter of so many. He had the mercenary's acute awareness that war was not personal. Men went where they were ordered and died for causes not their own and ideals they did not share. It could so easily be his men in the path of those rocks. His men, who were depending on him to see them to safety.

'Bring down the cliff,' he ordered, turning away from the flare of triumph in Needa's eyes, resenting her for putting this choice before him. He hated rushed decisions. It was why he had never wanted his present command. 'But not *on* the enemy unless you have no choice.'

SIX

SEDAINE RUBBED HER aching forehead and blinked gritty eyes. Her throat was scratched dry by dust and ached with thirst, and all her senses were worn thin by the demands of the delicate wards she had placed around the ruined shop. They could not hide here forever. She had sent Derias out after dark to scrounge for food, but they could not risk too many such forays lest they lead their pursuers to their hiding place.

They had to decide what to do, and the more time that passed, the more urgent that decision came. She looked at Derias, sitting against the wall with his legs drawn up and his injured arm resting on one knee. His eyes were closed but she knew he was awake, muscles too tense for rest. He was so tired. They both were. Her head felt heavy with lost sleep and her eyelids wanted nothing more than to slide closed, but she could not sleep, so instead she said, 'We could leave the city.'

There was a chance that word of what had happened had reached Galydon. If so, he would be coming for her.

Derias opened his eyes and looked at her. 'They will expect it. The gates will be too closely guarded.'

'I could hide us.' Though she had spent many years in Luen with Aarin's father, her first lessons in magic had been at the feet of the undisputed masters of illusions. For all that he lacked, her uncle's skills in glamours and deception had no rival. With no other demands on her resources, she could work a glamour that no one could breach.

Derias glanced swiftly at her, remembering, assessing, and she could tell he was tempted. Then he shook his head. 'They will be expecting it,' he said again, but she thought it was less from conviction and more from an inability to commit to a decision. It occurred to her then how young he was, and how little his life's training had prepared him for a moment like this.

She was about to try again, to insist, when raised voices floated down the street.

Derias tensed, hand edging towards the hilt of his sword, unsheathed on the floor beside him. He raised the other hand to his lips as he climbed silently to his feet and crossed to the boarded window.

The commotion faded as quickly as it had flared, the voices dying away, and she sank back with sigh. Derias stepped back from the window, suddenly decisive. 'We should –'

But she never heard what he thought they should do. The shouting was back, closer this time, close enough for her to hear what they said.

They had been found.

Wearily, hopelessly, she climbed to her feet—she would not be found cowering in a corner—and forced her will into the old door, unable to spare the energy to fashion any kind of assault. The door would only hold for so long. When they came through, she could not stop them.

Derias was at her side, his sword out. His face was grey with dust and fatigue and marked with dried blood. 'Get behind me,' he said again, and this time she did. But he could not save her either. There were too many.

The hammering came again, then Galydon's muffled voice shouting, 'Sedaine, open up!'

The wave of relief was so intense it made her stagger. Power dropped away, released in a rush, leaving her dizzy. They had come for her.

There was a thump of a body slamming into the door. 'Sedaine! It's me—Galydon. Open this door!'

Derias stepped back but he did not sheathe his sword, his face watchful and tense.

She took a deep breath and let the last of her hold on the door fall away. It splintered open with a crash and Galydon forced his way into the room. Clansmen crowded the street behind him, Kinseris among them, and she knew at once that he had tracked her here.

Galydon's eyes found hers and she saw what was usually locked down tight and hidden from view, and even at the end of her endurance her physical response was undeniable. He took two steps toward her, arm outstretched, then he caught sight of Derias and his face twisted with rage.

Sedaine caught his arm as he lunged past her. 'No! He's not with them.'

'Prove it,' Galydon snarled, brushing her aside, and she watched in horror as he backed Derias against the wall and raised his sword.

Derias didn't move as Galydon's sword came up to rest under his chin. Instead, he asked quietly, 'My brother?'

Gently, Sedaine pushed Galydon's arm down. She could feel it trembling with the force of his anger. 'He didn't know. He protected me.'

Galydon took a step back, breathing hard. So close, she could hear the thudding of his heart. It took all her self-control not to move closer, to press herself up against his warmth and strength. But Derias was standing there, watching them, fear and hurt in his eyes, and he did not deserve that.

'My brother?' he asked again, and so guarded was his tone that she could not tell what he was really asking.

Galydon sheathed his sword with a click. 'He lives, for now. Had she died, he would be dead.'

Derias nodded but made no other movement, as if he sensed that Galydon's leashed violence could erupt at any moment.

Morven's betrayal she would, she must, deal with later. Its consequences were too pressing to wait.

'Limina?' Limina, who had stayed behind to allow her to escape. If she had been hurt, if she had died, not even her affection for Derias would save his brother's life.

Galydon dragged his eyes from Derias. His expression was so bleak Sedaine felt her knees weaken.

He steadied her, gripping hard. 'She's alive. Limina's fine.'

But his voice and his eyes were irreconcilable with his words. There was something else, she realised. An ocean of anger, and behind it was something worse. This was not just for Morven.

'What is it?' she asked. 'What has happened.'

Galydon's hand tightened on her arm and he steered her towards the door, a silent look at Derias giving him permission to follow. 'Not here,' he told her grimly. 'Not yet.'

Sedaine looked at the man on his knees before her. On his knees, but not kneeling, shouting his silent defiance from the set of his shoulders to the tilt of his head as he locked his eyes on hers.

Her hands rested in her lap, pale and marked against pristine green silk. Today she had dressed like a queen because today she must dispense a queen's justice, before her lords and her people, and they must see her and know her for what she was.

Her vision was a blur of sound and movement. The great hall had been cleared of rubble, but it still bore the scars of when they had come for her. Two men, from her enemy's land, who had torn the palace apart to take down those of her own lords who had betrayed her.

The chamber was full today, as it had not been full for so many months. It was not the entire court, only as many as could be assembled at short notice, as many heads of Lothane's noble families as would obey her summons to bear witness. All here knew that she had gone to meet with Darred. That they also knew the outcome could be in no doubt. The returning soldiers would have spread the tale far and wide, and the hall was a susurration of rumour and gossip.

They also knew that Morven had allied himself with Lothane's enemy. And so today she must dispense a queen's justice.

But all she wanted was revenge.

I'm sorry, Galydon had said when he had told her. *I'm sorry.*

She did not remember the words he had spoken after that. She did not even think she had heard them. Because it was the look on his face that had told her. She hadn't needed the words at all, and she couldn't bear to hear them.

Did he see that? This man who glared at her from his knees, who had betrayed her to the enemy who had done this thing. Did he see it and fear what it meant? Or was he so blind to everything but his own ambition that he really did not know the danger he was in?

I'm sorry.

Abruptly she broke the contact, her throat aching on a silent scream. She had thought not knowing was worst she could face. She had been wrong. Not knowing meant hope, however slim. This… this was the end of hope. How many times did she have to live this same loss?

Derias had come to her the night before. He did not know and she had not told him, could not tell him. He had gone on his knees before her—he had begged her—to spare his brother's life. And she had given him the same terms she now gave his brother.

'My lord of Morven, this country needs you. I need you.' Somehow she didn't choke on the words. 'Will you recant your treason and stand with us against Lothane's enemies?'

Her voice did not shake. It was cold and deadly. Morven stared back at her, hard-eyed with hatred. He did not see. If he had, he would not be on his knees, he would be prostrate.

The silence stretched on. 'Perhaps you did not hear me, my lord,' she said, and no one there could have mistaken those words for weakness. 'Will you recant your treason and stand with us against Lothane's enemies?'

He spat on the floor.

A ripple ran through the assembled court. Behind Morven, his four remaining fellow conspirators also knelt. They did not share his defiance. Here, in her presence, they heard the threat. One tried to speak and she raised a finger, silencing him. Her whole attention rested on Morven. He must speak first. Their fate would come after.

'I will ask you once more, and once more only,' she said, her voice brittle. She would not look at Derias, standing just behind his brother. She could not. Pale and distressed, he reminded her too much of what she had lost, and her own pain flashed agony through her, hardening her heart to ice. Today of all days, there was no mercy in her. 'Re-swear your oath to the crown, to me, and I will restore your lands and your title and welcome you back to my side. If not, you give me no choice.'

'Will you bestow all my honours on my brother?' Morven sneered, breaking his silence at last, and his words were ugly, demeaning things. 'Take all that is mine and make it his?'

Derias, white-faced, made a strangled sound.

She looked at her traitor lord steadily, his bitterness and jealously exposed to wound the brother who adored him. If she could have hated him more, she would have.

'No, my lord. I will take your life.'

He did not believe her. She could see it on his face. The silence stretched on, her gaze implacable, and the sneering smile slipped, his face paled. 'You wouldn't dare.'

She could feel Galydon at her shoulder, tense and watchful. She could feel the fear and anticipation of the room, its attention rivetted on the drama before the throne.

'Yes,' she said. 'I would.'

At last he woke up to his danger, disbelief giving way to panic, and from panic to rage. But it was too late.

A flick of her wrist saw two guards move to stand either side of the kneeling man. Morven flinched away from them, his eyes wild with terrified fury. 'Kill me and you lose any chance you had of holding onto your throne! They will never stand for it!'

'Will they not?' she asked, surveying the silent ranks of courtiers. 'I see no one begging me for mercy on your behalf, my lord.'

Derias took a step forward. 'Your highness, please!'

Morven laughed. 'You think she will listen to you, boy? You think she cares? This is what you betrayed your family for! You are nothing to her— and you are nothing to me!'

And she knew then what weakness Darred had exploited to entice this man into betrayal.

Ashen, Derias stared at his brother. 'Leo…'

'Get out of my sight!' Morven snarled, too eaten up with bitterness to see the devastation on his brother's face.

'Enough,' Sedaine snapped, as Derias seemed to collapse in on himself. 'You have said enough, my lord.' And she nodded at the guards, who each took one arm and hauled Morven to his feet.

Derias looked desperately at her, his face grey. 'Please…'

'I'm sorry,' she said, as tears pricked her eyes and she had to look away. *I'm sorry.*

It was a poor repayment for the loyalty he had given her, for the devotion he had shown.

Morven spat curses at her as they dragged him out. No one else made a sound.

I'm sorry.

Derias dropped his arm to his side, his face blank with shock. Then he backed away a step, turned, and walked quickly from the room.

I'm sorry.

She turned to the four men who now faced her from where Morven had sealed his own fate. Swallowing her regret, her grief, she took a breath. 'My lords, this country needs you. I need you. Will you recant your treason and stand with us against Lothane's enemies?'

Because Darred had taken her child, he had tried to take her crown, and now, she was sure, he was coming for her country.

SEVEN

KALLIS LISTENED TO the brief report and waved the scout away, but he made no move to follow him back into the camp. He had no desire to be pestered with questions, or in fact, for company of any kind, and Meinor was more than capable of seeing to whatever needed doing.

There wasn't much *to* do, and that was the problem. Galydon had gone haring off to deal with a new crisis, following the main body of the army that had already decamped to return to Rhiannas, but they could not simply leave Vannarai undefended with Darred's army sitting just across the river. Since his force was the one in the defensive position, it made sense that he stay. It also meant that instead of a crisis to keep him busy, he was stuck here watching Darred do not very much and with far too much time to think.

Yet here he was, hiding from the few tasks he did have. Oh, he had sent regular patrols to keep an eye on activity on the far bank. He had even been down to the river himself—once he was sure Jeta was safely away, because he was too much of a coward to face her. To tell her what had happened, to admit that it was his fault, that he did this. Because he just wouldn't *listen*.

His hand curled into a fist. He would not think about that. To think was to feel, and if he let himself feel, he wouldn't be able to function.

If only the bloody army they were watching would do something, anything. They were too quiet when they should have been pressing their advantage. The withdrawal of half Lothane's troops should have been too tempting an opportunity to pass up, but they did nothing, and he did not know why. How significant was the destruction of the dragons? How badly had it affected Darred? He had no way of knowing and the only one who could have told him was...

454

No.

With a growl of disgust, Kallis abandoned his solitary vigil and stalked back to the camp. Callan emerged from a tent to his right, his arms full of soiled bandages. There had been a handful of injuries in the river camp in the chaos and panic of the dragon's thwarted attack. Most were not serious, but one young lad had tripped and fallen, breaking his lower leg badly enough that the bone had pierced the skin. With the boy unable to travel, and unwilling to leave him in Vannarai, Petrik had ordered him brought to their camp with a company of reinforcements. He had already taken a fever by the time he arrived, and Kallis privately thought him unlikely to survive. But Lysan had marched his brother into the tent where the boy lay crying for his mother and if nothing else, Callan was still here, and the boy might have a chance.

Feeling the prod of conscience, Kallis started towards him, intending to ask how the boy fared, when Callan was intercepted by one of the archers under Lysan's command. Kallis couldn't hear what the man said, but he had a clear view of Callan's face, and there was no disguising the shock that rippled across it. Or the speed with which he took off after the messenger.

Kallis felt a flutter of alarm. He could not imagine anything short of something happening Lysan that would put that look on Callan's face.

'Might be he'll live,' Meinor said, appearing at his side, nodding towards the tent Callan had just left.

His eyes on Callan's retreating back, it took a second for Kallis to realise he meant the boy with the broken leg. 'You've seen him?'

'Aye. One of us ought to.'

Kallis studied the larger man's carefully neutral expression and knew he deserved that. He was less sure he deserved the understanding that blunted the reproach. Then he sighed, rubbing a hand over his face. 'I'll see him later. Something I have to do first.'

But he had lingered in full view of the camp for too long, and one after another, minor problems came to him, which he dealt with in growing impatience and gnawing anxiety. When he finally arrived at the tent the brothers shared, he saw Lysan sitting outside, whole and unhurt. Alarm turned to suspicion. If Kallis didn't know him so well, he might have been taken in by his casual attitude. To his practised eye, however, Lysan was unmistakably on guard.

'Lysan,' he said pleasantly. 'Is Callan here?'

'Kallis,' Lysan greeted him in the same tone. 'I have not seen my brother since this morning.'

Kallis studied him. Lysan, with his sunny nature and honest face, was a terrible liar. And he knew it. There was a touch of desperation in his voice as he added, 'I thought he was with Bern.' Bern, the boy with the broken leg.

'He was,' Kallis agreed. 'Until your messenger found him.' There was a fraught pause, then he asked, 'What's going on?'

Lysan looked at him miserably. Losing patience, Kallis stalked past, only to find an arm barring his way.

'Don't go in there, Kallis,' Lysan pleaded. 'Not yet.'

Touched by a prickle of dread, Kallis gently forced Lysan's arm down and ducked inside. Callan looked up as he entered, then went back to cleaning his hands in a basin of blood-tinted water. Kallis looked from him to the figure on the cot, mercifully covered with a sheet. He felt a sudden, overwhelming desire to be sick. He closed his eyes.

'Sit down,' Callan said. 'It will pass.'

Kallis sank heavily onto the other cot as Lysan entered the tent behind him. It took a minute to get himself under control, and even then the surge of emotion closed his throat. 'How?' he asked finally. 'Is he –?'

'I found him when I returned from the pickets,' Lysan said. 'I don't know how he got here. I…' He paused, swallowing. 'I don't think he can speak.'

Kallis dragged a hand over his face, horrified. 'Merciful Maker, what have we done?'

For an answer, Callan flipped back the corner of the sheet, exposing the back of Aarin's head and shoulders. Given no warning to look away, Kallis found the protest died in this throat. Expecting the charred and weeping flesh of the body on the cliffs, he was confronted instead by livid, raw skin and puckered scarring. Scarring.

He looked up, astonished. He didn't need Callan to tell him what he was seeing was impossible. That Aarin was alive at all defied all knowledge, but there was simply no way the burns could have healed to such an extent in so short a time. Yet even so the disfigurement would be terrible.

'I cannot tell for certain,' Callan said into the silence, 'but I think that the healing process is only just beginning.'

Kallis forgot to breathe. 'What are you saying? Will he–?'

'Heal completely?' Callan shrugged and Kallis realised how tired he looked. 'I have no idea. I did not think, not for a moment, that this was possible.'

Because if you had you never would have left him there. He knew Callan well enough by now to guess just how much that thought must be tormenting him. It wasn't doing an awful lot for him either.

'Can you help him?' he asked, to force Callan to focus on the present dilemma and not the past mistake.

'Aarin must have believed so,' Lysan told his brother. 'He came to you.'

Callan's look told them he knew what they were trying to do. 'To affect the healing? No. Because that is none of my doing. All we can do is support his body while he recovers and give him a safe place to rest.'

That brought Kallis to a sudden decision. He turned to Lysan. 'Send a messenger to Galydon. Tell him what has happened—no, tell him Aarin is alive, but hurt. And tell him no one is to come here, not yet.'

Lysan was already leaving when Kallis called him back. 'This message goes to Galydon. No one else.'

Callan said, 'You think he won't have told them yet? Or you want to keep it from Darred?'

'I don't know. I don't like it, but this is about more than just Aarin's life. Galydon must decide who can know and when.'

EIGHT

THIS TIME DARRED came to him. Hanlon had been expecting it. He tried to tell himself he had not been dreading it, but that would have been a lie, and there was little room left for self-deception in his reduced existence.

There must be a price for what he had done. Davi had known it. So had the girl. But he had to stay here, not just for his son. Darred might allow him a lot of leeway in this strange dance of theirs, but there was one unspoken rule he would not be permitted to break. Darred might sometimes turn a blind eye to the comings and goings of his Farnorians, but no such grace would be granted should he attempt to leave. If he tried, he suspected he would discover that he was guarded by more than just men.

Besides, if he took to the sea now, Darred would know where to look for him and he would see what they desperately needed to conceal.

So he had steeled himself to meet his enemy and defy him, whatever the cost, but when Darred finally appeared after nearly two days, tired and pale and dishevelled, Hanlon almost did not recognise him. The unconquerable arrogance, the infuriating confidence, was utterly stripped from him. Instead, he seemed subdued, thoughtful, almost sane.

Hanlon looked at him and saw for the first time only a man. And hated him for it. His enemy had no right to seem so human.

Darred's face wrinkled with disgust as he entered the tent, and Hanlon hated the rush of shame for the conditions his enemy forced on him. He seemed to have nothing but hate in him these days.

A quiet command saw the guard secure the tent open, allowing clean air in, and the stream of sunlight cast Darred's face into shadow so that Hanlon could no longer make out his expression.

Darred contemplated him in silence for a long moment, eyes roaming around the tent, resting briefly on the patch of earth where the girl had lain. Then his gaze returned to Hanlon. 'I am not currently possessed of much patience, so let us not dance, Admiral, this once. What did she tell you? You did ask her, I presume, since you were good enough to help her escape.'

The girl had not been put with him by chance or carelessness. He had known that from the moment they had dragged her into the tent. And he had not meant to play Darred's game, not at first, but then she had spoken Kinseris's name and he had seized the chance she offered him, because there was nothing left to lose. And he would not throw it away now.

It was pointless to lie, but he lied anyway. 'Her own people were in the camp. They got her out.' He tugged at the chains that kept his hands secured behind him. 'If it was me, would I still be here?'

'So you know who she was,' Darred observed. 'And no doubt why she came. So, I will ask once more: what did she tell you?'

'That you made a mistake and left your enemy alive.'

He expected a spark of anger, but Darred looked amused. 'Kinseris was never my enemy, far from it.' There was a pause, then, 'He is my friend.'

Hanlon snorted. 'Aye, a friend. Like I am.'

Darred laughed softly. 'Just so. Do you have regrets, Admiral?'

'Aye,' he replied, watching his enemy. 'I will never feel the sea wind on my face again. I regret that. I imagine your own are more vengeful.'

'You would think so, wouldn't you? But no. What would be the point?'

'Of revenge? Isn't that why we're here?'

Darred's smile was devoid of warmth. 'Of course. I meant regrets. What can be gained from them?'

'Perhaps they make us human.'

'Indeed,' Darred observed with a touch of his old manner. 'Many things make us human, Admiral. Fear. Pain. Love.'

Cold dread squirmed in Hanlon's belly as Darred's eyes sharpened on him. His wrists protested as his fists clenched, straining against his bonds.

Darred saw it and smiled. If his smile had been cold before, it was wintry now. 'My patience, Admiral, is waning.'

'Will you take my other eye?' Hanlon growled, taking small pride in the fact his voice did not shake. The thought of it turned his bowels to water. The terror and pain of his maiming were too raw, and the fear of the darkness too great. Blindness would take from him everything he was, everything he loved. He could not be a sailor if he could not see. But he would never see the sea again, whatever happened here today.

Darred shook his head with a tired quirk of his lips. 'And make you useless to me? I think not, Admiral. I need your sight. I don't, however, need your thumbs.'

The swell of panic was so overwhelming he almost vomited as he contemplated something worse than blindness. It took everything he had to say, 'Take what you like from me. I will not tell you.'

Darred studied him thoughtfully, then he nodded. 'Very well.'

Hanlon felt dizzy. His heart was beating very fast. 'Just like that? You give up?'

Darred shrugged. 'Perhaps I won't take it out on you at all.'

The panic this time was worse than before, because he could endure anything, *anything*, if it kept his son safe from harm. But he could not give up so many lives for one, though Maker forgive him, he wanted to.

'Your choice, Admiral.'

Hanlon stayed stubbornly silent.

Darred sighed. He glanced behind him, out of the tent. The sun was past its height, the day well into afternoon. 'We leave tomorrow.'

'Where?' Hanlon asked, his voice husky. Darred must know already. It was the only thing that made sense.

Darred's teeth flashed white in a shaft of sunlight. 'You can't do anything with it, Admiral.'

'Then there's no harm in telling me, is there?'

Darred walked to the tent door, his back turned. And he said, without looking back, 'I find I grow tired of restraint, Admiral. And if the girl brought you a message from Kinseris, I suspect I may soon be pressed for time. It is time for Lothane to burn.'

NINE

THE RHIANNAS JETA returned to was not the Rhiannas she had left. The gates were closed and barred, and the walls more heavily manned than she had seen them, though the gates opened readily enough once her escort was recognised, and the royal flag was flying to indicate the queen in residence. Whatever Kinseris had feared, the city was still in Sedaine's hands.

Inside it was less reassuring. The signs of a fight were everywhere, and though most of the damage had been set right, bloodstains marked the cobbles and she saw more than one clansman bearing an injury.

Jeta waited patiently while the mercenaries exchanged news and orders and the clan captains organised their men. She had fretted the whole length of their journey, but now they were here she found herself reluctant to confront what she would find.

The morning after she had escaped from Darred, when she had woken to find the camp being urgently disassembled, Kinseris had told her what they knew, which was not much. He had been so careful with her, so gentle, and she knew it was because he believed Aarin was dead. But she did not believe it. She would not. If the dragon lived, Aarin would live. She was certain of that. And it seemed inconceivable that the dragon could be gone, that the immensity of its existence could be extinguished so easily. Because of her. Because of what she had done.

They had ridden together that first day and she was reminded of the journey from Ephenor, how careful he had been never to leave her alone, and the memory hurt, because then she had believed Aarin gone forever and she had not thought she wanted to live. Kinseris had given her back her life and for a while she had been happy—until that life was ripped away and Aarin had returned, and now it felt like every choice she made hurt not only herself but those she loved. But Kinseris was wrong about this. He had to be. She would *know.*

She could feel his doubt, his concern that she would not accept what he thought to be truth, but he had not argued with her. They'd had so little time. Not nearly enough to say all the things that needed to be said. She didn't have the words and she sensed that he would not speak until she did. That he understood better than she did that the space he had given her was what she needed, and she needed it still.

That first evening on the road, as most of the mercenaries had pitched a camp, Petrik had taken two companies and marched on through the night, setting a pace that the main force with its wagons and followers could not hope to match. Kinseris had gone with them. If Khiannas was truly threatened, he would be needed. She understood that, just as she understood that if it came to a fight, her presence would be a hindrance. They could not spare the men to protect her.

So she had stayed with the wagons and the other women, not because she wanted to, but because rash action on her part had already caused enough damage.

A captain detached from the group of the officers by the gatehouse and offered to take her to the palace. They went on foot, and she soon realised why. A clansman whistled low and long when they saw the state of the road leading to the palace. Jagged cracks snaked across the cobbled street, and the buildings on either side lurched at odd angles and crawled with craftsmen.

She stopped dead, anxiety transforming into alarm 'What happened?'

The captain glowered and spat. 'Mage craft.'

'Who –' But he had already moved away, and Jeta had to run to catch up.

Her alarm rose a notch when they reached the palace. One of the huge gates lay on its side as men worked to straighten warped ironwork. The other was being fitted back into new hinges. All around them stepped a flurry of grooms and unfamiliar servants, watched in grim silence by a heavy guard of mercenaries and garrison soldiers.

The clan captain, his duty discharged, took his leave as soon as they entered the courtyard, and for a moment she just stood there, unable to summon the resolve to confront what had happened. Someone bumped her elbow, and she stepped out of the path of two men carrying a chest only to find herself berated by another who nearly tripped to avoid her.

She was halfway up the steps when Derias burst out of the palace. He brushed roughly past, taking the steps at a run, his face bone-white and tight with distress. She called after him, but he disappeared through the gates and out into the city.

Just breathe. Find Kinseris.

The guards on the doors let her through without comment. She knew them both. Inside, the corridors were lined with guardsmen in royal livery and full of strangers, richly dressed in elaborate court finery. The Lords of the North had arrived.

She attracted a few disapproving looks as she made her way against the flow towards the main hall. In comparison to the spotless attire of the court officials and attending nobility, her travel-stained clothes were an affront, but no one stopped her. They barely noticed her.

Jeta was used to aristocratic company. She knew how they moved, how they spoke. The men and women around her were in a state of poorly concealed shock. She could hear it in voices that were a shade too loud and laughter that was too high and went on too long.

She quickened her pace, brushing too close to a woman in a silk dress who assumed she was a servant and started to complain. Jeta ignored her. The entrance to the audience chamber stood ahead. The doors were gone, the frame that had contained them no more than splintered wood in damaged stonework. Huge cracks snaked outward, leaking dust, and as she passed through the small antechamber she saw the hasty framework of planks shoring up the ceiling.

Just breathe.

The throne room bore even worse scars. Half the ceiling was gone, a latticework of ancient wood revealed through the gaping hole, and the walls were covered once more with tapestries, which she suspected hid more damage. Whatever had happened here, it had not happened today.

Sedaine sat on the throne, her face as white and taut as Derias's had been, her gaze distant. Galydon stood protectively beside her, talking quietly with Petrik, whose clansmen lined the room to either side. A group of men she didn't recognise stood under guard before the throne. She looked for Kinseris and felt a touch of panic when she could not see him. She knew what had caused the damage here and in the city. Then she found him, the sober colours of his clothes blending into the background as he stood to one side, watching.

No one noticed her as she slipped inside and threaded her way through the departing audience. Then Sedaine's head turned towards her and the distance fell away from her eyes. What Jeta saw there instead made her heart thud painfully. Galydon looked up, following Sedaine's gaze, and he fell silent.

Jeta looked from one to the other. 'What has happened?'

Her memory of what came next was never clear. She remembered the way Kinseris turned at the sound of her voice as though he had been slapped. She remembered Sedaine standing, and her sharp command to clear the room. She had a vague memory of Galydon leaving, perhaps called away. Later, she knew why. But the rest of what happened disappeared as though it had never been, because by then she *knew*, and the world broke apart.

She did not remember leaving the throne room. The next thing she was aware of, she was sitting in a chair in Limina's apartments and there was a cup of wine, half-empty, in her hands. The taste of wine was on her tongue, but she could not remember drinking. Carefully, she set the cup on the table at her elbow. Everything felt as fragile as glass. Her hand shook, the cup clattering out of strengthless fingers. Then everything unravelled, the shaking all through her, her breath stopped in her throat.

A rustle of movement. Someone knelt by her side. She heard her name, then arms wrapped around her, hugging her, rocking her, and she fell into them as the soundless wail she had been holding inside burst like a dam.

But it was not Limina who held her. It was Sedaine. Aarin's mother.

And that could not be right, because this was *her fault!* If she had not gone to Darred, Kallis would not have gone to the exchange and Aarin would not have gone after him. Sedaine had lost her only child because of what she had done, but there was no anger, no judgement, in the embrace that held her, only grief to match hers and a need to share it.

'I'm sorry.'

The words were mangled by tears, but Sedaine heard them.

Calloused hands enclosed her face, a cool forehead rested on hers. 'No. *No.*'

Sedaine's voice cracked on the word and Jeta had a sense of a loss so deep and awful that her own paled before it, the hurt of a mother for her lost child. She felt her own grip tighten in response, but she did not attempt to comfort what could not be comforted. Instead, in the other woman's raw, choking grief, she allowed the harsh vice of her own agony to find its release.

Time passed. There was a knock at the door.

Limina opened it. Galydon stood there. His face was tight.

He dropped to one knee by her side. By Sedaine. The queen tilted her face so he would not see her tears.

'Look at me,' he said, and Jeta saw Sedaine close her eyes as though steeling herself. Then, with a deep breath, she turned her head.

Galydon looked at Jeta to make sure he had her attention also. He smiled. 'He's alive. He's *alive.*'

TEN

IT SHOULD HAVE been simple. Retreat up the trade road, keeping the Caledani at bay long enough to reach the top of the pass, blocking it behind them. It *would* have been simple, Lorac thought bitterly, if they had gone a day earlier, maybe two. Now it was all a bloody mess and there was no point wishing things had gone differently. They had been too slow and the enemy too close behind them.

In fact, they hadn't been behind at all, or not all of them, and the ambush had fallen on them as the refugees were still clearing the top of the pass.

Lorac roared uselessly at his remaining men who were hurrying the exhausted Elvelians through the bottleneck. Too many were still milling around in confusion on the road just beyond the pinch point, blocking those behind from coming after, and he had sent Sem and two others forward to hustle them on. If they stayed there, they would all be crushed.

An ominous vibration rumbled through the stone beneath his feet. In the distance, crouched halfway up the opposite slope, he could see the cloaked figures of Needa's mages. He knew they had been working on the rock face all through the previous day and night, widening its faults, weakening the cliff, doing in a day what would have taken the elements years to accomplish. Brannick had warned him they could not precisely control the moment of collapse, which meant they had to move everyone through the danger zone as quickly as possible or risk disaster.

The Caledani above them were scrambling down the slope, dropping into the pass as the tail-end of the line of refugees broke into panicked chaos. A child stood alone in the centre of the track, face contorted in a silent scream. It should have been so bloody simple, Lorac thought bitterly as he plucked the wailing child from the path and thrust it into the nearest set of empty arms, before whirling round to defend himself against the rush of a blade.

His men knew their business and they were already cutting out the first few Caledani, protecting the stream of refugees, finally galvanised by terror to push their way forward. But the goat paths above were crawling with the enemy and it was not long before the weight of numbers forced his men back, cutting them off and forcing them in the wrong direction, back down the pass.

They were trapped. A company of Caledani were now between them and the safety of the far side of the cliff face. And behind them, cutting off their retreat, was the advancing main force of the enemy.

A figure was standing on an outcrop high up the opposite face of the pass, outlined against the sun.

It took a split second to recognise what had to happen, and only a second more to get his men moving.

By cutting them off, the Caledani had placed themselves in the direct path of the fall, but no one in the pass would be safe once the rocks came down.

Lorac could feel the eyes of that unknown watcher on his back as they broke into a run, back towards the startled enemy. One hundred yards, two, then three... Another rumble ripped through the stones beneath his feet, then a second, increasingly violent, and he screamed, 'Up!'

They scrambled up the opposite slope, hauling themselves hand over hand as fast as they could, angling up and away from the danger. The rumble became a crescendo. He watched in fascinated terror as the face of the cliff just dropped away, plunging in a thunder of violence and noise onto the road below. The dust cloud billowed up, choking his throat as the shockwaves made the ground buck and leap beneath his feet.

A boulder the size of a man's head tumbled away from the main fall and glanced off a rock to ricochet up the slope and crush a clansman an arm's breadth from his side. The blood hit his face in a warm splatter, almost emptying his stomach, and he turned his head just as another boulder, bigger by far than the first, rolled inexorably down the trade road and smashed into the advancing line of soldiers.

There was no time to think about what had happened on the other side of the fall, no time to grieve.

'Up,' he growled again, then coughed, hacking up grit and dust.

His men were already moving, stumbling up the steep incline. Below them, the cries of the stricken soldiers sounded harsh against the eerie silence that clung to the shattered ruins of the cliff. He stumbled, shrugging off a steadying hand, and twisted to stare back down into the pass, but the cloud of dust was too thick, shrouding what was left of the trade road in a dense grey pall. He could not see what had happened, or what they had lost.

ELEVEN

KALLIS PERCHED ON the edge of Lysan's cot and forced himself not to flinch from the barely healed scarring on his friend's face. Already it was immeasurably better than it had been. It was the internal damage that was taking longest to heal. This was the first time they had spoken, because until now Aarin *couldn't* speak, his throat was so badly burned.

Kallis cast a glance at Callan, who stood to one side, watching them with arms crossed.

Aarin sat on the other cot, arms wrapped around his knees. Every movement was stiff with pain, his skin a hideous patchwork of livid scars. Only his right forearm remained heavily bandaged, thrown up to shield his eyes. It had saved his sight, but in doing so it had taken the brunt of the wall of flame, the flesh burned down to the bone. If not for his link with the dragon, that injury alone would have killed him. Even with it, he was lucky not to lose the arm, and Callan thought it would take months to fully heal.

Kallis rubbed a weary hand on his neck. 'Aarin. I'm sorry…'

Aarin waved a hand in dismissal, every movement creaking. 'Don't…' The word rasped in his throat. 'Not… your… fault.'

That was too much. Kallis found his own voice cracking. 'I should have listened to you. I should never have gone.'

He knew now what had happened, how Jeta had managed to escape and had made her way back to Kinseris and Galydon mere hours after he left them. How he missed Galydon's message because he would not wait. How Callan and Lysan sent the messenger after him, then searched for him themselves. But none of it would have happened if only he had *listened*.

'I was angry. I wasn't thinking straight.' It wasn't much of an explanation, but it was all he had. He had let his hatred of Darred and his anger over Iraius's death, over Jeta's foolish sacrifice, cloud his judgement, and refused to hear what Aarin had tried to tell him.

Aarin's face twisted, scarred skin pulling on his mouth. An attempt at a smile. 'I know.'

Kallis looked away, sick to his stomach. 'We left you…'

'Didn't know,' came the raspy reply. 'Didn't… tell you.'

There was silence for a beat, then Callan said, 'Tell us what?'

'Hard to kill… together. I thought we could get through… get free. Thought I could… control it.' The words were breathless, strangled. He turned his head away. 'Make Darred think… won. Wrong. Killed them.'

Kallis didn't hear the choked grief, the piercing regret, he only heard the words that preceded it, and felt a swell of anger and revulsion.

'You planned that?' he demanded, sickened, reliving the horror of the burned body on the cliff. 'You…' Words failed to encompass the thought that anyone could plan such physical devastation. He swallowed. 'And you knew what it would do to you?' Because to plan such a death was bad enough, but to plan to live was beyond comprehension.

Aarin recoiled from his fury. 'Not a plan…hoped…all survive. Couldn't fight them.'

Appalled, it was Kallis who now turned away. 'You did *that* to protect Darred's dragons? The dragons that are *killing* us? I thought, we thought…'

'Kallis,' Callan said warningly.

But Kallis was too angry to listen. 'Did you hear him?' he demanded of Callan. 'He did that *to himself.*'

'I heard him,' Callan replied. 'Did you?'

Aarin said urgently, 'He thinks… I'm dead. Lost two. Be careful.'

Kallis turned back to him. 'What?'

'Darred…' Aarin took a breath, coughed, and there was a wracking pause during which no one spoke.

Callan said, 'Darred thinks he's dead. You have a window. Use it.'

The words sapped the fury, leaving nothing but the horror. He felt very tired. 'Aarin, what we saw…'

'What you saw... I *lived*,' Aarin retorted, and this time Kallis heard the emotion and saw on his face the terrible cost of both the maiming and recovery. 'Don't make... same mistake.'

But he could not stand it, so he left.

When Callan found him some time later, Kallis was already more than half drunk, sitting at the loudest, rowdiest fire in the camp. One hand rested on his bent knee, a flask held in loose fingers. He waved it at Callan who shook his head. 'Suit yourself.' He planned to get drunk. To wipe, if he could, the nightmare images from his head.

They sat in silence for a while, Kallis drinking steadily, until suddenly he sat up, hurling the empty flask into the darkness.

'I can't get it out of my head. Every time I close my eyes... no matter how much I bloody drink. And the smell...' Maker, the sickening smell of a charred corpse. 'And it was all a *trick*?'

'If it was a trick, it was all too real. Don't forget, I saw him too.'

Kallis recoiled, shamed. It was Callan who had carried Aarin's body from the dragon's back, who had kept him from looking too closely on the ruin of his friend. He looked away. 'How could he do that? Why?'

'What are you really angry about?' Callan asked. 'That he almost died, or that he lived?'

His head whipped back, eyes wide. 'Why am I angry? I listened to that boy yammer in my ear for a year about the magic and the dragons. And when I think of what we went through, what your people sacrificed.... That he could just go and throw that away. We need him!'

Callan shook his head. 'But this wasn't about us, Kallis. You listened to Aarin for a year—have you listened to him since he came back?'

'I –'

'Because if you had,' Callan continued remorselessly, 'you would realise that everything he has done, he did for them. And what you see as a senseless sacrifice is to him a tragic failure. Aarin's life has only one purpose and it is not to save us, but he is tearing himself in two because you don't understand that. He is here because of the dragons, Kallis. That is the only reason he is back, because Darred has found a way to enslave them. But now he is here, he cannot simply pursue his own aims and leave you unsupported—*because you keep asking him to help.*'

Shocked, Kallis looked up.

'The dragons died,' Callan said, harsh. 'And Aarin would have paid any price—any price at all—to prevent that. Except one.'

Kallis felt the blood drain from his face. Aarin had begged him not to meet Darred, to retreat into Lothane and leave Darred to him. But he had refused, because he had been so angry, so determined not to lose another friend. Too convinced he was right.

And because of that decision, Aarin had been denied the freedom to act without risk to his allies. And so, instead, to protect them, he had been forced into the sacrifice that had almost destroyed him and had killed the creatures whose lives he was dedicated to protect. Because the fire could not have touched him unless he let it, and why would he let it if not because he did not have resource enough to shield both himself and the army? And Kallis saw, finally, that Aarin had not sacrificed himself, but the dragons.

What you saw, I lived!

Those words, spoken in desperate rebuttal, took on a much darker meaning. Kallis had watched Aarin break faith with the dragons and himself to preserve the lives of his friends. And he had lived. Kallis knew he would find that all but intolerable.

Two dragons were gone but Darred believed he had wiped out his greatest threat. That might mean a reprieve, or it might mean all-out assault. He made a decision. 'We leave in the morning. Stay with him. Move about.'

Callan nodded. He had not needed to ask, that Callan would not have strayed from Aarin's side for anything. And he felt a little twist of guilt at that because he could not bear to stay.

The silence stretched, then Callan said, 'I think Jeta should come here.'

'What? I don't think…'

Callan ignored his protest. 'Lysan can bring her.'

Kallis thought about that for a while. 'I don't think that's going to work out how you expect.'

Callan didn't reply and Kallis had the distinct feeling he was missing something. He reached for the flask, cursing when he remembered what he had done with it. Regret led instantly to the memory of what he wanted to forget, and he sighed. 'I can't get it out of my head.'

After a moment, he felt Callan's hand press on his leg as he rose to leave. 'Neither can he. That's the problem.'

Galydon was there to meet them when Kallis and his men straggled into Rhiannas three days later. Kallis looked from the general to the extensive repair works in evidence all around them. 'I don't even want to know.'

Galydon's lips twitched. 'Nothing much to tell.'

'Yes, I can see that.'

He glanced towards where Meinor was talking to Petrik's second. Catching his eyes, Kallis signed a request. Meinor raised a hand in acknowledgment, and Kallis, one less task on his shoulders, turned back to Galydon. 'So, what now?'

Galydon glanced at the gallery. 'First, you need to see the queen, give her your news.'

Kallis winced. That was going to be fun. 'There's not going to be much left of me after that.'

'Just enough, with any luck,' Galydon said, 'because we have work to do.'

TWELVE

JETA WATCHED THE newly arrived mercenaries milling around in the courtyard. Kallis had disappeared inside with Galydon, who would take him to Sedaine. To Aarin's mother. After that, she would have to track him down herself. Kallis would run cheerfully onto the swords of his enemies before he would willingly talk to her about this.

So the quiet footsteps behind her some minutes later came as a surprise. But when she turned it was Lysan hovering on the threshold of the gallery, his demeanour uncharacteristically hesitant.

'Are you looking for me?'

'Who else?'

He drew alongside her, leaning his elbows on the balcony so she could see only his profile. 'I have a favour to ask you, from my brother.'

She had not been expecting that. 'From Callan?'

He shot her a quick, troubled glance. 'He needs your help.'

'With what?' But she knew.

There was a slight hesitation. 'With Aarin.'

A hundred questions hovered on the tip of her tongue, but she settled for the simplest. 'How is he?'

Lysan grimaced. 'I don't think I know how to answer that. It was... bad.'

He fell silent, and she saw on his face a pale echo of what 'bad' meant. Enough that she did not press him for details. Galydon had given them the bare bones of Kallis's message and there were some things she did not want to imagine. Instead, she asked, 'I can help—how?'

He smiled faintly. 'I'm just the messenger, but if Callan thinks you can help, he'll have his reasons. And he's usually right.'

She thought of all the ways she *wanted* to help, and all the ways Aarin might fight her, and wondered whether Callan knew what he was doing after all. She also thought about what it would mean if she went, and to whom, but she did not need to speak to Kinseris to know what he would say. 'When do we leave?'

Lysan flashed her a grateful smile. 'Tomorrow is soon enough,' he said. It was already afternoon and even with the lengthening evenings, they would not make it far today. Then he grinned. 'There's someone else I was hoping to see tonight.'

It took her a moment to understand, then her hand flew to her mouth. 'Oh Lysan, I'm sorry.'

'Sorry?'

'You don't know. Derias has gone.'

Raw and bleeding but still largely intact after his meeting with Sedaine, Kallis was ushered into Galydon's office, where he found the general waiting with Kinseris.

'I don't even have time for a rest,' he grumbled, taking the *kafe* Galydon offered him and avoiding Kinseris's eyes. He had no wish to repeat the conversation he had just had, and he was uncomfortably aware that Jeta would be waiting for him when he emerged.

'You can rest when this is over,' Galydon told him unsympathetically. 'We have decisions to make and they can't wait.'

'Do they have anything to do with the mess you made of the city?' His meeting with Sedaine had been painfully focused.

Kinseris winced, confirming one suspicion. Kallis pursued another. 'Where's Derias?' You couldn't usually go near Sedaine without falling over her chancellor, but today he was nowhere in sight.

'Now that,' said Galydon heavily, 'does have something to do with it.'

Kallis set down his cup with a pang of real regret. 'Tell me.'

Some of it he knew already, some he had guessed. But when Kinseris related the news that Jeta had brought with her out of Darred's camp—that he had not expected. Not that he was given long to enjoy the cautious optimism, as Galydon sketched the details of the rebellion that had nearly made it irrelevant.

'Wait,' he said, holding up a hand to stop the flow of words. 'She *executed* him?'

Galydon was frowning. 'What should she have done?'

'She needs Morven's resources,' he retorted. '*You* need them. Better than half our horsemen come from Morven's levies. Derias could have given them to you, but—and I can't believe I am saying this—*you killed his brother.*'

'You weren't there,' Kinseris said.

'Oh, I've met the man,' Kallis assured him. 'You forget how I've spent most of the last ten years. But we *needed* him.'

'That may be so,' Galydon said. There was no mistaking his feelings on the matter. 'But she had no choice, he made sure of that himself.'

And she had done it thinking Aarin dead. Kallis had to bear his part of the blame for that. Had Derias known? Had he understood why his brother had died? He rubbed a hand wearily over this face. What a mess. But it was done. Derias would come round, or he wouldn't, and in the meantime they had a hundred other problems to deal with.

'What news from Elvelen?' Needa and Brannick should have reached Lorac weeks ago.

Galydon shook his head. 'There has been no word. Since we do not yet face invasion from the west, we must assume they are holding.'

He did not ask whether they had sent scouts to find out. Galydon liked not knowing what was happening on his flanks as much as any commander. He would have done what he could to ascertain the situation on their western border.

'But Elvelen is lost.' It was the only conclusion.

'Elvelen is lost,' Galydon agreed. 'I think perhaps it was lost from the moment this started. We expected one kind of war, we got another. All that's changed is that now we know why, though it would be unwise to assume we understand all Darred's motivations. So, now we must find a way to defend Lothane on two fronts and hold it together until help arrives.'

'For four months? For help that may or may not come? If you're right, and he's about to move—and it is well past time—then four months is likely three months too long.'

Galydon spread his hands. 'Nevertheless.'

Kallis muttered his view on that. 'Do you agree?' he asked Kinseris. 'Is this it?'

Kinseris looked as tired as he felt, his fingers drumming a rhythm on the desk. 'What else can he do to her? As far as he knows, Aarin is dead, and though his gambit here may have failed, I doubt he cares. In all the ways that matter, he succeeded in his aim. Now she knows how fragile her grip on power is, and trust me, that is no small thing to live with.'

On that point, Kallis would not dream of contradicting a man whose experience was so much vaster than his own. He picked up his forgotten cup, but the *kafe* was stone cold and he spat it out in disgust. He frowned, massaging aching temples, then gave his considered opinion of the situation. 'We're fucked.'

When Lysan led Jeta into the little camp where Callan waited, it was almost full dark. Callan came to meet them. Even in the dim light he looked exhausted, his eyes smudged purple and red rimmed from lack of sleep.

'Nightmares?' she asked, surprised at the steadiness of her voice.

He nodded. 'Thank you for coming.'

What had he expected her to do?

A faint sound drew his eyes towards the tent. She hurried after him as he retraced his steps, but he held out his hand to stop her before she could go inside.

'Jeta –'

She knew what he was going to say. Gently, she lowered his arm. 'It's all right. Lysan told me.'

He shook his head. 'It is one thing to hear.'

Another to see. She had not wanted to imagine it, but it had been impossible not to. Seeing would be a relief. 'I understand.'

He studied her face for a drawn-out interval, but at last he seemed satisfied, holding the canvas aside to let her duck inside. Jeta stepped past him and barely heard the words he murmured before he left her alone. Her entire attention was focused on the figure on the cot.

Alone, Jeta watched Aarin for a moment, unmoving, taking in the raw scars that snaked up his neck and head, the uneven first regrowth of hair, and the rapid, shallow breathing that warned of unquiet dreams.

She forced herself to look without flinching, to take in every inch of the gruesome damage, to endure it and learn it so that he need never see the horror of it reflected in her eyes. Because she had done this to him, and he did not deserve her revulsion.

Then, as Aarin's breath hitched and his hands clenched, she slipped off her cloak and stepped out of her dress. Naked, she climbed into the bed beside him, soft, warm, and safe, and drew his scarred head onto her shoulder. The human comfort he would never accept from her awake she gave to him sleeping and felt him relax against her. And then, silently, she wept.

There had been many long nights in her life, but that was the longest. The bitterest. And yet she knew she would treasure it.

At some point she must have fallen asleep. The next thing she knew Callan was shaking her. He had one hand on her shoulder, the other on his lips.

'It's almost dawn.'

When Callan had gone, she sat up carefully, shifting Aarin's head to rest on the cot, still warm from where she had lain, and slid out from under the blanket. She dressed quickly in the pre-dawn darkness, one eye on the sleeping man. He had not wakened once in the night, though she had felt the moments when the nightmares came clawing at him, and each time she had held him close, speaking soothing, meaningless words until the flames and the darkness retreated. But all that would be undone if he woke and found her like this.

She slipped out of the tent to attend a call of nature, then joined Callan at the small fire and took the plate of food he offered her.

In the dawn light he looked even worse than he had the night before. 'Did you sleep?' she asked.

He shook his head. Brown eyes studied her in his turn. 'How are you?'

Callan must have sat with Aarin through countless long nights, through

478

countless nightmares. The thought caused a rush of sorrow, and she blinked, forcing a smile. 'Tired.'

Lysan joined them, yawning hugely and bringing the unfailing warmth of his presence to their bleak little gathering. As he wolfed down the cooling breakfast, Callan caught Jeta's eye and nodded towards the tent. 'He'll wake soon.'

She found she did not want to go back in, that she lacked the courage. But Callan had not brought her here just to steal into Aarin's bed at night and guard his dreams.

So when Aarin finally woke, she was drowsing in a chair by his side. Alerted by the change in his breathing, she turned to see his eyes open and watching her warily, whole and undamaged but clouded with sleep and pain.

He tried to speak, but the words would not come, and she averted her gaze as he struggled with his maimed throat. 'When... did you...?'

'This morning.'

He frowned in confusion. 'I dreamed... of you.'

The flippant, easy response died on her lips as she saw the raw hurt in his eyes. 'Callan told me about the nightmares.'

He did not reply to that, his eyes still searching her face. Then he rolled onto his back, the fingers of one hand twitching towards her. She reached out and slipped her hand into his and felt the answering pressure of his fingers. There were tears on his face.

'Thank you.'

THIRTEEN

JETA STAYED WITH them as Aarin healed. She went to him every night after he had fallen asleep and left each morning before he woke. If he knew how she spent her nights, he never said. She suspected that he feared that if he did she would stop coming, and that made her sad because she thought perhaps it was true.

Awake, he was frequently impatient and irritable, unwilling to accept help yet still in need of it. She had watched Kinseris recover from his injury, in fits and starts, in progress and regression, over long, drawn-out months, and she understood what she was seeing. She understood that pain, in and of itself, was as exhausting as injury, and that the frustration of doing nothing day after day would inevitably outpace Aarin's ability to be up and about. And also that it would pass.

This was faster, a process accelerated and supported by the link between man and dragon, but the dragon was also healing, and Callan had warned her that this made it harder for both of them—that it was not just Aarin's own injuries that lay behind his cut-glass fragility, but the dragging weight of Silverwing's hurts that could not be entirely blocked out. And while the death of the dragons tormented him, privately she thought it a blessing, because it gave him time to heal.

It gave time for other things as well, that she came to treasure. Things that had nothing to do with this war. Lysan joined them now and then, bringing supplies, helping them move. He brought news from Rhiannas and Kallis, amusing stories and army gossip, though he never stayed long. Just long enough, she thought, to reassure himself that his brother was finally coming alive again. If he had stayed longer, he might have seen why.

Aarin didn't do much talking at first. The effort was too painful and exhausting to sustain for long, and it was a while before she realised what he was doing.

It was Callan who finally showed her, one evening several days after her arrival. He was sitting cross-legged on the ground, patiently stitching a tear in a shirt as the light began to fade. Aarin was propped up against a tree not far from his side. His eyes were closed, but that could mean anything. She watched Callan idly as he examined the stitching. The light was disappearing fast and soon it would be too dark for such work. His frustrated glance at the sky said he knew it too. So it should not have surprised her when the little globe of light popped into being above his shoulder, except…

She cast a quick glance at Aarin. He hadn't moved, and the slight lines of tension of his face had smoothed out. He was asleep.

She sat up straighter. Callan was watching her with a pleased smile as the light flickered behind him. It was a little ragged around the edges, fading as she watched it, going down with the sun, but it was *his*.

'How?' She hardly knew what to ask. She had seen the closeness between them, she had felt Callan's need, and like Kallis she had misunderstood it. 'When?'

Aarin stirred, wakened by her movement, and his eyes were drawn at once to the light. He gave it an appraising glance, then looked at Callan with approval. Callan smiled in delight, so like his brother than Jeta felt a moment of bemused disorientation. Then Aarin settled back down and closed his eyes again without a word, leaving her desperate curiosity unanswered, but she saw the small smile hovering on his lips and decided it was a fair exchange.

After that, by silent consent, they enfolded her into their circle and it was then she realised that the long silences, the still moments between them, were not what they had appeared. But she was still on the outside, unable to see what they could see, so after a while Aarin began to explain. Haltingly at first, the words raspy and breathless, but gradually they smoothed out, as though just the use of them made it easier.

She found herself lulled by the sound, closing her eyes as he talked, imagining that she could see and feel the things he spoke of. Part of her could.

The part that remembered the sensation of his consciousness melding with hers for a brief instant in Redstone, the part that recalled standing at the vortex of the connection between man and dragon before he had left her so far behind.

So real did it seem, sometimes, that she felt almost as though she could touch it. It became a game she played with herself—if she could imagine hard enough, she could pretend she could follow them wherever it was they went. It was a nice game, and she thought perhaps that Aarin knew what she was doing because sometimes he chose little things that were easy to imagine.

Like the day he showed Callan how to make one thing look like another. How to take the Water that was all around them and use it to bend and direct the light to show a false image to the eye. He gave them both a pebble, one of the small flat flints that littered their campsite. She held that little stone in her hand, letting her body's heat warm its cold surface, holding in her mind the memory of the pearly-white quartz pebbles that adorned the paths of her mother's ornamental garden in Situra. She had always loved those stones, so smooth and perfect, almost translucent after rain.

And, quite suddenly, the warmth of her palm was no longer a passive thing. She felt it as it curled itself around the grey stone, smoothing out its rough edges and turning flat grey to twinkling white.

She gave a yelp of surprise. Aarin's eyes flew open and he saw the pebble in her palm, bleached white and winking in the sun. He looked from the pebble to her face, his shock as vivid as her own. Then he was smiling and laughing, and Callan was grinning at her. And she couldn't *believe* it. She felt giddy with shock, unmoored, disconnected from her body. It was both exhilarating and unsettling, as though she had gone somewhere infinitely strange and did not know how to find her way back.

A touch on her arm grounded her and she looked up into Aarin's eyes.

He pointed at the white pebble. 'Let it go now.'

The pebble faded back to dull grey and the euphoric dizziness receded. She clutched after it, suddenly desperate not to let it slip away, and his hand closed over hers, tight enough that she could feel the healing ridges of the scars on his fingers.

'It's yours now,' he told her, and she knew it was true and the panic faded. 'It's yours.'

And after that the world was changed.

It quickly became apparent that there was no great power waiting for her, that there would be no glorious flowering of a different destiny. But Jeta didn't care. She didn't want that. It was enough to taste it, to glimpse even so faintly the world in which Aarin and Kinseris lived, day by day. And it brought some choices into focus with a clarity she had not hoped to find because some things it did not change at all.

He never said so, but she thought that it was not the same with Callan. Now she knew what to look for, she could feel his hunger, his need for more, for all of it. She wondered whether the changes she had seen in Lysan, and why he never stayed with them long, were because of what he could see was coming. And she knew Callan well enough by now to glimpse the bitter tug of war as he struggled with his desire for what Aarin could give him, that he *needed*, and the brother who could not follow him on that path, and whom he could not leave behind.

If that thought was a niggling sadness, it was dwarfed by her joy in what her awakening did to Aarin. The discovery that she could learn, even a little— it acted on him like spring sun on cold earth; it brought him back to life. It gave him hope that he could once more belong here, that the dragons could once more have a place.

That had never been her dream, but now she dreamed it too.

And then it was gone.

One night Aarin woke screaming, raving about fire, incoherent, tears on his face, and it took both of them to calm him, to hold him down. And that was just the start.

Darred had unleashed the last remaining dragon.

Night after night, Aarin was ripped from sleep by the devastation of its fire as the dragon struck again and again, and they did not know who or where.

Lysan, returning hollow-eyed, told them of assaults in the north, of grain convoys destroyed and food shortages as Darred systematically attacked their lines of supply. The destruction of Kamarai had already cut off help from Elvelen, and now he razed the protected farmlands to the north in a fury of revenge, the arc of destruction sweeping down towards Rhiannas while his army tested the river defences to the south, stretching Lothane's forces almost to breaking point.

Darred was no longer playing with them. Jeta thought of Hanlon and his captain in that filthy tent. *Four months. Too long.*

Without Aarin to help, Galydon had stretched the mages he had to their limits. Unable to stop the dragon's attacks, he did what he could to minimise the damage, to conceal and protect precious supplies and move people from vulnerable villages into the bigger towns where mages could offer some measure of protection. Sedaine and Kinseris had leant their strength, but Lysan told them many had died. He looked sick, telling of it, and he did not stay.

She asked him about Derias, and he told her Derias had not come back to court. Nor had he responded to Sedaine's messengers. Worse, Morven's levies had withdrawn from their stations, and the clans Lorac had taken west remained missing. They were all running out of time.

Worst of all was the reversal it worked on Aarin. Whatever resilience those quiet weeks had given him, the dragon's onslaught stole back. Unable to sleep, barely eating, he retreated into himself and they could not reach him.

But they were no longer alone now.

The first morning after the nightmares returned, Callan and Jeta emerged from their exhausted huddle to find the dragon sprawled protectively around their camp, the tip of its tail curling inside the little tent where Aarin slept.

The shock made her stumble, and Callan steadied her, his attention rivetted on the sleeping dragon. Behind him, the clan sentry sat frozen in terror, his eyes wild, one hand paused in the act of reaching for a weapon.

'Don't,' Callan said softly, not to her but to the frightened soldier. 'It's not here for us.'

Jeta watched the rise and fall of the dragon's breathing; she could feel the heat rising from it like a vast furnace. The silver hide had regained its lustre. The blackened, flaking scales were the only sign of the injuries to its flank.

The skin beneath had knitted together so perfectly that not a trace of the wounds remained, and between the delicate, splayed bones of the wing stretched a fine web of new skin, pale and translucent.

As if sensing her attention, the dragon opened one obsidian eye, its gaze roaming lazily from her to the terrified clansman before coming to rest on Callan. Callan's hand still gripped hers, his fingers stiff with tension as he endured the dragon's regard. Then, with a snort that sent smoke curling from its nostrils, its head sank back down, the eye closing to the merest slit.

The mercenary let his hand drop, a heartfelt prayer to Tesserion on his lips. The dragon's tail twitched, and the clansman jerked back, prayer turning to curse as he overbalanced and landed on his arse on the hard ground.

Callan laughed, and there was no fear in it, only joy. And Jeta felt the tension drain out of her.

The clansman sat up, still muttering curses. But there was no further movement from the dragon, and with a last, suspicious glance, the man stalked out of the camp.

From then on, everything was different. The dragon reclaimed Aarin from her, reminding her of everything that had changed, of all the things they had gained and lost. Pushing her gently aside. But it could not prevent the intrusion of the war into their quiet little world.

It was time to face that. It was time to go back.

It was Aarin's decision to make, but it wasn't much of a choice. Jeta thought that to do nothing would kill him, and worried that anything else would do the same. Darred had exposed the fatal vulnerability. If Aarin had tried to protect the dragons almost at the cost of his own life once, the same weakness could trap him again and again. Defence was no defence at all, but attack was unthinkable.

Callan—calm, concerned, *practical*—was quietly persistent. They needed another way, and he forced Aarin to look for it, night after night. Aarin tried to ignore him, but he was too tired and Callan wore him down. Made him think, made him question, but it always came back to one thing—the same magic that joined Aarin and Silverwing gave Darred his link with Eiador, no matter the deception at its heart. To take one was to take the other.

'Could you undo what joins you?' Callan finally asked, a burr of frustration roughening his voice as they hit one more dead end. 'Break them apart long enough to give us a chance?'

Aarin hugged his knees a little closer as though the very thought was painful. His face was pinched with the exhaustion of too many lost nights. Though only the worst of the external scars remained now—a fading weal that emerged from his collar and snaked around the side of his head, and the injury to his arm that had not yet regained full function—his voice still rasped when he was tired, which was all the time now, and he was frequently breathless. 'No.'

'Why not?' Jeta challenged, sensing his refusal was all instinct. 'Because you don't want to?'

Aarin's eyes snapped up, full of angry denial. Then he sighed, resting his chin on his arms, wincing as he did so. 'How could I want to when I know what it would cost? But it is more than that.'

Callan, watching him closely, asked, 'More how?'

Aarin didn't answer, not at once, and Jeta thought that he would not, but then he surprised her.

'I swore an oath once, to Silverwing. When I asked him to do as the Arkni had done—to become as they were—because we were desperate, and I could not see any other way we could fight them.'

Jeta held her breath. He had never spoken of that time. Of what they had done. Of how they had died, nor why they had lived. Only for whom.

'He made me swear to destroy the magic of the Joining forever before I let anyone misuse it as the Arkni had done, before I let *us* misuse it, because he feared that we would lose control. That it would take us as it had taken them. And it nearly did. But this is not the same.'

They said nothing, just waited, and their silence forced him to answer.

'It's not the same because I don't know if they *are* misusing it. I don't know if they are using it at all. What Darred has done with Eiador, what he did with the other dragons—it is not a true joining. If it was, their deaths would have killed him. The devices still control them. And the devices linked the races even through the years of the Severing. If I undo the link now—even for a short time—it might do nothing at all to Darred's power, but it would destroy mine.'

And that he could not do, and they could not argue with him.

'It is the device that links them,' he said after a pause. 'If we want to break their connection, we have to destroy it.'

Her head came up. The words were bitter, and she knew he was remembering Redstone, when they had held Darred's dragon device in their hands and just threw it away. But they had not known then a fraction of what they knew now.

'Could you destroy it?' she asked him. Before, he had been adamant that even attempting that would be dangerous.

There was as slight pause, then he said, 'I don't know. And first I would have to take it from him.'

'You did before,' she pointed out, recalling his bloody fingers uncurling to reveal the silver dragon on his palm. The shock on Darred's face. A perilous stalemate only broken by Kallis's arrival.

Aarin shook his head. 'That was not...' The words trailed away, his expression thoughtful.

Callan was watching them curiously. 'Not what?'

When Aarin didn't reply, Jeta answered for him. 'Not real. Was it?'

'I made him think it was real,' Aarin said slowly, as though he were stitching the scene together in his memory. 'But he had already lost sight of it, otherwise I could not have done it. I showed him what he feared, and because he feared it, he believed it.'

She picked a pebble from the ground, began unconsciously to play with it, thinking hard. The flint flashed from grey to white and back again and he tracked it with his eyes. White again. She flicked it into the air and he caught it, left-handed. 'Could you do it again?'

FOURTEEN

DAVIYAN THREW A handful of coins onto the bar and they disappeared before they stopped spinning.

The old man gestured to the western side of the island. 'Came in a ten-day ago. Asking for word of your admiral.'

'How many?'

The man shrugged, his attention on the glass in his hand and the filthy cloth he was cleaning it with it. 'Only saw him.'

Daviyan eyed the rag with distaste. He put another coin on the bar, a silver this time. 'How many?' he asked again. He had disembarked at the island port this morning to be met with the news that Caledani were here paying a bounty for news of Farnorians. His little fleet would be at least two days in port, taking on water and food for the rest of their journey, repairing the damage done by a storm three days ago. They were short-handed. They had to be, for what they had come for. If there was going to be trouble, they needed to know the shape of it.

The old man paused, looking from the coin to the captain's face. Then he flicked the piece of silver off the bar and returned to his task. 'Only saw him,' he repeated.

Daviyan concealed his irritation by force of habit. The priesthood rarely interfered in the affairs of the islands that lay roughly halfway between their lands and Amadorn, but they had been known, from time to time when the pirates grew too bold, to crack down hard and without warning. He could little blame the man for protecting his livelihood. No one else was going to do it for him.

He was halfway to the door when the old man said, 'Left a name.'

He froze mid-step. So. 'Did he?'

'He did.'

Daviyan sighed. He turned, flicking another coin towards the bar.

The old man caught it in the cup. He grinned and told him the name.

The sun was high overhead when Daviyan reached the west side of the island. There was no harbour on this exposed stretch of coast, just a long swathe of golden sand interrupted by bays that were too small for the big trade ships, and a scattering of fishing villages that clung to the shallow inlets and supplemented their meagre living by trafficking the stolen cargos the pirates dropped into their bays. Compared with the busy eastern trade port, the west coast was a lawless emptiness. Usually.

Daviyan paused as he crested the dunes surrounding the beach and took in the sight that greeted him, aware of some emotion that he hadn't felt for a long time. It was only when the heat of the sand began to penetrate the thin soles of his boots that he realised he had not moved for several minutes. There was a man sitting in the shade beneath a palm, watching him. With a last look at the beach, Daviyan walked towards him.

The man stood as he approached. He was taller than he had appeared. 'Admiral Hanlon?' he asked, his heavy accent mangling the name.

'Not quite.' Daviyan looked past the man, surveying the activity on the beach again. They were here, in the islands, and suddenly four months had become two. A hopeless cause had become possible again—if he could trust this. 'Is this all of you?'

The man's lips quirked. 'Not quite.'

Daviyan could see faces at the rail as the small boat skimmed across the harbour towards his ship. They would have spotted him as soon as the boat cast off. He had been gone for hours. They would have worried. He understood that. It was why he had left orders that no one was to come ashore after him. The Caledani he had found might be friendly, but that didn't mean there weren't enemies here. When you made a career of fighting pirates—even if, or perhaps especially, at times you were a pirate yourself—

there were always enemies. And now was not the time to alert them.

Daviyan turned to the man sitting quietly behind him, his face obscured under one of the wide-brimmed hats worn by the locals to protect against the fierce sun. He had his reasons for that. He had not lived a life that made him trust easily, and his admiral, for all his guile, would never think to question such a long-standing loyalty. And Daviyan had to be sure. No one could expect otherwise.

The boat bumped alongside the ship's hull. Voices called to him.

'Remember,' he said, the words low enough that no one else would hear. 'Not until you are on board.'

Then he was scrambling up the side, leaving the other man to follow as best he could. He was not a sailor.

The two Caledani were waiting for him as he climbed aboard. Their loyalty, at least, he had no reason to question. It lay absolutely with the man who had engineered this meeting, on whose word they had travelled here. And that was the problem. There too many chances of betrayal in all of this. Too many people he was being asked to trust, without question. It was why he had brought the man from the beach with him, alone. If he was not who he claimed to be, they would soon know it. And then what?

The former Ancai, Kestel, watched him in silence, arms crossed, his expression questioning. The younger one, Trad, was fidgeting by his side.

Daviyan ignored them, turning to his mate to give the order to weigh anchor. The supplies had already been loaded and stored. They would have to complete their repairs elsewhere.

A thud told him his companion was aboard. He kept his back to the newcomer and watched Kestel's face, and he saw the moment the man removed his hat. Saw the surprise widen Kestel's eyes, then the smile, genuine and delighted. Daviyan felt something in his chest release, finally and completely, with that smile. It was real. He could believe.

He turned to the man he had been sent to Caledan to fetch, only to find here, in this island port, three weeks sail from the mainland. It still hadn't quite sunk in yet, what that meant. Two months, not four. A chance. He held out his hand and the other man took it. 'Welcome aboard, Captain.'

Then he left them alone to greet each other. Too many other things needed his attention, and chief among them the need to collect the men on the beach. He had thought about that the entire trek back to the port, because as miraculous as it was to find them here, there were also dangers in that, and logistical challenges. The priesthood would have spies in the islands. They always had done. And they were close enough to Amadorn for word to outrun them and carry warning to Darred. That couldn't happen.

He gave his orders quickly and precisely, and had the signal sent covertly to the other ships. They would straggle out, tonight and tomorrow, just as they had straggled in, and make their own way to the far side of the island. They could not afford to be seen as a fleet.

There were ways, if you knew them (which he did), to anchor safely off the bays on the western coast, and ferry goods and men to and from the shore. The pirates did it all the time. It was slower and riskier, especially when they had to move so many, but what they lost in time they would make up for in secrecy, and thanks to the strength of a loyalty he had not anticipated—that he suspected even Kinseris himself had not truly appreciated—they now had time to spare.

Daviyan felt a presence behind him and turned to find Kestel at his shoulder.

The big man's expression held more emotion than Daviyan had yet seen. 'Thank you.'

Daviyan grinned. He couldn't help it, his heart suddenly soaring with carefree, reckless joy to be at sea with possibilities and, impossibly, hope, once again before him. Then he shook his head. 'I would not have come. Thank my admiral. But we're not there yet.'

They weren't. But they were close.

FIFTEEN

LORAC SQUINTED AGAINST the too-bright sun. He had come to hate the light in the mountains. It was too white, too cold, and the days seemed endless. Maker, but he was *tired,* and he wasn't the only one. He rubbed his eyes, trying to blink away the fog of exhaustion. It was getting harder and harder to think. How long had it been now? He had no real idea, beyond too bloody long.

It had been too dangerous to try to scale the rockfall after the dust had settled, even if they could have risked descending back to the road, which was now crawling with Caledani. So they had continued up, hoping to find a way to circle around and then drop back down on the other side of the fall where the mages and refugees waited with a handful of his officers and the bulk of the clansmen they had rescued from Elvelen. But a jagged ravine, invisible from the trade road below, cut between them and the pass and they were forced to keep climbing to find another way.

He had managed to shout hurried orders across to Sem before a warning cry from the lookout below told him a pursuit was forming and they had had to move.

At first it had seemed impossible they could get so lost. They knew which direction they needed to go in, but first they had to lose the Caledani who tailed them, three days spent playing a brutal hide and seek that had forced them further and further from where they needed to be. And, when their pursuers gave up the chase, the mountains themselves conspired to hinder them, forcing them to backtrack, to go over and around, cutting them off with rockfalls or dizzying fissures. They had lost three of their number to slipped footings and another to injuries sustained by a falling rock.

And they had been lucky. They had water from the trickling streams of snowmelt, and a couple of Elvelians who had been cut off with them were from the mountains and knew which plants could safely be eaten. But a diet of little blue berries and nettle leaves would have been barely sufficient to keep his men on their feet, if not for the occasional luck hunting—small round mice, a squirrel or two, and once a fat, furry animal that looked like a large rat. Not that he would have turned his nose up at rat. None of them would. They were not quite starving, but they were hungry and exhausted. It was slowing them down and dulling the sense of urgency that should have been driving them.

He returned his attention to the argument. 'You're sure we can get through?' he asked the excited scout.

The man nodded. 'Yes. The gap is small enough to jump—I've done it—and the path beyond widens. It will take us down into the next valley.'

He had seen the proposed route, and the perilous leap required over a jagged crevice between two narrow ledges. But his scout was certain the valley beyond would finally lead them out of these accursed mountains. If he was right, it had to be done, because they had already delayed too long.

The spiralling argument faltered as he stood, feeling his knees creak, feeling tired and old. 'Enough. We're going.'

The two scouts saluted their captain. He returned it, brother to brother, and saw both men flush as the reminder hit home. They were not just soldiers, they were clansmen, and their clans were out there, waiting for them—their wives, sisters, brothers, children—and they had to get back.

At least, he hoped someone would be waiting. His last orders to Sem had been to move the surviving refugees down from the mountains to whatever succour awaited them in ravaged Kamarai. His men did not have the resources to do more for them, and anyway they were needed elsewhere. Sem's orders were to find Galydon or Kallis and failing that to return to Rhiannas. He had thought, at the time, that he and his men would only be days behind them, but between the initial pursuit and the treacherous mountains, days had turned into weeks.

It should have been simple. It was a refrain that haunted him, a mistake made from compassion that might well doom countless others. It had bothered him, at first, how the Caledani had got ahead of them in the pass. How they had climbed those high tracks in such numbers, how they had evaded his lookouts. But the possibility that they hadn't was much worse. In the dark of the night, shivering himself to sleep on an empty belly without even the comfort of a fire, it was the thought that haunted him—that something else was out there, hunting them.

He had not been the only one unable to sleep the night before the avalanche, nearly falling over Needa, still and alert in the dark on the far edge of their perimeter. He still got a chill remembering the faraway look in her gaze as she had glanced at him, then back out at the night.

'There's something out there.'

The words echoed in his head, the dreamy quality to her voice heightening his unease, even in memory. But when he had questioned her, she had just shrugged, uncurling from her crouch and brushing past him to return to where Brannick and the others slept. He had not seen her again.

The words had stayed with him. If she was right, if there was indeed something out there, something that might, perhaps, explain how their enemy had managed to flank them, they had seen no sign of it. Not here. But once or twice, outlined against the dark horizon, he had seen the orange glow of fire to the east and the distant spirals of smoke in the dawn.

They were tired, frustrated, and afraid. And they needed to get back. While there was still something to get back to.

SIXTEEN

JETA MADE THE return journey to Rhiannas on the back of the dragon, and it was beyond words. It was also cold and terrifying, the flight made uneven by Silverwing's still healing wing, and made her wish for solid ground beneath her feet.

She risked a glance downwards as they soared aloft, only to see the ground recede beneath them at a dizzying pace. It had taken her a long time to open her eyes again, to breathe past the nausea, to banish the image of that same ground rising to meet her as she tumbled through the sky. Jeta gripped tight to the ridges of the dragon's spine, letting the warmth from its fire ease her chill, and fixed her eyes on Aarin's back, looking neither left nor right until they were above the clouds and there was nothing to see anywhere except endless blue.

The blue was deepening to purple when the dragon banked, the steep curve tilting her sideways, and her scream was lost in the wind. Aarin glanced to the side, his back was rigid with tension, and even in profile she could see his frown.

Something was wrong.

Then the dragon was diving and wet chill clung to her skin as they burst through the obscuring bank of cloud.

The scene below was lit by the light of a hundred small fires. A long line of wagons lay upturned and ruptured, their contents scattered and many in flames. There were bodies among them, grotesquely splayed around the blackened ground.

They flew past, and one by one the fires winked out. She felt the rush of power that extinguished them, the wave of elemental Water channelled through the man in front of her. But they were low enough now for the stink of smoke and charred flesh to reach them, close enough to see that some of the bodies were not whole. Jeta looked away, her hands gripping the ridges on Silverwing's back until they ached—and saw over Aarin's shoulder the column approaching from the southeast. And, far behind them, the dark smudge on the horizon that was Rhiannas. Then they were past, and she sucked in the clean air, trying to clear the smell and the taste of the horror.

They flew towards the column of men and wagons marching from Rhiannas, who saw the dragon coming at them, silhouetted against the setting sun... and scattered.

At the first warning cry, the company broke apart, small groups moving in all directions like a many-pointed star, the empty wagons abandoned. As Silverwing dived lower, the nearest group stopped running and crouched, interlocking shields raised above their heads. She could feel the power on them, shimmering across their surface, a last desperate defence against the deadly fire of the dragon that had destroyed the convoy.

They passed overhead, sweeping towards the next group, low enough that she could see Kallis among them, and the fierce relief on his face as he recognised the silver dragon. Then he was lost from sight as they flew past and the dragon landed with a soft thud.

Aarin was shouting at them to go, and Callan wrapped his arm around her and slid them both down the wing. They had barely rolled clear before the dragon was aloft once more and they were flattened into the dirt by the powerful pulse of its wings.

A clansman helped her to her feet, then Kallis was there. He looked older, leaner, tired, but he was grinning. 'I have never been so glad to see you,' he said, clapping Callan on the back hard enough to make him stumble. 'When we saw....' He glanced up and back, shaking his head. His expression sobered. 'Is it still out there?'

Callan looked up, following his gaze, but Silverwing was already out of sight. 'I don't think so.'

Men were hurrying past them, heading towards the devastation spread across the road. Kallis watched them, and she was struck again by how tired he looked. How tired they all were. They reminded her Shrogar's people in the last days of the siege of Ephenor.

'We need to clear the road,' Kallis was saying to Callan as he began to follow his men. 'See if there is anything that can be saved. This is the third in a month...' He trailed off, and Jeta caught the sense of everything that went unspoken.

'We'll help,' Callan said.

Kallis nodded. 'I know.' Then he was gone.

Jeta watched him go. She did not want to follow. She wanted to go back to their little camp and hide.

Callan was watched with understanding. He said gently, 'We need to help them.'

She nodded, feeling sick. The last place she wanted to be was among that carnage, but she let Callan lead her towards the remains of the convoy.

Soldiers were already sifting through the smoking wreckage, searching for any supplies that had not been destroyed. They had rags tied across their faces and Callan gave one to her now and put one on himself, but it couldn't keep out the smell.

They reached the first body. It was some way from the others. She could not tell whether it was a man or woman, only that they had tried to run and there had been nowhere to run to.

She tried not to see it, to distance herself from it, but the horror of fire on human flesh... And it hit her that this must have been Aarin, before the dragon's gift had begun the healing, and then she was on her knees, weeping and gagging.

Callan was crouched beside her, one arm around her shoulders. His hands were trembling.

Aarin's name choked in her throat.

He looked away. 'Don't think about that.'

She wanted to wail. *How can I not?* But he was right.

'Come on,' he said, holding out his hand. 'Some of them might be alive.'

The nausea returned. There was no dragon to ease these wounds. If any lived... She swallowed. 'If there are...?'

Callan's face above the cloth mask held the same bleak thought. He didn't quite meet her eye. 'Then we'll see.'

Overhead she felt the passage of a dragon's wings. Then she saw Aarin talking to Kallis and wished he had stayed away.

A clansman gave a shout and began pulling aside debris from one of the wagons. He looked around for help. 'This one's alive.'

Aarin turned. His face drained of colour. Kallis took his elbow and steered him away.

Jeta followed Callan as he ran to help. The mercenaries had cleared the worst of the wreckage and she could see a body of a man curled inside the burnt-out wagon, his exposed side scorched and weeping. She thought the clansman had made a mistake, then the man moved and she saw his face, untouched but ravaged by pain.

Callan pushed her aside and crawled into the space by the man's side. Aarin was nowhere in sight. For so many reasons, he did not need to see any of this.

Callan emerged looking grim. 'He'll live.'

More soldiers came to extract the man from the ruined wagon and they carried him, gently, to where the new wagons waited. He screamed. Callan watched them go, his expression a strange mix of relief and guilt.

There were more dead bodies than live ones and it felt wrong to be grateful for it, but she was, because it spared them what they had to do. Callan's arms were red to the elbows and his face held the deadened look of a man who refused to think about what he was doing.

The clansmen moved the dead. They could not take the bodies with them. They had too few wagons, and those must carry the wounded and whatever they could save from the dragon's attack. In Lothane, they burned their dead. But not now, not yet. Instead, they busied themselves clearing the devastation, piling what little they could salvage onto the wagons and tending to the survivors.

At some point, the wounded were moved out and there was nothing more for her to do. More men arrived, and salvage became clean up as they worked to move the wreckage from the road.

She watched them until it was too dark to see, until finally her legs had had enough and she sat down where she stood, her back against what remained of a wheel. Exhausted. Numb.

A shadow approached, indistinct in the darkness, and crouched at her side. It was Kinseris. He must have come with the reinforcements but in the dark she had not seen him. He smelled of sweat and horses and burnt things and he looked tired in a way she had hoped not to see again. He looked like the others.

A sob choked her throat and she couldn't speak. The rush of emotion was overwhelming.

He held out his hand. It was black and filthy. There was a smear of dark blood on his wrist. He smiled slightly as she took it. 'There is nothing more we can do here, and you have done everything you can. Let me take you back to Rhiannas.'

Aarin watched as the soldiers finished loading the remaining wagons, Kallis hovering by his side. He did not look at where the bodies lay, awaiting the flames that would take them home to the Maker. Memories of his father's long-ago pyre mingled with those that were not his—of men and women killed in the war with Aarkan, their bodies consumed by the cleansing fire of their dragons in final farewell—and could not reconcile the healing power of that ritual with this deliberate, deadly savagery. And some things he could not think about at all.

Silverwing was far to the south and west, flying a long, slow route between Rhiannas and the river, guarding against further attack. But the dragon that had done this was long gone. Here, so close to the carnage, Aarin could measure in hours the time that had elapsed since the slaughter—easily long enough for the creature to be safely back across the river—but that did not mean it would not return.

He caught sight of Jeta's blond head among the soldiers, pillowed in exhaustion on folded arms. It was only her presence here—and Callan and Kallis—that had made him face this. The things he could not think about were too close, too raw.

The thought sheared away and he flexed the hands that had curled into fists. They were trembling, the right aching with a distant throb. Fatigue was dragging at him. By the wagons, he saw Kinseris help Jeta to her feet, and almost welcomed the confusion of jealousy and guilt, remembering the warmth of her body pressed up close against him through all those long nights.

A clansman approached, calling Kallis away. He threw a peremptory 'stay here,' over his shoulder as he left, as if Aarin had any intention of moving. There was nothing he could do to help, now Kinseris was here, that they couldn't do for themselves. The regenerative gift of the dragon that had allowed him to survive the unsurvivable would do nothing for those caught in the ambush, and the dead were beyond anyone's help.

He turned away, choosing to look instead through Silverwing's eyes as he swept over a country scarred by the demands of this war. And, far distant across the Istelan, he felt the shadowy presence of their enemy.

Kallis was back, the wagons almost ready to depart.

'What now?' Aarin asked.

'Now we do it all over again.'

Aarin glanced at him, seeing the bitter twist to his mouth. 'For how long?' Because they could not continue like this forever.

Kallis watched the filled wagons start to move out. 'Galydon is moving men and supplies south,' he said finally. 'Within a few weeks, Rhiannas will have been stripped of all but a skeleton garrison.'

Aarin frowned. 'Why?'

Kallis sighed, running a hand through his hair. 'The clans we sent to Elvelen have vanished. We have had no word from Lorac for weeks, and we've lost a good part of the lords' levies. Derias... We think...' He shook his head. 'We thought we could hang on, that help would be coming, but we've run out of time. It's fight or starve, Aarin. Or burn. And the longer we wait, the weaker we get. If we don't fight soon, it will be too late.'

'You cannot fight the dragon.' It was blunt and brutal, but it was also true. If they forced a confrontation with Darred now, the horror of the convoy would be repeated on a scale a hundred times greater. It made no sense.

'No, we can't,' Kallis agreed. 'Either way we lose.'

'Then why?'

'This is no longer about winning or losing. It's about survival now—the survival of Lothane.' Kallis stopped on a hitched breath and looked away. The lines of tension were etched deep around his eyes. 'The only reason we haven't lost yet is because Darred cares more about revenge than he does about victory, and more cities will burn, more people will die, the longer this goes on. And at the end—what is left then? Darred doesn't care. He'll burn it all down. But Sedaine does.'

Aarin felt cold. 'What are you saying?'

Kallis finally looked at him. 'She must save what she can, Aarin. If we can bring Darred to battle—one battle—perhaps we can end this, one way or another. If we lose, he's won. Lothane is his, we're all dead. There's no more revenge to take. Either way, his energy is focused on us. Who knows?' he added with a humourless smile. 'We might even win.'

'She could surrender,' Aarin said desperately. 'Stop the war that way.' But he knew she could not, that none of them could. Darred would destroy Lothane just to spite her. He would accept her surrender and betray it, as she had betrayed him.

The smoking ruins of the convoy filled the air with the smell of death. He imagined that death coming to Rhiannas, to the other towns and cities of Lothane, as it had already come to Kamarai and so much of the north. And he imagined what would happen to an army that stood in its way. 'There must be another way. He will destroy you.'

Kallis shrugged a shoulder. 'Maybe. Maybe not. This is not a grand sacrifice. He can be beaten; we *can* beat him. But only if we can even the odds.'

He had known it was coming; it was why he was here. Because he had to do something. But the gulf between their expectations and his freedom to act yawned cavernously deep.

Kallis's eyes were on him, measuring his reaction. 'You know what will happen if you come back with me?'

'I know.' He could feel it already—their expectation, their hope. Weight after weight piled onto the thread of his resolve.

'If you can't, if you won't…' Kallis stopped, embarrassed. 'You don't have to come. I won't ask it of you.'

Aarin looked away, unable to respond to everything that had gone unspoken in Kallis's awkward offer—the responsibility he felt for what had happened, the implicit acknowledgement of everything he had, until now, refused to hear. The tentative attempt to rebuild a friendship that had been stressed almost to breaking. The acceptance of Aarin's refusal and everything it would mean.

'It wasn't your fault.'

Kallis flinched. 'Yes, it was. I wouldn't listen. I didn't even try.'

'But you were right, too.' Because Kallis had understood much more clearly than he had that the terms by which he was prepared to engage left him dangerously vulnerable. But even so… 'I will not kill the dragon for you.' It was the one thing he could not do.

Kallis closed his eyes as he absorbed the blow, then his shoulders straightened and he nodded. 'I understand.'

'No,' said Aarin, 'you don't. I will not kill the dragon for you, but that does not mean there is nothing I can do.'

SEVENTEEN

THE LIGHT HAD been different the last two days as they descended from the higher peaks. The air was not as thin, and Lorac felt he could finally *breathe.*

It was late but he did not call a halt. As long as the daylight lasted, he kept his men moving. He had lost another two at the leap. Two more deaths on his conscience. And hunger and thirst and taken more of the wounded. Each loss was a raw wound, but it could have been worse. So much worse. The shadow that haunted his dreams felt closer now, just out of sight, and no matter how firmly he told himself it was a delirium of exhaustion, fear pressed at his heels. And so he pushed them on.

Night fell. His scouts drifted in and he sent them back out. It was stupid and reckless. The ankle-breaking rocks were behind them, but a man could still trip and fall in the darkness and be left behind. Better to stop, rest through the short night and start again in the dawn, but they were so close now, he could feel it.

The scouts confirmed it an hour later. A large camp, a mile south.

'Are they ours?' *Please let them be ours.*

'Aye.' The man was grinning. 'They're ours.'

Lorac turned away, dropping his face in his hands so they would not see the tears in his eyes. 'Then what are you waiting for? Let them know we're coming.'

The scout saluted, still grinning, and disappeared. Lorac bellowed his men back to their feet, moving them on with the promise of a fire, food, friends. They needed little encouragement. He had never seen exhausted men move so fast.

Then, out of the darkness, a voice called a challenge in unmistakeable clan accents, and it was the most beautiful sound he had ever heard. Not long after that they saw the glow of many fires and in a matter of heartbeats they were surrounded by the men of their advance guard and everyone was talking at once. Lorac shoved his way to Sem's side. The man was grinning like a loon.

'You disobeyed my order,' he growled.

Sem's grin widened. 'Aye. What did you expect?' He eyed Lorac critically, his gaze sweeping past his captain to take in the ragged, half-starved state of the men at his back. 'How about you berate me after some food, eh?'

In short order his men were seated around the scattered fires eating bowls of hot stew and laughing with friends and brothers they had feared they would not see again. Lorac barely tasted the food as it went down, savouring the warmth as it hit his empty belly. People were talking at him. Needa appeared at some point, and even her glower lacked some of its usual sting. But he could barely focus on their words. Food and safety were doing their work too well and his eyelids were fighting a losing battle.

He swayed. Someone took the bowl from his hand and replaced it with a blanket, and he was too tired to protest the handling. The heat of the fire seeped into his bones as he lay down. That night he slept like the dead and for once did not dream of his shadow.

They moved out the next morning. Waking was hard. Lorac felt every bruise and strain acquired over his weeks-long trek through the mountains. He wanted nothing more than to lie back down and sleep for a week, but they had lost too much time already. And too much else besides.

He received Sem's report in grim silence, heard from him the names of the dead they had left high up in the pass under the rubble of the cliff, and the scores of unnamed refugees who had died with them. They had tried to dig them out, Sem told him, and he could imagine that desperate effort. Could imagine the horror of crushed bodies and the grief of families torn apart by so many tonnes of rock.

Sem shrugged off his awkward sympathy. 'Then we waited for you. I know. You told us to go on –'

'I *ordered* you.' It was a point he felt deserved more attention, as grateful as he was to find them last night.

'Aye, you did. And once we realised you weren't coming, we took the refugees to Kamarai, just as you ordered.'

And then came back for them.

Lorac glared at the unrepentant profile of the Raven's captain and sighed. He wouldn't make the man say it. They had just lost the better part of three whole clans in Elvelen. If Sem had refused to give up on any more of their own, he could not find it in himself to discipline him for it.

'See that it doesn't happen again,' he growled, and ignored Sem's grin.

'Aye, captain.'

Lorac dismissed him with a disgusted wave and went back to worrying.

By the afternoon of the second day they had reached the Amadele and turned south along its banks, heading for the place where the river widened and grew shallow enough for them to cross. From there it would only be a day's march to the nearest of the border towns, where he hoped they would find news and supplies.

It was late in the day by the time they reached the ford, and Lorac almost ordered the men to make camp and wait for morning, but every instinct was drawing him east, back to Rhiannas, and with an urgency that overrode his natural caution.

Moving six hundred tired men and supplies across a river in the teeth of nightfall was not without risk. Had they not been his own clansmen, he would not have attempted it, but these men had crossed this river many times. They understood the way the ford shifted with the seasons and how to find the safest places to enter and leave the river, and the first party had already crabbed their way across with the rope while the end of the column was still arriving at the western bank.

A breeze was rising from the south as Lorac waded across, the cold of the snow-fed river biting through his wet clothes. Sem's Ravens were already setting up camp, but he resisted the lure of the fires, waiting on the bank for the last groups to start their crossing as night fell in earnest.

The wind grew stronger, gusting in eddies that raised white-tipped waves in the fast-flowing shallows. Lorac felt the hairs on his neck stand on end, and he waded back into the water, dragging the men out as fast as he could, screaming at them to hurry.

A cry went up from the camp behind him. A flash of light shattered the gathering darkness, and in the burst of brightness he saw the thing from his nightmares. A huge black shape outlined against the mage-light, so close he could feel the heat of its body as it swept overhead and hear the steady, rhythmic pulse of its wings.

The crossing turned to chaos. Men panicked, those still in the river stumbling and trampling their fellows as they tried to scatter. Lorac, caught in the rush, tripped and fell, and for a terrifying moment was held under the icy water as the oblivious scramble to the bank surged over him. Then a hand reached down and dragged him gasping to the surface, and he grasped Sem's arm with desperate strength and let the other man haul him upright.

Another flare of light. He saw Needa outlined against its glow and heard his own voice screaming at her as the dragon turned and dived.

Then the night was rent by an altogether different kind of light and the horror began.

EIGHTEEN

THE BOUNCING OF the cart on the cobbles of Rhiannas's main thoroughfare woke Jeta from her doze. It was morning, but only just. The sun, low in the sky, dazzled her eyes. She could not see Kinseris.

The city was awake and moving even at this early hour, but it was not the market traders setting up their stalls that caught her attention. It was the ragged procession of refugees lining the broad avenue. Wide-eyed children, their faces pinched with hunger. Women with tired eyes, resignation in their hunched shoulders. A few men, most grey-haired, their defiance broken by hunger, exhaustion, and loss. They gathered in groups at the entrance to side streets, or trailed doggedly along the road, heads down and silent.

As the market stalls gave way to the grand buildings of the nobility, the line of refugees continued, all the way to the gates of the palace itself, where they bunched around the gates as the mercenaries moved among them, allowing a trickle through, mostly those with small children, turning the rest away. Some would not leave, and she turned her face from a woman's desperate cries when a clansman shook his head and tried to steer her to one side as she beat at him with her fists.

The wagons rumbled closer and the mercenaries began to clear the refugees from around the gates. They were efficient but not cruel, and Jeta felt the weight of many eyes staring hungrily as she passed. Their accusing silence followed her as the wagons passed through the gates, then the clamour began again, the pleas for shelter, for food, for *help*. But she saw at once why the mercenaries were turning most away. There was no room.

The courtyard's fine colonnades where the nobility had once strolled had been converted for storage, piled high with crates and barrels, and new structures had been hastily thrown up either side of the gates, their dim interiors providing a glimpse of close-set cots and a handful of off-duty clansmen. Through the archway that led to the barracks, small children played while their older siblings and mothers sat in the shade of the buildings, working through piles of laundry or twisting rope with nimble fingers. Refugees, packed in tight into every corner, a testament to the destruction Darred was wreaking on Lothane.

The wagon rumbled to a stop and Jeta let a groom help her down as she looked again for Kinseris. He was standing several paces away, a clansman on either side, both talking urgently at him. She watched him deal with first one then the other, before a garrison officer she recognised took their place, leading him away.

Soldiers and grooms swarmed around her as they started unloading the wagons. She moved out of their way, unsure of her place in this unfamiliar version of Rhiannas.

Ahead of her, Kinseris stopped and looked back. Their eyes met. He said something to the garrison officer, a raised hand halting the flow of questions, and two quick steps brought him to her side.

'Come,' he said, drawing her with him.

The waiting officer gave her a curious look, but at a gesture from Kinseris he continued his litany of problems. In short order she gathered that the main granary was almost empty and the clansmen guarding the grain silos within the city walls were reporting attempts to break in; that there had been problems between the refugees from two neighbouring villages who had been housed together in the barracks (they had been separated); that a man whose name she did not recognise was complaining that the noise was interrupting his work; and the latest rotation of the Istelan's garrison had returned an hour ago.

Kinseris stopped, his attention sharpening. 'And?'

'The general is meeting with them now.'

They were inside the palace by this point, making their slow way through corridors clogged with people.

Kinseris glanced in the direction of Galydon's office, his face tense.

'Anything else?' he asked the garrison officer.

The man shook his head and received Kinseris's various instructions with obvious relief that someone else was making the decisions. He left them at the anterooms to Sedaine's private chambers, which had once been Derias's domain, but an older man Jeta did not recognise now sat at Derias's desk.

When he saw Kinseris, he started to rise. 'My lord...?'

But Kinseris was already hustling her past, pretending not to hear. 'Whatever you do, don't make eye contact.'

Jeta bit her lip. 'Let me guess. War is too noisy?'

'Too noisy, too dirty, too disorganised and too expensive,' Kinseris agreed. The words were exasperated but there was a smile in his voice.

She knew what he was doing because he had done it before, on the journey from Ephenor. When she had been lost and despairing and wanted nothing more than to be left alone to curl around her grief and forget the world. But he had not left her alone; he had not allowed her to give in. Instead, he had kept her by his side as he embarked on the enormous task before him, forcing her to confront all the complexities of living. Giving her a purpose.

This was both like and unlike that time, as much a mask for all the things that remained unsaid between them as a distraction from pain and fear. Even so, something that had been lost in Kas'Tella as his blood stained the floor of his sanctum had been found again here in the midst of this war, and he was sharing it with her now, just as he had done then. Because he had always known, somehow, what she needed.

She had been in a bubble after Vannarai, divorced from all its consequences, distracted by Aarin's pain from dealing with her own. But she could see the consequences now—in the faces of the displaced people on the streets, here in the palace, out on the road with the convoy, and so much more elsewhere she would never see. The horror of Darred's revenge, forced into the open. All the things Lysan had kept from them, until the point when even that kindness had been impossible.

'We didn't know,' she said in a small voice. 'Why did no one tell us?'

He sighed, the lines on his face etched deep around his eyes and mouth. 'What good would it have done? We have already asked too much of him.'

She heard the bitter note and understood. 'But you will ask more?'

He did not answer, but she saw the truth on this face—that they had to ask, and keep asking, because otherwise the suffering all around them was merely the beginning.

She thought of Aarin and the fragile peace he had found in the short weeks before it was snatched from him, and knew that he also had to do something. If only the help they needed and the help he could give were not so mismatched.

Her stomach rumbled, breaking the awkward tension.

Kinseris smiled. 'Are you hungry? There's not much, but we're not starving yet.'

The kitchens were even busier than the rest of the palace as they strained to cope with the demands of feeding so many, trays of oatcakes and flat loaves cooling on the long trestles. Kinseris led her to a quiet corner and pulled up a bench, fetching a handful of oatcakes and a flagon of wine.

She raised an eyebrow. 'Are you planning to get me drunk again?'

He laughed and pushed the oatcakes towards her. 'It's more water than wine. Besides, I'll be asleep long before you can challenge me to a drinking contest.'

He sat down with a sigh and leant back against the wall, closing his eyes. He had been awake all night, but his face, like Kallis's, betrayed an exhaustion that spoke of far worse than lost sleep.

Jeta put down the oatcake and stretched out her hand to his. 'Tell me.'

NINETEEN

THEY MADE IT back to Rhiannas without incident, their progress guarded by Silverwing's protective shadow far overhead. Aarin stayed on the ground with them, and Kallis knew it was not by preference, but only because of the reassurance his visible presence would provide. But he was clearly too tired to walk, and after a mile Kallis made him ride in the wagon beside Callan, who was already asleep, his face pale and filthy.

They didn't speak. Aarin had his head down on his knees, discouraging conversation, and Kallis had no desire to pursue the difficult discussion they had started by the convoy. He was here. For now that was enough.

They travelled through the night, the clansmen taking it in turns to rest in the wagon, and it was mid-morning as they passed through the main gates of the city and began the journey to the palace. When the wagon hit the cracked cobbles, Aarin climbed out and walked beside him. Callan slept on, sprawled in exhausted oblivion on the wagon bed, and not even the cries of the market sellers that lined the thoroughfare made him so much as twitch.

They were halfway to the palace when Aarin stopped dead, an outflung arm holding Kallis in place as the wagon rumbled past them.

Kallis took in his tense face, gaze turned inward, and felt the familiar flush of fear. 'What is it?'

Aarin's fingers flexed; he blinked, turned. 'It's coming. *Now.*'

Kallis couldn't move, couldn't think, his mind blanked by primal terror. They stood there on the street, with people moving on either side of them, living, breathing, going about their lives, while they were frozen in a silent nightmare.

Sound returned, a woman's laugh cutting through the ice, and he grabbed the closest man to him—a young lad in the uniform of Rhiannas's garrison. 'Sound the warning, get the people off the streets. Do it now!' he snarled when the boy just gaped at him. 'Now!' And shoved him into motion.

'How long?' he demanded of Aarin. They were still several minutes from the palace. *Maker.* It was happening. They had waited too long.

A bell started to ring, an erratic, desperate warning. Other bells joined in until the alarm rang out across the city.

The human swirl around them changed. Kallis was jostled aside as a man shoved past, dragging a child behind him. Shouts and cries rang out as realisation dawned and fear spread.

They had known this day might come. They had planned for it, drilled for it. Everyone in the city knew what those bells meant, what they had to do. But this wasn't a drill, and Kallis could feel the rising tide of panic spread through the streets as people were wrenched, from one instant to the next, from their comfortable day-to-day monotony to confront the unthinkable.

Get off the streets. Find a stone building. Take shelter. Prepare for fire.

'How long?' he called again, pushing his way towards the mage through the suddenly surging crowd. 'How close?'

Aarin cocked his head. He hesitated. 'Fifty miles? No, more. Soon.'

How fast did a dragon fly? 'Come on.' They had to get to the palace. He was not going to die here, in the street, with not even a chance to defend himself.

A harsh jangling of bells broke the quiet of the kitchens. Kinseris stiffened, oatcake forgotten halfway to his mouth. Silence fell, except for those bells, for a long-drawn out moment. Then a clamour of voices and movement, of fear and near-panic, as the whole palace seemed to spring into motion.

Kinseris stood. 'Come with me.' His voice was calm but urgent, his face oddly blank.

Jeta obeyed on instinct, rising and following him out into the hallway. Then she felt it, a distant gathering of power, pin pricks of focus scattered all around as every mage and magician in the palace and the surrounding city suddenly drew on their power. *On Water.*

She stopped, forcing Kinseris to a halt. 'What's happening?'

Footsteps clattered on the stairs. Limina rounded the corner ahead of them, a small, dirty child in her arms and a knot of refugee women around her. The former queen of Farnor wore a look of grim determination but her eyes betrayed her fear. Jeta's heart lurched. *The dragon.*

She looked wildly at Kinseris. 'Where are you going?'

He took her face in his hands and kissed her. It was a farewell. 'To help.' A hesitation, then, 'I'm sorry.'

'No.' It was a whisper, a plea. She had seen what dragon fire could do. He was not Aarin. He could not…

Aarin.

She tried to feel for the signature of his magic that she had come to know so intimately these past weeks. But she had neither the experience nor raw strength to cut through the confusion of so many sources of power.

She blinked, giving it up, and saw Kinseris staring at her, his eyes wide and shocked. Because he had just felt what she had tried to do, what she should not have been able to do, and in a moment of clarity she realised she had not thought to tell him *because it did not matter.*

A hundred questions rippled across his face as crisis surged all around them, but in the end he asked the only practical one, because they had no time. 'Can you shield?'

She shook her head. So he taught her, quickly and precisely, in the middle of that crowded hallway, buffeted on all sides by the fear and haste of those seeking shelter, how to capture and shape the energies she needed into a protective shield, just like the ones she had felt on the shields of the mercenary company that had responded to the stricken convoy.

As her fragile defences formed, he smiled with something as close to delight as the moment would permit. 'Hold it. Don't let go. Promise me.'

Then, taking her hand, he led her through the thinning crowd to the staircase that descended to the lowest level. Limina stood at its head, guiding the last of the women into the relative safety of the basement, watching her with an understanding that made Jeta's heart hurt.

I sent him out to die and I would do it again, because it saved countless lives.

She could not ask him to stay with her, to hide away when his power could help protect the many thousands who were defenceless. He might not be Aarin, he might not have access any longer to so much of his power, but what he did have was vast and deep and she could feel it now as she had never been able to feel it before. It would be needed.

'Go,' she whispered, and he smiled, his fingers brushing hers in farewell.

Then her resolve broke and she called after him, but it was too late. He had already gone.

Kallis entered the palace courtyard at a dead run to the controlled panic of well-practiced drill. Refugees were streaming out of the barracks, clansmen directing them into the lower levels of the palace, down into the service areas below ground, while servants closed the shutters. And on the roof, Kallis could see the outlines of dark shapes moving between the tall chimneys.

None of it would make any difference, but it gave people a purpose to displace fear.

Aarin stopped, his face grey and his breath rasping. His eyes were quartering the courtyard, looking for something, someone. 'My mother?'

'She's not here,' Kallis replied, trying to keep him moving.

Aarin shook him off. 'Where is she?'

Kallis saw he would not budge until he knew. *My mother.* He could count on one hand the number of times Aarin had called her that in his hearing. Of course this would be one of those times. And they didn't have *time.* 'North of here. The Lyne Valley. It… it was hit hard—whole towns destroyed. Half our mages are there now, to help protect what is left.'

'My mother is there?' Aarin demanded, incredulous. 'Galydon let her go?'

'I wouldn't put it quite like that. Aarin, come *on.*'

Callan, woken by the bells and the chaos, said, 'If she's there, she's safe for now. We're not.'

Kallis shot him a grateful look as Aarin finally moved, and he called out to mercenaries by the palace doors to clear them a path through. Then he hauled Aarin by his good arm, ignoring his protest, through the corridors and up staircases to where he knew Galydon would be.

A company of clansmen armed with war bows and spears crouched on the roof. Galydon stood among then, his cloak swirling behind him in the breeze. Beside him stood Kinseris.

It was hopeless, desperate defiance. The heavy steel-tipped shafts might be devastating against merely human enemies; against a dragon they would be little more than insect stings. As for the spears—if a dragon was close enough for spears, every man on this roof was already dead, and they all knew. But they also knew what it meant if the dragon came for Rhiannas. And so, here they were.

Galydon turned at his shout, and Kallis felt the force of his relief as the general caught sight of Aarin at his shoulder. Aarin here, now, meant that something would be saved. But how much? At Vannarai, the attack on the camp had been a feint, a distraction, meant to weaken and expose the true target. Against a concerted attempt to destroy the city, how much could he do?

They threaded their way across the roof. Aarin ignored the armed men as if they did not exist, which told Kallis just how effective he though they would be. He walked past the general to Kinseris and stretched out his good arm. With barely a hesitation, Kinseris clasped his wrist. Callan, following behind, took up station on Kinseris's other side. None of them said a word as they turned to face the south. As they faced the dragon.

Kallis stopped beside Galydon. They regarded each other in silence and Kallis found he did not have any words for this moment. He felt hot and cold, sick to his stomach, but also calm. There was a kind of release in knowing there was nothing he could do.

Then Aarin murmured something to Kinseris, and the priest replied, his words equally indistinct.

Galydon, who was closer, tilted his head up.

Through a break in the cloud, he saw it. High up, a sleek dark shape passing silently overhead.

Men around him muttered prayers; some were weeping. No one ran. There was nowhere to run.

Beside him, Aarin was gripping the parapet with his free hand, eyes tracking that deadly shadow from a face that still bore the fading scars of its fire.

The moments stretched, unbearable.

Somewhere in the city, someone was screaming, a strident wail that cut through the eerie silence. Aarin flinched, his fingers curling tighter around the parapet. But his eyes never blinked, his attention never wavered. Beside him, Kinseris and Callan stood as though carved from stone.

This time, the dragon flew low enough that Kallis could feel the pulse of its wings and see the scars on its scaled underbelly. It rolled as it passed overhead, regarding them from one unblinking black eye. Such a tempting target. The thought was fleeting and instinctive and followed hard by the realisation of just how catastrophic it would be, this moment, to give in to that temptation. He reached out and placed a restraining hand on the tip of the bow nearest him.

A single powerful beat of those wings and the dragon was past them and out of sight. Aarin released his grip on Kinseris's hand, breaking the spell. 'Hold your fire.'

A strong wind buffeted Kallis where he stood, then another, and he realised what was coming. 'Stand down,' he ordered the nervous clansmen just as another dragon glided into view, closer, lower, silver scales glinting in the sunlight. 'Stand down,' he said again, gently pushing down on the trembling bow under his hand.

As Silverwing disappeared along the path the other dragon had taken, Galydon released his breath with a sigh. There were tears on Callan's face.

Kallis caught Aarin's eye. 'Is it over?' It seemed impossible.

Aarin nodded, his gaze unfocused. 'It's gone.'

Kallis felt the tension drain out of him in rush, leaving him lightheaded and giddy. The reaction spread. He heard a shaky laugh and a few curses. It was no small thing to face such a death and survive. Some men rested their heads on their knees, others just knelt there, staring silently after the dragons. One man leapt to his feet and started capering around with delight, until another hooked his ankle and sent him sprawling onto his back, where he lay and laughed until tears ran down his face and the laughs turned to sobs.

Galydon put a steady hand on the shoulder of the clan captain whose men had just stood their ground in the face of the unimaginable. 'My thanks to your men, captain. You may stand down now.'

The captain nodded, his face pale under his tan, his hands visibly shaking. He rounded up his men, hauling the sobbing clansman to his feet and embracing him, their foreheads pressed together.

Then they were alone on the palace roof, alive, though the air felt too thin and every face bore the stamp of unreality—of life that somehow continued when they had expected to die.

Kallis cleared his dry throat. 'What happened? What did you do?'

Aarin exchanged a look with Kinseris. 'Nothing. It knew we were here, that Silverwing was here. Whether it would have attacked otherwise, or just came to look, I do not know.'

'But now he knows,' Kinseris said grimly, his eyes on Aarin.

'It seems to me that's no bad thing,' Galydon observed. 'If it spared us that. It's truly gone?'

Aarin gave a small shrug. 'For now. It's heading west.'

Galydon nodded, and beneath his rock-steady calm he too was deeply shaken. 'We don't have much time. Come.'

Kallis followed the general back into the palace and through the empty corridors of its upper levels,

'What will you do?' Aarin asked him.

'That was our warning,' Galydon said as he the flung open the door to his office. 'We must assume the dragon would have attacked if you hadn't been here. In which case, the waiting is over. Darred is coming. And I do not intend to yield one inch of Lothane without a fight.'

Footsteps pounded in the corridor. Lysan skidded round a corner, coming to a breathless halt as he saw his brother. Fear gave way to a relieved smile as Callan stepped past Galydon to embrace him.

Lysan murmured something, and Callan gave a shaky laugh, his face muffled in his brother's shoulder. Lysan hooked an arm around his neck, still grinning, and led Callan back the way he had come.

Aarin watched them go, then turned back to Galydon. 'What will you do?' he asked again, an edge to his voice.

'We take the fight to him,' Kallis said, following Galydon into the room. 'Like I told you.'

'You can't –'

Then Vianor was there, filling the small room with a swirl of black robes and his towering rage. 'This is madness!' He rounded on Aarin. 'You could stop this, and you're doing nothing!'

Galydon's hand on his arm was all that stopped Kallis going for the magician's throat. He shrugged it off. 'You're only alive, this moment, because of Aarin,' he growled. 'Try to remember that.'

'And we only face this danger because of him!' The old man was shaking with the force of his anger, or perhaps it was fear. He pinned Aarin with a fiery look. 'If you're too scared to face him, bring us more dragons to counter his. Give us the means to defend ourselves!'

Aarin didn't bother looking at Vianor, his face cold and remote. 'I can't.'

'Can't or won't?'

There was a fraught pause. 'Both.'

It was said quietly but there was a flat finality to his tone that Kallis had come to respect. It was not a lesson Vianor had learned yet.

'Does it matter?' Kallis asked, before Vianor could argue. 'If we bring the dragons into this, we unleash something we cannot hope to control.'

'But the dragons are in this, or have you forgotten?' Vianor retorted. 'And as long as they fight on the side of our enemies, there is only one way this ends!'

'You think the alternative is better?' Aarin asked him. 'The last time dragon turned against dragon, there was a war that laid waste to this world for generations and ended with the destruction of the magic. It took us three thousand years to even begin to heal that breach, and I will not allow you or anyone else to draw the dragons into your conflict and risk that happening again.'

'And if Darred had not already done so, I might agree with you,' Vianor shot back. 'But as it stands, the alternative is to let them destroy us. You could use their power to protect us, and you will not!'

'I already have,' Aarin retorted. 'But you don't want me to protect you. You want me to take their power and use it to kill your enemies, and to kill them in such numbers that it evens up the odds. And I…' The words seem to fail him.

Vianor's face was white with anger. 'Do you have any loyalty left in you for your own kind? *You swore an oath!*'

Aarin looked at him, but his eyes were far away. 'That *oath* ceased to bind me the day I died to fulfil it.'

In the silence that followed, even Vianor seemed to realise he had gone too far. Breathing hard, he said gruffly, 'I apologise.'

Aarin ignored him, turning to Kinseris. 'Within your Order, how many are priests?'

'In possession of a dragon device? Many hundreds.'

'And how many of those devices have you retrieved?'

Kinseris's expression was one of growing unease. 'Less than two hundred. That we know of.'

Aarin looked back at Vianor. 'I cannot bring the dragons here because they are not yet free. And I cannot bring them to you because they are not weapons to be summoned to your hand.'

'They are weapons to be used against us,' Vianor countered. 'Why should we not want to even the odds?'

'You think I can crook my finger and the dragons will come to me and obey my commands?' Aarin demanded. 'That those dragons not enslaved by Darred will fight for you *against their own kind?* What is your war to them?'

Exasperated, uncomprehending, Vianor asked, 'Then why are you here?'

'Not to fight your battles.'

Watching him, Kallis thought he had never seen anyone look so tired. Aware that his own transgressions on this subject were too numerous to count, he was about to steer the conversation to safer waters, but Aarin hadn't finished.

'What you do not seem to understand, any of you, is that the dragons are their own masters. They are not subject to my will, and they will never be subject to yours. Darred believes the dragons can be subjugated to a human will. That this is what the Joining does. But it is not. It is what *he* has done.

519

The Joining is a partnership. He could control those dragons because they were already shackled—*by their own choice and actions*—to the devices possessed by the priesthood. He preyed on their loss and showed them a false face. And he can do it again.'

The speech left him grimacing and short of breath, and Kallis's mind conjured horrific images of flames and burnt lungs. He glanced at Galydon, wondering why he did not intervene, and the general looked impassively back. There was going to be no help from that quarter.

'This is a new world, with new rules,' Aarin said, his voice hoarse. 'Where are the devices you took from the priests?'

Kinseris was looking shaken. 'In Kas'Tella. I could not risk attempting to destroy them. They are hidden, but…'

'They could be found,' Aarin finished. He looked grim.

'Is that even possible?' Kinseris asked, understanding what Kallis was scrambling to follow. 'They were wiped clean, blank. Could he use them that way?'

Aarin shrugged. 'I don't know. Nobody knows. That's the point. Those devices changed everything. It should not be possible for Darred to do what he has done, but they made it possible. And now, perhaps, every single dragon stands at risk.'

'What were you doing?' Kallis demanded of Galydon when they were alone.

The general quirked an eyebrow. 'I did nothing.'

'Exactly,' Kallis growled. 'Vianor —'

'But Vianor is right. He makes his argument badly, but that does not make it wrong. Aarin cannot hold himself apart from this and I cannot let him. He is part of it whether he likes it or not, and whether he likes it or not, he will have to pick a side.'

'He won't.'

Galydon shook his head. 'He already has. Darred threatens the dragons, so Darred is his enemy, just as he is ours. What he must work out now are the terms on which he can engage that enemy while keeping faith with himself.'

'And you think that *helped?*' Kallis demanded in disbelief.

'I hope it will force him to think, past pain and past guilt, about what he must do now.'

'Were you even listening?' Kallis asked. 'Aarin will protect the dragons at all costs—that is why he is here. We nearly lost him once already because I didn't understand that.'

'That was your mistake,' Galydon told him. 'But it was Aarin's also. We have different goals, but our enemy is the same. The way to one is through the other. If Aarin wants to free the dragons, he must first defeat Darred, and he cannot do that without us, or without sacrifice. He fears the risk to the dragons by involving them in this war, but the risk of doing nothing is far greater. You cannot fight a war without losses. I know that, and you know it. It's time Aarin realised it too.'

Kallis thought about his conversation with Callan and the bitterness of Aarin's grief. 'Maybe you're right, but even if you are, you heard him. He will never ask the dragons to fight for us.'

'As to that,' Galydon said thoughtfully, 'I wonder if he has even realised it is not his decision.'

TWENTY

IT WAS BELLS that heralded the end of the crisis, just as they had started it. Only this time it was a different sound that cut through the awful, waiting stillness of the palace basement, joyously chaotic, a clamour of relief. And yet for Jeta it brought no release. They had survived, but at what cost?

Limina gave a choked sob and buried her face in the tangled hair of the child on her lap, hugging the girl tight in trembling arms.

She looked up when Jeta stood. 'Wait. We don't –'

But she did not wait, she could not. She had to know, and she forced her way through the huddle of bodies back up the steps, and then she was flying through the corridors, racing her fear.

She emerged into the courtyard, blinking in the bright sunlight, and felt dizzy. It was untouched. People were spilling out of the palace and the barracks with shaky steps, looking around them in disbelief, unable to comprehend what had happened, and she pushed past them, searching all the time for a face she knew.

Through the growing crowd, she saw Callan and Lysan. Callan turned and saw her, and she flung herself at him, suddenly overcome. He held her tight while she wept, and she could feel the too-rapid beat of his heart thudding in time with her own.

'They're safe,' he murmured into her hair. 'They're safe.' Over and over, till her tears stopped and she pulled away.

'Where?' It wasn't enough to know, she had to *see*.

They couldn't tell her so she left them and went searching.

She found Kinseris as he reached the door of his room, one hand braced against its frame as if it were the only thing holding him upright. She called his name and saw him stiffen, saw the precious seconds of effort he took to compose himself before he turned, the attempt to mask whatever it was he was fighting.

She didn't let him. She walked towards him, slipping one arm around his waist as she fitted herself in the crook of his shoulder, and felt him lean into her, his head resting on hers.

'Come on,' she said gently, pushing open the door and walking them into the room.

He let go of her then, easing himself stiffly onto a chest, and after a moment's hesitation she sat down next to him. Not quite touching. The numbness was fading from his eyes, replaced by something else. Uncertainty, perhaps. And underneath it a bone-deep weariness.

Then he smiled, shaking his head. 'That was…' But whatever it was, he didn't have the words for it. The smile faded.

She touched his hand. 'What happened?'

He looked away. 'Nothing, nothing at all.'

But they had expected to die, and they had gone out to face it anyway. And it was now, when it was over, that it hit hardest. She knew that.

Kinseris sighed, running his hands over his face. 'We cannot risk that happening again.'

It was his tone rather than the words that sent a thrill of fear through her. 'What do you mean?'

He heard her fear, *of course* he did, but this time he had no ready answer for it. That scared her more than even the careful ordering of his thoughts.

'We cannot wait any longer,' he said at last. 'We're holding on. Barely. But any day now that might not be enough. If we wait, it won't be so much a defeat as a collapse. Darred is breaking us down, piece by piece, and we can't strike back. His army sits safe across the river while the dragon destroys us. We have no choice. Galydon has no choice. He must force a battle.'

We cannot wait any longer. 'Four months is all he asked for,' she whispered, remembering Hanlon and his captain in that filthy tent, of all they had given up to grasp the hope she had offered them. 'It has been more than half that. Give them a chance.'

He took her hand, drawing her gaze. 'Jeta. It's too long. There will be nothing left by then. We must draw Darred out. It's our only chance. We cannot go on as we are. There is only one way it ends.'

She had never seen him like this, too tired to dissemble. Even in Kas'Tella, as the council schemed and delayed and obstructed, when he had found his efforts thwarted at every turn, she had come to realise how carefully he had concealed his doubts. She had wanted his honesty, his trust, but now she found that she longed instead for the comforting mask, and realised, almost too late, that it had never been a lack of trust that had led him to shield her.

He must have seen it in her face. 'I'm sorry, I should not have…You asked me once to share my fears…'

She looked up at him, tears in her eyes. 'That was a long time ago.'

'I know. I'm sorry, for everything. Jeta —'

'Please. Let me speak.' And then found she couldn't. This wasn't how she had wanted to do this. It was too raw.

She saw the hurt bloom in his eyes, but he said only, very gently, 'You owe me nothing.'

You're wrong. But she could not say it, because she could not put into words just what she owed him, and it no longer mattered. She had already made her choice.

Kinseris saw the decision on her face. 'I understand. He has a prior claim…'

Her eyes flashed. 'Claim? No one has a *claim* on me.'

'I didn't mean…'

'I know what you meant,' she snapped. 'How do you think it feels to have two men so anxious to give me to the other?'

The struggle on his face was hard to watch. 'Jeta…'

'No. I am not a prize to be passed between you. Why do both of you think you can make my decisions for me? I am here because I chose to be, and I choose to stay.'

'He loves you,' Kinseris said quietly. 'And I know —'

'That I love him?' Jeta finished. 'And you think you will always be second in my heart.'

Kinseris's answering smile was rueful. 'I know I will always be second, that's why —'

Jeta put her finger on his lips, cutting off the words. 'Then don't be.' He met her eyes, not understanding, and she tried to smother her frustration. 'Do you love me?'

It was a question neither had asked the other. Love was a word they did not use. Two broken souls, coming together for comfort, had shied away from the demands of love. But what had seemed like a kindness she now recognised as cowardice. Aarin's return, so unexpected, had stripped away those comforting blinkers and forced them to be honest about what lay between them. About what they could have together if they allowed it, and which, she knew now, she could never have with Aarin.

She saw his hesitation and did not know whether her question had surprised him, or the memory of a dead woman would forever stand between them.

'Do you love me?' she asked again. He had not answered but neither had he looked away, and there was an intensity in his eyes that sent a flutter of sensation through her belly. Ever since Kas'Tella, when she had thought him dead and then not dead but dying, the realisation had been growing that this, that *he*, meant more to her than simply a safe harbour and a balm for her loneliness.

Here was a man she did not have to share with any other creature. She could not and would not deny that she also loved another. But she was practical enough to recognise that no matter how much he loved her, the one thing Aarin couldn't give her was himself. And he knew it. If only Kinseris would realise it too.

Just when she thought she couldn't bear the silence any longer, he smiled unsteadily. 'More than I ever thought I could.'

She buried her face in his shoulder. 'I love you,' she whispered and felt his arms tighten around her. Then she let the tears come.

Sedaine returned from the devastation of a dragon's fire to the celebrations of a city that had been spared the same fate. Darred could have marched his army right up to Rhiannas's main gate at that moment and no one would have noticed. Even so, when Petrik appeared to translate his men's garbled news and restore some order to the jubilations, she did not have the heart to reprimand him. They had had precious little to celebrate in the last few months.

The city shared her view, the outpouring of euphoria in direct contrast to the terror survived, and her progress to the palace was impeded by crowds thronging the streets. She couldn't share in it. A dragon had come *here,* to her city, and she did not know what had happened. She did not know how they had survived, and she refused to let herself guess the reason. To hope.

The clansmen at the palace gates were no more help than Petrik had been, and she was reaching the end of her patience when she saw him, walking fast away from the palace. He glanced neither left nor right and so he did not see her, standing in the doorway of the guardroom. She drank in the sight of him, so very alive, but so thin and pale that the angles of his face seemed carved from marble, his profile marred by an ugly seam of scarring. She wanted to call out, to go to him, but the words died on her lips as Jeta came flying across the courtyard in his wake, stopping him in his tracks.

She could not hear what the girl said to him, but she saw Aarin lean into her, saw their foreheads meet, and the careful way she touched him.

Then Aarin turned away and she could not see his face or hear his words, but she saw by the set of his shoulders that they hurt him. So like Ecyas in that moment. So like his father.

Jeta said something in reply and her smile was sad, her fingers brushing his as he pulled away. She let him go, watching as he walked away, out through the gates, and Sedaine wanted so very much to go after him.

Jeta turned and their eyes met in a moment of understanding, then she too walked away and disappeared into the palace.

Sedaine moved then, quick steps taking her to the gates, but the crowd of refugees clogged the road. She tried to push through them, frantic to find him, and was aware of a mercenary on either side, clearing her way. But it was too late. The road beyond was empty.

The clansmen escorted her back through the crowd. She did not hear the voices calling out to her, or feel the hands plucking at her clothes, only the irrational fear that she had just lost a chance that would not come again.

'Your highness?'

The clan captain's words were hesitant, uncertain, and she realised he had been speaking and she had not heard a word.

'Your pardon,' she murmured, forcing her attention back to him. 'Please continue.'

She could feel his sharp eyes on her face and smoothed away her anguish. Aarin was alive. He had come back. She would see him again. Others needed her now.

The captain cleared his throat and gestured to the palace, from which Galydon had emerged and was jogging down the steps towards her.

She nodded her thanks and went to meet her general, exchanging one agony for another. The breeze blew the strands of her long hair around her face as she accepted his greeting, her eyes searching his face and finding there something that made her heart start to beat faster. 'General,' she said formally, aware of the eyes on them.

'Your highness.'

They did not exchange another word as they walked together up the steps to the palace and through its bustling corridors. They did not speak as they came to her chambers and she dismissed the servants. And even when they were alone she found she could not at once find the words to break such a complicated silence.

Then the door clicked open, Kallis stomped inside, and everything else dropped away from Galydon's eyes except the war. She watched him shake it off, the ingrained discipline learned over decades, and made herself do the same.

She was dirty and tired; she had seen things in the last few weeks that would stay with her always. She was frightened and angry, grieving.

He saw all that and got straight to the point. 'We have run out of time.'

So. It had come. Though they had hoped for something different, Galydon had always planned for this. They were as prepared as they could be. But all that meant nothing if Aarin would not help them, and she had just seen him walk out of the gates and she had no idea what that meant.

Galydon was watching her, his eyes seeing too much. She took a deep breath, steeling herself to face it. 'Can we win?'

TWENTY-ONE

'TAKE ME AWAY FROM HERE.'

Nestled in the hollow at the base of Silverwing's neck, Aarin held on and closed his eyes as the dragon made his clumsy ascent, the still healing wing with its covering of fine new skin beating an uneven rhythm that skewed them sideways before the wind caught them and its power carried them up and free.

He did not look back as they left Rhiannas far behind. He wanted—no, he needed—to put some distance between them and the weight of divided loyalties. Of the strain of trying to balance what his heart was telling him and what his head demanded. Whether he wished it or not, he was being sucked deeper into a war he saw now there was never any way he could have avoided. But the weight of horror in the other memories he carried—of a war so terrible it had destroyed the old world—made it impossible to accept.

What went before is over and done, Silverwing told him now. *Those choices were not yours and they never will be. It is today we must fight for.*

Aarin rested his forehead on the dragon's neck, overwhelmed by the sorrow of it. *I cannot ask your kind to fight for mine.*

But you can ask us to fight for ourselves.

And if doing so means you must fight against each other? Just as before? What then?

Then we would be lesser for it, Silverwing agreed sadly. *But perhaps we might also be free.*

Aarin felt the tragedy of it tighten his throat. *I cannot…*

We cannot stay in the dream forever, Æisoul. The magic is healed. We long for Andeira, for home.

I know.

The collective yearning that filled Silverwing's words was almost physical. It made it even harder to say, *Not yet.*

Because no matter the choice before them—and he acknowledged there was a choice—the dragons could not simply return to the world. Not like this, not *now*. Not until he knew how to protect them.

I fear it too, Silverwing thought. *The chance that this human might take more of my kind and make them his playthings. But he cannot do it if he is dead.*

There was a primal savagery to that thought that made Aarin shiver, a desire to fight and kill that was the ages-old instinct of a predator.

And if you must go through your kin to kill him?

That is not your choice. It is ours. All you must do is let us make it.

But the consequences of such a choice were unimaginable in a world so changed. In a world in which humanity was no longer scattered and confined to small enclaves, but now sprawled across its surface in huge numbers. Where everywhere Darred could hold them hostage through the threat of death on a vast scale, and which Aarin had learned could only be defended against at crippling cost.

They cannot fight this alone.

He knew that was true.

They cannot win if we do not help them.

And the consequences of that loss, of Darred's victory, were equally unimaginable.

He had only one choice.

They were back in the dream; the pain fell away. Aarin flexed his right arm, feeling only the tug of half-healed scars and not the deep, throbbing ache that had plagued him, waking and sleeping. A weight seemed to lift from his shoulders as Silverwing flew effortlessly through the endless dawn, the healing wing forgotten, left behind like Aarin's own hurts. For precious moments, he just allowed himself to be, cradled in the welcoming embrace of the dragons.

But not for long. He had not come here to hide, and though the pain was forgotten, there was no healing in this place. It was time to use that.

They came again to Eiador's shadow, and this time Aarin allowed himself to see through Silverwing's eyes to the chains that bound the dragon to Darred's lie. Unlike last time, they did not try to break those chains, nor awaken Eiador to the deception that had stolen his will.

He traps himself.

There was great sadness in Silverwing's thoughts, an acknowledgement that here was a fight they could not win.

He traps himself, Aarin agreed. The chains were thicker and stronger. Almost solid in a world of dreams. Eiador had made them, and each time Darred pulled on them, they tightened. Yet there, perhaps, lay their weakness.

He remembered the feel of the desperate illusion he had wrought in Redstone, opening his hand to show Darred the device he had lost. *I made him think it was real.*

Could you do it again? Jeta had asked him. Could he? Here, in this place, the power of suggestion was dangerously strong. He only had to look at Eiador to see how it could be twisted, distorted. It was why he was so afraid—for all the dragons who remained imperilled by the devices still in the Order's hands, of his own failure to protect them. It was why he dared not allow their return, any more than he could risk once again confronting Darred in the dream.

And yet...

They cannot win if we do not help them.

He could not do again what he had done in Redstone. He could not take the device from Darred, not unless he once more gave himself into his power. And he could not take the dragon from Darred. He looked again at the chains and thought about their deadly foothold. Perhaps, just perhaps, he could take Darred from the dragon.

TWENTY-TWO

LIMINA WALKED BETWEEN the guards at the antechamber to the great hall and recognised neither of them. Inside, yet more unfamiliar faces stood in a loose ring around the room while Sedaine met with reassembled Lords of the North. It frightened her a little to have so many strangers near when the scars of Morven's rebellion were still visible. But these were not the lords' men filling the palace. They weren't clansmen either. Most of them weren't even soldiers, merely men wearing their uniforms.

It was an elaborate deception Galydon was orchestrating, stretched out over weeks, as he moved the bulk of Lothane's forces south without alerting Darred to where they were—or where they were not. Disguising their movements, filling the gaps they left behind, hiding his intention until the last possible moment. Limina did not know the specifics of his strategy, but she had known enough miliary officers to appreciate the meticulous planning that had gone into even the smallest of logistical details.

She watched him now, arms folded across his chest as he fielded one objection after another from Lothane's nobles, never losing his temper, never giving ground. And they would do what he said. They might argue and complain and drag their feet, but as long as Sedaine backed him, Galydon would get his way, and her lords would risk no disobedience with Morven's example to motivate them.

The price of that compliance was the vacant seat on Sedaine's right. Derias's absence was like a cut that wouldn't stop bleeding, his empty place at this gathering a bitter reproach. Sedaine would not speak of him at all, though her eyes strayed more than once to the seat that should have been his, and Limina worried daily about the rumour of Morven horsemen seen south of the river. She did not believe it—she did not want to—but when she had dared broach the subject with Kinseris and Galydon, their evasions had made her fear that it might be true.

Sedaine's steward appeared at her elbow. 'My lady, a message for you.'

Distracted, Limina held out her hand and the steward placed the cylinder in it. She looked at the seal and asked sharply, 'Who gave you this?'

The old man glanced behind him, his forehead furrowed. 'He was here a moment ago.'

Limina stared for a second, her mind blank, then she was outside the hall and flying through the corridors. Once she thought she caught a glimpse of someone ahead of her, disappearing round a corner, but when she reached it the hallway beyond was empty. Abandoning her pursuit, she ran up the stairs to the upper gallery and threw open the shutters that overlooked the courtyard.

She scanned the crowd until she saw him, a face from a past she had thought dead and buried, his burnished hair glinting in the sun. As though he felt her gaze, he looked up, blue eyes laughing as he sketched a wave. Then he was gone. And Limina was left with his message in her hands and a sudden, searing hope.

She found Galydon in his office sometime later, just returned from hours of tedious argument. He fixed her with a penetrating look, then stood aside and let her into the small room. Kinseris was there too, and she gave him a distracted nod.

'My lady?'

She handed Galydon the message. 'You asked me once… If anyone should make contact…'

He read it, then asked, as she had done, 'Who gave this to you?'

'A friend of my husband.'

'Do you trust him?'

'With my life.'

Galydon handed the message to Kinseris, who read it silently before returning it.

'Who else has seen this? Who knows what it says?' Galydon asked.

'Only me. And the man who brought it.'

'Are you certain?'

She nodded. 'As certain as I can be.'

'Good.' Galydon held the message in a candle flame, watching as it crinkled and blackened. 'See that it stays that way.'

Limina looked at him in astonishment. 'If it is true…'

Galydon smiled grimly. 'Precisely. *If.*'

'You don't believe it?'

'It makes no difference whether I believe it. I must be able to rely on it. This is not enough, do you understand?'

Kinseris leant forward, his hands resting on the desk. 'Limina, we must be certain. We must find him and talk to him. Who gave you this message?'

It was his hair that gave him away, glinting pale gold in the bright moonlight as he moved silently down the street and disappeared through the door of a house opposite. Limina watched him from the shadow of an alleyway and struggled to hold back the flood of memories—of Farnor, of *before,* of a dangerous, difficult man, devoted to her husband, so much so that where Daviyan went, she half expected to see Hanlon. Except, of course, Hanlon was dead. The only reason Daviyan hadn't died with him was because he had been with her.

'Get her out,' Hanlon had told his captain before he went to his ships, and she still remembered the look on Daviyan's face when he realised he was being left behind. She thought he had hated her then, but he had done as his admiral had ordered. He got her out. Then he had gone back, back into the chaos of Farnor's fall, and she had not seen him again. All this time she was sure he had died, yet here he was, and Maker, it *hurt.*

A hand closed over hers and she realised she was shaking. She swallowed past the painful lump in her throat and looked up at Kinseris. 'It's him.'

His searching gaze saw much more than she intended. 'I know.'

She did not ask how he had found this place so quickly, nor how he had known where to look. She had been aware, in a vague way, of what he had been doing since his arrival. And she knew enough of the life he had lived, and the world he had come from, to understand that it was an ingrained reflex, a survival instinct honed through years of living with constant suspicion, when knowing what those around you were doing and thinking was the only way to stay alive. But still, it surprised her.

They crossed the street together and stopped outside the house Daviyan had entered. 'Are you ready?'

She nodded. She wasn't, but what choice did she have?

Kinseris gave her a tight smile, seeing through her lie, and pushed the door open. He stepped back at once, hands raised, as a sword emerged from the entrance, followed by a harsh challenge.

Kinseris regarded the sword calmly. 'We need to speak to Daviyan.'

The response was immediate, a bristling of weapons and hostility as the owner of the sword was joined by two more and they spread out across the doorway. 'Who wants him?'

'Friends,' Kinseris replied, pulling back his hood. 'Allies, I hope.'

The man who had spoken spat on the cobbles. 'Ain't got no friends with your kind. Never will.' He exchanged a glance with his companions, who moved silently behind them. 'You shouldn't have come here.'

Kinseris sighed. He didn't move or speak, but he did *something*. The men stiffened, frozen in place by some invisible force.

'I'm sorry,' he said, sounding like he meant it. 'But we really need to speak to him.'

Then, taking Limina's hand, he led her between the restrained guards, who watched him with desperate, angry eyes, through the open door and down the steps. He did not try to disguise their arrival, making no effort to muffle his footsteps, and she heard a voice call out, 'Garath?'

Daviyan was in the room at the bottom of the stairs, sitting at a table with a flagon of wine. He was alone.

'Not Garath,' Kinseris said as he entered the room.

Daviyan tensed but he did not rise. One arm rested on the table. The other, she was sure, was holding a weapon. His eyes travelled up from Kinseris's pared down Lothani court dress to his desert-brown face and silver hair, and she saw the exact moment he realised who he was talking to.

Shock rippled across his face for an instant before he recovered his composure. He had always been so good at hiding his feelings. 'My lord, I did not know you.'

'No, I imagine you did not.' Kinseris said wryly. 'It has been many years and a lot has happened.'

Daviyan nodded, his eyes guarded. 'I am pleased to see you alive and well. We heard you had died.'

'And I thought you had,' Limina said, stepping into the room and throwing back her hood.

This time there was no disguising his reaction. He shoved to his feet, catching the corner of the table with his hip and sending the flagon crashing to the floor, his expression a complicated mess of emotions. 'Limina.'

He started to kneel amid the clay shards and the spilled wine, and something in her broke. 'Don't! Don't you dare.'

'Lim —'

'You left me!' She advanced a step, anger flying free. 'You let me think you were dead, and all this time… Was it you, Daviyan?'

He watched her warily. 'Was what me?'

For an answer, she slammed them down on the table—all those precious, hoarded messages that had found their way to her in the last two years. And most precious of all, the sketch Galydon had given her of Hanlon's sign.

Daviyan winced and looked away. He didn't say anything.

'You could have come to me,' she hissed, furious. She thought of that frantic flight from Farnor city as it burned around them, of the lonely journey across the war-torn Alliance states to Rhiannas, thinking she had lost everything she ever loved, even her unborn child. Of the struggle to put it behind her and build something new when her heart remained in the wreckage of her nation. 'I *needed* you.'

'No, you didn't,' he said gently. 'You never needed either of us. You always were entirely… self-sufficient. It's why we followed you.' He hesitated. 'It's why we loved you.'

She didn't realise she had moved until Kinseris stood between them, her wrist caught in his warm grip. Daviyan, his face flushed red where she had slapped him, was looking at her with something as close to compassion as she had ever seen from him, and she couldn't *bear* it.

Kinseris, his eyes dark with understanding, offered her the shelter of his body as she composed herself. She took a deep breath, feeling the tension in her chest release for the first time since Sedaine's steward had placed Daviyan's message in her hands. Without looking at him, she asked, 'Am I still your queen, Davi?'

His sharp intake of breath was answer enough. 'Always.'

'Good.' She met Kinseris's eyes and he nodded. 'Then, as your queen, I have some *requests* to make of you.'

She did look at him then and saw his blue eyes brimming with silent laughter. 'Of course, your highness. Make your requests.'

And Kinseris started to talk.

The moon was full and bright the night before her general left to go to war and Sedaine could not sleep. Tomorrow, Galydon would go south to meet up with Kallis and the army he had painstakingly assembled over many weeks, leaving her behind.

Because this was it. All these weeks of pretence, of hiding, of brutal punishment had been leading up to this moment, and she could not go with him. Here, at the end, her place was in Rhiannas. As her general rolled his dice and made his desperate last gamble to protect her country and her people, she had to hold them together while he fought so that there was a still a country left at the end of it.

But once he was gone, it would be too late. Too late to say the things she could not say, and he would not hear. The things that were keeping her from sleep and had led her to this door, where the light of a candle within told her the occupant was still awake, even late as it was. She rested her palm against it, then her forehead, eyes closed, and listened to the scratch of a quill over parchment. It took all her strength to resist the impulse to send tendrils of power to touch the man within. She would not invade his privacy like that.

The quill stopped. There was the sound of a chair pushed back and soft footsteps.

She jumped back as the door opened and Galydon stood there looking at her, something deep and impenetrable in his dark eyes.

'Your highness.'

'Please…' Her voice cracked. 'Sedaine.'

His head dipped, an acknowledgement but not surrender. 'Sedaine.' He stood back and held open the door, the smooth motion almost disguising the hesitation.

She brushed past him into the room, so close that she could feel his warmth, but did not take the seat he offered her. His desk was covered with documents, maps, lists, all covered with his small, neat script, and stubs of burned down candles stood mute witness to hours of work.

She looked from the desk to his face. He looked so incredibly tired. 'You should be sleeping.'

'So should you.' Then he sighed, exhaustion cracking his customary reserve. 'It is that hour of the night when I doubt every decision I have made. When I wonder what I have missed, or what I have not done, that could tip the balance.'

Without thinking, she reached out and touched his arm. She felt him tense, then his hand covered hers and her breath caught in her throat.

'Sedaine…'

She tilted her head and met the scorching heat of his gaze. He detached her hand from his arm, holding it between both of his. 'When this over, I will come back, I swear to you.' His fingers squeezed her hand then let it go. 'Until then… until then, I cannot allow myself to be distracted.'

I will come back. The one promise that no man heading to war could truthfully make. But it was also a plea, and she would not make it harder for him. 'I will be here,' she promised. Then she left him alone with his maps and his doubts, because all she could do was add to them, and he had a battle to fight.

PART FIVE

ONE

WHEN KALLIS ENTERED the old mercenary camp east of Forthtown there was little sign remaining of the attack that had so nearly ended in disaster—that would have ended in disaster had Aarin not been with them. His men had been here for weeks now, preparing for the army's arrival, and as the camp filled up he was glad that Aarin was out there somewhere with Silverwing, because if Darred wanted to end things quickly, there had never been a better time.

They had feinted, dissembled, distracted, but eventually they had to play their hand, and here they were. And now they had to be seen. As he stood in the centre of the growing camp, Kallis knew he was both an invitation and a trap. Today, the army came together, offering itself to Darred's much bigger force. Tomorrow, they would cross the Istelan and place themselves between that force and its way into Lothane. And once they were there, squarely in its path, Darred would have little choice but to attack—especially when they would make it so easy for him.

Well, that was the plan, and Kallis knew as well as Galydon how useless even the best plans were once the arrows starting flying.

The clan captains were arriving at the command tent. He should join them. He would. But once Galydon laid out his plan—or those details of it he was willing to share, because Kallis was certain that there were some things the general was holding back even from him—they were one step closer to making this real and he wouldn't be human if he wasn't terrified of what was coming.

The briefing had already started when he finally joined them. Galydon looked up as he entered, one eyebrow raised. Kallis ignored the question—

he was *fine*—and watched with arms crossed as the assembled captains learned their respective roles.

There was less resistance than he had expected. Hardly any, in fact. The problem of Lorac's absence and the question of who now commanded the clans had been solved by tacit agreement. They simply ignored it. Regardless of how each clan felt about their captain of captains, not a single one of them was prepared to accept the loss of so many without certain proof. Therefore, Lorac was still their chieftain and the bargain he had struck with Sedaine still held. Had Galydon been any less competent, Kallis suspected that might not have been the case, but even those who had resented his authority at first, accepted the orders he gave them now with barely a quibble.

Considering what those orders were, and how much their success relied on Aarin and the mages they had brought with them—on factors outside the control or comprehension of these men—Kallis considered their acceptance little short of a miracle.

But then, there were remarkably few alternatives by this point.

'Are we leading or being led?' Kallis asked Galydon once the others had left. It was the suspicion he could not lay to rest. What if they were doing exactly as Darred wanted them to? If he had manoeuvred them here as cleverly as they believed they had manoeuvred him?

Galydon glanced up from the pile of maps. He looked as tired as Kallis felt. 'Both, I suspect. But the result is the same. We must meet him, and even if we had a free hand to choose our course, I would make the same choice.'

In the end, Kallis had to agree. But Galydon was still taking a terrible risk by choosing to fight on the southern bank. It kept Darred out of Lothane, but their army would have the river at its back, giving them no direct line of retreat should the fighting go against them. But then, as he had said himself, this was the gamble to end all gambles. Battered, bruised, and pushed to the edge after months of bloody toil and deadly attrition, they had to risk everything on this, because they had reached a point where there was no other choice.

They had to fight, and Galydon had been ruthless. They could break or be broken, but whatever happened, they could not retreat.

Kallis felt the doubts rise, almost to his lips, when they heard shouts and the rush of many feet. He reached for his sword as Galydon strode out of the tent, then the quality of the sound reached him and he knew this was no attack.

Emerging from the tent he saw the Raven making his unsteady way towards them surrounded by a knot of jubilant mercenaries. The scout met his eyes and Kallis knew the celebrations would be short-lived. No man delivering good news had that look on his face. Galydon must have seen it too, because he neatly detached the man from his excited escort and shepherded him back to the tent.

Kallis followed reluctantly, a leaden weight in his stomach. He caught sight of Meinor, standing grim-faced at the back of the crowd, and gestured for him to join them. The clans needed one of their own to hear this news.

Inside, Galydon pressed the man into a chair. Even in the uncertain candlelight, the Raven's face was grey with fatigue and filthy with dirt and dried blood. His leather armour was blackened with what looked like scorch marks. Kallis closed his eyes briefly. When he opened them, Galydon was watching him with the same bleak realisation.

It was Meinor, looking down at the scout from his imposing height, who said, 'Make your report. What has happened?'

The clansman took a sip of the watered wine Galydon had given him and said in a voice that was emptied by exhaustion, 'The dragon. It came on us as we were crossing the Amadele. We were completely exposed. It slaughtered us.'

Memories of the boatyard returned in a black wave. Moments passed. Meinor was muttering a steady stream of quiet curses—or prayers, Kallis couldn't tell—as the scout sagged under the weight of his news delivered.

Galydon took the empty cup from his slack fingers and refilled it. As he handed it back, he asked, 'How long ago?'

The Amadele was a tributary of the Istelan that ran parallel to the Grey Mountains for much of its length. It was a ten-day march from their current position for men on foot, more with wounded.

The Raven shrugged again, beyond the ability to track time. 'Two weeks?'

Two weeks. Kallis felt sick. Two weeks ago, the dragon had come to Rhiannas and flown off to the west without touching the city. While they had been celebrating their survival, Lorac's men had been dying.

Then his attention snapped back to the exhausted scout as he said, 'I'm not far ahead of them.'

Galydon exchanged a wary look with Kallis. 'Ahead of who?'

Kallis felt Meinor poised by the door of the tent and signed to him to hold. Whatever else this man had lost, he did not think him so far gone that he would fail to deliver a warning of impending attack.

'Lorac. He sent me ahead once we had word you were here.'

At Lorac's name, Kallis was aware of a weight lifting, a shadow he had not wanted to acknowledge, even through all the weeks he had feared the clan captain dead. To know Lorac still lived was not simply a relief, there was joy there too.

Galydon caught Meinor's eye. The slightest hint of a smile curved his mouth. 'Take him,' he said, with a nod at the exhausted Raven. 'Get him food and somewhere to rest. Then go and find them and bring them in.'

Two hours later, Lorac limped into the camp with Meinor's escort, a healing scab on his temple and a muddy bandage round one thigh. Kallis saw a cluster of Black Ravens in the men around him as well as a scattering of other badges. There was not a man among them not sporting some injury. Some were barely upright.

The camp welcomed them in silence. Clansmen lined the perimeter earthworks and the routes between the tents, fists on hearts, heads bowed, as the ragged survivors returned to them. As Kallis watched, the commanders of Lothane's crown forces brought their own men to attention, offering their tribute to the dead. Even the soldiers of the lords' households, who usually tolerated the presence of the mercenaries with disdain, maintained a respectful silence.

Kallis walked a pace behind Galydon as he went to meet Lorac. The man looked as though sheer will was all that was keeping him on his feet. Kallis saw with a wince of pain that the man on his right who wore the armband of the Raven's captaincy was not the same man who had worn it when they left Rhiannas. That was a loss that had to hurt, and badly.

He did not hear what Galydon said to Lorac, but he saw the man straighten and a flash of life returned to his eyes. Then he waited, stifling his impatience, as arrangements were made to provide food and shelter to the new arrivals and tend to their hurts. Callan was already crouched beside an Eagle who had slumped to the ground, his fingers running lightly over the misshapen mess of the man's arm. Willing hands helped the man to his feet and led him away as Callan shifted his attention to a glassy-eyed mercenary hanging from the arm of another.

Lorac limped to Kallis's side. They did not speak. What was there to say? Callan glanced towards them and caught Kallis's eye, his gaze shifting to Lorac with a question. But the clan captain shook his head. 'Plenty hurt worse than me.'

Kallis kept his thoughts on that to himself. And when the last of the clansmen had been ushered away to sleep or eat, he knew better than to offer his assistance as Lorac limped beside him to Galydon's tent. Once inside, he could collapse. Out here, with all his men's eyes on him and so many reasons to despair, he had to be strong.

That collapse came almost at once. Meinor steadied his captain with a strong arm under his shoulder and helped him sit as Galydon handed him a cup. Lorac drank, then stretched out his leg with a hiss of pain.

'How many are with you?' Kallis asked, because someone had to.

Lorac stared at the cup in his hands. 'A hundred maybe, no more. The same again we left at the nearest settlement. The rest...'

Lorac's shrug conveyed an exhaustion that had gone beyond feeling, and that was a mercy. Meinor had gone white. His lips moved silently, his eyes on his chieftain.

Two hundred. Out of the twelve hundred sent west, only two hundred had survived. Almost half the fighting strength of the clans, gone.

Kallis had to force himself not to look away. Beyond conscious thought, he adopted the clan's posture of deep sorrow, soldier to captain. When his eyes met Lorac's, he found the gesture returned, brother to brother.

And then there was nothing more to do or say except give thanks that two hundred at least had survived. But it would not salve the pain of the brothers, the wives, the children left behind, or salvage a way of life that had lasted for more than two centuries.

The clans were dead. It had started at the Istelan, and it would end there too, but they would not go quietly. It was why they were here. Why injured, grieving men had pushed themselves in a gruelling march across the length of the country to join what must seem a hopeless fight.

Lorac took another sip and winced. 'I need something stronger than this.'

Even in the dim light, he looked awful, his face grey with pain, but his red rimmed eyes burned with an emotion Kallis recognised all too well.

'You should rest,' he said, unsettled by the force of that glare.

Lorac drained the watered wine and shoved the empty cup across the desk. 'Not until you tell me how you're going to beat him.'

Galydon met Kallis's eye with a faint shrug, but he did not waste words echoing Kallis's suggestion. What Lorac needed even more than rest was a purpose, so he gave it to him. Not everything, but sufficient to show the clan captain the outline of hope.

It was not enough. It could not erase the pain of what he had lost, but it was a start. As Galydon talked and Lorac listened, his questions becoming more measured, Kallis saw some of the reckless anger start to fade.

Lorac was frowning at the map. He traced a line that met the Istelan to form the point of a triangle right over Galydon's chosen battlefield. 'This map isn't worth shit. There's a stream here, and the land around it as it hits the river is a bog, marshland.' He indicated the fat end of the triangle. 'There's a nice slope he can send a charge down. If you make a stand there, you'll be trapped. He'll crush your right flank and force you back against the Istelan. This is not a good place.'

Galydon rolled up the map. 'On the contrary, it is perfect.'

'He'll slaughter us,' Lorac growled. 'If it's been wet, which it has, it'll be a mud bath as well as a bloodbath. We do not want to fight there.'

Completely undeterred, Galydon said, 'But Darred will, yes? And if we fight him there, we can control him. On open ground he has more options.'

'So do we,' Lorac insisted.

'But we are limited,' Galydon replied. 'We have fewer men, and they have Kas'Talani. More options favour Darred more than they favour us. Here, he cannot flank us. There is nowhere he can hide more men. And his path to victory is so obvious he will not think beyond it.'

Lorac was unconvinced. 'He will not need to. I know this country. You don't. I am telling you this is a bad idea.'

'And I heard you,' Galydon assured him with a slight smile. 'But that is the point. I don't know this country and neither does Darred, neither do his Caledani commanders, and neither do the Kas'Talani. That is their weakness. Their army will do what it has always done because it has always worked. And here'—he tapped his finger on the map—'we have a chance to turn that against them.'

'He will have Amadorian commanders too,' Lorac pointed out.

Galydon's smile widened. 'And we will show him he cannot trust them.'

TWO

DARRED COULD HEAR the argument before he even entered the tent, a rise and fall of muted voices that carried across the empty space around the pavilion. The tent doors were tied back because of the heat, giving anyone who cared to look a view of three of his commanders locked in undignified disagreement.

The flash of anger was sudden and dizzying. As fire flushed through him, his skin felt so hot it must burn. He had to ground the charge of power in the earth beneath his feet before he could regain control of himself.

He ignored the frightened glances of the guards outside the tent. Let them fear him. He knew what he was. What he was becoming. Only one thing mattered, and it was nearly his.

Through the open entrance he saw a fair-haired Amadorian officer arguing with three of his Second Army generals. One of them rattled off a string of angry objections in Safarsee and Darred felt a renewed burst of irritation that even after two years in Amadorn, so many of his commanders had failed to attain a basic grasp of the language.

The object of the tirade folded his arms over his chest and waited calmly until the words ran out, then responded in idiomatic low Safarsee, and not politely. It did nothing to improve his mood.

As his generals flushed, Darred stepped into the tent. Silence fell. 'Enough.' He pointed at the Amadorian officer. 'You. Explain it to me—what are they doing?'

The man indicated a point on the map just inside Lothane to the east of Forthtown. He cleared his throat. 'The latest reports have just come in. They are camped here.'

Darred studied the man in front of him as his commanders pulled the map towards them and continued to argue over it. His fingers tapped an impatient rhythm on the table. The news of Lothane's manoeuvring had started trickling in days ago, vague reports of troop movements with no clear pattern or intention. This was the first firm intelligence of anything more concrete, and he distrusted it. 'Why?'

'As a staging post for an invasion, my lord. Our intelligence suggests Lothane's forces are gathering there to attempt a crossing.'

Darred raised an eyebrow. 'An invasion? Really?'

'Yes, my lord,' the Amadorian replied, without a trace of irony in his blue eyes.

'I see.' Darred drew out the pause, a slight, mocking smile on his lips. The officer was one he did not recognise, but that was not unusual. The army had absorbed thousands of conscripts and he could not know them all. Nor, frankly, had he tried. It was for his Caledani commanders to organise and assimilate the Amadorians into their ranks. But there was something unsettling about this man, something in his manner, and his accent was difficult to place. Not Alliance. Possibly one of its border states. 'An invasion seems rather unlikely, does it not?' After the mauling Lothane had endured in the last few months, he considered 'unlikely' a generous assessment.

'If I may?' The Amadorian retrieved the map from the generals and spread it before Darred. His fingers traced multiple lines that ended at the camp. 'They have been massing their forces here for two days, drawing them from here, here, and here. What other explanation can there be?'

'To defend against our invasion?' Darred suggested. He could send Eiador to confirm the news, but now he knew for certain that Aarin was alive he had held the dragon back, and left the others where they were, safe in the Dream. Until all his plans were in place, he did not want to risk a confrontation between them. This action by Lothane—whatever it meant—altered his calculations, but not by much. He did not intend to allow anything to interfere with his revenge.

The man straightened, his hands clasped behind his back and his expression carefully blank. 'Of course, my lord. I'm sure you're right.'

Darred's eyes narrowed at the insolence, and he realised that it was about this man that he found so disconcerting. He wasn't afraid.

'We will know soon, my lord,' the Amadorian continued, the words cutting across Darred's blooming suspicion. 'I have sent the fifth division to scout the area. They will cross into Lothane to the east of the camp and assess the situation. They have orders to attack should conditions seem favourable.'

'Without my authorisation?'

The audacity was stunning. The fifth division. His precious mounted troops. He laid his hands on the desk, the surge of anger leaving him shaking. He was dimly aware of his commanders backing away as power slipped his control and spilled his rage into the tent. Then the sense of the man's words reached him, and restraint shattered. 'They will cross to the east?' Power lashed out to grab the Amadorian by the throat. 'How? *There is no ford east of Forthtown!*'

Heels dangling inches from the floor, face turning purple, the soldier tried to gasp a reply. Darred released him to fall in a heap at his feet. Chest heaving, the man looked up through a fall of blond hair, blue eyes laughing as his hoarse voice reverted to his true accent. 'How could... I know that...lord?' He rolled on his back, fingers sketching Hanlon's sign. 'I'm from Farnor.'

Darred felt an instant of icy shock, seeing at last the long hair and deep ship's tan. The sailor's grasp of Safarsee. Then rage drenched him. The Farnorian was dead even as he turned to where his commanders stood in mute terror. He grabbed the nearest. 'Call them back! *Call them back!*'

Eiador took to the air, powerful wings driving the dragon north, but he would be too late to prevent the unfolding disaster. Even as men scrambled to recall the advance, Darred felt the thunderous pressure as a wall of water built and built, a huge reservoir of raw power gathering in his enemies' hands, then its explosive release as the wave was unleashed to sweep exuberantly downriver. He watched through the dragon's eyes, powerless, as men and horses were washed away in a furious, foaming torrent.

The wave overflowed both banks, snatching at anyone too close to its shore, pitiless and impartial. On the south bank, the remains of Darred's mounted troops wheeled and stamped in close-quarters confusion as discipline dissolved into a desperate retreat against the weight of those behind pressing forward.

Then the arrows started.

Concealed under the eaves of the Grymwood, Galydon's archers unleashed a rain of death on the close-packed cavalry. They struck first at the rear, their shafts taking down men and mounts, whose dying churned up the boggy ground and snarled the retreat. As Eiador flew above the carnage, Darred watched a snorting, blood-mad horse crush its fallen rider's skull with its hooves, then fall across his body as its back leg snapped, its collapse entangling and pulling down another horse.

Trapped between their dying comrades and the swollen river, a group of riders charged at the trees, but the powerful shafts plucked them from their saddles. Horses shied as the forest bristled with spearheads, the ground beneath their stamping feet foaming with blood.

Almost blinded by fury, the best part of his cavalry wiped out, Darred sought his dragon's mind.

Burn it down!

As Eiador swept down amid a hail of arrows, his fire raking the forest canopy, it was turned and extinguished like a breath on a candle flame. Screaming his rage, Darred forced Eiador against the shield again and again, white-hot fire licking over the ancient trees and meeting the same impenetrable barrier. Arrows bounced off the dragon's scaled underbelly, one tore through the tip of a wing. A warning.

Aarin. Only one man could channel that much raw power and not face instant annihilation.

As Darred's control slackened, there was a strange *tug* on the bond that bound them. Eiador pulled up, turning in mid-air to direct his fire away from the trees. Furious, Darred tried to make him turn back, but the dragon ignored the command, great wings taking him, beat by beat, away from the forest. Away from the other dragon hidden under its canopy.

Aarin and Silverwing were here, and they had the power of a river in flood at their back.

Well, let them have this small victory. It would be costly. Because his enemy had shown his hand too soon. Eiador's flight had shown Darred more than just the slaughter of his cavalry and he now knew two things: that he could not trust his Amadorian conscripts and that the bulk of Galydon's army had already crossed the river.

Darred turned to the young Caledani officer hovering nearby. 'Ready your men, captain. I want that forest cleared. Take as many men as you need. I will send five of my colleagues with you. Burn it down around them.'

Let Aarin scramble to defend the Lothani against that conflagration and he would be quite unable to interfere in the battle Galydon was so obligingly offering him.

Because if he had made a mistake, Galydon had made a bigger one, and it had given him the opening he needed to crush them.

THREE

'THERE.' KALLIS LOOKED where the Hawk pointed and saw what he
had seen. He smiled. Darred had not disappointed. After the disaster on the
banks of the Istelan, he was sending his own soldiers into the Grymwood
after them. So far, Galydon's gamble was paying off.

'My countrymen have never fought in terrain like this,' the general had told
him, outlining his plan. 'Nowhere in Caledan are there such forests. They are
used to flat, open ground—arid land. If he sends them in after you, you will
have the advantage.'

The gamble had been whether Darred would also unleash his priests, and
it looked like he had—Kallis could see a handful of the distinctive Kas'Talani
robes among the assembling soldiers—but the mages who had dammed the
Istelan were in the forest with them. Their talents augmented by the wildly
flowing river, they would act as a counter to the deadly power of the
Kas'Talani. Or so he fervently hoped.

Kallis watched the Caledani for a few minutes more, long enough to satisfy
himself as to their numbers and intentions, then made his way back to where
Aarin waited with Callan's ever-present shadow at his side. 'He took the bait.
They're coming. There are Kas'Talani with them.'

Aarin nodded tightly, his expression distant, and Kallis turned from him
and began issuing orders for his men to pull back deeper into the forest. He
caught sight of Lysan among the archers whose skills had been used to such
devastating effect against the survivors of the flood. They would be crucial
to what came next, and he was glad Lysan was with them. His men were on
edge in the deep darkness beneath the Grymwood's thick canopy. They had
lived in its shadow and in fear of its legend their whole lives. Lysan hadn't

and likely wouldn't care if he had. His lack of concern steadied them, and they needed to be steady. *There are Kas'Talani with them.*

By the time the last of the clansmen had disappeared into the thick undergrowth, Aarin and Callan had gone. Kallis let his eyes linger on the place they had been, wishing he understood what they were doing, then crossed to where Meinor stood with a handful of Hawks and two of Luen's mages. 'You know what to do?'

Meinor grinned, his missing teeth showing as black holes in the low light. 'Aye, I know my business. You just make sure you know yours.'

Kallis gripped his arm and nodded towards the two mages. 'Stick close to them. Don't let them get killed.'

'And there I was thinking it was the other way round. Ah, don't fret. I'll give them back to you whole. Now get out of here.'

Kallis hurried after his men, catching up with them after a few minutes. It was slow going through the tangled forest, even with two hundred mercenaries trampling a path before him. He used his sword to cut through thick brambles and rotten, broken branches. There were few paths in the Grymwood, and they needed to leave a clear trail to follow in case the Caledani lost sight of Meinor and his men.

At its edges, the forest was a dark tangle of oak, beech and pine, but the further they went and the higher they climbed, the broadleaf trees thinned out until the tall pines clustered in close on either side. The sky was an eerie haze of fine needles and the leaf litter underfoot gave way to springy moss that cushioned his steps.

It was here that the path broadened into a track that could take two or three men abreast, and his sign to leave it.

Kallis scrambled up the slope to his left, pausing by a huge, old pine with drooping branches that swept outwards across the forest floor. Within minutes, Meinor and his band of Hawks appeared, jogging easily along the track, and not long after that, the faint sounds of the pursuing soldiers could be heard trampling their way through the undergrowth.

Kallis picked his way through the trees to where Lysan waited with a small group of archers. The commotion of the oncoming Caledani was unmistakable now, and Lysan flashed him a grin, his eyes bright with anticipation. At a sign from Kallis, he issued quiet orders to his archers that saw them spread out silently through the trees.

Kallis returned to the ancient pine, trusting its spreading branches to hide him as the vanguard of the Caledani came into view. They came cautiously, spread out along the track, eyes quartering the trees to their front and sides, but his archers were woodsmen. They knew how to stay out of sight. It wasn't long before the main body of the soldiers followed their advance guard.

Kallis waited until the bulk of the enemy had straggled past, then he stood, and the archers stood with him.

They fired two volleys in quick succession and retreated. Their arrows took down the men at the back almost silently. Almost. Three men fell dead, while a fourth rolled screaming on the path with a heavy shaft in his leg. Kallis waited just long enough to watch the confusion and panic spread out from the rear, then turned and hurried after the archers.

He caught up with Lysan, and the archer grinned at him.

'Think they'll follow?'

He shrugged. 'They might.' But he didn't think so, not yet. The unfamiliarity of the terrain would deter the Caledani from sending men in pursuit. If they did, he was confident his archers would lose them in the darkness of the forest.

His instincts were right. Their commander kept his men on the convenient path that took them on a curling route through the densest part of the forest. Meanwhile, Lysan's archers could move quickly to their next position and continue to harry the back of the column.

After the third attack, Kallis left them to make his way to where the main body of clansmen were waiting. The Caledani were waking up and adapting, the men at the rear walking with shields raised. It slowed them down, but the arrows were finding fewer targets, not that it mattered. The archers' priority was to cause fear and chaos, and they were doing that just fine, nervous confusion rippling further through the ranks with each hail of arrows. So, when the path eventually entered a gently sloping glade, the enemy column had lost all cohesion, and more importantly, *they were looking behind them.*

Kallis watched them come with Meinor, who had brought his little group safely back to their fellows just ahead of the Caledani advance.

As soon as the soldiers came into view, Meinor signed an order to the clan archers who lined the glade on either side, hidden by the trees. There was a yell, and Kallis saw a commotion break out at the heart of the advancing column—one final gift from Lysan's stalking woodsmen.

The clan archers struck a moment later, aiming for the priests. But the Kas'Talani had their guard up. Well warned by Lysan's harrying attacks, the arrows were deflected harmlessly off invisible shields. The soldiers around them weren't so lucky, however, and the priests' very act of defending themselves bought Kallis precious seconds.

'The closer you can get, the safer you'll be,' Galydon had told him. The priests' magic was most dangerous at long range, when they could strike their enemy without risk to their own side.

He didn't wait for the shafts to stop falling. The first volley was their signal, and the mercenaries burst from the trees, screaming their fury as they charged down the slope to crash into the disordered lines from both sides with terrible, desperate savagery.

No fury of fire met them. The air had the crackling, static feel of the depths of winter, as Kas'Talani power met the dampening force of the Istelan's furious flood, channelled through the mages who had come into the forest with them.

The enemy line flinched and recoiled. The failure of their priests was as much a shock as the suddenness and ferocity of the ambush. Terrified, disorganised, and too reliant on the Kas'Talani to do their killing for them, the Caledani broke. Kallis watched it happen, a slow-motion collapse that started from the already panicked rear and spread quickly to engulf the centre, where a handful of officers tried desperately to rally their men around the priests—who were finally throwing off whatever impediment the mages had brought against them.

Clansmen began to die, pierced by invisible weapons or burned alive by bolts of fire.

But it was too late. Even as the priests broke through the suppressive efforts of Luen's mages and released the devastating power of their magic, their troops were already dead or running.

'Back!' Kallis shouted, straining to make himself heard.

From somewhere to his left, Meinor was roaring the same order, impossibly loud, and the clansmen began to disengage.

Fire followed them, arcing overhead to explode in a tornado of flames amidst the summer-dry wood of the forest floor. Their orderly retreat became a terrified scramble. Kallis stumbled, smoke and sparks burning his throat, choking him, and saw the body of one of his mages sprawled at his feet, burned from the inside out.

Another mage was beside him, scrambling away from the enemy, a middle-aged woman with black streaks in her greying hair and blood on her clothes. Her face hardened as she saw the body on the ground, terror replaced by hate. She turned back towards the Kas'Talani, but he grabbed her by the waist and dragged her with him towards the safety of the trees.

Fire roared up all around them, finding ready fuel in the tinder-dry wood. The billowing smoke made it impossible to see where they were going, and men stumbled into each other, coughing and half-blinded. The woman pulled herself clear, waving an arm, and the smoke around them parted to give them a clear view of the way ahead.

And suddenly they were moving freely again. The tangled undergrowth slithered out of their path as they retreated from the furious flames—*which did not follow them.*

'Are you doing that?' Kallis asked, glancing over his shoulder to see the fire now closing in on itself—on the Kas'Talani priests who had started it.

The woman shook her head, her face strained. 'That's not me.'

'Then who —?'

'Not who. What.'

The roar of the flames intensified. Even at this distance, Kallis could see the terror on the faces of the priests as the fire they had started engulfed them.

He looked away, feeling a spasm of revolted pity as the Grymwood exacted its vengeance on those who had tried to turn their power against it. Then he put his head down and trudged after his men as they made their way back to their camp.

FOUR

IT WASN'T FAR to their temporary camp. Men straggled in and threw themselves to the ground, the exhilaration and relief of combat survived quickly giving way to exhaustion and reaction. Kallis stopped at the edge of the clearing as the flush of adrenalin drained away and left him unsteady and trembling. The heavy silence of the clansmen told him he was not alone.

He was in the boatyard when it was destroyed; he had seen the aftermath of a dragon's attack too many times. Galydon had warned him, in detail, what to expect. But none of it had prepared him for the terror and destruction just a handful of Kas'Talani had caused, even hampered by all the power twice as many mages could throw at them. And this was just the start.

He put his head down, resting his hands on his knees as he drew in a shaky breath. They had to do it again. A few priests were dead, but many more remained, and he had to lead these men straight into their path. But he thought he understood, at last, why Galydon had chosen that treacherous stretch of ground by the river.

The sound of retching drew his attention to the woman by his side, on her hands and knees in the dirt. Kallis snagged a waterskin from a passing mercenary, waiting silently for her to finish, then handed her the water. She took it, not meeting his eyes, and took a long drink. Then she staggered to her feet and stumbled away.

Kallis let her go. He forced himself to move, to concentrate on what he needed to do, not what had happened. Around him the mercenaries were doing the same, cleaning weapons, snatching precious moments of stillness.

Between Galydon's obsessive planning and the clans' practised organisation, they had fallen back on a well-prepared position, where water and food waited. If the enemy had found it… But they hadn't, so all was well. For now.

Kallis walked through the makeshift camp, handing out waterskins, reminding the men to eat and rest—to sleep if they could—that they were not done yet.

Lysan was waiting for him as he finished his circuit. He had a pack slung over one shoulder and his bow in his hand. He looked tense and unhappy.

Kallis, realising at once his intention, clasped his arm. 'Thank you,' he said, meaning it. 'Now go.'

Lysan hesitated, clearly reluctant. 'I should…'

Kallis shook his head. 'Go.' One archer more or less would make no difference now and Callan would be no use to Aarin if he was consumed with anxiety over his brother. And Aarin *must* succeed, or none of them would survive this.

He wanted to say more in case he did not survive to say it later. To acknowledge all they had been through together, but he didn't have the words, and someone was calling his name. And it was all on Lysan's face anyway.

'Go,' he said again. 'Keep them safe.'

Lysan nodded, and Kallis turned to deal with whatever it was that needed his attention. When he looked back, Lysan was gone.

It was a march Kallis had no wish to repeat—several hundred men, through the deep heart of the Grymwood, at night and at speed. Or at such speed as was possible under those conditions. Because if they did not manage to link up with Galydon's larger force before dawn, all their careful preparations would be for nothing.

They had fifteen miles to cover in a little under nine hours. By day, over good terrain, he would not have worried. Overnight, after a fight and with only a few hours of snatched sleep, through several miles of tangled forest, it was too tight for comfort. At least they were marching light, taking only their weapons and what water they could carry. Even at night it was stifling under the thick canopy, and tired, thirsty men would not make good time.

And they were not making good time. Kallis suppressed the urge to hurry the weary men. They had always known this part of the journey would be slow. Once they were out of the forest they could make up the time they had lost—assuming they did not themselves get lost.

Eerie mage-light lit their way, another reminder of the urgency of this march. Galydon's great gamble—the choice of the boggy ground against the river—relied on the presence of as many of Lothane's mages as possible. And better than half were currently marching alongside him—the men and women who had dammed the Istelan to such devastating effect, and who were currently guiding them through the Grymwood.

He saw Meinor waiting for him up ahead.

'Men need a break.'

Kallis bit down on a frustrated curse. Meinor was well aware of the stakes; he was also right. He reviewed his mental map of their route, fuzzy as it was. 'Another mile.' If they were on the right track—a big if—another mile would take them close to the edge of the forest. They could rest under cover of its canopy. There would be no stopping once they were in open country. The night was no protection against a dragon's eyes, and he did not know what Aarin had done, or where he was.

Meinor grunted an acknowledgement and headed back towards the front of the tired line, while Kallis wished for the hundredth time that Aarin was still with them.

It wasn't until he walked into the back of the man ahead that he realised they had ground to a halt. Someone was calling his name.

He pushed his way through the clutter of collapsed men to where Meinor was standing, hands on his hips, arguing with the mage at the head of their untidy column.

Kallis looked from one to other. 'What's the problem?'

Meinor growled and spat, gesturing ahead, and the mage directed his light at the man-high obstacle of fallen trees and overgrown brambles that blocked their path.

Kallis looked at it in silence for a few seconds, then he swore. He had spent two days walking this forest with Aarin, trying to get a sense of its scope, marking their route. This was not it. He swore again, with feeling. Somewhere, somehow, they had missed a marking or made a wrong turn and now it would cost them precious time. Too much precious time.

'Go back,' he told the mage. 'Take two men and find out where we went wrong—what we missed.' To the men closest to him, he said, 'Rest. Eat. We'll be moving again soon.' And heard the order passed down the line as his mind turned to worrying the problem of how to reverse their long, ragged column and backtrack over bad ground, in the dark, without losing even more time in the inevitable chaos.

He looked again at the obstacle, chewing his lip, and tried to orient himself in the darkness. But the forest was thick and unfamiliar, and he had no sense of their direction. 'Why are you still here?' he asked the mage who was hesitating by his side.

In the fey glow of the mage-light the man's face was little more than planes of shadow, but his unease was evident. 'We didn't miss any markers. Look.'

Kallis looked where he pointed and saw the sign he had carved into the trunk of a tree just days ago—the tree that now lay across their path, looking as though it had been there for months, years. He had a sudden, disturbing flash of the way the fire had closed in on the priests that had called it, and muttered a rare, heartfelt prayer. It seemed appropriate.

Meinor's eyes snapped to him, but Kallis ignored him. His mind replayed the way the forest had seemed to part for them even as the fire consumed their enemies. The memories were a jumble of confused impressions—could he trust them? Could he trust *this*? Could he afford not to? The one thing they didn't have was time.

Kallis beckoned to the mage. 'Come with me.' He turned to Meinor. 'Be ready to move. If I'm right, we won't be long.'

'And if you're wrong?'

Kallis cast a last, suspicious glance at the moss-covered trunk of the dead tree that had stood straight and tall just days ago. 'I don't think I am.'

With the mage by his side, lighting the way, he retraced his steps, scanning the trees on both sides. They had walked less than a hundred paces before he saw it—the broad, inviting opening on his right, wide enough for his men to walk comfortably two abreast. The sight sent an uncanny tingle down his spine.

Blowing out a long breath, he took a step onto the path, then another. Nothing stirred in the humid air. The trees were just trees, alive but not *alive*, despite the fact this path had not been here before. The mage followed him, unspeaking, and together they walked in silence to the first bend in the track. The path beyond it led on in the same easy fashion.

Kallis turned. 'Stay here. Keep that light high.'

The man nodded, his face tight with complicated emotion, and Kallis felt a twinge of sympathy as he headed back to where he had left Meinor. If they were going to do this, there was no point waiting.

FIVE

AARIN TESTED THE threads he had hooked around Eiador as the dragon unleashed its fire against the Grymwood. Gossamer thin, they lay unnoticed in a web around the dragon, snaking through the chains that bound him to Darred. Dormant. Waiting.

It was tempting to try to strengthen those threads, to bind them tight around the weakness of Darred's rigid grip, but he knew it would not be enough. To simply restrain the dragon would not work. The strength of the false bond would always be greater. No, to take Eiador out of the fight, Aarin would have to stand in Darred's place, to insert himself into the illusion Darred had created. To *become* Cadyr. And he had no device to help him, no connection to draw on. Just that delicate spider's web of masking illusion he had cast in the moment of the attack on the Grymwood.

He could have stayed with the army, spent his power and his strength trying to shield them from the fire, but that was too uncertain, too fraught with risk for him and for them. They needed to remove Eiador from the board and force Darred to fight without the dragon. They had to make this a battle they had a chance of winning because then, and only then, would he have a chance of getting to Darred himself.

Callan's fingers curled around his forearm, just as his own arm was held firmly in his brother's grip. Lysan had joined them little more than an hour ago, prompted by instinct to be where he was most needed. They could have attempted this alone—Aarin was almost certain that Callan could not cross over into the Dream, not without a bond to take him there—but Lysan's anchoring presence gave them a welcome safety net.

They were back in Lothane, Silverwing carrying them close to the western edge of the Grymwood but not within it. He could not afford to be distracted by what was happening in the forest. Though even here the echoes of violence reached him, and he had to spend precious effort blocking them out.

Callan's hand tightened on his arm, a steady reassurance. Aarin could not see his face, but he was grateful for the touch. He was afraid.

Left unchecked, Eiador and Darred between them would destroy Galydon's army. It would not matter how clever they were, how many mages and magicians they had, or how deeply they could draw on the furious torrent of the Istelan. To give them any sort of chance, he had to take away Darred's greatest advantage, but to do it he had to leave himself perilously exposed. He would have to work an illusion so strong and so perfect that it could not be pierced by even the most determined probe. An illusion so perfect it would allow him to step between Darred and Eiador and subsume, for as long as he could, their connection within himself. As he had once subsumed the magic of Darred's device in Redstone. And he had to stay alive to do it.

He did not know if he could step into Darred's place—Cadyr's place—and he did not know if he could hold it. But he had to try. And he had to do it now, before Darred turned Eiador against the Lothani forces Galydon was assembling on the southern bank of the Istelan.

We are ready.

There was hesitation in Silverwing's thoughts that went beyond an instinctive reluctance to put his mage at such risk. Aarin knew why. In attempting this thing, they had stepped from their role as protectors to collude in a deliberate deception. But Darred's actions and ambitions stood between the dragons and their return to Andeira; it threatened them all. And he hoped that by deceiving Eiador they might ultimately free him, though it would be to a cruel, cold grief.

Aarin allowed himself to slip into the dream. It was as easy as breathing now, to go between the *now* and the *then*, to move between the *here* and *there*. But this time was different. While Eiador's physical form might reside in Andeira, his ethereal spirit remained in the Long Dream. The dragon was neither here nor there, and to reach him, Aarin must be the same.

The pressure of Callan's hand receded as the dream opened up around him and the world faded, but it did not completely disappear—the anchor tying his physical self to Andeira, as Darred was the anchor for Eiador. A lifeline in case he lost his way and his self in the attempt.

Aarin had no device, and no connection. But he had something Darred didn't have. He had Lorrimer and Silverwing's memories of Cadyr. Where Darred had imposed his deception through the brute force of the dragon device, Aarin was capable of a much more insidious betrayal.

The memory of a laugh, spontaneous and free. Golden hair, streaming in the sun. A temper that flared hot and died fast. A final, impassioned speech against the division of the races.

Fragments of memory that unspooled into a true image of a man who had once lived and was again, for a moment, filled with life.

He stepped into that image, allowed its folds to mould themselves around him like a cloak, and showed himself to the chained and subdued creature that was at the heart of this battle.

Come, brother.

Eiador's head raised, his neck painfully weak, and joy suffused his eyes.

This was the moment of greatest danger—when two versions of one man vied for the loyalty of one creature. Joy turned to confusion, the dragon shaking its great head back and forth, agitation raking its limbs. And reached instinctively for the reassurance, the anchor, of the bond.

Aarin almost lost him then, as the false bond stirred and Darred's threads tightened.

But he *could not* lose. Too much was riding on this.

He forced a smile into his voice as he copied the greeting that Silverwing and Lorrimer knew so well, one hand curving out with an extravagant flourish. *Let us ride these winds together.*

It was that gesture, so familiar, so *loved,* that let him in.

There was no place for guilt or heartbreak. The trust and love that was extended to him was, this instant, nothing but a weapon.

He stepped into its embrace, opened himself to it, and before he could think about what he was doing, *pulled* Eiador deep within the circle of his own bond, walling Darred out and deadening the connection that lay between them.

The reaction was immediate, from within and without. As the surge of Darred's violent protest battered against the barrier he had forged, the full weight of another creature's presence where only one should reside nearly cleaved his mind in two.

He lost time. He nearly lost everything. As the unnatural, unsupportable dual presence ravaged his mind, he felt the barrier begin to crumble.

Then Silverwing was there, the force of his presence adding steel to Aarin's defences, calming the turmoil within to allow him to divide himself, to wall away one from the other and preserve his sanity.

A pressure on his arm. The sensation of sun on his face.

Aarin.

He tumbled out of the dream; he hadn't moved.

Callan was calling his name.

A storm raged inside, but it was distant, remote. And he was so tired.

Aarin dropped his head onto his knees, eyes closed, and slowly, methodically, reinforced the delicate wall that divided his link with Silverwing from the bond he had stolen from Eiador and Darred. That divided his self in two.

The warmth of the sun faded. The touch on his arm never wavered.

He looked up. His vision split and blurred. He blinked, tried again, and this time just two identical faces watched him with concern.

Callan glanced at the hand that still held his arm, then back to his face. 'Is it done?'

Aarin nodded.

Lysan gave a sigh and rocked back, releasing his brother to massage his aching hand.

Callan's grip uncurled stiffly and he grimaced as he stretched cramped fingers. His gaze swept over Aarin. 'Can you sleep? We will keep watch.'

Aarin shook his head. 'We must leave here.' Darred already knew what he had lost, he might already know how. Desperation would drive him to recover it. They couldn't take the risk that he had tagged their location in the instant that his link with Eiador had been shadowed, and they had already tarried too long.

The pulse of wing beats backed him up as Silverwing landed close by. *Quickly.*

Aarin let Callan haul him to his feet, then surrendered to instinct as he climbed onto the dragon's back and let Silverwing take him away.

Within an hour Kallis doubted his decision. After two he was sure he had made a terrible mistake. But there was no going back. The way was closing behind the end of his straggling column, the path disappearing in thick undergrowth that gave them no option but to go on. It reminded him of the torturous journey out of Ephenor, ensnared by the magic of Shrogar's tunnel that prevented their return the way they had come. Just so did the Grymwood guide them now, and he did not know to what or where. As the hours dragged on and the trees crowded close on all sides, he felt a sinking despair. There seemed little hope they could reach Galydon in time.

The first glimmers of dawn were already lightening the sky before the forest around them began to thin. *Too late. Far too late!* He forced himself not to snap at the slow pace. Not to give in to his seething frustration. Everyone was tired, and this had been his mistake. In his frustration, he nearly made another.

He stepped out from the treeline into the open without taking even the most basic precautions, in too much of a hurry to establish where they were. And, following his lead, the clansmen trampled their way out of the undergrowth in a widening arc. He barely registered the shout of alarm before they were facing a line of nervous crossbows. Several voices called a challenge, cutting across each other and adding to the confusion, as more clansmen poured out of the forest, and for an instant they hovered on the brink of disaster. In the uncertain light, no one knew quite who they were facing, and it was only Meinor's bellow to 'hold your bloody fire' that saved them from a tragic misunderstanding. One man released on instinct, throwing his arm up at the last moment so that the bolt sailed harmlessly overhead.

They had not expected to find pickets here, and the pickets certainly hadn't expected them to appear in their midst. Kallis looked around him in the grey dawn light and drew in a shaky breath as he realised why the lookouts were so tense. They had emerged from the forest on the very edge of Galydon's chosen battlefield when they should have been several miles away at least. They had emerged from a forest *where no forest had been*. And even as he watched, it seemed as though the undergrowth was already retreating.

He blinked and rubbed tired eyes. When he looked again, he saw only leaves stirring in the gentle breeze, a picture of innocent nature—and had the distinct feeling that someone, some*thing* was laughing at him.

Get it together, he berated himself savagely. *Focus.* Because as uncanny and disturbing as it was, the forest had brought them to where they needed to be, hiding them from unfriendly eyes, and he would take that, however it happened. All the same, he was happy to turn his back on the Grymwood as the officer in charge of the lookouts peppered him with questions.

As the long column emerged from the forest to find they were not lost, the mood changed. Men shucked off their exhaustion, and he saw Meinor moving among them, keeping them calm, focused.

It took several long minutes to untangle the details about exactly where they were and where they should be, and through it all Kallis fidgeted impatiently, resisting the childish impulse to spin around to try to catch the trees moving. He had more important things to worry about—getting his men to their stations, ensuring they were fed and could snatch a few hours of sleep. The coming battle.

As a guide was detached from the sentries to take them to the army, Kallis found his men neatly organised back into their companies. He rested a grateful hand on Meinor's shoulder. When his only response was a distracted grunt, Kallis eyed the big clansman, noting the pallor and his wild look.

His spine tingled. 'It's gone?'

'Aye.'

Kallis straightened his shoulders. 'Right. Good.' He was *not* going to look.

Meinor spat, but the effort lacked his usual scorn. 'Your boy doing that?'

That would have been an altogether less alarming proposition, and if it helped anyone to think that who was he to argue? He nodded, avoiding Meinor's gaze, and snapped, 'Let's go,' before anyone could question him further.

It was less than a mile from where they had left the forest to the main camp, by which time the sun had edged over the horizon, bringing a foretaste of its warmth. The camp was awake, and even at a distance Kallis could pick out Galydon, moving purposely through his men. A great cheer heralded their approach. What they had been sent to do was not common knowledge, so of course the entire army knew. That they had survived and were here was victory enough. The details did not matter.

Galydon turned at the roar of sound, and his face betrayed his relief. He clasped Kallis's arm. 'You cut it fine.'

'You have no idea.'

Galydon started walking, beckoning Kallis to follow. When they were out of earshot, he stopped. 'Well?'

Such restraint went into that calm question. Because the details *did* matter, and this was a crucial component of their strategy. They needed an early victory, and more importantly, they needed to show that the Kas'Talani were not invincible. And it was just as vital for the priests to feel their vulnerability as it was for Lothane's army to know they could be beaten. That they could be *killed*. Galydon had given Sedaine's forces every advantage he could, but they were still naked against the power of the priesthood. He needed the Kas'Talani to hold back, to fear the consequences of engagement, and fear it at least as much as they feared Darred.

As Galydon observed dryly, 'Let us hope they heed the warning.'

Because to deliver it they had risked their lives, and the loss of a good part of the clans that were left. And it had worked—thanks to an intervention they had neither foreseen nor planned for. Memory supplied the image of the fire closing in on the priests. Of the sight and sound of their terror. Kallis hadn't watched their deaths, but by now his imagination was more than capable of filling in the gaps. He shuddered. Any Caledani soldiers who survived the slaughter in the forest would carry its message, and he trusted that his own men were already doing the same.

Galydon fired questions at Kallis as they walked towards the place where they hoped they could decide this one way or another. He could see the river now through the morning mist, still running high and fast after yesterday's flood, and the ground beneath his feet was softer. It wouldn't take much to turn it into thick, treacherous mud, just as Lorac had warned. Terrible conditions for an army. But Galydon had wanted the boggy ground, just as he had wanted the river behind them, as he laced together a hundred tiny strategies to provide as much protection as he could against an enemy that possessed a power they could not match.

When Galydon's questions ran dry, Kallis voiced the one that remained. 'The dragon?' Because for all those clever layers of strategies and deception, everything depended on Aarin keeping Darred's dragon away from the battle, and they both knew it.

Galydon looked pensively out over the river. 'We have not seen it; it is too late to withdraw.'

In other words, they must simply hope that whatever Aarin had done had succeeded and move forward as planned. They had to fight the battle in front of them, and Kallis decided he would rather not know if the dragon were still free to rain down its fire on them. He had quite enough other things to worry about.

Kallis looked out over their chosen battlefield. The geography was terrible, but it was worse for Darred—it just looked better. The river at the back of Lothane's army gave them nowhere to go but getting at them in any numbers would be difficult.

'From up there he will think one charge will finish us,' Galydon said, shading his eyes as he gazed up the rolling slope.

Another of his gambles. Make the victory look so easy, men alone would achieve it. And it did look easy. Kallis had a sudden, hideous flash of the army drawn up at the top of the incline and swore.

Galydon smiled grimly. 'Just so. But then his men will be funnelled through here and with any luck they will trample themselves to death before they even get to us.'

Kallis looked where Galydon did, and he saw the point at which the onrushing charge would find itself caught between the treacherous marshland to the left and the Istelan on the right. Even so, it was a terrible risk. He would much prefer to be doing the attacking rather than waiting for an outsized enemy to come to him, but they had to bring this to a head. They had to get Darred to commit everything, and so they had to lure him in by making themselves vulnerable.

'I don't like it.'

Galydon was silent a moment. 'I like it better than the alternative.'

And since the alternative was waiting for the dragon to come for them, Kallis was unable to argue with that, but he found he liked their chosen ground even less in the cold dawn light with the enemy army almost within sight.

SIX

HANLON WAS BROUGHT before Darred on his knees and knew this was the end. No one had entered his tent for a full day. He was hungry and thirsty and covered in his own filth, but his heart was lighter than it had been in months, because he knew how to read the sounds of this camp, and they were *losing*.

'I thought you had forgotten me,' he sneered.

Darred turned. 'You will wish that were so, I promise you, Admiral.'

His face was white and strained and the madness in his eyes raged closer to the surface, but there was something else there too, something that looked suspiciously like grief.

Darred gestured to the guard behind Hanlon's shoulder, and his head was dragged back, a cold blade pressed up against his throat.

'I'm afraid I don't have time for our usual dance, Admiral, so let me tell you how this will go. You will give me the identities of your agents in my army—*all* of them—or I will round up every Farnorian in this camp and execute them in front of you. Then, when I have finished with Lothane, I will return to your precious Farnor, and I will burn every city and every village to the ground. There will be nothing left. *Nothing*. Do you understand?'

He did understand, and foremost in his understanding was that Darred could not have his son. If he did, the boy would be the one on his knees with the knife at his throat.

Something dropped away, deep inside. His son was dead. It was what he had feared these two years, and it hurt. It hurt a thousand times worse than the taking of his eye, but it was also peace. His son was dead, and he was, finally, free.

'No.' He couldn't give Darred what he asked, even if he wanted to. He and Davi had made sure of that. If he died now, he would die as he had lived. Unbroken. Defiant.

Something very dark flashed in Darred's eyes. The knife at his throat twitched as the silence between them stretched on and on, but Hanlon never broke that unsettling gaze.

Someone scratched at the canvas. A tentative voice called, 'My lord?'

Darred snapped his fingers and the knife disappeared. His eyes continued to bore into Hanlon's. There was no trace now of the mocking amusement that had characterised their prior interactions, nothing of the inexplicable tolerance that had preserved his life despite his provocations. He should have been afraid, but all fear had left him. His son was dead.

The call came again, and a snarl of impatience rippled across Darred's face. 'Enter!'

Sunlight streamed in as the tent door was pulled back and two men were escorted inside. They were wild-eyed and terrified, their clothing ripped and singed but still recognisable as the remains of Caledani light armour.

Darred's eyes narrowed. 'Who are these men?' The words were quiet and dangerous.

Neither spoke, and the officer who had escorted them in cuffed one around the head. 'Speak.'

The soldier drew in a gasping breath and Hanlon saw the glitter of moisture on his face. Tears.

'My lord, second *kyrta*, fourth *shu'un*.'

Hanlon watched Darred as the man identified his division and unit. He had gained a rudimentary understanding of how the invaders organised themselves, but he no longer knew their dispositions, so he searched Darred's face for a clue as to what this meant.

For several heart beats the only sound in the tent was the hitched breath of the man's companion. When Darred finally spoke, his words were cold and flat. 'Where is your captain? Where are my colleagues?'

The man looked up at him, tears on his face. 'They are dead, my lord. They are all dead.'

The silence this time was far from cold. Darred's expression never changed, but his white-hot rage scorched everyone in its radius.

Everyone except Hanlon, who threw back his head and laughed, offering a private salute to Lothane's general. It was what he would have done. Kill the priests. Challenge their supremacy, make an example of them. Make them *fear*. It was beautiful, and if he died this moment, so be it. He would die with the satisfaction of knowing his enemy had suffered a grievous defeat. It was a strike at the very heart of the army, and it would shake its confidence to the core.

The soldier flinched, his eyes darting from Hanlon to Darred. His companion hunched further in on himself. Whatever horror they had survived, the second man was still living it.

Then Darred did something unexpected. The blistering heat of his rage cooled. In two steps he had reached the survivors and grasped the spokesman's shoulder. The man controlled his instinctive reaction, but just barely. He was terrified, and Hanlon could not blame him.

'Fetch these men some wine,' Darred ordered. 'They have endured a great shock.'

As the officer who had escorted them moved to obey, Darred's fingers tightened on the soldier's shoulder, and only Hanlon could see the way his knuckles shone white.

'Are there any other survivors?' His voice was gentle, soothing.

The man shook his head. 'No others, my lord.'

Darred nodded, his head bowed in respect. 'Your sacrifice will not be forgotten. Who else knows of this?'

Hanlon felt the surge of alarm like a sickness in his belly. He tried to speak, to call out, but the words would not come.

The soldier bit dry lips, aware of danger but not its source, and walked straight into it. 'No one, my lord. We came first to you.'

Unable to speak, unable to warn them, Hanlon struggled against his bonds, but his movements were tied as tight as his throat.

'Peace, Admiral,' Darred murmured. 'Please, do not upset yourself.'

The soldier glanced at him, and Hanlon tried to force every ounce of warning into his one eye, but it was too late. Even as realisation dawned on the man's face, Darred was taking the cup of wine from the officer and holding it to the soldier's lips. 'You did the right thing, now rest.'

Wild eyes met Hanlon's over the rim of the cup, but the man had no choice. He drank. His companion, openly weeping, gulped the wine as though it would grant him oblivion, which Hanlon was quite certain it would.

Darred's back was to him, his face hidden, as he handed the empty cup back to the officer. 'Drink to your compatriots, who have given their lives.'

As the bemused officer, with a covert glance at the two soldiers—still alive and unharmed—refilled the cup and drank, Darred retired to his chair. He waved a lazy arm towards where Hanlon knelt in invisible chains, and the cup was handed over his head to his jailers. And all the while Darred watched with a look of fatherly benevolence.

When each had taken a drink, Hanlon waited for the cup to come to his lips, tears of fury burning his eye. *Not like this!*

Darred merely smiled at him and said softly. 'Oh, not for you, Admiral.'

Instead, he was forced to watch as Darred murdered the only witnesses to the Kas'Talani's defeat, and the advantage the Lothani had gained stuttered and died with the beats of their hearts. Forced to watch as first one then another crumpled over, pain lancing through their mid sections, horror darkening their eyes. Within moments they were on the ground, their bodies spasming in silent screams. The only sound was the drumming of heels and the scraping of fingers as one man tried to haul himself to the door.

Darred made no move to stop him; he made no movement at all. His eyes never wavered from Hanlon's, a slight smile hovering over his lips as though men were not screaming their silent agony at his feet.

Stillness returned to the tent. It took too long. Hanlon felt the vomit rise in his throat as Darred took everything these men had been and left them voiceless and helpless at their death.

When it was over, Darred rose. He pushed back the tent door, and through the sliver of daylight Hanlon glimpsed a party of Situran conscripts, saw their apprehension as Darred hailed them, saw their fear as they entered the tent and found the contorted bodies on the ground.

'An assassination attempt. There was poison in the wine,' Darred informed them. 'Remove the bodies and make sure no one comes in or out. Touch nothing. The wine might not be the only thing poisoned.'

'My lord?' One of the men gestured at Hanlon's bound form.

Darred spared him one brief, contemptuous glance. 'Gag him and leave him here. I'm not finished with him yet.'

SEVEN

KALLIS SLEPT LIKE the dead for two hours, and when he woke it was to find the enemy outlined against the sun on the crest of the hill.

'Time to earn our pay,' Lorac muttered. He leant on a crude crutch to take the weight off his injured leg, and he looked awful, his eyes red-rimmed and his face grey with exhaustion. Only the most seriously injured clansmen had not crossed the river with them. They hadn't marched the length of Lothane just to remain behind now.

'What pay?' Kallis eyed Lorac critically. 'How is it?'

'It hurts,' the clan captain replied, and Kallis wasn't sure he was talking about his leg.

'You shouldn't be here,' he observed, knowing it was pointless. What was coming would be brutal. A man who could barely hold himself upright may as well save the enemy the bother and slit his own throat. But he didn't *say* that, he merely thought it very hard.

'And where else should I be?' Lorac fretted. He pointed his crutch at Galydon, who was striding towards them. 'You think he's going to cower at the back?'

'He bloody well better,' Kallis growled. 'Or I'll knock him out and drag him there myself.' The last thing they needed was to lose their general because he was on the front line where he had no business being.

Lorac huffed a laugh and found something urgent that needed his attention in the opposite direction, leaving Kallis alone with Galydon.

'Drag me where?' Galydon enquired, and Kallis muttered something unintelligible as Lorac's laughter drifted over them.

Then the amusement faded from Galydon's eyes. He turned to stare out at the army forming up on the ridge. 'I hate this time,' he confessed. The quiet moments before the storm broke, when all there was left to do was question every decision and worry about all the things that could go wrong.

Kallis glanced behind to where Meinor and the other clan leaders were herding and bullying their own men into lines. 'It's what comes next that's worrying me.' They had spread the mercenaries out through the ranks, trusting their professional competence to steady the less experienced men, but the truth was that battle on this scale was beyond even their experience. The frightened faces looking back at him did not just belong to Lothane's conscripted farmers and untested garrison troops.

Galydon's tight smile was edged with bitterness. 'But then we are in the hands of fate.' Because not even he could control what would happen when the two armies met.

Movement on the ridge drew Kallis's attention. 'They're moving.' The words sounded surprisingly calm.

Galydon scrutinised the distant figures. 'Not quite yet. Walk with me?'

He walked along the length of the Lothani line as nervous men jostled each other into position. They watched his calm progress as the enemy ranks began to form into their order of attack, and if they were expecting a rousing speech, they didn't get it. Instead, Galydon surveyed his lines, inspecting them as if they were on a parade ground. Each man must have felt he was looking at them directly, and under his sharp gaze they grew still and stood straighter. Then he nodded, satisfied, and instead of fierce rhetoric, he gave them calm confidence.

'Remember, we do not attack. Let them come to us. Hold firm. Do not break, and we will win.'

So simple. Don't break. But it had to be simple. When the arrows were flying and blood started to flow and the horror and chaos of battle descended, it was a mantra to cling to. An anchor. A promise.

I hope you know what you're doing, Kallis thought as he left Galydon's side to take his place in the lines. Every instinct honed by a decade of fighting agreed with Lorac—this was a terrible position.

There was a distant roar and the Caledani advance began, a great rolling mass of men darkening the grassy slope. Kallis felt the visceral shudder that swept through the Lothani lines as they watched death come for them. A few men pissed themselves, but no one broke ranks. Not while Galydon stood before them, his back to the advancing enemy, holding them steady with his gaze.

There were too many of them. Kallis watched the enemy come and felt terror seize him. He knew without doubt that they had made a terrible mistake to think their thin lines could hold out against this monstrous force. And still Galydon stood there, his back to the enemy, the embodiment of confidence.

The controlled advance splintered as those at the front picked up their pace. It was not a charge, not yet, they were too far away, but they could see those fragile Lothani lines. They could see victory, and they wanted it.

The man next to him leaned to the side and vomited. Behind him, he could hear the sound of weeping. And still Galydon hadn't moved.

The close-packed ranks stuttered. The right flank stumbled and splashed into the stream, floundering in the hidden waterways of the bog. As men tried to claw their way back onto solid ground, they pushed the rest tighter and tighter into the narrowing space, and the weight of those coming behind created a deadly crush through the centre.

Then they hit the mud.

That wild flood had not been wasted. As the waters had thundered downriver, sweeping away the horsemen by the Grymwood, Amadorn's mages had harnessed its fury and used it to lay this trap. Because Galydon had quickly learned what the Kas'Talani had not grasped, despite their vast power. The priesthood might have access to all five elements, but no one could manipulate Water like those who had spent centuries restricted to its use. When the river broke its banks, Luen's mages had seized control of the flood. The ground beneath Kallis's feet should have been waterlogged and treacherous, but instead it was merely soft, the water that had soaked into it directed into the ground midway between the two armies, which quickly turned to a quagmire under the churn of so many feet.

The struggling advance slowed still further as men found their legs sinking up to their knees in the thick mud or sliding out from under them. Many fell and were trampled into the boggy ground by those behind, and soon the ordered lines were a staggering, heaving, mud-slicked chaos.

The men around him started to jeer and laugh. Kallis let them.

The front ranks reached the other side of the mud, and as their feet hit firmer ground, Kallis saw the thirst for revenge take hold.

Galydon finally moved. He turned, his arm raised above this head, and when it fell, so did the arrows.

The sky turned dark as the volley of shafts soared overhead, crashing down on men who had lost all discipline. The slaughter from just that first flight was terrible. It seemed to Kallis that the entire front rank shuddered and died, the advance coming to an abrupt halt, and they were close enough now that he could see their faces and hear their dying. Then shields came up, men bunching together to better cover each other as they forced their way forward, step by step, the ranks thinning as they had to pick their way over the bodies of their dead, and each successive volley found fewer and fewer targets.

The arrows stopped. There was no point wasting more valuable shafts. Kallis hefted his shield and adjusted his grip on his short sword. Now they would come.

It took several paces before the Caledani realised the hail of arrows had stopped, but when they did caution disappeared. If they had been angry before, they were mad beyond reason now. The roar of the charge hit Kallis's line like a wall of rage. Men flinched, the cheers washed away by fear.

'Hold firm,' he roared, and heard other voices up and down the line echoing the cry. He looked for Galydon and saw him being dragged back through the line by his own men.

Then there was no more time for words.

The enemy thundered into them like a storm against the shore, shields crashing against shields, weapons stabbing through the press as they heaved against each other. Then it was hot, close, terrifying chaos as the world was reduced to a matter of inches, a clawing, desperate fight for the next moment, and the one after that.

Kallis lost track of everything except the space around him and the men on either side. The weight of many bodies pressed against him, and he leaned into it. A spear jabbed at his legs, scraping against metal, and he brought his shield down hard, cracking the shaft as he stabbed with his sword. The man went down, his spear jammed into the mud, as the Lothani to Kallis's right staggered sideways. Kallis tried to sidestep but tangled with the spear shaft and fell to his knees, shield raised above his head.

Something hit the shield, sending vibrations down his arm and knocking him to the ground. And suddenly he was on his back amid a forest of legs and he was sure he was dead. Then someone stepped over him, covering him, and someone else grasped his shoulders and pulled him back, and he was scrabbling back to his feet, his breath coming in painful gasps.

He had lost his sword in the chaos and reached down to grab a broken spear from the ground, the movement saving him from a blade that came swinging at his head. He shoved up and forward, the spear held before him, and impaled the Caledani on the steel point. The shaft stuck fast and was pulled from his grasp as the man fell, so he took his sword instead and hurled himself forward.

The line moved with him, instinct driving them forward together, and their enemy gave. Just an inch, but it was enough. Kallis heard his own voice screaming as they flung themselves into that tiny space, shields locking together and thrusting ahead, as they gained one pace, then two. The line bulged, and for a moment, they were alone, surrounded by enemies. Then there was a roar, and the men on their left and right surged forward in response. The enemy were backing up, step by step, and the roar became a cheer, and there was clear air around him and he could breathe.

Hanlon lay on his side in Darred's tent all through the night, but no one came for him. No one came when the sun rose and turned the inside of the tent into a sweltering hell, and his thirst after two days without water became a torment that rivalled the taking of his eye.

He had long since stopped working at his bonds. The exertion had soaked the rope in sweat, which cut deeper as it dried, so he could only lie there, unmoving, as furious fighting rocked Darred's camp. He heard voices—Caledani and Amadorian—shouting commands over the roar of combat, but he could not make out the words. He only knew that, after a time, the Amadorian voices dwindled, and it was Caledani surrounding the tent. The brief flare of hope died; he no longer had the energy for despair.

The fighting stopped and footsteps approached. Two men ducked into the tent. He did not recognise them, but he knew who they were nonetheless.

'Admiral Hanlon?'

Hanlon would have cried if he had not been parched dry. His eye burned and stung. Not because this was a rescue, but because it was *revenge*.

The older of the two men crouched at his side. He was huge—taller and broader than Hanlon, who was himself a large man—and his skin was almost black in the gloom of the tent. The younger one, slight and wiry with a shock of dark hair, grinned at him from a sharp-featured face and handed the other his knife.

The blade slashed through the filthy gag. Hanlon spat it from his mouth, taking a deep breath of the fetid air. Then the black man cut the cords around his ankles and wrists and hooked an arm under Hanlon's shoulder and helped him upright. Even crouching, he was taller by Hanlon by a head.

'Do you know who I am?'

Hanlon spat again, trying to rid his mouth of the sour taste of the gag. The man handed him a waterskin and he drank greedily, then poured the rest over his head, revelling in the cool, clean sweetness. He looked up at his rescuer and felt a fierce smile crack his face. 'Ancai Kestel.'

'Just Kestel, Admiral. Come, let us leave this place.'

And together they levered him to his feet and waited through the rush of agony as the blood returned to his legs and he could stand unaided. Then they led him from his enemy's tent into the bright sunshine and his first taste of freedom in too long.

Outside, more men waited. A tall man with the Caledani insignia for captain on his salt-stained leather, and a slighter, younger dark-haired Amadorian in mud-stained riding clothes and no obvious military rank. He wore a strip of green and gold around one arm and the badge of one of Lothane's noble houses on his breast. That ought to mean something to him, Hanlon knew, but exhaustion was blurring his thoughts. There was no sign of Daviyan.

The Caledani captain stepped forward. 'Admiral Hanlon?' His heavy accent gave the words an odd inflection. He gestured at himself. 'Fylian. Apologies for not here sooner.'

Hanlon nodded, massaging aching wrists. He understood what he had heard now. Not an attack by Lothane's forces that had been beaten back, but the liberation of the camp by these men. Men whose arrival he had sent Daviyan and Amadorn's pirate fleet to secure, even when it seemed like they must be chasing a dream. 'There is no apology necessary, Captain. Only my thanks that you have come at all.' His eyes searched the faces of the men moving around them, but he could not see the one he sought. 'Daviyan?'

The Ancai—Kestel—shook his head, his face grave. 'I am sorry, Admiral. He is dead.'

The sun dimmed, the world tilted, as though its supports had been pulled away. *His* support had been pulled away. Daviyan, who had been at his side since he took his first pirate ship thirty years ago off the coast of Farnor and declared himself admiral of a fleet of two. Daviyan, who had fought beside him in every ship battle but one, who had patched up his wounds, sat drinking with him till dawn when his first wife died, and danced at his wedding—both of them.

'How?' he asked when speech returned. 'Darred?'

Kestel nodded. 'Let me show you what he died for. Come.'

Fylian was already walking. 'This way, come, Admiral.'

He followed. They walked past Darred's pavilion to where the main body of the newly arrived Caledani troops were drawn up in ordered ranks—*their* Caledani, that Daviyan had travelled halfway around the world to bring here. This was First Army of Kas'Tella, brought here against all odds on the strength of a promise made to Kinseris, and their ultimate commander was the man Kinseris had sent from Caledan to lead the defence of Lothane.

Fylian snapped an order as they approached the front ranks, which heaved and parted. The captain shouldered his way through the gap and Hanlon followed, the others behind him. A hundred paces ahead, a crude barricade stretched between two wagons, lined with archers. Behind it waited hundreds of Amadorian conscripts into Darred's army, confused and frightened to find themselves under attack from a force they had assumed was an ally.

'They have been left behind in reserve,' Kestel told him. 'But Darred will not call on them unless he has no other choice, because Daviyan made him fear betrayal. This is what he died for, Admiral. Make them yours.'

Fylian gestured towards the barricade. 'Tell them no harm, fight with us.'

Hanlon looked at the tense, nervous faces of his countrymen—they were all his countrymen now—and felt a rush of emotion that nearly undid him. *Thank you, my friend,* he said silently as he stepped forward. Filthy, maimed, degraded, undefeated.

'Men of Amadorn,' he roared. 'My name is Admiral Idaras Hanlon. You know who I am. You know what I have done. Now let me tell you what we will do together.'

He was a pillar of fire; he was molten rage. He was ice, a frozen wasteland.

Since the moment Eiador had been stolen from him, Darred could no longer tell where the anger ended and he began. And it was not just his control that was shattering, it was his desire for it. He *wanted* to let it out, to allow the rage to explode, to hunt down the man that had dared do this. To *destroy* him. To kill everything he loved. To let it all burn. To turn the whole world to ash.

Things were happening all around him. Things he should care about. Somewhere in the depths of consciousness, he was aware of urgent movement, of many feet pounding over hard earth, of shouting and chaos. But nothing mattered but this.

Frantic voices called to him. He ignored them.

'My lord!'

He saw the horror of his face reflected in the messenger's terrified eyes.

The man started to back away, but Darred's hand was round his throat. He squeezed with his power, the man's eyes bulging in his purple face, and tossed the corpse to one side. Then he was striding through the camp.

Nothing mattered but this.

The Kas'Talani were clustered together around his generals. Some part of Darred's mind recognised that they were grouped in battle formations. Five for the elements—four to shield, one to destroy. An officer tried to talk to him. Darred registered little more than the movement of his hands and lips. He pushed him aside, intent on his purpose.

The senior Kas'Talani saw him.

He was living rage; he was walking death.

The priest backed away, but Darred stopped him in his tracks, stopped and held them all.

'Leave us,' he barked to his terrified officers. They were already running.

He turned to the priests, finding the two he wanted, leashing them with cords of power and hauling them to their knees before him.

A trembling hand reached out to touch the dragon devices they wore. He stopped himself, a fragment of self-preservation intervening before he could immolate himself where he stood.

He could not do this, but they could.

'Bring over your dragons. It's time.'

EIGHT

THEY HAD FLOWN north, closer to Rhiannas. Silverwing would have taken them further, as far as the icy north coast and far beyond Darred's ability to strike back, but Aarin was aware enough to know they could not go so far. They would be needed.

He was not conscious of much else at first. The need to maintain two separate selves—to endure the presence of two dragons and their bonds—took his entire attention. He was vaguely aware of Callan and Lysan moving around the small camp as he laboured to place brick after brick in his internal walls. As he learned to separate the thoughts and feelings that were his and shuttered the tumultuous emotions that were not.

With each brick, his defences strengthened, but at a cost. To protect his mind and keep Eiador safely guarded, he also had to dampen his link with Silverwing. It was still there, always, the knot that tied them together, but their awareness of each other dwindled as he built his walls. To break through them without dire cause carried great risk.

For battering always at the bastion he had built was Darred. Just as his link with Silverwing could not be broken, so Darred's connection to Eiador would remain intact for as long as his enemy held the dragon's device. The loss of that connection was as much a deception as the face he had shown to Eiador, a deception Aarin had to maintain at all costs. But the furious insanity he now endured as Darred raged against his loss was a stark warning. The longer this went on, the greater the risk that he too would lose his mind and his humanity, as his enemy had done.

Time passed. The sun began to set and the sticky heat of the day cooled into evening. They did not light a fire. He ate something he could not taste and heard muffled conversation that gradually resolved into words.

'Can you sleep?' Callan asked again, sometime later.

But he was awake now and unwilling to chance his hard-won defences by sleeping.

Across from him, Lysan yawned. 'I must, or I will be no good to you.' He had been in a battle today. His face still bore traces of mud and blood.

'Both of you should sleep.' They were the first words he had managed in hours.

Callan looked sceptical, but Lysan was already stretching out. They were inside the tent. He did not remember that.

'I'm awake,' he assured Callan. 'I don't think I could sleep.'

But he had slept eventually. It was shallow and fitful, just enough to stave off the worst exhaustion, and when morning came his defences were still holding.

The enemy broke and the Lothani followed them. Kallis tried to stop them, but he might as well have tried to hold back the tide. Even as their officers bellowed at them to hold, men streamed past him, desire for revenge eclipsing everything else. The shrill notes as the signallers called them back went unheeded, and he could only watch as unfolding disaster threatened to undo everything they had gained.

The Caledani went back, but they didn't go far. Kallis felt sick as the apparent rout stopped, turned, and met the undisciplined Amadorian charge head-on. Then it was Lothane's turn to feel the killing force of short-range archery as crossbowmen rose from behind the Caledani front rank and emptied their bolts into the pursuers. They died by the score, cut down mid-stride as the first volley was followed by a second, then a third.

Then it was Lothane's army retreating pell-mell across the field, chased by triumphant Caledani, and now the lines that held their formation were at risk of being overwhelmed by their own side in their panicked flight.

Kallis heard Lorac and Galydon bellowing orders, saw the clan lines step forward then spread out, creating corridors through their ranks. The survivors barrelled into them, clawing their way to safety. The mercenaries funnelled them through, grabbing fleeing men and hurling them roughly past, their frustration and anger evident in the ungentle handling. Then they closed ranks behind them.

Shields came up, spears came down, as the depleted line braced for the impact.

It never came. The recklessness of that first wild charge had given way to cooler heads. With a discipline that reminded Kallis that these men came from the same school as Galydon, the Caledani pulled their charge a hundred yards from Lothane's front rank, their archers cutting down the last few fleeing Amadorians, jeering insults on their lips.

As the last man dropped and died a hush fell over the two armies. Separated by a hundred paces of mud and death, they faced each other over a sea of bodies from both sides. For a long moment, nothing moved.

Kallis felt a crawling trepidation, a sense of impending calamity. *They're waiting for something.*

Movement caught his eye, and he swore. A line of horsemen had appeared on the ridge, outlined against the sun, more and more appearing until there were so many that they were little more than an indistinct dark mass on the horizon.

Something had gone terribly wrong. The death on the banks of Istelan had been for nothing. There should not have been so many cavalry troops still living to assemble such a force.

Kallis felt the despair that swept through the hushed ranks, then, on its heels, a tangible girding of loins, a gathering of resolve, as men who had been fought to a standstill looked at this latest enemy and refused to give in.

The horsemen paused at the top of the slope.

'Come on,' Kallis growled. 'Don't make us wait.'

A lone rider trotted to the front and raised his sword in a salute, then the whole line wheeled around, and a thunder of hooves sent the horses down the hill.

A ripple ran though the Caledani army, confusion morphing to fear as the horsemen came on—aiming straight for the heart of their forces.

Kallis didn't understand what he was seeing. Neither did they. The cavalry charge hit the back of the Caledani advance like an axe splitting wood, boring deep into their midst. Swords flashed down and men died in a widening arc, and still they came on. The Caledani were pushed back before them like water under the bow of a ship, and for a glorious moment it looked like they would make it through.

Then the horsemen slowed, the sheer weight of numbers snarling their progress and the mud miring hooves in its deadly suction. A spear took down a rider near the front. Another was dragged from his saddle, disappearing beneath a flurry of swords. Their leader stood in his stirrups, sword above his head, urging them forward, but the Caledani were regrouping. More horsemen fell. The man at the front was almost knocked from his saddle by a spear that hit his sword, and Kallis lost sight of him as the sun disappeared behind a cloud and a wave of soldiers surged over him.

'Form up!' Galydon called from his right. 'Forward on my command.'

Because this was their chance, and they could not just leave the horsemen to die, whoever they were. Kallis elbowed his way into his place and men jostled and shoved and spread out, making room for the survivors of that suicidal charge to find their way back into the ranks.

But they were too late. Even as the clansmen stepped forward, falling into their positions to advance, Kallis saw the Caledani reserves arrive on the ridge where the horsemen had appeared minutes before. The sun, bursting out just at that moment, glinted off ranks and ranks of drawn swords.

'Tesserion preserve us,' muttered Lorac, staring up the slope. 'Where the fuck did they come from?'

Realisation hit hard. 'This is what they were waiting for.'

Lorac flashed him a look. 'What?'

'Forward!' Galydon roared, and the line lurched into motion. But they had all seen the new threat, and men started to fall out of formation, those whose nerve had finally failed. Kallis didn't blame them. His own nerve was none too steady. There were so many of them.

'Forward, you bastards!' Lorac yelled, using his crutch to force stragglers back into line. 'You fight or you swim! Now move!'

It was hopeless. If they had somewhere to retreat to, they would have broken right there, but they didn't and Galydon was hurling them into the teeth of the enemy's reinforcements who were pouring down the slope in the horsemen's wake. The exhausted Caledani parted for them, raising a ragged cheer as their reserves came to their rescue.

They were still cheering as those reserves turned on them and started killing, and for the second time that day, Kallis was unmoored by utter confusion.

'They're ours!' Lorac shouted in his ear. 'They're bloody well ours. Look!'

He looked, and he saw what Lorac had seen. Behind the screen of Caledani, the bulk of the men now savaging their enemy's rear were unmistakably Amadorian.

Their advance became a run. Lorac stumbled. Kallis grabbed him, hauling him back upright and locking an arm around his waist. He caught sight of Galydon, his face full of fierce triumph, then they were past him, and he released Lorac seconds before they slammed into beleaguered Caledani.

It was a rout. Or it would have been, if the Caledani had had anywhere to go. Instead, it was a slaughter, as the enemy were caught between Lothane's forces at the front, the Amadorians at their rear, and the horsemen still wreaking havoc in the centre.

Afterwards, Kallis could not clearly recall the minutes that followed their collision, only the hot splash of blood on his face and his arm rising and falling until the muscles seized and he couldn't lift it anymore. But by then there was no need. He staggered to the side, driving the point of his captured sword into the ground to steady himself, and looked around. There was no one near him.

He heard a whoop and saw the horsemen break free of the mud and burst through the disintegrating Caledani formation to sweep around in front of the exhausted Lothani. The leading rider pulled off his helm and Derias grinned down at him, a wild glee on his face.

Kallis caught his bridle, smiling in astonishment. 'I thought…'

The fierce smile on Derias's face faded. 'So did I, for a while.' He swung down out of the saddle and embraced Kallis. 'Then your friend found me.'

Kallis looked at him blankly. 'My friend?'

Derias grinned and waved his arm towards an approaching rider. Kallis recognised Kestel. The tall Caledani captain cracked a rare smile as he rode up, bleeding from a ragged cut above his knee.

Kallis shook his head. 'How –?' It wasn't possible. They should have been halfway across an ocean still. There was no way they could have been to Caledan and back in just three months.

More horsemen crowded around, and now Kallis could see the green and gold armbands they wore. He swung back to Derias. 'Found you where?' These were the missing Morven men, and for Derias to have brought them here, just at the right moment, it had to have been planned.

Derias was laughing, high on survival and success. He clapped his hands either side of Kallis's face and kissed his forehead. Then he spun away, leaping back into the saddle, a series of sharp commands bringing the milling men to order.

Kallis looked up wearily at Kestel. 'I have no idea what just happened.'

The big man leaned down and placed a hand on his shoulder. 'We just won.'

NINE

JETA WAS CROSSING the courtyard when she heard the scream, a long wail of pure terror. The sound froze her where she stood. Then it came again, and it was no longer a single voice but a chorus. In an instant, everything changed.

Fear spread like a contagion. As the bells called their deadly warning, panic took the city by the throat. They had faced this once and survived, but there was war in earnest now. They would not be so fortunate again. Rhiannas was under attack.

All around her people were running, shoving their way through the crowd towards the doors of the palace, trampling each other in their rush. She saw a child, no more than two, ripped from its mother's grasp and lost under the crush of stampeding feet. The mother's agonised scream went right through her.

She couldn't move. Frantic people battered at her, their fear demanding action, and she didn't know what to do. Then Kinseris was there, forcing a space around them, pulling her free of press, throwing his power around her like a cloak as his arm circled her waist, drawing her tight against his side.

He didn't speak, just hauled her grimly through the crowd, but when they reached the palace steps, she pulled away. He could not be here, with her. He could not spend his power to protect her when so many needed his help, and she could not hide with him and leave these people to their fate.

She pushed him away. 'No, go. Help her.'

She thought he would refuse; it was there on his face. But he had stayed behind to protect the city, to protect Sedaine, not her. And he couldn't save them both.

The handful of mercenaries who remained were taking control of the chaos, helped by the palace's depleted garrison, but more and more people were streaming through the gates, desperate for shelter, and they would soon be overwhelmed. The garrison captain was forcing his way through the crowd and up the steps, and Jeta pushed Kinseris towards him. 'Go.'

There was a stirring of power within the palace, a tiny trickle. Kinseris's attention flicked up to the queen's apartments and back to Jeta.

Something settled into her, delicate as silk but strong as steel. He tied off the shield, wrapping it tight like an embrace, leaving a part of him with her. And she knew he had made it that way so it would survive his death.

The thought caught in her throat, choking her resolve. She couldn't speak, but they had already said everything they needed to say to each other and more words now would just make this harder.

He understood. His lips brushed her hair, holding her against him so she could feel the steady beat of his heart. Then he pulled away, following that trickle of power, and disappeared into the crowd.

She snagged the nearest clansman. 'There are too many for the palace. Start sending them to the barracks.' The old palace wing that had once housed its garrison was good solid stone. If that counted for anything, it would offer almost as good a shelter as the palace itself.

The mercenary nodded. The clansmen started funnelling people through the archway, and Jeta went with them.

Sedaine heard the screams and knew what they meant. She did not need the bells that interwove their stark warning with the wave of terror rippling out across her city. She knew what was coming. She had always known it would. And, strangely, she did not feel fear, only calm acceptance. Her one bitter regret, she buried deep.

Limina put her hand on the wall, her face paling. She had lived through this once; there would be no miracle a second time.

Footsteps were pounding in the corridors outside. They had hardly any time, but she meant to use it, every second. Cupping Limina's face in her hand, she kissed her, letting their heads rest together.

594

'Thank you. For all you have given me.'

Limina pulled back. 'Don't you dare,' she said fiercely. 'I won't let you.'

Footsteps stopped at her door. Someone hammered at it, calling her name. She ignored them, sparing a trickle of power to hold the door closed.

Her fingers tangled in Limina's hair, catching on the strings of tiny shells. 'You make it sound like I have a choice.'

Limina caught her hand and squeezed it hard, tears running down her face. 'Please. I can't do it again. I can't just let you go.'

The hammering became more insistent. Vianor's voice demanded admittance. Still, she ignored them.

'But you will, because you're braver than me.'

A force other than her own pushed against her ward and she released it, letting go of Limina's hand as she stepped back.

Her garrison commander swung the doors open and Vianor strode in, his face white and his mouth set in a thin line. 'You will not go out there.' For once it was her uncle talking, not her advisor.

But it was not his power that had pitched against hers, and Kinseris entered the room on his heels.

His eyes met hers and he shook his head. 'It's too late for that, I promise you. He will no longer accept only your sacrifice.'

Too late. She closed her eyes for a heartbeat. 'Then give me another way.'

Don't think of Aarin. But the thought had already escaped her careful barricades, worming its treacherous way through her resolve. Because if there was any chance, any chance at all, that she might see him again…

She turned, walking across the room to throw open the doors to the balcony. The courtyard seethed with panic as people poured through the open gates, desperate for shelter.

Pinpricks of power were bursting into being across the city, but they were too few, far too few to fend off what was coming. *Take them,* she had said to Galydon of the mages. *You will need them more than I.* When he had refused, she had made it an order, and he had bowed his head and accepted—and then disobeyed her as only he could. For though there were too few, there were more than there should have been.

'Water,' said Kinseris, his thoughts following the same track. 'If these are the enemy's dragons, they are not truly linked. Without that bond, water is anathema to them.'

'Water,' snarled Vianor, fear making him savage. 'This is a land-locked city! How do we use water as a weapon?'

Sedaine ignored him, her eyes locked on Kinseris. As one they looked up— at the thick belt of cloud rolling inland from the eastern coast. 'Rain,' she murmured. 'We need rain.'

Vianor followed their gaze, aghast. 'You can't.'

'I must.' The impact of such a vast manipulation of the weather system would be felt for weeks, maybe months to come, but those were months they wouldn't have unless she did this.

Sedaine turned to the garrison captain. They did not have much time, but what they did have they must spend wisely. 'Send your men to clear the south of the city—pull everyone back from the walls towards the centre and keep open the gates to the palace grounds. The smaller the area we must protect, the better. We cannot cover the whole city.'

The captain nodded, clearly terrified. 'The villagers? They will want shelter in the city.'

'They stay outside.' *And there is no time.* 'The dragons are coming *here,* they are coming for Rhiannas. Anyone inside the city is in more danger than those outside. Go,' she snapped, and the man set off at a run.

Sedaine spun, looking for Vianor. 'How many magicians are in the city?'

The old man was pale and shaken. 'No more than ten, perhaps fewer.'

'Ten is enough,' she said. 'Listen to me, uncle, because if ever we needed your skills, it is now. I will bring the storm, but you must give it fury. It must be such a storm that these dragons will not dare it. There will be power enough to spare, I promise you. Can you do it?'

For once, he did not argue, merely nodded and left. And she knew he would give her the wildest storm in the power of his people, because though they were often at odds, their goal had always been the same.

She turned to Kinseris. 'I cannot do this alone. Will you help me?' She had seen what he had done on Galydon's orders to rescue her. Even without the device he had given up, he possessed a strength she did not have. A strength she badly needed.

Dark eyes met hers, so alike to Galydon's, and she saw a reflection of her own fear and worry. Her own resolve.

'Whatever I have to give, take it. It is yours.'

There was no time for thanks, already she was moving, and only then did she realise who was missing. *Limina.*

She had been here only moments ago, but the balcony was empty now but the two of them.

Kinseris saw her frantic glance and canted his head towards the courtyard. 'They are down there.'

Down there. Exposed. Unprotected. But she could not ask Limina to make a different choice to the one she made herself. Jeta was down there too. Kinseris flinched as he saw her realise it, and a moment of understanding passed between them, as each, separately, chose the path that would take them from the ones they loved.

Then there was no more time.

He followed her as she ran through the corridors to the staircase that led to the roof. 'You can control the weather?'

'Not the weather,' she replied, pausing at the foot of the stairs to let him catch up, his face twisted with the pain of old injury. 'The Water.'

He heard the emphasis but did not understand. Sedaine cocked her head, a wild, reckless smile on her face. 'Aarin's father showed me how.'

Aarin felt himself slipping as Eiador grew stronger. Given a respite from Darred's relentless drain, the dragon rapidly regained its strength. Hours dragged on, time without meaning. Everything that was not the struggle was a deadened haze. He had to hold on.

Silverwing was gone. Awareness remained always, a distant pulse, stretched out by distance. They were together. Silverwing and Eiador. Far away. So there was no one to give warning.

A twig snapped, shockingly loud. Then silence, unnatural and deep. Lysan tensed, his hand on the hilt of his sword.

Belated awareness of threat penetrated Aarin's tired senses, the presence of encroaching danger. Still reeling from the dislocation of two disparate identities, he had missed the approaching soldiers.

He groped for his wards, *but he had not set them.*

The mistake was like ice water, a paralysing chill.

'Stay here,' Lysan hissed, slipping his brother's restraining grasp as he rose to his feet.

Another mistake. There were too many.

'Wait,' he tried to say. He had to *act.* He had to *hold on.* The divergence lost him precious moments.

Lysan stalked towards the trees. Callan swore, torn, and Aarin found he was on his feet.

Movement helped, focusing him in the *here.*

He tagged the soldiers, one after another. They were all around them. 'Call him back.'

He slammed defences in place, putting an impenetrable barrier between them and their attackers. But Lysan, moving too quickly, was caught on the wrong side.

He let it go. It was too hard to think. There was twang of a bow, a cry, and a man staggered into view and collapsed to the ground. Then another.

Callan. He had Lysan's bow, but his face was a torment to look at.

Their attackers hesitated, wary of Callan's aim. Aarin lost sight of Lysan, but he could track his presence as he moved silently through the trees. Could track him as another of the soldiers died. But there were too many. They could not run. Silverwing could not get to them in time. If he did not do something, they would die.

If he did nothing, he forced Callan to kill for him.

Bile rose in his throat. Magic came from life; it should not take it. *He* should not use it to kill. But he had done it before for less cause.

The bow sang out again and he finally acted. One by one, he found them, then stopped the air in their lungs.

But he was too late. Lysan screamed and Callan roared with rage.

TEN

SEDAINE STEPPED ONTO the roof to see the south of the city burning. The fires leapt high as the two dragons flew through them, scaled bodies writhing in the flames. It was beautiful, but beneath that beauty, her people were dying. Her city was burning.

Cinders swirled in the air, catching in her throat. Her voice cracked. 'Help me.'

Kinseris took her hand. A great door swung open and a rush of pure, sweet power flooded into her, making her gasp.

There was a wild smile on Kinseris's face, the mirror of her own, as together they tapped a well that alone she could never have accessed. And such was the brightness of their power, blazing like a sun, that all the little suns in the city were drawn into their orbit, and she gathered them up like children, absorbing their power and flinging it outwards, towards the ocean where the storm clouds were gathering.

She *pulled* the storm, forged it, shaped it, and invited it to thunder its fury on the burning city. Forcing the dragons back, inch by inch, steam hissing from their heated hides.

The power filled her, and still she kept drawing on it. Kinseris's hand gripped hers like a vice, his fingers icy cold as the rain whipped around them, and he gave and gave through the link he had gifted her, and she *took*. They all gave, and she took from them all. Around them the air seethed with power as they were buffeted by the exaltation of the storm, the dragons wheeling and screeching just beyond the curtain of rain that encircled the city in its protective shield—as long as they could hold it there.

Pockets of flame were doused all across the south of Rhiannas. The bigger fires fought on, despite the downpour, coils of black smoke rising until they met the grey of the storm clouds.

Then the magicians joined the fray, their magic weaving in and out of her own, augmenting it, adding wildness to the rain, bringing the lightning crashing down, forcing the dragons back and back, giving them precious breathing space.

A wave of euphoria picked her up, and she rode it, a conduit for *so much* power, and all of its theirs and theirs alone. Then, just as violently, the tragedy of it smashed into her, the wave breaking, as she realised *how much more* they could have been—if the dragons that hunted them had been their partners and not their enemies.

As if to mock her, something sliced into that perfect wave of power, something malign and intangible that opposed her mastery of the storm. She felt it, not as a thing, but as an *unthing,* and knew at once what it was.

Kinseris felt it too, seconds later, and he would know it. His hand went rigid in hers, and he took two steps towards the parapet, eyes searching. She pulled him back. They could not confront the threat directly. It would jeopardise their control over Rhiannas's defence. All they could do was fight it, and she tightened her grip, like a fist clenching, and drew deeper of the willing resources at her disposal.

Beside her, Kinseris gasped, his heart stuttering. And still she took, straining to maintain the shield, casting her net wider as the resistance grew and a rising wind tried to blow the storm past them. The dragons, sensing the weakening defence, circled closer, braving the outer edges of the lessening downpour, their wingtips steaming as Water met Fire, their calls pitched between rage and hunger. The wind pulled the plumes of smoke high into the sky like a signal. If only there was someone there to see it.

Sedaine felt cold stone at her back and found herself on her knees, Kinseris crouched on her right, his head tipped back against the wall. He was still conscious, still giving, but she was perilously close to taking everything.

Jeta looked out on the courtyard from the window of the barracks, listening to Limina calm the frightened masses crowded in at her back. Her vision darkened as black clouds rolled in and thunder rumbled in the distance. The unrestrained energy of Water boiled in the air, a tidal wave of pure power that washed over her like a caress then bored straight into her being. She felt Kinseris in the flood, his warmth, his steady strength, his *love*. Then the storm broke over them with savage fury, a curtain of rain lashing down on the city, surrounding it, protecting it, and far away she heard the shriek of a dragon's rage.

Wild elation made her unsteady, tossed like a ragdoll on the wave of power that crested and crested but did not break, rising higher and higher as more and more mages drove their will into the storm.

The clamour of terror died to a whisper. Limina was beside her, fingers curled in hers, nails digging into her palm, but the pain was distant, as though her hand belonged to someone else, to another life, and still the wave grew, engulfing everything in its reach, and she had never felt such perfect joy.

The storm drove the dragons back, exiling them to its edges as it tightened its grip over Rhiannas. And for a glorious moment she knew they would prevail. That for as long as they could maintain it, the perfect harmony of intent would allow no chink through which the dragons could penetrate.

Then a discordant note entered the chorus of power, as though some of the players had fallen out of tune, dragging against the tide. The storm thundered on, its fury undinted, but the resistance was growing, and now she could feel the shape it, like absences in a pattern, concentrated on first one then another point within the palace grounds.

It was the absence that triggered the realisation—there were Kas'Talani here. *In the palace.*

No!

Rapture faded. The storm stuttered. The dragons, sensing weakness, circled closer.

'What is it? What's happening?'

Limina, clinging to her arm, sensed her panic. Saw with her own eyes the break in the clouds.

Then Jeta saw them, striding through the open gates, two dark shapes in magicians' robes. Lightning cracked, and the black shimmered and faded, the shapeless folds giving way for an instant to the midnight blue of a Kas'Talani priest.

Jeta looked around, searching for Vianor, for Kinseris, for the clansmen who guarded the palace, but the courtyard had emptied at the dragons' approach, the fury of the storm driving even the bravest to seek shelter.

A hand dragged at her arm, and she realised she was halfway to the door. Limina clung to her, holding her fast.

Sense returned. What could she do against Kas'Talani? But the absences were expanding, sucking in more and more of the power that drew the storm, dampening it. If she did nothing, they would smother it entirely and the last defence of Rhiannas would be spent for nothing.

Already she could feel the erratic shuddering in the great wave of power, felt the rising wind as it tried to blow the storm away. Kinseris and Sedaine must feel it too, but they could not break off their efforts to hunt down its source, and the magicians likely could not recognise it. Nor could they counter it. Like her, they lacked both the strength and the understanding of the Kas'Talani's power.

She felt hands on her shoulders.

'Jeta!' Limina was frantic now, her face close, her eyes searching. 'Talk to me. What's happening?'

She drew in a breath. 'There are Kas'Talani here. They will stop the storm, let the dragons through.' *If we don't stop them.*

Limina's hands fell away. She took a step back, turning so she was looking out into the courtyard, her eyes narrowing. Her voice was hard. 'Where?'

A gust of wind made the rain pound like hail against the window, then it blew past, clearing their vision for long enough for Jeta to grip the other woman's shoulders and turn her towards the threat, the two figures in black who were alone outside in the storm.

'The magicians?'

'They are *not*.'

Limina did not argue. She did not ask how she knew. 'What do we do?'

She didn't know! Jeta felt a wail of despair in her throat. What could they do?

A long, bone-shredding call echoed over the courtyard, closer than it had been. The rain was slackening, the thunder growing distant. A reminder of the fate that awaited them when the dragons broke through the storm.

She forced herself to breathe, to think. There was no power here that could challenge the Kas'Talani, even if she had been able to reach Kinseris. So they must use other means. Physical means.

A thought began to crystallise. 'If we can get close…' But how? To reach the Kas'Talani, they would have to cross the open courtyard, and the priests would not hesitate to strike down any threat. They would not fear discovery. They were too close to their goal. And even if they could somehow alert the garrison, a direct confrontation would trigger a slaughter. It might distract them for a moment, give Rhiannas's defenders precious breathing space, but it would be over too soon, a pointless sacrifice.

Limina glanced behind her at the cowering masses, then back to the priests. Her face was hard.

Jeta tracked her thoughts, horrified. 'The children –'

'Will all die if the dragons get through,' Limina said harshly. 'They deserve a chance to fight for their future.'

Rhiannas would burn. Aarin would die. Eiador would return to him.

The knowledge was a current of calm, of reason, in Darred's sea of rage. Inch by inch, he clawed his way back to sanity, or whatever version of it remained to him. He knew what he was becoming. He *embraced* it.

Darred stood on the ridge, looking down at the battlefield and the devastation of his forces. His Kas'Talani stood beside him.

Rhiannas would burn. Aarin would die. Now it was the turn of this insolent general and his army. Let it all burn. Turn the world to ash.

They had thought they could stop this. That their killing in the Grymwood would frighten and deter, that the power of the great river could shield and protect.

They were wrong. The deaths he had hidden, and already he could feel the Water draining away, pulled east, as Rhiannas sought to defend itself against annihilation. Soon there would be nothing left that could stop them.

'Destroy them,' he said softly.

And the Kas'Talani went to war.

ELEVEN

KALLIS TOOK THE offered canteen gratefully, the lukewarm water a balm to his aching throat. His mouth was filled with dust, as dry as the desert of his youth. Every breath made his thirst worse. He heard a mage say something about a massive drain on water, but he didn't know what that meant, only that it made him take another drink. He shook the canteen, realising it was almost empty. 'How many more of these do we have?'

The boy shrugged, and Kallis thrust the skin at him. 'Find out.'

The boy darted off. Kallis swallowed, then coughed. All around him, triumph was turning to unease as the strange sensation spread. He saw Derias wheel his horse around, snapping out an order to the nervous riders.

There was an odd pressure in his ears, then a flash like a bolt of lightning cracked down, and man and horse disappeared in an explosion of flame. One moment they were there, and the next…

He was on his knees. The world was a silent horror as the concussion from the blast took his hearing, then sound returned in a barrage of screaming men and horses as they plunged madly away from the blast site.

The Kas'Talani had entered the fight.

Kallis shook his head. The sound beat against him, unbearably loud. He staggered to his feet. The cloud of dust was thinning, drifts of smoke showing him a patchwork of chaotic images. He started to run, reaching Derias as another bolt smashed into the Lothani lines further to the west. Choking, his hand covering his mouth, Kallis turned away as his stomach heaved.

Where the fire had struck was a blackened crater as wide as a man, and in its centre lay Derias, choking on blood and terror, his body a scorched and bloody ruin.

Kallis stumbled to his knees, hands reaching out then holding back. There was no part of Derias that was undamaged and some parts of him were not there at all.

Derias gripped his arm, eyes wide with pain and horror. 'My legs… I can't…' His voice rose on a wave of panic. 'My legs!'

He tried to lift himself, to look, and Kallis pressed down gently on his chest. His eyes stung. There were tears of rage and hatred on his face. 'Don't.'

Derias saw the tears. 'Kallis…?' His voice wavered; underneath the blood and burns, he was very young and very scared.

Kallis shook his head, and his hand found Derias's and gripped hard.

Something shifted in Derias's eyes and his head dropped back. 'Tell her. I was angry… but I didn't… I never…' He choked to a stop, every shallow breath an agony.

A thunderous discharge shook the ground beneath them; the smoke was thick with screams.

Derias's grip spasmed in his. 'I would never…' he said again, eyes begging Kallis to understand. 'Had to let him think…'

Kallis thought of Sedaine's tight-lipped agony when the rumours had started. 'I know,' he lied, helpless. 'She knows.'

It was too late. Derias was gone.

Another bolt fell. Chaos turned to rout. Galydon's victorious army was rupturing, terrified men and horses scattering from the fiery death, their victory unravelling from one heartbeat to the next. They could not retreat with the swollen river at their backs. To form up on each other was to invite a Kas'Talani strike. But if they did nothing, it was over.

Kallis laid Derias's hand on his chest and stood, filled with cold fury. Then he looked up at the ridge and saw the most terrifying sight of the whole battle. The slope was alive with power, columns of fire rising thirty feet into the air, and beneath them walked the Kas'Talani. Even as he watched, he saw them shape that fire and hurl it at Lothane's forces.

Kallis looked desperately for Galydon—the second bolt had struck close to where he had been standing—but clouds of drifting smoke obscured his sight, and it was impossible to hear over the cacophony of terror.

A strike to his right knocked him to his knees, and a riderless horse reared out of the smoke, almost killing him right there with its flailing hooves. He grabbed the bridle, hauling the snorting, deranged beast to a fractious stop. A signaller's bugle swung wildly from its strap.

Nowhere to retreat. Too dangerous to remain together, even if they could. He swung himself up in the saddle, reaching for the bugle.

The survivors of the Caledani army were converging on the priests, seeking the shelter of their magic, desperate to flee the field of their destruction.

There was only one place the enemy's fire wouldn't strike at them, and that was in the midst of the enemy itself.

The bugle called the desperate charge.

Jeta watched the storm, waiting for her moment. As the wind gusted another sheet of rain through the courtyard, she used all the hoarded power at her disposal to do the one thing she could. As the lightning forked, she wreathed the barracks in a burst of illusory flame. And the screaming started.

As the women and children tumbled out to engulf the courtyard, the priests faltered, turning towards them. She could not fool them; she just needed to distract them. They would see through her unpolished illusion with ease, but only if they had time to *look*. And they did not give them time.

The wave of refugees flooded towards the two Kas'Talani in a chaotic rush as the barracks burned high for the precious seconds she could give them. Two clansmen emerged from the palace doors, waving their arms frantically, trying to turn the crowd back.

One of the priests hesitated a fraction too long, confronted not with soldiers but with ragged, terrified children. They reached him in tight-pressed rush, clawing at him, beating at him with their hands and their makeshift weapons. He went down, swamped by their desperation and fear.

The second priest, seeing the fate of his fellow, was not so tender-hearted. As the crowd engulfed him, he hurled the fury of the storm against them, a skin-shredding assault that threw them back.

Jeta was thrown from her feet to her knees. Screams filled her ears. She lost sight of Limina. She crawled forward, one painful inch after another, but the force that hammered at them was like nothing she had ever felt. Eyes half-lidded against the swirl of debris, she had to turn her head to gasp a breath. Her elbow gave way, dropping her on one shoulder. She could not go on. Jeta curled up on herself, hands over her head, and closed her eyes against the mass of huddled shapes all around her. *Let them not be dead!*

Then it was gone, cut off so abruptly that she lurched forward, her face striking the rain-slick stones. Pain blurred her vision, and when it cleared she saw the priest face-down on the steps, the back of his head a bloody ruin, and past him, her face shocked but determined, stood Limina, a mace hanging from her white-knuckled hand.

Her heart thudded a heavy beat, two, then a screech of fury went deep into her bones. *Maker, the dragons!* It had not been Darred controlling these dragons, their mages were right here. And only then did she realise what they had done. The dragon would feel the death of the priest that held its image— the priest it *believed* was the partner it had been unable to give up—and the madness of its rage was about to fall on them.

Frantic urging snapped her from the horror. Limina was beside her, tugging at her arm, as the terrified crowd surged. The clansmen were shouting, herding the panicked refugees back to the barracks. Heartbeat by heartbeat, the dragon drew closer.

'*Move!*' a voice roared from behind, strong hands hauling her upright.

She threw off the shock; they did not have *time.*

Limina was weeping. The pulse of heavy wings hit her back.

They were not going to make it!

'*Back!*' the voice roared again, and the clansmen scattered; the last of the refugees disappeared through the archway. A mercenary was beckoning frantically to them from within the shadow of its entrance.

The dragon swept overhead, the wind of its passing snatching her legs from under her. From her knees she saw it turn, looked into the black of its eyes.

A hand hooked under her shoulder and she was up and running. The dragon dived. The clansman who had hauled her to her feet pulled them sharply to the left, away from the barracks they could not reach and towards the stone colonnades.

Talons flashed, so close! The clansman shoved them, hard, and they tumbled under the shelter of the colonnade a split second before the dragon's strike, its tail lashing against the stone arch. A weight punched into her and bounced off Kinseris's shield. The force of it sent her flying. Her breath rushed out and pain exploded in her chest. She couldn't breathe. Then air returned, filled with dust, and she rolled onto her side, choking, coughing, unable to stop, and saw through the tears that streamed down her face the jumble of stone from the collapsed roof, mere inches from her face. They were trapped.

Kallis urged his terrified horse through the horror, death striking the ground all around, turning the world to a blackened ruin. Arcs of flame tore gaping holes through the men and horses on either side, but still they went forward. There was nowhere else to go.

The horse beneath him shuddered. He had time to register the spear that protruded from the animal's neck before its front legs collapsed and he was kicking his feet from the stirrups to jump clear as it slumped onto its side.

A spear struck the mud by his shoulder as he rolled, its owner collapsing to his knees with a blade through his throat.

The sword disappeared, and blood fountained from the wound, drenching him. Kallis looked up into Lorac's face and didn't have the breath to voice his thanks.

The clan captain was braced upright with a spear, his sword stained red to the hilt and the bandage on his leg soaked through. His men surrounded him—Ravens all, here at end—and the look on Lorac's face told him they were here for one thing, and one thing only.

A hand reached down and hauled him to his feet as another firebolt hit, so close that he was thrown back, his vision white and the world silent. Sight and sound returned in a rush, and through the gap that had exploded in their ranks, Kallis saw a familiar figure in black.

Darred walked through the maelstrom and everywhere he went, death surrounded him. Amadorian, Caledani—he killed them all, sheets of power crushing them, drowning them, tearing them to pieces.

And his eyes… If madness had a face, this was it.

There was a shout of rage. Lorac had seen him in the same moment. The clansmen pivoted to face their enemy. This was what they had come for.

Kallis lurched from his knees and hurled himself after them.

Darred saw them coming. His ruined face cracked open as he laughed, frenzied and inhuman. A sound from a nightmare. He threw his arms wide in mocking invitation, and the men at the edges of the gesture fell dead.

Lorac roared his fury, his sword in both hands, his injured leg forgotten. His Ravens spread out around him, a stalking, deadly formation, and still Darred waited.

The mercenaries closed and he struck them down with a flick of his wrist. He swatted them aside as if they were nothing more than insects. Kallis saw Lorac on his back in the mud, his leg twisted at a gruesome angle, his mouth open in silent agony as he tried to suck air into his crushed chest.

Kallis didn't know he was screaming until Darred looked towards him, his eyes black and empty as starless night.

He was lifted into the air, a pressure squeezing his throat, his feet kicking uselessly against empty air. Breath left him; panic took over. The vice tightened, pain exploded in his head, and he knew was dying.

The world faded at the edges. He clawed at his throat, desperate for air. All he could hear over the roaring in his ears was Darred's laughter.

Then there was only pain and blackness, his head spinning free…

Falling. Impact. Wetness on his face. Air. Precious and life-giving.

Kallis rolled on his side, choking, gasping, sucking air deep into his lungs. Lorac was lying beside him, his knife buried to the hilt in Darred's calf.

Above him, Darred was stumbling back, screaming his pain and rage, but Kallis only had eyes for Lorac. Blood spilled from his captain's mouth as Kallis reached out to grasp his hand. Lorac choked once, and his eyes fluttered and went still.

And the world went mad.

They carried Lysan to the tent, his blood running freely over their hands.

'You healed yourself,' Callan pleaded. 'Now heal my brother.'

Aarin looked at him in despair over Lysan's bleeding form. 'I can't,' he whispered. 'You know I can't.' The power that had healed his body from the dragons' fire had not come from him.

'Save him!'

Aarin met Callan's desperate entreaty and could not turn aside. He searched in vain for the dormant channels of talent that must exist within Lysan, as they existed in his brother. But where Callan's were close to the surface, open and waiting, Lysan's lay buried deep, and he could not reach them. In desperation, reached for Lysan through his brother, forcing his magic through the open door of Callan's waiting talent. He sensed the shock as Callan staggered under the onslaught of raw power, felt his heart stutter then restart, and feared he had gone too far. Then he felt, quite clearly, as Callan opened the way for him and gave his silent permission for Aarin to take of his very life to save his brother.

But even so it would not be enough. Aarin felt Lysan's mind brush up against his, felt the archer turn his eyes on him and felt him repudiate his brother's sacrifice. Then the contact was gone and Lysan's life was slipping faster and faster into nothing.

Desperate now, Aarin clawed after that ephemeral contact, using his own power to open up the dying man's vision, and as he did so he felt himself slipping, as though the very edges of his self were unravelling. A misty quality crept over his sight, and he forced himself to hang on, to reach further…

A furious rejection roared through his being as Silverwing thrust his presence between them, cutting the tenuous connection with a force that sent his physical body flying away from Lysan. There was a sensation of release as he felt something slip through his fingers, and he looked up from the floor into Callan's shocked and frightened face. Sensitive as he was, connected as he was, Callan could not have failed to feel the dragon's emphatic denial of what Aarin had tried to do. Then, as Aarin scrambled from his back to his feet, Callan looked away from him to his brother, who lay gasping his final breaths to the fast-fading pulse of his agony.

Arms rinsed with blood to his elbows, Callan clasped his brother's face between his hands. *'Please, Lysan!'*

But Lysan had already made the only choice he had left. Not even Callan could call him back now.

Aarin turned away, unable to watch, aware that his presence now was an intrusion. He stumbled from the tent, his own grief roaring in his ears, and it was only then that he realised what he had lost.

He reached for Eiador's bindings and they were gone. *Gone.* The shock stopped him dead. He felt again that sense of release, of letting go, and knew it had not been Lysan he had lost in that moment.

Eiador was free. Free to return to Darred. He had failed.

A ripple of nausea bent him double. As he sucked in a breath, he felt the desert-dry air catch in his throat. Alarm swelled to panic. Somewhere far away Silverwing was crying a desperate warning.

The world seemed to contract, pressure building behind his eyes, dimming his sight. He staggered to his knees, one arm locked straight all that kept him from his face.

Silverwing's panic hammered against him, but he could make no sense of it. A thousand voices screamed inside his head. Then the pressure released with a force that turned his whole world white.

TWELVE

BETANAS WATCHED THE last of the soldiers file out through the gates of Kas'Tella's military camp just as the dawn rays reached the outer walls of the citadel. These were the stragglers, the tail-end of a long exodus that had started so many months ago as a slow trickle, secret and hidden, but had become a flood his colleagues had been powerless to stop. They left behind them only bones and ghosts—empty structures, broken equipment, discarded uniforms. An empty pike where the camp doctor's head had shrivelled and dried in the harsh sun. A death that all Betanas's warnings and arguments had failed to prevent, and one that had turned simmering resentment into silent rebellion.

They had been clever, these officers. Hiding their anger, their treason. Hiding their desertion behind troop movements and training exercises, distant campaigns to remote provinces to investigate reports of unrest, things in which his brothers, so intent on undoing the catastrophic changes Kinseris had wrought, had little interest and paid less attention. Until it was too late to stop it and pointless to try.

He had watched them do it, from this window and others. He had given Fylian his orders from his own lips so many months ago, knowing what he did, choosing once and for all where his loyalty lay as he ordered the army to keep its promise to Kinseris, as he prepared to keep his own. And he would never forget the look in Fylian's eyes before he walked away. Haunted. Relieved. Sickened.

The chatter of voices rose behind him as his colleagues began to fill up the council chamber, taking their places on the rows of tightly packed benches. Never before had so many of the Order come together at one time, in one place. But this was important. A crisis, Casamir had called it. *Of our own making*, Betanas had added, but not out loud. He never disagreed with Casamir, not where anyone could hear, nor even in private, not anymore. He could not risk it. He could not risk *this*.

The sun was higher now, its glow encroaching on the inner courtyards. A man emerged from the shadows of the walls and walked swiftly across the empty grounds. The sun picked out the insignia on his ceremonial uniform—a general's braid on his arm. Betanas's eyes were old and it was a long way from his window to the courtyard, but he thought perhaps the man looked up, just briefly, before the angle of his departure took him out of Betanas's sight.

A staff banged three times on the floor as Casamir called the meeting to order. Betanas turned from the window and walked to his colleague's side, looking out over the packed ranks of his brothers, their faces turned to him, their voices stilled. Some faces he had known for more than a century. Others he had never seen before this moment. Some, a very few, still wore the dragon devices that had given the Order its power and then torn it apart. Those few would spread the word of what happened here today faster than any messenger could match. And he was glad of that. Because it needed to be known.

Kinseris would hear and he would weep, but Kinseris had thought he could curb a thousand-year-old hunger for power and remake the Order as he thought it should have been. He had to have known he would fail. Just as he must know that Betanas could not stand alone against the weight of his brotherhood. He had no choice. Kinseris would understand that. It was, after all, why he had made this last, desperate plan.

Casamir held out the staff, a look of elation on that old, cracked face, because this was his moment of triumph. Betanas placed his hand upon the gnarled wood as Casamir leaned in to accept his embrace.

Betanas's lips brushed that withered cheek. 'Forgive me,' he whispered.

The sun's ray hit the windows and flooded the floor of the chamber in golden light. As one the Kas'Talani bowed their heads in prayer. Except Casamir, who was staring at him in dawning suspicion.

It began as a distant rumble, like the first tremors of an earthquake far below their feet. He had time to turn his face one last time to the sun before the world exploded in fire and stone.

THIRTEEN

IN THE SKIES above Rhiannas, a dragon roared in rage and grief. Sedaine felt the pressure hit, a soundless thunderclap, as an immense shockwave seemed to flatten the whole world.

The impact hit the circling dragons, swatting them like flies. One fell into a spiral then righted itself, wings beating a drunken rhythm as it strained for height and disappeared into the disintegrating storm, heading away from the city. The other plummeted straight for the centre of the palace.

Kinseris doubled over, his mouth open in a silent scream, his hand torn from her grasp. The link shattered. Lunging, she screamed to Vianor, all control gone, but the magician was two floors below, out of sight and hearing, and the dragon was already on them.

A ripple ran through the world. A soundless shockwave swelled and retracted. Already prone, Kallis was hammered into the mud, his vision fading in and out, Darred's face above him a snarl of unseeing rage.

The wave burst. Darred staggered, his eyes wide and shocked, exposed and vulnerable for a split second. Kallis didn't hesitate. There were no second chances.

Awareness seeped back into Darred's eyes; his hand reached for the dragon on his breast.

Kallis gripped Lorac's dagger, dragging it free. Darred screamed, stumbling and almost falling, and Kallis launched himself upward.

Aarin's eyes flew open. He was face-down in the mud, dirt choking his throat, his fingers curled into tortured fists. He gagged, pushing himself to his knees, then the clamour exploded in his head and nearly sent him back down.

Shocked awareness came an instant later. He did not stop to question, or to understand. Reaching out to Silvering, he stepped sideways into the dream, and then out again, into utter madness. And left the way open behind him.

FOURTEEN

THE STORM FALTERED and began to die. From her knees, her head ringing with the aftershock of *whatever that was,* Sedaine threw herself forward, fingers scrabbling for Kinseris as the shrieking, screeling dragon plummeted out of the sky, punched from the air by the shockwave, a roiling, seething mass of wings and claws. Her questing hand touched his and she grabbed hold, weeping with fear and rage.

Kinseris jerked at the touch, his fingers latching onto hers, but before she could re-establish control, she felt him seize it from her, felt the shield of his magic form around her, protecting her, and *could not accept it.*

As the shield shaped itself, she pushed it back, drawing deep on Kinseris's own strength to take the defence he had fashioned for her and reject it. In the instant before the dragon hit, its body flailing wildly in its uncontrolled fall, she flung that shield as hard as she could. The shield hit the dragon, and the force of Kinseris's last, desperate defence deflected its fall just enough to prevent it crashing through the roof of the palace and onto the people sheltering inside. Its tail lashed out, striking the parapet in an explosion of stone. She felt something hit her and then she was falling, the dragon above and around her, down and down…

Kallis let his arm drop and staggered back a step. Darred was on his knees with the dagger in his chest, eyes wide and disbelieving, their brightness fading. Kallis went down on one knee, then the other, unconsciously mirroring his enemy's pose. Then Darred toppled forward and lay still, his face buried in the churned-up mud of the battleground, and Kallis raised his head.

The scream of rage almost shredded his flesh from his bones. The sky boiled, and visceral terror surged in response. Too late he remembered Aarin's warning—of the insanity that would consume the dragon on Darred's death. He turned, his sword arm rising slowly, pointlessly.

Then, out of nowhere, Aarin was beside him, dropping to his knees in the mud, one arm hooking Kallis round the shoulders and the other pushing his head down.

The blaze of flame passed over them, sucking the breath from his lungs in a blast of heat, *but it did not touch them.* He was on his back, blinking a red haze from his eyes. He saw the dragon wheel around for another pass, saw Aarin on his hands and knees beside him, half-stunned, and curled up against the horror that was coming. Then there was an answering screech and something massive and silver crashed into the maddened dragon. The concussion flattened Aarin into the mud as wings pounded and tails thrashed. Then Silverwing's greater bulk carried the other dragon away and Kallis fell back, releasing his breath on an explosive curse.

He looked at Aarin. The mage was bone white, his breathing shocked and shallow, and Kallis tried to imagine what it must have taken to throw himself into the path of that blast of flame. Then he saw where Aarin was looking— not at the disappearing dragons, not at Darred, lying dead at last, but at a coil of black smoke rising in the north.

Rhiannas was burning.

FIFTEEN

THE MERCENARY WHO had pushed them under the colonnade was dead, crushed when the archway collapsed. Jeta felt for him in the dark, her questing hands finding one arm and a shoulder. The rest of him was buried under the weight of fallen stone.

She edged back to where Limina was slumped against the wall. She was conscious, but Jeta could not tell if she was hurt and she had not spoken. They had been lucky. A column had fallen crosswise at the impact and must have lodged itself against another, stopping the roof from falling in on them. But the space was tiny and stifling, barely big enough for her to stretch out her legs. Sweat trickled down her back, and her breath came in panting gasps. She could not tell if it was panic or lack of air. Which only made the panic worse. They were trapped.

Everything outside was muffled. But the storm had rushed back to fill the absences the priests had made, and she could not hear the dragons.

A vibration shuddered through the stones. Something shifted, dislodging a stream of grit and dust onto her ankles. She groped for Limina's hand, dropping her head onto her knees, trying to breathe slowly, calmly. Trying not to move. The stones moved again, grinding ominously. Then she heard voices, muted and indistinct. Someone was digging them out!

She scrabbled closer, calling out. Silence met her pleas, then, louder, a man's voice shouted a question.

Crying, laughing, she answered, and heard a ragged cheer. Minutes later, a shaft of light hit her eyes and a small opening appeared in the wall of rock. She stretched a hand through the hole and warm fingers reached for hers as she took deep, gulping breaths of clean air.

Then the fingers released their pressure and a voice called, 'Stand back. We'll have you out soon.'

She crawled back to Limina, helping the other woman struggle to her knees and saw the filthy tear tracks on her face through the chink of light.

More voices joined the first as the mercenaries worked to enlarge the hole, caution abandoned. Then *something* pressed her back, down, and she felt a blinding pain as her vision darkened. A massive shockwave shuddered through the stones of their prison, a release of energies so vast that her mind simply shut down. Dimly, as though from a great distance, she heard panicked shouts and pounding feet as a rumble rocked the ground beneath them, showering her with shards of stone, then the whole front of their prison fell away as the pressure in her head released.

And she watched with horror as a great tangle of scales and claws fell from the sky and crashed to the ground in the centre of the courtyard.

An instant of silence, then the palace groaned like a wounded beast. Jeta threw herself back, across Limina, covering her head with her arms as huge blocks of stone rained down, engulfing them in a choking cloud of dust. The roof above them lurched with the impact, and she curled tighter round Limina, feeling the other woman tremble in her arms, the thud of her heart like a drum in her chest, and channelled all her strength into the shield Kinseris had given her.

But the roof did not collapse and crush them. Its tremors faded, the stones of their shelter shifting and settling. She sat up, dizzy with exhaustion and relief, the crunch of grit beneath her the only noise in a soundless world, and saw the unmoving curve of a dragon's back, its hide still steaming gently as the raindrops fell.

Jeta crawled out into a world painted in ashes. A layer of dust covered everything in grey, so thick that even the rain could not wash it away. The silence was absolute.

Then movement, as clansmen emerged slowly and hesitantly from the shelter they had sought, and silently ringed the shallow crater, the shock in their eyes reflected in her own.

In its centre was the smoking ruin of the dragon's corpse, its skull crushed by an avalanche of falling masonry, its deadly fire stilled forever.

But it was not the dragon that brought the tears to her eyes or Limina to her knees. Beneath its great bulk, wet with rain and blood, was an unmistakable, devastating sprawl of black hair.

SIXTEEN

THE DRAGONS CAME to Aarin on that battlefield as they had come once before, and their revenge was swift and deadly. Half-stunned, the Kas'Talani were plucked from the battlefield and carried aloft. Aarin averted his eyes from what came next, but he did not try to stop it.

Rhiannas was burning.

He had one arm under Kallis's shoulder, supporting most of his weight as the man sagged against him. Bruises were already blooming around his throat and the whole front of his armour was soaked in blood and gore. How much of it was his, Aarin couldn't tell.

Rhiannas was burning.

Darred was dead in the mud behind them, his body already lost and forgotten among the ocean of the fallen. Ghosts picked their way through the drifting smoke, blackened and blood-stained, eyes vacant. In the distance, Aarin saw Galydon's tall figure, his relentless energy for once replaced by stillness as he looked upon the horror of the battlefield.

Rhiannas was burning.

Silverwing landed before him. Kallis staggered free of Aarin's support, standing unsteadily. 'Go,' he rasped.

Galydon was making his way towards them, clusters of men straggling in his wake. More and more dragons flew down to land.

'No,' Aarin said, catching hold of Kallis before he could fall, and walking him to where Silverwing waited. 'We all go.'

As Silverwing leapt into the air, he looked back and saw the dragons dropping out of the sky amid the survivors, offering their wings to the stunned soldiers. Galydon was watching them, hands shading his eyes as a copper female lowered its head at his feet in invitation. Then Aarin lost sight of him as they soared up into the clouds.

Kallis sagged and Aarin felt a surge of worry. He never had discovered where all that blood had come from. But there was nothing he could do except wrap Kallis in the warmth of Silverwing's fire and stop him slipping from the dragon's back.

Now and then, through the clouds, Aarin caught glimpses of the other dragons, keeping pace with them as they flew on and on. Then, finally, he saw it. Rhiannas.

And all at once he knew what the defenders had done.

The city was ringed by storm clouds, obscured behind a curtain of rain, its edges smouldering stubbornly despite the deluge. And woven all through the storm, he could feel them, all the mages and magicians who had poured their magic and their lives into the last, doomed defence of the city.

His mother, Vianor, Kinseris. Even Jeta was there, faint as the touch of morning dew but as fierce as the storm. But they were all echoes, the storm they had called playing itself out without a guiding hand, and they were close enough now that he could see the ruin of the palace.

Kallis, seated before him, had seen it too. 'Aarin…'

There was pity and compassion in his voice and Aarin couldn't bear it, wouldn't hear it.

'Don't.' They were alive. They had to be, or what had it all been for?

Silverwing set them down on the deserted avenue outside the palace gates. Kallis slithered gracelessly down the dragon's wing and placed himself between Aarin and the gates. He put a restraining hand on his chest. 'Wait. Let me…'

Aarin pushed him gently aside. Through the open gates, he could see Jeta. She had her back to him, and there were other figures around her, all of them looking at something in the centre of the courtyard.

He picked up his pace, Kallis struggling to keep up. It was a dragon, and it was dead. And under it…

Jeta turned and saw him. Her faced paled, and he *knew*.

He was standing amid the rubble of the courtyard and he was back in his childhood home, safe in his mother's arms, her warmth all around him. The memories he had carried with him always enfolded him one last time then faded away. There were tears on his face, but he didn't notice. Instead, a loss he did not know how to understand opened up before him and swallowed him whole.

He had been seven when his mother left, when the world he knew broke apart. It had rained that night too, as his father held him in his arms, his hair plastered to his face by rain and tears, and they had watched her walk away into the night. *You will see her again,* his father had promised him. *She is leaving now but you will see her again.*

His father had been right. Fate had brought them back together, and he had wasted it. Because he thought they would have more time. Now he had no time at all.

The dragons circled overhead. He was vaguely aware of Kallis trying to calm the surge of panic the sight of them caused.

Silverwing touched his mind. *We will care for your dead and ours, Æisoul.*

He looked up as the dragons descended, gathering up the body of their kin, lifting it off the dead queen—off his mother—and carrying it away to care for in their own way.

Away.

His heart lurched. 'Don't take her!' The words were torn from him, aloud. He couldn't bear it. He could not bear for them to take her from him yet. He had thought they would have more time.

We won't take her, little brother. But she should not rest here.

He was only distantly aware of the restless movement around him, of the fear and consternation, as Silverwing flew down once more.

'Aarin?' Kallis was beside him, his name an urgent question.

He could not speak, but he managed somehow to convey to Kallis that they should not interfere as Silvering gathered Sedaine in his talons. The dragon cradled her like a precious child as he lifted her clear of the cracked and smoking crater and then laid her, light as a feather, on the untouched marble steps of her palace. Away from the filth and the blood and the devastation of Darred's final strike.

He did not remember moving, but the next thing he knew he was by her side, on his knees on the cold, slick steps, and he could, finally, take her hand.

We grieve with you, Æisoul, Silverwing told him. *Truly, she was worthy of us.*

I know.

He remembered her agony of doubt when the dragons had returned, but not to her. He had not tried hard enough to make her understand that it was never the rejection she had feared. And now he never could.

Kallis watched Aarin sink to his knees by his mother's body and felt a hollow weight in his chest. Sedaine was dead. After everything, Darred had had his revenge.

He felt his knees give and stumbled backwards, dropping onto the rubble of what had once been the eastern colonnade. After everything, it had still come to this.

A hand squeezed his shoulder, and he looked up into Jeta's tear-stained face. Someone else was missing. 'Kinseris?'

Her face cracked, tears spilling over, silver tracks through the ashes. 'I don't know.'

No more, Kallis thought fiercely. *Please, no more!* They had already lost so many, too many.

'He's not here,' Jeta sobbed. 'Why isn't he here?'

He stood, still wobbly, and pulled her into an embrace as she wept on his shoulder and tried not to think about the last time they had stood like this.

Over Jeta's head he watched Limina walk to where Aarin knelt by Sedaine. She laid a gentle hand on his arm, her words too soft for Kallis to hear. Then, behind her, the palace doors opened.

Kallis bent his head down to Jeta. 'Hey,' he said. 'Look.'

Vianor was framed in the doorway, his white hair wild and his black robes streaked with filth. And propped up in his arms was Kinseris.

As Jeta flew to Kinseris, taking him from Vianor and helping him sit, the magician stood staring down at his dead queen and Kallis saw such a spasm of rage cross his face that he was on his feet and halfway across the courtyard before the impulse had finished forming.

The magician took a lurching step forward. 'You did this!' he hissed at Aarin, hand raised to do *something,* and Kallis barrelled into him.

'Back off,' he growled, as Vianor's wiry strength pushed against him. 'Leave them alone.'

'She was my queen!' the old man said savagely.

Limina stood. Her face was very white. 'And he is her son.'

Her implication was clear, and Kallis winced as Aarin finally looked up, confusion and dismay on his face.

Vianor snarled, jerking himself free of Kallis's grip. 'It means nothing. She made sure of that herself.'

Kallis felt a knot of pain tighten in his chest. 'Shut up!' he growled, desperate to stop whatever it was Vianor was about to say.

The old magician shot Aarin a look of cruel triumph. 'She made Limina her heir. She didn't want you. She never wanted you.'

Limina dropped to her knees beside Aarin. 'A decision she made when she did not know if you were alive or dead. It cannot stand if you contest it.'

'Oh, it will,' countered Vianor. 'After you returned, your mother wrote you out of the succession.'

Kallis saw the impact of those words reflected on Limina's face as the shock blanched her white. She hadn't known that.

All Aarin said was, 'I know.'

'He is her *son,*' Limina insisted. She was shaking. 'It's his choice.'

Aarin shook his head. 'No, it was my mother's. And it was the right one.' He took Limina's hand. 'She was doing me a kindness, not an injury. Take what she has left to you. I think you already know it is not a gift.'

Vianor opened his mouth. Kallis bundled him roughly down to steps before he could spew more poison on their grief, and saw three men enter the courtyard.

Galydon, battle-stained and weary but imbued with the vigour of triumph. At his side were two men Kallis did not know, an officer in what was just recognisable as the uniform of Kas'Tella, and a heavy-set man who bore no badge of rank or identifying marks other than a raw and ugly scar where his left eye had been.

Galydon sketched him a tired salute before turning to the one-eyed man at his side and drawing his attention to where Limina was crouched beside Aarin. Kallis saw the man follow Galydon's gesture, saw some of the battle weariness lift from his shoulders, then he took a pace forward and bellowed, 'Woman. Your husband has returned.'

Limina froze with her back to them. Kallis could see the hand at her side trembling. Then, slowly, she turned, her face white. And the man, who must be Hanlon, threw back his head with a great rumbling laugh. 'You look as skittish as you did on our wedding night.'

The words jolted Limina from her shock. 'Your face would strike fear into any girl's heart,' she retorted, hands on hips, gaze roaming all over him. 'Better take my eye too if you expect me to live with it now.'

Hanlon laughed, arms spread wide to receive her. 'Ah, woman, I've missed you.'

And then she was in his embrace, tears pouring down the face he crushed against his massive chest.

Kallis smiled at their joy, and then his smile froze and died. Galydon stood in silence, staring at the place where Limina had been, the place where Sedaine lay, and in his blank face Kallis the agony of a man who had just lost his whole world.

EPILOGUE

AARIN SLIPPED SILENTLY into the tent. Head bent, Callan did not acknowledge him. His eyes never left his brother's body, lying where he had died hours before, and in his eerie stillness Aarin read all the despair of a man who no longer cared if he lived or died.

For Callan, weary of war and death, who wanted nothing more than to mend the things that were broken, the death of his beloved brother—his happy, laughing, carefree brother—had robbed him of the crutch that kept him sane in the midst of insanity. And Aarin, who owed this man so much, could not bear it.

Finally, with a stiffness that spoke of hours of motionless vigil, Callan looked up. 'There is nothing you can offer me that I want.'

Callan, the man who saw to the heart of everyone and everything, knew why he had come. And he was telling him he would not listen.

Aarin had thought of him once that he did not care if he lived or died. Meeting Callan's bleak gaze now, he recognised a man who knew exactly what he wanted, and everything in him rejected that choice.

'It is not mine to offer, but yours to take,' he said at last. 'And I think there was a time when you wanted it.'

His eyes once more fixed on his brother, Callan shook his head. 'What do I want with centuries of life when one more day is unbearable?'

If you want to help Callan, keep Lysan safe. So had Shrogar said to him months ago in Ephenor. But Lysan, who had understood his brother better than his brother had understood himself, had rejected their efforts to save him. In that fleeting instant of contact, Aarin had felt him make his choice, and he guessed that Callan had felt it too—the decision to free his brother from the last tie that kept him from seeking what he so clearly desired. But Callan could not accept that gift.

Tears in his own eyes, Aarin said quietly, 'Lysan didn't die for this.'

Callan's head snapped up, eyes dark with anger. 'My brother died for nothing at all.'

He wanted to say that it didn't have to be that way, that Lysan's sacrifice was worth something. Instead, he said, 'My mother is dead.'

The words came from nowhere. Callan stared at him, the anger fading.

'My mother is dead,' he said again, because it didn't sound real.

Something in him broke. And in breaking, it broke another dam, and suddenly Callan's face was wet with tears.

For Jeta, the aftermath of the attack on Rhiannas was nothing more than a series of splintered impressions. Aarin's grief. Vianor's anger. Kallis's defeated exhaustion. Sedaine's death.

She remembered how Aarin had slipped away and she had stopped Kallis going after him. How Galydon had stood there for what seemed like hours and she still could not bear to think about his face. How Kinseris had appeared, leaning heavily on Vianor, and when she had gone to him, he had kept repeating over and over, 'They're dead. They're all dead.' It wasn't until much later that she understood what that meant, and she kept her thoughts to herself. Because she was *glad*.

In the days since, swept up in frantic activity, there had been no chance to stop, to think, to sort those memories into any kind of order, because life went relentlessly on. There was a funeral and a coronation to organise, wounds to bind and damage to mend. And a new world to adjust to.

She found Kinseris on the gallery as she had known she would. She could not tell what he was thinking, but she knew what he was looking at. Out in the ruined courtyard sprawled the dragons. She could not count them, their long, muscled bodies entwined in a sinuous heap of shimmering scales, but she could feel the heat of them, even from here. More than that, she could feel their lure, the intense attraction that touched something primal within her that Aarin had awakened.

But it did not pull at her. It was not, she thought, a compulsion, as it was for others. It was a choice now, to accept or reject. Not like before, in the world these dragons had abandoned and was now lost forever, when it had been an imperative. And she had watched, when she could, as one by one the mages from Luen had been drawn into the courtyard like moths to a flame and picked their way through the tangled mass of dragons until they found their partner. She did not know how they knew, but they did. She only knew that their choice was not hers and never would be.

Her gaze shifted from the dragons to Kinseris, and she saw their longing reflected in his eyes. He could not hide it from her and did not try, and her heart fluttered with impending loss.

Burying her grief, her pain, she asked, 'Will you go to them?'

His hand tightened on hers, but he didn't answer for the longest time, nor did he tear his gaze from the dragons, hungry eyes drinking in the sight of them. Then, just when she thought she couldn't bear it any longer, he looked down and murmured, 'No, I don't think I will.'

He smiled, and the sun came out.

'Where shall we go?' he asked, sometime later when her tears had dried.

She smiled, leaning close, feeling his warmth. 'Back home.'

'To Situra?'

'No,' she said. 'To Caledan.'

'He's in there?' Kinseris asked the guards on the door.

They eyed him warily. 'Yes, my lord.'

'For how long?'

'Since last night.'

He put his hand on the door and both men stepped in front of him.

'I'm sorry, my lord. He said no one was to disturb him.'

Kinseris let his arm drop. They watched him from determined, nervous faces, loyalty holding them in place despite their misgivings.

He said gently, 'I think he's been in there long enough, don't you?'

They didn't say anything, but when he reached for the doors again, they moved aside.

Kinseris pushed open the doors to the great hall of Rhiannas and walked inside. A man stood in the middle of the room, his back rigid, his very stillness an eloquent sorrow.

As Kinseris stopped beside him, Galydon said, 'My place was with you. I did not want to come here. I did not want any of this.'

Kinseris searched for something to say, but he looked at the body of the queen and the words would not come.

'All this, for nothing?'

'No, not for nothing. She wanted you to save Lothane, and you did.'

Galydon shook his head. 'She *was* Lothane. And I did not save her.'

Kinseris did not, could not, look at him. 'If anyone failed to save her it was me.' He had tried. He had shaped the strongest shield he could and tried to give it to her, but she had rejected it. He had lived and she had died, because that was the choice she had made. But he would die himself before he ever told Galydon that. He had seen what neither of them had ever acknowledged; he knew what this was.

There was a scraping of metal and he looked down to see Galydon's sword in his hand, held out hilt first.

Kinseris looked from the sword to his general's face and shook his head. 'The Kas'Talani are destroyed. My time is finished.'

The sword didn't waver. 'You are not Kas'Talani. You never were.'

Not Kas'Talani. Free at last. 'We have been here before, you and I. I didn't want it then. I want it less now.' But there was a part of him that did, that would always crave what he had lost—a purpose, a place, power.

'You will take it,' Galydon said fiercely, 'because I need you to. You owe me this. Then let us go back there and build something together.' There was a fraught pause. 'I cannot stay here, and I am so very tired of death.'

Let us build something together.

Kinseris felt his hand close on the sword.

Kallis found Aarin two days later, climbing stiffly from Silverwing's back in the clearing behind the tent, the dragon's thoughts all guileless innocence in the face of Aarin's surprise.

They regarded each other warily as the dragon powered up into the air and disappeared.

'You left,' Kallis said eventually, his words devoid of inflection. His throat was livid with bruising, his voice as raspy as Aarin's had been.

Aarin nodded and moved to one side. 'I was needed here.'

Kallis looked past him to where Callan stood before his brother's pyre, and Aarin saw the impact hit him like a physical blow. He took a step back, turning his face away, and took two quick breaths. 'How?'

Aarin said bleakly, 'Protecting me.'

Silence for a beat, then Kallis drew a hand over his face, his eyes tight closed. 'We won,' he said after a while. 'So why does it feel like we lost?'

Aarin glanced at him, hearing the echo of his own thoughts, the echo of his own grief. 'It wasn't your fault.'

Kallis inhaled. 'Wasn't it? We should have realised what he would do. We should have protected her better.'

'She would not have let you.'

'She should not have had a choice!' Kallis retorted. 'It feels like it was for nothing. The war is over, Aarin. We won. I'm not about to die at any moment in any one of a hundred horrible ways, and yet I feel...'

'Lost?' After a moment, he asked, 'What will you do?'

Kallis didn't answer, his eyes locked on Callan's back as the flames from the pyre leapt towards the sky.

'You told me once you were going to retire, buy some land...'

Kallis snorted. 'You need money to buy land, and your mother wasn't paying me.' There was a pause, then, 'Sorry.'

Aarin waved the awkward apology away. 'I'm sure Limina...'

'I'm sure she won't. Derias... Derias mortgaged Lothane to the hilt. He didn't really believe we could win. There's nothing left.' He paused. 'It's not money I need.'

No, it was not money, or land, or retirement that would fill the gaping hole left by this war. 'A purpose?' Aarin guessed. 'Lothane is in chaos. All of Amadorn is. There is surely work for you here.'

Kallis didn't look at him. 'Darred is dead, and all the people who tied me to Lothane are dead with him. There's nothing for me here.'

'What about the clans?'

'The clans… I'm not even sure that means anything anymore. They need to work that out themselves. They don't need me.'

He lapsed into silence, and Aarin didn't try to fill it. Because it was the companionable silence of old, when he had just been a boy with an impossible dream, and Kallis a cynical, amused, rudderless ex-mercenary. Before power, revenge, and deadly ambition had torn everything to shreds.

The flames of Lysan's pyre burned lower. Callan still hadn't moved.

Eventually, Kallis said what he had come to say. 'Jeta is going back to Caledan with Kinseris.'

Aarin kept his eyes on Callan's back. They were leaving. He had expected it, he understood it. 'And you're going with them.'

He could feel Kallis's eyes on him, but he did not, could not, look round. They were not leaving him. In every way that mattered, he had already left them. But even so it was like a door that had been wedged ajar was finally closing and it was all he could do not to hold it open.

'There's nothing for me here,' Kallis said again. 'But in Caledan… I can help them rebuild. Maybe even find my people.'

He knew Kallis was waiting for a response, an acknowledgement, but the words wouldn't come.

'Will we see you again?'

'I think you know the answer to that.' It was the least that he owed her— to stay away and let her live the life she had chosen, not force her to question it.

'I do love you,' she had said to him when she made her choice, when she had said good-bye by the gates of Rhiannas.

'But you love him more?' He had not meant it to sound so bitter.

Her smile had been sad. 'He can give me more.'

It was true, and he had not told her how much he wished he could give her everything. It would not have been fair.

Kallis stood. 'So, this is good-bye?'

Suddenly there were tears in his eyes because he did not want it to be, but the fate that had brought them together was taking them now in different directions.

He held out his arm and Kallis clasped it, then the mercenary pulled him into a fierce embrace. Rough fingers ruffled his hair. 'Take care of yourself.' He glanced towards Callan. 'And him.'

'I will,' Aarin promised. 'You take care of them.'

Kallis laughed. 'I'm not taking responsibility for that.'

A gentle nudge and Silverwing drifted down. Kallis took a deep breath. 'This is the last time. I'm taking a bloody ship to Caledan.'

It was dark by the time Silverwing returned. Aarin felt him arrive and trudged to meet him. The dragon lifted his head as Aarin approached, obsidian eyes holding a question.

We're waiting.

For how long?

Aarin settled back against the dragon's side, looking down into the camp where Callan still knelt in lonely vigil. *As long as it takes.*

THE END

THE MANY SHADES OF MIDNIGHT

BRIVAR

It was the first day of spring when they met the woodsman a week out from Orleas. For Brivar, apprentice surgeon and cousin of the king's envoy to the erstwhile Duke of Agrathon, it was the day blue star-violet flowered, and he longed to abandon his diplomatic duty and pick some, because there is no more potent painkiller in all the land than the dried blossom of blue star-violet harvested on the first day of spring. More importantly, it was also the day he met the Duke of Agrathon. And that was the day his life changed forever.

Of course, Brivar didn't know that then. At the time, the directions the woodsman gave them meant only that they were saved from one more night of sleeping under the stars, though with the pace his cousin set, Brivar would have preferred another night on hard ground to the harsh ache in his thighs from so many hours in the saddle. And he quickly came to regret the lost opportunity to collect blue star-violet blossom on the first day of spring, because he would soon need it rather badly.

Perhaps that's what the woodsman was looking for, out here in the wilds so far from any settlement. Certainly, as he stood a little off the path, watching them with his hood drawn up, his stance was less easy than it should have been. Apprenticed to the guild of surgeons since the age of ten, Brivar was trained in observation. He knew how to read people, how they held themselves, how they moved and spoke, how to look for the truth beyond what words could convey—or conceal. His teacher, the Varistan Alondo, had a bad hip. Brivar always knew when it pained him by the way he walked, the stiffness when he sat, and those first few limping steps when he stood. Of course, he never complained or asked for help. Some people were too stubborn for their own good.

The woodsman looked like one of them. His attention reluctantly drawn from the temptation of blue star-violet, Brivar watched the forester spar with his cousin, observing the tension in his shoulders, the way he held his left arm close. An old wound, most likely, that had healed badly. Brivar observed other things about him, too. The half-hidden worn leather sheathes for paired blades. Only professional soldiers and duellists used such weapons. Since you were unlikely to find a duellist wandering the wilderness, he had probably once served in a kingdom army, which made sense since he knew where the Duke of Agrathon was holed up. Once King Raffa-Herun Geled's most trusted commander and confidant and now a renegade military captain whose fame had made him friends, and enemies, across half the continent.

And this one wasn't giving him up easily.

Brivar's cousin, the rather pompous Lord Sul-Barin Feron, had exhausted his meagre supply of patience. Brivar couldn't understand why the king had chosen him for such a delicate mission. As far as he could see, his cousin was without an ounce of either subtlety or tact, as demonstrated by the way he lost his temper and his dignity arguing with a woodsman in front of the entire royal embassy.

It had started badly when Corado, the half-Flaeresian captain of their guard, had rudely hailed the man walking the track ahead of them, asking him where they could find the Duke of Agrathon. He had followed this with a flick of his whip when his question got no response, an insult the man had sidestepped easily enough but which had done their cause no favours.

Ignoring Corado's glare, the man's shadowed gaze skimmed their party and fixed on the ostentatious figure of Lord Sul. "I don't know a duke."

This was not well received. "Everyone knows the Duke of Agrathon. He's in these mountains. Tell me where and you can go on your way."

It wasn't a threat, though it could be taken as one when considered alongside the guard captain's attempted assault. But Brivar had the distinct impression the man was amused rather than afraid.

"Who's looking for him?"

"The King," Lord Sul informed him with an arrogant tilt of his chin.

The man laughed. "Which one?"

"Which one? His king, man!"

There was a dangerous silence, which was almost certainly lost on Lord Sul. Then the man said, "The captain doesn't have a king. Best remember that when you see him, or you won't get far."

"I'll thank you to not give me advice," Lord Sul snapped. "Just tell me where to find him."

The woodsman gave a one-shouldered shrug. Definitely an old wound there, Brivar decided. He let his attention wander back to the carpet of blue star-violets as the man told his cousin what he wanted to know, and he wondered whether he would have time to pick some of the precious blossoms when they stopped for the night.

The woodsman's parting words put paid to that hope. "You'll have to hurry if you want to reach him before night falls. You'd be better off turning around and starting out again early tomorrow. You don't want to be out after dark in these mountains."

"I am well protected," Lord Sul answered haughtily, hauling on his reins to wheel his stamping horse around.

Again, that awkward shrug, but there was a different tension to the man now. A kind of watchful stillness Brivar had observed in many old soldiers. For the first time since their journey began, he felt a touch of fear.

His cousin, of course, was oblivious to such things, and was not a man to take advice in any case. He was already waving his escort on, snapping at them to pick up their pace. He did not bother to look at their guide as he rode past. He certainly didn't thank him.

Trailing at the back of the column, Brivar reined in as he passed. Careful that his cousin should not hear, he said, "Blue star-violet, dried in the sun and crushed into a paste with spring water, is an excellent pain reliever."

He sensed the man's surprise and kicked his heels into his horse. He hadn't gone more than a few paces when he heard him say, "I meant it about nightfall. It's not safe."

Brivar looked back, but the woodsman was already disappearing into the trees and his cousin was shouting at him to hurry.

They were spared the perils of the mountains at night, but only just. Emerging from the forests of the lower slopes onto the mountain track, the woodsman's directions took them quickly away from the main path into the depths of a canyon. The temperature dropped, the sting of cold edging Brivar's fingers and misting his breath, and the fading light brought with it the wraiths of his imagination, crawling out of the rocks and from behind trees until all around him he felt the presence of their midnight threat.

There was a flicker of movement ahead and they were no longer alone on the track. The lead horses shied and Brivar started so hard he nearly toppled from his saddle. But the figures emerging from the twilight were merely human in shape, though they were armed, and their spears were pointed with definite intent at his cousin's escort.

A woman stepped forward from the deep shadows lining the canyon walls. She pulled down the hood of her fur-lined coat to reveal a face that was as hard as it was young. "You've missed your way," she told them, an uncompromising note in her voice. "Road to Orleas is two miles back."

Lord Sul looked down at her with disdain. "We're not looking for Orleas. We're here to see the Duke of Agrathon."

She raised an eyebrow. "Agrathon is two hundred miles to the west."

His cousin, Brivar saw, had had enough. Ignoring the threat of the spears, Lord Sul stalked his horse up to the woman. "He's not in Agrathon. He is in these mountains. I demand that you take us to him this instant, in the name of King Raffa-Herun Geled."

The woman fixed Lord Sul with a level stare. "That name means nothing here."

Brivar heard a hiss of outrage from the guardsman to his right as his captain surged forward, sword in hand. There was an answering movement in the shadows and they were surrounded by drawn bows as well as ready spears. Brivar clutched the pendant of Yholis in his left hand and his voice shook through a muttered prayer.

"Hold!" The woman raised her hand and the archers stepped back, bows dropping but arrows still nocked. "Not here."

She made a gesture and one of the spearmen turned and disappeared through a cleft in the canyon wall. Brivar's stomach churned in an unpleasant manner. He thought he might be sick but he was too afraid to move.

Lord Sul snapped, "I demand –"

The woman put a hand on his bridle, her touch calming the nervous horse. "I wouldn't," she advised.

A tall man, his dark hair peppered with grey, emerged from the cleft. He was dressed in a black leather brigandine that fell to his knees, quite different from the short scale coats worn by their Avarel escort, and was pulling thick gloves onto his hands as he walked. He checked in surprise when he saw them, frowning at the royal standard that hung limp in the still evening.

Lord Sul nudged his horse forward. "Are you the Duke of Agrathon?"

The man gave a derisive snort. "No." And walked away.

Not to be deterred, his cousin kicked his horse after him. "We are here to see the duke on behalf of King Raffa-Herun Geled."

The man turned. His gaze raked over Lord Sul and his escort, resting a moment on Brivar's pale blue temple surcoat. "You're wasting your time. He's not here."

He turned to leave again and this time it was not Lord Sul who stopped him, but the woman. "At night, Esar?"

So, this was Esar Cantrell, foster brother to the man they had come to find. Brivar studied him as a whole welter of unspoken communication passed between him and the woman with the spear. Varisten Elenia said it was just as important to understand a patient's state of mind as their physical state, that it was often critical to their treatment and sometimes to their survival. You could read more than just pain in how a person moved and spoke, and watching Cantrell, Brivar saw a man who was tense, angry, and worried. And not at all happy to see them.

"Fine," he said, turning away. "But they leave in the morning."

Lord Sul, who was rapidly confirming all Brivar's fears about his diplomatic skills, announced, "We will not leave until we have seen the duke."

"You will," Cantrell said without stopping. "Or you can spend the night out here."

On cue, an eerie call echoed through the canyon. Not the howl of a wolf, which Brivar knew well, but a long, high wail that was picked up and answered by more voices until it was no longer possible to discern where it was coming from or how many there were. He found himself recalling all the lurid tales he had heard of the savage Lathai tribe who inhabited these mountains. From the tense faces all around him, he knew he was not the only one.

Lord Sul's mouth snapped shut on further protest. His horse stamped nervously.

"Your choice," the woman said.

He nodded, pale in the light of the rising moon.

Her face relaxed. "All of you, dismount. You need to lead your horses."

They didn't have to go far, but the path through the cliff was narrow and dark. At several points the overhanging rock would not have permitted a mounted man to pass, and the horses were skittish and hard to handle. Wailing cries followed them, nipping at Brivar's heels till his nerves were strung so tight and his breath so shallow he feared he might faint.

Then they were through and the glow of firelight and the cheerful sound of laughter dispelled the terror. It was dark now, the light of the fires burning away Brivar's night vision so he could see little of the camp itself. Cantrell had disappeared, but a red-haired woman led his cousin towards one of the deeper shadows that Brivar saw was the mouth of cave. It smelt of horses and other creatures, but it was big enough for them and their mounts, and it was dry and safe. At that moment, that was all he cared about.

More women entered, spears and bows strapped to their backs, and lit Isyrium bulbs so they had enough light to care for their horses. Brivar was a little shocked at such extravagance. When he tried to thank the woman who positioned a bulb for him, she merely shrugged as though it was nothing to adorn a cave in the mountains with luxuries that cost ten silver marks apiece in Avarel.

He had hoped for a moment of privacy to rub cannavery liniment on his saddle sores, but his cousin summoned him with a curt gesture and Brivar spent his last hour before sleep—and the last of his preciously hoarded liniment—attending to Lord Sul's comfort. He tried not to resent him for it too much. It was, after all, partly why he was here.

Apprentice surgeons were rarely called on to travel, and almost never outside Avarel. By requesting his presence in this embassy, Lord Sul had given Brivar an opportunity he would not have otherwise had, but the ache in his muscles went to the bone and it was a struggle to feel grateful. Once he exchanged his pale blue surcoat for a surgeon's green, he would either be appointed to a wealthy household as a personal physician or he would remain at the temple, tending to all those who came in need of care. He already knew which he would choose. If all wealthy men were like his cousin Sul-Barin, he would rather spend the rest of his days treating the city's street sleepers and factory workers.

Finally dismissed to find his rest, Brivar was too tired to do more than collapse into his bedroll, fully clothed. The night was cold and the stone floor was hard, but he fell asleep almost at once, only to be jolted awake some hours later by running footsteps and muffled voices. He grasped the thin blanket tighter around himself, ears pricked for inhuman sounds, his fear magnified by the fey light of the Isyrium bulbs that cast their eerie blue glow across the cave.

Then Cantrell's voice rose above the rest. "…what in Ithol's name did you think you were doing?"

A voice, rough with weariness, answered, "Testing a theory."

"Testing my bloody nerves more like," Cantrell growled. "You could have been killed."

The footsteps stopped. "Are they here?"

Silence, then Cantrell's curse. "So that's how they found us. What do you want us to do with them?"

Whoever he was talking to said something too quiet for Brivar to hear, then Cantrell, exasperated concern clear in his voice, said, "You're wrecked. Go to sleep. Let me handle the morning."

The response was muffled as they moved away, but before he dropped back to sleep, Brivar clearly heard Cantrell say, "Now, Alyas? Why?"

Dawn came early in the mountains. Sunlight poured through the gap in the curtain that hung across the entrance to the cave, burning bright against Brivar's heavy eyelids. He rolled over, every muscle protesting, and felt the sharp edge of stone between his shoulder blades.

"Ithol's bollocks," a gruff voice complained from somewhere behind him. "I've spent more comfortable nights in a Qidan prison cell."

"You've never been in a Qidan prison cell," someone else said. "Stop talking shit."

"But if I had…"

Then Corado's harsh voice snapped at them to shut up and Brivar buried his head under his cloak. Their escort captain was vicious and unpredictable. Brivar didn't doubt he knew what he was about, but he had a scathing contempt for his betters—Sul-Barin Feron excepted, for some reason—and an equal disdain for those beneath him. He was half-Flaeresian and a bastard, and no doubt that was the problem. It meant he had only one name in a society that based merit and honour on how many names a person could list after their birth name, though even the highest in Avarel were restricted to the formal use of just three (after the current king's grandfather, furious at the hours it took to announce his nobles at court, decreed that no man or woman in the kingdom could use more than names than the king and promptly shortened his own to three). Brivar thought he would be forever grateful that he had surrendered all names but his birth name upon entering the temple, and thereafter never had to worry about such things as whether the man he was talking to could count back twenty named generations or merely nineteen to determine who had precedence in any situation.

Brivar waited until Corado had left the cave before he unrolled his cloak and stood. The camp that had been wreathed in darkness the night before was revealed by the new day in all its organised chaos. Eyes like saucers, Brivar watched in fascination as men and women emerged from other caves on both sides of a wide, deep canyon like the one they had travelled through the night before. This one could be reached only via the narrow passage at one end, where they had entered, and a winding defile that led up and out onto the clifftops at the other.

Hide canopies shaded the cave entrances, which were hung with thick curtains. Canvas tents were dotted throughout the main clearing, some with their doors tied back to reveal neat bedrolls or stacks of crates. Even to Brivar's unpractised assessment, it was clearly a camp of some permanence.

"Impressed, are you?" Corado snarled by his ear. "Don't let it fool you. These are nothing but scum, and their captain is a charlatan. You'll see."

Brivar watched him walk away, hostility in every line of his body. If last night Cantrell had been tense and worried, Corado was a vibrating well of anger and aggression waiting to explode.

Brivar crept out to join his cousin, making sure he put several bodies between himself and Corado. They ate a cold breakfast alone, the residents of the camp keeping a wide berth. They had been given pails of icy water to wash with and a fire had been laid at the entrance to their cave, but they were otherwise left alone. No one spoke to them beyond what was necessary. It was clear they were not welcome.

They saw Cantrell once from a distance as he emerged from a tent, a lean, black-haired man by his side. Brivar watched them speak together before disappearing into the largest of the caves. Lord Sul was arguing with Corado loudly enough that his voice could be heard throughout the camp. Brivar saw several looks cast their way, and one or two frowns, and he studied their owners curiously as he chewed on his stale bread.

This was his first journey of any length outside Avarel, and his first outside the borders of Lankara, although that last point was disputed and rather fluid. King Raffa-Herun Geled and his father and grandfather before him claimed these mountains as part of their realm, as did the neighbouring king of Flaeres, and the territory passed between them on a regular basis, with little regard for the wishes of the Lathai tribe that called the mountains home. That endless feuding had something to do with the exile and disgrace of the former Duke of Agrathon, whose camp this was, but Brivar was too young to remember the details of a scandal fifteen years in the past and so far removed from his life. He had not been interested enough to find out, even after he had been assigned to this embassy. He regretted that now.

But though he might not be well-travelled, Avarel was a powerful trade city, and he was a surgeon. Many travellers came to the Temple of Yholis seeking solace and healing. He recognised Janath from far-off Qido, their pale hair braided and coiled above slanting cheekbones and sea-blue eyes, scattered among the more familiar sallow complexions of the central Ellasian nations, Lankara, Hantara and nearby Flaeres, indistinguishable except for their accents. There were even a few dusky brown faces from the southern steppelands. None of them returned his stares with friendliness, though there was no open hostility. They were, he thought, as curious as he was to see what would happen.

We will not leave," Brivar heard his cousin insist. Under the sun and after a night's sleep—*his* sleep cushioned by the bed of furs loaded onto his spare horse along with all the other luxuries of his rank—Lord Sul had recovered the nerve the evening before had stolen from him. "If he is not here, we will wait until he returns. I have a duty from the king, and I will see it through."

Brivar recalled Cantrell's lack of welcome and thought it unlikely such obstinacy would be rewarded, but his cousin would not be dissuaded.

"Which one of you is Sul-Barin?"

Brivar started, dropping his bread, and turned to see the dark-haired man standing behind him. Cantrell was a few paces back, arms crossed and brows drawn together in a frown. They both wore the distinctive long, flared brigandine, daylight showing the scuffs and small damage of long use. The speaker was smaller and lighter than Cantrell, all sharp angles against Cantrell's burly strength, and his manner thrummed with impatience.

There was an awkward pause. Brivar eyed his cousin warily as he retrieved his breakfast, noting the flushed face that boded ill. Newly come into his title, Lord Sul guarded the privileges of his rank like a jealous lover, and he was already smarting from their rough treatment. Now, with deliberate insult, he turned his back on the two men and continued eating.

Brivar's gaze slid back to the man who had spoken as an expectant hush fell over the camp. An alarming suspicion began to form.

The newcomer surveyed the back of Lord Sul's head with narrowed eyes. "I was told you had a message from Raffa and were most insistent."

Even Lord Sul could eventually recognise the obvious if it slapped him in the face hard enough. He surged to his feet, scattering crumbs from his lap. "Your Gra –"

He was speaking to the man's back as he walked away. "There are no titles here," the Duke of Agrathon called over his shoulder. "Come with me."

Lord Sul had planned this audience for weeks, down to the clothes he would wear and who would be with him. Brivar knew, because he had been forced to participate in endless rehearsals, his role—even his words—drummed into him over the course of their journey. None of those preparations included the king's envoy scurrying after the retreating figure of the former duke in the clothes he had slept in, having first offered him a grave insult, under the watchful stares of his mildly terrifying company.

Hurrying along at his heels, his heart thumping with nerves, Brivar wished he was back at the temple. He missed his masters and his fellow apprentices. He missed his patients, even the difficult ones. But most of all he missed problems he understood and knew how to deal with. It had seemed a great adventure when he had been assigned to this mission, carrying an appeal for help that surely no reasonable man could refuse. Their need was urgent and terrifying—he knew that better than most—but his innocent certainties had begun to fray the moment they arrived. There were currents swirling beneath the surface here that spoke of worse troubles and deep resentments.

The duke's quick steps led them into a stone basin, shaped like the amphitheatres of the ancients with smooth, sloping sides rather than ranks of stepped seats. The morning sun crept across the land from the east, cutting across the floor of the basin, casting one half into shadow and making the other a pool of light, where Lord Sul now stood, blinking against the brightness, exposed and unprepared.

Brivar edged to the side, out of the glare of the mountain sun. It was his testimony that mattered here, not his person, and his cousin was too focused on the grim pair facing him to object.

"So," the duke said. "Raffa remembers me. Should I be flattered? You seem to think so."

Brivar saw his cousin bridle at this casual use of the king's birth name, but he managed to curb his objection. "Your Gra —"

"I have warned you," the duke said, "not to use that title here."

Lord Sul seemed to be suffering from a rare moment of uncertainty. He floundered about for an acceptable form of address. "My lord —"

The duke's eyes narrowed. Behind him, Cantrell coughed, turning his head away.

Brivar felt a twinge of sympathy. By the king's order, exile had stripped both title and name from this man, and his cousin would never think to use one he had assumed for himself because Lord Sul was Lankaran nobility, and to him names were everything. Besides, he had come here—he had been sent here—to find the former Duke of Agrathon and rescind his exile. In exchange for his service, of course, but they were coming to that.

Corado, his eyes alive with hatred, leant forward and whispered in Lord Sul's ear, who, looking relieved, tried again with, "Captain." And ruined it with a bow barely less formal than for titled royalty.

The answering silence was long and awkward. Then the duke sighed. "Yholis have mercy, just get on with it."

Lord Sul took a deep breath, his hesitation falling away as he prepared to deliver the speech he had practised for weeks on end.

"Spare me the pretty phrases," the duke said with vicious timing. "Just tell me what he wants."

Lord Sul deflated like a pricked bladder. Brivar felt a spark of anger. His cousin was a pompous fool, but that had been cruel and deliberate. Greatly daring, Brivar said, "Your help, Captain."

The man's eyes snapped to him in surprise and in that moment Brivar knew him. The clothes and the voice were different, but there was no doubt this was the woodsman they had met yesterday—the same man, he realised now, he had heard arrive deep in the night. If his cousin guessed, he gave no sign of it, and since Lord Sul had all the subtlety of an uroc in heat, he could not have concealed his recognition. But to Brivar's eye, the stiffness of the left shoulder was unmistakable. They were one and the same, and now he could see the man's face, he liked less and less what he saw.

The duke's skin was so pale it was almost translucent, the lines of his face pared down to sharp angles and his eyes smudged in shadow. Brivar's gaze dropped to his hands, the only other part of the man he could see. His skin was stretched tight over prominent bones and had the blueish tint he usually only saw in starving street children. Whatever else he was—and he was certainly angry—he was also gravely ill, or Brivar had wasted the last thirteen years of his studies.

He raised his eyes and saw the duke watching him, an odd expression on his face. Cantrell, too, was staring at him, and his expression was much easier to interpret. Brivar had seen it too often in those who brought their loved ones to the temple.

"My help," the duke mused, his gaze still on Brivar. "With what could he possibly need my help?"

"Lankara is threatened, my lord," Lord Sul said, anxious to regain the initiative but forgetting his carefully planned speech. "A mysterious enemy, a horde of *things*. It has already devastated parts of Hantara and the Donea and the king fears Lankara will be next. Already we are seeing incursions along our borders. And…" he hesitated, his face paling. "It is not human, or no longer human. It spreads a poison wherever it goes, a sickness."

His voice faltered, the words falling flat against the duke's silence.

"A sickness?" Cantrell demanded. "What kind of sickness?" He did not look at his foster brother, but Brivar felt the sharp rise in tension.

Lord Sul focused on him with pathetic gratitude. "A terrible one, my lord. It transforms men and beasts into more of itself, if it does not kill them. Many have died, and many more have been consumed. It has already reached the borders of Lankara." He looked at Brivar, gesturing him forward. "The Temple of Yholis can tell you more, my lord. They have treated many with the sickness. They have even cured some. My cousin Brivar…"

Brivar took an obliging step forward, his mouth dry, aware of the weight of Cantrell's stare, waiting for the question he knew was coming. The identifying signs of the duke's illness were plain to see now he knew what he was looking for. The wound that bothered him was not an old one that had healed badly. If Brivar was right, it hadn't healed at all.

The duke stirred, silencing Cantrell before he could speak. "What does he expect me to do about it?" he asked. "And why? He was quite clear about how he felt fifteen years ago when he took everything from me. I cannot believe he has changed his mind. Why now does he ask for my help?"

It had seemed so simple back in Avarel, Brivar thought, watching his cousin's nervous face. They would find the former Duke of Agrathon and present to him the king's offer: a full pardon and restoration of all his lands and titles in exchange for bringing his elite military company to the defence of the realm. If he had given any thought to how that offer might be received, it was to assume it would be welcome. Now, as his cousin hesitated to even voice it, he knew it was dangerous at best.

Once again, Lord Sul took a deep breath. Brivar could not, at this moment, fault his courage. "King Raffa-Herun Geled wishes to convey that he bitterly regrets your quarrel –"

"Our quarrel," the duke echoed in a hollow voice.

"– and, further, that he desires to make restitution through the return of your family's names, lands, and honours, and begs you to retake your place at his side in this time of Lankara's need."

"Restitution," the duke said flatly. "Returning to me what is mine is hardly restitution."

"Your Grace…" Lord Sul stuttered, then faltered, realising his mistake.

But the acid didn't come. "Just go," the duke said. He ignored Cantrell's concerned glance, Lord Sul's gaping surprise, and turned on his heel and walked out.

BUY NOW FROM AMAZON

ABOUT THE AUTHOR

www.andeira.net

Printed in Great Britain
by Amazon

25587162R00371